DISCARDED

CASTLE CORNER

CASTLE
CORNER

---

by Joyce Cary

HARPER & ROW, PUBLISHERS

NEW YORK AND EVANSTON

First United States Edition 1963

Originally published in Great Britain 1938

Library of Congress Catalog Card Number: 63-20302

CASTLE CORNER

I

'And now to God the Father . . .' Old Mr. John Corner's voice rose as usual upon the phrase and paused there. For old John, at eighty-three, brought up in the eighteen twenties, God the Father was the ruling conception of life. God was Father of creation, the King was father of his people, and he, John, was father of his tenants, both English and Irish, especially the Irish here at Castle Corner. He found them helpless and foolish children.

Because of this habitual pause, lengthened by the old man's shortness of breath, no one at first noticed that he had stopped praying. He had turned his ear, thin and white as porcelain, towards the open window beside him, listening.

There had been in the last months a little difficulty with certain tenants, and old John had ordered their eviction for that morning. He was therefore attentive for any sounds from outside.

Inside the room nothing could be heard except the hiss of the urn on the breakfast table and the lap of small waves outside the eastward windows. A morning shower had just passed over towards the east, leaving the air as bright as water. The room was full of sunlight, warmth, glitter of silver and the white reflection of the starched linen, mixed on the ceiling with the silvery reflections of the lake outside the windows. If one looked to the east, the house seemed to float on the lough, sparkling yellow in the April sunshine; like the yacht of some legendary prince in a sea of Rhine wine. But if one looked out of the west windows into the dark green shadows of the trees and the mountain behind, one seemed to be in a forgotten castle where some sleeping beauty in her country stays might eat hot buttered scones for a thousand years and never hear a sigh, except from the chimney.

Prayers at Castle Corner were exhilarating or sleepy for visitors according to the weather and their views. Cleeve Corner, only grandson of the house, aged eleven, faced the water and he was effervescent with happiness. He was on his first visit to Ireland for nine years. He was at home for the first time in his life.

Cleeve's father, Felix, the eldest son, could not agree with old John on any subject, religious or political, and rather than quarrel with him, he had stayed away from home. Therefore Cleeve's life had been spent in cheap hotels and boarding houses, wandering through Europe, often with no companion except his mother, who, especially in his father's frequent absences, could talk of nothing save her own misfortunes.

Cleeve had been envied for his travels and he had sometimes boasted of his freedom, but he felt himself deprived. Like other children, he combined a taste for novelty with a strong dislike of change. He liked new things but they must be added to the old, already known and loved. Cleeve was always losing his old things; friends, toys, rooms, and he understood perfectly the meaning of home which was something always there and always the same; a secure possession.

That was why he expected to be happy at Castle Corner, which, as soon as his grandfather died, was to be his home. He was already taking possession of it. He had explored already attics full of old rubbish, cellars, every corner of the yards; and now at the idea of it surrounding him at that moment, he smiled into his hands all the time, and twiddled his heels with delight. He did not notice his grandfather's long pause, or the first small noise from outside which now began to grow into the silence of the room; causing his elders one by one to raise their heads.

He was interested only in the magic castle, the glittering room; a hole in the chair seat which already, in his two prayer times, he had enlarged to admit two fingers; in a piece of string dangling against his nose from the mantelpiece above his head.

What did it come from? He knew the mantelpiece by now; his mantelpiece at home. There were six glass jars upon it and two figures in green bronze. The jars all contained spills, buttons, bits of sealing wax, corks and string. This string probably came from the blue and white ginger jar, most precious of all to his aunt Mary Corner.

How dangerous to let a string hang like that. Suppose somebody ran against it by accident, what a crash, what cries of horror and anger. The very thought gave him a thrill; his heels jerked, he squeezed his thighs together. He had been told three times already that if he got into any mischief he would be sent back to England. He was on his best behaviour. The string tickled his nose. He thought of the pictures on the Chinese jar, the floating islands, the mandarin. His imagination travelled rapidly through China. He saw mandarins with long moustaches, prisoners in cages, junks. This very room might be a mandarin's junk, and he a mandarin among his silk cushions, his wise friends telling him stories of wonders.

Cleeve himself, though not the chief mandarin, was the mandarin's favourite. He was everybody's favourite.

He gazed with a smile of delight at the glittering water outside the window, and enjoyed this paradise of friendship and wisdom; his fingers rose towards the string; twiddled it, flicked it. The fingers were afraid of the string; but also they wanted to be active, to reach out, to explore. When the string slipped an inch, they jumped from it. But the next instant they had closed again. These movements were independent of Cleeve and his mandarins. The fingers were like an excited crowd of children gathered round a dangerous dog on a chain, who scatter with yells every time the dog rushes out of its kennel, and then at once come creeping back, a little nearer, a little more dangerously near.

Mary Corner cried suddenly, 'What is that?'

'God the Son and God the Holy Ghost, as it was in the beginning, is now and ever shall be, world without end, Amen.' The old man quickly finished the prayer in his thin voice; and shut the huge prayer book. The servants, that is to say, the three Protestant servants out of the staff of seven, got up and filed out of the service door; and at once, like a Jack-in-the-box, the pale little butler popped in again and broke up the row of chairs.

'What was it?' Mrs. Corner asked, turning to the man.

Her father-in-law, old John, and her husband, John Charles, or John Chass, as he was always called, gave her a discreet glance. Mary Corner was in her fifth month.

This was nothing unusual. Mrs. John Chass, in her nine years of marriage had been pregnant five times. But the only two children born alive had died at a few weeks and three miscarriages had been severe and dangerous. She was now forty-six, a year older than her husband, and the doctor had warned her against another pregnancy.

'It sounded like a drum,' she said.

'Why should anybody beat a drum at nine o'clock in the morning?' John Chass asked.

This was not convincing. Drums had been beaten during the land wars at all hours, to warn the people of an eviction.

'You're not going to evict those poor Foys?' she exclaimed.

'Not if we can help it,' John Chass said. He listened. 'Isn't that a yaffle at a tree. He sounds very like a drum.'

Mary Corner turned towards the old man, but he, having put the great Bible in the sideboard drawer, was slipping from the room. Doubtful and suspicious, she turned again to her husband. 'I won't have Kitty upset.'

Kitty was a maid, who had been nurse to the last baby, before it died.

John Chass, smiling at this domestic view of the matter, said in a soothing voice, 'No, no, we'll take care of Kitty.'

'Yes, but——'

At this moment a crash like a bomb made them all jump. Grogan, the butler, went down on his hands and knees, Cleeve's mother gave a loud shriek; Mrs. John put her hands to her breast and her long, plain face became set in apprehension and courage; the expression of one who has learnt what suffering means; and also how to face it.

11

Then suddenly Cleeve's mother shrieked, 'Cleeve!' The eyes of all turned upon the small boy, with his pale thin face and pale yellow hair, standing by the mantelpiece with a look of astonishment. The Chinese jar lay smashed on the fender.

'It fell,' he said. He was bewildered by this strange accident.

His mother flew at him. There were cries of anger and horror.

Mrs. Felix, a pale pretty little woman, very like her son, shook him by the arm. 'Wait till your father comes and he'll beat you.' Mary Corner, from the other side, protested, 'But, Clara, he didn't mean it.'

John Chass took a pair of field-glasses and ran upstairs to the book attic.

Its window, on the landward side of the house, looked out on the little park, full of sycamores, the drive, the post road, and beyond, the mountainous centre of Annish. The sun from the east, behind John Chass, threw the shadows of the castle chimney pots on the loose gravel in front of the house, and struck full upon Knockeen mountain, whose foot was at the road. In the soft morning light, Knockeen was all in the bright colours of a Victorian silk shop. The little fields of young corn, the potato gardens freshly ridged, were like patterns of moiré ribbon; the corn was like fine green plush; and above, the rounded top of the hill, bog and heather, was in the soft reddish brown, shot with magenta, of Mrs. John's best dress. One imagined a breast underneath its pale tight shimmer. Only the long oblong cuts of the turf banks and the clamps and stacks on the skyline broke the smooth curves, the soft colour; incongruous as drops of blood pressed out of some silk-covered, tight-corseted bosom.

The drum was louder. John Chass focused his glasses on the hill-top and searched the ground between the dark blobs of turf.

A clump caught his eye. It seemed to swell; to bulge. John Chass muttered in surprise. Suddenly he saw the black circle of the drum. The drummer was climbing the turf; now drummer and turf stood like a black, trembling drop. It shook to the drum-beat, loud and quick, like the pulse of an animal.

'I thought so,' John Chass said. 'I knew there'd be trouble. One good thing, the old man won't be able to do anything this morning, and if Felix comes to-day he'll probably put a stopper on it.'

It was characteristic of John Chass to hope that his eldest brother would stop the eviction, for though he had been his father's agent for eight years, he still did not care to oppose him. Neither did he want an eviction. John Chass was a man who enjoyed life so much that he detested any interruption of that enjoyment, above all, bad feeling. He liked to be on good terms with everybody, including himself. He loved people, sport, good company and probably he loved Castle Corner too,

12

without noticing it; as a man loves an old coat, and does not know his love until the coat falls to pieces.

He took after his father in nothing except good temper. He was a big man, with the handsome features of a classical Roman. His eyes were dark blue. His whiskers and hair, of a true auburn, were still as thick and curly as a young man's.

'Yes,' he said at last. 'I'll take five to one that it's old Mrs. Foy herself with the drum, and it must be two miles. Wonderful how they make glasses these days. They were worth every penny of twenty pounds, whatever Mary may say.'

A soft, quick breathing at his elbow made him glance downwards, Old John stood beside him. His chest fluttered, the breath whistled through his half-parted blue lips; something seemed to struggle in the wasted old body as if with a powerful enemy. But the eyes and the tall forehead, turned towards the drummer, were full of masterful assurance.

'They've got wind of it,' John Chass said. 'I suppose we'd better wait a bit.'

'What's the good of waiting—they won't learn.'

'It's Mrs. Foy herself with the drum—that makes it awkward.'

The faint voice breathed in answer, 'The women—what do they know about it.'

'Ah well, I suppose it's the last of her boys.'

Mary Corner saw her husband slip from the room and away from her questions; but she was for the moment concerned with something more immediate than politics or even Kitty; to rescue Cleeve.

'Nonsense, Clara, he couldn't help it.'

'You don't understand, Mary. He's completely spoilt and his father does nothing.'

Mary Corner was already between mother and son. Cleeve looked at her with a doubtful expression. He was not used to this ugly aunt, with her shrill voice; he knew that she was foreign and he found her odd both in voice and dress. The face with its bulging forehead, long, bony nose and projecting chin, surmounted by hair already mixed with grey; parted down the middle and turned back over the ears in two horn-like projections, still alarmed him. As for the dress, the tight-buttoned bodice of red rust, the broad skirts which might have hidden a crinoline; and the little silk apron with its six pockets, he knew it to be ridiculous. His mother had called it so.

Now while he gazed, still uncertain whether to cry or not, he saw the chin come forward, the hooked nose come down, the eyes close, in a look of extraordinary slyness. His own eyes blinked, his lips trembled.

13

'He's impossible,' Mrs. Felix said, 'and if you're going to spoil him too——'

Mary Corner, seeing Cleeve's uncertain lips was already in a panic. She could not bear to see a child cry. 'Never mind, dear, never mind.' She hastily caught Cleeve's hand and put it into the top left pocket of her apron. At the same time she made another face at him, and this time he understood it. It was a two-eyed wink which meant, 'We're together in this—rely on me.'

His fingers had already closed on a packet of sweets. Mary Corner always carried sweets in her apron pocket, for any wandering child whom she might encounter. He took out the paper and looked into it. Mrs. Felix gave a cry of indignation. Mary Corner soothed her. 'But it's his holiday, Clara. He must enjoy his holiday. What are holidays for?'

'But it's all holidays for the boy, Mary. And his father is just as bad. However, I can see it's no good me saying anything here.'

Mrs. Felix, having discovered this grievance, was able to console herself. She was a woman who needed grievances, for though they made her unhappy, they also made her occupation.

John Chass, coming into breakfast, was glad to see that the women were still busy with Cleeve. Unfolding his napkin, he smiled about him at the united family, with the greatest enjoyment of the field-glasses, of his good appetite, and of the pleasures of hospitality. 'Well now, Cleeve,' he said, 'what would you like to do to-day—there's plenty more bowls if you'd like to break them.'

Cleeve smiled. He knew already that John Chass was a joker, but he smiled carefully in case his mother should see him, and be reminded of the promised beating.

Under the drum-beat, falling from the air, the people ran out of their cottages, leaping crookedly like active black fleas across the lower bog. One in shirt and trousers was high on Knockeen; when in his scrambling hurry he put his hands to the ground, he looked like an Annish collie, black and white, frisking his tail; two or three more at the top stood staring at the woman with the drum. They were surprised to see her for they knew her well. She was Mrs. Foy herself, in the same brown dress and black shawl which she had worn to market this forty years; a quiet, decent woman. To see her on the clamp beating the huge, gaudy drum with canes, her knuckles already bleeding, was like seeing one's mother take command of armies.

The Foys were a well-known family on Knockeen. There had been eleven of them but five were dead, one was in a convent, and three had emigrated The only two left were the brothers Padsy and Con.

The two boys had taken over their father's farm on Knockeen, fifteen acres, but since Padsy's wife's death they had paid very little rent. Padsy was a hard worker but a bad manager and he had six children. Con handled no money. Then Con engaged himself to Kitty Egan whose sole fortune was six pounds, and set to work to build up a ruin still attached to one end of Padsy's cottage. The plan was that Con should take seven acres from Padsy, at two-thirds of the whole rent, and buy himself a pig and seed with Kitty's fortune.

This was a private plan because division of farms was not allowed even by Ulster custom, and though the Foys swore that the farmhad. once been two and was still two in law, they knew that old John liked large farms. He would rather lay two together than split one into itwo As soon as he saw the new house and knew that Con was getting married, he guessed their plan and challenged the brothers.

They denied it and there was angry talk. Old John accused them and they threatened the law and the League. He had answered by ordering an eviction for Padsy's arrears of rent.

Mrs. Foy, who lived with her sons, was a woman of over sixty who had worked about Knockeen for fifty years. Her hard, withered flesh looked like a piece of the poor ground of her own farm and her face, as she beat her drum, had no more expression than the two twisted fists whirling the canes. She did not speak to the watchers or look at them. She stood high up in the blue air, beating the drum as if by that alone she could save her home, her sons and herself.

Down below the lanes were blackened with the people hurrying towards the Foy holding; they pressed past the gates of the castle from whose white chimney-stacks the new morning smoke, as blue as the washed sky, trickled into the cool air. A policeman lounged at the gates; but the main column was already at the Foys. It stood at the halt in the open rough ground before the cottage; picked out a mile away by its new straw thatch, glittering in its eastern facet like topaz. Three men in bowler hats and dark suits, bailiffs, approached its door, a fourth turned aside to a window, stooped to peer, but the glass was obscured with thick sacking.

The brothers, taken by surprise, had stuffed sacking in the windows to hide their preparations for a siege. The cottage, lit only by the gleam of the holy lamp, one candle in a bottle and the glow of the fire, was like a cave full of excited gnomes. Con, the younger, small, long-armed, with long jutting chin, sprang from window to window, building them up behind the sacking with sods of turf. Each time he rammed in a sod he uttered a screaming curse against the police or the Corners. Con had sworn to hang for a Corner if they took away his house. His elder brother, Padsy, tall, fair, with vague eyes but an active positive mouth, was wedging a long stool against the upper half of the door. Meanwhile he never ceased protesting.

'I tell ye, they can't do it. It's unlawful for to do such a thing. Why shouldn't we build up a wee room. Sacred heart, what is it to ould Jawn if Con should live with his brother?'

Padsy, like other people, created an ideal world for himself, but unluckily he did not build facts into the structure. He was like a nonsense poet whose masterpieces are beautiful to the ear of a Chinaman but excite only confusion or wonder in those who know the language. 'But I'll tell ye it's young Mrs. Jawn has set him on till it because she's wantin' Kitty at the castle.'

'Aw, devil damn their souls to double burning hell,' Con screamed like a madman. 'They say I can't marry and they say I can't work. Why don't they cut us like stirks and sell us to the butchers?'

Padsy's children were running to and fro bringing the sods of turf to Con; except the eldest, Manus, a boy of ten, who knelt beside Kitty Egan in front of the holy lamp and the picture of the Virgin tacked to the wall above it.

Kitty was praying and she had brought the boy to pray because he was already noted for his piety, and it seemed to her that his innocence and his good looks, charming to everybody, would have a strong effect in heaven.

Kitty was a fair, thin girl of seventeen, with a freckled face, made pretty by its honest expression.

She prayed at great speed, with force and eloquence. 'Oh holy blessed Mother of Gawd, Mother of pity, who takes all the poor, motherless children to live in the boundless mercy of your heart, and to breathe the sweetness of your loving faithful soul——'

Kitty was a girl of nerve and fire, whose whole energy had seized upon the idea of love. The love of the Virgin, the tender love of her mother, of Ireland; these were the first openings presented to her imagination and her passion, and she had possessed them with ardour, so that the ideas of them in their turn had formed her looks, her expression, even her voice, which had now, when she spoke to the Virgin, her beloved Mistress, the caress of an adoring child.

'Save us, darling Mother, in this extremity——'

Manus, beside her, holding her by the hand, lifted up his face to the lamp and murmured in awe. He knew the whole of his rosary, and already he could read and write. Manus was ambitious to be a priest, and when, in chapel, he watched the priest in his vestments going to the altar, he had felt wonder that everybody did not want to be a priest; to work miracles, and to live in a house with a housekeeper and a glass-fronted bookcase full of books.

'Ave Maria,' he prayed, imitating a priest's chant; and Kitty implored, 'Holy Mother of Him that died by the bloody-minded men, save us from the stain of blood.'

16

Con, each time he passed, brushed rudely against her and muttered to himself. He was furious with Kitty. He had told her not to come to the house that day, and she had come, not to help, but to hinder, to object, and now to pray. What sense was there in prayers when he was being turned out of his house. 'To hell with you and Father MacFee,' he muttered. 'I'd rather have his curse than the Pope's medal.' Con was raging against injustice and Kitty could not tell him how to cure it, but only not to fight the police. There was no sense in any of the women, only fears and feelings. Look at Padsy's wife, who married him with nothing; the prettiest and sweetest girl in Knockeen. She had slaved for him but would she go to America with him when his father died and left him the money? She would not because she could not leave her father, or her sister, or her priest, and so she worked herself ill for him and the six children that God had sent them for their love, and the money was spent on taking her on pilgrimage to holy places, and the doctors, and now she was dead.

Con rushed to the bed and pulled out an old, single-barrelled fowling piece, which he charged from a gunmetal flask. It was a Corner weapon, by a London maker, in the best style of the 'forties, with long, tapering barrel and gold damascened lock. It had been handed down to Con by his father, a Corner gamekeeper; he had often poached hares with it. It would kill a duck at forty yards.

He laid it on the table and said to the back of Kitty's head, 'That's for your friends the Corners and the peelers. If Gawd won't give them what they need, it's up till the devil's friends.'

Kitty did not seem to hear. Her voice rose in a stronger appeal. But Kitty was a catholic soul; not only patient but resolute. A few minutes later, when Con was cutting a loophole in his own cabin, Padsy was surprised to see Kitty unbarring the door. He ran up to her. 'Holy Saints, ye can't go out. They're only waiting to push through.'

'It was just Bridgy here that wanted out.'

Padsy's second child Bridget, a black-haired little girl, turned up her black eyes to him through the rat tails of her hair.

'Ach, she can do what she wants within.'

'But, Padsy, she could slip through a wee crack. Mind now, Bridgy.' Kitty suddenly pulled the lower half of the door a few inches inwards; and the child instantly dived through.

'Sacred heart, what are ye doing?' Padsy hastily refortified the door. 'What is she to mind?'

Kitty made no answer. She went back to her prayers.

'Though indeed it's no odds,' Padsy said, 'for they can't do it. It's unlegal. And it's Master Felix will let them know it this very day.'

When Kitty put Bridget out of the besieged cottage, the police and the bailiffs, even the crowd, were already growing bored. Nothing had happened, no orders had come from the magistrates; and they began to think that nothing would happen.

The police were sitting on the walls with their caps at all angles; the boys were throwing stones at marks and the women had all gone home to their work.

The sudden appearance of a small, filthy child on all fours at the Foys' door was a surprise. Bridget was not timid, but she was shy, when she stood up and found several hundred pairs of eyes fixed upon her. She stared at the crowd and it stared at her. When at last she had made off at a slow trot, looking over her shoulder at the crowd, the bailiffs and the constables stared after her with equally blank faces.

Bridget knew the hillside as well as her own yard but she took no care to pick her way in the sheep tracks. She plunged straight downwards, careless of the heather stems which scratched her round feet and fat short legs to the knee. She did not notice them; she was absorbed in her task. Her orders were to go to the castle and to tell Mrs. Corner that Kitty Egan wanted to see her at Padsy Foy's.

Bridget was thought stupid. She would never learn anything, and she was singularly fond of dirt and fighting. She was as dark as a gypsy, a colour common in Annish where it is supposed to come from wrecked Armada sailors. The Armada sailors, those that escaped the Donegal rocks, went back to Spain, but the black people of Annish, as they are called, have perhaps some of the same blood. They are a tough race, inclined to keep their own council; jealous in love, and fierce in hatred; bringing to everything they do an uncommon energy and tenacity.

Padsy Foy's wife had been as dark as a Spaniard. Bridget was as dark and reserved and devoted to her purpose, whatever it was. Now, full of importance and resolution, she rushed through heather and whins like grass, to take her message into the castle which she knew only at a distance, as a place of mystery and terror, where the magistrate lived; and where the cupboards were full of silver plates and gold watches.

She approached from the shore; panting up through the trees, then trembling, she slipped from the stackyard into the coachyard. This brought her by way of a gate under the loft to the kitchen steps. But even Bridget drew back from the steps. She had never gone down steps in her life.

Castle Corner had a deep basement. It was a Georgian house built about 1760 on the site of the original castle and fort of 1615, and the deep gully of its basement was probably part of the original moat. The kitchen door was at the bottom of fourteen stone steps; Bridget shrank back against the wall in terror before this flight of precipices. Her lips shook but she did not cry. She knew crying would not help her.

She knelt down, put her fingers to her holy medal, hung under her frock by a string, and said a Hail Mary. Bridget was not so good a Christian as Manus, but she knew her prayers.

Then she turned face to the ground and pushed herself down the steps on her stomach, feet first. Her eyes were closed. She was in great terror. Half-way down she stuck for several minutes, but a boy from a window above uttered a loud yell, which caused her to jump up, whereupon she fell the rest of the way to the bottom.

Bridget advancing, bruised and filthy but still resolute, through the passage, was astonished by the castle kitchen. It seemed to her with its dim arched windows, high up in the dirty walls, its blackened ceiling, the bars of sunlight slanting through blue clouds of smoke and the glittering range at the far end, like a kind of church, a place of awe and marvels. It was full of people, like a church, and all of them turned their eyes upon her so that she felt she had done something wrong.

She recognized Sukey Egan at once. Sukey was the castle cook, Kitty's aunt; and one of the best-known characters in Annish. She sat now with her large bare arms on the table, drinking tea. Sukey had put herself at the side of the table so that a sun bar would fall upon her gold hair. She looked like a holy image with the golden fire round her pale, bulging forehead, and one could see that she knew it. But she had taken no trouble to look beautiful, she had screwed up her small face with its snub nose and wrinkled, freckled cheeks into a bitter expression.

Sukey, who had been twelve years at the castle, had just given notice. 'It's what they'd bury ye in the airth,' she said, 'and forget ye. But thanks be, I'm out of it this day week.'

There was a murmur of approval from the company and a ragged young man with broken, blackened teeth, spat at the fire and said that there was only one life.

'Bating Heaven,' said an old fisherman in the corner.

'And that's far enough.'

'Nearer than Ameriky.'

'Aye, for there's nothing to pay.'

'But Padsy Foy wouldn't go to Ameriky when he had the money.'

'The Foys have never been landless men,' the old man said, 'and faith, I don't think they could stomach the coming down into wages.'

Bridget, meanwhile, having pushed herself sideways between two of the visitors, had appeared at the corner of the table which was her own height. There she stood gazing at Sukey until Sukey's eye fell upon her and she exclaimed, 'Go wan out of my kitchen. Gawd's sake, it's Bridgeen. What d'ye want, Bridgy?'

Sukey pulled Bridget to her knee, and bent down her ear. But Bridget, in the excitement of her success, of the kitchen, had forgotten her message.

19

'Is she dumb then?' Sukey asked.

'She's afeard,' the old man said, taking the child on his knee. 'Tell your ould grander, Bridgy.'

But Bridget stared. Her body and her feelings were still excited with triumph and importance, so that her cheeks were flushed, her eyes bright, her chest thrust out; but her mind was empty.

'It'll be from Kitty,' the young man said.

'Aye, it'll be about the eviction. Kitty's up the hill this while.'

They all looked at Bridget, but without anxiety or urgency. They had been discussing the threatened eviction and the Foys for the last hour, with the detachment of Chinese philosophers regarding the moon. This was not because they were not concerned, The old man, for instance, Dan Egan, who was uncle to the Foys, was threatened with the responsibility for the whole family, should they be turned out. They had already claimed shelter from him as a family right. Dan was a widower who lived in a one-roomed hut, twelve foot by eight, on Ballycorner shore. He had barely room for himself. It was generally agreed that the descent of nine Foys of all ages would kill old Dan, and Dan himself had agreed that it had disadvantages. The toothless boy, too, Darcy Foy, was an orphan cousin who was dependent on Padsy for his bread.

Their detachment was fatalistic. As old Dan said, 'There's that many things can happen, annyway, that wan here and there doesn't make a differ.'

Cleeve had watched Bridget's approach to the steps with interest and sympathy; the sympathy of a puppy, which suddenly notices, in a world full of huge and dull human beings, another puppy; and instantly feels this other puppy's situation.

Cleeve had been sitting still for nearly five minutes, under strict orders to read his book, be good and keep clean until his father arrived to punish him for all his various crimes.

Within two yards of him his mother, in great excitement, was arguing with Mary Corner. He heard words like ruin, boycott, eviction, and he knew that his grandfather had just ordered his boots and the gig, and that he was going out to something like a battle. It was because of this excitement that he was ordered to sit still and keep by his mother's side. But it was agony to sit still at Castle Corner.

'Good gracious, Clara,' Mary Corner said. 'But what has it to do with me?' She took out her scissors from an apron pocket.

'But if they attack the house.' Mrs. Felix put her hand to her head in a characteristic gesture of despair.

Cleeve, not daring to move, watched Bridget from the corner of his eye. She had reached the edge of the steps. His breath stopped for he felt that she was holding her breath.

'If he'd only wait a few moments,' Mrs. Felix said, 'till Felix comes. He must listen to Felix.'

Mary Corner was threading a needle with a sharp eye and steady fingers. She answered calmly, 'Very likely, m'dear, but you know that anything we could say would not help matters. This is not our business, and we're better out of it.'

Mary Corner always made a strict division between man's and woman's business. She was half French, the daughter of a Waterloo captain, who, poor on his half pay, had settled in Paris and married at fifty-four a young French girl of good family and small fortune. Mary had been brought up in France and she was like a French Protestant, with that sense of order, logic, duty and subordination which is even stronger in French Protestants, with their Calvinist tradition, than in the Catholics. The whole of Mary's strong character and imagination had been directed into the idea of wifehood and motherhood, and she left politics to the men.

This appeared to her not only right but natural; the only possible arrangement. In her view, it was necessary for somebody to rule; and the happiness of women had to be in affectionate obedience, in child-bearing and in the love of children, because God had assigned their natures to love and their bodies to bear.

Her idea of life had not been changed by her experience. Her marriage had given no scope, such as a Frenchwoman of her quality had a right to expect, to her gifts and her careful education. She had been brought at thirty-seven from Paris and a circle of friends at once highly culti-vated and very simple, to Ireland of the 'eighties, in the midst of a civil war, to a society in which religion and politics took their most primitive forms, and the only other subject of conversation was sport.

She was loved but she had no sphere of duty except housekeeping; to provide large, elaborate dinners for sporting magistrates and to listen to their wives' scandal. Thus all her hopes were in children and while her nursery was empty she felt lost and wasted.

The doctor's warnings were nothing to her; she thanked God that at forty-six she had been blessed with another pregnancy. This for her, while she sat in the quiet drawing-room, was the centre of importance, giving meaning to her life and to all life.

Clara seemed to her a foolish and underbred woman without common sense, who did not know even how to be patient.

'I wonder,' she said thoughtfully, 'why Kitty hasn't come yet. She was going to cut out for me. If ever you should want a long frock, Clara, you should get Kitty to cut it out for you.'

Mrs. Felix pressed both hands to her head. She was suffering the bitterest grievance of some years and making the most of it. 'But, Mary, how can you sit there——'

21

An ear-splitting yell made her leap from her chair. Even Mary Corner started and exclaimed, 'Bless my soul.' Cleeve was seen leaning half-way out of the window.

Cleeve himself was startled by his own explosion. He looked round with the guilty alarm of the puppy who suddenly recollects where he is and what is expected of him by human beings.

For an instant mother and son stared at each other with mutual horror. Then Cleeve jumped up and bolted out of the room. If he had had a tail it would have been between his legs. But it would have started up again as soon as he was beyond the door. He plunged down the back stairs, reaching the middle landing with a crash. He had already learnt that the kitchen at Castle Corner was the centre of conversation and excitement.

'And who is this young sir?' Dan said.

'A new Corner for ye, Dan.'

'Indeed, young sir. Will ye be the ould captain's son?'

Cleeve, looking with interest at the old man with his one eye and his large Roman nose, said that he didn't know of any captain.

Darcy said, 'He's the son of Jawn Felix.'

'Jawn Felix,' Dan said. 'What, the ould captain's son's son?'

'Ach, not that John Felix. He's been dead these fifty years, but Jawn Felix the son of himself here.'

'He's the ould captain's son's son's son.'

Dan uttered a short laugh and exclaimed, 'Faith, I must be gettin' ould.' He spat on the flagstone and gazed at the spit for some time; smiling thoughtfully and gaily. Bridget stared at Cleeve with round eyes.

Old Dan turned his laughing face to Cleeve and said, 'I'm a Corner myself.'

'Are you Mr. Dan Corner?' Cleeve asked politely.

'Naw, me name is Egan and me mawther was a Kerly and her mawther was the daughter of ould Jawn Councillor up thonder in the hall.'

Darcy said solemnly, 'Aye, and she larnt latin with his own daughters.'

'A rare deed for a woman,' Dan agreed.

'Had he a lot of daughters?'

'Ould Jawn Councillor. He had as many wains as Nick's ram.'

'Aye—there's many of us might claim his blood.'

'But not the nose. Dan has the grandeur in the nose,' Sukey said, 'and well he knows it.'

Cleeve, startled by this rude remark, looked nervously at Dan Egan. But the old man had an imperturbable dignity. 'Aye, it's the Corner nose. And here's another,' putting his arm round Bridget. 'Here's your Cousin Bridgy, young sir.'

The group looked at the two children like an audience watching two small animals put into the same box; with speculative curiosity. Cleeve and Bridget stared at each other with blank faces.

Sukey gave a squawk of laughter. 'Is she too dirty for ye, Master Cleeve?'

Cleeve started and, recollecting his manners, took Bridget's hand and gave it two shakes. Then he seemed to reflect.

The gig wheels sounded on the loose sea gravel of the drive, beyond the high up windows; and Darcy exclaimed, 'Himself is away.'

'They'll murder'm,' Sukey said, and poured herself out another cup of thick black tea.

'I'm thinking we ought to tell the mistress that Kitty sent to her.'

'She'd never go the way she is. Jawn Chass wouldn't let her.'

'Aye, but it's more friendly.'

'But she might go too, and then what would himself say?'

Grogan the little butler came in for his cup of tea. He was pale and anxious. He was a Protestant and any trouble with the Catholic tenantry frightened him. To him the Catholics were a mysterious secret society as terrifying as the leopard clubs of Africa. He heard the arguments about Bridget's message, pondered for several moments with his head hung forwards and sideways and said then in his mournful but decisive voice, 'It's what you'd better be talking of it when the mistress comes.'

'Aye, let it fall into her ear.'

This suggestion was at once approved for its delicacy and politeness. Darcy especially, who was perhaps even more ragged than Dan and less well settled in the world, was struck by its excellence. 'Aye,' he said, 'That's the politer way.'

'But what was it Bridget was to tell her?' Grogan asked.

They looked round for Bridget. She and Cleeve had apparently melted into the air.

Cleeve, in fact, after a little reflection, had discovered how to enjoy Bridget. He had invited her to see the castle. At the moment, they were standing in one of the cellars; used for the storage of old lamps, broken fire-irons, holed saucepans put aside for the tinker. At first Cleeve had been disappointed in Bridget who stood without uttering a word. But already he had perceived that the stare expressed a fascinated attention and that his enterprise was successful. Now both were absorbed, unconscious of themselves. Cleeve was holding up part of an old brass lamp, a small scroll, at which both gazed. 'It's all made by hand, solid brass,' their eyes rounded at the glittering object, 'covered with gold. Real gold. That's real gold on it. That's why it isn't rusty. Gold doesn't rust, you know. If that were solid gold it would be worth a hundred pounds—more than that.'

There was a pause; Cleeve himself was carried away by the idea of this wealth. Then, seeing Bridget's eyes, he handed her the brass with a grand gesture. 'Would you like to hold it?'

She took the brass and gazed at it. Her fingers were full of awe and arched themselves delicately.

Old John, ill as he was, as soon as he heard that the eviction was resisted, made John Chass drive him to Knockeen. They arrived just after one. The young district inspector, glad to see the magistrates at last, walked to meet them in the lane. His smooth soldier's face with its official moustache, like a piece of uniform, expressed nothing, but his step was nervous. He shaped his course towards John Chass who had descended from the gig and who greeted him with a cheerful wave of the hand and the words, 'We've got a fine audience; that's one thing.'

'It looks like trouble, doesn't it? I was waiting to see you before we went any further.'

'We might go further and fare worse.'

'Annish has been quiet enough till now, I don't think you've had any trouble with tenants in the last five years.'

'No, indeed, and Con Foy is the best judge of a dog from here to Dunderry. If he wouldn't poach all the hares.'

'We ought to act at once, one way or another.'

John Chass looked this way and that, summed up the odds, and said, 'I think old Mrs. Foy has us beaten this time. As you say, shooting would spoil it all.'

He turned and walked back to his father. Mr. Corner, thin and white as old bone, had not come down from the gig. He could not walk far. Seated high up in his old black cape, with his black felt tall hat, he appeared even smaller than usual. His white face with its short straight nose was like a carved miniature.

John Chass and the D.I., standing at the wheel, explained their agreement.

Mr. Corner looked down at them, listening gravely. His manners, like his sense of duty and his religion, belonged to the old generation. Then he said, 'You want to run away.'

'We don't want to make trouble with the tenants.'

'The worst thing that could happen to the tenants is the dividing of the farms. If we allow that, they'll all want it and then we'll have the same misery and poverty here that ruined Connaught.'

'But, father——'

'Fifteen acres can't keep two families—fifteen acres of Donegal mountain.'

'It's only Con and Kitty Egan added.'

24

'But how long will it be that?' The old man glanced round but neither John Chass nor the D.I. needed to do so. They knew that every wall and bank for a hundred yards had its row of children. Children of every age, from one upwards, staggered, rolled, climbed, stared, played and shouted among the crowd; going about their own private affairs in their world, with as much detachment from the political ideas of 1890, and the problems of distribution and ownership, as the birds, mice and bees which everywhere flew out of the bushes, dived into holes and flowers. One might have said as the round brown heads started up every moment from a new hole, that the earth itself was throwing up crops of children, with no more regard for their provision than for that of the birds and the bees. This was the fact upon which Mr. Corner based his obstinacy, and if one had said to him, 'But if you turn these people out, they'll starve, anyhow,' he would have answered, 'God will provide,' or, 'we are all in God's hands—I can only do a plain duty.'

'Old Foy was a good tenant,' John Chass said, anxious only for peace.

'So he was. But the sons can't stay here. There's no ground for both of them,' and to the D.I. he said, 'We'll have to pull the roof off. I'm going to pull down the house in any case. Couldn't the men start at this end—it's a blank wall.'

Old John spoke like a ruler and he had to be obeyed. He was chairman of the bench, and in 1890 the Annish magistrates were still the rulers of the country. There were no councils.

Old John, throned on his gig, looking calmly at the crowd, the playing children, the police now tightening their belts and examining their carbines, was the Government. The D.I. was the Minister of War, the police his army. All present felt that power, not least old John himself. It did not frighten him. He was not a constitutional king. Not even Marx despised the democrats so heartily as old John Corner, and for the same reason, that they did not face hard facts.

The crowd, now gathered close, watched in silence the bailiffs fetch rakes, poles, and a long-handled pruning hook, but when they approached Con's new-built cabin and began to hook down the roof, there were sudden yells of 'Give them Martin, up the League.'

Martin was a district inspector of police murdered the year before.

Old John gazed round with an air of mild reproach; John Chass, looking embarrassed, smiled and attempted a joke; the D.I., with a marble face but very brisk legs, walked up and down in front of the police, who looked like men awaiting the dentist, some with resignation, some with ferocious resolution.

Sods and stones began to fly, the crowd pressed forward; the D.I. shouted; the police advanced and pushed it back. But at once there

25

was a rush from the other direction. John Chass had his hat knocked off, and old John was compelled to come down from the gig.

Ten minutes later the crowd had hemmed in the police, bailiffs and magistrates against the gable; and the D.I. had already given two warnings that he would fire, when the bottom half of the cottage door was opened and Kitty was seen creeping out of it. The sight caused at moment's pause in the struggle. Both sides for a moment thought that she had come to propose a parley.

Instead, Kitty ran down the road and up from the lane there appeared a small, cone-shaped figure in a brown cloak with a huge brown hat bent down at each side by a veil tied beneath the chin. Everybody recognized Mrs. John.

The two women approached. Kitty walking sideways in her excitement, waving her arms; Mrs. John gliding forwards with the peculiar step of one who had been trained for crinolines, and answering with the quicker, neater gestures of France.

In those days, especially in a Catholic country, a woman had a special character. A sacred immunity attached to her. The crowd parted for Kitty and Mrs. John, allowing them to approach the besieged group. John Chass came forward to meet his wife, reproving her. 'Now, Molly, you have no business to be walking all this way.'

'Good gracious, John, mayn't I see Kitty? I didn't know what had happened to her.'

Kitty and Mrs. John went to the cottage door and stood there knocking and calling for a long time. Meanwhile, for some reason, both the people and the police changed their minds about fighting; they all began to talk; to walk about. Some of them were even seen laughing as they described and acted some incident.

The D.I. and John Chass confessed, 'It's no go to-day.'

'We've got off very well.'

The old man, seated on the ground against the gable end of the cottage, understood also that an eviction was not possible that morning, but he did not admit defeat. He beckoned for the gig.

Meanwhile one of Padsy's children had let the two women into the cottage, their voices were heard arguing, protesting, and suddenly Con rushed out of the cottage with a gun in his hand, turned the corner by the gable and aimed it straight at old John at five yards' range.

Somebody beside him knocked it into the air before it went off; and two policemen caught him by the arms. He was shouting in a confused way. Kitty came running in tears, and made to throw her arms round his neck, but he pushed her away with a violence that made her stagger and yelled that he never wanted to see her again. 'Ye tricked me, the pair of ye,' and turning on Mary Corner, who was stooping down over

26

her father-in-law, he shouted, 'Ye knew I couldn't shoot a woman and so ye did the jawb for them—but I can curse ye.'

A silence fell on the crowd while Con was cursing Mrs. Corner. They listened respectfully as to a religious act, because the man was so angry that his words had power on their nerves. He only had time for the opening words, 'Curse ye in your house and in your life and your death, too,' before the police whisked him away and ran him down the hill.

John Chass, who had pushed up to his wife's side, took her arm to lead her away, 'You mustn't mind Con—he'll be sorry himself afterwards.'

Mary Corner was white; and she appeared more shaken than anyone would have expected. But she said several times while she was walking to the carriage, that Con should not have cursed her like that; she was surprised at him. She had thought he had better manners.

It was never known whether this intercession of Mary Corner were a stratagem to prevent shooting or merely an attempt to rescue Kitty. She herself said that she had come for Kitty because she was not going to have so good a girl brought into trouble, and probably this was the truth. It was in the character of her mind. But the people who knew that she had faced Con's gun in the cottage and told him that he would be stupid to get himself hanged, always gave her the credit of intervention and admired her for it. They wished to add a virtue to one they liked; for it was the more pleasure to think of her.

When the carriage and the gig had gone away with the Corners, the police marched back to Dunvil leaving the mountain men in possession of the field. Padsy was triumphant, for he said, 'We've saved the roof and Master Felix is on the sea that's the Home Ruler. Holy Saints, a grand man that would set himself right too.'

Felix's coming had been reported every day that week; but this time it was true. He was on the way. His boat from Liverpool made a good passage and at nine the next morning she was off Sandy Point, at the mouth of the great sea lough where she blew her horn for tenders. Steamers usually stopped opposite Dunvil, a small market town near the lough-mouth, to land passengers for Annish.

It was raining, but Felix was already on deck; to see for the first time in twelve years the first view of Annish which always seemed to him, because he loved it, the most beautiful in the world.

From this point it was like a high, mountainous island, shaped like a driving cog-wheel of an old-fashioned horse-mill, whose hub was the top of Knockeen, rusty like old iron; whose sloping spokes or stays were the ribs of high ground between the streams; and whose black, oily cogs were the wet points of rock projecting into the dark green of the Atlantic. All the colours, under the drifts of fine rain blowing like smoke across them, were darkly brilliant like leaves and stones under water.

As the steamer turned slowly round Sandy Point, the rocky cogs of Annish seemed to revolve northwards; the tender could already be seen creeping out from Dunvil.

When Felix turned again to walk the deck, he gave a sigh.

It seemed to him tragic that anyone having been born and brought up in a country so beautiful, so worthy to be loved, should not be able to live in it.

These regrets did not show in his face or movements which were always dignified. Felix was a very big man with a large brown beard, a large white nose, bony and sharp-edged; and gold spectacles. He carried himself like John Chass, very upright, but with a slower, heavier dignity.

Felix had early distinguished himself at Oxford, where all his friends predicted for him a great career, and where he had written, while still an undergraduate, a pamphlet called *Schopenhauer and Darwin. The will to live*. This work, published at his own expense, was expected by his friends, and even himself, to have profound effects on science, philosophy, religion and education. It was thought that religion especially could not survive such a revelation of its fundamental untruth. But unluckily nobody noticed its publication except one scientific newspaper which abused young Felix for trying to bring morals into biology; and a church weekly which called him an atheist equally ignorant of religious truth and scientific fact.

Moreover, owing to the excitement of composition, Felix had taken a third-class degree.

Since then he had eaten dinners for the bar, acted as secretary to a Liberal Member of Parliament, written articles in newspapers about science, politics, history and art, and travelled over much of the world. He was now forty-six and still dependent on his father. But he was still considered a man of uncommon sagacity, his good sense, his wide knowledge, almost as much as his imposing figure and large beard, his bass voice and spectacles, made him respected wherever he went.

The screw had stopped, the tender, a large open boat, pointed like a whaler at each end, whirled up behind the starboard plates. A rope flew out and fell across the steersman's knees, who belayed it to a thwart so that the big boat was jerked forward like a toy, crashing on the waves. The stewards appeared on the decks, ringing bells.

Felix, standing against the rail, did not hear the bell or see the tender because his eyes were fixed on the water, where a sunray was turning the rollers from hawthorn to absinthe. A broad band of sunlight fell across Annish itself and suddenly the whole dark wet mountain sparkled almost to the top with cottage walls, white glittering points to the edge of the clouds. There was no landskip like it in the world, where the cottages were scattered like daisies in a field.

Felix' rich lips moved under the large moustache. He was saying to himself as a reminder, 'Quite uneconomic.'

'Is that you, Felix?'

Felix turned round and saw before him a tall, thin man about forty years old, with a long, thin neck, hollow cheeks blotched with red like a consumptive's, ragged ginger whiskers, meeting a ragged moustache, and round, popping green eyes; eyes which one would expect in a lunatic.

'Is it James Slatter?'

Slatter gripped his hand and pumped it up and down. 'I came out on the chance to find ye. John Chass told me ye might be here. Be Gawd, you've come in the neck. The ould man will have us destroyed. D'ye know that they had the drums out yesterday and he's still wanting an eviction.'

Slatter spoke with a broad Ulster accent, and anyone, seeing his dirty tweeds and enormous boots, would have taken him for a small farmer. He was in fact among the richest men in the county. Slatter was one of those who made fortunes by buying up the estates of landlords ruined by the boycotts and rent strikes of the land wars, and he had long had his eye on the Corner property.

Felix, on his side, had already resolved to sell. He saw that any other course would be stupid, considering the political situation, the debts on the property, his own debts and his responsibilities to the family, especially Cleeve. He was determined that Cleeve at least should have a first-class education and the chance of happiness and success in the world. He did not like Slatter, but as he had said to his wife, 'Business is business, especially in this commercial age, and if that lunatic Slatter is prepared to buy the castle, I ought to jump at the chance.

He shook hands warmly with the dealer, in the way of business, and said, 'How are you, James?'

'We'd be well enough,' Slatter said, after a long description of his physical and political misfortunes, 'if they would only lave us alone. Lave us alone. That's all we're asking in Annish.'

They were sitting in the big boat which now seemed small under the steamer's side. It jumped under Felix while he gazed at the shore where rocks, cottages, bogs passed rapidly to the south until the castle bay opened. Castle Corner stood dazzling in the sun against the dark trees of the little park; a neat white house, with a grey slate roof. It seemed to stand in the sea. From one side a long wing ran out to barns and stables; from the other a small balustraded terrace.

Felix thought, 'What a setting for a house—and what a perfect house for the setting; and he felt that pain which belongs to the special grief of the exiled; who lose something more and nearer to them than any living kin.

'It's what the roof would fall on ye if ye coughed in the hall,' Slatter was saying.

'It's not the roof,' Felix said, reasoning with his own sadness, 'but Home Rule, for after that no one would buy the place.'

'Home Rule,' Slatter bawled. A look of terror and anger came into his eyes. 'There'll never be Home Rule. Nobody wants it.'

'Even now,' Felix murmured, 'I can't imagine why any man in his senses should invest in Irish land.'

But Slatter was not listening to him. 'Why can't they lave us alone?' he asked. His bulging eyes stared at Felix with angry wonderment. 'What ails them that they can't lave us alone?'

Felix well understood Slatter's feelings of bewilderment and disgust at the changes taking place in the world. He himself had the same feelings; and he would have liked to enjoy his life in peace. But unlike Slatter he understood why nothing could be left alone, why all over the world the same changes were taking place, smashing up all the old ways of life good and bad, customs, religions, economic systems, by a force as irresistible as that of a moving mountain; and he knew that this tremendous blind thrust, released by education and science, would go on until the whole world, as seen by Slatter, was overwhelmed and new forces had come to a new equilibrium.

This feeling of the impermanence of all that he saw about him never left Felix. It made him feel helpless. He was a Fabian and a Socialist; he had written and spoken for the social revolution; but he could not help noticing that the revolution, of which the social revolution was only a part, was very much more powerful than any of those who tried to direct it. What could men do in an earthquake.

'Why can't they lave us alone, Felix?'

'I suppose it's human nature that's the trouble.'

'Human nature be dahmed. It's that ould devil Gladstone.'

They had reached the old wooden pier at Dunvil, beloved of every Annishman, and Felix was gazing at the huge stones, covered with green slime, heaped between its black timbers to anchor them against the tides. The sound of the waves breaking among the stones and echoed from the deck above, affected him as certain notes of music touch the nerves, making people cry or thrill in spite of themselves.

With his good, wise air he climbed the pier. Several fishermen took off their caps, a crowd charged upon him. It was a deputation. Con, Padsy, Kitty, old Egan and a dozen of their cousins and children, all shouting together greetings, blessings and appeals. Kitty took his left hand and Dan his right. Kitty raised his hand between hers as if she would kiss it.

Felix did not understand at first what they wanted of him. He was too much surprised to find himself remembered.

Slatter bawled from behind, 'I've me own broom waitin' on ya.'

'But what can I do?' Felix asked Padsy.

'You won't let us be put out.'

Felix had forgotten that such rags existed and such appealing voices. 'But what chance have any of you on Knockeen? Take my advice and go to America. That's the place for a worker.'

'Oh, Master Felix, ye'll spake for me.'

Felix knew very well the danger of beginning his visit of reconciliation by a quarrel with his father. He shook his head and made for the brougham. 'Spake for us, Master Felix,' Padsy cried through the window as they drove away.

The voices mixed with the waves beneath the pier and all belonged to a past that he must put away. When had he first stared under the pier at the churning of the black waves on the green rocks?

'Yes, Irish land's done,' Felix said, mournfully admonishing himself. Slatter was in a rage. His green eyes bulged with contempt. He hated Felix for frightening him with Home Rule; but he despised him still more for depreciating his own property. 'But tell me this—if ye want to keep your money safe, what do ye buy. Isn't it land rents and mortgages and houses, and what's them but land?'

Felix said nothing. His silences contributed much to his reputation for wisdom. No man looked wiser in silence. He was trying to recall at what age he had fallen off the steps of Dunvil wooden pier into the sea. He distinctly remembered the slap of the green wave, and the grip of his father's thin strong hand, saving his life.

'What else is there that's safe?' Slatter shouted.

'Mosi Company,' Felix answered gravely.

Slatter was too astonished to speak.

'African produce,' Felix said. 'Soap and ointment. What's safer than a company providing universal wants?'

'Gawd's sakes,' Slatter exclaimed. 'African produce.'

'I daresay I could get you a share, James. I have an introduction to the directors.'

'I'm sure ye would,' Slatter said. 'Aw, and I'm sure there's a fortune in it if you're in it. For ye always knew your way about the world.'

The irony was wasted on the big man who did not even hear it. He was listening for the first sound of the castle gravel, the loose sea gravel of every Irish country house, under the wheels.

Just as the Foys and Egans received Felix as a saviour, so when he reached the castle everybody ran to the hall with excited and relieved faces. Old John, coming to receive his son, had an expectant and affectionate smile.

Cleeve, who thought his father the wisest and greatest man in the world, kept running round his legs like a puppy, catching sometimes a hand, sometimes his coat.

Mrs. Felix, kissing her husband eagerly, cried, 'At last—and quite time. Cleeve has been impossible——'

Felix greeted everybody with his grave, thoughtful air and said nothing. Then he looked round him and opened his lips. Everyone was silent.

'You've changed the pictures,' he said.

Everyone looked round at the pictures as if their arrangement had suddenly become significant. Felix, however, said no more about the pictures. He looked thoughtful and pinched Cleeve's ear, causing him to wriggle with delight.

The whole family conducted him to the drawing-room and drinks were brought. He chose brandy and soda, and John Chass, who always drank whisky and water, asked for a brandy and soda. John Chass kept smiling at his brother and his smile, though it was still gay and confident, appeared suddenly respectful and even shy, the smile of a dependent.

John Chass had been told that Felix would sell the property. Everybody in Annish knew that he had always declared his intention of doing so and Slatter had said a dozen times to John Chass, 'What'll ye do, Jawn, when ye lose your jawb.'

John Chass had always answered, 'I'll have to get another.'

But obviously he did not believe that he would be separated from his pleasant life at Castle Corner. He had no reason for this faith which was simply the confidence of a child, who, because it is alive and happy, imagines without question that fire won't burn it or water drown. John Chass' providence was the original providence, the original faith of life itself, the living cell. He said cheerfully to Felix, 'There's not many arrears nowadays. Except on Knockeen of course. But we mustn't talk business now,'

Felix said nothing and looked wise. He was feeling confused and sad.

The old man said in his thin voice, 'You heard of the trouble with the Foys?'

Felix took a sip, threw up his grand head and said, 'The Foys.' He was not going to be drawn into an argument.

'The farm is scattered all over the hill,' old John said, 'and Padsy could never make anything of it.'

'Poor Padsy.' Felix gave a mild sigh. 'I'm sorry for Padsy, and really I suppose if Con went there'd be no harm in letting Padsy stay. It's poor soil, but Padsy will break his heart if he loses it.'

Old John was much surprised. He frowned. But plainly he did not like to refuse Felix at this moment of reconciliation. He said at last, 'It could be managed, I suppose.'

John Chass, Mary, full of surprise and admiration, looked at Felix. Mrs. Felix looked round with an air of pride. Felix himself was looking out of the window. He sighed and raised his beard.

'And I suppose it's all the same in the long run,' he said, 'for the whole system is done for. Even land purchase isn't a real cure—though of course it's the best way out for the landlords.'

'Land purchase,' old John said in surprise. 'You wouldn't want us to sell?'

'The sooner the better I should say—before Home Rule comes.'

'Sell out.' The old man's surprise and indignation were plain, but such was Felix' prestige that no one perceived any danger. Everyone, including Felix, was calm and thoughtful. Cleeve said, 'You've got a new tie, Daddy.'

Old John, after a moment's thought, got up and left the room. He was greatly agitated. Half an hour later, he ordered the carriage and went into Dunvil, and from Dunvil to Dunderry.

There was now some slight alarm in the castle. Mary Corner disappeared into her own room, John Chass went out with a fishing rod, Mrs. Felix lost her temper with Cleeve and demanded that he should be beaten.

Felix now also showed signs of anxiety and concern, but this was on account of Cleeve. Felix's chief interest in life was Cleeve's education. He saw in the boy intelligence, affection, vitality, a gay spirit very easy to lead by sense and kindness; and he was ambitious for him. The idea of beating Cleeve always horrified him. On the other hand, it was bad for the child to see his parents quarrel, and it would be still worse for him if Clara, as she had threatened, demanded a separation and took Cleeve with her.

This difficulty had occurred a hundred times and always threw Felix into extreme distress; nothing depressed him so much.

It was solved in the usual way. After several hours' reflection, he sent for the boy to the bedroom and appealed to his good sense. He explained why the authority of mothers must be supported and why, therefore, small boys had to be beaten.

Cleeve did not at first agree.

'But, Daddy, I didn't do anything.'

'After all, you know it's not nearly as bad as the dentist.'

'But, Daddy, I do so hate being beaten.'

33

Felix, weakening every moment, hastily bent him over his knee and said, 'And you'll be brave, won't you?'

He then gave him four smacks with a slipper, hard enough to satisfy Mrs. Felix who was listening on the stairs.

'There,' Felix said with a deep sigh, 'that's over.' He looked sharply and anxiously at Cleeve. But the boy, out of consideration for his father's feelings, restrained his tears to a grimace or two.

The incident, as usual, greatly increased Felix's love and respect for Cleeve and Cleeve's admiration for his father. He felt how wise and also how big and strong he was.

Old John came home late in the evening; exhausted but in his most cool and formidable temper. The next morning the Foys were evicted by a small party which took them by surprise at dawn, pulled down Con's house and unroofed Padsy's.

Padsy, his old mother and six children went to Dan Egan's. Kitty, sewing a baby's frock at the castle wept so much that Mary Corner ordered her a tonic.

Con was lucky. He got only six months for assaulting the police instead of five years for attempted murder. But it was understood that the Corners did not want to press the case against him.

Old Mr. Corner during the struggle with the Foys had shown un-expected strength; but after the eviction he became very weak. He could not dress himself without help. Only his will was still strong. He would not stay in bed, he continued at work and he refused to see the family doctor from Dunderry. He wanted to die in peace. But he himself made this impossible by an odd stroke of pride. One day John Chass asked him if he had been hurt at the riot; people were saying that he had been hit by a stone; and this rumour made him extremely angry.

Perhaps he was moved by some distant relation of the idea which causes Eastern potentates of divine origin to deny that bullets can wound them; that makes Western kings give out reassuring messages when they are attacked by illness.

He sent at once for young Doctor Hanna to examine him and contradict the rumours, and this was the end of his peace.

Hanna was the young dispensary doctor, lately appointed by old John's influence and perhaps he chose him because he thought that he would do what he was told; but of course to Hanna the case was simply a case; an important one.

He was a tall, raw-boned, red-faced young Dubliner who still had the manners of a student. He affected a kind of brutality and he used to shout at old doddering women, 'Go on then, there's nothing wrong with you at all.'

He was, however, very keen on his work and he would visit his

34

poorest patients twice a day. He would say to some trembling little boy ten miles out on the bog, a creature as wild and easily scared as a mountain hare, 'That's a grand osteo-myelitis ye have—that's an arm that ought to be in Dublin. But what do you care about that?'

He was a sociable young man and he liked to go to parties when he would sing sentimental ballads in a roaring baritone, sometimes with great pathos and sometimes with an exaggerated emphasis which seemed to be making fun of them and himself. In fact, he was in that stage when a man is looking for his place in society but doesn't quite know how to find it or how to adjust himself to it.

Hanna, when he was sent for to the castle, came rushing from Dunvil and his voice began to rumble even in the hall. He boarded the house like an admiral taking charge in wartime. He talked to Mary all the way upstairs, asking her questions and saying, 'Ah yes, ah yes. It's what ye'd expect. Ah well, I'll just have a look.'

But in five minutes he came quietly to her in her own room and said, 'He won't let me examine him at all.'

Consternation had overcome his social improvisations, so that he appeared what he was, a good-natured country boy, inexperienced and simple-minded.

'But what did he say to you, doctor?'

'He just made me look at his back and then he told me to tell everybody that he wasn't hurt anywhere. But, Mrs. Corner, he can't go on like that. He'll have to let me examine him.'

The family saw that Hanna must be given his rights and Mary interceded for him. The old man submitted at last in order to save himself from more trouble. But he never reconciled himself to the doctor's visits and he would say when he heard his step on the stairs, 'Is that the young man again?' with emphasis on the adjective.

'And how are we, Mr. Corner? That's a great pulse ye have now—we're doing grandly the day.'

'Yes, I'm going on well.' No one could tell from the faint voice and expressionless old face whether this was a joke or merely a sop to please Hanna. But one day, after he had been interrupted among his business letters, he seemed forcibly struck by a new idea and he said to Mary, 'What a vanity it all is—vanity of vanities.' His voice included all life, Hanna and the estate business in one item. To old John, the next world was as solid and real as this one. He had a faith which now at its proof surprised Mary and John Chass, who believed themselves to share it. But their surprise showed that in fact their own creed was already dissolving away, attacked by corrosives of whose action they were not even aware.

Mary even tried to console the old man, as if he needed consolation for escaping out of the world of the land-wars into paradise.

35

'But, Papa, it isn't vanity to save us all from the Land League, and pay off the bank.'

'It will all seem very silly to me in another week or so,' he murmured thoughtfully, fixing his eyes on the air.

He was now too feeble to walk but he had himself dressed as usual and every fine afternoon he was carried to the terrace. He would sit there in a long cane chair, with a very tall hat on his head and a plaid across his knees, listening to Mary reading *The Times* or the Bible. Mary was his closest friend in the family because he respected her. One day when she was looking for one of his favourite passages in Isaiah, he said to her, 'I suppose you'll be glad to leave Ireland, Mary?'

It was understood by both of them that she hoped to leave. She wanted above all, if God gave her a child, to bring it up away from Irish conflicts. But she did not like to tell the old man that Castle Corner was exile to her.

'It'll all go,' John said in his faint voice.

'Good gracious, Papa, you mustn't speak so. Just when you've got us settled again.'

'It'll all go. Felix would sell and Charley would waste it.'

'But, Papa, Felix is a good man of business.'

'Have you found the place, my dear?'

Mary was glad to read for she did not know what to say,

'At that day shall a man look to his maker—
'And he shall not look to the altars, the work of his hands, neither shall he respect that which his fingers have made.
'In the day shalt thou make thy plant to grow—but the harvest shall be a heap in the day of grief.
'The nations shall rush like the rushing of many waters—but God shall rebuke them and they shall flee far off, and shall be chased as the chaff of the mountains before the wind.'

It was a fine August afternoon, with a breeze from the lough scarcely strong enough to bend the dry flower stalks of the grass between the flagstones. The waves breaking below the shore were so small that they could not be noticed above the smooth water until they suddenly lapped upon the stones. The boys, home for the summer, were shouting somewhere in the grounds. Cleeve's voice could be heard shrieking, 'Oh, good, oh, awfully good. Do it again.'

'And like a rolling thing before the whirlwind—
'And behold at eventime trouble and before the morning he is not.'

Mary paused at the end of the verse, and the old man meditated for a long time, then he said softly, 'Remind me, my dear, to remind Charley about the new handle for the chaff-cutter.'

36

His mind was continually on estate business and he still read all letters and gave all directions.

He spent an hour one afternoon arranging with John Chass for the cutting of a new drain on Knockeen moss; which left him so exhausted that he could not speak. Mary seeing his lips move bent down and heard him whisper, in an apologetic tone, 'A waste of time.'

He looked round at the shining water, the balustrade, the bowing grass stems and then towards the end of the house, the drawing-room doors and his own rooms above, shook his head and whispered with profound conviction, 'Vanity of vanities.' Then after a long pause he turned his small, shrunken face towards Mary and said in a stronger voice, 'It's a bad world—I wouldn't live my life again—even with all God's help. How can anyone live in such a world without God? Felix may try but he won't succeed. No, these young people—they can't understand. But when they do they'll be glad to come back to God.'

It was understood at last between him and Mary that he wanted to die and she did not trouble him with encouragements; but to visitors he used the formula that he had discovered. He said that he was going on well.

James Slatter in these weeks was in such excitement that he seemed drunk. He was one of those men, common enough in Ireland, who are always in a simmering condition. He would rush in every day to stare at old John and cry, 'Aw, Mr. Corner, it's turble to see ye like this. Wouldn't ye get a specialist. Thon Hanna's nawthin' but a play boy. But faith I brought one down for one of me gyurl's whoopin' cough at ten guineas and I had her put under the tinker's ass for a shilling and which of the asses cured her I couldn't tell ye.'

He would waylay Hanna in the drive for the latest bulletin, which was usually bad. Hanna always took a bad view of his patients when he was not speaking to them.

Thus Slatter grew every day more hopeful and as he was a perfectly honest and simple man he did not try to hide his feelings.

He would rush up from the castle to the rectory, where his nephew Philip Feenix lived, and burst in with the exclamation, 'He's done, Philly—he won't last the week.'

Philip Feenix was the son of the rector. He was a good-looking boy of sixteen, quick and friendly, very popular everywhere, and Slatter was devoted to him. For years he had boasted about his good looks and intelligence saying, 'The wee boyo has everything in the world—looks and brains. Begob, a real bit of blood.'

Slatter's father had been a farmer and the Feenixes were from the south, but Slatter had found a pedigree joining them to some ancestors of the Corners. Slatter had a great admiration for that family and especially for John Chass.

'It's a queer thing,' he would say, 'but the wee boyo grows like the Corners. He has the profeel of John Chass already. But it's what ye might expect.'

No one saw this likeness except Slatter who perhaps wished his adored Philip to be a Corner for the same reason that he had set his heart on owning the castle.

Slatter, who was a widower with two daughters, had tried to adopt Philip in order to make him his heir. Old Feenix, who did not care for his brother-in-law, had prevented the adoption, but he could not prevent him from showering the boy with presents and carrying him off every day to his own house. He had had to allow Slatter to pay for Philip's education at an English public school because he dared not disappoint the boy by a refusal. Thus Philip was already more Slatter's than Feenix's; he admired and respected his old father, but he was far happier with Slatter, who gave him everything he wanted, and talked to him on equal terms.

Slatter's passion for the boy had never known reticence. He had always told him his hopes and fears, his clever deals; the latest jokes at the magistrate's meeting; but during these weeks when old John was dying, and he saw the castle property at last within his reach, he was like a young girl in the first excitement of love. He walked about smiling or frowning at his thoughts, and he thought of something new every minute, which had to be told to Philip.

He was in terror for one afternoon that old John would get well. He had no reason for his belief except that a pig dealer in Connell's bar reminded him that old John's grandfather had lived to ninety, but it sent him flying to the rectory for the consolation of his darling's company. Another day he woke up with the conviction that Philip would go into the church.

Young Philip had once talked of going for a missionary. He was an adventurous boy who liked the idea of foreign parts and he had a natural ambition for glory. About fifteen, when he began to distinguish himself in the second eleven as a slow bowler, he thought much of the glory of the missionary, and he would have liked to give his life for Christ.

He saw himself going up some African shore, with the cross in his hand, among savages, and then they would spear him or preferably torture him to death while he smiled at them and forgave them in Christ's name; he felt his strong love rush out towards the savages while they laughed at his agony.

Feenix was eager to see his son in the Church of Ireland, and he had begun in the last year or two to direct his mind towards the problems of faith, and their correct answers.

Father and son would sit in the musty dark study of the rectory, which was a dark, damp little house under the trees behind Ballycorner church, and Feenix would deliver his exposition.

Feenix was a very tall, thin man of sixty, with a long thin face. His face always had the same expression of calm melancholy and he spoke with a mellow, sleepy voice like the lower notes of a wood-pigeon.

'We see therefore why God, ómni-pótent as we must believe Him, created the world full of evil and cruelty. For without evil, there would be no overcoming of evil, no moral triumph.'

Feenix, who had lost his pretty young wife in the first year of marriage, who himself had been buried alive in Annish for thirty years, spoke eloquently about the triumph over suffering.

'The typical glory of the Christian and the highest experience possible to mankind.'

Philip sitting with a serious, reverent expression, feeling that his life of devotion had already begun, would look out of the window at the damp garden under the dripping trees, where every kind of weed flourished and every useful shrub, vegetable or flower rotted away, and think of glittering strands.

'But it is the éscható-logy, the four last things: Death, Judgement, Heaven and Hell—absolutely necessary as we see, to complete the scheme of Divine Justice and goodness, when as the preacher says, all tears shall be wiped away——'

Philip reflected dreamily, 'I must choose a rocky place for the landing—they would want a memorial church and it couldn't stand on sand.'

Slatter went regularly to Church and he admired his brother-in-law's learning and goodness.

'Aw, a real scholar,' he would say. 'There's the manny to twist the Pope's tail.'

But he also despised parsons for their poverty and their virtue, which prevented them from being fine fellows like his ideal, John Chass. He despised Feenix especially whose stipend was very small and virtues great.

'The ould stick,' he would shout. 'The haff of him is hell-fire and the rest is German blather.'

He used to warn Philip against the Church and his father's wiles. Slatter looked upon the Church as a trap; and he was suspicious of all services; including the civil service and the army. He thought of them all as traps set to catch fools or innocents and use them.

'Ye know, Philly,' he would say, 'ye have to look out for yourself in this world—once a parson, always a parson, and the parsons is like ould maids—they'll always be telling ye that they wouldn't be anything else for the world and that there's no blessedness like being without a man,' he winked. 'It's just that ye need to keep your eyes open.'

On the afternoon when, after three whiskies with John Chass at Connells, he had the sudden conviction, arising from nothing, that Philip would be a parson after all, he climbed to the rectory in such a hurry that he arrived speechless. As usual, he went to the study window, and poked in his head.

No one would have expected to find father and son in the study at that hour, but they were there; and Slatter felt at once that providence had sent him for a purpose. This must be a critical interview. In fact, Feenix had been talking about the moral consciousness and Philip had been dozing a little. At the sight of his uncle's red dripping face and alarmed eyebrows, he jumped up and said, 'Here's uncle.'

Feenix was already looking at Slatter over his spectacles, with tranquil resignation. 'Good afternoon, James,' he said.

'What are ye doing in there on a day like this,' Slatter cried. 'Aw, come on out, Philly, come on over—haven't seen ye for a week.'

Philip, who had been at Carnmore every day of the holidays, and who had undertaken to spend that afternoon at home, looked at his father. Feenix, seeing the eagerness in the boy's face, said, 'Don't stay here for me, Philip—I may go out myself.'

'There'y 'are, Philly, your father doesn't want ya,' Slatter cried, and as soon as they were in the fields together, walking towards Carnmore, he squeezed the boy's arm and said, 'Ah, these old wans can't be bothered with boys—they'd liever be at their books.'

Carnmore, built by Slatter on his marriage twenty years before, was a big square barrack, painted butter yellow, with chocolate drip stones. It was like a giant doll's house and everything about it glittered with paint and polish, its brass doorstep, its windows, its new London furniture and gilt frames. Slatter admired it greatly and he had often remarked that what the castle wanted was a lick of paint.

Now standing in front of it with Philip and squeezing the boy's arm, he said to him slyly, 'That's better than any of your rectories and your bishoprics, too, or whatever them fellas live in with the wee skirts.'

Philip looked pensive. He did not want to be a rector or a bishop, but a missionary. Slatter looked at him with tender anxiety, clutching his arm and stooping down to his level. 'And ye know, Philly, when ould Jawn goes, I'll have the cassle. I have the option of it now from thon fule Felix. And what I have is for you, Philly. Mind that now.'

Philip said nothing. His ideas at that time demanded poverty rather than riches, and Africa rather than Annish.

'Aw, Philly, there's no whale could swally Jonah or much else of what they tell ye.'

40

The boy flushed slightly. 'Father says the whale was a ship.'

'A ship—haw, haw—but it's their jawb, ye know, their jawb to think them things up.'

Old John grew so weak at last that he submitted to go to bed; but he remained calm and busy up to the last day of his life. Half an hour before he died, when Mary was reading to him from his favourite psalm eight, he held up his hand and beckoned John Chass to bend down his ear to his lips. John Chass heard the whisper, 'Don't forget the big drain on the moss——'

John Chass assured him that the drain would be dug out that very day, and he made a signal to Mary, who continued, 'What is man that thou art mindful of him, and the son of man that thou visited him.'

Old John's lips moved again, but no one ever knew whether he said drain or amen. It might have been either.

The will was to be read on the afternoon of the funeral, and Cleeve was told to go for a walk on the shore with his cousin Harry Jarvis.

Harry Jarvis was another Corner cousin. His parents were in India and he spent his holidays at Castle Corner. He was a short fair slim boy with a hook nose and very blue eyes; and already, since he was to be a soldier, he carried himself with a swagger. He also used very bad language and he would say to Cleeve, 'Curse my soul if you aren't the bloodiest little blithering idjit in the universe—excuse me, old chap, if I express myself in a friendly manner.'

Cleeve worshipped Harry who seemed to him the bravest and the wisest of beings.

Harry was fond of practical jokes. He had sent Cleeve to ask the cowman for a pint of pig's milk and he and Philip once shut him up in the old oven at Carnmore and forgot him, so that he was discovered half suffocated. But these attentions only increased Cleeve's love, like that of a puppy who is walked on.

Cleeve, on the funeral day, found Harry still in his blacks with a bowler hat on his head, walking through the yard carrying a fishing rod.

'Where are you going, Harry?'

'Shooting,' Harry said. His pale thin face, which had by nature a resolute expression, was marked by tears. Harry though fifteen years old had wept violently at the graveside. This had surprised people who had not supposed that he loved his grandfather so much. Harry himself had been surprised and now he disdained to wash his face; he was in a mood of defiance.

'But can you?' Cleeve asked.

Harry said nothing and walked down the drive. Cleeve, still feeling shy of fishing on a funeral day, said, 'Perhaps Philip could come, too.'

'We don't want a bloody mob.'

41

But Cleeve ran into Carnmore and brought out Philip also in deep black. Luckily Slatter was out. He was mouching about the castle to catch Felix as soon as the will was read.

Philip would not fish but he agreed to join the party and the two Slatter girls came with him.

Margaret and Constance Slatter were then fifteen and twelve. They were brown girls with brown eyes; Margaret, or Maddy, had a sharp nose and little eyes which gave her a quick, sharp look in contradiction to her buxom figure. Constance, or Coo, who had a small flat nose and big eyes like a cat, was a dreamy little girl. Their lives were incredibly dull. They never went away and their only treat was tea at the castle or sometimes a trip to Dunderry. Slatter had a great contempt for his girls and once when he came upon them unexpectedly at the castle, having tea in Mary Corner's sitting-room, and sitting close together on the old broken horse-hair sofa, with their scones in their hands and their feet turned under them, he had shouted, 'Gawd's sakes, look at the ould maids.'

But Maddy and Coo thought themselves lucky girls to have such a rich father and a good house. He told them so himself and they believed him.

All the children were excited by the funeral and this accentuated their characters and made them talkative and affectionate. They walked up the lane all talking at once, except Harry, and huddled together as if joined by a bond.

They described to each other the funeral, though they had all seen it, repeating the same things over and over again. As children they were all interested in facts. They felt the importance of them; not as facts but as means to their own security and happiness.

'The gloves gave out,' Maddy said.

'But Pappy took three pairs,' Coo said.

'Can you take as many as you like?' Cleeve asked.

'Mr. Felix didn't wear a band on his hat,' Philip said.

Harry was in the middle and the two girls who had been in love with him for years pressed against him at each side and even inclined their heads towards him. Cleeve stumbled at his heels and Philip walked half in front of Maddy, with his shoulder almost touching her chin.

They passed a cart full of the tenants from the funeral; farmers in tall bowlers and their wives in black bodices as hard and solid as coal scuttles. Harry swore and said, 'It was my own grandpapa—so why shouldn't I fish.'

He objected to the farmers staring at him. Maddy boldly pressing his arm said, 'Never mind them, what do they know.'

Maddy had no shame in her love for Harry. She was always taking his arm, or putting her hands in his pockets, and pressing herself up against him. She didn't know why she shouldn't enjoy her love, for Harry did not trouble about it.

'It was a grand funeral,' Coo said with a sigh. 'Far better than the other one.'

'Coo's only seen two funerals,' Maddy said.

'Except dogs.'

'Except dogs.'

Cleeve was talking all the time. He was not so much interested like the girls in hats and gloves; or like Philly, in the distinguished guests; but in the fact that his grandfather had not wanted to live his life over again. He had heard Mary Corner tell this fact to his father; and his father answer that he was not surprised.

But Cleeve was astounded. He wanted also to enjoy the pleasure of giving the information to the rest and astonishing them. Nobody paid any attention to Cleeve's shrill outcries. But they were nevertheless recorded by the ears of the unlisteners and Philip suddenly said, 'They're saying Mr. Corner was glad to die.'

This fact from Philip was so interesting that it caught everybody's attention. It produced a silence while all the children examined it, judged it and tried to feel its significance for themselves.

'He was so lonely,' Maddy suggested, 'and old, too.'

'He wasn't happy in himself.'

'Perhaps it wasn't true—you know the tales they tell.'

'Anty Jinny at the other funeral had a wooden foot,' Coo said. Coo's remarks were unexpected because her mind hopped the intervening train of thought. But her friends understood her. Philip said, 'Aunty Jinny was an old maid.'

They had reached the first pool in a hollow among rough grass and tufts of rushes, a field belonging to old Dan. Two miserable cows which could find nothing to eat stood and watched the children from a distance with stupid, mournful eyes. The clouds which had been a light bluish-grey like pigeon wings, were now thickening into an opaque yellow grey like new spun raw wool.

'All her life she was unhappy,' Maddy said.

'Then it was her own fault,' Philip said severely. Harry pushed his bowler to the back of his head and threw his fly across the pool.

'Women are different,' he said. The two girls looked at him. Coo's eyes seemed enormous with enquiry.

All except Cleeve had reached the age a little beyond that of confidence. Cleeve, like puppies, kittens and small children, was sure of happiness as of air and light. Life itself secretly assured him of it. But the others had begun to notice other people, even grown-up people, as separate persons and to see that they sometimes failed to enjoy their lives.

43

'Poor Anty Jinny was poor, too,' Coo said.

'What difference does that make,' Philip said. 'Missionaries are poor, but that is the happiest life you can have.'

'There are four hundred million heathen in China,' Cleeve said, but no one paid any attention to him.

The clouds had turned brown and at the same time Knockeen mountain behind darkened to a strong blue and seemed to come nearer with a sharper edge; so as to hang over the dirty, worn-out field. The field was now as dark as sea moss; a dark green so thick it seemed to throw green fire into the cold heavy air. Large drops fell into the pool, making circles like rises. Cleeve protested. 'But it's raining.' He hated rain like a cat. Philip turned up his collar and looked at the sky with indignant surprise. The two girls drew together and Coo, apprehensive of thunder, took her sister's hand.

'We ought to go in,' Maddy said, as the eldest girl present, responsible for clothes and health. But no one could make up his mind to leave the rest.

'That was why Anty Jinny was an old maid, because she was so poor,' Coo said.

'She could have married a missionary if she'd been good enough.'

'It's not raining on me here,' Cleeve said, under a small bush. No one answered him, but after a moment they gathered under the bush, all except Harry. He with his pale face and the stains of tears still under his eyes, continued to fish. It was obvious that he was ready to get wet.

Maddy and Cleeve looked at him with admiration; Coo with wonder. Philip stood frowning. He was still troubled by the suggestion that old John had not enjoyed life. He knew that he had been a good Christian and a good man, greatly esteemed by his father, so that his unhappiness could not have been a punishment.

Slatter, having made an excuse to call at the castle for an umbrella at four o'clock, was probably the first person outside the family to hear the stupendous news that the whole Corner property had been left to John Chass.

Felix had only a legacy of five thousand pounds and the forgiveness of debts amounting to another five thousand.

Slatter went straight to Carnmore, where he knew Philip was to have tea. He wanted to tell him about this catastrophe, and on the way he told everyone he met, farmers, labourers, even a man breaking stones at the corner of Knockeen lane.

'D'ye know what—old Jawn has left the cassle to Master Jawn Chass.'

He rushed into Carnmore bawling 'Philly, Philly,' and when he was told that the children had gone out with Master Harry, he burst out, 'Couldn't he wait then?'

He jumped on the outside car which had taken the servants to the funeral, and made the man drive along the lane until, standing up in his seat, he caught sight of Harry's bowler and the black coats under a bush.

'Aw, that's the way of it—what do they care for anybody,' he cried, as if appealing to heaven. He jumped down and rushed at them through the whins, with his swinging, crouching walk which was like a ploughman's. 'So that's how ye go, Harry, fishing, and your granddad's eyes not cold. But what's the good of talkin' to ye, the way your anty spoils ye.'

Harry, without paying any attention to the man, made another cast among the circles of rain on the pool, which had turned as black as the mountain. Slatter turned upon Philip. 'Philip, arn't ye ashamed of yourself—in your blacks. Get along with ye.'

Philip, like other affectionate and generous boys, had his pride. He did not like to be abused; and now he did not hurry to move. But Slatter, turning crimson with rage, suddenly bawled at him, 'Aw, Philly, ye're the grand man then, but who bought your Sunday suit. Go wan then, go wan to Afriky, whenever ye like. Go wan and be the Holy nose among the niggers—the sooner the better.'

Philip, red with astonishment, now went to the car, followed by the two girls. But the whole way home Slatter continued to shout at him, 'I'll not keep ye, go wan then, the sooner the better.'

At Carnmore, in the drawing-room, he brought the whole party to tears. Philip kept on repeating, 'But I don't understand,' and Maddy cried, 'Oh, Pappy, he didn't mean for to leave ye.'

'Go wan then,' Slatter yelled, crimson and perspiring. His tall hat, almost entirely covered by its black band, was still on his head. He moved his long arms in a frenzy of despair and protest. 'I don't want ye, I don't give a dahm for anny of ya.'

Maddy clung to him on one side and Coo on the other, crying, 'Oh, Pappy, he didn't mean it.'

At last he rushed out of the room. Maddy then explained to the bewildered Philip, 'It's because he's so fond of ye, Philly.'

Afterwards, in fact Slatter came to Philip at the rectory and apologized. He shed tears and said, 'Aw, Philly, it's because I love ye, I wouldn't have ye wasted, ya see.'

Philip was astonished to see this tall, whiskered man in tears for him. He felt his responsibility towards him, and he saw that it would not be possible for him to be a missionary. But he gave up the plan easily out of affectionate gratitude to the man who loved him, and even depended on his love.

45

Old John's will astonished the countryside as well as the family. Mrs. Felix wanted to go to law against John Chass and Mary, and Felix was more astonished than anybody else, so that for once he showed an extraordinary agitation. He was impatient with his wife and walked about with hasty steps; his nose was pink with anger and his eyes had the expression of surprise and dismay that one sees in those of an animal which has received an unexpected wound.

'Of course this must be your home,' John Chass said. Felix went out for a walk. Everybody was in consternation.

But he came back full of energy and resolution. 'The luckiest thing that ever happened to me,' he said. 'But I'm sorry for you, Charley.' He looked benevolently at John Chass through his spectacles. 'Take my advice and sell out now. Otherwise it's a life imprisonment. Land's done, Charley. Business is the only thing. And we've got to think of our families.'

His proposal was that John Chass having sold out, should join him in a West African business, and he pointed out the enormous profits which were to be made in African produce.

'The Mosi Company wants capital, I know, and one could probably get in there.'

'It'll need considering,' John Chass said.

'We've no time to wait if we want to get into the Mosi. In business, you know, time is money.'

Felix was so impatient to start his new life as a business man that he would not wait for John Chass to make up his mind. He wrote at once to the directors of the Mosi Company, which had been advertising for additional capital. He was greatly pleased when they sent him a warm invitation to meet them.

Felix had visited the coast but he had not heard of the Mosi Company there. His opinion of its prospects was founded on an advertisement in a financial newspaper and as he said, he wanted fuller information.

The senior partner, a Captain Braun, lived at Cheltenham. He was a little round-faced man with pink cheeks and a white moustache, who admitted, in the first minutes of Felix' call, that he had inherited his share of the business, and did not know much about it. His deference to the visitor as a business-man amused Felix, who thought, 'And this is how our business is run, by directors who don't know the difference between a balance sheet and a profit and loss account.'

They sat in a small, high but well-proportioned room in an Italian villa which opened by a flight of steps upon a neat garden. The garden was full of roses and delphiniums; bright-coloured flowers which with the short, well-watered grass and the new gravelled paths gave an effect of gaiety and security. Felix's eyes turned continually to this charming

English garden. He had never had time to have a garden but now he thought, 'When I have made enough to retire, I shall arrange to have a garden like that opening from my room.'

'I suppose this room is due south,' he said, looking at the sun which fell on the round table covered with the official papers.

'South-west—nice outlook, isn't it? Are you fond of gardening?'

'Not gardening. But I like a garden.'

Felix turned over a paper. 'And this is the last report.'

'Last but one. You see that gross profits were up, but expenses went up, too. I don't know if that's the rule, I don't understand these things.'

'It's very common,' Felix said. 'It's what you'd expect.' He read the paper with a frown, throwing up his head with a critical air. Then he laid it down and said, 'I can smell the roses from here, charming—charming.'

This interview gave Felix a very favourable view of the Mosi Company, but he took care not to show it. He said that he could not make a decision until he had seen the other partner, Mr. Wilkie. 'As you know, Captain,' he added smiling, lest the captain should feel hurt by this suspicious policy, 'in business we go on Descartes' principle of doubting everything until it is proved—even your excellent company.'

Mr. Wilkie, the junior partner, lived at Wimbledon. He was much older than Braun; a pale, gloomy little man who had bitter complaints against the markets and the Government policy in Africa. When Felix discovered from the last printed report, already a year old, that the company had made a loss in that year, he said, 'It's an up and down trade, Mr. Corner, as you know, and we have a great deal to contend with.' He seemed almost ready to cry. Felix had to encourage him by pointing out the enormous prospects of the West coast trade.

'Yes, there are prospects, and risks too. Big risks, as you know, Mr. Corner. Look at that loss of a whole year's trade because the people would rather fight each other than sell their nuts or hire their dugouts.'

'A business like this depends on transport,' Felix pointed out, 'and I am inclined to suspect if you'll excuse me, Mr. Wilkie, that your transport wants reorganization.'

Mr. Wilkie agreed. But reorganization needed capital, and capital was scarce on the Mosi. People were afraid of the risks.

'There's always risks,' Felix said, and he added with a faint habitual sigh, 'There's not much security anywhere these days.'

They reviewed the finances of the company. Mr. Wilkie said that it needed at least ten thousand pounds new capital. But Felix was not perturbed. He knew his Annish farmers who always asked three times what they expected. He suggested that three thousand would be ample both for new stock and new transport.

Negotiations lasted several weeks and they were twice broken off by

Felix himself, who having discovered that the company had had a bad half-year, seized his chance to drive a hard bargain.

'It seems rather unfair,' he wrote to John Chass, 'to take advantage of them, but *à la guerre comme à la guerre*, as Mary would say. And if you'd like to edge in another thousand, I'm pretty sure I could arrange it.'

The final bargain was struck in October. Felix and John Chass between them invested six thousand pounds, and Felix secured the appointment of local agent, at five hundred a year pay with commission. He sailed at once, for he was anxious to see the company's properties; and especially to get rid of the local agent, a certain Major Kentish, who had not even sent a report for the last year.

II

FELIX LEFT ENGLAND in November, 1890, with three thousand pounds' worth of stores, and reached Mosi mouth on the fourth of October. Kentish, ordered to meet him there with a barge to carry the stores, did not appear and, Felix was forced to hire six dugouts to take them up the Mosi, in full flood after the rains.

Felix had once spent two months in a coast town of stores, agencies, where all natives were servants or labourers; cut off on all sides by a web of rivers, whose gloomy waters poured away through the tunnels of the forest, unmapped and often unnamed. He had found beauty in the forest flowers, but none in the rivers. Their gloom, the thickness of their water, their sudden unexpected floods, when they poured away through the dark green tunnels of the forest, was merely strange or terrifying.

Now for day after day he travelled through the gloomiest and thickest of these streams, the Mosi. It was like an immense ditch whose muddy water ran with the smoothness and weight of hot beer between perpendicular walls of dark green, a hundred and fifty feet high.

Nothing was heard or seen except an occasional parrot far up in the green tops of the forest. If there were small birds, their twitterings did not reach down into the underworld where the dugouts crawled like water beetles from morning to dark, and seemed to be still in the same

48

place, opposite the same muddy banks, the same mud-caked trees. No natives were seen except at the stations or on the hulks, which at that time often served for stations on the oil rivers; and every day they became fewer. On the seventh day, only one was reached; a tumble-down mudhouse on a low island, half flooded. This was called the Empire Oils and Transport Company. As Felix' dugouts drew into its rotten landing stage, a thin little white man, bent like a question-mark, was carried out of the house in an armchair made of two packing-cases.

From this chair he grinned down at Felix and called out, 'You're Wilkie and Braun, are you?'

'Mosi Trading Company.'

'Ah, yes, that's what they called it when they sold out to the flats.' He turned back his wasted lips in a grin. 'Sounds better. So you're going up to sack the major.'

'Do you know Major Kentish?'

'Do I? We all know the Major.'

'He doesn't seem to take much interest in his work. The company hasn't had a report from him for a year.'

'I haven't sent a report for four years. Poor old Major—I don't suppose he can write.'

His face with its small bones and flat nose was full of intelligence and malicious amusement. His name was Pepper. He asked Felix to stay as long as he liked, but Felix, who was paying seven pounds a day for transport, would spare time only for a meal.

They sat at table in one end of the big mudhouse, divided from the store by a wall of mats. The floor was uneven mud; at every light puff of the hot wind, a fine golden dust drifted from the thatch roof. Pepper, propped in his deal armchair, fired out his questions.

'Bringing in new capital, that's it, eh?'

'You look as if you needed some capital.'

'We do. We haven't paid a dividend for seven years.'

'Mosi has been paying pretty well.'

'Braun brought in new capital in '86 and he's been getting some back.' Pepper grinned. 'Look at me, I was the flat who brought money to this concern in the same year. They made me local agent at four hundred and commission with leave on full pay. I've never had any pay, but leave—that was the real joke.'

'Haven't you had leave?'

Pepper gave a scream of laughter that turned into a scream of pain. His boys rushed to lift him. Felix saw that his wooden seat was full of round holes, all sizes. Pepper continued to moan while the boys carefully replaced him in his chair.

'I'm afraid you're ill,' Felix said.

'Boils.' Pepper made a grimace.

'If I were you, I'd go home, even if I had to take the fare out of the stock.'

'Stock.' Pepper began to laugh again; the boys approached uneasily. But he suddenly took control of his laugh. 'Stock, there hasn't been any stock for two years.'

'How do you go on?'

'Like this.' Pepper grinned at Felix's surprise. It was delightful to him to see the horror and bewilderment of this large, confident, fresh-faced man. He enjoyed the triumph of every old-timer, over the tenderfoot; and that triumph is always the keener when there are horrors to tell of.

'These chaps keep me,' Pepper nodded towards the boys, 'and the boatmen do a bit, too, farming and fishing.'

'Without pay?'

'Yes, but I look after 'em. If I weren't here they'd soon get chopped up by some of the local tribes, the Mosi chaps are all man-eaters. But they know that if they shoot me, the gunboat may come along to shoot them.'

Pepper mused, grinning at the idea of his own situation. Then suddenly he looked grave and thumped the table. 'All the same, Mr. Corner, there's fortunes to be picked up on the Mosi. I always said so and I stick to it. For a man with capital, real capital.'

'You must have the capital,' Felix agreed with the elation of one who had it. He could hardly wait for the end of the meal, and when Pepper asked for books, anything to read, he could not wait to open a box. He gave him the book from his pocket, a copy of the *Stones of Venice*.

'The *Stones of Venice*,' Pepper said. 'What's that—architecture.' He seemed disappointed, and looking down from his armchair, still supported in the air by the two boys, at Felix in his dugout, he said, 'You haven't got anything about science, have you?'

'I'm afraid not.'

'Pity, I wanted to do a bit of science—keep in touch.'

Felix was paddled away. Looking back, he saw Pepper, aloft in his chair, thoughtfully staring at the *Stones of Venice*. He held the book open in the middle, high in front of his nose, in the attitude of one not yet decided to commit himself to a new course of study.

On the eighth day Felix passed no station at all and no habitation, it was not until the evening of the ninth that his headman, turning to him at a bend in the stream, said, 'Wilkin Braun, sah.'

Felix turned and saw, close to him, the hulk of a schooner lying across shallow water, with a lift of the bow and a list to port, she seemed to be a long low island. She still carried stump masts, and lying canted in the sailing, under bare poles, before a following gale.

50

The dugouts turned and working against the swirl of the current, gradually forced their way round the tail of the island and under the schooner's stern. Felix looking up saw the name, '*Maria Fry*, Bristol.'

From this view the illusion of a ship at sea was spoilt by a landing-stage and several sheds built on piles against the starboard side. Stage and sheds were falling down. Long black holes appeared in the roofs where whole planks were missing and part of the stage was under water. The station appeared like a deserted ruin, half buried in mud and powdered with the tropical dust of rottenness.

Felix gazed in surprise. The canoemen themselves were silent, looking at the desolation with curious faces. The headman gave a loud shout. Half a minute or more after this shout, long after it had died away in muffled echoes down the river, the station was suddenly filled with running, staggering figures hurrying confusedly in all directions.

An old negro, wrapping himself in his cloth as he ran, came six steps towards the stage and then turned back. His cloth fell off and sixty canoemen laughed together with a sound like a bush fire in dry branches. A little white man in a dressing-gown and slippers made a dart from the store and gazed at the boats. He was a short, stout man with a white bald head, pink cheeks and a large white moustache; a head and face that might have belonged to any senior military club or Cheltenham boulevard. At the canoemen's laugh he popped into cover like a startled mouse. A moment later the shining head was seen rising cautiously above the stern rail of the *Maria Fry*.

But as Felix landed on the stage, which was empty, both the old negro and the Major, by a simultaneous inspiration, came running towards him. The old negro held up his cloth with one hand and cried, 'Oh sah, welcome sah, God bless you, Oh Jesus.'

Major Kentish, with dressing-gown flapping round his white legs, was too excited to make himself clear. 'Awfully sorry—touch of fever—no idea—Joe here will explain—Joe—Joe.'

'Majah,' the old negro, grabbing his cloth, turned in the wrong direction.

'Tell this gentleman, Mr. Corner you'll excuse me if I go back—a touch of fever—but Joe knows all about things. Excuse me, you'll have dinner.'

But though the Major thus handed over his responsibilities to Joe, he continued to trot at Felix' heels while they inspected the ruinous stores, the rotting stage, the island itself which seemed to be dissolving into the Mosi.

Felix did not need to criticize this ruin or the Major, who, staring with his round brown eyes at each broken roof and mud pit, exclaimed with a desperate honesty, 'Rotten, isn't it—awful. A perfect disgrace,'

51

and then turning to Felix, he would mutter, as if untrustful of his own excuse, 'The tropics, you know—plays the devil with woodwork.'

He was like a little boy expecting to be beaten and trying to avoid punishment by confessing his fault. Even in his eyes, turned anxiously towards Felix there was a childish fear. Felix already felt the need to stiffen himself against Major Kentish. He said to himself, 'Business is like war—you have to be ruthless.'

'And why is there no oil in store, Major Kentish?'

'No stock, sir. We've been out of stock for eight months. The trouble here, sir, is the want of capital.'

'Yas, sah, we no got nutting—no gin—no clot—not nutting for nobody.'

They entered the ship by a door through the leanto into the hold; where two ladders led to forecastle and cabin. Felix examined the hold, driving his penknife into the rotten timbers. This greatly troubled the Major. 'Superficial,' he burbled, 'she's sound underneath—last a hundred years.'

The cabin was painted white, with muslin curtains on the windows. Four water-colours of African scenes hung on each side of the forward bulkhead; regimental photographs mounted in faded ribbon had been pinned beside the stern windows.

'Not too bad.' The Major looked anxiously at Felix for appreciation. 'Make things homely.' He twitched a curtain straight and looked at the effect. 'Only thing you want is a fireplace.'

He did not ascend to the deck where Felix looked with surprise at an enormous wooden bed erected forward of the mizzen, on the hatch combings. It was about four feet high, eight feet long and six broad. Its net, of white coarse muslin, slung from a sailcloth awning, resembled the large square cover net used to protect soft fruit from birds.

While Felix was staring at this immense bed, he heard a muttering at his elbow, a mutter so faint that it was almost inaudible. 'More homely, you know.'

Felix, looking down, caught again the childish, terrified appeal in the brown eyes, and again he stiffened himself against the Major. 'The boats will have to go back to-morrow, so I'd better write my report at once.'

The Major became incoherent and fluttered round his legs.

'Yes, to-morrow, I suppose so—they can't wait, of course—in the cabin, sir. Yes, ink and paper.'

Felix wrote his report while below, the canoemen unloaded into the hold. At each crash of a case thrown down, the whole ship trembled and Felix' pen jerked. He wrote in short phrases, terse and napoleonic. 'All buildings must be replaced—enormous scope for expansion—the Mosi a veritable artery of commerce—a new launch is absolutely necessary with an efficient engineer. Branch stations should be at once pushed out into the Laka district, at present untouched.'

These phrases, scope for expansion, artery of commerce, which he had never used before and which he would have despised, came to his pen as if they had waited for it on the office paper. They belonged, it seemed, to the very idea of business; and Felix writing them, unconsciously assumed a severe and formidable expression, like a Napoleon of commerce, photographed for the newspapers. Interrupted by a scuffling noise at the door, and urgent whispers, he turned with an impatient, majestic frown. A black girl, thick-set and heavy breasted, with a broad, heavy face deeply marked by small-pox, was kneeling at the doorway. She looked at him with a nervous humble expression, and meeting his eyes, quickly looked down and picked at the rotten fibre of the floor. A small girl of seven or eight, squatting beside her, continued to stare at Felix, wrinkling her eyes as if at a glaring light.

'What do you want?' Felix asked.

The woman crouched lower; the little girl twisted up her face and eyes as if cold water had been dashed against them.

Felix shouted for his boys. At once both Joe and the Major appeared from opposite sides of the door, pushing their heads round the frame. Then old Joe said in a trembling voice, 'This woman wash for you, sah.'

At that time on the coast, washerwomen fulfilled the duties of a mistress; but Felix in his dignity as agent chose to overlook this understanding.

'Do I need a washerwoman?' he asked.

'Oh, I think you'll need somebody, sir, excuse me, such a good chance,' the Major exclaimed.

'How much does she charge?'

'You think six pounds too much?'

'For a month or a year?'

'Oh, sah,' Joe laughed, 'for whole woman. Six pounds for buy her and small girl, too!'

'Do you deal in slaves here?'

'Oh no, sir, excuse me, you don't understand,' the Major fell into panic. 'It was some Laka fellows brought her—she was in the chief's house but she got into some trouble or other. If we don't take her, I'm afraid they'll use her for a sacrifice.'

'Dis one very cheap—fine strong mammy.' Joe pulled the woman to her feet and turned her round, poked her in the breast, sides, thighs. 'Clean strong woman, sah, worth ten pounds, more with chile.'

'She is a slave, in fact.'

'Oh no, excuse me,—lump sum in lieu of wages, call it what you like.' The Major in his desperate effort to explain his feeling that a woman bought by a white man for his mistress was not a slave in the same sense as one bought by a black one for the same purpose, or for labour, became incoherent. His cheeks grew purple, sweat broke out on his white forehead. 'Excuse me, sir—quite a different thing—depends how you treat 'em.'

Felix answered coldly that he could not buy a slave, and the two men withdrew in discouraged silence, pushing the woman and the little girl in front of them.

Dinner he ate alone. The Major, apparently depressed by the rejection of the washerwoman, had retreated to his cabin, opening off the saloon. The cabin had lost its door, and each time Felix' eye fell on it, he saw the dressing-gown with a pair of small pink hands folded across it. The fingers were twitching and jumping, but not a fold of the dressing-gown moved.

'I'll see him after dinner,' Felix reflected and took another stiff whisky. The more he saw of the Major the less he liked the idea of sacking him. The man was so helpless, so obviously inefficient.

It was a clear night. The moon at three-quarters had risen over the forest, but it was not yet high enough to throw its rays on the river. It reached only the trunks of the masts and fell on the opposite cliff of the river gully, turning the precipices of green to the colour of grey screes. The river below could only be heard. It was like the noise of blood heard in a shell.

'An artery of commerce,' was the phrase that came to Felix' mind; but the movement, the noise, the cliff of leaves like stone, the steel-blue sky opaque with the colour of transverse moonbeams broken upon its floating air dust, had nothing to do with commerce. Felix walked quickly to and fro. He was full of the excitement of his enterprise; but it was a free elation. He had written his reports and his letters. 'Dear Charley,' 'My dearest boy, this is a very interesting place,' he had ceased to make plans of conquest and now he was enjoying the excitement of them, the pleasure of his fancy.

A voice muttered behind him, 'Beautiful night, sir—a thing you don't forget—a wonderful view from this point—it grows on you.'

'Yes, it's a good moon. By the way, Major, didn't you get orders to return home—the boats leave at dawn, you know.'

'Home, yes, I believe I did. I was wondering if——' The voice faded. The Major disappeared.

The moonlight was falling on the water, making a glittering smooth path to the *Maria Fry*. On each side of the path the river was a deep reddish black. Felix stared for a long time gazing at the black stream below the whitened trees and thinking with a dreamy satisfaction, 'An artery of commerce.'

54

He turned briskly and noticed that the moonlight was now falling on the great bed, making its net like a floating white cloud, suspended above the deck.

'I'll have that down,' Felix thought. But approaching it on the way to his cabin, he saw a movement behind the net and stooped to peer. A young woman, fair and handsome, with small neat features; a girl from some northern tribe, sat within and stared at him from her black eyes. A yellow baby of about two years old crawled across her feet, and seeing the white man's face, stopped with one hand in the air, like a startled puppy.

Felix was surprised. He stared at the girl and she at him. He felt a warmth beside him and he heard the Major's asthmatic breath. 'The missus, sir—ha, ha.'

The net was pulled up and the Major drew out the baby by the arms and held him for Felix' inspection. 'Poor little beggar—good eyes though—don't often see such eyes—intelligent, too, you wouldn't believe.'

'I didn't know you had a family.'

'Ha, ha—these things happen.'

'You've made a regular home for yourself out here.'

'Ha, ha. Hardly a home. Nothing like home. But still, you know, I used to look forward to going home but now I don't somehow care about it so much. Of course I could get a job down river, but it's not so much the missus—ha, ha—or this little beggar—ha, ha—as the whole place—the whole thing.' He jerked his short arm in a semi-circular sweep including the sky, the ship and the river, with a final twist of the hand perhaps intended for the cabin below. 'It gets you, sir—that's it— it gets you in the end. Of course I know I can't stay—but it gets you.'

Felix reflected a moment. Then still with his napoleonic air he said, 'There's no great hurry, of course—I daresay there'll be another chance by the end of the month.'

The Major broke into profuse thanks, more embarrassing than his distress and at every minute as if in explanation of some lamentable weakness, he exclaimed, 'It gets you, sir—that's the truth of it—I don't know how it is—but it gets you.'

Felix stood reflecting. 'Or should we say rather that you get it. After all, the scene itself is not an active partner in the relationship.'

The Major looked at his new master with surprise. He did not know what he was talking about but for that very reason he began to hope. He approached with his anxious, supplicating air. 'It gets you in the end.'

'It's what you get that's so important, I suppose—what you get to begin with.' Felix drew out a pipe and leant against the columns.

55

The Major sat down on the bed. He began to feel at home again. He felt, he did not know why, that Felix was not so ferocious as he looked. His pipe, too, was a curly one. That was a hopeful sign.

Con was due out of gaol in the spring of '91, and there was a subscription among the magistrates to send the Foys to America.

They were miserably poor, but Padsy would not agree to leave Ireland. Neither would he accept road work, and since he was little seen at home, it was thought that he was making poteen.

The truth was that he had found a piece of waste land on the back of Knockeen mountain; two roods of cut out bog studded with rocks as big as boats, and he had convinced himself that he had a right to it because some Foy had cut the turf. Also he believed that if he could cultivate it for six years it would be his in any case.

This might seem a poor hope in Annish, but the patch was well hidden among the rocks, where no one would look for a farm.

Meanwhile Padsy was happy. He was no longer a landless man, and every day before it was light he and Darcy stole miles though the mountain and spent the next twelve or fourteen hours breaking the rocks with sledge hammers and wedges, building a wall and clearing the ground at the same time.

If anyone passing to look for a stray sheep should call to him, 'You'll be run out of that, Padsy, as soon as himself or old Slatter sees ye,' he would answer firmly, 'They can't do it—it's unlegal. I've a right to it, and I can prove it.'

He would turn to Darcy, 'It's Foy land this hundred years.'

'Aye, Padsy, we'll stay.' Darcy did not agree with Padsy's notion of his rights but politeness to his benefactor devised this form of agreement. Darcy himself, who was much poorer than Padsy, who wore the clothes Padsy left off and who did not even own a spade, had passed a wretched time after the eviction, when Padsy had not known what to do with himself. But now he was even happier than his master who had the anxiety of defending his rights. In that cold wet winter, when both were working up to the knees in the long drains, Darcy might have been seen dressed in nothing but a pair of trousers with one leg ripped open and a torn cotton shirt; so whipped and frozen by wind and rain that his skinny legs and arms had taken the colours of dead flesh, purple and scarlet like those of a frost-bitten corpse; but he himself, being asked by a passer-by if he didn't feel cold, would stop and reflect before answering, 'It's a soft day, the day. But hasn't it the right to be this time of year.'

His view was that the day, since it was a day spent on Padsy's ground, ought to be defended from rude criticism. About his own legs and arms he had as little opinion as sensation.

But at night he and Padsy were so tired that coming down the mountain they could not feel their bodies, so that their heavy boots, swinging out from the downhill into the air, seemed to bring them home by gravity. They would stagger to Dan's in a kind of trance, and Darcy, creeping into the cowshed, would fall down suddenly against the old cow as if shot down; asleep before he touched the floor.

Padsy, older and tougher, would stagger to his place by the fire and collapse into himself, with his long neck hanging out like a dying camel's, and his long arms, stained as black as blood, hanging out over his knees till his fingers nearly touched the floor.

Then gradually he would discover that Manus was reading; and after he had gazed at the boy for a long time, he would distinguish separate words and echo them.

'Saint Bridget, having given herself to God, built a cell for herself, under a great oak, which place was therefore called Kildare or the cell of the oak——'

'Having given herself to God,' Padsy's voice said, like an echo from a cave.

'One evening, Saint Bridget was sitting with a nun called Dora, a holy woman who was dark. It was in the evening when the sun had just gone down and they talked of the love of Jesus and of the joys of paradise.'

'The joys of paradise,' Padsy echoed.

'And they were so full of the sweetness of their thoughts that the whole night passed before they knew.'

'The whole night passed——' Padsy said, now surrounded by a pool of bog water as if he were slowly bleeding in the firelight. He would stare at Manus through half-closed eyes as if at something far off from him. 'Sacred heart, the boy's a wonder to read.'

It was understood that Manus was to be a priest. He would go to college at the end of the year, or sooner if there should be a vacancy.

Manus was the glory of the Foys in Dan's house. He was the one who had the best of the food and the only pair of boots on Sunday. The Foys made the more of him because they were in misery. Old Dan himself was starving, his stomach and his cheeks had fallen in. The only money coming to the house was from Kitty Egan, who was nurse at the castle.

Mrs. Corner's baby had been born in September, and both mother and son had nearly died. It was said that only Kitty's nursing saved them, so that more than ever she was a person of consideration at the castle, and when she asked for broken meats or old clothes for the Foys, she always had them. She dressed them all that winter and made Bridget a first communion dress out of an old skirt that Mary Corner had worn as a bride.

Padsy had a fright one day when he was discovered in his squatter's hole by young Phil Feenix. They looked up from their digging and saw the boy standing on the rocks above them with Breedy Macan, who was the Slatter's yard boy, Padsy began to shout, 'It's me own land, it's Foy ground, sir.'

'I don't think anyone else will want it,' the boy said.

'But they might now if they heard of it.'

'I won't tell anyone, Padsy.'

After that Philip came often to Padsy's hole, as he called it. He liked to sit in the high place, which seemed to be in the middle of the sky; to look out over the little fields far below and to chat with these people who were so friendly and so peaceful in themselves; who knew what they wanted. Philip had learnt in his English school that the Irish peasantry were to be appreciated; that all country life and country work was noble and admirable, and so he felt a strong affection for the people and for their work.

Slatter used to say, 'Ye can do anything with education. Look at Philly—he might be a jook's son instead of old Willy Feenix in his holy nightshirt.'

Slatter's admiration for Philip increased as the boy grew taller, better-looking, better-mannered; but also he became more anxious about him. He would send for the doctor if Philip cut his fingers; and there was a terrible scene at the end of the year when the boy asked to join the army class. He wished to be a soldier, like Harry Jarvis.

'So that's the way of it,' Slatter bawled. 'I've paid five hundred pounds to make a snawb and a fool of ye—but go wan then. I'm not stopping ye. Go and dress yourself up like a hoor's pin-cushion and get your throat cut by the boors or the injuns.'

Afterwards, of course, he repented. He came to the rectory and shed tears. 'Aw, Philly—why would ye want to leave me and get yourself killed in some fule's play.'

Slatter had a peculiar view of the army, common to his class, which was really that of the dealers, publicans and big farmers, a real bourgeoisie. The peasants enlisted, and their families said with easy acceptance or pride, 'Pat's gone in the regiment,' or 'Mick's away to the fleet,' to them these were livelihoods. The landlords sent their younger sons into the services, for the honour of them. But the class between had a great contempt for anyone who was fool enough to serve the State, especially in the army, where pay was small, and a man might get killed.

Philip did not give way at once, and this made him feel selfish because of Slatter's despair. When he gave way and saw his uncle's gratitude, he felt that he had done the right and good thing; in fact, Slatter sang his praises all over Annish—'Aw the best-hearted wee boyo in Ireland.' He gave him a watch and a sixteen bore gun. But Philip, in spite of his good conscience, felt foolish as if somebody were laughing at him.

He was snappish with the girls and disappeared for whole days with Breedy and the new gun on the bog or the mountain. He did not shoot much; he preferred to lounge in Padsy's hole or to sit under some rock with Breedy and discuss the affairs of the country.

Breedy was the son of a tinker, a castaway from Dunderry who had attached himself to Carnmore as yard boy and to Philip as gun carrier. He had raw red hair, a nose like two holes in his face, a large gap-tooth mouth, and he went in the dirtiest rags. But he was popular with Slatter because he knew some scandal about everyone in the countryside and he knew how to commend himself to young Philip by talking to his mood. He used to say to Philip, 'Oh, Mister Slatter is the grand man, but he needs a clever wan to manage him. He has poor Miss Maddy distracted. It's a pity ye wouldn't be at home all the time.'

Breedy's system was a double one; flattery to the self-importance of present company; and depreciation of all the rest. He knew that people, especially the gentry, liked to feel important.

Con came out of gaol in March, but he would not see Kitty, and when he reached Dan Egan's on Ballycorner beach he sat down with his hat on and refused to speak to anybody. But it was seen that he had nothing to say. Con did not think a great deal, but he felt strongly, and his feelings were wont, as soon as they sprang up, to run into ideas of action. But now he had no ideas of action. His feelings turned into walls. He had meant to shoot old John and old John was dead. Kitty was a traitor.

When they told him that there was money to take him to America, he made no answer, but he allowed old Dan to take his ticket and gather him a box of clothes.

There were nine emigrants from Knockeen and Dunvil going by the same liner; all the Foys and Egans came to their farewell party, and they lit their bonfire on the shore below the castle. Dancing began at six o'clock.

Sukey Egan in the castle kitchen was dancing; both she and Jebb, the coachman, had been drinking from one o'clock in sympathy with the ideas of a party. Grogan, on the other hand, carrying his little head slouched, as if he had ice on his back; and Peggy, the new housemaid, who was a Plymouth sister, looked as sour as pickled cabbage. Grogan and Peggy both feared an attack on the house, and it was always Grogan's conviction that the Catholics would murder him.

Grogan was asked afterwards why he had not warned his master, to which he answered with his usual suffering look, 'I had it in mind but it seems it wasn't meant for me to do it.'

Grogan, rescued from a Dunderry slum by old John twenty years before, had worshipped the old man, but he had little confidence or respect for anybody else. He was an extreme protestant; belonging to no church; but he read his Bible every day, and sometimes he would be heard groaning in the pantry, though no one could know whether his grief was for the world's wickedness and folly, or for those of his family. He had a brother in the army and a sister in Liverpool, who were both always in trouble and always sponging upon him.

Grogan's doctrine, like old John's, was that all things were pre-ordained, and this was perhaps why he did not repeat to John Chass the local gossip about an attack. The Corners certainly heard nothing of it. They were going out to dinner, six miles away, an hour's drive in the old carriage. John Chass in his shirt-sleeves, was walking about the upper passage, singing softly:

> St. Patrick was a gentleman
> That came of decent people,
> He built a church in Dublin town,
> And on it put a steeple.

John Chass was never so happy as when he was giving or expecting a party.

Now and then he paused to shout, 'Grogan, Mary—where are my shirts with the little collars.'

But Grogan was below stairs closing and barring the shutters and Mary was playing with her baby.

> His father was a Shaughnessy
> His aunt was an O'Grady.

Exhilaration flowed out with the rich, contented voice through the house, making Mary say to the baby lying on her bed, 'Who's that, m'dear?' and Cleeve in the nursery smile at Bridget and say, 'That's uncle. They're going out to dinner.'

John Chass was among his possessions which he was revealing to Bridget Foy, come for her communion dress to be tried on. Bridget made no answer. The dark little girl never spoke while she padded after her host from one corner to another, but Cleeve felt that she was admiring and therefore he was happy.

'It's rather convenient,' he said, carelessly pulling out a drawer and banging it to again. 'That's all for soldiers, and of course the rocking-horse is a safety one. Would you like a ride?'

Bridget silently climbed on the rocking-horse and Cleeve gave it one

60

push. Then at once he went to the far end of the room to point out the picture of Nelson. 'Come and look—it's rather valuable. The death of Nelson.' Bridget climbed off the rocking-horse and padded across the floor.

John Chass' voice was heard calling, 'Molly, Moll, aren't you ready yet?'

Kitty came in briskly and picked up a shawl from in front of the fire. Her eyes were red with weeping. But her manner was brisk. She stood for a moment turning her face towards the window, where framed in a corner of the pane, she could see the minute dancers, two hundred yards away, on the concrete foundation of the old boathouse which was their dance floor. The little fiddler's arm seemed no bigger than a fly's leg.

Kitty made one step towards the window; but turned quickly as Mary Corner came in with the baby. 'Kitty, Kitty, now I must go, but you'll be careful that he doesn't lie in a draught.'

'The wee darling.'

Both women looked critically and eagerly at the baby as if it was something good to eat but novel to experience. Mary and Kitty were both among those women whose imaginations were always excited by a baby.

It was a small, white, very thin baby, with large blue eyes. At six months it was under twelve pounds weight. It was, however, very active and good-tempered. Now, wrapped up in numerous fine shawls, it was like a parcel from which its arms stuck out like pegs, and its two round eyes, of which the blue seemed to have soaked into the white, like paint not yet dry, gazed out between two folds, with intense but calm curiosity.

Its name was John Chesney; Chesney after its maternal grandfather; and it had been called Chesnay or Chay in the house. But the kitchen called it Shon or Shony, and already it was known as Shon.

John Chass' voice, rising from below, was heard again. 'Mary, the horses will be eating Jebb if you don't come now.'

The change of name from Molly to Mary was a warning of impatience. Mary kissed Shon on both cheeks, like one saying good-bye for ever on the way to the scaffold, and went quickly out. A moment later the heavy carriage wheels sounded on the gravel of the drive. As the front door banged, Kitty stood still for a moment with the baby in her arms; she was breathing quickly. She looked at the window; then suddenly she laid Shon face downwards on the rug, in front of the fire and said to the children, 'Watch him for me a wee minute. Master Cleeve, and you, Bridgy.'

Cleeve, who had now reached the nursery screen, answered politely that he would watch, and as soon as Kitty was out of the room he showed his *savoir faire* and the opulence of the nursery by scattering a few rattles, balls and painting books on the rug.

Shon, holding up his head with a jerk, and striking out his arm with stiff fingers like cribbage pegs in mother of pearl, at once began to jerk in the leaves of a painting book. The rustling fascinated him. His lips sucked in and out, his eyes stared, his feet kicked, he dribbled with curiosity and the excitement of his deeds. Kitty, with a shawl over her head, was flying along the shore as if pulled by elastic. Cleeve had gone back to the screen. 'And that's the Jersey Lily.'

The two children stared at the photograph of Lily Langtry painted on the screen in a fan-shape composed also of Lady Randolph Churchill and the Countess of Warwick. The centre of the fan was Peter Jackson fighting Frank Slavin, with an unusual number of fly blows on his chest.

'They're famous beauties,' Cleeve said in a serious voice; 'people stand on chairs to see them go past.'

Bridget stood silent and motionless, but Cleeve knew that she was breathless with attention. He looked round affectionately at the room which he had scarcely noticed before; at the pictures dimly seen in the glow of the fire, already fading, so that Little Red Riding Hood was only a red cloak, the Queen at Osborne, a blue garter; the Death of Nelson, a pair of breeches; and the meeting of Blucher and Wellington had disappeared altogether in its corner. He felt a warm tenderness even towards the hole in the carpet and the burnt hole in the table-top where so many cavalry charges had come to disaster.

'It's nice here,' he said in a tone of a discoverer's appreciation. Years after, he remembered the castle nursery as he saw it that evening by the light of the fire, and of Bridget's silent attention.

'Do you like it?' he asked her.

Bridget said nothing. The question surprised her as if the word like did not apply. There could be no liking in her for the treasures of the castle, but only intense curiosity mixed with some awe. Bridget did not talk much, but her imagination was active, and for the last year it had been occupied with the castle. Old Jebb, who hated children, was tired of driving her from the yards.

Her ambition was to see the drawing-room at which she had only peeped through the windows.

It was now dark; the fire was dying; and the flicker of the bonfire could be seen on the ceiling. Cleeve, growing bored with Bridget, went to draw back the curtain and gave a cry of surprise and delight. He saw the great bonfire waving in the wind like a ragged scarf of fire; the sky and sea behind dark green; the long thin waves breaking in glittering ruby and the dancers red and black like demons, jigging on the pink square among the rocks.

Close below Harry and Phil were standing with their guns, looking in the same direction. They had been on the mountain all day. Cleeve flung up the window and called 'Harry, Harry, wait for me.'

Harry did not hear him, and he turned to rush out of the room. Suddenly the baby choked and he perceived that it had managed to bite a bell from a rattle.

Cleeve said, 'Oh damn it!' and darted at the rug. He tried to gouge the bell out of the small flexible mouth with its pin teeth. Shon, to his great relief, submitted without a protest; dribbling in streams, wildly waving his stiff arms. His round, blue eyes, fixed on Cleeve's face, seemed to forget everything else but the excitement of seeing this new object before them. They forgot the mouth; the arms, the kicking legs; the wriggling toes; and even Cleeve's finger, so that when, looking still dirtier because of its wetness, it came out with the gilt bell, the mouth continued to wriggle by itself, while the eyes gazed eagerly seeking, and the frantic hands still investigated bells, the rattle and the painting book.

Cleeve threw down the bell and ejaculated, 'You'll stay, Bridgy'; then he rushed down the stairs shouting for Harry.

Bridget tiptoed upon the landing, and stood motionless for several minutes, listening. Then she slipped downstairs, as silent as a shadow, and opened the drawing-room door.

The thick yellow flames of the coal-fire still lighted the room, glittering on polish, glass. Bridget closed the door behind her and leant against it.

Cleeve was in terror that Harry and Phil would disappear before he reached them. He burst upon them from the yard door head first, almost diving down the rocks on his head. 'What is it? What are they doing?'

Harry caught him by the arm to save him from a fall; he was talking seriously with Philip about politics, and especially Parnell. They put their guns in at the coach-house window and walked along the shore towards the fire.

'He's a bloody traitor,' Harry said, not indignantly but as if stating a fact.

'But he made the party,' Philip said.

'Are you going nationalist, Philly? What will your uncle say?'

'I don't care what he says,' Philip said with dignity, 'he doesn't understand the people.'

'Are you a Home Ruler?'

Philip did not answer this because he did not know what he was. He was doubtful in all his beliefs, and therefore in himself. His Uncle James, for instance, had proved right about religion, that it was full of tricks; that he had been a young fool to swallow the fairy tales in the

Bible. But he still had his own feelings; about Ireland and friends like Breedy and Padsy. He could be sure of them. They liked him and trusted him, and he was eager to deserve their trust.

'Anyhow, Parnell's done for—the priests have finished him,' Harry said.

'But don't you think they're the finest people in the world?'

'The Foys? Yes, I liked the Foys—but it's only Con going.'

'I meant not only the Foys—the Irish people.'

Philip's enthusiasm surprised Harry, to whom the Irish were like members of the same family. He thought about his liking as little as a brother. He said that they were bloody good fighters, anyhow.

Philip stood looking at his friend with a kind of anxious pleading look. He wanted somebody to agree with him in his enthusiasm; to assure him that he was doing the right thing. All day he had been trying to get Harry to say that he, too, loved Ireland, and the Irish people. He wanted to talk about it to somebody; to realize it and enjoy it and feel its grandeur and importance.

But Harry would not use words like love, and he had an objection to all poetical ideas.

'Look at Kitty,' Cleeve said, pushing his head between the two boys. Neither paid any attention to the child. They were occupied with serious problems of life.

They stood now within ten yards of the fire. Con was dancing at one end of the concrete slab and Kitty at the other. She was dancing prettily but weeping at the same time, and when every now and then she put her hand to her hair to see that it was not falling down, she pressed it also over her forehead as if her head was bursting. She looked the whole time at Con but it was plain that she did not dare go nearer. Con did not look at her; his eyes were half closed.

His black Sunday hat hung upon the very back of his head, as if he had grown a peg there. His arms were crossed, his legs were jerking and kicking like machinery; from his mouth, pulled out at one side, came pants and howls; sweat stood in beads upon the deep corrugations of his little forehead. When one looked at the despair of Con's face, his legs were enough to make one cry. In them was the desperation of his obstinate misery. Cleeve felt the power of the sight; and stood fascinated.

Con and Padsy, Kitty and Rifty were dancing to the fiddle; but beyond them at the fireside, a group of young men and girls were sitting, close together as starlings when they perch in the cold night; and singing to a slow mournful tune.

Some of the men were emigrants. One could tell them by their Sunday suits; and the girls were all wearing shoes and stockings. All were losing brothers, sisters, sweethearts, and as they sat in the bright

64

light of the fire, which made their faces look as smooth as young children's, one saw the flames glitter on tears. They sat quite still. All their violence was in their voices. Nothing moved but their lips and their quivering eyelashes when they held a top note, forcing into it all the might of their sadness in order to feel its pain.

'Sad was the day we said farewell.'

The discordant voices were like cracked flutes, shrieking fiddles, flat bassoons; a hurricane of despair that made one's nerves shake like twigs in a gale; caught the breath in one's throat; squeezed the tears out of one's eyes.

Old Egan, perched on a rock, nodding his head, his stick and his feet to the rhythm, was weeping, though without tears. His mouth twisted from a little round hole to an oblong and then to the shape of a Greek tragic mask, with two round holes at each end and a narrow strait in the middle, while he let out broken howls.

'Fare-hoo-well, dear native land, to thee,' and wiped his nose on his forefinger. Then seeing the two boys, he waved the forefinger in front of the famous nose, as if to say 'Follow me, and you can't go wrong.'

Harry Jarvis smiling, began to sing, but at the first sound of his own voice, uttering the word Farewell, his throat closed; a sharp painful contraction squeezed his chest; tears rose to his eyes. He was overwhelmed in the pain of loss, of separation; and when he sang 'Erin,' though it was a word from poetry, a ridiculous and mamby pamby word, it brought such love rushing into his heart that the rocks, the seaweed, the concrete slab and a piece of an old boat, all he could see of Ireland; and the bodies and voices of the singers, because they too were part of Ireland, were more dear to him than anybody he had loved; even than his Aunt Mary. He could have put his arms round the nearest rock and squeezed it to him.

Suddenly he caught Phil's eye, fixed upon him with an eager, anxious look, and he saw that Phil was going to make another more urgent appeal. He realized that his feelings had probably betrayed themselves. He forced a smile, turned quickly away, and strolled behind the singers. What an escape! He looked round to make sure that Philly was not yet on his tracks.

'And what are you doing there, young Cocky?'
He looked up startled, and saw half a dozen boys above him on the ledge. They were village boys. He recognized Breedy Macan. He had played with most of them and run beside them panting after the greyhounds when his uncle coursed the mountain hares. But now as he saw at once they were themselves looking for game. The use of his nickname

was a challenge and his nose went up. 'Why shouldn't I be here on my own ground?'

'Your ground, is it?' one of the boys said, in a quiet, relishing tone. 'I thought it was Egan ground. I'm tould all Annish was Egan ground, and Inishhowen, too, before anny of you Englishmen knew how to cook your meat.'

'I'm as good Irish as you are,' Harry said, 'and better.'

'Put him in the ground if he wants it,' a voice shouted.

'Up the green,' Breedy yelled. 'To hell with King Billy.'

All Harry's excited feelings rushed out of him in a new direction. 'To hell with the Pope.'

Every head turned as if pulled by a string, and on forty faces, flame colour in the fire, one saw astonishment, fury, exaggerated by the strong shadows into grotesques. Somebody gave a curse and whirled a stick; a dozen came leaping over the rocks.

Harry ducked under the stick and disappeared as if into the ground. He knew every crack and hole of the rocky shore.

'The cassle!' Breedy yelled. 'The cassle!'

'To hell with the Pope.'

The heads turned round to the north. The boy was forty yards away, on a big round stone. They rushed after him with yells of rage. Breedy, in an ecstasy of delight, yelled, 'To the cassle,' and seeing his master, young Feenix, standing at a distance with a bewildered expression on his face, he picked up a stone and threw it at him. 'To the cassle!' he howled. Breedy was a natural revolutionary; he hated all the rich.

He did not see the effect of the stone because just then the whole mob, turning towards the house, rushed over young Feenix, so that when it had passed nothing was to be seen of the boy but his legs waving in the air from between two rocks.

Cleeve was already a hundred yards away, running for his life. He had never been so frightened.

Many Irish houses then had iron-lined shutters, but the Corners had been popular landlords and the house had not been attacked since the rebellion of '98; their shutters were light wood panels which burst open at the first shower of stones. Some of the mountain boys climbed into the lower rooms, and it was certain that the house would have been wrecked or burnt if it had not been for a strange and lucky accident. John Chass, for the first time in many years, had an attack of nose-bleeding on his way to the party, and came back for a clean shirt. Mrs. Dow, from the lodge, met the carriage with the news that the emigrants were attacking the house, and he ran down the drive just as some of the boys in the drawing-room were throwing out the small ornaments from the tables. At the sight of John Chass the looters, outside and in, bolted

66

through the trees. Mrs Dow was heard screaming after them, 'I know ye—I can see ye—Pat, I can see ye—Bridget Foy.'

John Chass meanwhile ran round to the waterfront. Luckily his sudden appearance on the bank top, in the light of the fire, with his evening cloak streaming behind him, and his tall hat held out in front of him, had the effect of surprise. It was a theatrical entry, and John Chass, by an instinctive stroke of art, had already begun to speak. His lips were seen moving before anyone could hear him.

The voices were heard already saying, 'Whist—yous'—and the shouts died.

The speech was a chaffing speech, as it had to be in the circumstances, and it served its purpose. A few more stones were thrown in the front, but when the police arrived, twenty minutes later, the crowd was already placable. The great part of it had not intended harm.

It was extraordinary how much damage had been done in a few minutes, not only to windows, shutter-cases, and furniture within, but even to roofs and spouting. It was already plain that repairs would be expensive.

Shon had been found asleep on the floor, among broken glass and stones, with the rattle in his hand. Mary Corner and Kitty, having each thanked her own god for his safety, put him to bed. It was not till the next morning they perceived that he had eaten nine gilt bells.

The morning was grey. Showers fell from low clouds which seemed to have no edges. They were in dissolution before they were born. The lough was like grey granite, flecked with sparks of white and crystal; and the Derry hills were pale heaps of ashes, smoking cold mist. The Allen liner moving slowly towards the sea with its load of emigrants, was so sharp and clear cut in these drifting vapours, that it seemed like one of those half models cut out of wood and brightly painted, which, stuck on paper seascapes decorate the walls of old merchant captains.

Like a model, it fixed the eye. John Chass gazed at it from the terrace with a thoughtful interest, as if he remembered his own travels; the schoolchildren stared at it from all the roads with fancies reaching out for the high seas, America, riches; Kitty looked at it from the nursery windows with eyes so swollen with weeping that they were like slits. But at the same time she was crying out blessings upon Shon. A chamber-pot was in her hand: the first bell had been found. 'Ah, the cliver wee manny—look ma'am—and he smiling like an angel from the holy crib.'

Kitty was perfectly able to be heartbroken and joyful at the same time, because there was no falseness in her. She never dramatized herself. The horn of the steamer blasting good-bye to the tender as it rounded the cliff was like a slow explosion in her brain and heart, disintegrating her life, but she was still smiling at Shon, delighting in his feat.

John Chass watched the liner turn west and disappear slowly; then he put up his mackintosh collar and stooped towards the ground. He was seeking his lost property and already he had made a sport of it. He had bet the boys sixpence that he would find more loot on the terrace than they on the drive. His bag to that moment was two silver medals. But Harry had picked up a gold miniature trodden into the gravel by the front door.

There were still a dozen small objects missing, miniatures, snuff-boxes, and two antique watches, from a glass-covered table in the drawing-room; which had been broken by the fall of a shutter bar.

Mrs. Dow said that the thief was Bridget Foy. 'It's bound to be Bridgy,' she said, 'for thon wain's the biggest thief in Annish—she's always in the gyarden or the yards.'

No one had ever seen Bridget steal, or caught her with stolen goods, but now it seemed to everybody that she must be a thief. 'She's the very shape of a thief,' Mrs. Dow said. The sergeant made a note that Padsy's Bridget had been seen running from the garden immediately after the robbery.

It was true that Bridget had picked up a locket under the drawing-room window; a small, flat gold case set with a monogram in diamonds. She had hooked it to the string of her holy medal, beneath her shift; and now, while she dozed on a sack of straw among her brothers and sister on the floor of Dan's cottage, her dirty hand still clasped it through her frock. Six children were sleeping in the one-room cabin, which was still in twilight. The floor was covered with a heap of rags from which came sighs, broken words; an arm was thrown up and a sudden twist opened a gap through which one saw the pale oval of a child's face with open mouth and tight shut eyes. Old Mrs. Foy snorted and moaned from the box bed. Padsy, who had been out all night with Dan on a long line, was sorting his share of the fish among the rocks. Father MacFee came stepping through the mud with trousers rolled to his ankles. He was a small, thin, pale man. His eyes, behind his gold spectacles, were the same colour as the grey shower falling on Knockeen behind him. They were cool, mild, soft eyes, but when the priest spoke his voice was decisive and confident. He spoke very fast. 'Good morning Dan, and to you Padsy, it's a sad thing to lose Con. That was a terrible affair last night at the castle, and I hope no one from Ballycorner had anything to do with it. We may thank God no one was hurt.'

Padsy, throwing down the skate from which he had just cut the wings and rump, came slowly towards the priest. 'It was that young fella Jarvis, your reverence, that was shouting injuries against the Pope; and the Dunvil boys got to clodding a few rocks.'

'Never mind how it began, I'd be sorry that anyone of you had part in such a disgrace, even if it went no further than throwing stones. But the sergeant tells me this morning that things were taken—robbed from the house.'

'I wouldn't put it beyond some of those Dunvil spalpeens.'

Father MacFee looked keenly at Padsy and said, 'Some gold medals and lockets and a watch were taken, and some of those who took them were seen.'

There was a short silence. The children, waked instantly by the sound of the priest's voice, soft as it was, crowded in the door, looking up at him. The faces of the little ones were full of perplexity and awe. The father was a living god to them, but he was also a little man in a black hat and dirty boots.

Father MacFee raised his voice. 'Now I saw Mr. Corner just now and we had a little talk and I said that the people had been excited last night, no doubt, and not themselves; and he said true, and he'd be sorry to make a court case of the robbery, and if the things were brought back he'd say no more about it.'

'There's noan here,' Padsy said shortly, wiping his nose with his bloodstained hands. He looked sidelong at the priest. Padsy was a Parnellite, and for the last six months he had been suspicious of the priests.

Father MacFee looked down suddenly on the children. 'Some of your children were seen near the house, Patrick.'

Bridget detached herself from the little crowd and walked slowly out of the door, past the father and round the corner. All watched her, and Padsy suddenly called 'Bridgy.'

Bridget darted round the corner, her father flew after her. But instantly on turning the corner Bridgy squatted quickly down. She raised her eyes to her father's face as he came thudding round the corner. He stared down at her, taken aback; then said firmly, 'That's no place to do it. You're old enough to know that. Go wan over there behind the wall.'

Bridgy disappeared, with a modest air, behind the wall, and then, beneath its cover, quickly put half a mile between her and Ballycorner. She stayed there until she saw Father MacFee walking up the road, with his long scissor-step, which seemed to strain his short legs, towards Knockeen.

Bridget was in terror, for she knew nothing was hid from God and that Father MacFee was God's representative. Father MacFee was even stronger than God, for when he made the little bells ring on Sunday in Ballycorner chapel, God came down from heaven into the bread and wine on the altar. If Father MacFee's eye had fallen upon her, he would perhaps have seen the locket under her shift and the sin in her heart. She looked inland. The spire of the chapel stood up from the glen of Knockeen; and she knew that Father MacFee lived in the slated house next down the lane from the chapel. She thought, 'I'll go now and throw the jewel through the window.'

She pulled up her dress and shift to her neck and held out the locket. She looked at it with awe, not feeling the cold rain which drifted against her bare body. In the cold grey light, the diamonds had no sparkle, the gold was less bright than the gilt tinsel on the holy picture. But Bridget knew that the little stones were diamonds, the pale yellow metal, dimmed with her sweat, was gold. Her eyes were full of wonder while she gazed at the mysterious treasure. She knew what a halfpenny could do; but she could not imagine the power of gold except as a vague glory. All this power and the glory of it was in her hand.

A gate creaked and rattled; two thin cows came into the field and wandered among the bitten grass and the tufts of rushes. They did not even look for food in this field where they had been starving for two months. Old Dan hobbled after them and began to rebuild the gate, whose bars fell apart at each opening. Bridget in one gesture dropped the locket so that it swung against her chest, and smoothed down her clothes. Then she darted to the hedge; fell on her face; and with the quick wriggle of a terrier, slipped between the roots and rolled down the bank into the lane.

Father MacFee, not a strong man, walked eight miles that morning. But he was very successful. During the next two days, nearly all the objects taken from the castle were returned; from anonymous parcels, left on window-sills, in doorways, or even in chapel. Old John's gold watch was found in a sugar bag at the foot of the chapel cross. Only a miniature, two lockets, a Crimean medal and an ivory fan were still missing, and of these the miniature was sent back three months later in a parcel from Boston.

Father MacFee's powers had stretched, by means of some family letter, three thousand miles across the Atlantic, into the slums of an American city. He was congratulated by John Chass in person, who would have liked to take the oportunity of making friends. He pulled up his dog cart one day beside the priest and asked him to come in to luncheon. But Father MacFee began to excuse himself.

'Why is it that you won't come into my house?' John Chass had asked. 'Old Father Maccarty that was here before you came in to dinner every week, and I can remember well the punch we made for him; rum punch to his own recipe.'

Father MacFee answered politely that he was a busy man; perhaps there was more work in the parish these days than in the time of Father Maccarty. John Chass looked down on him with a puzzled and humorous look—his usual expression in the face of religious or political difficulties—and said, 'Well, it's a great pity—I'm sorry for it.'

Father MacFee had a smiling air, unusual to him. He allowed a little pause, to show that the subject was ended, and then spoke of the weather and the good catches of herring, which, he hoped, would pay some of the half-year rents. John Chass touched Kitty Grey on the shoulder and, as he darted forward, catching his whip-lash with a skilful twist of the wrist; swaying to the roll of the cart on the camber of the road, and feeling all through him the delight of his smart turn-out, his skill and the easy quick motion, he thought 'politics—politics—the ruin of everything.'

But Father MacFee did not know why it had become wrong for him to sit down at table with a Protestant landlord. His Church was now emancipated, respected by the British Government; more rich and powerful than ever before; but every year it drew farther away from sympathy with the Government; so that even its ultimate nerves, the priests and curates, shrank as if by instinct from the company of heretics. It was as though the Church were withdrawing behind walls; and as it grew in strength, so it became more self-sufficient and more isolated.

Father MacFee did not think much of politics, or the Home Rule party led by Parnell, heretic and adulterer; but he felt the rising power of his Church and rejoiced in it, for the salvation of the world.

'No more prayers at the castle, they tell me,' he said to himself as he hurried along with awkward strides. 'No more Bible.' He felt pity and contempt for these protestants whose faith, if it could be called faith was melting like a sand-castle.

'Darwinism,' he thought with contempt. But his stride grew longer, more irregular. The very idea of Darwin made him angry, not because there could be danger to the true faith from biological theories about the origin of species, but because they might mislead the ignorant.

Father MacFee, a very good-tempered man, grew hot and red with anger when he thought of the enormous power of atheism and the ignorance and weakness of the faithful. Every newspaper from England and America, every book carried poison, heresy, atheism and temptation, and every year there were more to read them. Even the little bare-foot children in the mud cabins were learning to read. Father MacFee was strong for education. He was a school manager, and he was strict even with the poorer parents, like the Foys, who always had excuses why their children, especially the girls, should not go to school that day, because there was no one else to drive the cow; or to mind the baby. He insisted that Bridget, who had never been to school at all on the mountain, should go now, though she was already ten and in two years' time she would be free.

71

But just as Father MacFee, when he refused John Chass' invitation, obeyed some slowly rising force, from outside himself, a warlike spirit refusing to fraternize with the enemy; so when he spoke of the importance of education, he obeyed some other power, some quite different power which he did not examine, but which had been growing slowly for a hundred years, until it was irresistible. But where did it come from? It was not a force of nature, like the increase of population or the swelling of the tree trunk which throws down a wall. Illiterate people did not ask for schools and children did not beg to be sent there. Spain, Italy, Brazil did not cry out for education. And what a danger and a nuisance it could be to the young, especially before they had judgement. It was not a week since he had taken out of the hands of a twelve-year-old boy, a favourite pupil, Manus Foy, an American magazine, containing, under the guise of a scientific article, an attack on miracles, Lourdes and many of the chief wonder-making relics. Luckily Manus was one of those rare boys who seemed, from their earliest years, proof against infection. He had even found new faith in the discovery that the Church had enemies.

'But, Father,' he had said, 'why do they tell such lies about Holy Mother Church?'

'Because they hate her, my son.'

'Why, what harm have we done to them?'

'The wicked hate the Church because she wants to cut them off from their darling sins.'

'But, Father, their sins will take them to hell.'

'They know it, but they are too weak to save themselves; and so are we, Manus, without God's grace.'

'I suppose that is why Christ was sent to save us, Father.'

Father MacFee made a kind of leap at the recollection of this answer, so that, coming into a puddle, he was splashed to the fork. But he did not notice it. He saw once more the child's white face, like that of an infant Samuel. 'What beauty,' he thought; 'the beauty of an angel,' and he was filled with ecstasy. Father MacFee had a touch of the mystic which did him no good with the bishop. 'Of such is the kingdom of heaven, and it is a heavenly privilege to know them.'

One day, however, a month after Parnell died, there was an article in an American paper saying that the priests had killed him and ruined his party. Manus tried to despise it, like the others attacking religion, but he could find no answer to it. It was not a religious article, but political. One could not answer it by faith.

Manus was in such excitement that he could not eat, and when he waked up at night, because of his excitement, he did not know what to do, and he could not go to sleep again.

One morning, when he and Bridget were carrying a bucket of

potatoes from the mountain they saw Father MacFee's wet umbrella standing open in a blink of sun at a cottage door. His voice came from within.

Manus stopped and looked at it, and seeing the wet gleam he suddenly spat upon it; then in a panic, he hurried on, dragging Bridget.

He looked at Bridget fiercely across the bucket and to his surprise she appeared calm and undisturbed. It was not a month after her first communion.

'Those wans murdered the chief,' he said.

Bridget answered in her hoarse voice, which always seemed rusty from lack of use, 'He wouldn't know.'

'He wouldn't know what?'

'Father MacFee wouldn't know about the umbrelly.'

'He didn't see.'

This was obviously not what Bridget meant, but she said no more till they reached Ballycorner and had put on the dinner to boil. Manus and Bridget were minding house. She then came close to Manus and looking at him with a round eye she said hoarsely, 'Ye needn't confess it neether—for he wouldn't know.'

Manus did not like this reference to confession. He was shocked by something in Bridget's triumphant eye and harsh voice. He was a little shy of Bridget especially since the talk about the robbery at the castle; for she denied that she had been anywhere near the castle that night and he had seen her going into it. He made no answer to her, therefore, but went out to look for some of his new cronies, Rifty Egan, who was the new stable boy at the castle, and Breedy Macan. The spit on the umbrella had been an inspiration due to the wet, but it opened the way to imagination and energy. The next night, Manus, with four others, after fighting the Healyites on Dunvil green, went up to the parochial house and broke three windows. Father MacFee was inside eating his tea. He ran out and though he did not catch the boys, he recognized Manus by his patched shirt. He challenged him the next morning. Manus looked up at him with his brilliant eyes and opened his lips to say that he would do it again to the murderer of Ireland's chief. This was what he had decided to say. But he could not utter a word, and afterwards in confession, he confessed the sin and was absolved. Padsy paid for the windows out of Con's next remittance.

There was no more talk now of Manus going to college, and Padsy used to exclaim that it was a fairy had got into the boy when he went to the fairy fort above the Point; and that he'd never be right until a wise woman made a cross on him with a red-hot poker.

Manus did not seem different. He ran about like other care-foot boys. But he felt his difference, not as if a fairy had got into him, but as if he had got into some narrow place and couldn't get out. He was checked on all sides, and even in his love of the chief and his hatred of those who had broken his heart, he was held back. He could not strike at Father MacFee. Holy Mother Church stood between them. A blow at a priest fell upon one's own head. It was turned back by that strong invisible wall which stood round on every side.

Father MacFee had compared Holy Mother Church to the heavens. It was like the eternal crystal of the sky through which God's love, the strong beaming light of his countenance and the warmth of his grace, was poured upon his peoples and the fields of their hearts; to make grow there in hundredfold increase the sweet swelling grain of grace and the food of blessedness.

It was true. There was no break in that crystal dome, standing upon Peter's rock. For Peter and the rock were in the Bible itself, written by God in Latin. The dome might press upon you like the sky on a hot June day, where if you looked at it, you could see the sun in its crystal like a candle in the thickness of a tumbler, hot rays twisted in the glass; but though you ran about inside it like a fly under a tumbler, you could not escape. There was no crack anywhere. The warning of the Angel Gabriel, the Birth, the Death, the Resurrection and the Rock of Peter and the Keys of heaven and hell, these were the inner wall and behind them stood the millions of angels and the saints, turning down the rays of their swords and their spears with points clearer and sharper than the stars.

All day Manus was flying round this crystal dome looking for the smallest crack, so that when anyone saw him running along by the turf banks, with his feet red with bog water, and his face splashed with bog mud, and called out 'Hullo, Manus!' he would wag his head in silence, forgetting the names of his own cousins and uncles.

But this was not much noticed because it was well known that all boys about thirteen and fourteen lose their manners and run about as if they had been bitten by a hornet.

At Christmas, Father MacFee, in a long and powerful sermon, warned his people against the Parnellites. 'Enemies of Holy Mother Church, who in the name of a heretic seek to destroy the very soul of Ireland, her Christianity.'

He also warned his people against secret societies which he said were the curse of the country and a danger to the young.

Manus Foy's Ivyleaf Boys was one of many new gangs. Nobody knew how many there were or what they were all doing. Breedy Macann belonged to a society which robbed turf stacks and took the lead from the roof of Knockeen Hall. On a dark night every corner had its whispering group, which fell silent when anyone came near; so that a passer only saw a dark mass as if the wall and a bush or two had fallen into the road. But if he went close to see what the obstruction might be, he would suddenly feel the warmth of bodies and see half a dozen pairs of motionless eyes fixed upon him. Only strangers went to look at these natural phenomena of the countryside. Annishmen walked quickly past on the other side of the way with their eyes held straight before them.

Father MacFee and the papers said that the country was disturbed. To people in towns and in places like England this seemed a far-fetched metaphor. But to anyone who lived in Annish, and heard the bushes muttering at night, saw lights like eyes flash suddenly from a mountain top and close again, it did not seem like a metaphor at all.

The builders who repaired the castle after the convoy riot said that the roof was full of rot and the chimney stacks ready to fall. A general reconstruction was necessary.

John Chass sent up the gardener with a bucket full of cement, but he could not afford rebuilding. Gradually he was running into debt and though he had already borrowed a few hundreds from the bank, he did not like writing the letters. John Chass, in his first borrowings, was like a little boy learning to swim. He made a few hurried strokes and came out gasping. When at the end of '92, Felix cabled for another thousand pounds to meet some crisis on the Mosi, it was as though he had been thrown suddenly into deep water. He sent the money to Felix because he always felt that Felix, as the eldest brother and a man of noble character, had a better title to it than himself, but he exclaimed to Mary that they were being ruined. 'We can't afford to keep up the place any longer. The debts are killing us. I hate debt—there's no peace with it, and if we go on we'll be ruined in no time, and God knows what will happen to us.'

Mary, delighted by this unexpected prudence in John Chass, begged him to go to the lawyer and ask for advice, Hardy, the lawyer, and Mary were old friends and they knew each other's minds. Hardy's scheme was also Mary's, to sell the whole Irish property at once and to keep only the English land, which was nearly all let on leases due to fall in within the next fifteen or twenty years. Hardy calculated that the rental value, then less than three hundred a year, would rise by six or eight times on reversion.

They agreed also that the best market for the castle property was in England, where it could be sold as a shoot.

Hardy then made enquiries, answered advertisements and after five months in March, '93, he actually had an offer from a man called Benskin who for some years had been one of the Corner tenants in the West country. He paid a few pounds a year for shooting rights in a small wood near Porriton.

Benskin was well recommended by the English agent, who described, him as one of the new South African millionaires, and wrote that he was a friend of General Pynsant, a well-known west country man who had bought much land from old John in the 'fifties.

Benskin's first offer indeed was for the whole property in England and Ireland, for which he offered a very good price. But he was told that the English land was not for sale.

John Chass, having made his great decision, had been in very good spirits, but now, after five months, he seemed surprised by the offer. 'That's a good day's work,' he said, 'but I suppose those millionaires have money to burn.'

On the next day he could not eat his breakfast, and Mary soon noticed that he was ill. She sent for Doctor Hanna, who prescribed iron, and they all agreed that the tonic had a good effect. Nevertheless, the patient grew thinner and more restless. He wandered about the house and yards all day, staring into corners that had been forgotten for fifty years. He had the vague expression, the calm air and the flabby white jowl of a man dying of a quick cancer.

One evening, he wandered about six o'clock into the night nursery. Most of his aimless wanderings ended at his wife's elbow, wherever she happened to be; like those of a child who doesn't know what to do with itself.

Mary and Kitty were bathing Shon in a tub. Each was protesting against the other's presence, and now that it was time to take Shon out of the bath, each spread a towel across her knees.

The boy, two and a half years old, pretended not to notice these preparations. He never wanted to leave his bath. He peeped over his shoulder with an obstinate and suspicious expression. His hand still pushed a boat under the water, but he was preparing for battle.

'I'll take him, Catherine, for you know you mustn't get wet.'

'Oh, mam, it's not me has a silk petticoat.'

'You've got your cough, you silly gel, and you know very well you ought to be at the 'ospital now.'

'Oh, mam, but there's nawthin' the matter with me, only a wee cold.'

In fact, Kitty had been ordered to the hospital six weeks before; for Doctor Hanna suspected her of consumption. But Kitty made excuses every day. She could not leave Shon.

John Chass, having looked round the nursery, at the bright coal fire, the cot shining in the flames and upon the two women, as they sat at each end of the tub, went to gaze out of the window at the yard. The moon, throwing the shadow of the loft up to the foot of the pump, gave it the importance of a monument. It's solid round-topped pillar stood up like the holy stone of a primitive cult. Among the turf stacks in the next yard, so black that they seemed to scintillate on the eyesight like the intense darkness of a cellar, two small active figures suddenly dodged. Old Jebb complained of the Parnellite boys who used the stackyard for their secret meetings. A scythe blade had been buried in the turf and the muttering voices frightened the maids coming home from Dunvil by the back avenue.

Manus Foy and Breedy Macan were there almost every night, making their plots to avenge the beloved chief. John Chass watched the two black, active figures slip into cover, but he did not think of his turf or his maids. He had a quiver of recollection at the memory of his own childish games among the turf stacks, when he and Felix, patriots for France, had stormed the Malakoff to cries of Vive l'Empereur.

A fearful yell of rage made him turn. Shon, held in the air between his mother's hands, struck at her with both fists. He was murderous. Mary laughed at him and said, 'Bless us, what a rascal it is.'

Kitty, defeated, had left the room. She could not bear to see another woman bathe the baby which belonged to her.

John Chass sat down heavily in her chair and said, 'Why wouldn't you let him enjoy himself a wee bit longer?'

'Ah, the rascal,' Mary laughed, 'because he's not going to catch his death however much he likes it.' She put down Shon still fighting and rolled him in the towel, stifling his yells.

'Where's Kitty?'

'She's gone for his supper.'

'The poor gyurl wanted to bathe him, for she knows she hasn't long now.'

'I won't have her getting wet with that cough. She's killing herself.'

'It's Con that's killing her.'

'Nonsense, John. Don't speak of the man, She put him out of her head two years ago. Good gracious.'

'She might put him out of her head and not get him out of her chest, poor gyurl. It's Con that's destroying poor Kitty.'

Shon had suddenly come out from the towels and he uttered another yell. His mother seized him, turned him like a parcel, sat him up and rubbed his head; the yell died into a wail. He caught sight of Mary's cameo brooch, a favourite toy, and grabbed at it.

'It's a pity she didn't go to America after him,' John Chass said.

Kitty came in with a silver bowl, and Shon was handed to her. Her sharp face at once relaxed into happiness. It was perhaps her last night, but she knew how to enjoy it because all her life of a poor girl was floated upon insecurity.

Mary went to dress. There was a dinner party and afterwards the young people were going to dance. Sounds of a fiddle and an occasional shriek from the kitchen told them that the music had already arrived.

'Benskin's man is coming down from Dublin to look at the roof,' John Chass said through the dressing-room door.

Mary came to the door and looked at him with a face as sharp and pale as Kitty's. 'Are you sure you want to sell, John?'

'Hardy says we can't go on. And then there's Shony. We agreed that he mustn't be tied down here in the bag end of things.'

'Yes, there's Shony.' She disappeared. Francie had come to do her hair. Francie was Kitty's fat sister, who had been second housemaid, and who was to be nurse when Kitty went to hospital.

'We're lucky to get out of it,' John Chass said.

Mary was sitting at her glass without seeing it. She knew that John Chass was appealing to her, and she could not bear to refuse him. Whether it would be better for him to lose the house and be unhappy or to stay and go bankrupt she could not tell, but it seemed to her that no good could come of unkindness. Everyone has a different faith and in the final analysis Mary Corner's was probably kindness. Her god was a commander-in-chief, one greater than Wellington; or perhaps the King of kings, with more quarterings even than the Chesneys, but her creed was love. She believed in a providence that enjoined and sometimes even rewarded love. Had she not enjoyed the supreme happiness of loving, the only happiness of her life?

She came suddenly to the door, fully dressed, and said to John, struggling into his coat, 'Don't let Hardy and that African man make you do anything stoopid.'

'But Hardy says——'

'Hardy. Good gracious, it isn't Hardy's house. What does he know about it?'

'Well now, I've thought that myself.'

He looked at her with such an excited hope that she would have smiled if a smile had not been rude. Her question was answered.

'I wouldn't sell for Hardy.'

'And what about the bills, my dear?'

'We must do without some things.'

John Chass at once thought of half a dozen economies; two horses instead of a dozen; Grogan and Jebb to go; letting off the lodge and the paddock; but every few minutes he said, 'All the same, Mary, it can't be done, and Hardy will tell you so. It's no good dodging the plain facts.'

Mary said nothing but after a while she heard John Chass whistling for the first time in a month; and she felt the queer sensation of those who are compelled to know by experience how strangely men are constructed.

From the distant nursery came the voice of Kitty singing to Shon, who always demanded a song with his supper.

78

> *Old Dan Tucker was a great big nigger,*
> *As big as me and a great deal bigger:*
> *Out ob de way, old Dan Tucker,*
> *You're too late to come for your supper.*

Shon, beaming with delight in her lap, could not be persuaded to open his mouth for the spoon in front of it. 'Again, again, Kitty.'

'Open your mouth then, darlint.'

Shon, without taking his eyes from Kitty's face, opened his mouth and allowed the bread and milk to be stuffed into it. Kitty sang:

> *Some stirabout and a mutton chop,*
> *And a nigger's mouthful of slipperty slop,*
> *Out of me way, old Dan Tucker,*
> *You're too late to come for your supper.*

'Again, again.'

Kitty laughed and kissed him. They were both as happy as they could be; Shon in getting the familiar song; and Kitty in singing it. It might be the last time for Kitty, but the immediate pleasure like the immediate duty was enough. For the rest she trusted to the Blessed Virgin and the Holy Saints.

The next day John Chass visited Hardy and the castle was withdrawn from sale. Benskin, who was just about to leave for Ireland, behaved very well. He made no claim for damages, and he offered a surprisingly high price for the English reversions alone. But he was told once more that they were not for sale.

III

Mrs. felix died suddenly in '95 of a chill caught spiting a wet field in thin shoes; and Felix came home from Africa in the next month. He was greatly distressed to find himself so relieved by her disappearance.

Having come home he stayed for nearly a year, partly to see Cleeve and partly on business. The Mosi Company was now in great difficulties and though John Chass, since debts had become inevitable, made no difficulty about borrowing money, especially for Felix, he failed to raise another loan at the bank. John Chass' creditors were already growing alarmed.

The Mosi directors therefore, since there was no other means of obtaining new capital, decided to float a public company, and they looked for a new director of known integrity and wealth to join the board. As Felix said, 'Business in the last resort, rests on confidence.'

Unluckily no leading financier would agree to give his name to the new Mosi Company. Felix, when he came to stay in Ireland for the summer, was still unprovided.

'You'd better ask our own millionaire,' John Chass suggested.

'I didn't know you had one.'

'Benskin has taken Knockeen Hall and the mountain.'

'Who's Benskin?'

'One of these new South African millionaires that are buying up everything and everybody. But you'd better look out for him—he's a real schemer.'

Benskin had taken Knockeen Hall, a shooting box on the mountain, in the previous year; but he had not used it. This year he had arrived with a party of six which had made more excitement in Annish than any visitors since the Duke of Connaught. On the first day of his arrival, there were at least a hundred people on Dunvil pier waiting for the foreigners to land. The castle party, come to meet the tenants, could not reach the steps. A solid crowd six deep stood gazing inwards at a lady in lilac silk, who stood on the staging.

The two Corners, with their height, could see her over the heads of the crowd, and John Chass said, 'That must be the great Mrs. Pynsant.'

'Who's she?'

John Chass did not answer. He was gazing at the lady, who was certainly a new species in Annish; and enjoying the aplomb with which she challenged the stares of the crowd. Smiling and conscious, but conscious like an actress who makes of the consciousness itself an additional charm, she glanced carelessly here and there with her handsome brown eyes, moved her shoulders in their long sleeves and raised and turned her chin with the gesture of a magnificent bird about to preen itself. She seemed to say, 'Look at me if you like—I'm worth looking at. I know how to be looked at and all of us are pleased.'

This performance was astonishing to the Annishmen who had never seen even a play, but it delighted John Chass.

'A real London charmer,' he said, smiling at Mrs. Pynsant, and then, as a small man in a blue suit came to the step, 'And here's the wee schemer himself.'

John Chass, from the very beginning, took a kind of chaffing enjoyment in Benskin's party and Benskin himself, as if like English people with foreign lords and celebrities, he could not take them quite seriously. He was even amused by Benskin's various efforts to possess himself of his property, as a man is amused by the antics of an intelligent dog trying to take a biscuit out of his pocket.

Benskin was a middle-sized man, broad shouldered and short legged, in a shabby blue suit and a bowler. He was, in fact, extremely like any of a hundred small farmers in Annish; with a brown face, sundried and shiny across the cheekbones and the bridge of the nose; a brown moustache, a shelving forehead, deep set hollow eyes, a slow heavy walk.

'You wouldn't take him for a millionaire,' John Chass said. 'Not that he is one. Hardy says he's not even very rich. I suppose he's going to make a fortune out of us, if he can.'

John Chass laughed at this idea. Meanwhile Benskin took the lady's forearm and guided her through the crowd. A schoolgirl, of about fifteen, running after him, took his other arm; and the three advanced unconcernedly upon the crowd which divided before them. John Chass came forward to shake hands. But even then he could not help smiling as if the whole ceremony were comical.

Benskin had made another offer for the Corner property, about a year before, when he took Knockeen. He did not talk business to John Chass on this occasion, but he examined the castle, walked all over the farms and the mountain, and went to a Dunderry lawyer for an opinion on Annish land. He also tried to pump him about John Chass' financial position. He asked a Dunderry coal merchant to shoot, and remarked to him what a pity it was to see a beautiful old house like Castle Corner falling into ruin.

Probably in England such discreet enquiries would have seemed normal and correct; nothing would have been heard of them; but in Annish they might have been shouted through a megaphone. They reached John Chass on the same day, who enjoyed them greatly.

Slatter, of course, was the chief tale bringer. 'The dirty little thief,' he would shout. 'He'd steal a chicken's teeth while she laid him an egg. Watch out for him, Jawn.'

Slatter was in terror that Benskin was going to outbid him for the castle. One day, however, Benskin asked Slatter to dinner at Knockeen, let him win two games of billiards, filled him with liqueur brandy and said to him, 'I hear you're interested in Irish land, Mr. Slatter. I must say I wouldn't like to own anything in Ireland in these times—this shooting lease is quite as far as I'm going.'

Slatter was relieved and delighted by this tactful announcement. But this did not prevent his telling the story next day to John Chass himself at the castle, where they were entertaining the Knockeen party to tea. 'You see, Jawn, he knew I'd made an offer and he was just tellin' me that if I let him have the breast he'd leave me the pope's nose. Aw, Jawn, ye can't beat him.'

They were standing at the drawing-room window looking out on the terrace where Benskin was walking slowly up and down with Jarvis. John Chass gave a loud laugh, and stooping to peer at Benskin under the curtain, said with great appreciation, 'You'd have to get up very early to be beforehand with that wee schemer. Look at him there getting round young Cocky.'

Harry Jarvis had just come on leave from his regiment; his first leave. He had grown up like his grandfather, small, lightly built, with sharp, aquiline features, very blue eyes, a resolute and serious air. His small, reddish moustache was curled up at the ends. It was not a Kaiser moustache, but it sprang from the same idea; the German army, in those days, was the centre of military inspiration. Harry's fingers were continually twirling and smoothing the little moustache while he talked; with that special kind of earnestness and impatience which belongs to young men when they discover the responsibility of life.

Harry had just realized that his beloved Castle Corner and the family property was going to ruin; and he was both astonished and enraged by his uncle's folly. He could not understand how any man in his senses could behave so stupidly.

But also he was astonished like most serious young men in their twenties by the inefficiency and carelessness of nearly everybody. He had, as it were, come out of the nursery and perceived, to his amazement, that the grown up world was full of rascals and fools. Harry was already a warm friend and admirer of Benskin's, who had not only devised a plan for extricating John Chass from his difficulties, but who agreed with him that the Government was feeble, the War Office hopelessly inefficient; and that the resources of the empire were being wasted by selfishness and lack of imagination.

'They don't seem to see the opportunities,' Benskin was saying in his grave, soft voice, and he turned to Jarvis with a characteristic bend; a kind of deferential sideways bow which seemed to say, 'Excuse my presuming so far.' He was an extremely polite man, with the formal manners of a European.

'They see all right,' Jarvis, with a melancholy expression, gently curled his new moustache. 'They couldn't help it,' and he added severely, 'It's pure bloody slackness, that's all.'

A girl came out of the French windows and ran up to them. She was a square-shouldered, buxom girl with dark brown hair and very thick eyebrows; her round, rosy face had an expression as English as its colour; a look at once confident and friendly; as if she found the world simple to understand and easy to enjoy.

She glanced laughing at each in turn and said, 'Hullo, Harry! Hullo, Theo!' Jarvis answered gravely, 'Hullo, Stella!' and seeing his serious face she at once became serious and waited to see what the men were talking about.

'Not so much slackness perhaps as simply having a good time,' Benskin said. 'That's the danger of success—the very fact that people have more money and leisure and freedom to amuse themselves is a danger. I suppose all democracies commit suicide that way.'

'Got to keep up your standards,' Harry agreed.

'And that takes some self-sacrifice—but people ask, why should we sacrifice ourselves?'

'Got to be made,' Harry said, 'or everything'll go smash.'

'Look at school,' Stella said, glancing at Harry for his support.

'Yes, or a regiment.' Harry and Stella Pynsant were already close friends. Stella, though she was an only child and an heiress, had that simplicity and self-confidence which was seen only in young girls from the schools of the time, very strict, evangelical and decidedly sentimental. Stella, however, had a frankness of her own, due probably to the fact that she was an important person in her own world. She did not trouble to hide her pleasure in walking arm in arm with her two friends, in being the union between them, and in feeling herself part of their serious and important world.

'That's the difficulty,' Benskin said. 'When people get too comfortable they must keep things up, and everything needs keeping up.' He glanced as if by chance at the house, and Harry said gloomily, 'Yes, that's the trouble here, nothing's kept up.'

83

'It's such a beautiful house,' Stella said. 'It would be simply a crime to let it go to pieces.'

'But what can a chap do?' Jarvis asked, half turning to Benskin, whose silence agreed with sad and polite deference that a chap could do nothing with a man like John Chass.

All of them looked at the house as if at some neglected and deserving veteran, and Stella repeated in a tender and affectionate tone, 'It's a darling house—I love it.' It was obvious that she did really love the house. She was ready to love anything.

John Chass peeping under the curtain said, 'There now—they're saying that I'm letting the house go to rack and ruin,' and he and Slatter, looking at the three solemn faces upturned towards the roof, exploded again. 'Ah, the wee schemer,' John Chass murmured, tearful with joy. Schemers were always greatly appreciated in Annish.

Felix and John Chass had meant to discuss the Mosi business with Benskin, and Felix had brought his official portfolio from his room. 'If anything will get him in,' he told John Chass, 'it will be the prospectus. Business men love statistics, and I have enough to convince anybody.' But up till the moment he had been too much interested in a discussion with a certain MacEwen and Mary Corner to look for Benskin. MacEwen, a tall, thin man with a long, thin face was an Indian civilian on leave. He took great interest in the colonies and he was the kind of listener that Felix enjoyed; a man of knowledge and judgment.

'Conditions on the Mosi are a bad joke,' Felix boomed, 'and you can't tell what's going to happen from one day to the next.'

Felix' beard was now streaked with grey, and his stomach had become larger. In his mourning he looked like an archbishop; Mary and MacEwen were listening to him with deference. 'As for the traders,' he exclaimed, 'you couldn't hope to see a finer collection of blaggards as we keep on the Mosi—the best of them are the slavers.'

'Slavers, Felix,' Mary said with surprise.

'My dear Mary, we all deal in slaves. I bought a girl myself to do the washing. If I hadn't she'd have been sacrificed to some god or other—or sold to someone else—no one thinks anything of it—when slavery is established, it seems the natural thing.'

'The natural thing,' MacEwen murmured.

'Certainly!' Felix' eye brightened, his head rose as he saw before him a promised land of enquiry and discovery. 'What could seem more natural. You might even call it an idea of nature like the family and the tribe, one of the earliest social ideas. Ants keep slaves, Every tribe of baboons is in subjection to old man baboon, and it must have been the same with men until some busybody said that it was a scandal. Then of course they all saw it.'

'You think so?'

'In time.'

'A long time.'

'Yes, but the point is that they had to see it in the end because it's a fact that wouldn't let them alone.'

A boy whom Felix did not recognize; a tall youth with a slight dark moustache, who had been standing close behind Mary Corner, said suddenly in an English voice and with a slightly condescending manner 'The Southern States of America didn't see it like that.'

'Oh, but I think they did—that's why they were so angry. They were frightened. The truth, when it comes out, is always rather alarming.'

MacEwen asked if there was such a thing as political truth.

'Call it moral then—it's the same thing in the end—politics is only the expression of moralities.'

'Rather conflicting moralities.'

'Oh, everything from the tenth century up—or the first if you bring in the political religions.'

'Rome?'

'Good gracious, yes,' Mary exclaimed, 'Those Italians.'

'All religions are political.'

'And all politics are religious,' the Anglo-Indian remarked.

There was a slight pause while the three contemplated the pictures which they had rapidly sketched. In each expression, Mary's vivacious, MacEwen's concentrated, Felix' lively and amused as by his own dexterity, there was the same quality of a special enjoyment, like the restrained but keen excitement of polite children at a rare treat. In fact, it was extremely rare for any of the three to enjoy an exchange of ideas.

'The conflict of beliefs,' Felix said. 'The battle of ideas. That's the real struggle for life. The dinosaur put its faith in size and the tyrannosaur trusted to teeth.'

'The lobster was an odd inspiration—but I suppose you would say that lobsters aren't true.'

Felix laughed. 'The lobster got stuck because he ran up against the truth—the scientific fact that if you put your skeleton on the outside, you can't develop very far.'

'Would you say that religions tend to put their skeletons on the outside?'

'All except the ones that haven't any bones at all.'

'Those aren't religions strictly speaking.'

'But the fascinating thing,' Felix smiled with pleasure at the sight, 'is to see the big fundamental discoveries suddenly appear. Watch a new moral truth smashing its way into politics and economics and upsetting

everything and everybody. Look at the idea of employer's responsibility
—the Factory Acts and so on.'

'They've certainly smashed the old providential school——'

'Providence has been running away ever since—though I suppose it
had all the most powerful people in the country with it.'

Felix, looking round, again caught the eye of the young man fixed
upon him with a peculiar eagerness and anxiety. It was an expression
which reminded Felix of some of the faces on the *Maria Fry* on a
morning when he dispensed simple medicines and gave advice to the
sick. He had seen river pagans, slowly rotting with leprosy or eaten
away by dysentery, gaze at him with the same intensity while he gave
them directions and medicines. He found himself talking more and
more for the young man's benefit: 'Or look at education. When I was
young, even thirty years ago, people still said that it was wrong to
educate the poor. They got very angry with the Government for
forcing parents to send their children to school. But now it's obvious
to everybody that deliberately to leave children uneducated, even on
the highest economic grounds, is a moral crime. It's obvious even to
the Czar. He talks about education, at least.'

'Is that what you call a moral truth?'

'Kant would call it so, as I suppose you learnt, Watty, even at
Cambridge—it's a law of universal application,' and he looked at the
young man as if for support. Mary Corner also looked at the young
man and said, 'Philip is going to Cambridge.' She wished to bring him
into their conversation.

Felix vaguely remembered the name Philip, but he could not recog-
nize the face, and especially the look among the young men in Annish.
He was about, however, to give him an encouraging smile, when
MacEwen said, 'Ideas change.'

'Not that kind of idea. It can't. In fact, I suppose that ideas like
that—ideas of universal justice and peace and security are the only
permanent things in the world, so that in the end they are bound to be
realized.'

MacEwen smiled sceptically. Like all men with practical experience
of Government he was sceptical about permanent systems, fixed
constitutions. 'The golden age—a bit utopian perhaps.'

'But, my dear Watty, you can see the thing happening—you can see
one final idea after another appearing—you can even get a glimpse of
what the ultimate structure of society will be like—when it gets a solid
structure of permanent true ideas—ideas that square with facts.'

Felix grew warm and serious. His idea of the inevitable golden age,
though he had no hope to see it, was dear to him. He lived in this ideal
future as others live in an ideal past; the age of faith; or the age of
romance. One of his critics said that Felix Corner's idea of the golden

age was simply a universal Oxford; a world of quiet colleges, gardens, libraries, parks and streams; peaceful and secure; where the worst conflict would be a college football match or a difference of opinion between rival schools of philosophy, and the limit of freedom would be the same as that which at present restrained dons from murdering each other, stealing each other's wives, levying forces to devastate each other's gardens, or aspiring to the glory of dictatorship—a mere disinclination—a disinclination for these amusements.

'A permanent society!' MacEwen said. 'You'd need a very rigid kind of Government.'

Benskin and Stella had joined the party, and stood close behind MacEwen. Benskin looked at Felix as if to say, 'I believe you wanted to meet me.' But Felix was preoccupied; it seemed to him that the conversation was very much more important than his business with Benskin. It was a serious matter to discuss serious questions. He answered MacEwen with energy, 'I don't mean a rigid structure for society. That's no more necessary for a real society of interests than for an ordinary middle-class family, so long as its income and manners are reasonable—so long as it has some foundation. After all Watty, what you call civilization is simply floating on bog; any small child can dig under it with a tin spade.'

'And all the children do dig—of all ages.'

'They all do, except the owners of the mansion that's getting undermined.'

'Which is all the present governments and religions.'

'Yes,' Felix' eye happened to fall on the attentive Benskin 'and the millionaires—they can hear the picks going day and night. Why, their own children dig—it's an instinct to dig.'

'Exactly, that's why I doubt your permanent society.'

'But you can't dig bed-rock, Watty. No one tries to dig away the anti-slavery laws or even popular education. You wouldn't be able to dig up universal peace if we had it, any more than you could start a war between Kent and Sussex. But of course that's a long way off. I suppose the next idea that's going into the foundations is the abolition of poverty.'

'What a good idea,' Stella said with surprise. Benskin bent his neck sideways like a canary looking at a doubtful seed; Slatter turned his head suspiciously from the other end of the room, and Philip, starting like a child caught stealing fruit from the table, strolled carelessly away. But he could not stay away. A minute later he was again at Felix' back; apparently looking out of the window, but actually listening to the boom.

'If you can't defend slavery and illiteracy, I don't see how you can defend poverty. It's exactly the same thing expressed in economics. Poverty is oppression. It will have to be abolished.'

'Abawlish pawverty,' Slatter shouted, poking his head forward between Benskin and Stella. Jealousy for Philip had brought him to hear the talk. 'Abawlish pawverty—did ye ever hear such dahm stuff— and who's goin' to work if he gets his keep for nawthin'.'

Philip was already at the far end of the room. He had long learnt to avoid argument with his uncle on any subject; the result was only confusion. He went quickly out at the French window to the terrace and so among the trees towards the mountain. He wanted to think. He had not understood all the talk, but what he did understand was that according to Felix Corner certain ideas in the world were right and others were wrong; and the right ideas were bound to win in the end. Victory was certain to one side; and it was the side of the poor. He felt an extraordinary excitement.

Slatter had not noticed his nephew's disappearance. He had received too great a shock. He glared furiously at the astonished Felix. He could barely speak for rage.

'Abawlish pawverty—my gawd—and that's what ye tell them—and that's what ye call socialism.' He turned his furious imploring eyes towards Benskin. 'Why can't they lave us alone—what good does it do them—what do they get out of it—nawthin', nawthin'.'

Felix, taken aback by the man's vehement despair, hastened to reassure him. 'But, James, there's no immediate danger.'

'No danger—my gawd, no danger—with wages up a shillin' a week at every hiring fair in Annish—eight shillin's a week is what they ask now—no danger.' His voice was full of amazement and terror. 'It's just the talk that is the danger—and how can ye stop a fule from talkin'— how can ye stop it.'

Harry's infatuation for Stella Pynsant was a joke to everybody. He was seen every day walking about Knockeen with his solemn, fierce air and his smartest norfolk suits, waiting to catch the girl after breakfast or lunch. Then they would play tennis or more often march through the fields arm in arm, serious and absorbed, discussing the ruin of the Corners, the melancholy condition of the world and the need for loyalty and self-sacrifice to save it.

'We want more men like Benskin, ready to give their time and money for public service.'

'Poor Uncle Theo is awfully worried about things in England—the Prince of Wales you know—they say he's still playing baccarat.'

'It's not so much the game,' Jarvis said, who had lost ten pounds at *chemin de fer* on his last mess night, 'as the people he plays with.'

'That's what Theo says, he's letting everything down.'

They walked on in silence, full of gloomy forebodings and the delight of each other's sympathy.

Harry had never met anyone like this girl; he was astonished by her intelligence. They agreed about everything. But also he thought her the most delightful and honest person he had ever known. The candid look of her brown eyes when she turned them towards him, full of affectionate sympathy and confidence in his affection, made his pulses jump, and he thought, 'What a darling she is—what extraordinary luck to meet a girl like that—unique in every way.'

But his face would continue grave and thoughtful while he continued the discussion. 'I believe in missionaries myself. If our religion isn't good enough for export, what is it good for?'

'That's perfectly true. It's a perfect disgrace the way we call ourselves Christians and do nothing about the heathen in Africa or India.'

Stella delighted in her friend because he was at once sensible and serious and because he did not treat her like a young lady, with smirks and compliments. She admired him for not being silly with her, as she put it. She spent all day with Jarvis, walking or playing tennis, sailing on the lough, until the affair was a scandal even in Dunderry and everybody said, 'But of course her mother is a thoroughly bad lot—you know about—yes, that story—well, if the Prince couldn't do with her——'

In fact, Mrs. Pynsant did not seem to trouble her head about this flirtation. When local ladies gave her hints about the gossip, she smiled at them and answered, 'But they're so happy—it seems such a pity to worry the child with ideas.'

Mrs. Pynsant's smile, full of good nature, and her habit of talking about everything without the least reserve, overwhelmed even Mrs. Duff, the most formidable dragon in the county. It said clearly, 'My good woman, how absurd you are and how provincial.'

But one wet afternoon when she was sitting in the little parlour at Knockeen, bored as only town women can be bored at a shooting party, she saw her daughter coming through the garden and Jarvis' back disappearing among the trees.

The girl, dripping wet in her school mackintosh, with raindrops on her cheeks; and on her snub nose, pink with exercise, was smiling to herself as she came through the gooseberry bushes. This smile, which in the last week seemed entirely to have changed her whole expression and especially the shape of her rather thick mouth, amused Mrs. Pynsant. She entered through it into the girl's feelings; the supreme and unique happiness of a friendship which had the force of love without any of the selfishness and hysteria of passion. She understood it, but she did not intend it to continue. Mrs. Pynsant also had her prejudices. Schoolgirls could not be allowed to fall in love.

'And how is your bo-hoy to-day?'

The girl jumped as if stung, and her face turned dark red. She frowned in angry confusion at her mother, and said in a stupid voice, 'Wh-at?'

'How is your Irish bo-hoy? I believe that's what they're called.'

Stella said nothing. She grew still redder, and her eyebrows rose from the frown into a kind of wondering confusion.

'It's quite a case with the bo-hoy isn't it?' Mrs. Pynsant said.

'What do you mean, mother?'

'Has he proposed yet?'

'Don't be——' the girl burst out angrily; then suddenly went out of the room. But it was noticed that she was very ready to spend the next morning with the Slatter girls, and when Jarvis came up in the afternoon she did not go out with him.

Cleeve, who had not been to Ireland for four years, since his mother's final quarrel about the will, arrived on Saturday in the highest spirits. He ran all over the castle on the first afternoon, shook hands with everybody, and exclaimed with delight, 'Everything's just the same.'

Nothing, of course, was the same. To people in Annish the changes of four years were too many to tell; but everybody smiled at the queer-looking boy with his long nose and thin legs; it was seen that he was not yet, like Harry and Phil Feenix, at a responsible age. Cleeve himself felt grown up. He considered that his education was finished and hoped to persuade his father not to waste any more money on his schooling. Meanwhile he intended to begin life. At tea-time seeing through the window Francie and Shon coming back from their walk, he exclaimed, 'Is that Kitty, but she's quite fat.'

'Good gracious Cleeve. Poor Kitty's in America two years with that Conor Foy. That's Francie.'

'Francie. But I knew Francie quite well.' He rushed downstairs to cut off Francie and Shon outside the kitchen door.

'Yes, it's Master Cleeve, Francie. Back in the ancestral home. And how are you, Francie, ticklish as ever?'

Francie giggled. Shon was standing on the top shelf of the iron framework always known as the rattantoo, from Mary Corner's French *retient-tout*. The rattantoo was a favourite fort with small boys at the castle. Shon gazed down on his cousin with a solemn expression. He was a small pale little boy with thick brown curls and prominent grey eyes.

Shon had been excited for a week about Cleeve's coming; he had scarcely been able to sleep or eat for thinking of the arrival of his cousin from England. He had no idea what kind of experience Cleeve would bring to him, but he had felt that it must be good and extraordinary. Francie's voice alone had assured him of that.

Now he was puzzled. He could not find within himself any great happiness and the dark passage with its sharp sour smell, the dirty whitewash of the walls, the whole surrounding frame of his life, were the same as before. Already his hope was fading. He looked doubtfully at Cleeve.

Cleeve, who took interest in children only when he had time to spare from his own enjoyment, caught the child's eye and held out his hand, 'And you're Shony—you don't remember me, do you?'

'Look where I am,' Shon said. He fell back upon making his own pleasure, according to his nurse's and his mother's instruction in make-believe.

'I hope you're kind to Francie.' Cleeve put his arm gingerly round the girl. 'We're old sweethearts, aren't we, Francie?'

'Go on, Master Cleeve.'

'It's a tower,' Shony said thoughtfully.

'Lave me be, Master Cleeve. I can see you're a bad one.'

This was not so. Cleeve had not before squeezed any girl; he had wished to do so but he had found a great obstacle in his way: that he feared to give offence, to hurt anybody's feelings, including his own. But Francie had appeared to him like an inspiration. She was an old acquaintance; she was fat and good-natured; above all, she belonged to the family.

At Castle Corner, Cleeve had quite a different idea of himself than of the young Mister Corner who had lodged with his mother in three rooms over a chemist's shop in remote Somerset, opposite the methodist chapel. At Castle Corner, he saw himself the young prince among his people; and because of this conception, he was bold, easy, and full of a warm tender affection, like that of every man towards his possessions. He loved the castle, the country, his Uncle John and his Aunt Mary, because they belonged to this delightful scheme of things, in which he was Master Cleeve Corner; that was why he boldly squeezed Francie Egan.

Francie gave a squeak and said, 'Go wan now.'

'It's an island,' Shon said.

'And how bad are you, Francie,' squeezing so hard that his own face turned red.

Francie, giggling wildly, broke away and rushed down the passage into the kitchen. Cleeve, equally delighted, turned and rushed up the steps without even noticing Shon on the rattantoo.

But Shon had not noticed the departure of Cleeve. He was too busy with the exploration of his desert island. He stood still in the mouldy

91

twilight of the passage, with his head among the cobwebs on the dirty ceiling, and thought, 'I'm Robinson Crusle—this is Robinson Crusoe.' He stood breathless, enquiring into the sensations of Robinson Crusoe and seeing how he liked them. It was important to get them right. He wanted the real thing.

Cleeve squeezed Francie again that evening when Shon was being put to bed; and on the next morning he hastened to the nursery as soon as he was up. He was already flushed and smiling. But when he went up to Francie, who was giving Shon his breakfast, she said severely, 'None of that now Master Cleeve. Do you forget what day it is?'

Shon, looking at him with interest, asked, 'Don't you have to go to church?'

Cleeve was surprised. He had forgotten that it was Sunday. Cleeve, like Felix, had no religion. He said, 'Oh, is it? What of it?' He went out with the nonchalance of a free man.

He wondered if he would be expected to go to church, and as if by unconscious habit which had lain dormant for four years, he turned abruptly in the passage and opened his cousin's door.

Jarvis was standing before his wardrobe glass in full hussar uniform, with busby and sword. His attitude as Cleeve impulsively threw open the door, was imposing; his chest thrown out, his nose in the air; one hand on his sword, the other curling up his little moustache.

Jarvis was in a melancholy frame of mind. He had not seen Stella for four days and he could not understand her sudden change of mind towards him. He turned towards Cleeve with a grave and dignified air.

'I'm awfully sorry, Harry, bursting in.'

'Don't mention it, old chap.'

'Does one go to church?'

'Unless one happens to be a bloody atheist.'

Cleeve was startled. He said politely, 'I don't mind going.'

'Very kind of you, old chap. God ought to appreciate it.' He threw off his jacket and said, 'You won't be troubled with family prayers, however.'

'Needn't one go?'

'They're stopped, old chap.' He spoke gloomily. 'Too much trouble, I suppose—after three hundred years.'

Cleeve looked grave and went out quietly as if from the presence of a mourner. In fact, Harry Jarvis felt extreme bitterness on this subject. It seemed to him that everything precious and unique, the old ways at the castle, the castle itself, was going to the devil; because no one would take the trouble to keep them up. He had spent all the evening before trying to make his uncle understand that Benskins' plan for the estates; the sale of the English property, the liquidation of the Irish mortgages

92

and the investment of the surplus in sound gold mines, suggested by Benskin himself, was the only chance of salvation for the castle. But his uncle had only laughed and said, 'So he has got round you too.'

'But, Uncle, he's not getting round anyone. What's wrong with a plan like that?'

'Indeed, I'm sure it's very right for Benskin.'

'And for us too.'

'The wee schemer,' John Chass burst out laughing. 'James will laugh to hear that.'

When Harry had tried to press his point he had received one of those heavy snubs which John Chass could deliver when he was pestered.

Harry was bitter still at the recollection of it. It seemed that he was obliged to stand helpless and watch the ruin of everything he loved.

Harry Jarvis had a strong sense of the past. His romantic feelings had been turned into the idea of antiquity, and anything old was beautiful to him. To see an old custom die was for him like seeing an old and glorious hero leave the world; and to feel deprived of that glory. He had suffered as much for the end of the prayers as for the death of old John.

'Look at that,' Harry said, showing Cleeve the old family service books in the drawer of the sideboard, and he called indignantly to Mary in the hall, 'Look at Grandpapa's Bible, Aunty.'

Mary, in a fluster because it was not certain whether Shon had not a cold, rushed to look and screamed, 'Grogan, Grogan, didn't I tell you not to put your corks on the Bible.'

Grogan put his pale face through the door to deny indignantly that his corks ever touched the Bible. They might fall indeed on the episcopal prayer book beside it. But Mary was already back in the hall, calling for Francie to bring a muffler.

To Cleeve, smiling, the house had a delightful sensation which he decided to call in his new novel, just about to begin, 'Sunday morning at the castle.'

It was a sensation of mixed urgency, blue clothes, bowlers in the hall, shouts and clattering hoofs from the yard, maids running up and down stairs with capes, clothes brushes, prayer books and umbrellas.

'Did he cough just now, Francie?'

'Oh yes, mam.'

'Why didn't you tell me, good gracious?' She turned upon Shon who was running round and round the hall, shuffling his feet on the pavement and looking into the air with an expression of intense pleasure. He was a train and he was watching the steam come out of his own funnel.

'Put out your tongue, Shon.'

He put it out in passing, without ceasing to enjoy the steam.

'It's not what you'd call a rale cough, mam,' Francie said, beginning to think that Mary did not want Shon to have a cough.

Mary, having lassoed Shon with the muffler, pursued him round the hall.

'Now here's the station, good gracious are you going past the station. Harry, can you whistle for the child.'

Harry, standing with his grand air, a bowler of the latest fashion tilted slightly over one eye, pursed up his lips and without the least diminution of his sad dignity and Sunday reverence, whistled sharply and said, 'Tang. All change.'

Shon stopped. Mary tied the muffler.

'You're not taking the boy to church,' John Chass said from the back passage. He was wearing his smoking cap; a sign that he did not intend church.

'Of course I am.'

'With that cold?'

'You know yourself he ought to go to church. How do you feel, m'dear.'

Shon, slowly becoming aware of his own existence, turned his attention to himself, and said, after a close examination, that he felt very well.

'That's a good child,' Mary cried. Her anxiety was relieved. She was no longer flustered between her anxieties for Shon's physical and moral welfare.

Harry said sadly, 'It's a funny thing, Aunty, that you're always in a fuss about Shon's going to church and you never troubled about the prayers being stopped.'

'What, Harry? M'cape Francie. No, stand still, m' darling or you'll get too hot. Grogan, Grogan, tell Sukey there's something burning. Bless my soul, Harry, of course little boys must go to church, you wouldn't have me bring him up a heathen.'

Mary Corner had no leisure to be troubled about the prayers. She had felt the loss once as sharply as Harry himself; but for her it was so far away that she could hardly recall it. A thousand years of domestic history with all its cares and catastrophes separated her from the convoy riot.

Cleeve was interested to see that John Chass had also given up going to church.

'I thought that magistrates always went to church,' he said to his aunt in the carriage, as they drove away.

'They should m'dear, but in the last few years some of them have been getting lazy. Your uncle, of course, can't always come because the pew is so horrid draughty it brings on his lumbago. But Colonel Duff and that wretch Slatter don't even send their carriages, the stoopids.'

'They certainly are stupid not to support their own church,' Harry said.

'You're quite right, m'dear, but the truth is people are much too comfortable these days to do half the things they ought to do.'

But on this occasion both the Slatter brougham and the Duff landau had attended church. There was also the hired carriage from the Hall bringing the Benskin party, which was standing on the gravel in front of the porch.

Harry had hoped to catch Stella, because it was his last day and he wanted to say good-bye to her. But Mary Corner suddenly called out to Jebb, 'We can stop here, Jebb.' The carriage was pulled up. Mary Corner did not like Mrs. Pynsant and when Cleeve asked 'Who is the lady in the wonderful hat?' she answered with a little grimace, 'What you call a beauty. Don't jump, darling, or you'll break your legs.'

Shon was already in mid-air; but having jumped he became at once sedate. He had learnt how to go into church, and he enjoyed the practice of that art.

Mary Corner's tactics were successful. The Pynsant party had already disappeared. Harry, even by a dash which imperiled his dignity, could reach Stella's side only at the top of the aisle. He touched her arm and whispered, 'The last day.' The girl turned to him with a strange look of confusion; frowning and ashamed; but before she could speak, Mrs. Pynsant glanced round and at once her cheeks grew crimson; she scowled at her mother, and stepped into the pew with a haughty air. Harry was left to enter the castle pew after Mary.

The farmers who had waited for the castle party to take their seats moved up the aisle and filled the next pews. But the attendance was thin. The brougham had brought the two Slatter girls, but the Duff landau had been empty. It stood outside with the brougham, the castle barouche, the hired landau, Lady MacEwen's victoria and six outside cars to show the papists that the protestants were loyal to their religion. The whole congregation did not fill the first eight pews. It had come to a service of duty and instruction and to a sermon by the Reverend Feenix.

Feenix was famous for his scholarly and philosophic sermons. He preached on this occasion about the moral consciousness, showing that self-sacrifice and altruism of any kind was against the purpose of a godless nature, 'For as we know, my friends, to use the great shibboleth of these confused times, what is called pro-gress has been founded solely upon the struggle for existence; upon pure selfishness. What, then, has the scientist to say of this scientific ano-maly, my friends, of

95

altruism. For ob-serve, even the smallest good act—the least por-tion of unselfishness in any act, is to-tally inex-plicable upon the scientific hy-po-thesis of the struggle for existence.'

Mr. Feenix had his own method of pronunciation. He made short vowels long and long vowels short. He also anglicized all foreign words and talked of feet for fête and caif for café.

'My friends, the moral consciousness, however weak, is a fact suf-fi-cient to destroy all the vast edifice of the Darwinians.'

Mary, who knew all his sermons by heart, watched him with a round, abstracted eye. She was thinking, 'Poor man, what misery to see his son taken from him by that savage at Carnmore. And now the boy doesn't even come to church.' She was astonished at the idea of such an unhappy life; and her face grew every moment more mournful; her eyebrows rose; her pale grey eyes seemed to sink into their hollows, 'And if he had not come to Annish, perhaps he might have been a bishop and Philly saved from wasting himself.'

Shon played with the sequins of his mother's cloak, and thought a thousand things in a moment. Harry Jarvis sat bolt upright with folded arms; his chin was aimed at the preacher, across the high shining tower of his fashionable collar, like a gun. But his eyes beneath his half-closed lids, were turned upon the back of Stella's head two pews in front. He was thinking tenderly, 'Someone's upset her—some of these damned old cats.' The idea of blaming the girl was impossible to him, in the nature of things.

Maddy and Coo did not let their eyes wander. Hands in lap they sat gazing at the preacher whose arguments had no more meaning for them than Chinese; while Maddy's colour slowly deepened. Doctor Hanna coming in late had placed himself beside her, and this was the second time he had thus stalked her to church. He had also looked at her in a peculiar manner, smiled at her twice and tried to speak to her alone, on his last visit to Carnmore.

Maddy was now twenty-one, a strong, deep-breasted girl with big hips, a figure extremely fashionable and attractive to young men at that time. Her cheeks were pale and her nose sharp, but it was a face full of competence and good nature and several young men in the last three years had made approaches. But they found that Maddy withdrew before them; she avoided them even before they had discovered their own intention. A glance would make her turn pink and at dances she preferred married men or old friends like John Chass. She was a girl made for love and so she was extremely sensitive to all its manifestations.

Cleeve, with his eyes fixed sharply on the preacher's face was still enjoying his boldness with Francie. It had been quite easy after all. Perhaps he might go further next time.

96

'For, my friends, love itself by its very existence in the world of creatures is the proof of God's love towards them—and now before I conclude, I must refer to the to-pic of the coming feet—for the Eastern missions.'

Mr. Slatter's coachman and old Jebb from the castle, left their carriages to the grooms and walked across the fields to the chapel. But it was so full that they could not get in. Old Jebb, to keep his buckskins clean, sat upon the coping of a grave, and Slatter's smart young man put down his white mackintosh on the grass. There were fifty or more, kneeling in the porch and among the graves. They had come to a miracle; to the real presence of God; and at the first sound of the bell through the door, they stooped their faces towards the grass. Bridget Foy bowed so low that a long elf lock escaping from her shawl swung against the tombstone against which she knelt. She murmured with the hill people about her, 'Caid meel failta, aheerna.'

Only a few old mountain people in Annish spoke Irish, but the greetings were still used by the young ones, and it was the custom to welcome God among his people in the ancient tongue, 'a hundred thousand welcomes, Lord.'

As Bridget spoke, she bowed down, she felt the nearness of God, and she wished she had been able to get into the chapel, so that she might have seen him. But she had been ashamed to go into the chapel in bare feet now that all the girls from Dunvil and even Ballycorner had their new boots.

She slipped quickly from mass, although Father MacFee had warned the people that a young man would speak to them after mass about the new society for teaching the Irish songs and the old language.

Bridget did not care for Father MacFee, since the day of that confession, next after the famous convoy which broke the castle windows. She had gone in terror, and he had asked her at last, 'Is that all you have to tell me, my daughter?'

She had been in such fear then; she was so sure that he was laying a trap for her, that she had wanted to confess. She tried to tell him that she had stolen the jewel. But some force was too strong for her; a bitter sullen obstinacy locked her throat. She could not make herself give up the treasure which her hand had snatched.

'Is that all, my daughter?'

'Yes, father,' she whispered.

Then he had absolved her, and she had walked out into the sunlight of the churchyard among her brothers and sisters, her aunts, various uncles and friends, waiting languidly their turns in the box. Her wits were stiff and numb. She could not think or smile, and when Manus spoke to her, she stared at him blankly. But gradually life returned to her and then it seemed to her that it was a new kind of life. She was filled with astonishment; and the sense of this difference. She stood blinking at the sky, a barefoot little girl in a Sunday frock of blue serge, and thought, 'I bate him.' She grasped firmly this notion. 'Father MacFee never knew about the jewel at all,' and she felt a new over-powering triumph, a secret power. But then suddenly she remembered that she would have to take communion. That, in her sinful state would be a still more horrible sin. God would destroy her for it.

She looked round as if for escape. But already the bell was ringing; her father beckoned her.

When she had felt the wafer upon her tongue, she had felt it like a burning acid and almost screamed. But in the fraction of a second she perceived that it was not hot and acid but cool and dry. It dissolved. It went into her, carrying through her the blessed holy being; and God did not strike her dead.

For weeks she expected some blow; some illness; some sudden misfortune; the punishment of God. But she was not punished, and gradually she began to understand that she had cheated God as well as Father MacFee.

Now for five years she had triumphed over God. Often she made bad confessions for the pleasure of them, the triumph, and each time she took the bread she felt the glory of her deed, to steal from God his own power; and defy him.

'Father MacFee,' she thought with contempt. 'What's the good of him with his wee, soft voice and his smile.' She picked her way among the stones of the lane.

Three paces in front of her walked little Jebb in his gold-bound hat; his long black frock coat and silver buttons. She knew by that uniform that the Corners were likely to be at church; and that they could not go home until their coachman had returned. She followed him; keeping her distance to avoid his notice. She was secretive in all her deeds.

Six young men appeared below at the bend of the lane carrying a green banner with words painted upon it in gold. Bridgy could not read, but she had seen the banner before and knew that the words were in Irish. The young men belonged to the new Gaelic Society. They were all known to her and she darted aside into a potato field to avoid them. She was angry at this hitch to her project, and when they were past she flew on with angry feelings. Jebb was out of sight. 'And what good is Irish, onnyway? They don't speak Irish in America or London.'

Bridget had dreamed of America ever since Kitty had sent back pictures of herself in a silk dress and long French boots; but when Con had offered her the price of a ticket, she refused it. She had refused also to go into service; even as kitchenmaid to her Aunt Sukey at the castle

Yet she was angry when the people called her a lazy, dirty slut, for it seemed to her that her life was full of activity. She dreamed all day and even when she fetched the water for the potatoes or blew up the turf ash in the morning, one could see by her thoughtful expression and the look in her black eyes that her actual business was something quite different. She would go five miles to a wishing well; or a wedding.

Bridget was now fourteen; a slim strong girl with a white face, thick black eyebrows, and short Roman nose, dark red lips; the face of a Spanish Foy.

'A dirty class of bawg-hopper,' Sukey said of her, and it was true that Bridget was dirty. Why should she wash when in imagination she could be a princess at no trouble at all.

She was too late at the church. As she came from the potato field, the footman shut the door of the carriage and climbed on the box. Jebb lifted his hands, and the two bays, impatient at their long wait, came rattling and pounding over the road, making the huge old barouche swing and roll on its C springs like a boat towed rapidly over a rough sea. The dust rose in thick clouds on the hedge, on three little boys rushing to climb on the back axle, and on two others crouched in the lane, who were shouting with all their might, 'Whip behind, Oldy.' Old was Jebb's nickname, meaning in Annish, Owl.

Bridget jumped on the bank, careless of the brambles that tore her legs; but she was able from the bank to look down into the carriage and to catch, as it rolled past, a glimpse of Mrs. Corner's long chin and set mouth under the wide-brimmed hat; beyond her, the profile of a long nose, a short chin, and Shon's face and gazing eyes, alone on the front seat.

She jumped down and hurried through the field. 'A nose like a snipe.' She remembered Francie's description of Cleeve and tried to recall the boy who had played with her in the castle cellars.

She could remember nothing about him; but her family had never let her forget the time when she had lurked every day, month after month, behind trees and walls about the castle, to catch her beau again. She had forgotten Cleeve, but since his coming she had been full of a secret feeling about him; an excitement which grew. She laughed and thought, 'What a nose.' There were springs in her legs, and for the first time in days she noticed the cool sunshine of spring. It glittered on the lough below like diamonds among gold. Cleeve was already part of a dream so glorious that it transformed the world itself, and herself in the world.

It came into her head, as if spontaneously, that Sukey at the castle wanted a kitchenmaid. Sukey was without a kitchenmaid six months in the year, because of her temper and her heavy hand.

Bridget felt a strong disinclination to work. She had paid no attention

99

to her father's abuse or Father MacFee's advice. But now she thought, 'I might go down to the castle some day and see Anty Sukey.'

She did not intend to go soon; she was enjoying herself too much. The idea of Cleeve and the idea of work at the castle did not connect themselves in Bridget's mind, for she was not accustomed to a train of thought. Her thoughts were like bubbles rising to the surface of a bog pool. No one could guess, least of all herself, from their appearance, whether they arose from one cause at the bottom, or several different centres of fermentation.

At the beginning of May, Rifty Egan approached Francie with the news that Bridget might take a place in the castle. Francie said that she wanted no Foys in the castle, but she was afraid to stand in the way of that dangerous clan. She spoke to Peggy in June, who spoke to Mary Corner in the same week.

'She a dirty slumgalloper, mam, but it would be a Christian act to give her the place, for the Foys are starved.'

Mary Corner then approached Sukey. 'Susanna, I've found you a kitchenmaid and you ought to be thankful.'

'If it's thon Bridgeen, I'd rather a tinker from the road.'

But Mary Corner insisted, and on the first of July, Sukey, who was almost as glad of a grievance as an assistant and a victim, received Bridget in the kitchen.

At this time Cleeve had been back at school for two months, Jarvis was with his regiment, Felix alone of the visitors walked on the terrace and boomed about the arts of commerce or the decay of morals, arts and manners.

But Bridget did not trouble about the disappearance of Cleeve, because Cleeve had not been in her mind. She had come to the castle as she had gone to the barouche, on impulse.

She found herself at once in a hard place. Sukey did not forget that Bridget was a niece as well as a kitchenmaid. She had a double title to abuse her. But Bridget, who had lived all her life in dirt and misery, was as hard and patient as a mountain ass. She never defended herself, and never complained; she was silent, busy and attentive. She worked from before dawn till after midnight; and she never forgot an order or a lesson. She had the memory of the illiterate; of a savage who has to carry the whole knowledge of his tribe in his brain. She was a treasure to Sukey, as everyone but Sukey admitted. When Sukey, in the rage which always possessed her before a dinner party, slapped Bridget's face for dishing up a clear soup with bubbles of grease still floating upon it, she said, 'I didn't larn yet to clean the soup, anty.'

It did not astonish anybody that an idle, dirty, worthless girl should suddenly become a hardworking, respectful servant, because everyone

100

in Annish was accustomed to see such a change of nature. As old Dan said, 'It's what the growin' girls take a wish to be doin'.'

Bridget herself had no consciousness of reformation. She did not notice any break in activity, but only a change. Once she had been busy on the hills, taking a can to Padsy, or bringing the turf back; now she was running in and out of the scullery, the cellars and the yards. She was still busy all day long; not only with her hands, with her eyes, ears, smell, taste and mind. Everything was surprising to her. She had thought that at the castle she would have to do with the gentry; but she never saw them. She took her orders from Sukey or Grogan or Peggy and never left the kitchen except to creep to her attic. The castle, she found, was in three parts; the kitchen where Sukey ruled, the house, where Grogan ruled, and the rooms where Peggy ruled. When Sukey screamed for Peggy to take away her cans from the fire, Grogan would say, 'She's in the rooms.'

'I don't care where she is, but if she doesn't take away her cans from off me range this minute I'll put me poker through them.'

Sukey had fought Peggy for five years on account of her hot-water cans; and Grogan for sixteen because he hung his master's wet clothes in front of the fire. The cans were full of dents given them by Sukey with pokers, iron spoons, fish slices, frying pans and stove lids; and she would tear down John Chass' shooting jacket, stockings and shirts from the drying rails and kick them about the floor, ejaculating at the same time, 'Hell to your sowls, go wan to your own place.'

Sukey was in a passion three times a day before each principal meal, but after meals she was mild and sad. She would sit then with big, golden arms on the table, drinking tea as black as floor stain, and mourn her fate. 'What life is this for annywan of Gawd's creatures. Ye wouldn't wish it to the limbs of hell. But she has me notice. A month from to-day and be damned to himself and his denners.'

After dinner Sukey usually got drunk. She slept in a cellar at the end of the kitchen passage; or if she were drunker than usual, on the kitchen floor.

She had a bedroom in the wing; but she never went to it. She said that she preferred to be near her work. It was Bridget's last duty, after washing-up the dinner things and cleaning the servants' boots, to push her aunt under the kitchen table so that no one should tread on her.

Sukey was quick to understand Bridget's merits as a quick and hard worker and though on principle she never praised her to her face, she would hold her up as an example in order to depreciate others. 'Ye may call her black, but she's the only Foy in this world that knows how to do an honest jawb of work—she's an Egan in her elbows.'

One day, in order to throw a special gloom upon some of her numerous relations calling upon her in the kitchen, she even declared that she would make Bridget her heir. 'She's me own niece and the only wan in this world that ever cared for me—any bits of things I have and me mawther's ould ring will go to Bridgy, black as she is.

But she made up for this rash generosity by driving Bridget from morning to night. The girl, since in those days a kitchenmaid was regarded as the cook's servant, never had a day out. This did not trouble Bridget. She put all her interests in the castle. Once a month, when Darcy or Manus came to take five shillings of her wages for the support of the family, she heard the news of Ballycorner as if from a world's distance.

Padsy Foy had been for four years in his bog hole undiscovered by Slatter or any agent; though all Annish knew where he had squatted. He had now a patch of oats as well as potatoes in the gaps between the stones, so that he spoke of his farm. An Annish farmer could not respect himself without a field of oats. He had also built a house out of the broken rocks and thatched it with rushes. It was eight foot long by three foot high to the eaves and about two yards wide. From a little distance it looked like a heap of stones with some tufts of withered grass upon them.

In this hut, whose walls without cement let in daylight at every chink, Padsy and Darcy used to lie on a wet day, chewing tobacco and discussing their affairs. There was no chimney, so that the turf smoke made a thick fog within before it found its way through the walls and the small holes serving as windows. Whenever this fog grew suffocating Padsy, coughing, would gasp, 'Ah, but shmoke is a grand thing for the throat.'

'It is so,' Darcy would agree. 'It clanes it and it's good for the eyes too.' Darcy did not believe or disbelieve this, but his principles were loyalty to his benefactor and courtesy to all the world.

There were many visitors to Padsy's hole, as the people called it. A month did not pass without three or four. Poachers like Breedy Macan dropped in, and sometimes a distiller with a keg of poteen.

Phil Feenix came often in his holidays. He delighted in the high lonely place and the appreciation of his friends. He would sit for an hour on a rock, talking about the beauty of Ireland and the wrongs of her people. His voice rose and fell like a poet's, and Padsy and Darcy, who had a natural love of enthusiasm, had a great admiration for him.

In '95, just after Felix' arrival, he began to talk about education. 'What we want in Ireland is better education. That's the important thing. Of course it will come—it's inevitable. But it ought to be pushed on. The people have a right to it.'

'Sacred heart, young sir, and that's a fact,' Padsy would cry.

'Education is a weighty power to those that has it,' Darcy would say,

102

who could neither read nor write; and afterwards he and Padsy would discuss young Feenix for two or three days, and every hour or two Padsy would straighten his back, spit and exclaim, 'A grand young fella—but it's what all these Feenixes is a bit quare in the head.'

Darcy would say thoughtfully, 'He's quare and sensible too. For education is a grand ploy to the high up wans that don't need to work, and they'd miss it surely in their long days.'

In August Feenix was on the mountain nearly every day. Padsy and Darcy had never seen the boy so excited and restless. His whole manner was changed. He seemed more like one of the local nationalist speakers than a poet, except that he did not talk nationalism which Darcy and Padsy understood, but economics and revolution.

He told them that poverty was as bad as slavery; that it was a crime that anyone should be poor. Padsy and Darcy, seeing that this strange doctrine was dear to the boy, threw warmth into their agreement. 'Sacred heart,' Padsy cried, 'that's a true word. Holy Saints and so it ought.'

'It's the trade is the wealthy art,' Darcy said. 'Look at Joe Giveen with his son goin' for a doctor.'

'Yes, and whose money is paying for him. Your money, poor people's money. Look at you working twelve hours a day on land not fit for rabbits and starving on it; and look at the rich who don't even know how to be happy with all their money.'

He stood above them on the rocks, like a prophet, and no doubt he felt like a prophet. His eyes were full of conviction; his gestures were those of a conqueror. 'Poverty's got to go, and it will go—quick and soon. For if they don't abolish it by law, there'll be a revolution. People are getting tired of such nonsense.'

Padsy and Darcy gazing up at him with grave, sympathetic faces were now slightly beyond their depth.

'They talk about the way we shoot people in Ireland,' the boy exclaimed. He threw his gun across his shoulder and his fingers went to his black moustache which was now growing long enough to be curled up at the ends. 'But what are you to do with fools who can't see a thing as big as that and go on standing in the way.'

He marched away across the moor with his gun on his shoulder and Breedy trotting beside him. There was a long silence in the potato garden, and then Darcy said admiringly, 'Aye, it's a wonder the way he's grown this last year.'

'But why would he talk that way of me ground?'

'It's what he's been trained in England. He doesn't rightly understand annything.'

'Is it a kind of Fenian he is?' Padsy wondered.

'A Pro-testant Fenian maybe or Ivyleaf boy.'

'I'm thinking we'd better watch out for that fella.'

'It's the way that ould Slatter doesn't give him a fair crack of the whip.'

'Naw then, Slatter's a grand fella. He's done bravely. They say he's the richest man in Donegal. In Donegal. Holy saints. Naw, naw, he's a grand fella. But them Feenixes is all as mad as a Meath filly.'

This discussion lasted them, since there was no other visitor, till harvest-time in September, when old Mrs. Foy and all Padsy's children crept up in the early dawn to save the oats; Padsy cut with his scythe, the old woman and Darcy gathered the sheaves, laying their heads one way, and Annie plaited the straw ties.

It was a poor crop, but even to the children, hot and tired and with the wrinkles already in their foreheads, the idea of harvest was important and exciting. They worked hard and in silence without bickering.

About eleven o'clock when Padsy was calling for his whetstone, a shout was heard, and running with Darcy to the rock ledge on the east, they saw a long line of guns advancing obliquely through the heather. Benskin, John Chass, Slatter, MacEwen and Felix were all easily recognizable in the strong light. Shoots had passed near the rocks before, but this time, the line extended on the left beyond the rock.

'The fules,' Padsy said. 'Don't they know there's never a bird this side of the broo.'

'It's thon millioner,' Darcy said. 'He doesn't know annythin', but how would he?'

'Sacred heart, but they'll be on us. Go you down and lade them by the other side. Tell them there's no birds here among the stones. I'll creep across and whustle the dawgs that way.'

'But, Padsy, they're shootin'.'

Pellets rattled on the stones as a bird went over, Darcy, crouching to peer between them, jerked back his head like a dog hit on the nose, and said, 'They're too near.'

'Aw Gawd,' Padsy cried. 'What's a few pellets and me to lose the land. For the love of Gawd, Darcy—ye're spry and small——'

Darcy could never resist an appeal. He scrambled upwards. But the moment his head appeared above the stones and against the skyline there were three simultaneous shots. He fell back with his face running blood. Padsy in the act of creeping out by the far side, darted back to him, whispering hoarsely, 'Are ye kilt?'

Darcy lay apparently dead. Padsy took him by the legs and drew him into the hut. A moment later a dog ran sniffing through the hollow and jumped into the heather at the far side of it. The line of guns went leisurely strolling past. Benskin, who skirted the rocks on the south, looked curiously at the small hollow field full of potatoes, and the stone hut which seemed like some neolithic relic; but he did not stop. Slatter, on the north side, beyond the boulders which formed the back gable of the hut, did not notice the field in the half minute during which it lay open to him. He was looking along the line at John Chass who had just shot a bird rising from the very summit of the hill. Suddenly he gave a yell.

Slatter was in great excitement. He was continually shouting and waving his hands to the indignation of MacEwen, who accused him of frightening the birds, and to the amusement of John Chass. But Slatter, who cared nothing for sport, continued to bawl his comments.

'Aw, Jawn, look at that, thank Gawd I'm not a bird in front of your gun the day.'

Slatter was always ready to glorify his hero, and the more he robbed and possessed him the more he loved him and admired him. But John Chass was in fact not shooting so many birds as Benskin or MacEwen. He was a good shot; at snipe no one could beat him. But walking up grouse, early in the season, he could miss simply from lack of concentration, because he was admiring the sky or thinking of a good joke.

To-day he had scarcely used his gun, leaving the birds to his guests. He was enjoying himself too much to trouble about shooting. The pleasure came partly from the weather, partly from the harvest, but its foundation was money at the bank. This had come from Benskin, for though John Chass would not agree to sell him anything, he had suddenly discovered that it was possible to borrow from him without any troublesome legal arrangements, without even a mortgage. A simple I.O.U. had been enough. The money had been paid within an hour of his first remark about the limitations of his bankers and it had not only given him the sense of security and happiness which always came to him with money to spend, but it had enabled him to subscribe three thousand ordinary shares in the new Mosi Company. The Mosi flotation, a month before, had not been very successful. Benskin had refused a directorship and the shares were already at a discount. But John Chass' large subscription had pleased Felix and strengthened his position with the rest of the board; and John Chass considered that these results, even if the new company did not immediately fulfil the director's hopes, were well worth the outlay.

The whole transaction had delighted him; for though he saw Benskin's motives clearly enough, he appreciated his quickness, his immediate grasp of a situation, and above all, his superiority to convention.

'That's what it is to deal with a real man of affairs,' John Chass reflected, as he strolled through the moor. 'No fuss, no flurry, and everyone pleased. Ah, he knows how to do these things—two words from him are worth a Cunningham acre of lawyers' parchment; he knows his job, the wee rascal.'

He stood for a moment watching the dogs, leaping over the heather tufts as they quartered the ground. Their eagerness and excitement made him smile with pleasure, sympathetic and chaffing at the same time; as if part of his feeling, too, was in their anxious noses and joyful preoccupation. When over the hill two birds soared upwards, his gun was under his arm. It was Benskin who fired alone.

He turned to apologize for taking John Chass' bird.

'Aw, never mind, sir,' Slatter shouted. 'Mr. Corner thinks little enough of a grouse. Did ye ever hear about the hare that he shot in the road?'

The party was closing in for lunch. John Chass, opening his breech to take out his cartridges, laughed and said, 'Now, James, that's an old story.'

But Slatter preferred his old stories. He had perfected them until they had for him the quality of ritual, of hymns and prayers. He expressed through them his feelings of wonder and also supported a certain scheme of things; that scheme in which John Chass, the castle, the landlords and himself had their functions and value. 'Never mind if it's old,' he bawled, 'for it's true, and I'll tell ya, Mr. Benskin—he shot this hare from a dogcart—from the back seat of a dogcart—and what with? I ask ya, what with?'

'A fluke,' John Chass said, smiling the same smile that had chaffed the earnest dogs.

'With a rifle,' Slatter bawled, 'a hare, with a rifle—from a dogcart down the church lane that has more holes in it than Oliver Cromwell's nose.'

Benskin said politely that this was a remarkable shot; and Slatter, thus encouraged, began another story about John Chass' wit. 'Did ye ever hear what he said to ould Cousin Dan, as they call him, about the herrings that didn't have any roes.'

John Chass laughed and warned him, 'The ladies, James, the ladies.'

Slatter looked round in surprise and seeing his two daughters approaching with Cleeve between them, he exclaimed in disgust, 'Ladies, ye mane the ould maids—and where's Philly?'

He was depressed that Philip had not come to lunch, and enraged by the presence of the girls, who at once placed themselves on each side of John Chass, a favourite with all the Annish girls. He scowled at them, but as usual they did not seem to notice his disgust. To Maddy and Coo their father was like weather, to be endured with the same patience. Like Annish peasants, they had the air of patience and a deep preoccupation with urgent and fateful matters.

106

Maddy indeed was preoccupied with a great affair, for there was no doubt that Hanna was courting her; but it was not a preoccupation of mind. She could not think of marriage because such thoughts were improper and also disgusting, but she liked Hanna, she was eager to be a married woman, she waited patiently for the great thing that was coming to her, like a stroke of fate. It would befall her, she felt, like birth or puberty, in the course of things.

Maddy had grown rosier and plumper lately. She was a handsome girl; but patience was still on her mouth and eyes, and on Coo's, even while they flirted and laughed with John Chass, who was making them taste his whisky. Their faces seemed to say, 'This is a holiday, something special, and it will soon be over.'

Benskin, looking gravely at the view, also had the look of the peasant on holiday. But John Chass and Felix, glancing now and then affectionately towards Cleeve as he helped Dan Foley to serve the lunch, had quite a different expression, as if holidays were the natural lot of mankind.

Slatter soon forgot his irritation and told some new stories. Like the larks, of which two or three were singing in the deep air opposite their place on the mountainside, he felt the secret influence of the harvest; and could not help uttering his pleasure.

It was a warm, sleepy afternoon in which even the sea wind had a soft touch. The few clouds were like enormous fluffs of down drifting at random in warm eddies. The sea had no steady beat like a pulse; its little confused waves, far below, murmured like sleepy children.

Felix, leaning against his turf bank, felt the happiness which he knew how to appreciate, peace and the beauty of his own country. Underneath him, spread out like a school map, were the little fields and cabins of the Corner lands, surrounding the small dark island of the sycamore wood in which the roof of the house was glittering like a carving of dark topaz in a green velvet cushion. Beyond it the pale green lough rose up towards the blue shore of the county Derry; and beyond the lough to the north, the dark Atlantic like a mountain of solid unpolished sapphire level with their own brown mountain.

Down below there were harvesters in every fourth or fifth cornfield. Small black figures could be seen tying the sheaves and piling the stooks. But the Annish harvest at that time was silent. There were no reapers and binders and the one horse-cutter in use that afternoon was behind the mountain, where it made a sound like a drowsy mosquito. Everywhere else, scythes or sickles were at work, making less noise than the talk of the women and children, which was itself drowned by the larks.

John Chass, who was looking through his fieldglasses, first at one farm and then at another, handed them to him. 'Look, Felix, past the rock, d'you see two cows? Well then, don't look at them but a little higher up you'll find an old man in a blue waistcoat—he's cutting rushes with a sickle.'

'Yes, I see him.'

'Is it Dan or isn't it?'

'It might be old Dan——'

'I'm sure it's old Dan—d'you see the grand way he addresses himself to the rushes?'

Felix agreed that it must be old Dan and John Chass claimed a bet of a button from Coo Slatter. John Chass was also enjoying the view of harvest, but his enjoyment was more particular than his brother's. He liked to distinguish each harvester and when he had recognized him he took down his glasses and smiled at the minute speck with as much pleasure as if he had picked up a sovereign.

Felix did not go with the shooters after lunch. He had promised himself a walk among the farms, to see the harvesters and to meet old friends among the tenants. But when he had gone ten or twenty paces, looking round him already with that keen appreciation which was heightened by the knowledge that he would be leaving in the next week, he found Cleeve trotting breathless beside him.

'May I come, father?'

'Of course, of course.' Felix, who had expected Cleeve to stay with the girls, was pleased and touched by this mark of preference. It struck him also that this walk gave him an opportunity of a serious talk with the boy. It was agreed that he should go back to school; but Felix knew that his own influence was greater than any school. All Cleeve's letters to Africa assured him of it. He would get an excited note from him beginning 'Dear Father, what you say about chapel services has given me quite a new idea about religion,' when he could not remember a word of his letter.

This had made him cautious and lately he had avoided expressing religious or political opinions to Cleeve until he had had time to form a complete plan for the boy's education.

The important thing was to give him faith, that work was worth doing, life worth living, in this age of decadence, when religion, art, politics and letters all seemed equally confused and contemptible.

The problem was difficult, and unluckily Felix, not having expected Cleeve that afternoon, had not had time to solve it. He pondered it now as they walked forward across the moor in silence.

Cleeve said with respectful enthusiasm that it was a nice view.

'Awful hard work for these poor chaps,' Felix sighed. 'There's a smell of thunder, too.'

They both stood apparently thoughtful. Cleeve, in fact, was not thinking about anything. As always with his father he stood expectant, receptive; waiting for the wisdom to be poured into him.

A shout made them both look downwards. Somebody in the track a hundred yards below was waving to them.

'It's Doctor Hanna,' Cleeve said. 'I can see his red face. He seems to want us.'

They went down to Doctor Hanna who was seated on a farm pony, bareback. His long legs almost touched the ground.

'Which of ye bagged Darcy Foy up there?'

They stared at him, waiting for the news. Hanna had the country fashion of leading up to a climax.

'I'm told it was the neatest bit of work for he only had his head up half a second and he doesn't know himself who snapped him off.'

'Is someone shot?'

'Darcy Foy, if you can call him someone, poor fella,' and Hanna described the accident. 'He was lying out there in the heather for some reason—we'd better not enquire into that,' meaning that Darcy and Padsy probably had a still in the mountain. 'But the eye's gone and he's lucky to be alive.'

'I'll go to him at once,' Felix said.

'There's no harm in that because young Philly's up there and he'll be talking his poetry to them.' Poetry for Hanna was any kind of political or religious doctrine suggesting the improvement of anything or anybody.

'Where is he now?'

Hanna waved his arm and the twig he was using for a whip towards the top of the pass between Knockeen and Benargus, where, in the nick of the trail against the sky, a few figures could be seen. He then kicked up the little mare and rode on without another word. Hanna in the last months had begun to affect a rougher manner, to put a little more definition into his chosen character of the hearty fellow with no nonsense about him, who knew what he wanted and went the shortest way to it.

Philip had arrived at the pass with Hanna and as soon as he saw Darcy lying in the road with his face covered with blood, he began one of his speeches against the landlords and the rich.

Probably it was mere shock that carried the boy away but his fervour was very embarrassing to the small farmers and labourers gathered about the Foys. They wanted to discuss the more important question as it seemed to them then, of Darcy's predicament, and moreover, they had long made up their minds that young Feenix was up to no good.

They did not know the word Socialism, but they recognized the creed and they disliked it very much. Annish farmers were landlords and conservatives in all their instincts. They wanted Home Rule to give them more land and better markets, but they didn't want any innovations; they had only admitted Swedes and Aberdeens after a long hesitation. The Dunderry boys might break windows for Holy Ireland, for that was a religious act; but this boy's talk was dangerous and probably immoral. It might even be against property. But they were too polite to show their disapproval, and so, though they spoke among themselves about Darcy, they did so in soft voices, turning away from the excited Philip.

'Make up your minds,' said one, 'for here's Master Felix coming up, and you must know what to tell him.'

'It was the millioner shot him,' Padsy said. 'The wee brown wan.'

Darcy, who lay against the roadside with his left eye in bandages, protested in a faint but resolute voice that he would prefer John Chass.

The gathering reflected. In its harvest rags it looked like a gathering of scarecrows, but its dignity as a council was not impaired either by rags or Philip's intrusion. The oldest, and most statesmanlike, carrying a heart-shaped potato spade, was dressed chiefly in old sacks.

'If ye can't make up your minds,' he said, 'then lave me to speak and the rest of ye hold your whist.'

'I'd liever take Jawn Chass,' Darcy said.

'But the millioner would pay ye better,' another said, a little hairy mountain man, with a face like an Aberdeen terrier. Even his nose was blackened by hair. 'But why wouldn't ye put it on the lot of them? For there's great generosity in a man when six more will be shaking down the pounds.'

'Naw, naw, I'll have himself if I may.'

Darcy spoke as if he were choosing a wife against his parent's advice. There was a touch of passion and obstinacy in his voice. In fact, Darcy, to whom all the known world was personal relationships of various kinds, did obviously feel the same kind of motives, in this important choice, as an Annishman choosing a bride. He looked for one with a fortune; but he was not going to attach himself for money alone.

But Padsy was still urging Benskin with excited cries, when Felix and Cleeve came up the road, and several voices said, 'Whist ye now. here's the ould beard.'

Felix, having enquired from Darcy how he felt and expressed his sympathy, looked round the gathering through his spectacles, raised his beard and said, 'And you don't know who shot him?'

'It was the millioner,' Padsy said.

'But are you sure that he was carrying a gun?'

110

There was silence. Then the statesman, resting his broad-headed spade on the ground, like Nestor's spear of office, said, 'The truth is, sir, that we thought to do the best we could for him, for ye know, your honour, Darcy Foy's poor enough—he'd a hard time of it with two eyes, let alone the wan.'

'You think you'd better choose the richest.'

'He wouldn't miss it, sir.'

'He would not. If you could fix it on Mr. Benskin it would make Darcy's fortune.'

But Darcy murmured that he would prefer John Chass. 'Saving your honour's presence, he's the man I'd choose. I wouldn't be costly till him neether, if he had me in the stables, for I'm a good man to work. Ask Padsy here.'

The meeting pondered. No one saw any humour in a situation on which Darcy's future life depended. Felix said at last, 'I'm sure my brother would be very willing, Darcy, but you know he's not a rich man.'

Just then young Philip on the bank, who had stopped talking on Felix' arrival, jumped down and said, 'I was just telling them, Mr. Corner, that this sort of thing has gone on long enough—really it's too absurd if it wasn't so horrible.' The boy stammered and turned red in his excitement of conviction and enthusiasm, and each time he looked round, repeating that it was absurd, impossible, that this was the time to make a definite protest, his eyes sparkling with a kind of triumphant confidence, the assurance of one who knows his facts, returned to Felix with the same affectionate air of the disciple.

But nobody else spoke, and all faces expressed embarrassment. The farmers looked blank and wooden; Felix was gloomy. He was alarmed by this violent talk. He felt that trouble would come of it and he liked peace and quiet. He felt guilty and disgusted and he was greatly relieved when the cart came up to take Darcy to hospital, and young Philip elected to go with it.

He parted from the council suddenly, as if there was a mutual agreement to bury an unlucky scene, and walked off so fast that Cleeve was trotting behind.

'I never knew,' Cleeve said with admiration, 'that Philly was such a firebrand.'

'Neither did I,' Felix said gloomily. 'I'm afraid he won't do much good to himself or to anybody else.'

'But don't you agree with him?'

'What could he do in Ireland—most of those fellows can't even read,' and he added, 'Education is the revolution they want—it's the only real revolution anywhere. But it takes a long time.'

He sighed. 'It's a pity if Philly breaks his head on a brick wall—he's the best of the young ones round here. But it's a bad time for the young ones—a third-rate age all round.'

They walked on in silence for the next ten minutes; Felix gloomy and agitated, Cleeve full of enjoyment in the day and the walk.

Felix, looking aside to greet a passing countryman, became aware of Cleeve's presence; and of his animated, pondering expression. He was instantly reminded of his responsibilities towards the boy, but he could not recollect what he had been talking about. After a little reflection, he said in a solemn and encouraging voice, 'Well, Cleeve, you have your life before you—and a very interesting life it ought to be in these up and doing times. Yes, I envy you, starting now. Have you any idea what you want to be?'

Cleeve had no idea. In fact, he did not want to be anything, which would prevent his enjoying life. But he could not say so. He said only, 'No, father.'

'H'm, we must talk it over some time—it's quite time you made up your mind.'

Cleeve thanked his father warmly for the walk, and his gratitude was real. He always enjoyed being with his father and he was greatly interested by the notion of a third-rate age. But it did not depress him to live in it. Nothing could have depressed Cleeve at that time.

John Chass, having money in the bank, made no difficulty about taking Darcy into the stables. At the same time Padsy's farm was discovered; not by Benskin, who never interfered in Irish affairs which he regarded as past help; but by himself in person when he went to see how Darcy had contrived to be in the way of the shoot. But this difficulty was solved very easily; Padsy was allowed to stay on this ground for three loads of turf annually. This arrangement involved giving Padsy turf rights on the neighbouring bog as well as the land, and it excited as much rage in Slatter as if his own property were being given away. But John Chass, having money in the bank, smiled at him.

Slatter just then was in a very afflicted state of mind on account of Phil's ungrateful conduct. The boy declared that he would not go to Cambridge to waste money on a useless education. His work was in Annish among the people.

Slatter was at first stupefied. He could not express his rage at such contemptible foolishness; such romantic nonsense. Then he exploded. There was such a battle in the Carnmore drawing-room that Hanna, calling as usual in the afternoon to look at Maddy, found the two girls in tears, Slatter hysterical and Philip speechless. He had given up the attempt to explain himself. Probably he realized that he could not do so.

'The people,' Slatter bawled. 'Is it Padsy Foy and Breedy Macan—they need friends, do they? I'll tell you what they need—someone to leave 'em alone. That's all—to be left alone. Leave 'em alone and they're happy enough, and why won't ye leave 'em alone—why won't ye?' he screamed, 'except that I've spoilt ye, ye dahmed Englishman, the same as Felix Corner was spoilt with dahm nosy notions—go wan then and warm your shirt with Padsy's fleas for ye won't do it at Carnmore. Go wan out, ye dahmed yawping galumph, for ye're worth nawthin' to Gawd or man.'

He used to come to John Chass or Mary Corner for sympathy and stand in the middle of the drawing-room with melancholy eyes and hanging lips, firing out ejaculations every five minutes like a geyser boiling with rage and despair. 'It's what these young wans don't understand annythin'—and so they upset everythin'—just kick it over like a baby kickin' at the pot—and why, because they must be doin' somethin'. That's all, they must be doin' somethin'. Aw Gawd, if Philly had been put to the fields at nine years old, then he wouldn't be so dahm full of his kickabouts.'

At that time the Irish question gave as much excitement to millions as a war. It was a battlefield open every day to the humblest where he could distinguish himself. In Dublin thirty thousand Parnellites with ivy leaves in their buttonholes, execrated by fifty thousand Healyites, went to the chief's grave. In Dunvil boys stoned each other. At Aldershot an Irish regiment broke into civil war, but united in the first week of the general election to fight an English one.

Harry Jarvis, still youngest subaltern in his regiment, also got himself into trouble at that time when a certain well-known General visiting the mess, happened to remark in the ante-room that the Irish though fine soldiers were children in all practical affairs. This, of course, was the doctrine of the time. It was common form, and the General was surprised and hurt when an Irish voice from among the crowd of young officers standing modestly in the corner asked him if he had ever been in Ireland.

He answered politely that he had been in the Curragh, to which the subaltern replied that the Curragh was an English camp and no one could believe anything they said there about Ireland.

This caused an astonished silence. But no one could believe that a subaltern would mean to insult a General, and the General himself, a man much more of the world than the regimental officers, remarked that you certainly had to be careful in buying horses there.

The correct and necessary laugh passed off an awkward moment, and the adjutant hastened to talk horse. But at dinner that night, when the President of the mess raised his glass and said to his opposite number at the foot of the table, 'Mr. Vice, the Queen,' the General, who sat on the President's right, was seen to be in difficulties. The officers were already on their feet, glasses in hand, but the General was still struggling in his chair. His face turned red, his eyebrows rose in amazement, and he ejaculated, 'Damn it.'

At this moment Jarvis, from among the subalterns, was heard to say in a reproachful voice, 'The Queen, General.'

The General made a powerful heave, a sound of tearing cloth was heard; he rose with a furious curse, and all the officers hastily exclaimed, 'The Queen, God bless her.'

It was found that some sticky substance on the General's chair had glued him to his seat. His overalls were ruined. He was, however, extremely good-natured about the accident. No one can be more genial than a General visiting his old regiment.

The colonel was not so good-natured. He, like everyone else, had heard Jarvis' voice with its Irish accent say, 'The Queen, General.' He made enquiries. The orderlies swore that the chair had been clean half an hour before dinner. The sticky substance was collected and sent to the M.O. who reported it to be cobbler's wax.

Nothing could be found against Jarvis except that his batman had been sent to the store for cobbler's wax a few minutes before dinner. The General, like a sensible man, strongly advised the colonel to take no action at a time of political excitement. But the colonel had already taken a dislike to young Jarvis who had a peculiar manner to all superior officers; a kind of exaggerated promptness which seemed derisory. He was obviously one of those youngsters who naturally hated all authority, and the colonel, perceiving this, sent for the young man and advised him to exchange. Where would he like to go? The West Indies or Sierra Leone.'

'You don't take to me, sir?' Jarvis said politely.

'I'm afraid not. You've had several warnings now and I tell you finally that you're not doing yourself or the regiment any good at present.'

'I've done my best, sir, for the regiment, but of course I'd prefer a black one.'

The result of this repartee, delivered with a certain intonation, was that Jarvis was sent home on unlimited leave until he could be exchanged or seconded.

Annish was surprised by this event, because everyone had said that young Harry was the very man for a smart soldier. There was much curiosity to see how he would take the sudden end of his career. But as usual he would talk volubly about everything except what the gossips wanted to know.

A little earlier he might have enjoyed a local success with the nationalists, as a martyr, but it was now the end of October and the political excitement, the gust of national feeling, which had altered his

114

career, was over. The Home Rule government had been defeated and all at once the young men who had been raging through Annish with drums and banners began to talk about crops, girls, and jobs. There was a revival that winter, all over Ireland, of religious ardour, and great competition to carry the banners in the religious processions. Also there was increased emigration and Father MacFee preached several sermons against dancing, and against the licence of the young people courting in the lanes.

Manus Foy was bitter against those who forgot so easily the memory of the dead chief. He himself never let the thought of Parnell's wrongs out of his mind, and every day while he toiled over the mountains with turf or potatoes or a string of fish from old Dan, he made it a practice to call up before his mind a picture of the chief's agony; and then he would turn his mind upon the prosperity and security of those who had betrayed him, like Father MacFee and Joe Giveen, the local nationalist.

Manus had learnt from Father MacFee of the exercises of the Jesuits, who in their retreats fixed their minds deliberately for days at a time; upon each of the sufferings of Christ; upon the scourging, the agony, the passion. He had once practised such exercises on Knockeen, and now, looking at the ground, he thought of Parnell's twisted face in the coffin; and looking across the hill slope at the parochial house beside Knockeen chapel, he thought of Father MacFee eating buttered baps and drinking his tea in the front room.

To Manus it was the worst treachery to desert the chief because he had been defeated in death as well as life. He felt such hatred now for the traitors that he knew he must kill them.

Manus' boys used to meet in a cave behind Ballycorner, or often in the castle yards where they passed for Rifty's friends; no one troubled them among the stacks.

Manus resolved to execute the traitors on October 6th, the date of Parnell's death, but it was found that on the next day, the seventh, there was to be a dinner party and a dance at the castle, to which the District Inspector of Police was asked. Rifty brought the news and he promised to lend Manus a gun that night from the castle gun-room. He would hide it in the last turf stack which was already broken.

But when Manus came to the house at eight o'clock neither gun nor Rifty were to be seen. It was stormy, a wind was rising, and Manus was afraid his band would be dispirited. Six had come. The little party wandered among the trees for an hour, staring through the unshuttered windows of the house at the gentlemen in long, square-tailed coats prancing under the candles in the arms of panting girls.

The Ivyleaf boys looked with wonder at the girls' naked shoulders and the frocks cut low to show the valley between the breasts; at the

115

flashing of rings and brooches, the grinning teeth and crimson faces of Duff and other magistrates, usually seen in the dignity of power.

'And that's what they do with the chief cold beneath their feet,' Manus said.

The youngest of the boys, aged ten, who had been gazing with a smile, now changed his expression and looked timidly at the leaders as if to apologize for his forgetful pleasure.

'Blasphemous,' Manus said. 'May they rot in hell!' He glared angrily at the whirling crowd. He felt the bitterness and pain of this injustice to the dead; that the living should frivol as if they had never suffered and died. 'We'll not be lookin' at the traitors,' he said. 'Come, boys— to the stacks.'

Rifty had not forgotten the day but he was not sure if he wished to murder anyone. Rifty could never make out if the heroes, like Parnell and Manus, or the jokers like Breedy Macan, had the better part of life. This uncertainty made him distrusted by both parties. At the moment he was dancing in the kitchen with Sukey's party, which was even more gay and noisy than that of John Chass. The rule in the kitchen was to drink early in the evening; but in the house men were not expected to be in drink before midnight. Therefore the noise in the kitchen at ten o'clock drowned even the sea which was thundering on the shore like big drums.

Rifty had Bridget for his partner but Bridget was even more stand-away than usual. When he squeezed her waist in the corridor, she coolly removed his arm and said. 'Noan of that now.'

This was unusual for Bridget, though she never showed affection to Rifty, liked to be squeezed. Rifty was suspicious. He looked for a rival, and when, after the dance, some of the gentlemen and ladies, including John Chass himself, with Cleeve and Stella Pynsant came down to greet Sukey in the kitchen, he watched Bridget closely.

The kitchen party climbed on the kitchen table, pushed to the far end, and stood against the wall three deep, leaving the middle of the floor for the gentry, who stood looking about them with smiles of curiosity, calling out, 'Is that you, Paddy? Is that you, Francie?'

Sukey, in her apron, received her guests at the stove. When John Chass shook hands with her and congratulated her on the supper she shouted at him, 'Ah, but it was the ould wan was the masther.'

'Well now, Sukey, and we all know who's the mistress.'

But Sukey was not to be soothed by flummery. 'It's the wan that never saw a kitchen,' she said, 'Gawd help the rest.'

Sukey, more than half drunk, was sweating so much that she seemed to have been under a fountain. Her cheeks were coloured and shining like a pink blancmange, melting in the heat.

When John Chass had gone, her eyes fell on Slatter standing alone in the middle of the floor, at which he was gazing with a thoughtful air. He was in his usual dirty tweeds; he had refused the dance because Philip did not want to come to it. Now he had come because he did not know what to do with himself. Philip would not speak to him and their quarrel had now continued for two months. 'He's killin' me,' Slatter had told Hanna, John Chass, everyone who would listen to him. 'He's killin' me and after all I've done for him—aw, childher are cruel, they don't think of annyone but themselves.'

He had been following John Chass about most of the evening, in search of sympathy and now having followed him into the kitchen, he stood, seized with an overwhelming fit of misery, not noticing that he was alone.

'Is that you?' Sukey stared at him. 'Faith, I've had three other magistrates to shake me hand the night and they was rale gentlemen, too.'

Slatter started, glanced at the woman with his unhappy eyes and ejaculated in a voice as rough as her own, 'Aw, ye're drunk, Sukey.'

'Better drunk than damned,' Sukey said.

' 'Aw, and well ye'll burn.'

The crowd along the walls were laughing except Bridget and Rifty. Rifty's eyes were fixed on Bridget, and Bridget's on Cleeve, while he stood at the door pointing out to Stella the high windows dashed by the sea spray, and the forest of rusty hooks in the ceiling.

Bridget's eyes were wide as if they were trying to embrace some large and difficult visual idea; Rifty's had a sharp and doubtful expression. He could see but he did not want to think of what he saw.

Slatter, slouching to the door, pushed his way through the young people. Cleeve and Stella, leaving the door free, went through the passage. Stella, on Cleeve's arm, was laughing at him. She had been laughing at Cleeve and his droll remarks and his bad dancing all the evening. She had danced with him all the evening in order to avoid Harry Jarvis.

Stella had not seen Harry for eighteen months and since then she had grown up. She was sixteen, high up in her school, and she did not like flirtations. When Jarvis wrote to her, she found his letters absurd or annoying and she did not answer them.

He was ridiculous in himself but more ridiculous in his love. What could be more ridiculous than a man in love? He seemed to have no shame in making a fool of himself; no pride. As she whirled in Cleeve's arms, steering him and supporting him with her own strong arm and sure balance, she looked continually at the young soldier, standing by the wall in his three-inch collar, his minute tie, his long shirt smooth as china, the stiffest shirt in the room, and his tight waisted coat. His face was gloomy, and his nose, forced into the air by his collar, aimed far

117

above the heads of the whirling crowd, which he ignored. He was the picture of the rejected lover; a creature so abject that Stella felt angry with him. She loved everybody in the room, Cleeve, Mary Corner, old Duff, young Duff, the Slatter girls, everybody except Harry.

Stella was an affectionate girl. Her expression had that self-forgetful and friendly interest which only belongs to girls of her kind, in whom passion is still a diffused sentiment; a tenderness which is given even to strangers, dogs and things. Stella's glance at the kitchen ceiling had been affectionate. She had been prepared to love that dirty ceiling, and now she was in love with the drawing-room, with Mary Corner moving anxiously through the room, with Shony in black velvet and silver buttons, dancing a reel of his own invention in the hall; and John Chass carrying about glasses of whisky, fans or dropped gloves; or whirling Coo Slatter in the Blue Danube.

John Chass was always sent by Mary to dance with wallflowers but he himself enjoyed entertaining them.

Coo's screams of terror and ecstasy while she was whirled gave him great pleasure, and made Stella smile fondly at them.

'Who are you f-flirting with now?' Cleeve gasped. It was an hour after supper.

'Your collar's melting,' Stella said.

'That's because I've drunk too much.'

'You mustn't get drunk.'

'Oh, but I must. Ha, ha.' Cleeve uttered a feeble laugh.

'If you do I won't dance with you.'

'I'd rather get drunk any day—it's a m-most glorious feeling. Ha, ha.'

'That's not very nice to me.'

'No, no, I'm serious. Ha, ha. It's not a joke. Ha, ha.'

Getting drunk had just revealed to Cleeve the extraordinary happiness of the world. He saw that it possessed all the means of happiness, that they existed always and everywhere, in kindness, friendship, beauty, cold roast partridge and champagne; in the sound of music, and the fall of the sea, the sparkle of lights and of girls' eyes; in every kind of delight offered to the heart and senses and mind of lucky people's long life.

'What darlings women are, made for joy,' he thought, clinging to Stella and thinking of his Aunt Mary's unselfish love, of Maddy, Coo and Stella with their friendly confidence. Even Francie, with her soft breasts, was mixed into the idea of women's delightfulness, which for Cleeve belonged to all the girls as one; so that by his tenth dance, he did not know whether he was clinging to Stella, Maddy, Coo or the disdainful Miss Duff, to whom he revealed also his discovery.

'Glorious—absolutely glorious—seriously. Ha, ha.'

118

He caught sight of Coo and Maddy standing in a corner half hidden by a curtain, and he felt astonished and anxious. His face assumed the grave look of the drunk man who is shocked by the unfestive. How could anyone fail of happiness in this marvellous world? What held them back from its delights? He felt that there was a fault somewhere, an enemy.

'What's wrong, Coo, lemme get you a drink,' he said. But he found that he was dancing with Stella. He had meant to ask Maddy but it did not matter.

'Oh, it's you, Stella. What a dear you are.'

'Thank you, Cleeve. That's very complimentary.'

'Yes, and f-fat. I like f-fat girls. Isn't it g-g-glorious to-night. Oh God, I f-feel so funny. Ha, ha. I'm f-fearfully drunk.'

'You're not really drunk!' The girl looked at him anxiously. It was her first Irish dance and she had never before seen anyone drunk at a dance.

'Ra-ather, ha, ha. Of c-course I t-told you. Oh God, I feel sick.'

'You disgusting pig.'

'Want to get out.'

Maddy Slatter, who had stood for an hour against the wall in her best frock, cut down from her mother's bridal dress of 1863, came up and said coolly, 'Let me, Miss Pynsant.'

Maddy was quite accustomed to drunk men of all ages and classes. She took Cleeve, now beginning to droop, by the arm, and led him towards the door. Stella, seeing that a drunk man was not necessarily horrible, at once recovered from her horror, took Cleeve's other arm and said in a matter-of-fact tone, 'What shall we do with him?'

'The field's the best if he's going to be sick.'

'Is he going to be sick?' Stella repressed another moment of disgust.

'I should think so,' Maddy said, with a professional glance at Cleeve's pallid face, glazed eyes and hanging neck. 'Oh, dear, the tide's in. We'd better take him through the yard.'

They went back through the coachyard and the stackyard, passing first between the double row of hay and corn ricks, and then among the turf stacks, each as large as a cottage. The yard was closed by a nine-bar iron gate opening on a paddock. At this gate Cleeve uttered a loud peculiar noise which caused Maddy to whirl away her skirts. She said to him, 'Catch hold of the gate, Cleevy, or can't ye grip?'

Cleeve could still grip. He took hold of the gate and stooped. Maddy put her hand on his forehead. Her face in the moonlight was grave and calm, like that of a mother comforting a sick child. Stella, too, became grave and calm. She was not disgusted any longer even by Cleeve's loud and violent retching. She took his arm and put her left hand over Maddy's which supported his forehead. 'Poor Cleeve,' she said.

'It's bad,' Maddy said sadly. 'All the boys here go drinking and it's the roon of them.'

Cleeve raised his damp and livid face and rolled his eyes. He was looking about him at the stormy sky and the stacks, the three-quarter moon, and the big rollers advancing in an endless train towards the beach.

'U-s w-wondu-f-ful,' he stammered. 'My God—it's wonderful.'

It was a sky common enough in Annish about the end of the year, in a strong north-westerly wind from the Atlantic, clouds as big as mountains complete with heather, rocks, precipices and glittering lakes, whirling upwards from the black edge of Knockeen like dead leaves, the moon sailing backwards between them and suddenly darting down a brilliant glare like a searchlight, the shadows charging across woods, bogs and stacks like cloaked witches running. When the moon came out, the black, confused lough suddenly became glittering pattern, and the stacks took shape like a primitive village.

The village boys were seen sitting in a row on the last broken stack, already half used, and Cleeve staring at them in his wondering delight and surprise muttered, 'Glorious—it's w-wonderful.'

Maddy said to Stella shyly, 'I suppose you've travelled all over the world.'

'Only France and Italy—I did just glance at Germany once. Have you done much travelling.'

'I went to Liverpool when I was a wee gyurl.'

'G-glorious,' Cleeve muttered, staring vaguely at the boys who stared at him. His head was whirling, the whole world seemed to him in a whirl of excitement and beauty, girls, drink and happiness; and the horrible sensations in his stomach could not prevent him from enjoying them. He knew that this was a glorious evening of which he would boast and so he felt its glory.

'L-Lovely night,' he said politely to the boys in his rôle of the Corner princeling.

None of them spoke, but he did not notice their rudeness. He was feeling another qualm. It caught him; he fell forward; Stella quickly took charge of his forehead, anticipating Maddy, and her face, as she looked down upon her charge, like Maddy's before, was wise and patient. But Maddy looked at Stella with a longing envy. 'Italy and France—and ye're at school still. What all will ye see before you're done?'

Harry's voice came from behind. 'Can I help, Miss Pynsant.'

This was the first time that he had called her Miss Pynsant and Stella felt another pang of annoyance. She said coldly, 'No, thank you, Mr. Jarvis, we can manage perfectly well.'

'I think he'd be better in bed.'

Maddy agreed with Harry, but Stella would not give up her new post as good samaritan. She said to Jarvis, 'Why don't you and Miss Slatter take this dance.'

Jarvis, surprised, offered his arm to Maddy and carried her away. She was ecstatic but she did not show it. Neither did she utter a word to her partner until at the end of the dance she said, 'That's done now,' and plumped down in a chair against the wall. She refused even a drink, and sent Jarvis away with the words, 'Go you now and see after Miss Pynsant.'

Maddy still thought Harry the most charming and handsome man in the world but she was perfectly resigned to his loving somebody else. She was even eager to help that affair out of her affection for him and her admiration for Stella.

Harry insisted on bringing her a lemonade before he went to look for Stella, and this completed her happiness. She sat by herself in the empty drawing-room smiling pensively in the sense of this kind attention, of Harry's charming ways.

It was then that Hanna came in. Hanna had been watching her all the evening and as soon as Maddy saw his peculiar expression now, the same apologetic chaffing grin, with which he sometimes ended a pathetic ballad when it had made him husky, she knew that her moment had come. She put down her glass on the floor and waited for it. She was neither frightened nor confused.

Hanna sat down on the next chair to the right and said, 'Miss Margaret, but why wouldn't I call you Maddy?'

That was what Maddy had expected and she said, 'You might.'

There was a pause. Maddy waited confidently. But just then she felt something heavy on her waist above her left hip. She realized that Hanna's big hand was creeping round her.

Maddy had not expected this. She had expected some kind of speech or declaration. She was startled and gave a vigorous jerk away from the young man. He laughed in an exultant manner and tightened his hold, whereupon Maddy turned scarlet, gave him a furious poke with her elbow in the chin, and exclaimed in a desperate voice, 'What d'ye mean?' Then she jumped up and rushed into the hall to find Mary Corner or John Chass for protection.

Hanna, surprised, took a slow turn up and down the room. 'The darling wee gyurl,' he thought, 'she's scared.' This idea gave him pleasure and brought a tender smile to his lips. 'I won't try again now— there's time enough, God knows.' He looked round for a man to talk to and a drink. Hanna on the whole preferred men to talk to. He had a manner for men though he hadn't yet made up his mind how to deal with girls.

121

At the stacks Manus walked up and down with folded arms, or stopping before his followers, who sat like a row of schoolboys on the low wall of the turf, he turned his face towards the sky, like the picture of Father Murphy at Vinegar Hill. He was acting his dramatic part, but it was not an actor's part. It was real, and so it had a quality of interest and excitement beyond acting.

The boys muttered together. They, too, felt the excitement of the work. They knew that this was not a game. Even the youngest knew that boys of thirteen and fourteen had fired ricks and houses and shot down grown men in the land war. They had a different feeling from English boys because they had a larger grasp of power. They did not think of shooting sparrows but men.

They did not feel the cold while they sat in the flying shadows, listening to the sea, the bursts of music coming in gusts between the waves; they looked at the few passing guests who came now and then to smoke or to pumpship among the stacks, with indifference or disdain, as men of power look upon triflers.

Just before eleven Rifty came, but without the gun. He had failed to get it.

'Since Kitty went to Ameriky it's hard for me to be up in the house.' He offered them half a bottle of whisky.

Manus was angry at the boy's light excuses and half smile. He said severely, 'Ye've broken your oath to Ireland and that's death. Tie him up, boys, and we'll put him in the bay.'

Rifty then looked serious. But when two of the boys stepped up to take him, he gave a jump and disappeared in the shadows.

'We'll deal with these traitors when we get our gun,' Manus said.

'I know where you'd get a gun,' the youngest boy said.

'Spake then, MacLoughlin.'

'There's Master Phil Feenix little gun that Breedy could get.'

'And where's Breedy?'

'May be in Carnmore yard or maybe here if he came to dance.'

Breedy was not found in the castle yard. Manus said, 'Then it's up the hill, boys.'

The boys in a close dark group moved up the hill. Now and then they passed some courting men who drew aside for them and affected not to notice them. It was obvious to any Annishman by the boys' silence and their closeness as they walked, like one black body in the dark, that they were not mere schoolboys prowling the roads for lack of other amusement, but a political body, dangerous to meddle with.

Breedy was found at Carnmore but he was with his master. They were sitting together in the harness-room, under a stable lantern, smoking and chatting while Breedy cleaned the guns.

Philip was dressed in his oldest tweeds, as if in deliberate contrast

122

with the dancing men at the castle. His moustache now nearly as big as his uncle's, a ragged black moustache, his rough, long hair, his open shirt neck made him seem like the bold, swaggering kind of small farmer who shouted about the pubs on Dunvil fair day. He had come to look like that from wishing to do so, a desire that Breedy recognized though he did not know it himself.

Breedy was as quick as any Annish boy to know another's mind. He felt every thought and motive of this high-nosed, lonely young man of twenty; his boredom, his disgust with his own place in the world; his romantic affections; the quick sensitive feelings which made him sympathetic and dissatisfied.

Breedy himself had no sentiment. He was a tinker born. He would flatter Philip all day with great pleasure; squinting up at him through his mat of hair and crying out, 'Aye, sor, it's a poor country and we're greatly put upon, but what can we do for ourselves. We're too wake. It's only the gentlemen like yourself and Mr. Parnell, gawd rest his soul, that can do annythin' with the villains that do be robbin' us.'

When Manus whistled Breedy into the yard, Philip came to the door. He stood aloof, ferocious in appearance, but shy and cut off. He wanted to follow Breedy, to join in the country boys' secret talk, as he wanted to enter into their interest and their lives, but he feared to be unwanted.

Breedy gave a laugh and turned to him. 'It's what they want to have a bit of a joke with Joe, sor.'

'What, with Giveen?'

'Aye, the ould thief—we were going to give him a bit of a fright for the way he robs the people.'

'Is he the man that puts out the sprigging at threepence a dozen?'

'Aye, and pays the poor gyurls in rotten male.'

'He needs a warning, a roll in the ditch wouldn't do him any harm.'

'Aye, you're right, sor. So I'll just be going along with the boys now.'

'Do, and good luck to you both. But why the gun?'

Breedy had picked up the sixteen-bore. He laughed and said, 'It's what we thought we might skeer him a bit, too. Ah, we'd only be showing it till him.'

Philip hesitated. The boys looked at him, Breedy with a little grin said, 'Ye naydn't be afeared, sor. Nobody'll be hurted. The police won't be in it.'

This remark was perfectly successful. Philip remarked with careless contempt. 'The police—I'm not troubling about them.' He made a vigorous gesture, throwing out his arm and jerking his head like Slatter. 'You can shoot the old blaggard for all I care—he richly deserves it.'

The boys disappeared at once into the dark. Philip was left feeling like a leader of the people fierce and resolute. This partly solaced him in his loneliness; in the sacrifice of the dance and the loss of Breedy.

Breedy, though his pocket was full of Phil's cartridges had no intention of committing murder. His scheme was to loot. As soon as he reached Giveens he gave the gun to Manus. It was Manus who charged it.

The store was in darkness. The boys pulled their caps over their eyes and Manus tied a rag across his nose and chin.

He then banged on the door with the gun butt. He was calm and resolute for he felt the grandeur of the moment and the greatness of his destiny.

A woman opened the door, carrying a candle. Breedy, Manus and four more rushed past her into the house. Breedy turned through a side door into the back room where he expected to find the cash box. Manus and the others rushed upstairs. The girl below gave a scream and Mrs. Giveen began to scream also in the front room.

As Manus pushed open the bedroom door he saw Giveen in his nightshirt, trying to climb out of the window. He had one leg over the sill. Manus pointed the gun and ordered him to put his hands up. Giveen, who was a large fat man, tried to do so, but the fold of his nightshirt had caught beneath him, and he could not lift his hands above his ears. His struggles to do so, and his babble of prayers and moans, annoyed Manus by their lack of dignity of the noble Parnell.

'Giveen,' he said, 'you betrayed the chief to his death. The men of Ireland have tried you for a traitor and ordered you to die. Come down out of that.'

Giveen suddenly threw himself out of the window. Manus rushed to the window and fired at him as he rolled in the muck heap below. At the same moment a boy's voice from below shrieked, 'Peelers.'

Manus let the gun fall, dropped from the window-sill, took a running kick at Giveen as he lay howling in the midden, and then bolted for the moss.

Ballycorner moss was full of drains and turf banks where an army might have hidden. But in fact no one looked for Manus there because the police did not arrive for an hour. They were fetched by Mrs. Giveen. Giveen himself had a broken leg and a dozen pellets in his left buttock.

Cleeve waked up with a splitting headache and a foul mouth, but he felt at once the elation of a triumph. 'What a night,' he reflected. 'Glorious, my god, terrific.'

He began to form a description of his experiences for his new novel; the masterpiece which was to be written as soon as he had time. 'Richard Rowallan was a man who, as they say, could hold his liquor. He could drink a bottle of neat whisky without the slightest detriment to his dignity of the grand seigneur or his coherence of speech. Yet in this very immunity was a danger——'

Cleeve uttered an exclamation of surprise, got hastily out of bed and vomited. He put his hands to his eyeballs and thought again, 'What a night—terrific.'

He was surprised to see that it was three o'clock in the afternoon, and he remembered that there was a tea-party somewhere. But he did not choose to move. He lay back with a languid smile; enjoying his recollections, and the relief of his stomach.

Harry's step went down the corridor. Cleeve called him, but receiving no answer, put on a dressing-gown and staggered to his cousin's room.

'What a night,' he said, grinning. 'Glorious.' He felt like a hero from the battlefield, exhausted but triumphant and he wanted notice, applause.

Harry said nothing. He was changing his tweeds for his neatest and smartest suit. He picked up a collar. Cleeve, suddenly forgetting himself in friendship, said, 'If the Pynsants are going to be there, I should choose a lower collar.'

Harry stopped in surprise and looked coldly at Cleeve. 'What do you know about it?'

'Only that Stella asked me why you wore such extraordinary collars.'

'As it happens, old chap, everybody in London wears collars like this—they're the right thing.'

'Oh, yes, it's only that Stella was amused.'

'My dear old boy, women never know what's right and wrong in men's clothes.' Jarvis reflected a moment and said indulgently, tenderly, 'Why should they?'

Then he put on his highest and most fashionable collar, his grandest tie, and set out for Carnmore. He was feeling resolute and greatly excited. Stella had avoided him; she had barely spoken to him during her visit, and he saw that she disliked him. This was a disaster which he had not expected but it filled him with resolution. He was not going to lose a girl like Stella, who, every time he saw her, seemed more beautiful, sensible and kind.

He asked himself how he had offended. He had stopped writing at her own request; but his letters had not been indiscreet. He had not written love letters or expressed anything of his real passion. He concluded that the girl had met other men; was attracted by somebody else, someone perhaps of the fashionable young soldiers and writers who always surrounded her mother at home. This idea increased his resolution to strike a decisive blow.

The tea-party at Carnmore had been planned for a month and Maddy had been allowed to visit Dunderry by the mail car to choose the best cakes. Mrs. Pynsant had accepted Slatter's invitation and though he had abused her for a year, saying that Mrs. Pynsant was nothing but a mumped up hoor, he was now in great excitement. This led to another quarrel with Philip, who refused to attend the party. Philip that

125

morning was in his most revolutionary mood. He was walking about the yards in his dirtiest clothes with his pipe sticking out of his mouth like a gun from a barbette. Now and then he shouted through the stable for Breedy, but Breedy had not arrived.

It was a warm, damp morning when nothing stirred but an occasional rook flopping in silence high up through the white sky, and sometimes a maid throwing a cabbage end among the chickens. A bucket clattered in the stableyard, but the sound only intensified the oppression of the day; everything, the rook, the sky, the yards, the very air seemed full of a boredom more acute than pain.

Philip felt the boredom but only as a keen young horse feels the weight of a rider. He was not oppressed by it, but excited. He was restless with eagerness to do, and it seemed to him that the whole world was open to his energy. Look at the poverty and ignorance in Annish alone; the political lies, the religious lies, the mean, stupid hatreds and national jealousies.

His opportunity was immense, and these giants against which he was to fight, big as they looked, were bound to be defeated.

That was the delightful thought; as encouraging as that of Clive, Pizarro or Kitchener; that the enemy, however numerous and powerful in offensive, was in fact so out of date in equipment, so completely absurd in its theory, that it could not stand a battle.

'I used to think of being a missionary or a soldier,' Philip thought, 'but this is where my work is cut out for me—better than any foreign mission or soldiering abroad. Of course Parnell failed. But Parnell had no education and no idea of economics. Besides, what folly to mix himself up with women.'

An outside car came into the yard, and thinking that some guest had arrived, he slipped into the back room, out of the visitor's sight. He was in no mood for visitors.

The car belonged to the D.I. who had come to see Slatter. He brought Philip's gun, which had been recognized. Slatter, holding the gun, stood in the hall, staring like an apoplectic. 'Was he there?'

'They say not. We caught Rifty this morning, and according to him, the gun was only borrowed.'

'Are ye going to take Philly up?'

'No.' The young D.I. looked politic. He was the statesman of the moment. 'It's not even necessary for him to appear in court. That's to say, we could give Murphy a hint to leave his name out of it.'

Slatter pondered. Then he said, 'And Joe not much hurt?'

'No, except for the leg.'

Slatter looked from the gun to the officer. Then he exclaimed, 'Naw, Playfair, don't keep his name out of it.'

'You don't want it—his father seemed to think——'

'Aw, lave old Wully be. What's he know about Philly. Wait now, hould this till I come back.'

He walked through the yards, bawling, 'Philly.' A stable boy told him to look in the lamp-room.

Slatter burst in upon his nephew who, standing before the fire in a ferocious attitude, pipe in mouth, received him with a look of dignified contempt.

'They've murdered Joe Giveen,' Slatter bawled.

The young man stared and then slowly his cheeks seemed to sag; the pipe dropped. He sat down in a chair, and turned his face away.

'And the fules left the gun on the floor,' Slatter bawled. 'The polis will have them all for they know every gun in Annish and Donegal, too. Poor Joe, Gawd rest him, thrown out of a window in front of his wife and butchered like a sheep, and what for, seven shillings out of the till and a bottle of whisky. But thank God they'll hang for it—the dirtiest, manest deed that ever was done in Annish. They've got some of them already.'

Slatter, seeing Philip's increasing pallor, shouted louder and grew more indignant. He described the crime, Joe lying on the dung heap with a broken leg, imploring for mercy, and the gang kicking him.

Maddy came to the door and put in her head. 'Pappy, here's a carge and I think it's the Pynsants.'

'Go wan out,' Slatter shouted, furious at this interruption. 'Can't ye do annythin' without me. What's the good of ye, at all.'

Maddy went back to receive the guests. She shook hands with each and said, 'Pappy will be here in a minute.'

Shouts came from the back passage; the D.I. walked up and down with an embarrassed air; the guests, Duffs, MacEwens, stood in the hall listening to Mrs. Pynsant make conversation with Jarvis.

'So you want to go to that horrid West Africa.'

'I had my choice of Africa or the West Indies.'

'But it's such a terrible climate in West Africa.'

'I thought Africa seemed the most likely place for a scrap.'

'With France?' Stella suggested.

'France or Germany. Things are waking up all round.' Jarvis struck a characteristic attitude, chest and right leg forward, chin in air. 'Everyone's on the grab as fast as they can go, and there's bound to be trouble when France and Germany, or France and ourselves say snap at the same moment.'

'I hope you will have your war soon,' said Stella.

'My dear Stella,' Mrs. Pynsant protested. 'Why are girls so bloodthirsty, Captain Jarvis?'

But Jarvis, like Stella, did not care for this kind of trifling conversation. He said, 'I think Miss Pynsant is right. A war would clear the air.'

127

Maddy and Coo, who had been whispering together in a corner, now asked Lady MacEwen and Mrs. Pynsant simultaneously to pour out the tea. Polite exclamations rose on all sides. Jarvis said to Stella, 'Have you seen the garden.'

'Isn't it raining?'

'No, not much, anyhow.' He had placed himself behind her and now advanced, driving her before him by some power which she felt and resented. She felt that if she did not go he would touch her arm or body, and she was afraid of his touch.

Lady MacEwen began to pour out the tea. Colonel Duff spoke of the crops and especially the backwardness of farming in Annish. Lady MacEwen, with her mad eyes and wild hair, cried that the poverty was as bad as that of an Indian village. Maddy and Coo had once more got into a corner. They were not holding hands but their arms touched.

They did not know how they had come together again in this manner, and Maddy realized it. 'Go on and talk to them,' she whispered.

'But Pappy isn't come.'

The tea-party was a failure. Annish parties were of two kinds; roaring parties at which everyone made a great deal of noise, laughed at nothing, ate and drank too much; at which the gentlemen refused tea and went to the study with the host, returning still redder, noisier and more reckless-looking; at which Colonel Duff told barrack-room stories in a brogue, John Chass cleared the room for a carpet dance and the girls who had come to tea were rescued by their mothers at midnight with all their buttons off, their tapes burst, their hair down, their heels off their shoes and large rents in their best frocks; or they were failures, at which all the guests looked as if they had just been sentenced to death by slow torture, and Colonel Duff talked about the crops. Castle Corner parties were all in the former class; Carnmore and Duff parties in the latter. Colonel Duff was a teetotaller in his own home.

Meanwhile Jarvis and Stella had reached the garden. It was a small, walled square with cinder paths, gooseberry bushes and a half-dug potato patch with withered haulms behind the dead stumps of the herbaceous border.

'It's very nice,' Stella said, 'but perhaps we ought to go back to tea. It looks so rude.'

Jarvis had planted himself in front of her. She was angry and ashamed.

'I've been trying to get you alone for a fortnight,' he said, 'and this is probably my last chance,' and he said then what she had dreaded to hear, that he loved her and that he would never love anyone else.

'I suppose that your mother thinks that you're too young to be proposed to, but I know that you've forty times more sense than most

128

women will get in their lives if they live to be a hundred, and as I'm going away for some time, I'd like to know if I have any kind of a chance for you. I'm not asking you to say yes to me now, but only if you think you might ever say it.'

Stella turned a dark red to the forehead. She was astonished; her feelings were thrown into confusion as if by an outrage. She did not know what to say and her pulses throbbed. Suddenly she felt furious. Stella, like other girls of her strong life, had a quick temper. Her thick brows drew together; her eyes sparkled and she muttered, 'How ridiculous—and why do you wear such awful collars?'

Jarvis was startled. He put his hand to his collar and said, 'It's the usual thing.'

'It's ridiculous—don't you know what people say—that you're like a donkey looking over a white-washed wall.' She hurried off towards the house. Jarvis did not follow her. He reflected for a moment, touched his collar again, made sure that his tie was in the right place, and walked slowly home.

He was confirmed in his view that girls did not understand men's fashions, or what became a gentleman. But this did not alter his affection for Stella Pynsant. On the contrary, he loved her better than before; this odd prejudice, this sudden spite against a collar, were what are expected in a woman. They were for some reason charming.

When the D.I. was summoned to the back room, he found both Slatter and Feenix in a tearful state. The gun was lying on the table.

Philip was still trying to explain himself; but every time he began a new sentence, Slatter, full of tender kindness, shouted, 'Aw, never mind, we understand. Aw, we know ye didn't mane annything.'

He turned to Playfair. 'Ye know he wouldn't hurt a fly; the best-hearted boy that ever was, only too aisy led.'

Playfair gave the young man a sensible, mild lecture on the danger of encouraging such as Breedy, and Slatter answered him, 'Aw, he'll give ye no more trouble.'

'But, Mr. Playfair, it's not a question of giving trouble.' Philip tried again to explain in a dignified manner that he had no responsibility for this disgusting and ridiculous affair; that it had nothing to do with his political ideas, but looking at his uncle's affectionate, triumphant face, and the policeman's calm, soldierly one, he realized that explanation would not be understood. He therefore remained silent, and looked as far as possible as if he was perfectly well satisfied with his own conduct, whatever they might say or do.

Manus was not arrested till the end of the week. He was betrayed by some unknown person, suspected to be Rifty Egan. The trial took place at the next Dunderry assizes. Breedy was given six months, and Manus a year. Phil Feenix made a good impression in the witness box until under the cross-examination he admitted that he had been in the habit of talking to the country boys about means of improving their lot.

'You discussed revolution with these unhappy boys?'

'No revolutions.'

'Let us say you approved violence and murder——'

Philip's counsel intervened for him. But the court was against him. Everybody who saw the ragged Breedy and Manus in the dock was against the young man who had led them astray. He received a severe reprimand from the judge who said that he was either a knave or a fool, certainly a coward, and that he ought to be in the dock instead of his unfortunate victims.

Thus Philip had not yet succeeded in finding an explanation, a defence. For a long time after the trial he was not seen at all about the lanes. He hid himself in the rectory or in Carnmore. Country people who caught glimpses of him, slipping from one to the other, reported that he did not even give them a greeting.

This, of course, was also a method of defence; a blow for dignity and self-respect. It was a kind of policy.

Slatter did not hide his satisfaction with the results of the case. 'A prawvidence,' he said. 'Aw, we'll have no more of all that Fenian talk.'

IV

ONE FAIR DAY in Dunvil, there were sixteen drunks before the bench; and John Chass, acting as chairman during the illness of old Mr. Duff, asked, 'Is it for the Queen's Jubilee or old Bob Duker?'

Bob Duker was the village idiot; an old man who bowed down before everybody who passed him on the road, and got drunk whenever anyone would treat him to liquor. When the crowd, a large one, had finished laughing, the prisoner in the dock, an old mountain man, shouted, 'Naw, your honour, it's Con Foy's,' and roared with laughter, turning twice round in the dock to see that everyone had noticed his joke.

'Which Con Foy is that?' John Chass asked, and the prisoner shouted, 'Con from Ameriky—Con, the millioner.'

'What, is Con back?'

'Is he back!'

'Ah! it's like that, is it? Then I suppose you'll be here again unless I make an example of you. Two and sixpence.'

Con, in a blue sack suit, a turn-over collar and a blue satin tie with a nugget pin, was sitting in court among a close pack of his friends. He did not join in the laughter. His expression was contemptuous and now and then, twisting his mouth sideways, he made a sardonic comment upon the magistrates, and the proceedings.

Con, who had stayed in America after Kitty to wind up his business, had been in Annish for a week.

On his first day, he and Kitty had walked up to the old cabin in Knockeen. Nothing was left but the chimney gable in a sea of nettles. Con and Kitty stood hand in hand among the nettles, surrounded by the respectful crowd of their relations, and sang

> To the dear home that bore me, a stranger I came,
> And the hearthstone was wet with the tears of the rain.
> Oh, soft winds of Erin that sigh for my grief. . . .

But at the first line Con broke down and cried. Kitty however smiled at him and went on singing. Con turned to the crowd and began to shout at them. The song faltered and died.

'What's the good of yous, standing there and singing about Airin.

131

There's none of you worth a cent or there wouldn't be a Corner in Annish or an Englishman in Ireland.'

He cursed them for an hour, and afterwards at Giveen's, the cross-road store on the Ballycorner road, which was a news exchange for the townland, he cursed Giveen himself, who was the nationalist organizer.

'You and your party, and your Home Rule Bill that the English lords threw out in your faces. What happened to the English when they tried to grab the States? We beat them out of that in six weeks. Washington had their whole army down on its hunkers and beggin' for mercy in the first month. But in poor ould Ireland it's you wans that beg.'

Giveen, behind the counter, with the face of a good-natured greedy baby, said smiling, 'I won't deny it, Mr. Foy. I won't deny a word of it.' He took up a packet of tea and hopped it over a tin of beans; then pushed the beans behind a bottle of port. Giveen always played leap-frog with the tins and packets on the counter when he talked politics; looking down at the tins and then up at the audience with a little fat smile, as if the management of people and opinions was as easy to him as the arrangement of groceries.

'But I think you'll admit some progress—there's the land purchase now——'

'Damn the land purchase. Are you going to pay John Chass for the land he stole from you?'

But this was exactly what Annish men were eager to do. A farmer who paid twenty pounds rent and who saw the chance of reducing it to fifteen and buying his farm at the same time, was not much interested in Con's politics. For Con, Ireland was now a mystical vision formed slowly for years in the smoke and stink of his saloon; for Annish men, she was the ground they tilled. When Con talked politics in the bars, the people looked shy. Politics was a dangerous subject then in any place where there were bottles and glasses to be thrown, for though Parnell was dead six years, his name still provoked a riot every November. Barmen would rather discuss the approaching Jubilee or the prices for the Derby. But though they found Con changed, a foreigner, who found no good in anyone or anything belonging to Annish, they respected him as a man, who, if not a millionaire, carried a belt full of sovereigns, stood drinks to all comers; and who was prepared to settle in his native place.

He offered for Giveen's, and when Giveen refused to sell, he bought a field from him, on the other side of the road, less than a hundred yards away, and proposed to build a rival store there.

'Giveen's,' he said with scorn. 'If you took Giveen's to Ameriky, they wouldn't use it to spit in. It isn't a store, it's a swindle. I'll build you a store that is a store.' He went to a builder and ordered estimates and plans. He found out a shop in Dunderry where Kitty and Bridget could learn, for a small premium, the grocery trade. But Kitty, ever since her baby had been born, had been ill with a cough and fever, and Bridget would not leave her work at the castle with her Aunt Sukey.

Bridget's young energy of mind always had new fields of exploration and excitement opened to it in Sukey's kitchen for it was the central news exchange. It was Sukey's fort or dun, where, according to a custom as old as the Irish kings, all her kin had right of entertainment. There were often fifteen people to tea, and their talk was different from the cottagers' because it was prompted by the servants, who discussed the scandals of the house and of the world; stories more strange and fascinating to Bridget than the tales of the fairies.

'Did ye see thon woman in her diamints?' Padsy would say. Padsy, now once more a landed man and a tenant, came often to the kitchen, and he liked especially to talk of Mrs. Pynsant. 'Aye, a terrible rich hat she had the day. They say that wan has been in king's bosoms, no less. The prince, I mean.'

'Aye,' Darcy said, 'those great wans has their own ploy.'

Bridget, sitting humbly in the dark corner by the scullery door with her Cousin Rifty, her head against the wall, would feel each word of power, diamonds, king's bosom, like separate tremors in her body.

Annish had long discussed Benskin, but the idea of Mrs. Pynsant was more popular. Father MacFee had preached twice about Mrs. Pynsant, not by name but innuendo, on the text of Jezebel. He knew the force of this rival power contending with him for the imagination of the people.

'But they say the Prince run her out.'

'And I'll not blame him,' Sukey said. 'I was watching her there with herself on the terrace. There's no flesh for a dacent house, with the pushed up front of her as bold as two cannons on Dunderry wall, and the back of her buttocks wagging like a duck's rump.'

Padsy spat. 'A right folly-me piece. And be gad, it was a great wan follied her. She could tell ye a tale would make wars.'

Rifty's hand was creeping round Bridget's waist. She did not usually permit liberties to Rifty, for though he was now accepted as her boy, she was like other girls of strong sex, ticklish and modest. Her modesty was physical as well as religious; it was like the jump of a nerve. But now she was a king's mistress and Rifty's hand was useful to her imagination, which was not more particular than diamonds and a courtly squeeze upon a golden throne.

There was a double semi-circle round the fire; including six Egans, old Daniel, Padsy, Con. Con was often in the kitchen, for though he hated the Corners, he did not look upon Sukey's kitchen as Corner ground.

Con, by right of wealth and rank, sat in the middle of the front row, with his hat on. He gave now and then a snort of derision; threw out a bitter comment: 'Prince, d'ye mean that Jairmon?'

'A pity they didn't take a Foy for the jawb,' Sukey said.

Old Daniel quickly diverted the quarrels. 'We all hear that the Prince is a gay bucko that doesn't suit the ould Queen. But she was a gay wan herself in her young times.'

'It's in the blood bedambut,' Sukey exclaimed, 'and it's the gay blood is the best too.'

'Aye, and you were the gay wan, Sukey.'

'I was that. I could dance down anny wan from here to Dunderry.'

'It's the little legs are the best for that work,' Darcy said with the air of a specialist. 'They're not so weighty in the lifting.'

'Troth so, and I'm gye strong in the hips yet.' Sukey's voice rose like a keen. 'And here I am for twelve years in the smoke and the dark and the grief of work in this divil's hole that nearly has me spoilt. But I told herself not a day beyond the Jubilee, to hell with it. And then ye'll see me in the world again.'

There was a short silence, but no one smiled at Sukey. All of them had an acute sense of Sukey's tragedy, who had been a pretty gay young woman; and who was now, at fifty, a swollen, pimpled hag, dreaming of the escape which for some reason she could not accomplish.

'I tell you what, Anty Sue,' Con said, 'when me and Kitty has our new hotel built, we'd give a dance only for you.'

Sukey turned to him with her swollen, dirty face. 'Make it after the Jubilee and I'll dance ye like a may midge in the day of resurrection.'

It was past six, already dusk. Grogan and Mollie came clattering with the tea-things from the house; and carriage wheels made a twisting shadow on the wall as they passed the high windows on the drive side, with the sunset in their spokes. Bridget, tight-squeezed by Rifty against the stones of the wall, was floating in a gold coach with her royal lover; her white limbs were smoothly caressed by silk.

Shon ran in at the door and scrambled among the chairs. Shon liked the kitchen company better than any, and he had leave to come downstairs on any evening after his tea. He had never been shy, and now he shouted for his favourite Sukey, who received him with cries of welcome. 'Come awn, Ducky, and see who's here. Who's that now.' She turned him towards Kitty.

The child looked at Kitty, and everyone could see by his face that he did not approve her white, thin cheeks and sharp nose. 'Don't ye know her—that's Kitty that rared ye.'

Kitty gazed at the boy with an eager intensity of love, with her cheeks still further drawn in, her compressed lips pushed forward, her eyes large and bright.

134

'No, of course he doesn't know me,' Kitty cried. 'Hadn't they all forgotten me?'

Shon, after consideration, offered his hand. 'How do you do, Kitty?' Kitty caught him in her arms and kissed him. 'I'm doing well, honey, when I see you again.'

'Here's wan that wasn't so shtruck with Ameriky,' Sukey said.

'Ach,' Con said, spitting; 'Kitty was always fretting for Donegal.'

'America was a great rich land,' Kitty said, 'but I never felt me living there.'

Shon had discovered the baby sitting on the rug against her knees. The baby, a year-old girl, white as milk and blue-eyed like Shon himself, clenched its fists, squared its shoulders and stared at him with concentration.

Sukey made a signal, drawing the attention of the company to the children; like a showman displaying his pets. Shon, who like other small boys, was interested in babies, put out his finger. The baby grabbed it and frowned. Shon, surprised and delighted to find intelligence in the creature, shook the finger up and down and smiled. He blushed with pleasure.

The company stared from all sides as into an arena, where two small pet animals, domesticated among men like dogs and cats, played for their amusement. There was as much interest and pleasure in Con's face as Kitty's or Sukey's, for he did not think of Shon as a Corner, but a child. All the ugly, twisted worn faces relaxed, grew self-forgetful, unguarded, childish, like faces at a pantomime.

'D'ye like her?' Sukey cried suddenly.

'It smiled at me,' Shon said, looking round with a triumphant air, like the discoverer who feels that he has made his discovery, that he has created something, and he asked, 'Can it talk?'

'Naw, not yet. Ye wouldn't expect it.'

'Can it think?'

'Aye, well enough.'

'What does it think?' Shon stared at the baby, which stared at him.

'She thinks you're a nice wee boy.'

'Has it got a name?'

'Teresa is her name. D'ye like that name?'

'It's thinking all the time,' Shon said with surprise, and then he added, 'Is it a she?'

Everybody burst out laughing. Shon looked round in surprise. He could not understand why this sensible question was funny. But he did not resent the laughter any more than an intelligent person resents the chattering of monkeys. He did not pretend to understand grown-ups.

'Perhaps Kitty'll give her to ye for a wee wife,' Sukey suggested.

Shon looked doubtfully at the baby which, still gripping his finger, blinked twice and belched.

Kitty laughed and hugged him. 'Naw, Kitty'll give him to no one—for he's my own sweetheart. Didn't I christen him and shortcoat him and take him through his measles.'

Shon looked at her with surprise. He had always supposed that Mr. Feenix had christened him. The truth was that he had been twice christened, once by Mr. Feenix and once by Kitty, who had carried him into chapel one afternoon, said a rosary over him and marked his forehead and his breast with holy water. No catholic nurse in Annish that had any goodness of heart, would allow the baby in her charge to go to hell or the fairies for want of a little trouble on her part.

'I thought it was Mr. Feenix christened me,' Shon said.

The company winked at each other. It was understood that no more should be revealed. Con spat and said easily, 'Aye, maybe that one greased ye for the devil; but we'll see ye in the good place yet, and then ye may thank Kitty.'

Kitty's cough grew worse. The doctor said that she ought to go back to California; but this advice made both Con and Kitty angry. They agreed that there was nothing wrong with her.

One day in the castle kitchen, when Con was telling American stories, presenting them to the company as a good-natured missionary throws jujubes to savages, and the company was enjoying them, like savages, out of politeness, Kitty, forcing a big laugh for her husband's humour, coughed and spat blood. It flashed red across the fire and fell upon the hearth where it lay black.

'Tch, tch,' Sukey said. 'That's a bad cough ye have.'

'It's a wee catch in the throat,' Con said. 'But it's nawthin'.'

'It's the laffing is the shtrain,' Darcy said. 'An ant of mine in the county Derry spat blood for forty years, but it was laffing kilt her in the latter end, when she was bringing to mind some ould sight of a boy falling off an ass cart in Carn.'

'She's thin,' Sukey said, looking closely at Kitty.

Con put down his feet and turned like an angry terrier. 'Now, now, lave her be. There's nawthin wrong with her at all.'

'What did the doctor say, then?'

Con jumped out of his chair in a rage. 'Ach your Annish doctors? D'you call them omedauns, doctors. Tell me this, where could Kitty be better than here? Wasn't she born and bred in Annish?'

'That's a true word,' Darcy said, 'for it's reasonable.'

This speech had effect. All reflected upon it. Darcy, who had just come in from driving the gig to Dunderry and back, on special errands for Mary Corner, was already respected by all except Sukey. It was

136

seen that he was a responsible man, a man of character. Many people said of Darcy that he was greatly changed from the ragged mountain boy on Knockeen. In fact, Darcy had not changed except in his dress, in the black patch over his left eye, and in responsibilities. It was the responsibilities that made people see and hear him in a responsible connection.

'It's nature,' Darcy said. 'For why, as they say, would Gawd make water if the fish could fly.'

'You're right, Darcy,' Kitty said. 'Sure I was made for Annish, and I'll stay in it now.'

'Aye, ye might stay in it,' Sukey said, with emphasis on the in; and then as usual, when she had planted a hard blow, she jumped up and bustled about, shouting and abusing Peggy. 'I'm sick and tired of the cans. I don't care if they're for the master's bath or how he cleans himself, his tongue is long enough, Gawd save him. Bridgy, take away these cans and be quick about it, ye gawpy; out of my kitchen.'

Bridget, like a sensible girl, always took the cans away when she was told, and when Peggy, in her turn, abused her, she did not defend herself. One day she boldly took the cans to the bedrooms, and Peggy, conciliated by her humbleness, did not forbid her. She was even glad of her help. So Bridget was able gradually to attach herself, as can carrier, to the bedroom landing. Four people on that landing took a bath every day, and each bath required a huge can of hot water and another of cold, to fill; and four slop-pails to empty. In a week the rooms were as familiar to Bridget as a factory to a workman. She knew John Chass' shaving glass and silver shaving case, his rows of boots with their trees, as well as the rocks in Ballycorner bay.

She had tried on Mrs. John's boots and she had seen, for the first time in her life, her own back, in the double cheval glass.

For a long time she stared at herself, raising her arms and moving her body inside its creased dirty print, and when she looked again at the face which belonged with the back, she stared at it for ten minutes in wonder, as if it, too, were a new thing.

It seemed to her a beautiful face; the loveliest that she had ever seen. Even when she smiled, it was still beautiful, because luckily she had only lost four teeth and they were at the back. She felt such pity for this beautiful face, belonging to a girl who had no one but such as Rifty to admire it, that she was ready to break her heart. Her pity was deeper than grief; it was deep in her body, in her heart and in her blood. It was a pain through her whole body, which held her still in its over-powering sorrow for the miracle of beauty wasted.

Peggy's rattling heels sounded in the corridor, and she jumped for her pail. There were two baths to empty; the nursery bath and Master Cleeve's.

137

Cleeve's was her favourite room, and she knew all his possessions better than he did himself. She examined his brushes, shoes, hairwash, toothpaste, underclothes, books, the photograph of his father, the letters in his pockets. She touched the writing on them, which appeared to her like the random tracks of an inked fly, as if to understand them by touch. She handled his pyjamas, shirts, ties and hats, and even the pillow and eiderdown on his bed, in the same curious manner. Her fingers parted like mouths trying to form a question. But no question was asked and the sheets gave no illumination.

When Cleeve went back to school in September, she still visited his empty room to dust the bedrails; and to shake up the pillows which had supported his head.

She had been surprised by his going, but she awaited his return with that patience which will wait a lifetime because it expects nothing, consciously.

Cleeve left school at Christmas. There was talk of his going to Oxford or learning some profession, but he saw no reason why he should continue his education when already, after two years in the sixth at Ruffton, he knew everything about the world. As for a profession, life was too precious to be wasted, especially for one with so delightful a home as Castle Corner and a masterpiece to write.

His new novel about a Roman youth called Manlius, who discussed philosophy with his friends, was in its sixth chapter. As soon as he came home he put a table in the book attic, ordered a large bottle of ink and sat down to compose an important scene in which Manlius revealed the secret of life to his friends.

'The young man, beautiful as a god, reclined upon a couch of gilt wood, adorned with sardonyx and jasper. The beautiful Phryne, Grecian virgin, recently purchased for a high price in the slave market of the Forum, lay in his bosom; the charming and talented Rubilia supported his head against her breast. Having sipped from his cup of a single carved emerald a draught of the pure Falernian, Manlius answered his friend, 'Rather it seems to me that the five senses of man are like the five chariot horses of which the driver, intelligence, necessarily keeps control for his own safety and joy.'

Here Cleeve noticed that the sunshine was pouring through the window; and heard from the yard the dogs barking; sign that John Chass was going out snipe shooting on the bog. He perceived that to-morrow it might rain, snow or freeze; and he remembered the beauty of the bog in sunshine; the astonishing blue of bog pools under a clear sky; the green of the moss cushions. The pen fell from his hand and he rushed downstairs calling for his boots.

After all it rained. The shooters were caught in the midst of Ballycorner moss and soaked to the skin. But what delight to defy the weather, to come home wet and heroic, to be sent by Mary Corner to a hot bath, and afterwards while the rain dashed on the windows and the waves pounded on the stones below, to sit in front of the gun-room fire and eat fresh hot soda scones, dripping with new butter, while John Chass told stories, Mary Corner sewed a missionary shirt and Shon fought the Battle of Waterloo on the floor, complete with a one-legged lifeguard for the Earl of Uxbridge.

Cleeve never forgot the gun-room teas as long as he lived. They represented for him a concentration of the special happiness belonging to his years at the castle, the noise of the sea and the sea appetite, the sense of home, of old traditional hospitality, which seemed to impregnate the very chairs, so that the broken springed old armchair had more rest and welcome in it than the latest upholstery, and above all, the watchful affection of Mary Corner, which was not only a practical assurance that one would be spoilt in every possible way, but an ideal happiness to know and feel; like the sight and presence of love.

During the last fortnight of the year Cleeve was too much occupied with life to write about it. The weather was open, the snipe were on the bog, Carnmore woods were full of woodcock, and he borrowed six months' pocket money in advance to buy a gun of his own.

It was after shooting his first snipe with the new gun, and falling up to his neck in a bog-hole that Cleeve came in one evening at half-past four to find Bridget smoothing down his sheets.

He was surprised to see a new maid, and looked at her from the door. Bridget gave him a shy glance across the bed and said, 'Ye'll be wanting your bath, now, sir.'

'Yes, if you'll tell Peggy. You're new here.'

'Naw, I'm not new. I'm Bridget Foy.'

'I've not seen you before.'

'I've been in the kitchen this while.'

She glanced at him again with that look which all over the world says to a boy, 'I'm interested.'

Cleeve's response was as quick as any Annish boy's. He stared at her, flushing slightly, and said, 'It's funny I missed you.'

'I only came into the rooms this two months.'

'And you're Francie's sister.'

'Naw, I'm Francie's cousin. Am I like Francie?'

'I can see a likeness.'

'A bad one then.'

'Oh no, you're prettier than Francie.'

Bridget tucked in the blankets for the second time and said, 'Is that the way they talk in London?'

139

This was the second move of courtship in Annish. After the glance, the compliment from the man; and then the snub.

Cleeve, eager and serious said, 'But it's true—and I don't care for London. I'm as much Irish as you are.'

'Thon's a grand rich town. I suppose it's the richest town in the whole world.'

'I'd rather be here in Annish.'

'Why so?'

'The people are so much nicer, so much more friendly.'

Bridget glanced sidelong at the boy. She met Cleeve's eye, also sidelong. They looked at each other steadily for a second, like two birds; and although Bridget's glance, like a hen sparrow's, was cool and curious, and Cleeve's, like a cock's, was doubtful and enquiring, they were at once in a new relation of cock and hen. Cleeve turned red, pushed out his chest a little, adjusted his tie; and then with a foolish grin said, 'Do you always make my bed?'

'I don't make it. I turn it down.'

He came near her with the same foolish air. Bridget sedately left the room. But on the next day when she took the cans, Cleeve was in his room, and after that, they met every evening and talked about the wonders of England and the charms of Annish. Cleeve told Bridget that now he had left school he would never leave Annish again, for it was the most beautiful place in the world, with the most charming and beautiful people. He was going to write books about it.

He actually began a new novel, about Annish, in which the young master of the castle fell in love with a beautiful peasant, and their marriage, by uniting protestant and catholic, made peace in the land. 'Cornelius Carthew was lying on the sofa in the great hall. His wound was not yet healed and his head was supported tenderly against the breast of Nora Macconnelogue, while he spoke for a long time to the remorseful tenants. The senses of man, he said, were like the five sails of a boat, which properly managed would carry him swiftly to rich herring grounds. Nora Macconnelogue, beautiful and wise, with all the unspoilt nobility of the peasant, could scarcely refrain from tears at these words.'

It turned out, however, that Bridget had a very low opinion of Annish; she would only talk of England, and so Cleeve was obliged to talk of it.

Bridget, from the beginning of her long, devious approach towards Cleeve, had no more scheme in her head than a moth's when it flies to the light. She talked to him about London, just as she had peeped into the drawing-room, with no conscious ambition or greed. She was surprised when Cleeve suggested that she ought to seek work in London.

She was surprised by all Cleeve's suggestions, while he courted her every day at bath-time, but as soon as he had made them they seemed perfectly reasonable to her.

'A pretty girl like you, ought to go on the stage.'

'What would I do there?'

'You're much prettier than plenty of girls that get a hundred pounds a week.'

Cleeve was sitting beside her on the bed, holding her round the waist. This was now permitted by established custom.

'They wouldn't pay me that,' Bridget said.

Cleeve squeezed her and said, 'Not to begin with, of course. You'd begin at ten or twenty.' His hand shifted up through her bodice. Bridget caught his wrist and said, 'None of that now.'

She knew as well as any sparrow how to drive the cock mad for her. She had made Cleeve mad, and while she sat calmly beside him she could feel his heart pounding, and see his red face and foolish grin turned towards her like Rifty's or any of a half dozen others. She was used to the phenomena of love in boys, and they did not alarm her.

'Are ye going to behave now?'

'I wasn't going to hurt you.'

'Hurt enough if I know annything.'

'Wouldn't you like to go on the stage, Bridgy?'

'Would that be in London?'

'Of course it would.' Cleeve began to describe the glorious career of a London actress, with a hundred pounds a week, a carriage, and her photograph in the shop windows. Actresses could marry anybody; a lord or a millionaire.

'Me, marry a lord!' Bridget said.

'Why not? The others have.'

Bridget reflected, but because all this was to happen in London, it seemed already credible. She said, 'Am I pretty enough for a lord?'

'Of course you are. You're beautiful.' Again his hand was pushing into her bodice. Bridget, pondering, did not seem to notice it. She said thoughtfully, 'If I'm pretty enough for a lord, amn't I pretty enough for you, Master Cleeve?'

Cleeve laughed again, and said that she was pretty enough to marry anybody, then quickly he asked her if she liked chocolates.

'I do, but ould Giveen will ask ye saxpence a quarter and I wouldn't have ye waste your money.'

Cleeve nevertheless bought her chocolates; and the next day, a pair of stockings. But when he tried to take a kiss for them, she threw them in his face.

141

Mary Corner took Kitty a bottle of her paregoric which was a well-known remedy in Annish. Shon and his mother delivered the bottle one morning from the governess cart, and Shon, by his special request, stayed to hear old Daniel tell stories about the Firbolgs and to make experiments on the baby Teresa.

Doctor Hanna, shooting with John Chass on the mountain, warned him not to let Shon go too near his old nurse; but when John Chass told Mary that there was danger of infection, she answered indignantly, 'You don't expect me to tell that poor girl that she's not to see Shon. It would break her heart.'

'It's only that Hanna thought he might catch the cough.'

Mary was distressed and therefore excited. She was always mysteriously troubled by a question like this, as if she feared that there might be no answer to it. She used an argumentative tone which was rare with her. 'I'm surprised that Doctor Hanna hasn't more sense than to suggest a thing like that. I'd have to forbid Kitty the house, and how can I do that after all she's done for us and Shon.'

'It would easily make trouble with all the Egans,' John Chass said, anxious to make things smooth again for Mary and himself. 'Con would never forgive us. Besides, half Annish is coughing this time of year.'

'I'll go and see Kitty myself and take her another bottle.'

John Chass was already easy in his mind; for his faith was in a deeper providence than Mary's. He was sure all his life that no misfortune could happen to him, by an optimism that was part of his strong flowing life. But Mary had no peace. She returned to the subject again and again. John Chass, prepared to sleep, would suddenly hear, 'Was that Shon coughing?'

'No, no, how would he be coughing?' John Chass yawned with a noise like the pant of a hippopotamus and said sleepily, 'There's the rain now to lay the wind, thank God for that.'

'I wonder has Frances shut Shon's window.'

'Of course she has—trust Francie to look after her own comfort.'

There was a short pause. John Chass, preparing again to sleep, murmured, 'Nothing like a little rain to sing you to sleep.'

'I don't believe Francie——'

'Ah, Mary, now, don't be worrying about windows. Go to sleep, my dear.'

John Chass was a good sleeper, but he could not sleep unless Mary went to sleep also; Mary was already out of bed. In her long nightgown frilled to the ears and her frilled nightcap, she looked like the old woman who lived in the shoe. John Chass, with a groan, hastily pulled the sheets up to his chin, saying. 'Oh well, if you must go, you must. But why would you let your place get cold after half an hour warming it.'

The window in the night nursery was closed, but Mary stayed to look at Shon. She had gone for that. She stooped over the bed, shading the candle from the boy's eyes with her small bony hand, twisted with rheumatism, and gazed earnestly at the face on the pillow, the lips still babyish, the long lashes. Shon was her life, and only to look at him gave her usually a happiness that could not be described; a complete happiness beyond the imagination of one who has only created a masterpiece or possessed an empire. But now her happiness was broken by a mysterious confusion in her mind; an oppressed guilty feeling.

They told her that Kitty was dangerous to Shon, but to see Shon was Kitty's last great happiness, and she understood well in her own head the cruelty of refusing to let her see him.

Mary Corner as a child had been taught by the evangelistic preachers of her church that God was love; and all her woman's instinct agreed with that doctrine. The faith of love was as deep and strong within her as her life. She could not do a cruel act. She could not believe that good could come from unkindness.

Yet, as she looked down on Shon she felt a dark, painful confusion which had destroyed her happiness for weeks past, a sense of bewilderment and guilt.

She could not pray for help because she did not expect God to interfere in the world; she did not know even what to pray for. She was cut off in this strange confused suffering which could not be defined, a fear greater than understanding.

In the deep of the night, John Chass once more found himself awake. He knew what this meant, that Mary was also awake. For if Mary waked, even though she lay as still as a corpse, John Chass, by some telepathy of discomfort, also waked. He could not bear that anyone near him should be uneasy.

'Can't you sleep, Molly?'

'I was thinking that we ought to try balsam for Kitty.'

'Wha's that. Ah, go to sleep, my dear. Time enough in the day to do your sick visiting.'

'Shon was there again this morning.'

John Chass pressed his repeater under the pillow. It rang four silvery notes in A, and a single C. 'Bless my soul,' he said, 'half-past four and you talking about Kitty.'

'How could I tell Shon that he's not to see Kitty when she's always asking for him? And the poor girl so ill.'

'I'm sorry about that,' John Chass sighed. 'Has she tried porter?' John Chass considered porter a remedy for all female illness. 'I'll tell Grogan to send her a keg.'

But it was an hour before Mary went to sleep, and then she turned and groaned in such a manner that John Chass, though sleeping, also groaned, tossed, and, waking in the morning, declared that he hadn't slept a wink.

Mary was already hurrying away to see Shon washed and dressed; and to look at his tongue. John Chass sighed and said, 'There's waste of a good night.'

It was a dull morning. Sky and lake were in one shade of dirty grey. The trees, not yet budding, looked as wet and dead and rotten as driftwood. John Chass, seeing this dismal landscape out of his window, raised his eyebrows and it was only after some reflection that he said, 'This should be a good day for Dunderry.'

Dunderry meant a visit to the club, a call on the Dean, much talk with friends of whom some, no doubt, would be persuaded to come home to dinner. John Chass stropping his razor, suddenly burst into song.

One day Cleeve caught Bridget in the doorway of the attic stairs with a can in each hand. He squeezed her against the wall of the stairs and kissed her until he was tired, and after this he grew bold with her. There were struggles in which she needed all her strength to hold him away. She was sometimes frightened of him; and she was fearful that they would be caught. One day Peggy came upon them in the housemaid's closet. She was calling from the stairs, 'Master Cleeve,' but the boy, struggling with Bridget, did not hear her. Bridget jerked herself away and pushed him into the passage.

'What is it?' he asked Peggy.

'Ye're wanting in the house.'

Cleeve, still red and glowing with his feats of courage and enterprise, brushed his hand over his ruffled hair and ran down to the hall.

It was the day of the road sessions when the magistrates allotted road contracts for the quarter, and John Chass, having heard appeals at Dunvil all the morning, had just returned home with his friends to celebrate their release from court. The hall was crowded with men, talking noisily together. Beyond the hall the corridor of the north wing was full of farmers in their best clothes gathered round the open door of the room which Grogan, following old usage, called the courtroom, and John Chass, the office. For magistrates, even in Annish, were influenced by the time-spirit, and in a hundred small ways deprecated their power.

The farmers were petitioners either for recommendation to contractors; or, if they had succeeded in obtaining contracts, for some relaxation in their tenders. John Chass' voice could be heard now and then from within the room, in gusts of expostulation, consolation, congratulation, between the roaring waves of broad Annish vowels which filled the passage.

Sir Walter MacEwen was in the office with John Chass, but the other magistrates and their friends were gathered in the hall where Grogan, with a tray of small glasses filled with neat whisky, zigzagged from group to group, lifting up his face sideways and saying sadly, 'Wull ye take annything, sor?' Grogan was a strict teetotaller.

The air smelt of dust, frieze and whisky. Faces were red, and voices were loud. Everybody was smiling, chattering; and those who had nothing to say or to laugh at, were smiling to themselves and looking alert; just as stray dogs rouse up and lift their tails when the pack gives tongue.

Slatter, already half drunk, was bawling some joke about a bet; Duff, possibly drunker, but more civilized, stood smiling and screwing up his eyes with a critical air. But his tongue, unknown to him, gently licked the ends of his bristling moustache, wet by his whisky.

Philip Feenix, too, standing over against the wall, had a glass of neat whisky in his hand. He drank among the magistrates; but he did not speak much. With his rough, dirty tweeds, his big black moustache, his ferocious air, he had an appearance which alarmed timid strangers. When he did speak, often in a strong Annish accent, he spoke to the point.

'Don't ye trust any of them—a lot of thieves and blaggards.'

This development in young Feenix, even his dirty clothes, against which Slatter sometimes protested, his savage manners, and the whisky, though nobody had foreseen them in the nice English schoolboy of two years before, surprised no one in Annish.

'Ah well,' people said apologetically, 'it's natural enough.' They felt in some vague way that nature, the nature of people and things, had formed a set of patterns for conduct which were not easy to avoid; and that any young man like Philip, put on the defensive, might have taken the same attitude, even to the whisky.

Mary Corner stood at one side, out of the crowd. She had stood Shon, at his own request, on the hall table to look at a picture which Benskin was admiring. It was a portrait of the first John Corner, of Castle Corner; called John Recorder because he had been Recorder and M.P. for Dunderry. Benskin was advising that the picture which had lately been brought down from the back attic to the hall should be repaired. Benskin's interest in the Corner things and history had made him a friend of Mary Corner's, who felt the man's sincerity and simplicity. She had long been won over from her first suspicions of him.

It was said that Benskin had two ways of accomplishing his purpose; he blarneyed the strong ones and frightened the weak. But the fact was quite different. He admired and liked strong people and showed his

145

admiration; and he disliked weak people and quickly grew impatient with them.

He liked Mary Corner for her character, and his admiration for the old house was sincere. He knew from several experts that it was an admirable specimen of its period.

As Cleeve appeared from the stairs, Slatter shouted at him, 'Come on, young fella, I've got ye a jawb to be a millionaire—what d'ye say to that, now?' and pushed him towards Benskin.

Benskin gave him a slight, stiff bow, but continued to listen to Mary Corner. who was telling him the history of John Recorder—how as a younger son he had left the west country with a Beresford cousin, and had received his land from another west country man, Chichester, upon the undertaking to maintain in Annish a fort, a bawn, and thirty-five swordsmen.

Benskin, Shon and Mary all looked at the canvas which represented, under a black surface like that of a dirty frying pan, the dim picture of a hook-nosed man in a breastplate, carrying a rolled paper in his hand. In the right cheek there was a small round hole. A tablet bore the legend, 'John Charles Corner, M.P., 1592-1641.'

Mary Corner looked with calm pride. The hero, because he belonged to John Chass and to Shon, had her own loyal devotion. Shon gazed with round eyes, and a slight frown as if perplexed. It was he who had made the small hole with a new arrow, last Christmas. He knew now that it had been a wicked deed to shoot the canvas, and he was trying to find out why. He looked round at his mother like a child in church who sees the people kneel and suddenly feels anxious, even alarmed, in case he should prove to be different in some way from others.

'A pioneer of empire,' Benskin said softly, looking at the dim, brown face, which seemed to hide behind the canvas as behind three centuries. 'It's an extraordinary thing,' he turned suddenly to Mary Corner with a little sideways inclination full of deference, of anxiety to please, 'how many of them came from the west country, Raleigh, Drake.'

Shon turned round and fixed his eyes on Benskin's brown face as if to say, 'You, too, reverence this black thing.'

'The old boy did pretty well for himself,' Cleeve said, dissembling his pride.

Benskin at once turned to him with the same quick, polite inclination. 'He deserved success. A man of the imperial spirit.'

Shon, seeing the terrier Spot running among the crowd, gave a yell and suddenly leapt to the floor. Mary Corner, alarmed, cried out, 'You naughty boy, you'll break your leg,' but Shon was already darting among the crowd, with loud yells, as if the energy baffled by grown-up ideas had broken out in another direction. Mary, knowing by the very sound of the yells, reckless and defiant, that Shon was bursting with mischief, moved quickly after him. Benskin stooped towards Cleeve and said, 'And the spirit is not dead—Rhodes of course.' He paused.

'Do you know Cecil Rhodes?'

'I've met him. A very great man.'

'He's made millions, I suppose.'

'He cares very little for money. His only ambition is to serve the Empire.' Benskin looked at Cleeve attentively; his small blue eyes were never careless or vague. He looked at everything and everybody with concentration; avoiding rudeness by the poise of his head, which seemed to say 'Excuse me.'

'You have been in Africa?' Cleeve said.

'Yes. Would you like to go to Africa?'

'I hadn't thought of it.'

Benskin answered that there were great openings in Africa for young men with the pioneering spirit. He continued to study Cleeve.

Benskin was one of those, like Rhodes himself, for whom at that time the Empire was a sacred cause. The Empire brought peace, prosperity and free institutions wherever it went. What more could people want?

He had sent many young men to Africa during the last three years. His patronage, through his companies and his friends, was large. But he was particular in its use; he looked for imagination, for the imperial spirit.

'There are enormous opportunities in Africa,' he murmured. 'It's the last great continent still open to the pioneer, to men like Rhodes, and my friend Dr. Jameson.'

He talked about Rhodes, Kitchener, Lugard; and Cleeve saw contemporary history in a new light, which fascinated him. His boy's mind loved the pattern, the clue. 'You think Africa is Ireland over again?'

'And America. Except that the Americans wiped out the original inhabitants.'

Cleeve stood smiling with the expression of one who looks at a neat diagram solving a problem. 'Do you think we ought to have wiped out the Irish?' he asked.

Benskin was shocked. 'No, no, that kind of conquest is bad, even economically. Rhodes is a Home Ruler, for instance, and in South Africa——'

'A Home Ruler.' Cleeve was still more interested. He adjusted this new pattern of which he had taken hold.

All round them glasses clinked. John Chass had returned among his guests; his voice, which had the quality of welcome as a violin has that

147

of passion, could be heard saying like an accompaniment to the uneven chatter. 'But where's your glass—you can't go yet—another wee one.'

Slatter was still shouting bets. He had challenged John Chass to drive tandem to Dunvil and back within ten minutes each way, and the match was for that afternoon. Dunvil was slightly over two miles.

'Will ye give a pound for every minute over the ten, each way?' he shouted.

'I'll give you five,' John Chass said. 'Five pounds a minute.'

'Naw, naw.' Slatter was a nervous better.

'I'll take ye in tens,' Duff said.

'D'ye want him to kill himself?' Slatter shouted.

'Faith and he wouldn't mind,' an Annish voice said from the corridor. Duff's jealousy of John Chass was well known.

'Ten pounds a minute,' John Chass said, 'for every minute under ten going out; and every minute under ten coming home.'

The crowd streamed towards the yard. Cleeve and Benskin followed slowly. 'The spirit of adventure,' he murmured, 'the spirit of the pioneer, that's what we need to keep alive. In this country, I'm afraid, it's dead.'

John Chass loved to take a party to his stableyard. He stood now, in his grey pepper-and-salt cutaway, flat-topped grey felt hat and loose grey trousers, cut in the fashion of his fashionable youth; and looked about him with a smile of pleasure at the white walls, newly lime-washed for the spring, the little clock tower over the coach-house whose hands had stood at five minutes past eleven for many years, the neat green doors of the stable. Neither was he disconcerted when he turned towards his guests, to hear their approbation of the white walls, and found them all conversing about their own affairs. He continued to smile and raising his head he examined the sky and the mountains behind with as much delight as if they, too, had been his. It was a fine spring day such as he loved. The sky was barred with narrow white clouds like strings of enormous white geese flying towards the west, and like geese upon a green, their whiteness made the colour beside them seem so vivid that the eyes blinked. The blue seemed to be alive, as if it were made of glittering blue particles which projected their blueness into the eyes, dazzling them like rays. A cool breeze blew back the elegant locks of John Chass's whiskers; and suddenly turning to the tall grave Sir Walter, who, in his black coat, stood as usual aloof, wrapped up in his thoughts he said, 'Did you ever see such a sky? It gives you an appetite even to look at it.'

'A drinkatite ye mane,' Slatter roared. He seemed like a lunatic in his excitement.

Darcy and the stable boy, young Rifty, led in the tandem from the outer yard. The wheeler was Grey Lady, a famous trotting mare which had cost John Chass a hundred and forty guineas, the leader a young gelding called Dapple.

Dapple had a coat like a grey seal in colour, but in texture much finer. It was as if each separate hair was chinchilla. The creature's round flanks flashed silver under the harness and the blue of the sky was reflected on its broad croup and the thick muscles of its crest. The shining ponies, the new tandem cart, whose wheels threw off cool sparks from their bright varnish, were a work of art, complete of its kind; bright as jewellery; beautiful as youth; sophisticated as an expensive toy; perfection such as only appears at the crown of its period; and embodies its essential in a permanent and unsurpassable form. It was said that the carriage and pair was the typical and most beautiful creation of Victorian art, and that the tandem, even in its name, was already rococo, facetious and therefore decadent. But the tandem belonged to a different line of development from the family carriage. It was not, in spite of its name, a distorted pair. It was the descendant of the gig or trap; it was the high art of the dogcart; made at once as dangerous and as beautiful as dogcart driving could be.

It was an art understood and appreciated in Annish. The farmers, standing by the back wall, burst out in exclamations so loud that they seemed like applause. Shon, walking in front of Dapple with his father's gig whip in his hand, was now extremely serious. His cheeks were flushed with excitement, and he gave every now and then a half skip; but he carried the whip like a piece of regalia, and when he looked round at the tandem, his eye was critical as well as anxious. This was a grown-up interest, full of beauty and excitement, demanding knowledge, skill, courage, into which he entered without any difficulty. He could easily feel the importance and grandeur of tandem driving, and the greatness of his father who drove one.

'No imagination,' Benskin was murmuring. 'There's no big grasp of possibilities. But of course, this country is finished in any case. There's no future here for anyone.'

'You think they'll get Home Rule?'

'No, I mean our work's finished here. The people are prosperous and when they get the land under the act they'll be at peace. The Irish farmer is shrewd enough to know that his future is in the Empire. But for a young man who wants to make his way and do something that matters——'

'Like Harry Jarvis!'

'Yes. All the young men with any enterprise are going to Africa. They feel that big things are going to happen there. In the sixteenth century it was South America and the Spanish Main; in the seventeenth,

149

North America; in the eighteenth, India; now it's Africa, and now is the time to go.'

Dapple reared, and bucketed, striking sparks with its hoofs. Slatter, shouting and backing, obliged the crowd to fall back behind him. Shon called out with an important air, 'Now Dapple,' and Darcy ran up and down beside the new outfit in a state of the highest excitement. Darcy was in full livery, ready to take his place on the back seat, and he had put on the pink shade over his eye, only used for important occasions, instead of the black one. He carried in one hand the tandem horn which he had just brought from the harness-room and he was using it like a field-marshal's baton to direct Rifty. 'Hould him, hould him then, Rifty, don't ye know he's not fit to be driven at all.'

Old Jebb, in undress of trousers and cardigan jacket, standing aloof by the coach-house with a face of disgust, shouted, 'Ah, ye can let him go. He'll go to hell, annyway.' Jebb objected to the tandem rig because it had caused already many accidents to his horses and gear. But he was furious to see Dapple as leader horse; he had said that Dapple would never be fit for a tandem.

'Ah! they'll never go togither,' Darcy agreed, like a loyal lieutenant. He made a sweeping gesture of despair with the horn.

'He'll kick the teeth out of the mare.'

'He'll go mad at the bridge. He could never bear to see the wather!' tossing up the horn as if it were a symbolic sponge.

'Ye think himself will be killed,' Slatter shouted at the old man.

'It won't be his own fault then if he isn't.'

Slatter, now at a safe distance, gave a roar of laughter and shouted, 'It was me bet him he wouldn't drive the little devil for leader.'

'Gawd forgive ye, Mr. Slatter, for putting him upon such a foolish notion.'

'Ye hear that, Jawn, ould Jebby says ye're a fule!'

John Chass paid no attention to this cross-talk. It was the usual method at the castle of criticizing the master and mistress, and probably one of ancient tradition, for all autocrats are accustomed to it. John Chass' good nature allowed his servants rather more freedom than usual, but nobody except strangers was surprised to hear his servants discussing him in his presence. He himself noticed these remarks as little as a preoccupied nurse attends to the babble of her charges. At the moment, they pleased him. He laughed and said to the old coach-man, 'Go on with you, Jebby. If you had your way, I'd still be driving the old nanny in the go-cart.'

Grogan had brought his coat. He eyed it warily, and pulled down his broad white cuffs. It was always a struggle for John Chass, on account of his large arms, shoulders and chest, to put on a top coat.

150

'Of course, you'd only be on probation for the first year,' Benskin was saying.

Cleeve thanked him politely. In fact, he was scarcely listening to this offer of a career. His smile of respectful gratitude which deceived Benskin was for the picture of Ireland and Africa changing places in the historical scene which had for a moment assumed the form of a dance, and so acquired a classical beauty; like the yard, the tandem, and John Chass' top hat which gave him so much pleasure.

'It's very good of you, Mr. Benskin,' he said. 'I shall certainly think of it. Do you think he will manage it in the time?'

'I beg your pardon,' with a deferential bend.

'Get to Dunvil in ten minutes.'

'I hope so.' Benskin was shocked by this levity in the midst of a serious discussion, but his expression showed nothing but calm and judicious reflection. 'The road is fairly good, of course—but there are the hills.'

John Chass, having fought his way into the box coat, looked round for his whip. Shon, who had been waiting for this moment, handed it to him. His expression as he looked up was that of a worshipper. John Chass bowed towards him as he always bowed to anybody when he said 'Thank you,' and touched the boy's cheek with a finger. Shon flushed pink, and overcome, ran back among the crowd. Even his run, at this moment, was hieratic; slow and high-stepping.

'Ten pounds a minute,' John Chass said, turning towards Duff. 'From here to Connell's bar.'

'Ten pounds a minute,' Duff said, 'there and back.'

'And me, too,' Slatter squawked, like a crow with a pebble in its throat. He was choking with excitement.

'Ten pounds to you,' John Chass said. 'That's two separate bets, on two separate times.'

A hoarse voice bellowed from the back, 'Anybody give me two to one on his honour. Two to one that he's there under the ten minutes,' and a roar of voices broke out.

John Chass had climbed into his seat. He bent forward from the waist to take the reins from Darcy, who nimbly jumped up behind. But even as he crossed his arms he gave a shake of his head as if to say, 'What's the good of talking.'

Duff looked at his watch. It had been synchronized with the clock at Connell's in Dunvil, where Connell himself was timekeeper. 'Off,' he shouted. Rifty jumped away from Dapple's head, and at once it reared up.

Jebb gave a yell, and the horse bolted for the archway. The light cart, passing one wheel over the drain in the middle of the yard, and missing the pump by two inches, rocked like a boat in a beam sea. John Chass, smiling with tight firm lips and set jaw, balanced to its swing and kept his eye on the gate. Dapple was bolting; Grey Lady was not bolting, but she was in a fast hand gallop and feeling irresponsible. The leader almost bumped the off wall of the arch, but John Chass brought it safely across in its next stride; Grey Lady went straight on; Jebb waved both his arms like short wings, and gave a dismal cry; and the cart, just about to strike its right hub against the corner, suddenly tilted outwards at an acute angle, missed the wall by half an inch, and disappeared like a tin can tied to a mad dog's tail. It seemed to flash through the air, leaving an instantaneous snapshot of John Chass' broad back and high hat, framed in black and white under the shadow of the arch, like a daguerreotype, and Darcy, with open mouth and wild eyes, grasping at the seat rails with both hands.

Jebb let his hands fall, spat and uttered three loud curses. Then he walked over to the yard gate and picked up half a brick, fallen, perhaps that night, from the top of the arch. He held it up before Cleeve and Rifty and croaked in his angry old man's tenor, 'Is it the devil or who is it that gave him his luck?'

It was obvious that he resented the injustice of John Chass' escape. He threw the brick over the wall with an energy of anger surprising in so old and flimsy a man. Everybody else in the yard appeared to be drunk. Farmers, magistrates were shouting, laughing, all talking at once. Cleeve darted into the house and upstairs to the attic. He almost knocked Bridget down at the top of the stairs as he rushed towards the bookroom.

The bookroom window, a little dormer in the roof, looked over the drive to the high road. Cleeve threw open the dirty casement, and turned his eyes towards the afternoon sun behind Knockeen. The road, winding up the hill a mile away to the left, was bare; but two carts were drawing into gates, and the drivers, who had jumped down, could be seen dragging furiously at their heads and beating their legs. A boy on a wall was whirling his arms like flails.

Suddenly the tandem flashed into sight, it was more brilliant in its miniature. The strong, slanting light glittered upon it like the ray from a microscope. It raced up the hill a minute golden horn flashed in the hand of the minute Darcy, black-coated on the back seat. He raised it to his lips and then took it away again. The tandem vanished over the hill; and down through the soft air floated the three gay notes of the horn, left behind.

Cleeve stood breathless. He could not express his delight at the completeness, the beauty, the humour of the thing which would have made him laugh if it had not been for the exciting beauty.

He could feel somebody pressing beside him in the narrow dormer, to look through the same pane; and he knew that it was Bridget, but

152

he could not give her his attention. He pushed his head out of the window as far as he could reach and shouted at the top of his voice, 'Hooray!'

When he drew it in again and turned his head, he met Bridget's eyes, looking at him with an enquiry. He took her in his arms and squeezed her so hard that she cried out, 'Stop that now,' jerked herself free and ran across the passage into her attic. Cleeve rushed after her and threw himself against the door.

'Away now; are ye daft? Somebody's coming.'

'Let me in, Bridgy. They're all in the yard. It's quite safe.'

Cleeve had never dared to attack Bridget in her own room; which was next Peggy's, but now he saw his chance, and the idea of it made him reckless. He charged the door again; thrust his foot across the jamb.

'I'll scream out,' Bridget cried.

'Let me in—I won't hurt you.'

'What do you want in for?'

'I've got something to tell you.'

'Tell me then.'

'I've got a present for you, too.'

The door opened a little. Bridget had by now accepted not only the stockings, but a gilt brooch and a lace handkerchief. She had even begun to ask for presents. Her ambition was to own a pair of drawers with lace trimming. 'What kind of a present?' she asked.

Cleeve flung himself against the door and it opened before him. But Bridget instantly had her hand against his chest. 'Is it the wee drawers?' she asked.

'I haven't got it here.' Adroitly he pushed her backwards against the bed so that she fell on it. Bridget was surprised. She knew herself Cleeve's equal in strength. Now he was on top of her, crushing her, butting her nose with his head, tearing at her skirts.

'Holy Blessed Mary.' Bridget was more angry than frightened. She took the boy by the shoulders and pushed him away. 'Ye'll marry me then?'

'Of course I will.' Cleeve was taken by surprise. But he did not hesitate to promise, and the promise was given honestly. He wanted Bridget at that moment more than anything else in the world, and as for the future, he was confident that it could not fail to be delightful, whatever he did. His whole body assured him of it. It couldn't be doubted.

Bridget stared at him. 'Now at once will ye?'

'As soon as we get to London.'

'Swear it by the Holy Mother and the Blessed Jesus.'

'Of course I will.'

'Then we'll wait till London.'

Cleeve lost his temper, and made for the door. 'Good-bye,' he said coldly.

The strategy was old, but not to Cleeve and Bridget. Bridget was taken in like other girls because the threat might be true. She became apologetic, pleading. She caught hold of his coat-tails and said, 'Ye're not huffed at me.'

'Let me go. I can see you've just been making a fool of me.'

Bridget held him firmly. She recognized a crisis. 'But now, how can I let ye do so,' she begged, 'and we not married. It's a sin.'

'I've told you I'll marry you.'

'Telling's no doing.'

Cleeve pulled away his coat and went to the door. Bridget darted after him and put her arms round his neck, smiled in his face. Even Cleeve in his anger was surprised by the change in the girl from the sharp, watchful prude to the tender lover.

'Ye won't go.' Suddenly she kissed him.

Cleeve sulkily returned the kiss and consented to be led to the bed.

'I wouldn't dar do such a sin as that,' Bridget said, smiling at him. But also she was trembling. She was cold with terror and resolution.

Cleeve sulkily stroked her leg and said, 'It's nothing if you really cared for me.'

She gave a deep sigh and said, 'It's quare and hard to please yewans.'

Cleeve, understanding that this was a surrender, climbed upon her. She submitted to him with quiet patience; only once protesting when he tried to unbutton her bodice. She blushed then and said with mild indignation, 'Ye'll not be seeing me. Do ye take me for a pig or a cow?'

Afterwards, while she sat carefully brushing down her skirt with her hands, she looked at him mournfully and said, 'And that's all for what ye'd put my soul in hell.'

Cleeve wore the characteristic expression of the male, man or horse, in his place; at once surprised and wistful, like one who has accidentally committed a murder. He sat down beside Bridget and put his arms round her waist. 'But I do love you.'

He felt that he had better do so.

John Chass reached Connell's bar in eight minutes twelve seconds, and at once turned about. The bystanders, still lingering from the sessions and now running together to see the rig, startled Dapple in turning, and obliged John Chass to continue in another whole circle. Thus he lost half a minute. Another half-minute was lost at the first

154

cross-roads where young Breedy, with a load of turf, trying to drag his jennet out of the way had made the brute jib. After that, John Chass took his corners so fast and fine that Darcy had no breath for the horn. The thing tooted like a dying soul.

John Chass was a classical driver. He held his body perfectly still as if it were part of the cart; and the movements of his left hand, holding the reins, or his right, when he picked up the whip, were exactly calculated to fulfil their purpose in the simplest and neatest manner. He used his whip, too, in the manner of the old school. No one ever saw him lash at a horse. Now, when he needed to send Dapple into its collar, he picked up the whip from its bucket; threw out the lash, and touched the horse under the trace, on the quarter, with the extreme tip of the cord; caught the lash on the stock and dropped the whip back into the bucket with a succession of movements so smooth and precise that they seemed one. Neither did John Chass ever show any satisfaction when he took each corner a little faster than he had ever taken it before. He was always grave when he drove; just as he always wore his best hat. Nevertheless, he was enjoying the supreme pleasure of his life; the concentrated pleasures of artistry, drama, and danger. The mystic who combined the projecting of visions with nervous exaltations was not happier, or more self-forgetful.

Darcy with his last breath blew a desperate blast at the last corner. They whirled into the straight past Giveen's Store, and the Castle Corner Post Office. The crowd of watchers at the castle gate could be seen waving sticks and hats. John Chass looped Dapple's near rein round his forefinger to hold him out from the right-hand corner into the drive. At the same time he gave the horse a hint, by a slight touch on the right rein, of his intention to turn.

The gate stood back between two curving walls of rough stone. But the tandem from Dapple's nose to the tailboard of the cart was more than twenty feet long; many feet more than the width of the opening at its widest. It was necessary, therefore, to let the leader trot almost to the wall before turning him sharply to the right.

To carry out this feat at speed was a fine point of driving; to perform it with a young fiery horse like Dapple for leader was a challenge exactly to John Chass' taste. It required, in the highest degree, calmness of mind, delicacy of touch, a reckless nerve.

Keeping the left rein looped, he drew Dapple slightly back to take the weight from the long traces; then, when the horse's chest was within a yard from the wall, he unlooped the near rein with a single movement of his finger, and raised his wrist sharply; Dapple whirled round, flew through the gate. But it was now bolting. It galloped obliquely through the gate and jumped the low wall in front of Dow's lodge; Grey Lady pulled up against the wall, fell with it, and the cart, running one wheel up the steep verge in front of the wall, turned over. Darcy, still grasping the horn, fell out upon the loose gravel; John Chass into the mud at the side of the drive.

Grey Lady struggling to her feet, received Dapple's first kick in the chest and at last, losing her self-control, let fly at the cart.

The crowd, posted along the drive among the trees, came running; but long before they could reach John Chass he had scrambled to his feet. He glanced at his horses. Two boys had already freed Dapple. Grey Lady was on her feet. Nothing was in danger but the cart. He picked up his hat and whip and walked down the drive. One cheek and shoulder were plastered with mud; his hat was smashed so that it was like a hat in a comic picture; yet in every part of the man, in his easy walk, his smile, the cock of the smashed hat, even the slant of the whip, there was the dignity which is supposed to belong only to conquerors. It was not less dignity because John Chass was laughing at himself.

Slatter, standing right in the middle of the drive, stared at him in wonder. Eyes, mouth, bent back, pushed out neck, asked, 'How does the fella carry it off? Is he a fool or a twister?'

Cleeve was mad for Bridget. Even though he crept into her room every night, he would spend all day prowling after her, lying in wait on the stairs to squeeze her. He would pounce on her in the upper passage, drag her into the book attic and throw her down among the piles of old *Strand Magazines*. He was in a frenzy, ready to murder her for the least resistance, clawing at her dress and trying to tear it from her. The *Strands* cascaded on every side in clouds of dust while sneezing, panting, quarrelling like two cats, the young creatures fought and struggled together. Cleeve's face expressed his rage and exasperation; Bridget, her savage obstinacy.

Cleeve was enraged by the girl's modesty, the fierce prudery of a Catholic peasant. He did not realize that Bridget had never seen herself naked even in a bath and that the sight would have shocked her. But he hated this idea of hers which forbade him to possess the sight of her beauty not only on personal but ideal grounds. He would ask her fiercely what could be wrong in letting him see her. What was beauty made for except to be seen. His anger was general, like Shon's when he protested that Padsy's Art killed a crow on Sunday.

Cleeve hated everything that stood in the way of enjoyment, but for Bridget, soaked in the mediæval faith, for whom Heaven was behind the blue sky which she saw every day, and hell beneath the ground she walked on, so that volcanoes spurted its flames, and miners in deep shafts sweated for the heat, every one of her actions was religious. Though she had sinned with one part of her, she was a good Catholic

156

in every other part. She defended every inch of her bare skin like a separate maidenhead.

Bridget was a desperate sinner. She had made bad confessions and escaped punishment. She was in a condition dreaded by any Catholic priest who knows the satanic pride and enormous ambition that can grow in the human soul which has defied God and escaped. But she was a Catholic sinner, Catholic flesh.

When one night she had said her prayers before the crucifix on the wall, and drawn out the fine stockings, the gilt ring with glass diamonds, the photographs of Belle Bilton, and Dolly Tester who had married a lord, she would say, 'Gawd helping, with the face and shape of me, I might do better than Master Cleeve.'

But after seven weeks, when she knew herself pregnant, she gave up the grander dream. She told Cleeve that he must marry her at once. Cleeve answered that he could not go to London till his father had sent the money.

'You'd better get it quick,' Bridget said, 'for I'll soon be big and what will they say to you then?'

But Cleeve was in a difficulty. He had no money; and no excuse to ask for money or to go away from the castle. He had already refused politely Benskin's offer of a job, and it was understood that he would stay at the castle until he had found out what he wanted to do.

He knew, of course, that he must marry Bridget, but he felt an extraordinary inability to contrive the means of doing so. His brain became confused whenever he thought of it; his very legs and arms felt stupid and he did not know what to do with himself. He could not write, read or shoot. He slept like a drugged man and woke up with a headache. He possessed Bridget in an angry, obstinate way and when he had had her he felt disgusted with her. He moped all day with a resentful, surprised expression on his face; the expression of a young dog which has eaten too rich food and doesn't know who is responsible for making it feel sick. One day, Mrs. Pynsant, meeting him in Dunvil and turning upon him that fascinating smile, full of sympathy and also challenge, which she had ready for all males, cabmen as well as princes, said to him. 'So you don't want to go to Africa?'

'No, do you think I was very rude?'

Cleeve, who greatly admired Mrs. Pynsant, felt guilty of a lack of consideration to her friend, but she answered, 'I think you're quite right but don't tell anybody else.'

Mrs. Pynsant asked this as if it were a confidence torn by sympathy from the bottom of her soul. She had used the phrase so often that it had the force of art. It made Cleeve flush with surprise and pleasure. He said impulsively, 'I've been longing to meet you.'

Mrs. Pynsant answered, 'Yes, why didn't you? I've been so bored.'

'But did you expect me to?' Cleeve was surprised. The lady had been six weeks in Annish without paying the least attention to him.

She answered, 'I think civilized people ought to support each other in the country. Tell me, what do you do with yourself all day in a backwater like this?'

Cleeve, perceiving instantly that Annish was a backwater, answered that he read a good deal; and sometimes he went shooting.

'But then at Oxford I suppose you get tired of clever people, or are you one of the naughty ones who play baccarat and come to my receptions in green ties.'

Cleeve at once saw that he must go to Oxford. He said, 'But I'm not at Oxford yet—I'm not going till October.'

'You must come and see me in London. Stella would be delighted.'

Lady MacEwen, with wild hair and wild eyes, came out of the drapers and Mrs. Pynsant, taking Cleeve's hand raised it as high as her heart, gave him the look of one torn away from her dearest friend by cruel fate and wrinkling her nose in a smile, said, 'There, I knew I'd be dragged away. But remember.' She paused and looked very serious. Then she dropped the hand and undulated down the village street beside Lady MacEwen.

Cleeve went home from this three minutes' conversation in a state of excitement, which turned his stupid, confused dejection into an active despair.

When he came to Bridget's attic that night to pacify her with ribbons and promises, and to make love as carelessly as how d'you do, he felt betrayed and lost.

The dirty, stuffy little room with its characteristic smell of the peasant, unwashed sheep wool and old sweat, in which he had delighted, now revolted him. He quickly left Bridget to stand at the window and breathe clear air. It was a night such as he had loved to see from Bridget's window. The moon and the evening star, high above the roof, were like drifting fires on the water. The red eye of the Red-man lighthouse began to turn over against Dunvil pier. The waves of the lake, glittering like dark scales, ran in endless series towards the rocks below; on one side green black in the cold moonlight, on the other splashed with crimson and magenta from the shade of Mary Corner's lamp in the drawing-room, where no doubt she was reading *Ivanhoe* to Shon.

But Cleeve was gazing at women like Mrs. Pynsant in drawing-rooms full of splendour, talking with brilliant and witty young men about art, love, books and the great world. He was crushed by the sense of waste. He had wasted his life, and the idea of this waste, filled him with despair like a corruption of the flesh. He felt weak and ill.

Bridget made no complaint of Cleeve's indifference to her. A lover is not the centre of a Catholic girl's interest. She takes a wider grasp of

158

life, even when she is a sinner. She was happy by herself, seated on the bed among her toys, her ribbons and photographs. She would stare for an hour at the pictures of girls, who, starting as farmers' daughters or barmaids, had become rich, titled, glorious.

No one could describe what Bridget saw in these smiling faces. The vague, enormous sensation of triumph and glory passed slowly through her rapt muscles; like the undefined greeds of a Genghis going out to conquer a civilized China whose magnificence was only a word to him but a word charged with meaning for a conqueror; and she could not tell herself what she saw with her black eyes, opened to their widest upon Kate Vaughan, Belle Bilton, Dolly Tester who was a marchioness.

V

Jarvis was staring across the Niger from the deck of the *Maria Fry*, towards Laka. Jarvis had never heard of Laka till that morning, when after coming two hundred miles, on shooting leave, to see his Uncle Felix and to bag a croc or hippo, he had for the first time been brought face to face with a limit to the Empire; the frontier.

Since that moment he had spent most of his time staring across the river, examining it with fieldglasses, or climbing the foremast to see from above if there were any gap, through its green wall.

This excitement in the young man had caused the liveliest anxiety both in Felix and Captain Pooley, who was in command of the nearest troops. They stood beside him, with the Major, looking at him while he examined the Laka bank. Felix said, 'I'm afraid we're not allowed to land on the Laka side—the Laka chief is rather exclusive.'

Jarvis made no answer; he stepped along the deck to peer from a new angle; the three heads turned after him.

'Mustn't let him do anything silly,' Pooley said, and Felix, an old friend of Pooley's, raised his beard in reassurance. 'You can trust us to look after that—a row with Laka would finish us here.'

'Absolutely do us in,' the Major agreed. 'We can't afford to have any trouble with old man Laka.'

Laka was unknown and forbidden land to white men. The British troops had taken Oyo to the south; the French were in Dahomey on the north; but the whole of Northern Nigeria was still under its native rulers; priest kings, pagan and cannibal chiefs; and in the north, the Mahommedan emirs.

France, Germany and England were all encroaching on this rich country; but in a manner peculiar to the time. No one wanted war, and each knew that war might come at any moment over some frontier clash in Africa; yet each continued to advance as if by some mysterious compulsion.

They were, in fact, compelled by many forces; by national feelings in the people, released by popular education; by ambitions and weakness of governments; by the ambitions of colonial soldiers and officials; and of course by the imperial idea of national glory.

But below this idea there was the master faith of the age; the idea of

160

the struggle for existence; the survival of the fittest; the idea that some power in nature itself, a scientific providence discovered and proved by Darwin, had ordained progress by universal war. The imperialist god of Darwin, the faith of war and competition, pervaded all books, newspapers, speeches, board meetings; all the million schools of the new educational systems where science was thought of as truth; even the very missionary meetings, which assumed the white man's right to Christianize the world. It gave to the hunt for markets and the wars of the stock exchange the dignity of moral virtue. It made the ruin of an industry and the destruction of a thousand families of workpeople, a noble and godly act. It was so strong that it ruled even statesmen who had been brought up to believe in another one, in a quite different providence which was supposed to have designed all things for brotherhood instead of competition. It compelled Gladstone to send armies to Zululand, Afghanistan and Khartoum, he had to obey its command expressed through its millions of slaves, or he would have been driven from government. He stayed in order to compromise with the idea; but he only succeeded in hampering its operation; in producing defeat; and so exasperating its believers and increasing the violence of its operation.

On the faces of Felix, Pooley, even the Major, turned towards Jarvis now, there was the same expression of deprecation, almost of timidity, as if they felt a moral inferiority in the presence of his energy and boldness, his ideal activity.

'There's a creek over there,' Jarvis said, 'where a boat could run right in.'

'Well—three men were shot from that bank last week,' Pooley said mildly.

Jarvis turned his sharp eyes on the captain, a tall, thin, melancholy man with a long neck and a prodigious nose. 'British subjects?'

'I believe they were,' he admitted.

'Why didn't the gunboat come up?'

'Well, you know, everybody's been warned to keep away from that bank. Our orders are to let Laka alone.

'Government orders,' Jarvis said with bitter contempt. 'You can bet your life that this bloody Government is not taking any chances.'

From the starboard side came a loud hissing noise. A cockney voice shouted, 'Wot oh, she bumps,' and a woman yelled angrily.

Felix looked anxiously to starboard; the Major gave his little cough and said, 'Friend Hatto has brought company,' and then meeting Felix' eye, slightly shook his head as if to say, 'Oh dear, it's just what we feared.'

The truth was that this visit of Jarvis to the *Maria Fry* which seemed so simple to him, had caused as much excitement to his hosts as if he had been a young duke visiting poor relations in the country. Felix had had his beard trimmed at the first hint of it; explaining to the Major, 'He's a great friend of my boy's you know—and rather a particular young man—a bit of a dandy. Quite a good thing, I always think, in a young man—I was that way myself when I was the same age.'

Since then extraordinary preparations had taken place on the *Maria Fry*—the decks had been scraped, the bulwarks repainted, the boys drilled, and now on the great occasion, not only Felix and the Major, but even Captain Pooley, who usually dined with them in old pyjamas, were in full mess kit, freshly washed and starched to such a degree that Felix was afraid to sit down.

The entertainment had begun well; none of the servants had dropped plates or shouted insults; if it had not been for Jarvis' unexpected interest in Laka, the two housekeepers would have been extremely well pleased. But they had not counted on a visitor.

'I thought Hatto was down river,' Felix said.

'So did I. But it's always the way—I mean—if you don't expect a chap.' The Major faltered. Jarvis had already crossed the deck. A small steam launch had come into the landing-stage, steered by a white man in a torn cotton shirt, and an enormous white hat, finger marked all round the brim. He was chaffing a fat negress in the bows of the launch, who had apparently been thrown down by her collision with the stage.

'Go on then, spoil it all—wot's the good of trying to please a woman.'

The negress in a fury clambered to the stage and rushed towards the joker, who at once dived into the cabin amidships, wriggled with acrobatic agility through a narrow door into the bows, sprang ashore and darted into the store. The woman laboured in pursuit; growling like a leopard.

'Amusing chap,' Felix said at his nephew's shoulder. 'A well-known character on the oil rivers; Hatto.' He smiled as if to say, 'You mustn't take him seriously.'

Cocky was not interested in amusing traders and their public buffoonery. He said, 'The launch must be useful. Whose is it?'

'Hatto is the agent of the Transport Company.'

'I must ask him about his launch.'

Yells and shrieks broke from the leanto. Cocky stepped back from the rail. The Major, with a horrified face, murmured an apology, and rapidly descended the ladder, into the leanto. It was full of women, exiled from the deck for the evening. Lilly, the Major's girl, was sitting on the counter swinging her legs. She looked sulky and impudent. Dinah, Felix' woman, was wandering about the room with a serious and troubled face. The shy slave woman of five years before was not so shy but she was still a washerwoman, and this made her feel humble and uncertain of herself. She was afraid now that she must have offended. Other men's women, Bobs and Lilly, did not work, drank gin every day, and wore silk clothes, so that she was ashamed among them and thought, 'I'm not clever enough with my white man, and I'm ugly, too, perhaps he will throw me out.' She turned her large soft nose full of holes like a glazed pepper pot, her long crocodile jaw, towards the Major with an anxious air, as if fearing some new, unexpected slight.

The daughter Bandy, now fourteen, a small, slim girl with bandy legs, was examining herself in a looking-glass. She was stark naked, and as she held the glass on a level with her stomach, turned upwards to show the underside of her small hard breasts, shaped like pears directed straight outwards from widely separated points on her chest, her expression was intensely curious.

Hatto was crouching behind the counter while the negress Bobs slashed at him with a roll of blue cotton cloth. After each blow he popped up his head and bawled, 'That's it—go on—another.'

'My dear old chappy,' the Major said. 'My dear Bobs.'

'Dear's the word—dear at any price. Let alone the gin.'

'My dear old boy,' the Major implored, 'if you wouldn't mind, the fact is—we've got visitors on deck—two officers.'

Hatto looked at him and said, 'ole Pooley.'

'No, no, that's just it—one of 'em is Mr. Corner's nephew, and he's a friend of Mr. Corner's boy at home.' The Major's voice begged Hatto to understand this delicate situation. 'So we were putting the mammys down below.'

The Major need not have been alarmed. Hatto at once understood him. He stood up and tucked in his shirt. His expression changed in a moment to an alert, serious air. 'Why didn't you tell me before?' he ejaculated. ' 'Ow did I know they was gents coming.'

Bobs, whose near presence was like a hot wave of gin and sweat mixed, made another swipe at him, knocking off his hat. He turned upon her and said briefly, without anger, 'Stow that, Bobs.'

The woman muttered and swung the bolt. But she did not strike.

Hatto kept his woman in order.

'And look at me shirt,' Hatto ejaculated. 'I can't go up like this. Why didn't you tell me——'

The Major soothed him with the promise of a shirt. But he still complained that if he had been warned of the presence of gentlemen, he would have put on his party suit, and left Bobs behind.

Hatto was the new agent of the Transport Company, in succession to Pepper, dead in the last year. He was a little dark man with a bulging forehead, a protruding chin and a flattened nose, of which the tip covered the middle of a black moustache waxed into two long points. His tall forehead was wrinkled like a monkey's, but his age was probably not more than twenty-five. He was an old soldier who claimed to have been a sergeant-major, but who was said to have deserted from the ranks.

Hatto had come out to make a fortune. 'Two years is my limit,' he would say. 'I got a wife and family to think of. I told my Dysy I'd be back before Christmas.'

His wife Daisy was as well known on the oil rivers as himself. When Hatto was drunk he was always talking of Daisy's charms, he would pull out her picture and hand it round the party, and declare tearfully that she was the finest little girl in England, and that he was a b-bloody fool to leave her and come out to such a godforsaken hole.

Sober, he was as energetic as a summer fly. He had already, in fourteen months, trebled the turnover of his company, which even on the Mosi had been looked upon as dead.

He was one of those men who can work fourteen hours in a tropical sun, drink and yell and play the fool all night, and go out in the morning refreshed and full of new expedients for making money. Already he was dealing with Hamburg direct for his trade guns, and buying gin at the same time, transactions, needless to say, which would not appear in his reports, or yield a dividend to the company.

Nevertheless Hatto was very strict in his moral ideas. He would not allow any jokes about his Dysy or about the Empire and now, even when the Major had brought in a new shirt and allowed him to wash in his cabin, he was nervous of meeting the gentleman. He anxiously twisted the points of his moustache in the glass before he said at last, 'All right, Major, now for it.'

On deck, the servants in clean singlets were handing the gin and fried yam chips. Their gestures were dignified. Pooley and Felix, standing against the pale glow of sunset, had the same air of ceremony.

Hatto, dodging about the hatchway, stiffened again at the sight of this gentlemanly group. The Major went forward. 'Captain Pooley—Mr. Jarvis of the Constabulary—Mr. Hatto.'

'Pleased to meet you, gentlemen.' Hatto shook hands with a jerk like the second movement of a present arms.

He then pulled up his trousers with both hands, gave a loud cough, such as club stewards use before announcing the next dance and said, 'A nice evening, though 'ot. I might say——' He was going to say that it was extremely hot, using the ordinary ranker's adjective, but he recollected himself in the middle and turned it into 'F-uggy.' He then coughed again, turned slightly red and looked sharply round him.

Jarvis asked him if he had ever visited Laka.'

'Laka.' He jumped round, and stared at Jarvis. He seemed to bristle with excitement, the long points of his moustache rose as he squeezed up his lips. 'Do you want to get into Laka, sir?'

'I'm told it can't be done.'

'Don't you believe it, sir, don't you believe it.' Hatto rose on his toes; a trick of Jarvis himself, so that the idea occurred to Felix, in the midst of his consternation, that all men of his type, reckless and ambitious, had the same natural tricks. 'That for a f-funny yarn,' this narrow escape checked his enthusiasm and Felix said hastily, 'I believe dinner is ready.'

The dinner had been laid abaft the cabin under a stern awning. The table with a white cloth, a jam-pot full of flowers in the middle, folded napkins, had the same English correctitude that informed the dress and conventions of the party. It was a table which belonged to the idea of hospitality invented and imposed by civilized women all over the world. The dinner began as if ladies had been present, and Hatto, still abashed, himself introduced the subject of the Prince of Wales. This was followed by an account from the Major of his uncle, Lord Porriton, who had just given up the Porriton hounds after twelve years. 'It was Porriton got me this job through the Chorleys—do you know the Chorleys of Porriton, Mr. Jarvis? Charming people—they buy a lot of our kernels— for soap I believe. Mrs. Chorley was a Bentley!' The Major then went through the connections of the Chorley family.

Meanwhile sherry was poured out for the soup; a West African brand which tasted like sulphuric acid mixed with cooking brandy.

Hatto and Jarvis were separated by Pooley but now Jarvis was noticed to be talking to Hatto across Pooley.

'Three cases a month we pay old Laka.'

'Tribute?'

'No, no, it's blackmail really—all the chiefs 'ave to get paid so they won't come and cut our f-froats—froats. But wot I say is—'ow long are we going to put up with it—ignorant savages wot don't even know 'ow to do the best for themselves.'

'Have another sherry, Cocky,' Felix broke in.

' 'Olding up progress.'

'A sherry for Mr. Jarvis.'

'And wot's the good of it,' Hatto cried, rounding his eyes in amazement. 'Wot's the f-fools—fools I mean—of Government think they're doing in 'olding us up 'ere just because a silly old nigger 'as the jimjams about 'is jujus. Because they can't. No one can't. It's a law of nature, that is, get on or get out.'

'And you think you know a guide to Laka,' Jarvis said.

Pooley turned his long neck in appeal towards Felix, who began to talk about the political situation; the scramble for Africa; the danger of a European war, etc. His tone was detached, so that the party now drinking whisky with roast guinea fowl unconsciously took the same

165

dignified attitude of statesmen in council. But what they said, though thrown into an important and dignified form, was what they always felt; Hatto spoke of progress, Jarvis of the cowardice of the Government, the Major quoted various peers; and Pooley, who believed in the second advent of Christ, and the end of the world in 1897, remarked in his gentle, pensive voice that he had no choice except to obey orders. The whole conversation, like the service of the meal, was a kind of religious ceremony, enjoyable as social ritual.

Only once was the dignity interrupted when Bandy suddenly put her head out of the darkness behind Jarvis' chair and exclaimed in a shrill, childish voice, 'Papa.'

Bandy was used to call Felix Papa, and about this time in the evening she usually came to sit on his knee and steal food from his plate.

Her voice caused Jarvis to look round. Luckily at the same moment the girl was grabbed from behind by a servant. She disappeared with a cry of protest and the Major continued quickly the political discussion, which had reached the Egyptian campaigns, by remarking that his uncle Lord Porriton's father had once entertained Mr. Gladstone to tea at Porriton Hall.

'Gladstone sold Gordon,' Jarvis said. Gordon had always been his hero. He thought of him as a man completely without selfishness or fear, and now at his name his voice rose, full of passionate anger. 'He betrayed him, the finest man and the finest Christian that ever lived.'

This exclamation, by its unexpected force, made a minute's pause after which Pooley said politely that Gordon's death was probably unavoidable. It had been predicted.

Felix opened his mouth to speak and all, deferring to the prestige of the sage, turned their perspiring faces towards him. But he only smiled in the manner of the genial Prime Minister, and drank more whisky.

Felix had meant to point out to Jarvis that Gordon was a highly dangerous example for a young soldier; but he was still sober enough to realize that Jarvis, in return, would merely despise him as a moral weakling. He sighed and filled his glass.

Dinner had reached the pudding course; plum pudding with brandy sauce, washed down by four-finger whisky. The convention was still as European and dignified as the meal. Perspiration started from the Major's bald head, which seemed to be boiling on the fire of his face, while he related for the third time a story about the Prince of Wales at Ascot in 1889, or perhaps it was in 1879, and Pooley—whose greenish face was like a window-pane in a shower, was explaining why the world was bound to come to an end next June. Hatto was telling the party about the dangers of a German competition and Jarvis was drawing maps on the tablecloth.

But West African dinners are long. There are no women or billiard

166

tables to take the men from their glasses; unless they play cards they can only talk and drink. Felix detested cards which seemed to him a waste of precious time when a man might be thinking, and no one else proposed them. An hour after the pudding, at half-past ten o'clock, the party still looked like statesmen, but drunken statesmen. The table was in disorder, all except Jarvis, who had drunk nothing but one glass of gin, whose ideas were so exciting that he did not need drink, were talking loudly and at once. In the background half a dozen women were putting their heads under the awning and uttering shrill cries of laughter and coquetry. A few minutes later, Bandy slipped her thin body under Felix' arm, put her arm round his neck, sat upon his knee and took a sip from his glass. Then laughing and rolling her eyes at the company, she pushed her face into his beard. He, holding the girl with his small hairy hand, was having a serious discussion with his friend Pooley on the deepest subjects.

'But what I always say,' he said earnestly, while Bandy, giggling, buried her face in his neck, 'my boy Cleeve—got to look for facts— truth,' and the thoughtful soldier answered, 'That's it, Mr. Corner— why, I didn't understand anything till I got Mr. Cashman's book.'

'Education is everything.'

'Exactly. How was an ordinary chap like me to guess that everything depended on the ten toes of the prophet Daniel?'

Jarvis and Hatto had their noses together at one end of the table, upon which Hatto was drawing with a fork. The Major's fair girl, Lilly, sitting beside him, turned her sulky face towards Pooley, to whom she had taken a dislike because of his long neck. Bobs was lurking in the background, scowling at Hatto with a suspicious, resentful, but un- certain expression. She was not yet sure that she might interrupt him. Dinah, walking timidly to Felix' side, crouched on the floor beside him and put one arm across his knee. Dinah really loved Felix because she needed him and she thought about him all day.

'A sound foundation in fact.'

'The ten toes of iron and clay and the ten horned beast.'

'No good expecting the bloody Government——'

'My dear chappy, it was the Duke of Clarence who——'

'No m-muddle. It's fatal to m-muddle a child. Now Gordon started in a muddle because the Bible itself——'

'Just my case. I really couldn't make any sense of religion until Doctor Cashman——'

'What I say is, if you don't push, someone else will——'

'And so I told my boy Cleeve——'

The voices blended into a quintet which made a pleasant kind of music to all their ears. It seemed to each that he was surrounded by sympathetic and understanding friends.

Dinah, encouraged by Felix' genial smiles and conversation, got up and gingerly sat on his knee. He put his arm round her and continued to explain his system for the regeneration of the world by a rational system of education in those ideals of happiness compatible with each other's existence; the education he was giving to his son.

But though he continued to speak about Cleeve's education for a long time, he had more and more difficulty in remembering whether he had actually given Cleeve an education, or whether he intended to do so. He could see also that Hatto and Jarvis were now drawing maps together and this caused him a vague uneasiness. He felt that he must take some decisive step to prevent something or other.

Then suddenly Bobs darted forward, seized Hatto by the hair. Felix made a great effort to say 'Go away,' but to his horror only uttered a loud laugh. Then he caught a glimpse of Hatto hitting Bobs on the nose, the Major clasping Hatto round the neck, and Pooley bending slowly towards the floor, from the middle, like a melting candle. The table tilted up and in one tremendous landslide bottles, knives, forks, glasses, flowers all shot down upon the top of Hatto and Bobs kicking on the floor. The Major was seen under the tablecloth making the motions of a submerged swimmer.

Felix was still roaring with laughter. He was shocked by the laughter and he continued making efforts to explain the importance of a good education which would have prevented General Gordon from believing himself to contain the voice of God; but he could only effervesce like a champagne bottle and laugh.

Felix waked in the morning with a headache so severe that he did not care to move his head. It rested on some soft substance which he knew to be Dinah's breast. The dawn was breaking. The stars lost their glitter so quickly that it seemed as if a vapour had passed over them; a mist so dark that it could not be distinguished from the translucent darkness of night except by its opacity.

The edges of the river gulf, ragged as Donegal cliffs, grew from this opaque darkness, as if solidifying within it. Then suddenly the lightness of the sky was seen as a difference of tone. It appeared as a long, crooked streak of pallid grey, like washed-out ink, and from this cold grey a cool reflection, rather than a breeze, seemed to fall upon the schooner's deck.

Felix received it on his forehead, as he accepted Dinah's breast, with the humble gratitude of a tired man, who is surprised by any kind of beauty or comfort. It was as though he did not feel entitled by right either to the peace of this cool mild dawn, or the patience and elasticity of Dinah's flesh. He perceived that he was lying in the large bed called the family bed. This had been dismantled for Jarvis's visit and disguised under canvas, but apparently the women had pulled off the tarpaulins and rehung the net. He thought, 'What cheek, Dinah needs a snub. She mustn't get spoilt like these other miserable creatures.'

But he did not move. His head was splitting and he was overwhelmed with a sense of futility and shame. He resented this feeling. Why should he mind what young Jarvis thought of him?

He heard Hatto's and Jarvis' voices.

They passed the end of the bed; by moving his eyes he could distinguish Hatto with a black, bristly chin and a black eye, and Jarvis' sharp features, smooth and shining from the razor.

Hatto was speaking in the brisk, respectful voice of a sergeant to a company officer. 'Don't you worry, sir. If 'e don't turn up in a brace of shakes now, I'll go and get 'im.'

'Perhaps I'd better come with you. What's the fellow's name?'

'Jingler is the name 'e goes by.' The pair crossed towards the rail. But Felix hearing the name Jingler instantly knew what was in the wind. Jingler was a famous character on the Mosi, where he visited the various stations, begging for beads and tobacco, singing rude songs, and dancing obscene dances. He also acted as pimp, carried messages and undertook delicate negotiations with pagan chiefs, otherwise unapproachable, about trade, guns and gin, subsidies. He was looked upon by traders and soldiers as an amusing buffoon. In fact, as Felix knew he was a recognized poet of the middle Niger valley, known to every tribe for hundreds of miles, and passing safely among them even in wartime. They gave him passage, just as in the old days all the warring tribes of Greece or Ireland gave safe conduct to the wandering poets who brought them amusement and carried their fame. Jingler was probably the only man on the Mosi who was capable of acting as guide in the hostile pagan districts beyond the river; Laka and the islands.

Felix thought in panic, 'Cocky's off.' He jerked up his head. Hatto and Jarvis were sitting on the rail. Cocky called out, 'Good morning, Uncle. How d'ye feel?'

'Not very gay.' He collapsed on Dinah. He felt confused. He thought, 'After all, what can I do—if he didn't make trouble someone else would—it's in the very air.'

He allowed the argument to die away, out of all thoughts, into the skilful hand of Dinah, erudite in its art.

When he woke up at eight after a refreshing doze, he heard that Jarvis and Hatto had already gone ashore with Jarvis' orderly, servants and three loads.

'They're up to something,' the Major said. 'They had that tall chappie with them in the blue beads.'

'Jingler. Yes, I shouldn't wonder if Jarvis tried for Laka.'

169

Felix was standing naked on the deck. Dinah brought a bucket of cold water, gently pressed down his head to the level of her waist and poured the water over him.

'Good God!' the Major ejaculated. 'I hope not. He'll get us all murdered.'

'Yes, that's one way of looking at it.' Felix conceded the point. 'But on the other hand——' He prepared to give the opposite arguments their due; ideal compulsion; the evils of exclusive nationalism and so on.

Dinah brought the other bucket and bent her master to receive it. Her air was proud and though she did not smile, happiness shone upon her ugly face. She delighted in the glory of serving her white man. To serve was itself a kind of possession.

Laka town consists of many compounds among the high jungle, and at this time of the yam planting there was no guard on the roads because the international law of the country, strictly observed, forbade war in planting and harvest.

At sunrise Jarvis and his party were already in the centre of the town, opposite the chief's house.

Laka villagers were not early risers; they didn't like to come out until the air was warmed by the sun which did not reach into their clearings until seven or eight o'clock. It was the small children, in Africa as in England, who stirred first like the animals and who ran out, fully awake in a moment to take up again as soon as possible the delights of life; the study of the world; and the exploration of novelties like trees, wind, rain and dirt, or forbidden areas. It was the Laka children, exploring, who first saw the white man explorer. They were greatly astonished, and stood for a long time with unwinking round eyes watching him. He was a small, thin man with yellow hair and a red moustache shaped like a bull's horns. His nose and chin were thin and sharp; his face was very pale; his eyes sky-blue. He was dressed in a yellow shirt, yellow breeches and yellow boots. His yellow helmet stood behind him on a folding-table on which was spread an enormous piece of paper made up of smaller pieces, some white, some yellowish, some blue.

A soldier with two guns, one on his back and the other in his hand, and a Yoruba boy in a man's vest, stood beside the table, under a locust tree. They looked frightened.

The children were fascinated by the white man's strangeness. It was frightening and wonderful to them. Some of the little ones, because of too much fear, uttered shrill cries and ran away, weeping. Others, older ones, because of more wonder, began to approach him. They did not approach directly. They slipped to one side or the other, they pretended to be looking elsewhere, but they came nearer; like small deer which, compelled by their own fearful curiosity, come nearer and nearer to a hunter dressed up in odd garments, until he can shoot them from a few yards' distance.

One boy crept to within ten yards from the right where he stood peering from between two huts; another group of four led by a small but very active child of about eight approached from behind the locust tree. The leader, at each cautious step, held out his hand, palm downwards, as if to warn his followers.

This boy was wearing a rag of chief's cloth round his neck. He was, in fact, one of the chief's many sons; his name was Azai.

Azai had almost reached the tree when the white man turned round and saw the party. Two at once ran off; a third fell down flat on his face; Azai, seized with terror, turned to run, but could not bring himself, as a leader, to do so. He stood, therefore, on one leg, with his head and eyes twisted towards the white man; his eyes opened so widely that they caught the pale sky like projecting lenses and glittered as if from their own light. When the white man smiled at him, his lips parted in a grimace of terror, so that his teeth could be seen between them. His body shook. Azai was helpless with fear. He did not think or feel; he simply waited, breathless. The white man said something, and then, seeing the boy's fear, turned his back and stooped over the paper on the table. Azai felt warmth throughout his body like relief. His lips closed and his breast filled, lifting up the blue rag. His eyes blinked quickly and he gave a deep sigh. Then once more he looked at the white man, the smooth skin of the forehead wrinkled. If he had had eyebrows they would have been raised to their height. He looked sad from his expression which was an appeal for support. But he was alone; even the boy on the ground had silently disappeared. Azai looked at the white man again and his head came forward as if drawn by an electric pole. Then he looked round again with an imploring face, which said plainly, 'Save me, somebody. Come and help.'

The white man began to whistle softly. Azai started, gazed at him, and took a step nearer.

At Azai's step, three or four small figures appeared from the shadows of the bush; the boy between the huts came into the open. Azai made another step, and at once there were twenty children in the open space, with their eyes fixed on the white man. Azai looked round, and three disappeared. He stepped a third time and the boy from the huts laughed. Smiles were seen at once in every part of the clearing; the bright teeth shone at a distance. Not all the children were smiling. Many were still grave with terror and fascination. But at least a dozen had lost interest in the white man and were beginning to enjoy a game. They were inventing a game as a ritual out of their wonder and fear.

Azai remained grave and absorbed. He stared at the white man with greedy, searching eyes.

171

The boy from the grass hut laughed aloud, and made a kind of dance step. Giggles were heard on all sides. The white man jumped up. A fearful screech sounded through the clearing. The first woman, the first mother, had come out from bed. At once, all the children, like chickens at the warning cluck of the hen, flew to the nearest cover. Their looks were horrified with fear. Azai ran faster than any. His legs twirled over the ground like a running chicken's.

But at the same time the woman's cry brought out all the other women. Sleepy, rheumy-eyed, they put out their startled heads and gazed. Some of them, more intelligent, went in to ask the men what to think of this strange event. The men came out; soon every hut door held its five or six faces looking over shoulders like a family group. They did not know what to think. Their faces were as blank as pumpkins.

When the white man looked up from his paper, saw that the village was awake, and called, 'Bring me the chief,' they did not even show a change of expression. They might have been stone deaf.

Jarvis looked round then and asked, 'What is the name of the river here?'

Jingler stepped forward, grinning, struck an attitude to show that he did not take the whites seriously, and shouted, 'This white man wants to know the name of your river.'

No one answered from the huts but the soldier, in an extremity of terror, licked his dry lips and said, 'Gell, sah,' Gell meaning in Laka, a stream.

Jarvis politely thanked his orderly and wrote down, in a beautiful script, 'Gell River,' that was to say, 'Stream river.'

Jarvis was a keen mapper. He had had, however, unusual difficulties with his latest map. He had found it impossible to use a plane table in the high jungle, and he had had to rely on dead reckoning for distances; also it was hard to find out the local names of places. He was obliged to stop every traveller and to ask at every hut for names.

But villagers did not always understand what a strange white man meant by pointing at the earth and uttering a sound like a dog's bark. They answered sometimes, 'I don't know,' or simply, 'Dirt, grass.'

Thus one saw on Jarvis' map such places as Town Town, River River, Idontknow Village, Begyourpardon Rock, which was an important landmark, Dirtland, a fertile and prosperous tract on the River Water; and Forgodsakeplease Lake, which was surrounded by swamps and ought to be avoided by transport columns.

The map was ambitious. It covered not only Laka but Daji Emirate to the north. No one at that time had ever visited Daji, and Jarvis had relied on Jingler and other native travellers for the description of it.

172

But he had entered in the margin scrupulously, 'Distances in Daji and the position of the smaller towns, provisional.'

When Jarvis had printed Stream River he stepped back to admire the effect, and whistled softly to himself for some time, while he touched up the foliage of his dense bush, put a few more reeds into the swamps, and caterpillars among the hilly district. The soldier and the boy watched with a quivering, imploring wonder like that of dogs surrounded by a bush fire, who watch their master drink his morning tea.

It was a chilly morning. The village in its clearing among the high jungle was still in blue-green shadow, like a town submerged under a very clear but cold sea, a hundred and fifty feet deep. Above, on the surface where the sun was glittering among the tops of the trees, birds were chirping and darting as if in another kind of world altogether; full of life, beauty, social excitement. It dazzled the eyes to see the glitter of the leaves, springing under the impatient feet of birds, as they suddenly took a fancy to dart into the sky; or returned, on another impulse, to preen and dance.

In comparison, the creatures below, peering from doorways and green coves of jungle with dull eyes, moving sluggishly from one shadow to another, seemed like a kind of fish people; beings but lately generated out of mud, cold and stupid as octopuses, crawfish.

But at last the doorways and coves became more crowded, bodies touched and warmed each other. The sun, which seemed like the birds full of joyful energy, springing into the sky, slanted its rays into the clearing. The blood began to flow into sleepy, cold brains and brought ideas which passed as if by contact of flesh. A voice said, 'Get round behind them.'

Another added, 'Kill the soldier first; he has the guns.'

Twenty minutes later these notions belonged to everybody; spearmen began to gather at the far side of the clearing, cutting off the white man and his party from escape. None of the spearmen had orders to do this public service. They obeyed an idea in them as strong as an instinct. Their wonder at a strange thing was long dead and nothing remained but the fear of it, the hatred of it for disturbing their apathy; and the notion soaked into them by a million years of such fear and hatred, that all new things were bad, all strangers dangerous.

The chief of Laka, a man of sixty, thin, wrinkled, had stood for some time in the porch of his compound, among astonished slaves and courtiers. He had the look of an old Pope. He was actually supreme spiritual head of Laka, as well as autocrat. He combined, as logic demands, the Pope and the Emperor. He was called King of the World and he believed himself to be the greatest king in the world.

But his brain too was slow and cold. The news of the white man's coming had astonished him. Now at last when he stepped into the open, and looked at Jarvis for the first time, his angry stare was mixed with irresolution.

Jingler, recognizing the chief, made a slight bob, struck an attitude and sang:

> '*Behold the great king of Laka,*
> *Son of the Drum and father of fish.*'

The chief waved his hand and said, 'Who is the white man?'

'His name is Jar-vis. He is a soldier. The soldiers call him the cock.'

'Did you bring him here?'

'No, lord, he came,' and to Jarvis he said, 'This is the king of Laka. He salutes you.'

Jarvis, giving a light upward touch to his moustaches with his forefinger, put out his right leg, raised his nose and said in a clear, loud voice, 'Chief of Laka, your men have lately shot arrows upon the Yorubas who trade on the rivers Niger and Mosi. This is wrong and must not happen again. For the Yorubas are the children of the great white queen, the queen of England, who is also my queen. She is the queen of the world and she has ordered that all men be at peace and observe justice and do not shoot at traders anywhere. For all roads, all rivers, all seas shall be free to all men. And if you, King of Laka, shoot again at her children, she will send her soldiers to put you out of your chiefship and punish your servants who shoot.'

Jingler sang his translation, a short translation, stating only that if the Lakawa shot Yorubas, the white man would shoot them. This was received with astonishment and anger. Spears suddenly bristled out of compounds and bushes. The chief's face crumpled into a grimace of rage.

Jarvis, during Jingler's speech, lowered his nose, scratched it, glanced at the map with affectionate longing, and pursed up his lips to whistle, but recollecting himself just as Jingler finished, unpursed them again and continued, 'On the other hand, chief,' he paused and half turned to Jingler. 'Also will do. The great white queen sends me, her servant Jarvis, to offer to you also her friendship and protection that you and your people may also enjoy peace and safety which you certainly need, for the Emir of Daji is coming south with a large army.'

The chief, now fast coming to his senses, made a gesture of fury; the councillors uttered cries of indignation. Jingler interpreted quickly, 'The white man says, "Daji will eat you." '

'My queen will protect you from all enemies, if you are friends with her and don't shoot at any more traders.'

'He's a bit mad, of course.' Jingler said, shrugging his shoulders. He was growing alarmed for his own safety.

174

'But if you are not friends with her, she will have to make a new chief at Laka.'

'He's only a boy, as you see,' Jingler said. 'He's not a big captain white man but a small soldier white man. He's only got forty soldiers.'

The chief opened his mouth and shouted, 'Why did you bring him here?'

Jingler said hastily to Jarvis, 'The king say thank you. He go send letter. We go chop now. He say good-bye, thank you very much.'

Jarvis at once walked up to the chief, took his hand and warmly shook it. The cries of rage which were now sounding on all sides of the clearing were changed to a deep murmur of horror. The chief of Laka's hand is never touched.

This extraordinary incident, producing a new shock of wonder and horror, prevented Jarvis from being killed on the spot. The chief shrank back as if to fall into his councillor's arms. Jarvis said earnestly, 'Good-bye, chief, but remember what I've said. You had a warning before. This is your last chance. We don't want to put you out, but if you make any more trouble, out you go. Tell him, Jingler.'

Jingler said quickly, 'He say good-bye, king. I tink we go now.'

Jarvis, with a last friendly shake of the limp hand, and a short smile, friendly but firm, then marched off. The boy and the soldier had already rolled up the map and folded up the table. They followed so close upon their master's heels that the table was overlapping the top of his yellow head, like a moving verandah. Jingler, shrugging, grinning, turning from side to side, with the apologetic airs of a keeper, brought up the rear.

All were much startled, when, at the first bend of the track, Azai popped out of the undergrowth and then, terror-stricken to find the white man almost on top of him, froze. Jarvis, with a smile, saluted him; the boy, suddenly recovering himself, darted off like a rabbit and dived once more into the undergrowth. But when Jarvis passed, he popped out again and stared after him; grinning from ear to ear. Then he performed a dance, to relieve the happiness of his feelings, excited by his own boldness. Jarvis' own walk as he quick-stepped down the track, smiling to himself, was also full of elation. He, Azai and the other children had all enjoyed themselves.

There was no pursuit because the chief, overwhelmed by the last outrage, forgot to order it. It seemed, therefore, to many of the Laka people that the white man enjoyed the magic protection of some powerful god. The same notion had given power to many missionaries, whose lives were saved in the first place, like Jarvis', by the shock of their appearance and conduct.

Jarvis' letters from Africa were news for the whole household at Castle Corner. Mary, to whom they were addressed, read them in the nursery to Shon, Francie and Peggy, and quoted them to Sukey and Molly; John Chass read them at the breakfast table, called up Grogan to hear the more exciting parts, and quoted them afterwards to Jebb, Darcy, Foley and any tenant who happened to meet him that week. He also brought them up at magistrates' meetings, on any subject that might be before them, such as cottages for labourers, or repairs to school buildings; beginning 'My nephew Harry tells me that in Africa——' and then he would soon be in the middle of Cocky's latest exploit.

MacEwen, whose two sons had followed him in the Indian service, would sometimes in his modest way speak of their deeds in India, so that the others saw clearly through the old man's clear mind a work of empire which was also a work of civilization; and added to their natural expansive feelings a moral self-respect. The Annish magistrates, old Colonel Duff, who had fought at Inkerman, little Machale, a catholic archæologist, who spent ten hours a day examining the credentials of the Irish saints, Machugh, the banker, Slatter, John Chass, turning upon them all his affectionate, careless smiles, in the midst of their boring routine; questions about Padsy Foy's debt to the loan fund or the smoky chimney at Knockeen national school, would suddenly feel the imperial grandeur in which their office shared; so that Padsy, attending to explain why he could not yet pay for the bag of Indian meal advanced to him for the winter, would find himself among proconsuls instead of the gentry. The proconsuls were kinder than the gentry, for it was beneath their dignity to haggle with a poor wretch about fifteen shillings' worth of meal. On the day before the jubilee, indeed, John Chass and Sir Watty between them not only paid off Padsy's debt but gave him half a crown to drink the Queen's health.

Padsy drank the health and though he abused the imperial glory, he took his share of it. 'And who,' he asked, 'are the men who won their damned empire? who was it bate the Aygyptians and the Zulus, but Wellington and Kitchener, and the both of them Irishmen? And now they've got young Cocky at it too, to fight the blacks for them.'

'Aye,' said old Dan. 'Maybe young Harry will be a Jubilee Jook too, and why not? He's good blood in him.'

'Fourteen kings at the wan time, thon would be a noble sight.'

There was a pause while the company regarded the fourteen kings. They sat with their heads almost in the roof, for since Padsy had become a regular tenant of land, he had brought his family to the mountain to his own house and his own property. This removal had disadvantages for the walls were not yet watertight and though a chimney had been built, it would not draw except in a northern gale, which is a rare wind in Annish. Also since there was not room on the floor of the single room for the whole family, two of the children slept under the bed, and old Dan had made himself a kind of tent of sacks against the gable.

Old Dan, whose quiet cottage on the beach, where he had lived for seventy years, was now to let, had insisted on coming with the Foys. This had been already bad for his health; he was growing very rheumatic from sleeping in his tent among the mountain clouds. But the old man said to Hanna, 'It's my own life, and I'd liever use it with the wains up here than down me lone on the beach.'

'They say,' he said, 'ye couldn't buy a lobster the day in London under a gold pound.'

'Holy Ho, a turrible rich town.'

'Why wouldn't it be? Sacred heart, isn't it the robber of the whole world? Where is our riches gone? Down there on the strand King Fergus of Annish ate his herring from a gold plate and threw the plate to Shawn Egan for the price of his dinner.'

'Aye, them were the grand days of Ireland.'

Old Egan spat, and said in his soft gay voice, 'All lands have their days of jubilation, and it seems that we are past our kingly time. We are an ould people.'

Another spit hissed upon the fire and a deep sigh was heard. One of the children, the little girl Annie, eight years old, who lay in the mud floor against the wall had a violent fit of coughing. She coughed every ten minutes, and each time her whole flimsy body was shaken and her face was twisted as if with rage and despair, but instantly, at the end of the fit, it recovered its childish shape of calm patience. Annie blamed no one for her cough and she took the world as she found it. Now while she sweltered beneath a heap of rags, she was happy listening to the talk. The kings and their golden crowns passed through her vision and enriched her comfort with the sense of glory and wonder.

'And who won it for them?' her father shouted suddenly. 'Who does the fighting for them? Where would they be without the Irish soldier? Isn't the Irish regiments well known to be the bravest in the whole army? Look at the Connaught Rangers and the Fusiliers!'

'Why wouldn't they be?' old Dan sighed. 'Didn't the Irish bate the whole world in the days of Finn?'

'Aye, we did, and we do still, and this is the world we tuk, the British Empire.' Padsy's voice rose, he drew up his long back, and glared about him like a field-marshal from his charger, his ragged moustache, beaded with porter, trembled with excitement, and his pale eyes, surrounded with the wrinkles of his long misery, were full of triumph. 'It's the Irish Empire. What else!'

177

'Bedam, but you're right, Padsy. For we tuk it. Aren't we the fighting men of the whole world?' This was a mountain visitor.

Annie had another fit of coughing, and her father stooped over her to raise her head. At last she was able to spit out the phlegm upon the rags. Padsy wiped her lips with his finger and kissed her forehead. 'Poor wee darling, does it hurt ye?'

'Will I have a mug?'

'A mug? What kind of a mug?'

'A jubilee mug with the Queen on it and gold.'

'Of course ye will. Didn't himself promise every wan of yous a mug, with gold on it? Why wouldn't ye have a mug?'

'It was Uncle Con was sayin' that we had no right to take them.'

'Ach, never mind Con. And is it big Giveen? To hell with him. What right has he to stint ye of a mug?'

Big Giveen, the grocer, and the nationalist committee had refused a subscription to the jubilee fund, giving an example which had to be followed, so that the total was smaller than was expected. John Chass, who was chairman of the committee, had already ordered mugs and buns for all the schools in Annish, and quantities of whisky and porter, so that he found himself responsible for a large debt.

'It's lucky,' he said to Mary, 'that I'd got that affair settled or where would I be now?'

He had just completed the sale to Benskin of the Porriton reversions and some land at Motcombe. This sale, suddenly accomplished after John Chass had sworn for seven years that he would never alienate the English property, had greatly surprised his friends. John Chass himself had been surprised to find out how easy it had proved in the end to carry out the transaction. He felt none of the expected regrets. He had not lost even a wink of sleep. Indeed, he congratulated himself on a decisive act which had not only freed him from debt, including his debts to Benskin, but had won Mary's approval. For it was understood that he would now clear the Irish property, pay off the various mortgages, including Slatter's, and sell his Irish land to the tenants, in exchange for a sound Government security.

In John Chass' mind this scheme had already been carried out; the ready money period had begun.

'You may as well have that new carpet,' he would say, 'for the money's there.' A credit balance at the bank made him careless of small payments. He sent Harry a gold hunter for his birthday; he bought Shon a steam engine, and himself a new tandem cart. He set up a new flagstaff on the terrace and bought a brass cannon to salute the Queen. He advanced Cleeve ten pounds, and he gave Mary a pair of diamond ear-rings. Mary Corner now began to protest. 'Good gracious, bringing me such things—how much did you pay for them, you stoopid man?'

178

'Ach, Molly, what's a pound or two out of the thousands—you wouldn't complain if I gave out sixpence from a pound in my pocket.'

'But you don't tell me these only cost a pound or two—I'll be afraid to wear them.'

'What does it matter, Molly, what they cost?' John Chass said, who had spent a hundred pounds on the diamonds and twenty on having them set to his mind. 'They're bought now, so that's over. What does it matter?'

'Of course it matters.'

But John Chass, who always hated to hear money talked of, and especially the cost of a thing bought, answered coolly, 'Indeed then, I must change them, for there were others I liked more—they were bigger—and while I'm in Dunderry, I may as well order a new set-piece too for the old one's a ruin.'

Mary knew that he would carry out this threat, because he had already proposed a new set-piece. She therefore agreed to wear the ear-rings, and John Chass, for his part, commanded a search for the old set-piece. It was found at last in the coach loft where Jebb had hidden it, and when he was asked why he had not revealed it at once, he answered, 'Thon rubbish—it was thrown out this ten years.'

This set-piece was a portrait of the Queen, in a framework of lamps, used for a triumphal arch over the castle gate in the jubilee of 1887. It was hung out now below the drawing-room windows, over the terrace, one fine evening at the end of May, for John Chass' inspection.

The canvas was like a wornout oilcloth partly buried in a huge bird-cage of rusty wire, which had supported the candle lamps for illumination. The Queen's head in the middle, three times life-size, had lost all features except the nose, which was like a little pink map of England, surrounded by a sea of dirty grey and white. The crown had been overrun by the widow's veil; and the garter ribbon was green with mould. There were two bullet holes next the nose. Some Irish patriot had used it for a bull's eye during the last celebrations.

John Chass examined the portrait with delight; for he remembered it as an old friend. 'It's better than I thought,' he said. 'It only wants a touch.' He reflected and suddenly exclaimed, 'Where's the paints? Hi, you, Darcy!'

Darcy, as always, in his livery hat, ran from the terrace wall, where the outdoor staff, in gradation of domesticity, the stable men at the wall, the gardeners across the gravel, and the farm workers among the trees, were watching. When it was perceived that John Chass himself was going to repaint the Queen, excitement spread rapidly as far as the main road and Ballycorner. Padsy Foy and several children suddenly appeared on the shore; half a dozen mountain men from the turf carts, and a well-known tinker, joined the farm hands.

179

A ladder was set up; Molly and Peggy carried pots of paint of all sizes and shapes, age and dirtiness from the carpenter's shed and set them out on the drawing-room window-sill. Rifty was sent flying to Giveens for linseed oil, and there were loud shouts of despair when Sukey, coming up from below, screamed, 'Who am I to have turpentine? Turpentine is butler's stuff.'

Grogan, who, with Darcy, was holding the ladder, answered patiently, 'All I am having is in the wax this while; couldn't ye send Bridgy?'

'It's not Bridgy's nayther,' Sukey bawled.

'Well now, how are you, Sukey?' John Chass said. 'How's that old stove. Has it been smoking at you again? It's a strange thing how the spring gets into the stoves.'

'Bridgy' Sukey bawled through the top of the kitchen window. 'Ye're wanting for some damn fool jawb here up.'

Bridget, in her sacking apron, walked out on the terrace. Her face was as white as soap. It was the first time in six weeks that she had left the house. She stood wiping her steaming crimson hands in the sacking while Grogan and two or three men gave her simultaneous directions.

'Try Giveen's and if there's noan at Giveen's, take the mail cyar to Dunvil.'

Curious eyes stared at the girl from all angles. Gossips for at least a month had declared that she was pregnant; either by Rifty, Cleeve, Grogan, or John Chass himself; but it was not yet believed by everybody.

There was a silence while the girl walked across the terrace towards the drive; the mountain men, always more curious in scandal because of their lonelier lives, pressed up to the wall to stare at her. But Bridget, walking slowly, carried herself with her usual grand dignity, and her hands were still beneath the sacking apron, throwing it forward. Nothing could be detected. A little mountain man gave a short laugh and spat as if in appreciation of craft.

John Chass was now ready to ascend the ladder. As soon as he grasped the sides and put his foot on the first rung, loud cries of warning broke out from Darcy below, Molly and Francie at the windows, and even from the carters and the tinker.

'Mind yourself, sor.'

'Sacred heart, it's slippin—he's kilt,' from the shore.

'Hould on, Darcy, ye gomeril.'

There was not the least danger; these cries represented the sympathy and politeness of the onlookers, which were so strong that far away among the trees, the farm hands and the carters repeated among themselves, in voices not even meant to reach John Chass, 'God save us, he'll be down. Holy Mary, he's losht.'

180

John Chass dipped a brush in the nearest pot and drew a broad blue stripe, the colour used on all Annish cart bodies, across the garter ribbon; there was at once a dead silence. Darcy bent his head back so far to see the effect that his hat fell off. But he did not notice it now; his feelings were elsewhere.

Cleeve had been so depressed for the last fortnight that his aunt had made him take iron. But the iron had only given him spots and increased his depression. He felt cut off from the graceful accomplished world of Mrs. Pynsant.

He had borrowed the ten pounds in order to fulfil his promise to Bridget. He had not the least idea what he would do with Bridget in England or how he could support her; he was sick of Bridget, and the only reason why he did not hate her was his inability to be unreasonable. But he had never thought of breaking his promises to her. He knew that he could not escape a scandal and he preferred not to think of the future. Instead, he thought of Mrs. Pynsant and the society in which she glittered.

He wandered about the house all day with his hands in his pockets and a mournful, stupid air. He wandered now through the rooms, vaguely surprised to find the house empty, and coming into the dining-room, was startled by a loud hiss.

The blue yard-cat stood cornered on the side-table. Cleeve jumped and the cat jumped, raised her tail, curled her back. They stared at each other. The blue yard-cat, whose life ambition it was to establish herself in the house, had probably never reached the dining-room before. She had seized her chance after years of watchfulness.

Cleeve had chivied her a dozen times from the hall or the kitchen passage, but now, he turned away. He was detached already from Castle Corner. The cat's back sank; her tail drooped in the middle; as Cleeve went out to the terrace she turned again her curious whiskers to the dishes left from breakfast.

Cleeve was surprised to find a crowd on the terrace. He looked wondering at John Chass above him on the ladder. The Queen was now in the brightest colours available to cart, door, agricultural machinery, and boat painters. Her face was salmon pink, her eye, larger than a breakfast cup, pure cobalt, her hair white as a binnacle, her crown as yellow as a carriage wheel spoke; her robe as red as a new cart tail. The background was the same chocolate brown as the pantry doors. The spectators stood motionless; Darcy's hat was in the hand of Mary Corner, who stood at a little distance with Shon. She was looking at Shon, who stared with wide-open eyes and arched brows, in a state of such excitement that he could hardly breathe. Darcy was still craning his neck; Grogan looked upwards over his shoulder; old Jebb, in the

181

middle of the terrace, by the new flagstaff, had his toothless mouth wide open. For once Jebb, the only completely wretched creature in the house, or perhaps in Ballycorner, had forgotten his misfortunes, his rheumatism, his lost bets, and even himself.

Cleeve looked at him with vague surprise; perceiving that something extraordinary had happened to the old man but not asking himself what it might be.

'Out of me road there—ow, but thon man's a majiker—look at that hair—ye could comb it.' Jebb waved him aside.

Cleeve, astonished, stepped away. But now he perceived what was going forward; the rapt faces turned upwards, the absurd picture, John Chass' curved back as leaning outwards he studied the effect of his work, and he was filled with impatience and pity. He remembered Mrs. Pynsant's voice when she uttered the word backwater, and he felt cut off, wasted.

He was astonished now at the pitiful appearance of everything; the terrace, with its cracked slabs, the very lake, pale green in the cold morning light, and the pale whitish sky, shallow and of an even tint, seemed provincial and mean. The castle had suddenly become a small old house with crooked chimney pots and cracked stucco, John Chass, his aunt absorbed in Shon, Darcy, Jebb, squinting Molly, fat silly Francie, creatures as limited in their lives, barbarous and pathetic, as animals behind the bars of some neglected provincial zoo. They were not even beautiful, sleek creatures; not even with the possible exception of John Chass, good specimens of their several species.

What would Mrs. Pynsant, from the midst of the season, think of this scene? and at the word season, there rose before his imagination a delightful though indistinct picture of vast rooms in gilt and crimson, crowded with the most brilliant and charming people in the world; the women all beautiful, witty, sympathetic, and above all, intelligent; the men famous in history, art, literature; cosmopolitans to whom the whole world was a playground.

He was jostled in the back; a murmur had arisen; Shon, holding his mother's hand, suddenly leapt into the air as from an electric shock; and Mary, looking at him, laughed like a young girl, with a sudden irresponsible chuckle. Cleeve gazed at them blankly. He had again forgotten them. He wandered towards the sea.

John Chass had just put in, with careful strokes, a fine line above and below the eye, which was plainly his favourite feature. After he had studied this effect for at least a minute, during a silence like that of a bull-fight audience which sees the matador point his sword, he raised a round tool, a new brush charged with white, poised it and then with a single bold sweep, dashed in a highlight upon the top of the eye; a blob of glittering white boat enamel somewhat larger than a billiard ball.

182

Shon gave a shriek of excitement, and seized his mother's skirts; loud cries arose from the park and three or four including Padsy on the shore uttered sudden shouts of laughter; the laughs which mean in Annish that words fail; one of the carters threw his hat on the gravel, and old Jebb at the flagstaff with bulging eyes, dribbling jaw, screamed, 'She's livin', by Jasus,' to which Darcy replied, with mild reproach, 'Ah, and better than life.'

John Chass again held up the brush. It seemed that he was about to make another stroke. At once other cries rose; indignant warning cries.

'Lave her now, sir.'

'Ye'll spoil her.'

'That's the last touch.'

Darcy, looking anxiously upwards, called, 'Wull ye come down now, sir?'

John Chass hesitated. He was plainly inclined to make some further experiment upon the eye, of which the success had been so startling. He looked down and asked, 'What about that turpentine? This white is too thick.'

'There's noan turpenteen,' Jebb bawled. 'Bridgy's intil Dunvil for't and she'll not be back for an hour.'

The cries increased; Padsy in his anxiety, was climbing the terrace wall, the carters threatened with whips and arms. All were in fear to lose something precious to them. John Chass turned his flushed face over his shoulder, smiled and said, 'You think she'll do, boys.'

A tremendous yell answered him. 'She'll do.'

John Chass descended the ladder, but not with the same dignities which had saluted his going up. For those that were not still gazing at the masterpiece, were disputing about its protection from the weather.

'I'll put a rickcloth on her,' Jebb shouted.

'But it will blaw agin her and spoil her.'

'Aye, it's boards ye want. Get a dure,' Darcy suggested.

The people were now on the terrace; even the tinker and the mountain men; they swarmed across its sacred flags as if by conceded right; and what was strange, no one found this extraordinary, except Peggy, who in her indignation, went into the house. Even Grogan, with his strict views of deportment, found it natural that the cause of art should override the laws of etiquette. John Chass himself, standing back from the ladder and gazing aloft with a smile in which self-satisfaction and self-mockery contended, was jostled by ragamuffins from Knockeen moss and his own farm hands, running from side to side to find the best angle for study; or by the experts surrounding Jebb. 'A dure, how would ye fix a dure?'

'Hang it on a ladder, bedambut.'

A boat painter from Dunvil, a pale little man in a dented bowler, was saying to Mary Corner, with an urgent anxiety, 'It's the varnish, Missis Corner, wull bring her up like a Dunvil bap—but spreading varnish, Missis Corner, is work for a serious hand, and I'd be afeared if himself was to try it.'

The pale, worn face, as full of hard and long experience as Mary's own, had the grave urgency of a saint's, who fights for the holy kingdom. 'Ye see, if she's not dead dry, ye'll get a bloom on her.'

'I won't let him spoil it, Mr. Macconnell—no one shall do the varnishing but your good self.'

'Thank you, ma'am—not but what himself is a cliver man; we all know he could do annything—but a varnishing jawb like this is a more serious kind of thing.'

'He shan't touch it, Mr. Macconnell, till you come.'

It was tacitly agreed between them that John Chass was not a completely serious man; and in fact, the character of everyone in Annish was so well understood by a shrewd community whose chief pastime was discussion, that there was very little hypocrisy even in loyalty.

John Chass, his genius in all the arts of life, his dislike of trouble, his generosity, which was half the vice of self-indulgence, and partly carelessness of money; and the vein of self-mockery, purely Irish, which ran through all, sometimes appearing like the vital flaw which ruined a nature meant for great achievement, and sometimes like the essence, the life blood, of a real greatness already possessed, had been analysed over a hundred cottage fires for years.

The news that Bridget had gone to Dunvil had a surprising effect on Cleeve. He rushed into the house and packed his portmanteau. Within ten minutes, not having yet formed any definite plan of action, he was saying good-bye to his uncle and aunt.

'But you can't go now,' Aunt Mary cried, 'without anything to eat.'

He poured out explanations, lies came to his lips as if by themselves. He had forgotten an engagement in England; he had bills to pay in Dunderry; he must go to Dunderry at once and catch the boat. His excitement impressed John Chass, who sent Darcy to harness Dapple for the car; and Mary, at last persuaded that the boy was resolved to go, only begged him to wait a moment, and ran into the house. She came back in three minutes, and kissing him, slipped a small packet into his hand. 'God bless you, m'dear, and remember I know what boys want. Write to me if you need anything.'

The packet, when Cleeve opened it on the car, half-way to Dunderry, contained some of his favourite currant biscuits, and a five-pound note.

Bridget, returning from Dunvil on a turf cart, with the turpentine, did not learn of Cleeve's departure until the afternoon, when Peggy,

184

enjoying her after-lunch cup of tea, told her to go and fold away the blankets in number three.

'Are they for claning then?'

'I've no doubt they'll need it, but they're putting away because thon young smiler, Master Cleeve, is away by to-night's boat. Didn't ye see him go?'

Bridget made no answer, and curious eyes examining her face could find no change in it.

Cleeve, with fifteen pounds in his pocket, went to London and took a room at Smith's Hotel in Mayfair, even then extremely expensive. But he had heard of it as fashionable.

The manager and clerk were slightly surprised by the boy's dress and also his old school box, but his manner was so assured that they did not even ask for references. In fact Cleeve, who had always been a sensible boy, had never seemed so sensible, so responsible, as during this period of lunatic behaviour.

He called on his first afternoon at the Pynsant's house, in Portland Place. Mrs. Pynsant was not at home. Cleeve was not surprised. He reflected that so charming and sympathetic a woman would seldom be at home. He went for a walk in the park and afterwards, since it was a sixpenny day, visited the National Gallery, to see the copyists at work.

On the next afternoon when he called at Mrs. Pynsant's, he found a carpet across the pavement; a canopy over the door. A gentleman in a tall hat was at the door, speaking to the footman. Cleeve confidently ran up the steps.

'Mrs. Pynsant is not at home, sir.'

'But isn't she giving a party?'

'Not at home, sir.' The footman was indignant.

Cleeve was so surprised that he thanked the man and turned away. He noticed that the other was also descending the steps; they glanced at each other and were about to turn in opposite directions along the pavement, when the stranger hesitated and looked again at Cleeve; then suddenly smiled and approached him.

'Excuse me,' he said; 'are you a friend of General Pynsant's?'

'I know Mrs. Pynsant.'

Cleeve, now that he observed the stranger, noticed that he was extremely shabby. His hat was too small, his hair too long, his coat too big. He thought suddenly, 'I believe he's just a beggar or out-of-work piano-tuner.'

'Excuse me,' the other said, 'I believe we're going the same way.' He drew up to Cleeve, then suddenly introduced himself, 'My name is Porfit.' He took off his hat.

'Mine's Corner.' Cleeve, suddenly impressed by Mr. Porfit's

confidence, his brilliant smile and easy politeness, took off his own hat. They shook hands. They walked along together and Mr. Porfit began at once to talk in a lively and well-informed manner about the affairs of the day.

As Cleeve said afterwards, even at this first meeting with Porfit, he had a unique impression of the man which was not to be referred only to his lively talk or his very expressive features, but to something which could only be called personal magnetism; an electric quality of his whole activity, not especially attractive, but exciting. He began at once to take a lively interest in Porfit.

He was a short, thick-set man, with a large, pale face, a pugnacious rather flat nose, and a long chin. His brown eyes were peculiarly bright and his mouth, a very well-formed mouth, had a humorous expression even when he was abusing the Government. All his features were extremely mobile. Cleeve, thinking that he must have met at least a Cabinet Minister was listening to an impassioned attack on landlordism, with a most respectful air, when suddenly the other mentioned the name of Pynsants, whom he accused of turning people out of their houses on his estate, on political grounds.

'He calls himself a Liberal but he is worse than some of the Tories. He won't even hear an appeal. I've called twice now about some of these poor people in Motcombe——'

'But excuse me,' Cleeve was shocked, 'I told you I was a friend.'

'I thought perhaps you might mention that I asked to see him—you can't trust these servants.'

'Oh but——'

'Well; I mustn't trouble you,' and they walked on again, while Porfit continued to speak in the same good-humoured way about the tyranny of the landlords. He pointed out that England, supposed to be a free country, was actually governed by the rich and the landlords.

But Cleeve, though two minutes before he had listened to the same arguments with most respectful interest, was now shocked by them. He was violently repelled by Mr. Porfit. He was furious at the suggestion that anyone should ruin anybody in England, and above all, that freedom did not exist there. Cleeve had always felt a strong secret reaction against any attack or slur on freedom, just as if to attack freedom was to aim a blow at himself, and at the moment, when he was exulting in all his senses at the sensation of escape from Bridget, he was especially touchy on the subject. He looked angrily at Mr. Porfit and said severely, 'But that's not true. Of course it's a free country.'

He walked indignantly across the street; and when he came again the next day, at his usual time, saw Porfit standing in the street opposite the General's door, and realized that he had just made another attempt to call upon him, he was so shocked that for some time he did not care

186

to approach. The spectacle of this shabby little man, with his creased frock coat, standing beneath the magnificent façade of the house, in the bright May sunshine, filled him with disgust and anger. What persecution. What an outrage. Why didn't the police stop it?

He didn't like to meet the man again. He strolled down Regent Street and back.

This time Cleeve was lucky. Porfit was still on guard, but as Cleeve approached, he saw a little old man come panting and staggering along the pavement to the bottom step, where he paused to gather strength for the ascent.

Porfit took off his hat and held out a letter. Cleeve suddenly perceived, half by recognition, half by guess, that this was the famous General himself, the hero of the Mutiny and the Crimea. He sprang forward to the rescue. Loyalty already distilled from his excitement by Jubilee warmth, thrilled in his veins. He blushed, took off his hat and said 'Sir.'

The General did not look at Porfit, and though the letter was held in front of him, at a level with his chest, he also ignored that. He panted at Cleeve, ' 'Scuse me—who's it.'

'My name is Corner, sir.'

'Corner, Corner? West country?'

'No, sir, Donegal.'

'What, what, you from Castle Corner—Jack Corner, old friend of mine.'

'My grandfather, sir.'

'Come in, come in.' The old man took his arm and turned to the steps. As he did so, he brushed aside Porfit's hand and letter with his chest; he staggered through them as if they did not exist, so that Cleeve, in spite of his irritation with the man, felt for some reason guilty and ashamed. He took care, on his part, to avoid jostling him, as he stood there, hat in one hand, letter in the other.

But the old General, clinging to his arm and panting up the steps, continued to talk of Castle Corner. He did not even refer to Porfit.

Both doors now flew open. Cleeve, instantly forgetting Porfit, found himself in a high, dark hall. He felt such excitement that his mouth was dry. His own strong emotion took him by surprise. He could smell a perfume which suddenly he knew to be Mrs. Pynsant's. They were slowly climbing the stairs; the old man, still holding his arm, panted and talked without stopping. It seemed that John Corner had been a great man to the General. 'Gave me a lesson I needed—when I needed it—made a Christian of me.'

A door opened at the top of the stairs and Cleeve, looking across the landing as he slowly mounted the last four steps, saw Mrs. Pynsant, wearing her hat, among a group of five or six men and women who stood about her like attentive courtiers, with the bland and rather blank faces of courtiers accustomed to polite waiting about. She herself was talking with animation to two singularly tall young men standing one behind the other on her left hand; one red-faced and burly; the other pale and stooped. Both had green ties of different shades. Redface was smiling with bright teeth; pale-face seemed about to weep. Helen Pynsant, with her chin raised towards Redface, was laughing and shaking one hand in the air, palm upwards in a characteristic gesture, meaning, 'I needn't say any more to you, clever man.'

Benskin was standing on the outskirts of this group, and Cleeve's curious eye photographed at once the uneasy pose and expression of one who is out of things. He felt surprised to see the great and austere Benskin so abashed.

Benskin had always been a joke to Helen's friends. It was exquisitely comical to see this uncouth idealist attempting to reform Helen Pynsant, and to know that he was paying not only for the privilege of being snubbed but also of supporting his rivals. One of Helen's best-known extravagances was the debts of her young men. Thus Benskin and his friend and partner, Nussbaum, who were then supposed to be paying between five and ten thousand pounds a year for her clothes, card debts and jewellery, were also subsidizing the young soldiers who came running to Helen every time they had had a bad Derby, or young poets who wanted to publish.

Helen Pynsant, who in the provinces still had the name of a social leader, in London filled a doubtful place between several sets, none of them much distinguished. Sets were even then not sharply defined, but each had a clear nucleus. Thus it was not possible, if it ever had been possible, to mark the limits of a set. The most exclusive, the dowagers of the old Queen's court, merged by relationship of all kinds, family, social and religious, into a dozen others, into sets so large and vaguely qualified that they became classes. But the centre was always known so that a phrase like the Marlborough House set or the racing set called up certain names.

But Helen's name belonged to no such group; and most of the groups remembered her as a failure. She had begun as a member of the exclusive set to which her marriage entitled her, but she at once shocked the pious dowagers. She had then been met very frequently at parties where the Prince was a guest; for a few months she was supposed to be the favourite; but as suddenly she was dropped.

The story was that at Ascot she had been indiscreet enough to poke her friend in the back with a parasol. Whether this were true or not, all Helen's friends knew that she was capable of such an act. Her friends called her impulsive her enemies said that she was underbred, essentially vulgar; she herself liked to think that she was above convention.

But certainly her lack of calculation, from whatever cause it arose, gave her a kind of sincerity. She was often true to an impulse, and this distinguished her among women who were true to nothing. Benskin, who thought her a woman naturally true and noble, led away by bad friends, had some excuse both for his devotion and his anxiety to prevent her from some serious scandal.

Cleeve himself was out of things. The General had not entered the drawing-room but, turning aside, brought him into a tall, dark room, where he had been sitting ever since, hearing about the greatness of his grandfather and the degeneracy of the present times.

'There's no religion any more—no honesty either—it's all money—these randlords, as they call 'em.'

The old man had crumpled into a large armchair. His folded face, with its shaking dewlaps, swung down and forward on the weak neck. The skin, soft, dry and yellow as old washed-out linen, creased all over, was stained with yellow-brown blotches; the bloodshot eyes swam in a bright moisture. He uttered a deep raucous sigh, 'I'm glad to hear Mr. John is still alive. Keeps you up to the mark, Hey, I hope so. No cutting prayers at Castle Corner. I can remember when he had me out of bed by the legs for morning prayers. Had to go in my dressing-gown. Christmas time. Nearly got pneumonia. But he was right, by Gad. Bend the twig. A real Christian, and a real gentleman. He put me on the right path, for one.'

Cleeve was surprised; but suddenly he understood that the old man was talking not of his uncle, but of his dead grandfather. He opened his mouth to explain; but the old man's voice rose. He was growing eloquent while he found himself again, in memory, at Castle Corner of the eighteen forties among the sound low churchmen of the old Protestant ascendancy, when, as it seemed to him, men had been men, strong in belief and courage, sure of themselves and their god; and women, good, beautiful; fit to be worshipped.

Cleeve's mind wandered. He heard again 'Christian gentlemen,' and names which were to him merely words from a history primer, Havelock, Lawrence; and then again, degeneracy. No one was left to hold a candle to those two great-souled men. The nation had lost its soul, its honesty. 'Rotten to the core,' the old man muttered. The swimming eyes gazed through Cleeve, the hanging mouth, with the blue crumpled lips, the long white hairs of the moustache trembled.

Cleeve did not trouble to listen. He knew that this belief was an obsession with old men, and he was sure, also, by an instinctive faith which he had never examined or doubted, that it was nonsense. The world was improving all the time. No one could stop the irresistible progress of the world towards universal wealth, happiness, freedom and comfort; and anyone who attempted to do so would be thrust aside.

His mind wandered. He studied curiously the big room, fifteen feet high, with its enormous doors and window-frames, painted chocolate brown, its huge cornices and ceiling in deep plaster relief, its dark-red walls on which hung Victorian portraits; great gilt-framed oblongs of oily black in which nothing could be seen but a small face, red or white; and perhaps a hand, a fan or an open book; and then again his eyes returned to the little dried-up man in the chair, with his hollow, mournful face; and he thought of the dead beetle whose shrivelled body lies in the shell of a walnut upon whose sap it has lived.

The words, 'vulgar—pretentious' passed lightly over his mind. He could see that the old man was now in a rage. 'Look at it,' he exclaimed, jerking out a claw.

Cleeve, startled by this spasm of fury, turned to follow the pointing finger and saw for the first time, against the end wall of the room, a piece of furniture of a kind new to his experience. It was a settee in pale yellow oak, of which one arm was the top of a bookcase and the other was joined to a large wooden bin; possibly a waste-paper basket. The front legs projected four feet into the air, where they ended in flat shelves, supporting two pewter flower-pots. The back was decorated with squares of pewter and blue china. Cleeve looked from the settee to the stately, pompous room, with its red walls, and rich, confident mouldings, and perceived with interest that they had nothing in common. They arose from ideas as different as those of a bishop from a geisha.

Cleeve, at first glance, disliked the settee. It gave him the same uneasy sensation that he had felt once, when, at parties, he saw other little boys trying to attract attention by noisy, vulgar behaviour.

'What they call modern,' the General choked. 'Look at it—vulgar—pretentious—decadent.' He was so angry that Cleeve was afraid he would have a fit. He murmured, 'It's a bad colour.'

But he felt suddenly a strong boredom. The word decadent excited in him a secret protest, as if it had been aimed at him. He was all at once disgusted with the old man and his excitement, with the old man's room, and his old ideas, with everything old; and beneath his disgust, rising up like a wave or life itself, an exhilarating confidence in his own power. It seemed to him that he could remake the whole world to his own taste.

'Rotten all through—no beauty—no truth—all show and grab.'

'I rather like it all the same,' Cleeve said, smiling at the old man. He was surprised at himself; but he was bored, and also he was filled with this secret excitement to destroy, to knock down; like the baby who

190

throws down the pile of bricks that another has built for him. 'It's rather jolly, don't you think?'

The old man, whose face was now purple, stared at him dribbling; a strange inarticulate sound came from his throat. Cleeve thought with horror, 'I've killed him,' and he said again, because he could not help it, 'So much more cheerful than the everlasting mahogany.'

He held his breath for fright; his smile became a grimace.

Suddenly the door was opened, a wave of noise broke in like the fall of a sea; and thrown up as it were on the crest of the joyous wave, Helen Pynsant came floating in, with Redface, who opened the door for her, four ladies, and Whiteface, who followed behind.

Cleeve had already sprung, with guilty relief, away from the old man. Helen Pynsant greeted him with a dazzling smile, raising his hand as high as her chin, and ejaculating, while her eye affectionately embraced him, 'It can't be you——'

Cleeve, entranced, did not know that this was Mrs. Pynsant's greeting to all those whom she did not recognize.

'You don't mind my calling?'

'I'd be very cross with you if you hadn't—but have you had any tea. What have you been doing with the poor man, Robert?' Then at once without waiting for an answer, she turned to Redface and raised her hand towards the settee. 'There, Mr. Cross, I appeal to the expert.'

The big man spread his chest, showed all his teeth in a smile and said, 'A fine specimen.'

'Robert, you see.' Helen turned towards her husband.

'Of a fashion now somewhat demoded,' the young man continued. 'I should date it 1885.'

Two ladies laughed, and one said, 'So it's not modern after all.'

'Of course it is.'

'Cockeye furniture is all the go,' another said.

'Mrs. Bill is right,' Redface declared. 'Assymmetry in furniture is still the mode—or the go.'

Whiteface, who appeared to be very young, now remarked in a solemn and sad voice from behind the ladies that the settee was perfectly horrid.

'Oh, Cobby,' Helen cried in surprise, 'you don't mean that.' She looked anxiously from the settee to the group. Her expression was serious. It appeared that she was deeply concerned about the settee.

'A most corrupt piece,' the boy called Cobby continued. 'It is really disgusting.'

There was a short silence. Then the red-faced woman called Mrs. Bill said in a hoarse and nasal voice, 'Wot's he talking about, Helen?'

'He says my poor settee is improper.'

191

'A piece in fact,' Redface said, and Helen gave a delighted laugh.

'But it is a charming settee,' one cried.

'Cela n'empeche pas,' Redface said, making Helen laugh again.

'General, you can't really dislike it?'

'Of course, it wouldn't do for Osborne,' a little sharp woman said.

At these words the whole expressions, looks and voices of the party instantly changed. Helen lost her serious artistic air; the four ladies all began to speak at once with voices full of eagerness and laughter.

'But it would be perfect. The old dear could put her chicken bones in the bin.'

'And her prayer-book in the other cubby-hole.'

The old general who had struggled to his feet in the presence of the ladies, stood among them, turning his watery eyes about him. His cheeks were purple, but he seemed more confused than angry; and with his shrunken body, which made him shorter than the shortest of the women, he seemed like a small, bewildered street child among gorgeous tormenting schoolgirls.

'But it would have to have the legs draped—in crape.'

Cleeve only now grasped that all these jokes were being aimed at the Queen, who till that moment, had seemed to him above criticism; the great and noble Queen Victoria. He broke into delighted laughter, so loud and innocent that all the ladies' faces, pretty, ugly, thin, fat, but all with the same smart expression of insolence and self-satisfaction, were turned towards him. He had already caught the vein, 'And six portraits of Prince Albert instead of the pewter plates.'

Nobody laughed at this because Cleeve was not known. Even Helen Pynsant did not laugh, because she could not yet remember the young man. But because she was good natured, she smiled at him and said, 'How very unpatriotic of you. You ought to show more respect to our good old Queen.'

'Rather too old perhaps.'

The ladies looked severe; they thought this disloyalty vulgar in a young man whom nobody knew. But Cleeve, who never perceived when he was snubbed, continued to make old jokes about the Queen, and to laugh at them, while he gazed at Helen Pynsant's eyes, chin, nose and the broad shape of her bosom in its wave of pink silk, with an ecstatic grin.

The ladies moved away; Helen Pynsant said smiling, 'I'm afraid you are a terrible cynic,' and put her hand into the sleeve of the red-faced young man. They went towards the door. But Cleeve followed, still smiling, as if drawn by a string.

Mrs. Pynsant, seeing now that the young man must be got rid of, turned to him suddenly, held out her hand and said, 'Forgive me if I have to go—but you will come to my reception next week—the twenty-fourth. I'm counting on you.' She pressed his hand and at once went through another door with her train of ladies and the red-faced man.

Cleeve, not at all put out by this dismissal, which seemed to him quite natural, ran downstairs, but half-way down, hearing a step behind him, he turned and saw the pale-faced Cobby following him.

Cleeve waiting for him smiled like a small boy and asked him, 'Aren't you wanted either?'

'I have paid my call.' His air would have frozen anyone but Cleeve who cried, 'I say, isn't she a stunner?'

'Do you mean Mrs. Pynsant?'

'Of course. Do you know her well?'

'For twenty years,' the other said, as the footman came forward with his beautiful tall hat in one hand, a tall hat of rather French pattern, narrower at the top than the bottom, and Cleeve's dusty bowler in the other.

'But how old are you?' Cleeve asked in surprise; a question which in the presence of the two footmen made Mr. Cobby become even paler. He ignored it and turning to the door gave Cleeve his back. But when he reached the pavement Cleeve was already at his elbow smiling at him with the utmost affection and crying, 'But I say, is she your aunt or anything?'

'My relations with Helen Pynsant are purely platonic.'

'Oh, it's only that she called you Cobby.'

'My name is Chorley—Cobden Chorley.'

Chorley walked on in lofty melancholy. He obviously detested his Christian name as much as his youth.

Cobden Chorley was a young man who had lately come from Porriton where his family had been neighbours to the Pynsant family for several generations, to Oxford, and at Oxford he had found that Helen Pynsant's name, among a certain fashionable and æsthetic set, carried weight. He had therefore boasted her acquaintance and called several times in Portland Place. He had also found it correct to fall in love with her. Two fashionables and three of the æsthetics were in love with her.

The two fashionables, both of St. Mary's college, were fashionable in love; that is to say, they talked as if they could go to bed with the lady whenever they chose; the three æsthetics were æsthetically in love; one heartily in the early Rosetti style; one diabolically in the symbolist manner, and the third, Cross, perversely so, in a condescending manner. He described the lady as such a boy at heart.

Cobden, who already felt the need of forming a style of his own, therefore fell in love with Helen beautifully. He worshipped her with an austere and unselfish passion, expressed in numerous triolets. He had at that moment a triolet in his pocket which he had intended to give her as soon as he found her alone.

Unluckily she had been in that frivolous mood when she preferred Cross and her smart friends, and Cobden was still deeply hurt by his dismissal; his dignity had suffered and dignity was more precious to him even than to other young men because his whole life was a dignified attitude. It was because of this fundamental need to defend and restore dignity that in spite of his distrust with the barbarous Cleeve he said to him now, 'I always avoid Helen Pynsant when she is with men like Cross or women like Mrs. Bill; they laugh at her worst faults.'

'But I thought she was charming.'

'She is a child. All women are children. That is at once their charm and their failing. They have the beauty and the cruelty of irresponsible nature.'

'Are you awfully fond of her?'

'Of Helen Pynsant?' He raised his thin eyebrows and pursed his childish lips, like the lips of a melancholy cupid, and said, 'Speaking strictly, I cannot say that I admire Helen Pynsant. She is, after all, merely a smart woman who happens to have a little more intelligence and taste than some of the others. Nor do I admire her beauty, which is already rather full blown. But I adore beauty in Helen Pynsant. I could contemplate her little finger for hours or the marvel of her nose.'

Cleeve wanted to laugh but the serious and melancholy gravity of the young man made him feel that laughter would be out of place in his presence, as in church. He said, 'But isn't it the same thing?'

'I see you are not acquainted with Plato?'

'Plato—I read some of the Republic at school.'

'I hope you will do some more next term,' Chorley answered, taking a final revenge for his dignity, 'and now I fear we must part.' He held up his ebony and silver stick for a hansom.

'But I must see you again,' Cleeve cried, to whom Chorley was a fascinating person. 'At least you'll be at Mrs. Pynsant's reception.'

'Certainly not,' Cobden answered. 'I never go to receptions—I would sooner find my mobs in Trafalgar Square where the human animal is at least instructive.'

The hansom drove away; Cleeve returned to his hotel in great delight. Life in society appeared even more exciting than he had expected. He had not only won another smile from Helen Pynsant; he had entertained her with his conversation, and he had made important discoveries about the world. Queen Victoria it seemed, was quite exploded; the jubilee was only a new joke. He had overcome them both. A whole age, a great empire lay conquered beneath his feet.

Hotel bills were nothing to him, he did not intend to pay his bill in any case, because he saw that he must at once buy a frock coat, a silver and ebony cane, and patent leather boots with tops of lilac cloth.

Bridget in Ireland had vanished from his thoughts even more completely than if he had merely failed to remember her. His happiness had abolished her, as the sight of a birthday table cures a child's stomach-ache.

Although Cleeve managed for three weeks to avoid paying his hotel by giving references to John Chass and to Benskin, and to obtain his frock coat and two other suits of clothes from a good tailor, on the same references, he was obliged to pay cash for his new hat, his ebony stick, his patent leather boots and his hansoms. He could not resist hansoms. Thus on the morning of Mrs. Pynsant's reception, when the cashier brought him a bill of seventeen pounds and asked for an immediate settlement, he had only three shillings and tenpence in his pocket. This did not trouble him. He was not going to think of bills on the day of a party. He promised the cashier a cheque that afternoon, spent the morning in the national gallery, and took lunch in a bun shop. He economized on lunch in order to have enough for a hansom to Portland Place, which left him with ninepence.

Money was well spent on the hansom. He was supremely happy from the moment of his arrival at the canopy and the red carpet, which seemed to him to have been laid down expressly for his pleasure.

Porfit was at the door but Cleeve ignored him. Somehow he had perceived that he did not matter; that no one troubled about him. He greeted Helen Pynsant at the top of the stairs and the tottering General behind her with the confidence of a house friend, and sauntered into the crowded drawing-rooms. They were already so tightly packed that he could hardly make his way among the guests.

On every side of him he seemed to recognize duchesses, countesses, beauties of society, and men noticeable at first sight for their aristocratic distinction, or striking intelligence. Every moment he recognized some face from the illustrated papers, of a cabinet minister, a celebrated wit or a famous beauty. One group in the corner, of a tall man with a brown vandyk beard, an aquiline nose; a shorter, stouter woman, majestic in carriage; and a beautiful girl with a long, oval face, violet eyes and high arched brows, with that dazzling fair skin which is seen usually only in young children, he thought to recognize from a newspaper picture as a certain grand duke, then visiting London for the jubilee. The fair girl was obviously a princess.

He was fascinated by the idea of the fair princess, and his eyes continually turned towards her. He felt a touch on his sleeve, and found Stella beside him. She was now as tall as he, a broad-shouldered and deep-breasted girl with broad rosy face, snub nose and thick eyebrows like partridge feathers. She was dressed like a schoolgirl and her thick brown hair was in a club. He exclaimed with pleasure at seeing her, and she, blushing a little at his frank delight, said gravely, 'Why didn't you tell me you were coming? Now I have to go.'

'Oh no, why, I haven't seen you for a year.'

'I'm only up for the dentist. Are you all right?' She asked this with the air of the nurse or responsible elder sister, which now she always assumed to Cleeve.

'Absolutely.'

'You've had tea? Has anyone introduced you to anyone?' Cleeve was surprised to see Stella so serious and grave, but he remembered that she was now a prefect at her school. He answered untruthfully that he had had tea but that he knew nobody. Stella looked round and said, 'It's such a pity you came on a gatherum day.'

'Gatherum?'

'That's what mother calls it.' Stella looked round. 'They're mostly stockbrokers and doctors and artists and people from Porriton up for the Jubilee.'

'But Stella, don't I know that man over there, in the corner, the awfully handsome man with the brown beard. Isn't he the Grand Duke of Something?'

'Grand duke—oh no, he makes soap. Oh dear, I must go. Are you sure you don't want anything?' She touched his sleeve.

'Only to talk to you.'

'But I can't stay. Oh, Cobby, there you are.' She quickly introduced Cleeve to the tall, pale young man, standing wedged between two ladies at a couple of yards' distance, and said to him firmly, 'Mind you look after him, he's Irish, and tell Lucy he's a friend of mine.' She then edged quickly away.

Cleeve struggled to the side of Cobden Chorley and cried, 'You said you weren't coming.'

'I'm not here,' he answered. 'I only came in with a message.'

'You don't like the gatherum day—or the soap boilers.'

Cleeve described his mistake and pointed out the grand duke in the corner.

'My father,' the young man said gloomily, and before Cleeve could invent any apology, he continued, 'Apologies may be spared for the sake of both our dignities. But we had better obey Stella.'

He then led Cleeve to the corner and presented him to Mr. and Mrs. Chorley and Lucy Chorley, as a friend of Stella's.

'Oh, but I know all about you,' Lucy said, and then stopped, recollecting perhaps that what she knew of Cleeve was not a drawing-room story.

'Did she tell you anything about a dance?'

196

Lucy seemed to be laughing though she uttered no sound. Her cheeks became pink.

'Stella's Irish stories are after all Irish stories,' Mr. Chorley said quickly and smoothly. 'But what a beautiful country you have, Mr. Corner.'

'So green,' Mrs. Chorley said, raising her hooked nose. She dropped the remark like an absentminded hawk which lets fall a prey because it has thought of something forgotten at home.

Mr. Chorley, with the same swift and urbane manner of the European prince, was saying how much he had enjoyed his one visit to Ireland.

Cobden, having got rid of the barbarian, stood aloof, gazing at Helen Pynsant, three yards away, while she talked to a young soldier and the usual group of three or four smart women of her own kind. Cobden's message was still in his pocket, but he did not know if he would trouble to deliver it. Could any woman appreciate his poems? He doubted it.

The boy's attitude as he gazed was perfectly that of the contemplative philosopher, but his expression to those of Helen's smart friends who noticed him at all was very diverting. Like a 'hungry little boy screwing up his eyes at a bun,' one said.

'Somebody else's bun.'

'And the policeman looking.'

'Oh, is he here?'

'You mean the prop—the General's probably in bed.'

Benskin, who had once been saluted by the local Conservative newspaper in Porriton as a prop of Empire, was often called the prop by Helen, who found in the name a neat mixture of the wooden and the moral.

Helen was telling the young soldier that he must buy Klipspringer. This was the mine which at that time, on Benskin's advice, she was urging upon all her friends. She spoke with her usual air of interest in the person and the subject, but she noticed her friend's glances, and carelessly glanced aside. This glance took Cobden by surprise; and for an instant Helen saw something childish and longing in his pale stare before it became again a mask.

She continued her lecture on gold mines, as against horses, as investments for young guardees with debts, but her interest was suddenly diverted towards Chorley. She had not before paid much attention to the serious, melancholy boy. He was simply one among the very young adorers, the innocents who, fresh every year, worshipped her respectfully for a month or two until somebody told them that all devotion was ridiculous, or they set up a mistress.

But now she was suddenly sorry for young Cobden, and also she was curious. How young he was. How young was he? Turning a few minutes later to move from the room, she brushed against his shoulder as if she

197

had not seen him; then suddenly turned her eyes upon him and touched his hand. 'Bored? I know, poor Cobby—but wait for me. I must see you.'

The effect was even better than she had expected. The boy flushed up to the eyes; he looked after her with an expression of confusion and surprise. Helen felt at once that special excitement which was so delightful to her, because it was not sought for. The highest stakes at bridge could not give it to her; only something unexpected; fright or sometimes a love affair.

But she took care not to go back into the drawing-room. She did not want the boy to follow her about. She knew what Mrs. Bill or Hetty had been waiting for years to say; that Helen Pynsant was getting old, she was coming down to boys.

Cleeve, near the window, was still talking to the Chor.eys. He had never met people so charming, good-looking and intelligent. He felt a kind of perpetual surprise in them, and especially he kept looking at Lucy Chorley as if to say, 'Isn't she too good to be true?' This expression of Cleeve's and its meaning was probably understood; few pretty girls have not had experience of it, when, in their best frocks, they meet country cousins. It is very flattering and Lucy Chorley, catching Cleeve's eye, blushed slightly and looked at him with frank kindness. Both of them smiled, apropos of nothing; the conversation was a serious one. Mr. Chorley was talking about Walter Pater, lately dead. Chorley, like many who then showed Pater's influence, seemed eager to deny its power. The prophet of the 'eighties was already crowed down by Kipling, even for those who detested Kipling.

It was getting late and most of the guests had left the big drawing-room on the first floor when Mrs. Chorley said, 'Hadn't we better go now, Adam?'

Mrs. Chorley and Lucy both together glanced out of the window and then Mr. Chorley began a new speech. 'No, they may call Pater the typical man of his time, but was he? He despaired of his time and I should say that this was a period of general optimism. Things are going ahead in every direction. Pater was always looking back to Greece and Rome. Of course his philosophy of seeking beauty, of living in the beautiful moment——'

'It's no good waiting for that man to go away,' Mrs. Chorley said, suddenly impatient. 'Especially if he's waiting for us.'

Chorley paid no attention; Lucy flushed slightly and fixed her eyes on her father. It was plain that Mrs. Chorley's remark was felt to be tactless.

In fact, the Chorleys did not want to meet Porfit. They had succeeded in dodging him by a lucky entrance and they wanted to avoid him again. Porfit's campaign against what he called the landlords and the landlords had been embarrassing to Chorley who was a friend of both Pynsant and Benskin. They sat together on many Liberal committees, and Benskin was a large subscriber to local party funds. Benskin, since his purchase of the Corner leases, was Chorley's head-landlord; they were fellow directors in the Granport Printing Works and fellow debenture holders for the Liberal Club. They belonged to that network of business ties which in a country district before the war still formed an unseen economic framework often stronger than political connections.

On the other hand, Chorley, like Porfit, was a Nonconformist, and there was still a deep division, even in Chorley's mind between Church and State Liberals like Pynsant and Benskin and the chapel Liberals like himself and Porfit, a religious and fundamental difference.

He was therefore in an uncomfortable position, when Porfit from the chapel pulpits in the General's own village, abused him as a tyrant. But he never referred to it and Mrs. Chorley's tactless speech disconcerted him very much. Lucy, quick to feel his discomfort, and understanding his difficulty, came to his help by continuing the discussion. 'But would you say, Papa, that Pater was a kind of mystic?'

'Pater was certainly a mystic in one sense——'

'You could easily slip out when he goes down the street,' Mrs. Chorley suggested. Luckily before anyone had to notice this painful suggestion, Benskin came in. He seemed to be in a hurry. He saluted Mrs. Chorley and then said abruptly, 'Where's Cobden?'

'He went out, I think.'

'I was told he was here—you don't know, in fact, where he is.'

Benskin spoke sharply and looked at Chorley with an irritable frown as if accusing him of some neglect or carelessness. Benskin was easily annoyed by Chorley, whom he looked upon as a hypocrite and a shuffler.

In this, of course, he was wrong. Adam Chorley was never a hypocrite; though he was sometimes perplexed between conflicting responsibilities.

'He had to go back to Oxford to-day,' Lucy said.

'Yes, I suppose he has to sleep at Oxford.'

Mr. Chorley, not at all put out, said, 'Young men at Oxford like to go their own way.'

'I wonder if Oxford likes that so much,' he added, 'if you want to avoid your friend below, you can go out at the back—by the mews.' He then walked out, leaving the Chorleys much surprised.

Then Chorley said easily, 'A first-class chap, Benskin.'

This phrase so exactly hit off the necessary compound of forbearance and condescension that even Cleeve could appreciate it. He smiled at Chorley in frank admiration. The big man, with his most grand ducal air, remarked, 'We can only enjoy what we put into the moment and Pater could not put into his experience the quality of faith, the dynamic, shall we say, of the Christian belief.'

'I'm afraid he was really a very unhappy man,' Lucy said.

'The old tragedy of the man without faith, without God.'

Both he and Lucy looked sad; and Cleeve, who had shifted his admiring gaze to Lucy, now suddenly finding himself out of key, quickly assumed a mournful and pensive air.

Benskin was going upstairs towards Mrs. Pynsant's sitting-room. His information from Mrs. Bill, who had stopped his brougham to impart it, had frightened him very much. 'Mind Helen doesn't make a dam fool of herself with that boy.'

But the sitting-room was empty. Helen never used her sitting-room for experiments, but a certain dingy little writing-room on the half-landing which was not entered once in a month, and from which any approaching step could be heard on the stairs. Here, at the moment, she was sitting on an ancient couch with young Cobden tumbled across her, his arms round her neck, his head against her breast and his long legs trailing on the floor. The experiment had been successful—much too successful. She had not dreamt of anything like this. She had intended a little serious flirtation. She had wondered at most if the boy would dare to take a kiss. What a surprise when, without any pre-liminaries but a declaration which might have been composed by Oscar himself, this gawky, long-legged youth had begun to fumble at her clothes and she had perceived, with a shock of astonishment, the enormous audacity of his intention.

It was inconceivable that the boy should mean what he seemed to mean; here in her own house, with the servants still rattling the cups and plates of the reception just below; and her maid expecting her any moment to be dressed for dinner. But suddenly she realized that Cobby, unlike the guardees, was a highly innocent person; he knew nothing of the real world; he was capable of anything.

Then suddenly, still in her astonishment at the boy's boldness, she perceived, with terror, that he was nearly in hysterics. She imagined the consequences. She had had to go to the rescue, once when in his excitement the boy nearly fell off the sofa, again when at a critical moment he found himself still entangled with clothes. His face curled up then as if he would weep with humiliation. Only her most adroit and tactful intervention had saved a double catastrophe.

Now it appeared that he was overwhelmed for the third time by the mere experience. Helen herself was flushed and breathless. She did not know whether she ought to be amused, furious or triumphant. What an explosion. What a pity she could not describe the scene to Mr. Cross

200

or Mrs. Bill. It would require different treatment for each taste but how much they would appreciate it.

She gently stroked Cobden's head and said for the third time with a maternal tenderness, 'No, Cobby, you mustn't blame yourself—I ought to have foreseen this.'

Her sympathy was sincere; she was grateful to Cobby. He had given her a most unusual experience.

A quarter of an hour later, Benskin, still moving about in the lower rooms, saw Helen and young Cobden descending the stairs together. One glance at the couple told him what had happened. He had seen Helen before at such times, when she reminded him of a cat that has just had a meal of fish. Her eyes had a look at once sleepy and sly; her lips curled up at the corners; her cheeks and even her body seemed fatter, softer, as if she had melted a little on the surface.

She smiled at him, enjoying his helpless anger and said in a soft, lazy, fat voice, 'So there you are, Theo. What a pity you didn't come in sooner. Cobby and I had a nice little cup of tea by ourselves.'

Cobden said nothing. Apparently he could not trust himself to speak. He had the pale, bewildered look of a man who has just recovered from a fit.

Porfit disappeared at a little after half-past six, and five minutes later Chorley remarked that it was really time they were going. They offered Cleeve a lift in their cab; and when Cleeve mentioned that he did not want to go back to the hotel because he had nothing to do there, they asked him to dinner. Somewhat later in the evening, Cleeve mentioned that he was anxious to visit the West country and he asked if he could call on the Chorleys.

'We should be delighted,' Chorley said. 'We go home to-morrow.'

'But you must promise to come,' Lucy said.

'What time are you going to-morrow?' Cleeve asked, and it appeared that he was tired of London; he might be leaving almost at once.

Cleeve, when he went back to his hotel, had an unpleasant scene with the cashier who demanded immediate payment. Cleeve promised payment, but declared that he had mislaid his cheque book. Next morning before breakfast he put on his clothes over his pyjamas, two sets of underclothes and two shirts, put his toothbrush and razor in his overcoat pocket and walked out to a pawnbroker, where he raised seventeen shillings on his watch. He bought a large cardboard box for sixpence; went to a public lavatory, took off his superfluous underclothes and packed them in the cardboard box. He then joined the Chorleys at Paddington, where he borrowed five shillings from Adam to make up his fare.

The whole of these expedients, together with all those tricks, dodges and evasions, which Cleeve had carried out every day since his flight from Annish, required no premeditation on his part. He performed them, as it were, by a natural routine; as a baby, in a certain state of its being, begins to suck or crawl or talk. Some private intelligence inside him perceived what had to be done for his general purpose, and promptly suggested the right procedure, even to the correct nonchalant smile which makes an hotel manager hesitate to call the police.

It was not till the afternoon that the Chorleys having entertained Cleeve to tea, found that he had come to stay the night. He asked where he should put his luggage. He was at once shown to a room.

Mrs. Chorley, indeed, now made a protest. She asked who this young man was, and how long he was going to stay.

'We needn't discuss that until he has some money to go away with,' Chorley said.

'Poor boy,' Lucy said. 'What on earth could he do?'

Cleeve was already a responsibility to the Chorleys who were not only extremely kind people, but forethoughtful.

Mrs. Chorley opened her mouth to say something but she thought better of it. She had long given in to her family, who not only did what they liked, but had such excellent reasons for doing so. Even when she felt sure that they were not doing what they liked, they would always find reasons for it; in fact, they then found their most overwhelming reasons. She went out to arrange for Cleeve's sheets.

Lucy laughed and said, 'I was so terrified mother would say something about the poor boy's luggage.'

Chorley looked grave. 'Yes, she looked at it once or twice. But you know, Lucy, it's rather odd that he should have nothing but a cardboard box.'

'Oh, why?' Lucy asked. Lucy was already Cleeve's champion, not only because she liked him but because she suspected that he was in some kind of difficulty. 'After all, father, one mustn't forget that he's Irish.'

'Yes, of course, there is that.'

To Chorley, as well to Stella and to Lucy, the fact that Cleeve was Irish entitled him not only to special consideration but sympathy, as if he had suffered a wrong for which they were partly responsible.

Cleeve upstairs was walking about his room with a smile of delight. It was a large, square, high room, with tall windows and walls. Rugs, curtains, chair coverings were in bright chintzes. Reproductions of Burne Jones and Rossetti and several Arundel prints hung on the austere walls, which in contrast with the hangings reminded one of a monastery. A bookcase was full of recent novels and new poetry by Gissing, Meredith, Francis Thompson, Yeats, Patmore. There was also a Bible in Morris binding. Copies of the last volumes of the *Yellow Book* and of the *Foundations of Belief* lay on the bed-table. It was like many thousand bedrooms in the houses of well-off cultivated people in England at that time, but to Cleeve it was so novel and exciting, that already London, the frock coats in Portland Place, even Helen Pynsant, seemed ordinary, crude and far away. As for Bridget and Castle Corner, they were at such an inconceivable distance that they never occurred to him at all.

Cleeve never forgot his first impression of the Chorleys' 'You see,' he used to say, 'I had never before been in a house where any kind of idea or any form of art was taken seriously, and the effect was like the discovery of a civilization, a real civilization.'

On Jubilee day Shon was in bed with a feverish cold, and he could not see the Jubilee. But he was rebellious, he pestered Francie to be allowed out of bed, so that she sent for his mother to come and comfort him. Mary Corner, fetched upstairs from her dinner party, sat for a long time with the child, patting him and soothing him. As usual, she did not try to pretend that he was not suffering a misfortune.

'It's a sad thing,' she said. 'But if you got up, you might catch a chill and then, good gracious, you might die and wouldn't that be a stoopid thing to do for a few fireworks. Then you'd never be a soldier at all.'

'But Mama, a Jubilee is so special.'

'Moll,' John Chass shouted.

'Now, darling, I must go and you'll not pester poor Francie any more?'

'Molly!'

Mary jumped up hastily and kissed Shon. 'I know you're a brave boy and not a little stoopid.'

Shon, in the act of complaint, raised his eyebrows and thought of not being stupid. But the idea did not attract him.

'Mary.'

'God bless you, my pet.' She went quickly out.

Shon rejected stupidity and seized upon courage. For a long time he practised bravery, and uttered no complaint. But the heavy feeling of loss and waste which pressed upon him continued to increase. He did not even know what a Jubilee was like. He did not care to miss anything, but a Jubilee, he knew, was something extraordinary. He lay on his back, gazing at the window; listening, all his senses were stretching out to explore the Jubilee and experience it.

At ten o'clock the fireworks began to explode, the band struck up; shouts were heard from the watchers among the trees, and Francie, sewing by candlelight, grew restless, looked at the window, and uttered deep sighs.

Shon, hearing the sighs, turned on his side, and began to breathe regularly. Francie tiptoed from the room and descended the back stairs like an avalanche.

203

Shon jumped out of bed, put on his red flannel dressing-gown and his slippers and stole down the back stairs to the yard. It was full of carriages, cars, traps. Shon stopped in front of the rows of vehicles and thought, 'These are for the Jubilee.' He waited a moment, expectant for the new sensation. 'What a lot there are,' he suggested. But then, he had seen the yard as full before. He ran thoughtfully out into the park.

There were many country people under the trees in the park; smoking and talking together. The flat arches of the sycamores under the moonlight; the groups in the intersection of the irregular transepts, with their pale faces and bristling moustaches, their long black Sunday coats with braided tails swinging over their buttocks and crossed at the points like a crow's wings, their black Sunday bowlers cocked at all angles, made a scene like midnight mass and fair day combined. The murmur of the voices, too, punctuated by an occasional sharp spit, was as much of the chapel as a fair day, but livelier than either. It mixed with the quick, sudden rustle of the leaves overhead; but it did not agree with the monotonous rustle of the waves beyond the terrace, running up on the flow. It was lively and uneven, and while they spoke the people continually moved their heads and bodies, looking on each side of them, jerking themselves suddenly round at the hips, in fear that something new and interesting might be happening behind them.

But Shon knew them all, and he had seen their Sunday coats.

He gazed for some time with interest at two small children sleeping on the grass between the wheels of a tilted ass cart. They were two of the Foy children, and one of them had a sore nose. But they gave nothing except the idea, 'They're missing the Jubilee.'

Two ragged men staggered slowly past, holding up a third, extremely drunk. They were mountain men; and their serious faces were hollow and resigned, only their eyes were curious. They stopped to allow the drunk man to vomit, supporting him carefully and tenderly in the right position; and one of them, looking round while he paused in his duty, caught sight of Shony and saluted him gravely with the usual sideways nod.

At once the drunk man, feeling by sympathy his friend's glance, jerked up his face and turned it, still pouring with the sweat of his agony, in the same direction. His bright, swimming eyes met Shon's and they stared at each other for a moment, with the same eager enquiry.

But again a spasm took him. He tumbled forward from the waist as if his joints were broken. Shony had seen hundreds of drunk men, on fair days and feast days, but he looked closely and attentively at this one while he retched and groaned, his crimson face swinging, his long forelock hanging below his nose. He thought, 'He's enjoying the Jubilee; this is the Jubilee.'

A row of heads behind the terrace wall followed Bridget, while, in a borrowed cap and apron, she walked among the guests with a tray of glasses.

'She hasn't been to confession for nine weeks.'

'Is that so? Devil receive us. Then she's done for.'

'Wait till Sukey or Padsy throws an eye on her length of string.'

'Aye, there'll be murder.'

'Ah, the poor wain—it's hard for a gyurl to be spoilt by the wan wee nip.'

All were sympathetic. The church was so strong against Bridget that the people felt little spite. Bridget was in the place of a highwayman on his way to Tyburn. The respectable might scowl, but the young and generous felt sad for her and were ready to throw their flowers into the cart.

Bridget carried herself proudly enough while she followed Grogan among the groups. Balancing the tray she leaned backward from her powerful hips from which her strong round body stood up like a tree from its sinuous roots. Her round breasts, firm and large, as she threw them forward, strained at her black frock. The round neck, smooth and creamy as new stone, carried the head with its strong round chin and the mass of black hair, in the pose of that dignity which, by the nature of the human creature and the laws of balance, must belong to a pregnant woman; a grand and original dignity.

'Ach, look at her then, the stays are breaking out on her.'

'Naw, it's her apron blawing.'

'Whist now, there's Sukey.'

Sukey and Con were pushing through the crowd together. Sukey was in her print dress as she had come up from her kitchen. Her red hair blew out like flames, and her face was flaming with drink. She reeled along, swinging her arms like a guardsman and screaming at the crowd greetings and insults mixed. Foys and Egans swarmed after her. Kitty, Francie, red with giggles and porter, old Dan, with his fallen-in cheeks and bloodshot eye, already exhausted, gasping at every step; young Rifty, in a blue satin tie from John Chass' castaways, and a collar burst from it's stud; winking one minute and looking solemn the next.

Rifty under some small suspicion, among a dozen others, of seducing Bridget, could not make up his mind whether to own the deed for a bold glory or deny it for a pious and respectable one. He could not tell whether this charge were the opportunity of his life or a dangerous slander. This confusion had made him seem, during the last few weeks, more foolish than usual.

Con was last, with his bowler dangling from the croup of his long head and his nugget pin up to his jaw, turning this way and that, and jerking out his hand to be shaken.

He was like a weary king, doing his duty. He did not look at the shakers or smile. His face was hollow as if he had a wasting disease; and he was always full of bitter words. He had given up his plan of building a store in Annish, on the grounds that the people were not fit to appreciate a Christian store, and every night, when he stood treat in some bar, he abused the Nationalist Party, the British, Doctor Hanna who wanted to send Kitty back to America, the Corners and even his own people. He said now, twisting up his face as if he had something bitter in his mouth, 'This is the way we boycott the Jubilee—we're the brave boys in Annish.'

A voice behind said, 'Is it Bridgy? She's as fat as a bonham.'

'Why wouldn't she be fat?' Con said. 'She'd rather ate Jawn's mate at the castle, than mine.'

Alarmed and curious faces turned towards the group. Everybody was anxious to hear what would happen when Con or Sukey discovered Bridget's state.

'Aye, as fat as a wee sow,' Sukey said.

'Will that be ating spuds or apples?'

This was a question from Breedy, who was always full of reckless malice. The drink was running down his cheeks in thick white drops.

'There's noan apples now,' Sukey said, and two or three called out to Breedy, 'Go wan now.'

'Quit yer codding.'

They pushed him towards the south, saying, 'Ye'll find the keg at the corner.'

'Is it Bridgy's keg?' he exclaimed. 'But that's the leaky wan.'

'What's that?' Con said, confused. Sukey made a plunge after the fellow and screamed, 'Ah, ye dirty devil, and what sort of a drip are ye to be dropped in a medical hall. Let me at him, the pig's dung. But what did he mane at all?' She looked round with open mouth and astonished eyes. Suddenly her expression changed and she cried, 'Look at him, the darlint. Has he come to his Sukey.'

Shon, in his red flannel dressing-gown, wriggling between the legs of the crowd, had caught her eye. She stooped simultaneously with Kitty beside her; Shon, without looking at them, raised his elbows ready to be lifted.

Francie gave a cry of dismay and rushed forward to seize the boy, but Sukey thrust her back with a push like a mule's kick. 'Ach, leave him be, Francie. Let him enjoy himself this wan time.'

Kitty had already lifted Shon. She said to Sukey, pleading, 'Give him to me.'

Sukey scowled, then suddenly waved her hand, giving up her property in Shon to one more needy.

Kitty pressed Shon tight against her thin breast and said, 'My heart's blood, did ye come to see your Kitty?'

'No, the Jubilee.'

'What kind of talk is that about a dacent gyirl,' Con said bitterly. 'Now in Amurika a fellow who talked in that way——'

'This is the Jubilee, isn't it?'

Sukey gave a shriek of laughter, and kissed Shon's flushed cheek. 'Isn't he the prince?'

'The nose of old Jawn himself,' Dan Egan declared, raising his own Corner nose. His chest filled out. His lips smiled.

A mountain man, even more ragged then he; a Foy cousin, who was like a bundle of dirty rags from which peered two little eyes like black currants and a hairy black nose over a moustache like the whiskers of a tom cat, said gravely, 'Aye, a child has great gentility in his loveliness.'

Shon was staring at the erratic moving figures on the terrace; and behind them, at the waves advancing slowly and methodically, like an army in ranks, with glittering helmets and dark green bodies, towards the terrace wall. He stared at each familiar object in turn with the same eager enquiry, as if asking, 'Are they different?'

The drawing-room which could be seen from the outside like an illuminated tank full of gorgeous Japanese fish, trailing flounces and ribbons of brilliant colours, now appeared in turmoil. The flounces swirled. New parties had arrived. Grogan dived out of the door bent double, grasped the handle, and stood in the receiving attitude; upright as a soldier from heels to shoulder, but meditative from the neck upwards in a favourite pose which seemed to say. 'Have the workers of iniquity no knowledge.'

The men in their black and white uniforms, the women in their silks and satins, streamed out upon the terrace.

These were parties who had dined elsewhere; at the Duffs and at Carnmore with Slatter.

John Chass, coming out last with Mary, stopped in front of the doors, silhouetted against them. He looked round and raised his hand; Grogan turned round and called out, 'Whist ye.' There was a quickly-spreading silence, so that all at once the sea could be heard sounding in monotonous cadence like a large muffled clock. A horse whinnied suddenly from the stables in the dark behind.

'My lords, ladies and gentlemen,' John Chass said, 'I would rather say my friends and neighbours, this is a great and happy day for all of us who are proud to call ourselves Her Majesty's loyal and devoted subjects.'

A catcall from the trees was drowned by cheers and claps not only from the terrace but from the shore and from behind the wall. The Annish people were nationalists to a Catholic; but as Catholics they were not jealous of rank nor did they think that self-respect forbade them to be polite. They would have greeted the Shah of Persia or the King of Siam with equal cordiality.

'Five hundred million people join this evening in gratitude and affection to one who for sixty years as queen, wife and mother, has given us all an example of duty and devotion——'

'Gawd bless the ould skate,' a drunken voice exclaimed from the park. 'I gave her a leg at the Alma and here's my hand now.'

Darcy and Jebb passed along the wall pouring neat whisky into mugs and tumblers. Old Jebb, lame in both legs, groused and grumbled at each step. Jebb hated the Jubilee because he had it fixed in his head that the Queen's picture would be spoilt by the heat of its illumination. Actually some blisters were raised on the new paint and Jebb's last days were poisoned by a savage quarrel with Grogan who had arranged the lights.

'Jubilees be damned,' he muttered; missing with the whisky all those who seemed to hope for it. Darcy, on the other hand, was full of responsibility and solicitude. 'Where's your mug, Anty Sukey?'

'At the far end from me ass, Master Darcy, and that's the other way from yours.'

Darcy, who did not like to be insulted in his livery hat, turned round and called out in an offended, pompous tone, 'Hi, you, Bridgy, bring your anty a tumbler.'

Bridget came with her tray of glasses. A dozen hands were thrust out to take them and Sukey said, 'Faith, Bridgy, it's thrue what they say, ye're as round as a blather of lard.'

Bridget did not seem to hear. She walked slowly along the wall. She had avoided coming near it; but now that she was there, under the stare of eyes, she did not mind them. She did not mind anything or anybody. She had no will, no purpose. She knew that Cleeve had deserted her, and she did not hope to escape disaster. She was sure that nothing could save her and this assurance rose from within her, as strong and convincing as the ambition which, three months before, had informed every cell of her body. Bridget did not know why she had dreamed or why she was now hopeless. She could not understand anything that had happened to her and she did not try. She did not want to think about it at all. Her weakness of the illiterate peasant, credulous in a world of fantasy, was now her strength; the power of an ass to bear the stick, though it beat him to death on his feet.

'Our hearts go out to her,' John Chass said in his clear, loud baritone, 'and hers, we know, is with us.' His voice conveyed perfectly the rich and sanguine character of the man, his instinctive confidence in the rightness of things, as established by natural providence, and also his delight in that rightness; in all the things of life, and especially the pleasure of entertaining so large a party. 'Who has seen the British reign of toleration and justice extended over half the globe.'

'And haven't we ryalty to ourselves,' old Dan said. He took up Shon's hand and offered it to public view like a treasure from his own collection. 'See that hand, the true share of ryalty. I have it myself. A thrue Corner hand.'

'Aye, a princely beauty,' the ragamuffin said. 'Thanks be to Gawd I saw that one for I never seen him before.'

'The ould stock' Dan, who seemed ten minutes before the ruin of a man, had miraculously filled out till he seemed almost the figure of John Chass. His chest swelled; his nose stood up. He graciously bent his head and slightly waved Shony's hand towards the circle, making them free of it.

'Aye,' said the mountain man with the singing voice, 'and they may talk of their kings and queens but the Corners were lying in their beds of down when Adam milked the first cow for their breakfast.'

'The Corners are the biggest robbers in Annish,' Con said, 'but why wouldn't they rob ye when ye let them.'

'Thrue for you, sor,' the mountain man answered. 'Robbers they are, ryal robbers. Didn't they shteal all Annish?' He turned round. 'All Annish.' His voice made a joy and marvel of conquest, which was, of course, imaginary. The Corners never stole all Annish.

'A kingdom,' Dan said gently turning Shon's hand in his huge dirty paw, 'and this wan will have it.'

Once more the eyes stared at Shon with enquiry, with an eagerness beyond curiosity; as if each man was striving to comprehend within himself a quality, a power, and a beauty.

It was the mountain men who burnt alive the Corner children in the rebellion of 1641. That was the other side of reverence.

Shon paid no attention to these remarks. He was used to their kind from his first years, when Kitty took him to Ballycorner in the perambulator. He was staring at the castle, where an unseen hand, carrying a taper high up between the windows of his father's dressing-room, was lighting fairy lamps. The bright curving lines quickly formed this shape.

209

The taper then wrote underneath these words, THE QUEEN GOD BLESS HER; but almost at once some of the lamps went out, so that small gaps appeared both in the outline above and the letters below, which read:

THE QUEEN GOD BLESS HER.

The taper had now descended to the ground. A voice behind Shon read out slowly, 'The quare god bless her, a quare enough wan.'

'A Pro-destant wan.'

Several voices laughed and Con said bitterly, 'Ach, ye may laff but what do ye do?'

'And who is that?' Sukey said.

Kitty, who had never taken her eyes from Shon's face, said softly, 'Who is it, my blessing?'

Shon thought that it looked like a coal scuttle but he felt that it would be wrong and stupid to say so. He murmured 'The Jubilee.'

Sukey gave a scream of delight and cried, 'Ah, but you're the smart wan.'

Old Dan, seeing the child's perplexity, instructed him. 'The Queen of England, master Shony, your own queen.' The Queen was not his queen, but he wished Shon to enjoy his own possession.

Shon glanced at the old man and then at the lights. 'My own queen.' He began to feel a share in this greatness and importance. His eyes widened, his eyebrows rose, his lips parted; he breathed, 'My own queen.' He gazed, throwing his feelings into this new idea, his own queen, his own part in imperial glory.

Old Dan, Sukey, the mountain men, watching his face, perfectly understanding the process which they could not describe or explain, which their minds did not even notice, smiled. Kitty, gazing with wide bright eyes, had a smile of ecstasy. She was lost in the happiness of her love.

Shony on the day after the Jubilee was found in high fever. His cough returned with violence. No secrets were ever kept at Castle Corner and it was soon known that he had broken out of bed; but neither was anybody, even Francie, blamed for it, because Mary Corner saw that this was a disaster. Mary Corner in a disaster was like a soldier with his back to the wall, too preoccupied and concentrated to think of blaming anyone for bringing him there.

Shon was luckily a good patient. He had been ill before and he knew how to do it; and he was an independent child and felt in illness an obligation to nurses. He was polite even to those he loved like his mother and Francie.

He now took great delight in the Jubilee and knowing that it had been an important event, he considered it his most important experience. Seeing a picture of the royal coach in the *London Illustrated*, he enlarged his ambition to drive like his father into one to be the Queen's coachman and spent most of his time practising with a toy gig whip. He would try to touch up the end of the bed with the tip of the whipcord, and catch the lash neatly on the stock. Even at night, when coughing kept him awake, he would flick it in the dark; and when the night nurse complained, Mary Corner said, with the calm, almost joking voice of a leader in a forlorn hope, 'I'm afraid it can't be helped just now.'

It was from the first realized by everybody except John Chass that the boy was dangerously ill. John Chass, though he had a natural repugnance from the sick and the unhappy, was sympathetic with them also from a natural sympathy. The conflicting instincts produced a breezy manner in the sick room and John Chass told his best stories to the greatest sufferers. He believed greatly in presents for sick people and the sicker they were, the larger his presents. He had brought to MacEwen, when in the crisis of pneumonia, after influenza, a box of five-inch cigars, which, as the man was unconscious, he gave to Lady MacEwen with the explanation, 'They'll be something to look forward to when he gets up again.'

He brought presents for Shon every day, mechanical toys, a new rocking horse, enormous illustrated books of horses and the British navy, for all of which Shon thanked him politely and affected a desire, until he was out of the room, when he returned at once to his whip practice. He wanted to master the whip.

John Chass himself was busy, luckily, as Mary and Hanna agreed, with urgent business and estate work. The urgent business was concerned with Cleeve who, it seemed, owed sixty pounds in London and had bilked his hotel. Benskin had paid the debts but John Chass was determined to repay Benskin, and he was also disturbed by the idea that Cleeve might be forming extravagant habits.

'What you have to remember,' he wrote to the boy at Porriton where he was still with the Chorleys, 'is that debt is ruinous to any kind of peace of mind.' He repeated to Cleeve, in fact, his own creed of an earlier time, feeling like other teachers that he must give the best and soundest instruction, the most general rule, whatever his own special experience might be.

The estate work was the deepening and enlarging of the little harbour below the terrace, which had to be done in fine weather. He spent every day among the workers there, in his oldest clothes, stepping over the boulders with a long measuring rod, or a bottle of whisky. His idea was to make the harbour fit for a steam launch. Lord Watlington had lately bought a launch and John Chass always had a little jealousy of a

211

man whose family had not lived in Annish for more than a hundred years.

'We need a launch,' he said, 'for picnics. With a launch we could go where we liked, any day, along the shore. It seems to me that picnics are getting into a rut and I'm told that some of the girls would rather play tennis. That will never do. They'll never get husbands at tennis.'

Meanwhile he saw an improvement in Shon every morning, until the last, when Grogan came running from the house to call him, from the rocks. Grogan had not found time even to put on his bowler.

'But he can't be worse, Grogan. He was so much better yesterday.'

'The mistress sent for you to come, sir.'

'It's always up and down with children.' John Chass laid down his rod and clambered slowly, with Grogan's help, to the terrace. 'The great thing in these cases, Grogan, is constitution—and the boy has a great constitution.'

On the top step of the landing he met Francie, weeping, and patting her on her fat shoulder, said, 'There's no need for that, Francie, my girl. The child's constitution would pull him through worse than this, and if he's a wee bit down to-day, he'll be up to-morrow.'

Shon, indeed, like other consumptives, had flashes of energy and would suddenly begin to chatter, laugh; make plans for the future. But he was wasted to a thinness only seen in young children; he seemed transparent as if his limbs were made of cartilage. His face, growing thinner and sharper had become the small image of his cousin Harry; resolute and fine, but more tranquil.

When John Chass was summoned, he had just had a hæmorrhage. The sheets had been changed and he lay propped up on clean pillows, with a face like thin wax.

His deathly look startled John Chass, but at once, hearing his father's voice, he opened his eyes, smiled and tried to sit forward. He enjoyed his father's visits more than anybody's; because John Chass would talk to him about fine points of driving, shooting, and tell true stories of great feats in these arts.

His mother, sitting beside him, put out her hand to prevent his leaning forward and said, 'You must lie still, my dear.'

Mrs. John was almost as white as Shon and she had already in her face the lines of old age; the look of one who habitually faces the end of things. She said to John Chass, 'He was just going to say his prayers.'

'Yes, yes.' John Chass, confused, bent over to kiss the boy's forehead. 'But Mary, are you sure he wants to say prayers at this time of day.'

'Mamma thought I'd better because it's the last time.'

John Chass could not speak in his astonishment and anger. He looked furiously at Mary, who was putting Shon's hands together. She said, 'I told him.'

212

'Told him what. But what do you mean?' and breaking into French, 'Have you no sense to frighten the boy so? It's cruel, abominable.'

'But it was necessary, John. How could one hide such a thing from him. And he was not frightened at all. Look at him,' and then in English, she said to Shon, 'My darling, you mustn't be frightened, you trust in God to keep you.'

She put his hands together and prompted him, 'Our father——'

It was true that Shon was not frightened. He did not have a clear idea of God but he knew how to die. It was something between a solemn kind of party and being in church. Toys were allowed but prayers were also said, like a grace. Decorum was necessary but otherwise a boy could amuse himself or practise his skill.

'Hallowed be thy name.'

John Chass was crimson with indignation at the sense of outrage. He knew what would happen; that this sort of thing would be too much for him.

'Thy kingdom come——'

John Chass choked; tears jerked down his rosy cheeks.

'Thy will be done,' Shon said in his clear voice. Mary's lips moved with his, and her cheeks trembled; but no tears ran from her eyes, red with sleeplessness.

When Shon had finished, he asked for his whip. John Chass went to the mantelpiece and brought it to him, muttering indignantly that he would soon be up and then they'd go for a good drive in the new dog cart.

Shon looked up at his father and his lips parted. Both were afraid that he was going to say, 'You know I'll never get up again.' John Chass seemed to shrink and Mary touched Shon's shoulder as if to warn him. But the boy said only, 'I won't play with it. I just wanted it.'

'Ye'll soon be well again now,' John Chass said, with a kind of gasp. 'Won't you, my darling, and then we'll go and have a grand drive and you shall carry the big whip.'

Shon raised his eyebrows and looked at his father doubtfully, but he felt the pressure of his mother's hand, squeezing his, and he said politely, as if the hand reminded him of his manners, 'I should like that awfully.'

'Yes, with the new whip,' John Chass said, 'and we'll go tandem, and I tell you what, my heart's blood, we'll have a new boat too—a steam boat.'

Shon said that he would enjoy the steam boat greatly; he fully understood that his father, in this crisis, needed humouring.

'With a brass funnel, begad, like a real admiral's boat. We'll have a brass funnel to it, my darling heart, won't we, now, yes, and brass rails—you see now, Mary, there's the colour in his cheeks, and he's laffing at us."

Shon, after a moment's hesitation, smiled and said, 'Yes, a brass funnel.'

He was calm and happy; he had a complete grasp of the situation. His only moment of distress was when a few minutes later, Mary, hearing Doctor Hanna on the stairs, went out of the room, to ask him if an injection could be given.

Shon, dozing, waked up, found her absent, and suddenly cried out. He was afraid that she would not come before he had died. He explained taking her hand, 'I hadn't said good-bye.'

A few minutes later he had another fit of coughing; blood flowed from his mouth, he was dying. He could not speak, but when his mother stooped to kiss him he pursed up his lips dutifully like one saying good-bye and thank you after a party.

Shon's funeral brought a large attendance. It happened that there had been no big funeral in Annish for seven or eight months, and so the people were glad of an event. Cleeve came, of course, from Porriton, but also Slatter returned from Bath, to show his proper feeling and to use his mourning hat band.

The tenants came from the farthest glens; from the Lake of Shadows thirty miles beyond Knockeen. Some of them, Irish speakers from beyond Mawlin Head, had not been seen at the castle for twenty years. They waked all night in the castle kitchen; and the next day, after the funeral, they were still lingering about the scene of their meeting. A funeral in Annish, especially a child's funeral, gives strong feelings more exciting and deep than anything except an election. It touches a man's bottom nerve. It goes deeper even than a glass of whisky and sends him home with the feeling there are great things still in the world.

Shon's funeral had been a grand experience. No one wanted to end it. The old men were still seated in the castle kitchen on the second afternoon, talking of other deaths, all the visitations of fate; of cows that aborted, and debts and emigrations; and the young ones were as restless as they always are at the end of a party, when no one wishes to say good-bye and go away into his ordinary loneliness.

Breedy Macan was in and out every moment, full of excitement which changed every minute from curiosity to mischief and back again.

He said, grinning at Bridget, 'It's easy to lose a wain these days and easy to get wan too.'

Bridget went into the old back kitchen where she was baking a scone in a pan over the turf. She was turning her scone when Sukey took her by the arm and screamed, 'Is it true what they're saying?'

She looked Bridget up and down and then stared into her face. Bridget, who had prepared no defence, who had simply waited for the catastrophe, turned red and smiled foolishly. Sukey gave her a slap on

214

the side of the head and then tried to drag her out of the door, screaming 'Get out, ye bitch—out of me kitchen.'

Bridget fell down on her knees in the doorway, and Sukey, taking her by the hair, beat her over the face and head until she was tired. Bridget made no attempt to defend herself, even by lifting a hand.

The visitors, crowding from behind, peering over Sukey's shoulders, did not interfere because the quarrel was a family one. Family feeling in Annish is extremely strong in both directions.

When Sukey was tired of beating her niece, Bridget got up, with the blood streaming from her nose and mouth, went back to the scullery, looked at the scone to see that it was not burning, and then picked up a hot water can and set out for the stairs. It was time for the gentlemen's hot water.

She was a little confused by the thumps on her ear and jaw; she did not understand that she was bleeding. Peggy, meeting her, was just pushing her into the housemaid's closet when Mary Corner, in her new black dress, came upstairs and cried, 'What's all this, Margaret?'

Mary's hair was white and her cheeks the colour of bone. Her sunk eyes were scarlet as if cut round with a knife and she looked at fifty-two like a woman of seventy.

No one had seen her cry and on the very afternoon of the funeral she had begun, as before, to run all over the house and scream up and down the stairs her enquiries and reproaches. She had no affectations in her misery.

She ejaculated now at sight of Bridget. 'What have you done to yourself, gel. There's blood on your face. Your nose is bleeding.'

'It's nawthin' mam.'

'Nonsense. Look at your nose. Good gracious, come here into my room. Lie down flat on the sofa, till I put a piece of blue paper on the roof of your mouth.' She looked in an apron pocket for a piece of blue paper.

Meanwhile Cleeve was waiting in his bedroom for his hot water. He leant against the bed with his hands deep in his dressing-gown pockets and gazed at a hole in the shabby carpet. He felt ill and exhausted. The funeral had been an agony. It was as though the words themselves and especially the sounds, the music, the roll of Mr. Feenix' voice had struck directly upon the nerves of some mysterious animal inside him, making it cry out with his lips and weep with his eyes. It had frightened him and humiliated him to feel himself helpless in the tearing claws of this grief, stirred up and maddened by words and an American organ. It was a horrible experience.

He was exhausted and he felt depressed and apprehensive. He had not seen Bridget and he did not think of her, but he felt her now like something in the air, something that belonged to Castle Corner, and all his memories of it, dripping trees, the bog in winter, the little waves hissing among the stones on an empty shore, showers out of an Atlantic cloud falling on the broken pump in the yard, the tune of the fiddling tinker that beat his ass to death. He was oppressed by something like his funeral grief; a barbarous disquiet from which he looked back to Lucy Chorley and his happiness at Bellavista like a fallen soul gazing at paradise. Bellavista seemed now full of a lovely serenity and brightness; it was like some pre-Raphaelite panel, a Perugino on a wedding coffer, showing a sky full of sunshine without any sun to make a shadow, and below, fields and streams as smooth and scentless as jewels.

There was a knock on the door; it was immediately burst open and Peggy staggered into the room with the huge bath can. She placed it neatly in the middle of the bath, by a swing which seemed to pull her whole flimsy body out of shape; and then, still panting, spread a clean towel over it.

She said sharply, red and bitter with exertion, 'The cold is in the jug, Master Cleeve, and Sukey has been beating Bridgy. She's with the mistress this minute.'

'Beating Bridgy, why?'

'You should know that.' She went out with a kind of angular rheumatic flounce.

Cleeve felt confused but calm; as if someone had said to him, 'You can only die once.'

He walked calmly to his aunt's room and he would perhaps have remained calm, if opening the door he had not come plump upon Bridget stretched on the sofa at the foot of the big bed, with blood on her swollen lips. Then again, he was gripped by a nervous pity and horror; by natural sympathy; and he cried out, 'Oh, Aunty, it's not poor Bridgy's fault.'

Mary, who was peering into the medicine cupboard over the wash-stand, turned red in astonishment and cried sharply, 'What's that, what are you talking about, boy?'

Cleeve was confused. He did not know what to do and he felt acute misery. He stared stupidly at his aunt, and after a long moment said in a fluttering voice, 'It's really my fault.'

'What do you mean? You didn't hit the poor gel, did you? Your fault?'

Cleeve felt that it was not all his fault; that the affair was in fact very complicated. It needed careful explanation. But the moment he said, 'It's all my fault,' a way opened through the confusion and the difficulty. All was made simple and happy. He had only to confess and accept his fate.

'No, it's my fault. I promised to marry her—and I will marry her.'

The very words were salvation. Cleeve, as he spoke, seemed to be rising from despair, as if angelic wings had raised him. He felt mastery and even triumph. Even his features became calm and noble; his expression had something of Lucy Chorley's. But it was necessary still to make Mary Corner understand the situation, and when she did so at last, and Bridget, with another wail, had confirmed it, she was not at all impressed. She burst into loud scolding. 'You ought to be ashamed of yourselves, both of you. I'm surprised at you, Cleeve, you silly, silly boy—I don't know what your father will say. And you, Bridget Foy, a great gel like you. I thought you had more sense. Good gracious me.'

Bridget, still lying flat, as she had been ordered, began to sob, and Mary, already softening, cried, 'Now, that's enough. It's no good crying now, you silly child. That won't do any good. And I suppose it's no good asking what you're going to do next, for you don't know.'

Cleeve still clinging to his new moral grandeur drew himself up and said again, 'But Aunty, I said I was going to marry her and I mean to.'

'Stuff, you silly boy. Good gracious indeed.'

'But I will. I want to, I promised her.'

'Did he promise you, Bridget Foy?'

Bridget uttered a kind of wail which seemed to be an affirmative. She was now suffering wretchedness. The mistress' scolding kindness had removed her apathy, and she was extremely sorry for herself.

Mary sat down, overwhelmed. She asked, 'And did you believe him?'

'I did, mam.'

'Oh dear, that gels can be so silly; and Cleeve, you're a very wicked boy. Go away, go away now. I don't want to look at you. Go away and leave me till I know what's to be done with this poor silly Bridget.'

'But Aunty—I tell you I want to——'

Mary stamped her foot and cried, 'Haven't you done enough of what you want. Go away, you nasty boy.' Her voice and look were so fierce that Cleeve, though with a dignified and noble expression, did leave the room.

But he was angry and hurt, for it seemed to him that he was doing the right thing, the only possible thing which could relieve the situation, and give it some nobility and moral grandeur; something, for instance, which the Chorleys could approve and even admire.

He dressed quickly and went to look for John Chass.

John Chass was in the court room with a mass of papers, and a glass of whisky in front of him. He, too, seemed older, and his mourning made him seem smaller and more compact, as if sorrow had physically pressed upon him.

John Chass, in fact, had shown more grief than Mary at his son's death. His large face had become deeply creased; and for some days he had gone about with a stupefied look, as if from a heavy blow on the skull. Something of that look still remained; but already the eyes were bright and intelligent, the mouth had expression. It was as if an irrepressible spirit were already peeping through the mask of despair.

He spent most of his time in the court room, looking through his bills and examining long due creditors' accounts. The family in the house and kitchen had been impressed by this reform. But the truth was that John Chass at this time attended to some unpleasant business, partly because it was unpleasant and so, to his instinct, appropriate to a mourner, and partly because he had nothing else to do. He did not want to go fishing, or sailing or driving; and he could not find, for the moment, any pleasure in his books, even in Nat Gould. He was extremely glad to see Cleeve; and this pleasure did not leave him when he grasped, as he did very quickly, Cleeve's errand. He shook his head indeed and said, 'This is a bad business. One of Padsy's daughters, too. Dear, dear.'

'And of course I'll marry her, Uncle.'

John Chass was smiling. He said, 'Well, well, well. I wouldn't have thought it of you.'

'I meant to marry her even at the beginning.'

'Is that how it came about? You shouldn't have told her that.'

'But I meant it.'

'She ought to have known better, and so ought you. Well, well, well, I'd no idea of it. You young rascal.' He gazed at Cleeve with a brightening eye. His voice and look had never been so affectionate towards his nephew. 'But you know,' he said, as one instructing youth, 'things aren't what they were. This will cost somebody fifty pounds, and maybe more than that.'

Cleeve repeated with emphasis his resolution to marry Bridget. He was bound in honour to do so. John Chass was not incredulous. He understood Cleeve far better than Mary, because he was more detached. He said with respect and sympathy, 'I'm sure you would—it's a very right feeling, too.' He looked thoughtfully, almost piously at the whisky decanter, and with a reverent gesture poured out a weak whisky and water. 'Yes, a very proper feeling.' He pushed the glass towards Cleeve. 'A wee drink—it will do you good.'

Cleeve pretended not to notice the drink. He said again, 'It's the only right thing to do.'

'Well now,' John Chass said, 'now you mention it—it mightn't be just the right thing for Bridget—to be taken out of her class and religion, too. I don't suppose she can even read or write.'

'She can learn.'

'Why should she learn anything after she's married. It's not in reason that she would take that trouble for what she's never missed. And what will you do to keep a wife and family?'

'I could take a farm.'

'You could take it, but would you make a living out of it?' John

218

Chass said, mildly expostulating. 'It would be no life at all either for you or Bridget.' He pushed the glass towards Cleeve as if to say, 'Drink and be reasonable.' After a little reflection he said, 'Well now, I am thinking—you said once that you'd like to go to Oxford.'

'I can't do that now. I shall have to work at something.'

'You might work at Oxford. Yes, it's not a bad notion of yours, now I think of it. And you could choose a profession afterwards.'

'But, Uncle, how can I go now?'

'Well,' pushing the glass, 'I suppose your father and I could manage it between us.'

Cleeve wanted to repeat that he would marry Bridget; but when he met John Chass' eye he felt small and ashamed as if, after all, his decision to marry Bridget was not particularly noble, as if there were some humbug in it. He was even afraid that John Chass might be thinking of the word, though he knew that he would never use it. He sat white and shaken; feeling so unhappy that he was ready to cry.

John Chass pushed the glass against his fingers and said in his good-natured voice, 'I know how you feel—it's a very proper feeling—but the question is now—what's the best thing to do?'

'I'm afraid I couldn't think of Oxford,' Cleeve said.

'Well, you'll have this place some day, I suppose, and it's only right that you should get something out of it now.'

'It's awfully kind of you, Uncle.' The glass was in his hand. He took a sip. The grandeur was dying before John Chass' eye; and in its place, to Cleeve's surprise, was a sensation of power, almost of self-respect. 'But how,' he asked, 'could anyone leave Bridget in her terrible position?' John Chass said that of course she would not be left in it. 'Perhaps,' he said, 'we could send her to America, or Liverpool, with capital to set her up in a little shop—say a sweetie shop. Do you know, though I hardly like to suggest it, I believe the best thing for everybody would be for you to catch the next boat to England. You might go back to your friends the Chorleys for instance.'

Cleeve took another sip with complete dignity. It had somehow become possible for him to preserve his moral triumph and also to escape from marrying Bridget.

John Chass developed his theme. That Cleeve, for Bridget's sake, should remove himself and leave the way open for a husband more likely to bring her happiness. 'Of course, the matter would have to be kept quiet.'

Cleeve looked doubtful, pursed his lips and sipped his glass as if it had been the cup of Socrates. 'I still feel I ought to marry her,' he said, 'but it's what you think, Uncle, would be best for Bridget.'

Within twenty-four hours he was sitting at Lucy Chorley's feet, in the drawing-room of Bellavista, listening to Chorley's reading of *The Coming of Arthur*.

Meanwhile Mary and John Chass, who was completely revived by the interest of the negotiation, visited Father MacFee. On the next morning Bridget was sent off to confession and communion. She was absolved and reconciled to her church.

Father MacFee flatly rejected the plan of sending Bridget out of the country, to America or England. 'A very bad plan,' he told John Chass, 'which might well be the ruin of both mother and child. Far better for the girl to feel disgrace here than to go away among strangers where there'd be no one to know how or what she did.'

Father MacFee never liked to lose a parishioner from under his eye, and his power of direction.

'Then we must see if we can marry her,' John Chass said. 'Where are our bachelors. There's Grogan, Darcy; Rifty used to be a sweetheart of hers.' He went to find Rifty, who was in the yard strapping Dapple.

Rifty knew, of course, what was coming to him. The whole castle had followed the affair with breathless interest. When John Chass, who, by inattention, had placed over his mourning an old brown hat, appeared from the back door by the gunroom, Rifty gave a hiss like a whistle and threw himself upon Dapple with a fury that made the horse's tail jump at the root with nervous satisfaction.

John Chass stopped by the pump, and looked up at a pigeon on the hay loft. Then he looked all round him, at the sky, the buildings and finally, the pump. His expression was one of pleased surprise. Rifty, hissing like a railway engine, tore at Dapple's round, muscular croup. The horse, delighted by his violence, bent its neck and nibbled at his hair.

'That's the good lad, Rifty,' John Chass said. 'Tear into him.'

'Aye, and he's worth it. Look at the coat he has."

'It's quite time you had a bit of a rise, Rifty. Indeed, you're old enough to be married.'

'Thank you kindly, sir. But as for being married, that's all a tale.'

'I used to see you going about with Bridget Foy.'

'Aye, so I did. Houl up.' Rifty struck Dapple on the nose to save his left ear from its teeth. 'But then, sir, ye know, there's been things said about wee Bridgeen.'

'Is that so—but if Bridgeen had a fortune to her, you'd find that no one would say things about her.'

'If what they say is true, they might be joking me, sir—fortune or no.' Rifty continued all the time strapping Dapple's grey and black coat, and presenting to John Chass only his right ear and sharp-edged profile. This was not awkwardness; it was tact. In Annish it was the thing to give delicate negotiations a light and easy touch by carrying on some other occupation at the same time. Farmers in the market would whittle sticks or mend their whip lashes while they came to grips over the odd shilling.

John Chass admired Dapple's coat and patted its croup. Then he said, 'Well now, Rifty, you know they wouldn't laugh at any man that made his fortune by a good match.'

'They wouldn't if it was enough of a fortune,' Rifty agreed.

'She'll have forty pounds on the day she's married, and no one would call that a joke.'

'Faith, sor, ye don't know them, they'd be joking me for two times that and a heifer.'

'Would they joke you for fifty?'

'Deed and they would, sor. It's not that I'm craving the money, sor, but I wouldn't be dishonouring marriage and Bridgeen herself or you, sor.'

'What I think is this, Rifty, that your sense of humour is too delicate. There are plenty at the back of Knockeen who would laugh down Bob Duker himself if they could jingle twenty pounds at him.'

Rifty turned round at last and faced his master. 'Ah no, sor,' he cried. 'Ye know I'm fond of Bridget, and ye wouldn't be putting a stranger on her.'

This was a good argument. Marriage in Annish might involve calculation, but it was not all calculation. The people were poor; they knew the value of money and that other things being equal, an ugly wife with forty pounds and a cow was more likely to bring happiness than a pretty one with nothing. But they didn't marry without affection and knowledge of each other. Rifty knew that John Chass would not wish to marry Bridget to a stranger.

The bargaining therefore was soon over. Rifty accepted eighty pounds with a heifer, a sow in farrow, and the tenant right of twelve statute acres on Knockeen; a fortune which would put him far beyond the reach of laughter. The marriage was settled. Padsy, who had heard nothing of the affair, at first objected to the match; then finding Bridget's case, tried to beat Rifty for seducing her. Afterwards he told everybody that Rifty was a blackguard who had not only seduced Bridget but whose motive had been the seizing of her fortune. Con, of whose reactions everyone had been afraid, was drunk when he heard the news. He had been drunk for a week. He said only after long consideration, 'Good luck to the young devil if she knows what she wants for none of the rest of ye know annything.'

Bridget herself made no objection to the match. She refused, however, to speak to Rifty; so that Sukey, abusing her night and day, had the excuse of calling her sulky. But the girl was not sulky; she would not speak because she could not. She was one of those who earn the

221

reputation of sulks when in fact they have no feeling at all; no sense of grievance; only discouragement and hopelessness.

But she responded to the will of others. At the wedding when Father MacFee asked her the usual questions she gave him the responses which belonged to those questions.

The marriage feast continued for two days and a night, with dancing and drinking; and it was only ended then because Father MacFee, scandalized, came to Knockeen and told Rifty that he would denounce him from the pulpit if he opened another bottle or knocked another keg.

But Rifty was in triumph. From that time he was a changed man. He walked differently, he spoke differently; when he made a bargain in the market he slapped hands in the style of a big butcher or farmer. Wherever he went, one could see in his face and bearing the gay astonishment of his exaltation.

VI

CLEEVE THOUGHT OF Bellavista as an earthly paradise of peace and only gradually he perceived that the Chorleys, except Cobden, were extremely busy people. Their continuous activities were not noticed because they performed them unobtrusively, as if, like priests engaged in some ceremonial, they must not be seen in a hurry. They were never impatient or brusque, yet each had a crowded engagement book and each morning there was a new problem about the day's plans, who was to have the trap and who the carriage, how Mrs. Chorley was to reach the shops, Lucy her two different committees, Chorley his meeting or the works. Every day, too, there was a crisis; something unexpected; a visitor from America to be met at the station, or a change of plan by some visiting preacher, and this upset the whole programme. Old General Pynsant's sudden death at the end of July caused even a visible perturbation in the family. Cleeve for the first time saw Lucy agitated as she passed through the big drawing-room. He was so surprised that he asked her what was wrong.

'Have you seen Cobden?'

'He went to the summer house just now with some books.'

'Oh dear.'

Mrs. Chorley came in with her anxious face. 'And if Cobden is going into town——'

'He's in the summer house and he took his books.' She turned again to Cleeve. 'Did he have a portfolio—a big black thing?'

'Yes, I think he did.'

'Then that settles it,' Lucy said in a tragic tone. 'We'll send the wire by the trap and I can't go to the station.' Seeing Cleeve's face, her expression changed, became tranquil and she said, 'I'm sorry—its only plans.'

'When are you coming for that walk?'

'Any time you like—in five minutes.' She slipped out with her mother and their voices receded. Twenty minutes later she was walking in the garden with Cleeve as if she had nothing else to think of.

'Why mustn't Cobden be disturbed when he has his black portfolio?' Cleeve asked.

'Because it means that he's writing his poem. Poor boy,' she sighed, 'it's giving him the most awful time.'

223

'What sort of a poem is it?'

'A triolet. He always writes triolets.'

'He's good at them, is he?'

'I really think he is. I think they're rather wonderful. Of course they're agony to do. But I suppose they wouldn't be worth doing if they weren't.'

'Triolets are rather limited, aren't they?'

'That's why they're so hard—they're so challenging as Cobden says.'

Cleeve still felt that a triolet could not be great poetry, but his admiration for Cobden, who was already an Oxford man, and his affection for all the Chorleys, forbade him to say so.

'But, Cleeve,' Lucy argued with his silent doubt, 'suppose Cobden did a really perfect triolet; perfection is, after all, the only standard of quality.'

'So you think a first-class pepper pot is greater than a second-class cathedral?'

Lucy reflected. Her eyelashes, in the sun, made a violet shadow on her pale cheeks, now once more bright with her quick blood. 'I'm quite sure our Morris sugar sifter is far greater than Milan.'

'I see what you mean,' Cleeve said, pressing her arm and gazing at her cheek with delight which was full of laughter. There was no awe in Cleeve's affection for girls. But neither was there condescension nor jealousy. That was why he was attractive to women of character.

'But you don't agree?'

Cleeve turned his attention upon the idea and noticing it clearly for the first time, felt a sharp stir of interest. 'It's certainly interesting, but there's something rather odd about it. One ought to know about it. One ought to know about it, things like that.'

But before he could discuss it Lucy murmured, 'I wonder would you mind—I have to go in for a moment.'

He was surprised to find himself near the house. Lucy had imperceptibly directed the walk that way so that now she could break it off gently, easily. She disappeared, of course, for the rest of the day; but the smoothness of the disappearance made it seem that there was no break in their tranquil happiness together.

Cleeve was used, of course, to the notion of country house obligations. John Chass had his official duties, and his shabby court room in the back passage was still a nerve centre of government; Mary Corner had her sick visits, and when he went to see Stella Pynsant at the Pynsants' place, New Grange, about four miles on the other side of Porriton where, in the absence of the new made widow on a yacht in the Mediterranean, she was spending her holidays with a school friend, he was asked sometimes to help in the delivery of parish magazines. Stella also went to first-aid classes and taught in Sunday school.

But the Corners and Stella performed these duties as a matter of course. At Bellavista they were discussed at every meal; they were regarded as the most important things in life; and everyone who came to the house seemed to take the same attitude towards life, that it was a field of political and religious endeavour. Everyone had a feeling of responsibility towards the world, and even when Lucy played the piano in the evening to some visiting preacher or M.P. the listeners had the air of performing a duty to music; a pleasant and elevating duty, but still a duty.

There were visitors every day, and all were received in such a manner that Cleeve at first supposed them to be equally important. He was surprised to find out that one dignified gentleman, chairman of Lucy's library committee was a Porriton draper. A little old Welshman called Jones, with the face and head of a miniature Socrates, who walked through Bellavista as if he owned it, turned out to be the editor of the *Porriton Gazette*, of which Chorley was chief proprietor.

Old Jones came every Saturday evening, and treated Chorley like a small boy. 'My dear Adam, what stuff you talk. I don't know what your father would have said.'

He was greatly excited about a county council election for Motcombe. The old General's death had left a seat vacant, and Benskin was proposed for it, but the very idea horrified Jones.

'One of the worst of the Kaffir drivers,' he barked.

'He's given a good deal to the party.'

'I always wondered how we took his money,' and he sat with his mouth open and his thick white eyebrows in the air, visibly wondering. He had a habit, like many old men, of leaving his mouth open after he had uttered some emphatic speech, as if he had suddenly been taken with a doubt of its value.

But Jones did not wonder long. He quickly closed his mouth again, frowned and snorted at Chorley, 'That chap Benskin is a menace—he thinks money can do anything. But he'll get a shock at this election. It's the first time he's come out into the open and it'll be the last. Young Porfit tells me that all the Motcombe chapels are against him.'

Chorley defended his friend in a good-humoured way, saying that the important thing for Liberals was to pull together on the big issues like Free Trade and Home Rule. Then he suggested, as usual after dinner, a little music; Lucy, without making any fuss went to the piano and all the visitors broke off their conversation and threw themselves into attentive attitudes, opening their hearts and minds for the message no doubt intended for them. Even old Jones in his highest indignation against the landlords or the Government, never interrupted music unless

225

it was definitely unclassical, and when Lucy had finished, he said thank you in a tone of reverent gratitude.

These thank-yous after music at Bellavista had the quality of amens. Cleeve was astonished one Saturday evening to hear that old Jones was a devoted atheist.

'I thought he was a preacher.'

'Yes, he's a Free Trade preacher.' Cobden was exhausted after a terrible struggle with the rhymes for Helen. Lucy looking at him sympathetically said, 'Go to bed, Cob, you're worn out.'

They were in the hall, each holding a bedroom candle, and Cleeve was waiting for Cobden to go upstairs in order to say a private good night to Lucy. He hoped sometimes that he might dare to kiss her but he had not yet dared. He gazed at her now and was struck by her exhausted look in the upward light of the candles. Her eyes and cheeks were hollow. It was as though one saw beneath the young, smooth skin the harsh, angular shape of some gothic saint as carved on a tomb.

'Lucy, it's you that ought to be in bed.'

She smiled at him, surprised by his solicitude for her. Most people took Lucy's unselfishness for granted but unselfish people appreciate a thought for them even more than the selfish who demand notice. They receive it so seldom.

'Lucy also has a Liberal conscience,' Cobden said. 'She won't live long.'

'What nonsense, Cob.'

'And she saw her friend Mr. Porfit this morning—that always leaves her jaded.'

'My friend Porfit.' Lucy turned pink.

'Half Porriton admired your smile to-day when he took off his hat.'

'Well, if you're talking nonsense.' She turned as if to go upstairs.

'Is Porfit an admirer?' Cleeve asked.

'I hope not.' Her voice was startled. She looked at Cleeve and seemed about to say something more, then suddenly put out her hand, 'Good night, Cleeve.'

'Good night, darling.'

There was a slight pause. Brother and sister had the air of avoiding comment or glance. Then they looked at each other, and Cobden said, 'Good night, darlint.'

This made Cleeve's embarrassing tenderness into an Irish whim. But Cleeve did not accept the position of celt. He said, 'No, I meant darling.'

'You'd better go, Lucy,' Cobden said. 'The young man grows particular. It's worse than Porfit.'

'Oh Cob,' Lucy protested. She turned and slowly went upstairs. She seemed suddenly as tired as she looked.

226

Porfit at that time had just come to live at Porriton. Although he was already a well known lay preacher and radical speaker in the West, and many of the radical clubs were talking him into parliament, he was still in deep poverty. His father, dead three years, had kept a small stationer's shop in Motcombe, but the business had gradually failed in the hands of the widow. It was said that the landlord turned the Porfits out and that this was the beginning of Porfit's bitterness against the landlords, and especially his attacks on the General which were supposed to have hastened the old man's death. In fact Mrs. Porfit left merely because she could not pay the rent; and Porfit's attacks never reached the ears of the General, already ill. What actually happened was more interesting. Porfit, not at the time when he left Motcombe but six weeks later, went there on Sunday and preached a sermon calling down God's anger upon the bloody minded and the oppressors, especially the landlords. Three days later the General was found dead in his bed at New Grange.

Benskin, whom Porfit had mentioned by name as one of the oppressors, was told by his agent that this incident might cost him his seat on the county council. 'It's had a terrific effect round Motcombe.'

'But Porfit knew the old man was dangerously ill. I happen to know he asked Dr. Brown.'

The agent shook his head in admiration. 'I might have guessed it. That chap's a wonder. And he's got the chapels with him too. It's lucky he's not eligible for the council himself. That's one advantage of his leaving the place. But I shouldn't wonder if he stood for the Porriton council against Chorley—he'd win too.'

'He wouldn't stand against another Nonconformist.'

The young agent winked. 'Wouldn't he? Give the chap a chance at anything. It's a good thing he's broke.'

Porfit, in fact, was looking for a job. One of his first applications was to Chorley for regular work on the *Gazette*. He wrote and also called.

Porfit was always glad to be going to Bellavista. His admiration and affection for the Chorleys, their house and everything about them, dated from the time when, as a choir boy, he had come there on the annual festival of chapel choirs. It was one of his earliest recollections, and the most generous. A child has a long memory for his first generous expansion of spirit; and Porfit was a man of strong sympathies and affections. He really loved the Chorleys. They, not Pynsant or Lord Porriton at the Hall, were the great people of his social idea. Porriton Hall, New Grange, and other great houses, with their large gardens, parks, galleries, stables, disgusted him. He called their owners robber barons, and asked why Porriton should be allowed to keep five hundred acres of good land for his deer; or the General to employ thirty

227

gardeners to grow plants that God had never intended to be seen in England. But he could find nothing immoral in Bellavista where there were only four gardeners; and no menservants in the house.

He exulted, too, to think that the Chorleys, Nonconformists like himself, were better looking and better educated than any Tory magnate in the district; that Adam Chorley had been to the same Oxford college as Lord Porriton. He was fond of comparing Lucy Chorley with Stella Pynsant and saying, 'When you see them together, you'd think Miss Chorley was a princess going out with a servant girl; and if you talked to them you'd be sure of it.'

That was why the sight of Bellavista as he went through the fields, made him twirl his umbrella and smile to himself.

The Chorleys were still at breakfast. It was Lucy who, glancing out of the window, first saw Porfit and who exclaimed, 'Oh poor Papa—Mr. Porfit.'

Mrs. Chorley looked anxiously at her husband and said, 'At least you can get it over.'

Chorley had already heard from Porfit asking for work; and he found it difficult to refuse him in his extremity. Husband and wife had discussed the matter for half the preceding night. The debate, like all in the Chorley family, had been complicated and anxious; because so many things had to be considered. Mrs. Chorley had no sooner pointed out that Porfit had slandered Benskin, than Chorley reminded her of his justification. 'Though two blacks don't make a white. Porfit, however, is essentially sincere and he has made great sacrifices both for the chapel work and the Party in Motcombe.'

'Isn't there any room for him in the works?'

'I thought of that. But then if Benskin comes in——' and they found themselves discussing another urgent and difficult problem; Benskin's offer to finance a reorganization of the works.

Benskin and Chorley were already fellow directors in several local companies, but Chorley felt that there was a difference in sitting on the same board with the financier, and taking him into partnership. On the other hand, Benskin's offer was a very good one.

'The fact is that Benskin has money to spare and it's all new money. He's been investing right and left for the last five years. I'm told he owns half the ship yard at Granport.'

'All from the one mine—but of course it's a gold mine.'

'The Klipspringer is one of the richest—a fountain of wealth.'

For a moment they both contemplated the idea of a deep, dark hole in Africa, spurting up a shower of gold which was now falling upon Granport and Motcombe and Porriton; upon all the west.

Chorley gave a sigh and said, 'But there's something I don't like about the idea of a partnership.'

'Tainted money,' Mrs. Chorley said hopefully. She thought this was the right phrase.

'Yet you know, my dear, that money itself is strictly impersonal. Old Jones is rather absurd with his talk about tainted money.'

'And you do want somebody to help you at the factory—someone to take responsibility when you have to be away on the committee——'

Chorley's public work grew every year; and lately, the member for Porriton, old and slack, had delegated more and more of the local party routine to him.

'Perhaps Mr. Porfit could be employed as a sub agent?' Mrs. Chorley suggested.

'I thought of that, but is he the kind of man who ought to be representing liberalism—officially. You know what the G.O.M. thought of that kind of demagogue—that he is ultimately a danger as well as a discredit to his own side.'

Nothing was decided in the long conference, tiring to both, but exhausting to Mrs. Chorley, whose object, in all such discussions, was to agree with her husband. Once or twice, she grasped at a proposition as at a raft, but always it broke up in her hand, dissolved into the surrounding lucidity in which she swam. Chorley was always very clear and definite in speech; it was his decisions which were elusive.

'Poor papa,' Lucy said. 'Now's the time to escape.'

'Escape!' Chorley looked surprised. 'But why should I run away from Mr. Porfit?'

'Porfit!' Cleeve jumped up and looked out of the window. 'Why, it's the piano tuner.'

Lucy smiled at him. 'What do you mean, piano tuner?'

'That's what I thought he was when I met him in London. Why,' he asked, sitting down again, 'do piano tuners look like piano tuners?'

'They don't,' Cobden said sadly, 'except for the purpose of breakfast epigram. Have we decided who is going by the trap?'

'I can walk,' Mrs. Chorley said. 'I'd like to walk.'

'My dear mother, you know that can't be allowed.'

'But I like walking.'

The family paid no attention to this remark, and Mrs. Chorley returned to her silent preoccupation. This trance of Mrs. Chorley's, when she raised her hook nose and gazed out at the air over people's heads, intimidated strangers with the idea of lofty thoughts not to be disturbed; but it was in fact a trance of worry about plans, meals, visitors, Cobden, Lucy, her husband and especially time tables. Mrs. Chorley had once been the resolute woman she looked, but family life among the Chorleys, the endless difficulty of making decisions when each member of the family had to consider all the rest, had long broken her nerve. The question of who was to have the trap, who the brougham, at what time and where, was not decided when Chorley got up and left the room.

'Poor papa,' Lucy said. 'Poor Mr. Porfit always puts his teeth on edge.'

'Why does one hate Porfit so much?' Cleeve asked.

'But one doesn't,' Lucy protested.

'No, I suppose you couldn't hate anybody.'

'If she did, she'd be afraid to admit it,' Cobden said getting up from the table.

'How absurd—why should I be afraid?'

'Conscience.' The melancholy voice floated back through the door. Mrs. Chorley sighed and murmured something about the trap; Lucy coloured and said, 'Cob is rather too silly. I'm sure his conscience is much more troublesome than mine.'

Breakfast was over; the family dispersed, and in a moment it seemed as if the house was empty. The sunlight bars falling through the very tall windows of the ground floor, on bright carpets, gilt frames, palms set on marble pedestals, on the Thorwaldsen, the Canova in the long drawing-room and the Venus de Milo in the hall, seemed to illuminate some royal museum palace before any sight-seers had arrived.

It was the tranquillity of Bellavista which was for Cleeve its characteristic. Even the servants, all women, had a gentle, quakerish look, which was as different from the professional reserve of a conservative and Church of England maid, as the calm of a mystic from the imperturbability of a judge. They seemed to rejoice with the visitor, while they wished him good morning with the tea, or told him that the bath was ready.

At this time in the morning, no maid was even seen. They had got up at five to do the cleaning. Lucy whose duty it was to arrange the flowers moved silently over the thick carpets. She, too, appreciated the peace of the house, even though she knew how much maintenance it required. On this morning she brought in lilies, and having filled a great blue and white jar in the drawing-room, she passed like a ghost, in her muslin frock, through the connecting door into a small sitting-room or ante room between the drawing- and dining-room. Here she stopped abruptly. Any other girl would have exclaimed. She saw beneath the portière of the half open door, a man's legs.

Suddenly she recognized Cleeve's slippers, trodden down at the heels. She coloured with mischief and glided towards him, smiling and holding her armful of lilies out of harm's way. The boy, stooped down, was peering through the crack of the door Feeling Lucy's warm body leaning over him, he made a gesture of caution. Lucy peered through the crack into the hall. Right opposite their spy hole, across the broad polished floor of pale oak, Porfit was seated on one of the hall chairs

230

placed for the more humble callers who were told to wait. Apparently Mr. Chorley had not yet sent for Porfit. He was still waiting, but with the most amiable patience.

He sat squarely on the chair with his legs apart and his hat crown upwards between his hands. His eyes were turned towards the Venus de Milo, on her pedestal at the foot of the stairs, with a broad smile; a smile so ecstatic, so naïve, so unexpected on the shrewd, intelligent face of the preacher, that Lucy at once broke into silent giggles. She felt Cleeve's back vibrate and heave beneath her, a kind of whisper broke from him; and in horror of his being overheard, she tried to put a hand over his mouth. He turned and seized hold of her, choking, gasping, weeping, shaking all over; they clasped each other tightly, while lilies rained on the carpet round their feet. Then suddenly, as if in flight, they both ran into the garden.

Half an hour later, when they had recovered, and walking arm in arm through the rose garden, seriously debated Cobden's passion for Helen Pynsant, and his genius as a poet, Lucy raised her eyes and said, 'Oh dear, there he is again.'

Cleeve looked and saw the small, black figure going up through the meadow. In the long, black coat and the top hat it resembled a beetle with an absurdly small head and one broken leg. The broken leg was the umbrella trailing behind. It had an incongruous look on the bright spring green of the aftermath; like a dung beetle on a flower petal.

'Oh dear,' Lucy said, 'how wretched he looks.'

It was true that Porfit looked wretched. His dragging steps, hunched shoulders, the trailing umbrella, all expressed misery, and in a manner which was somehow comical. The man's depression had the same quality as his pleasure; something naïve, exaggerated, which made one laugh; not with contempt but with condescension, as at a child. 'By Jove,' Cleeve said, 'what a hump. Look at his back —visible despair.'

But Lucy had disappeared. Cleeve was not greatly surprised. Lucy, merely getting up to close a door, did so with such smooth and sudden deftness, that her whole movement went unnoticed. He strolled towards the house. She came swiftly upon him from its far corner and said in a voice of tragic intensity, 'Papa couldn't give him any work. I do wish we hadn't laughed.'

'We'll hope we won't see him again.'

'But, Cleeve, he's had the most awful struggle—and he's so good— he really is good—he gives all his life to making things better.' Seeing Cleeve's surprised face, she said, 'Oh, of course, I don't like him exactly.'

They walked in silence under the apple trees, with their ripening fruit. Cleeve was waiting for Lucy to make some confidence. He could feel that she wanted to speak. But suddenly Cobden was seen coming

231

from the summer house, with his black portfolio. They turned aside to avoid interrupting a poet's meditation, but he waved his hand in reassurance and came towards them.

'He must have finished,' Lucy said. 'Isn't that splendid—he was absolutely stuck last night.'

'Is that what was wrong?'

Lucy took Cobden's arm with an affectionate look. 'You've finished it, darling.'

'More or less.'

Cobden had the air of a man so worn out by effort that he could not enjoy triumph. He drew a paper from the portfolio. Brother and sister, their heads close together, looked gravely at it, and Cleeve, for the first time, saw a likeness in them, not in their features, but in something beneath the features, beneath the skin, the characteristic look of the devotee.

'It's not worth much,' Cobden said.

Cleeve read out the verses.

> *Where still the bright Ilissus flows*
> *The silent poet feeds his sorrow:*
> *Though vanished is the voice he knows,*
> *Where still the bright Ilissus flows.*
> *Though every day he needs must borrow*
> *The necromancies of the morrow,*
> *Where still the bright Ilissus flows.*

'You chose an easier rhyme this time.'

'Yes, borrow and sorrow. I chose those old hacks on purpose. The precious, don't you think, is really too easy, and besides, it misses its aim. The ideal work of art, as someone said, is the cut jewel, great concentration of value, in the simplest form. A still and gem-like flame.'

He looked again at the verse, and his lips moved. He shook his head. 'Too verbal—too noisy.'

'But it's awfully good, darling.'

At this praise Cobden became still more distrustful. He frowned and tore up the paper. 'Too, too horrible—quite bouncing.'

The baby is boy was born Tuesday christened Finian becas I cud not call him Cleeve he is beutiful boy blue eyes like you you wud like to se him Bridget.

This letter in a dirty envelope addressed to Mr. R. C. Corner, University, Oxford, England, was handed to Cleeve in the porch of St. Mark's.

232

'It's been going about some time, sir. They sent it to University College,' the porter said.

It was the first day of Cleeve's first term, and he had the feelings of a ship-wrecked traveller among a tribe of cannibals. He murmured an apology to the porter for troubling him; and reading the note, he was conscious only of a vague irritation, as at a foolish irrelevance, Castle Corner had nothing to do with the shipwrecked traveller. All that former life, sharp in memory, was as strange as if it had happened to somebody else; to baby Cleeve, to little boy Cleeve, to schoolboy Cleeve. He felt no responsibility for anything that had happened in that former life.

He stuffed away the note with a furtive gesture, hiding it from critical eyes. For he was surrounded by other shipwrecked men of the world; other new boys; watchful, uneasy; tentative even in their smiles.

They were waiting for the Dean to lead them to the Sheldonian for matriculation. All wore gowns. Some had borrowed old torn gowns and carried themselves with the nonchalance which they supposed to be the correct thing. But these even more than the others had the air of new boys studying a new code. Even in the toughest there was something young, nervous and seeking, as if they felt a little lost; or as if, like hermit crabs who have just grown out of one shell, they had been left soft and defenceless until they discovered another. Their eyes all seemed to be looking out for a clue to the right kind of shell; the varsity shell, impervious to the larger and fiercer enemies which might be expected in varsity waters.

The feeling, moreover, was very reasonable, because none of them probably had brought from his public school any belief, religious or political, solid enough to stand criticism. It was a time when school masters and even school chaplains did not like to commit themselves until the fog of dogmatic battle had begun to clear; and the fog continued to grow thicker.

Cleeve, looking round for solid ground, had discovered already among the freshman the former captain of his school, Stanlake, a heavy, good-looking boy expected to take a blue. Cleeve had admired Stanlake as he admired everyone with a certain force of character; above all, independence. It was obvious that Stanlake had no perplexities, or fear of his own inadequacy. This was his fascination for Cleeve, and he had been thrilled, on the evening before, when Stanlake, meeting him in another freshman's room, had greeted him by name: 'Hullo, Corner; I didn't know you were coming to St. Mark's.'

They had talked then for ten minutes about tutors, about the chapel services; and Stanlake had advised Cleeve to row because rowing was unpopular, and the college, he happened to know, wanted rowers. Cleeve had promised eagerly to row.

Cleeve had been trying to catch the hero's eyes for several minutes and now, just as he hastily put away the dirty and intrusive envelope from Ireland, he succeeded. Stanlake noticed him and Cleeve smiled. The hero, to his surprise, at once responded with a friendly grin.

Cleeve pushed towards him. Just then, however, the Dean, a dark young man, small and nervous, came among them and said in a high voice, 'Shall we go on?' He walked hastily away from his charges, his long gown billowing behind him as he turned across the street. The party trailed after him, and Cleeve, waiting to join Stanlake as he came out of the door, suddenly saw Cobden descending from a hansom at the gate.

Cobden had come from town where he had spent the night.

He was dressed in a dark tight-waisted suit, strange to the eye, at a time when men had no waists to their coats; his long pointed boots and dark yellow gloves gave him a foreign look. His pale face had a look of knowing gloom. He seemed like one who knew all life and found it everywhere contemptible. He saluted Cleeve by raising his ebony cross-headed stick, and called out as if they had been alone, as if the freshmen did not exist, 'There you are——'

Cleeve stood smiling before him. He felt now the distinction of being Cobden's friend. Cobden paid the cabman and strolled along the pavement beside him, talking of his visit to town. He had seen an Ibsen play, and some extraordinarily beautiful curtains in Regent Street. The curtains had struck him as more important than the play; they gave an experience more serious, more fundamental. They would go with Beethoven. Cleeve must see them.

Cobden's conversation was perfectly audible to the freshmen. Stanlake was at his elbow. Curious glances were directed at him from all sides and Stanlake gazed sidelong with the peculiar blank expression of a child faced by some new and strange phenomenon. He was not hostile; only watchful and suspicious. His judgment, as a new boy, was suspended, waiting to be given a new form.

Cobden, languidly strolling forward with his crutched stick held before him like a processional cross, had now got upon his favourite subject, the philistinism of the English. The curtains, so far, the shop people said, had won no real appreciation. But what could one expect. 'The only arts really understood in this country are military ceremonial, racing and certain games. Government perhaps, and a few poets. Shelley, Dowson, Lionel Johnson. I'm not sure that our greatest genius wasn't Brummel.'

'Who was Brummel?'

'Good heavens, have you never heard of Brummel—inventor of the dress coat?'

'The dress coat?'

'Which conquered the whole world and remains, after nearly a hundred years, the only dress coat.'

'You mean tails,' Cleeve said. He was more and more impressed by Cobden's calm indifference to public opinion. He felt now that Cobden was a man of power and independence.

'And yet, you know,' Cobden said, 'when we call the dress coat an inspiration, we ought to remember that it is based upon classical principles. It is, like all great art, the embodiment of the topical in the eternal. Look at the topical element in this case; the conformation of the figure, and then consider the dress coat. It is short in front to lengthen the legs and to give the effect of the high waist. All the greatest sculptors'—Cobden's eyes passed carelessly over the group, without seeming to see them—'from Pheidias, have lengthened the legs above the proportion of nature in order to obtain the proportion of beauty—the platonic ideal, we might say—the absolute proportion. But I forget you haven't done any philosophy yet.'

'I did some Plato at school.'

'Ah yes, the text.' He dismissed this schoolboy exercise. Cobden, though Cleeve had never seen him so confident and eloquent, still had his weary air. 'Brummel, in fact, perceived that the law of beauty was a law by itself—an ideal form quite separate from natural phenomena. He improved on nature—he lengthened the legs in front. It is true that had been done before—in the fifteenth century—to understand Brummel's genius, we must look from behind. See,' his voice rose, easily dominating the whole party and probably reaching the dean bustling timidly in front—'what he did with the human bottom'—he paused upon a note of disgust and contempt for this crude natural form. Cleeve caught a glimpse on Stanlake's face of wonder and confusion; the Dean darted forward still more rapidly, 'Which, I need not say,' Cobden continued on a falling cadence, 'has been the unsolved problem of tailors from the earliest times. Tails—what a discovery—a real idea of genius——'

They had reached the Sheldonian and the crowd passed into the brown twilight of the theatre; Cobden stopped in the door and said, 'I suppose you must go through with this absurd ceremony.'

'I suppose so.'

'Come to lunch anyhow—I must show you my Baudelaire.'

A week later St. Mark's College was surprised to see Cleeve walking about in a bright blue suit, with an electric blue tie, a grey bowler of unusual shape, brimmed like a jug, and trousers so tight that his little legs seemed like those of a rickety stork. This appearance excited contempt and anger, especially among the freshmen, who had already

235

reformed themselves on new models, which, since they had been taken chiefly from each other, were very like the old.

These freshmen would now have torn Cleeve and Cobden to pieces if it had not been for one doubt. All of them knew from legend and especially the comic papers that it was usual at Oxford to wreck the rooms and tear the clothes of unusual and unpopular persons; but they had already discovered that the legends and comic papers were not always right.

In *Punch* and their father's stories, Oxford was all sprees, practical jokes, drinks, smokes and riots; it proved to be a quiet little country town peppered with twenty colleges as different from each other as the different houses of a public school, in which intercourse was highly formal. One was called upon. One returned calls. One was asked to breakfasts more grave and formal than any family meal at the vicarage. The noisy men who shouted in the quadrangle at night were possibly bloods whom it would be an honour to know; or possibly nonentities whose acquaintance would damn. Society was much more complex than at school, and much more critical than any in the world. There were a hundred different sets and the great man of one set might be unknown to the others. A the blue might be unknown, even as a blue, to B the scholar, or the hunting man. Moreover all the colleges were different. Millionaire X who was courted in St. Ebbe's for his money, might be barred in St. Mark's for his accent. Lord Y at ease in St. Mark's would be stared at in St. Ebbe's like a freak of nature.

St. Mark's was a county college to which generations of Squire Westerns had come up from the shires. It was full of passmen who walked about the quads on a hunting morning in buckskin breeches and pumps, with fifteen inches of hairy calf, or woollen drawers, sock suspenders and bright silk socks, between. In this dress, with a chamois leather waistcoat, a rough tweed coat, a stock and a gown, they would even go to lectures. But the gown was usually as neat as the breeches. Those freshmen who had carefully procured ragged old gowns, were already trying to live them down. In St. Mark's, it was bad form to affect the hearty and the undergraduate of the comic papers was looked upon as a tout.

St. Mark's scorned St. Mary's which was full of millionaires and the beerage; and St. Nimrod's, which was also a hunting college, but whose men, when drunk, broke windows and ragged rooms.

St. Mark's, of course, also got drunk, broke windows and lit bonfires, at least once a year; and once or twice, when the boat was head of the river, wrecked the lavatories and bombarded the garden railings with jordans filled with burning methylated spirit; but all in a spirit, so one was told, as different from that of St. Nimrod's, as the unbending of a gentleman differs from the debauch of bumpkins.

Nevertheless this tradition or idea was passed on to freshmen. At various breakfast parties, when they spoke of the expediency of crushing the æsthetes; some second or third year man would say 'Yes, Chorley is a bit trying—I daresay any other college would have his bags off. But for some reason, I don't know how it is, we don't do much of that sort of thing in St. Mark's.'

The interesting event was that most of the freshmen not only threw away at once their moral desire to punish Cobden and Cleeve for their impudent difference of dress and opinion; but saw that this tolerance was the right thing, that it was something to be proud of. As a St. Mark's man, one boasted of the superior civilization of one's college and looked down upon the provincial colleges whose eccentrics were ragged merely as eccentrics. One was as perfectly sure of one's superiority in this respect as a civilized man is convinced of his superiority to the baboon.

Odd fish of course were ragged at St. Mark's almost every year, but public opinion did not approve of raggers and so the feeling of superiority remained. Moreover, Cobden escaped during his whole four years at Oxford, and this was to St. Mark's credit because he was very provocative. He displayed his contempt for all except Cleeve so openly that one might have thought he was seeking the martyrdom which two other æsthetes often achieved at St. Nimrod's, which was not even their own college. They went there, they said, to visit the great Cross, but they managed always to be caught in the quad by the most ferocious Christians—one of them was stripped twice in the same week.

Cleeve, like Cobden, loved to speak of Oxford as a provincial backwater, to hang Beardsleys in his room, to despise Christians and the footballers, and at least twice a week, he went to town with his friend as if returning to civilization. They had in fact nothing to do in town. They did not know the artists and poets even of their own admiration, who at that time kept their court in various pubs and garrets. In the absence of Helen Pynsant they often spent the whole afternoon walking solemnly and haughtily in Bond Street until they were tired out and glad to be seated once more in the train at Paddington.

Yet it seemed to them that they were favoured beings, and though Cobden Chorley was at least as melancholy as he seemed, could not sleep, agonized over his trivial rhymes and had moments of suicidal despair, he would not have changed places with the most contented rowing men in college. For he believed that he knew a greater truth; and that his life was nobler, more rational.

Cleeve, of course, had no wish to be a martyr. He had no notion of his unpopularity, and he was never more happy in his life. He had for Cobden, during at least the first six months of his æsthetic phase, a devotion seen as a rule only in religious converts towards the teacher who has given them for the first time a key to life; and like a disciple he wanted to lead others into the same promised land. He liked to explain in Hall, to a couple of horsy Etonians and a Rugby Christian that everything was art in some form or another and that the English were bad at most of them, including religion; and he wrote to his father in Africa that the only really great men of the last century were Walter Pater and Oscar Wilde, and that he did not think he would be able to stay long in Oxford; the dons were too provincial, especially in dress.

Felix, in reply, wrote that these views were extremely interesting; that the rains on the Mosi were late; and that he hoped Cleeve would not forget to send a Christmas letter to his Aunt Mary.

A huge new building in red brick was rising in a field at the end of Chorley Road. It was the new Chorley factory, designed by a London architect, with terra cotta pillars, vases, and balustrades. All the chapels in the district were proud of it, declaring it much more handsome than the new Porriton Brewery. The brewers were church.

Porfit preached a sermon on the contrast, pointing out that the Chorleys had never made the mistake of throwing away the substance of the spirit for the shadow of mammon; they never rated their gain above things of good report. Porfit used this phrase rather than beauty; because he knew the word beauty was suspect to many of his hearers.

He sent a copy of the sermon, written out by his mother in round hand, to Chorley himself; and meeting Lucy one day, going with her mother into the chief drapers' at Porriton, he congratulated them both on the public spirit of the firm.

After this, it became a usual thing for the Chorley ladies, when they shopped, to find themselves accosted by Porfit, now growing shabby, with frayed collar and broken cuffs. But always he had the same gay ecstatic smile on his pale face, while he stood, hat in hand and made his compliments.

'A beautiful day, ladies, worthy even of your countenance.'

Mrs. Chorley, with her fierce stare, would answer, 'Oh, good morning, Mr. Porfit,' and march to her brougham. But her march was a flight and Lucy in the rear guard was obliged to be doubly charming. 'But how lucky to see you, Mr. Porfit. I hear you made a splendid speech at the Free Trade Meeting.'

Porfit began to look for these short tête-à-têtes with his princess. He found out that on market days she was often alone. Mrs. Chorley, though not a vegetarian, could not bear to see the beasts driven to the pens, for she imagined them already slaughtered. On three successive Wednesdays, Porfit was able to waylay Lucy in one shop or another, and hold her for five minutes by his rapid and resourceful talk. He

238

would begin with the compliments which he obviously thought the proper things for young ladies, and go on to the affairs of the party or the library committee; of which they were both members. He was a good talker. He had the faith and enthusiasm which gave to everything he said the nervous force which moves the nerves. He had always moved Lucy. But soon he began to make confidences about himself; ask for the girl's approval; and once he said, 'What you think, means a great deal to me, Miss Chorley.'

'Oh, I hope not,' she had said, and she had seen at once her mistake, her confession. She felt his eyes on her and her cheeks growing pink.

She was delighted to hear that Cleeve was not going back to Ireland, and she waited eagerly for his return. But in the Christmas vacation Cleeve went to stay with the Pynsants at New Grange. Helen Pynsant was at home again and she was beginning to entertain, discreetly but extravagantly. Cobden went to see her almost every day, saying, 'I think I'll run over to see what Cleeve's doing.'

Lucy, therefore, continued her round of duties alone. This did not seem to her a hardship because she was used to the idea that Cobden and Cleeve, when they talked all day about a picture or a poem were doing something important and necessary, but she felt her loneliness. She felt sometimes as if she were surrounded by enormous spaces of vague warm kindness in which she hurried from one thing to another like a distracted fly. Nothing was solid there but duty which could only be recognized as duty if it was a trouble. Lucy and Cobden had had a careful religious training in moral responsibility. They had been taught to ask themselves what was right and wrong, and to do the right. But they were well-educated, on modern lines, and whereas all the little Baptist children in Porriton back streets had been taught exactly what was right and wrong; knew for instance that it was wicked to drink beer, to smoke, to play cards, to go to theatres, to look at naked statues, Adam Chorley, himself brought up by his father in this creed, now smiled at it. So that Lucy and Cobden, in effect, had no positive instruction except to be kind, to be honest, and to listen to God's voice. The very Bible had dissolved away beneath their childish feet, into the higher criticism.

Cobden, from the age of fifteen, had troubled his parents greatly by his moodiness, his mysterious weeping fits, and his reserve which even their affection could not penetrate. He had withdrawn into a desert of loneliness where he lived like a hermit. He was still a stranger to his family. Lucy, with her gaiety, her sense of humour, had seemed to escape this mysterious neurotic condition. She had only suffered a brief period of ill-health, about seventeen, when she had starved herself during Lent into anæmia. She had taken a fancy about the same time

239

to High Church services. But her father had proved to her the fallacy of authority in religion and she had been cured of her anæmia by the Armenian atrocities and local committe-work.

One day Cleeve, looking for the library, which was in the upper story of the draper's, came upon Lucy in the back entry, and found her with Porfit.

'Hullo!' he cried in surprise which revealed all his youthful contempt for the vulgar. Porfit turned quickly, clapped on his hat, and walked off. He, too, had been thrown off his balance.

'I say, was he worrying you?' Cleeve cried.

'Oh no!' Lucy was pink and breathless. Suddenly she took Cleeve's arm and said, 'You don't mind hating people, I suppose?'

'You hate him, do you?'

'But I don't—how could anyone hate poor Mr. Porfit.'

She gave a sudden deep sigh; so unexpected to Cleeve that he looked at her curiously.

'If he's being a nuisance——'

'Oh, but he's not—of course not.'

Cleeve looked severely at Lucy and said, 'You Christians are hopeless.' As an aesthete Cleeve despised all self-sacrifice.

'But, Cleeve, I'm not—not a real Christian—I only wish I was—it makes things easier.'

'Easier—to be a Christian.'

A customer came into the entry and looked at them curiously. Lucy said hastily, 'I ought to be going. I must meet Papa.'

It was raining, and Cleeve put up his umbrella as they walked over the deserted pavement of the sleepy little town.

Lucy took Cleeve's arm, a bold act in the market place, and said, 'I wish you had come to us.'

'So do I. I wanted to, but Mrs. Pynsant asked me, and I hadn't the nerve to plant myself at Bellavista again.'

They had reached the *Gazette* office. The brougham was waiting, but Chorley had not come out. Lucy stopped on the wet pavement and turned towards Cleeve under the umbrella, 'It's not too dull for you.'

'But I love it, you know I do.'

Cleeve meeting the girl's eyes looking at him with a peculiar brightness and steadiness, suddenly forgot his æsthetic wrath against Christians and his preoccupation with the rain dripping on his beautiful trousers; and remembered how fond he was of Lucy; how pretty she was and how close to him in friendship. All this was plain in his expression, and they looked at each other with the sharp enquiry of intelligent young people who ask, 'Would we be happy together—is this my chance?' It is a look seen commonly enough even between strangers in trains and buses; more common in girls than men. It is quite different from the exchange between the simple souls who wait for love to befall them, to whom each meeting is itself romance.

'Are you having an awful time?' Cleeve said.

'Good Heavens, no.'

'You need somebody to look after you, Lucy.'

Lucy looked away and her lips parted; suddenly Cleeve felt alarmed and said hastily, 'I mean as a friend, of course.'

They stared at each other; Cleeve as suddenly ashamed as he had been alarmed, said, 'But, darling Lucy, you see——'

To his surprise, Lucy began to laugh. Her laughter was not like Stella's sudden noisy explosion; it was a silent throb, which made her thin shoulders shake, and her cheeks, sometimes also her nose, pink. Her eyes closed, she showed all her teeth and poked forward her head as if to hide something indecent and shameful. But she could never control these sharp silent fits. Cleeve, whenever Lucy laughed at him, at first looked blank and then laughed with her, enjoying her pleasure with that deep affectionate sympathy which always lay between them.

Chorley came out of the office with Benskin who often looked there for his friend when he had business to do. He was interested, too, in the *Gazette*, which he had once tried to buy; but though the *Gazette* had been losing money since Gladstone's defeat in '95, Chorley did not like to lose control of a paper founded by his grandfather.

But he had a perpendicular wrinkle in his forehead as he came out of the office; and his quick walk told observers that he was worried. Benskin's face as usual looked like a rough carving in old teak; of a sad monk. He handed Lucy into the carriage with a deft hand.

They were going to Bellavista for luncheon. Cleeve jumped on the step and shouted through the window, 'I must see you, Lucy.'

Chorley's troubled eyes and Benskin's sad ones jerked towards the boy, as if he had fired a pistol in the closed space of their reflections.

Lucy blushed and smiled; her face was also full of surprise, but before she could answer, Chorley recovered his presence of mind, and asked Cleeve if he would like to come to lunch.

'I can't,' the boy said in a voice as if he were surprised by his own regret. 'I've got to go and see some blessed old church with Cobden and the Pynsants.'

All understood why he could not break this engagement, to entertain Stella while her mother flirted with Cobden.

'A pity,' Chorley said. 'Come to-morrow then,' and they drove away.

Porfit, having turned the corner between the draper's and the county hotel, made directly for the open country beyond. His mind was full of the ambition and admiration which moved him at any contact with the Chorleys, especially with Lucy. He thought how she had coloured when he had said, 'The battle for human freedom is a true work of the spirit,' and he felt the complex thrill of the preacher, the artist who creates and forms emotion. That look, like others of Lucy. had told him something about her. He did not examine his knowledge; Porfit never analysed his feelings, or his motives. But he felt a sudden encouragement. His admiration for Lucy, for years, had been the worship of a subject. But in the last few weeks, since he had met her often, another feeling had started up in him. He saw again her look, like that of any of the girls who sat beneath him at meeting, and turned up their startled eyes towards him when he shouted and thumped the desk. 'Freedom under God—that is a word greater than Empire.'

He smiled as he picked his way along the kennel of the muddy lane. He was in a slum. The slums of Porriton, as of most country towns, were at the centre. Next to the big shops of the High Street one found lath and plaster tenements two hundred years old, so foul and verminous that the lanes themselves seemed to have the heavy stench of bugs. These houses were also the most crowded, because they were cheaply rented. Every room had at least one family; and usually a large family. The idea that twelve persons of all ages sleeping in one ten foot room, was a matter of grievance, or even of comment, had not yet struck anybody. Porfit himself, stepping aside from the filthy babies rolling in dirt which was half sewage, and past the bulging houses, breathing from every door and window smells fouler than any from a sewer, was concerned only to keep his boots clean, and not to pick up vermin by contact with any of the inhabitants. They, for their part, young women with faces as pale as turnips, and a few old men past work, crippled, twisted, stared at the young man in his black overcoat and tall narrow bowler, with a kind of blank nonplus. No decently dressed stranger could pass through a Porriton slum, in those days, without abuse of some kind, often a stone in the back. But the slum tribe, in spite of their apartness, knew Porfit. Some of them had heard him speak against the brewers and the Tariff Reformers. They took no interest in his speeches; they looked upon him, and all the chapel folk in the little streets beyond the slums, as snobs and probably grabbers. They hated the chapel folk, even more than the rich, and much more than the great ones, like General Pynsant and Lord Porriton, whom they had never seen and whose lives they could not imagine. They felt no envy of a paradise beyond their conceptions. But they knew that Porfit always had enough to eat, a bed to himself, and they hated him. On the other hand, they were used to him. He was a familiar object. The conflict between their hatred and their feeling that he had in some way a right to be there, produced in them the peculiar looks of frustrated disgust

242

and aborted rage which are familiar to every clergyman or district visitor in a slum.

But Porfit's smile was not the hearty grin of the curate; it was absent-minded; as free of motive as the expression of the lane itself; its cracks, its dirt, its grey walls, which looked like the under vaults of a tropical jungle, dark, dirty, cut off from the sun, the old battlefields and corpse ground of a forest whose upper branches, far above, were engaged in another battle for life in the free air. He, for whom the slum was a kind of local hell for the improvident and the godless, noticed the looks as little as the children. He was absorbed in the quickening of his life, the expansion of his dream, a release like the opening of leaves in the air.

Porfit knew his power. No man who has held an audience, or silenced and subdued a hostile audience; a triumph won without arms, by simple force of character, against an irresponsible mass, can fail in the sense of his own power. It was his sense of caste, his social modesty that had prevented him from social ambition. But now suddenly, like a revelation, not to his mind, but to his feelings, it was suggested that Lucy was not unattainable.

VII

Jarvis won his first African distinction in Jubilee year when, as an officer of the new West African Frontier Force, he was mentioned in dispatches for intercepting slave raiders on the northern Mosi. The invaders, under the famous war chief, the Emir of Daji, came from the great Daji plain in the north. Turned back from the Mosi, the Emir came south and set up his war camp at the edge of the Laka swamp, threatening the pagan districts to the south, and all the northerly branches of the European traders. Three of these were in Laka itself. Hatto had made immediate use of Jarvis' first exploration of Laka, to open a branch there, with a negro in charge. He himself, of course, had been forbidden to enter; but when the Transport store had been established for six months, he had asked leave to visit it, pointing out that unless he could make such visits from time to time to examine the stock, he would have to close the store.

The chiefs' wives enjoying a shop for the first time in their lives, were sulky at the very thought of losing it. Even in Laka, women have the influence of their sex, strong especially with chiefs, who have time to amuse themselves with women. Hatto had leave to pay one visit a month for one night. After his first visit he stayed for a year, and by that time there were two other stores in Laka; old Joe from the Trading Company, who built the first hut for his company by the town creek, had already been succeeded by the Major who was in turn succeeded by Felix.

Felix came also to stay one night and to inspect his subordinate's books, but he had stayed for more than a year.

The trading stations were now familiar to the Lakawa, who went there every day to shop or gossip. They no longer looked with fear or hatred at the white men who were seen to be harmless and contemptible creatures, ugly, dirty, without religion or morals.

The women were used to seeing Bobs chase Hatto through the compounds; or in return, get her weekly floggings. They understood the comedy of the little man's antics; and Bobs' tragedy; and laughed at both. They appreciated Hatto as a clown; Felix they despised. He, too, was abused by his wife; but not like Hatto, for a joke. Felix never flogged Dinah, who had become huge and fat, and behaved like a jealous tyrant. She dressed in silks and dominated the whole household and the store, ordering everybody about.

Felix himself was never seen in the store. He would wander through the village in ragged trousers, patched shirt, gazing now at a weaver, now at the children with a solemn absorbed expression; or he would sit all day in his hut among a litter of boxes and papers smoking green native tobacco in a brass elephant pipe and gazing at the wall. Even Mosi traders were shocked by Felix' dirt and idleness. The Major, visiting him with his son Christy, now a lanky little boy of seven, butter coloured, would look round the hut with alarmed eyes and murmur, 'My dear Chappy, you need a change, come to us on the Mosi for a little holiday—my dear boy,' and afterwards in order that young Christy should not take harm by the bad example, he would tell him that Felix was a very good man, a very nice man.

The Major was strict about Christy's education and took care that he washed his ears and said his prayers every night. In his next visit to Laka, he left him behind with old Joe, his spiritual director. As he said, 'He's beginning to take notice of things.'

The Major was too polite to remonstrate with Felix, but Hatto, now a leading man in the district, selling his gas pipe guns to all the great slave raiding emirs of the north, could not bear, as he said, to see a real Oxford gentleman like Mr. Corner go native.

Hatto often remonstrated with Felix. 'If you'll excuse me, Mr. Corner, it's a pity to let things slide—we white men in a godforsaken place like Laka 'ave to keep up our standards specially as the Government don't give us no support. It's a duty. And wot's more, goin' native is bad in itself—it always leads to a narsty end.'

'Going native.' Felix was greatly surprised. It did not seem to him that he was changing in any direction. He was simply living his life as it came to him.

'Of course, Mr. Corner, we all know you've 'ad your troubles with your boy and all—but look at your beard, down to your navel—and you 'aven't changed your shirt night or day for a month. And look 'ow you spoil your mammies. I tell you wot it is, Mr. Corner, wen one of these nigger women loses her respect for a chap, she poisons 'im off.'

'Troubles,' Felix said, wondering what he meant. It was true that the Mosi Company had again failed to pay a dividend; and that Cleeve had been a disappointment; that he seemed to be making as big a fool of himself at Oxford as he had in Ireland. But Felix did not know why these private misfortunes should affect his habits of life. He was indeed glad that business in Laka kept him out of England; for he felt that a meeting with Cleeve might embarrass them both. It was lucky he was so busy. He would not like to seem unsympathetic with Cleeve's friends or notions, however foolish.

245

'My Dysy has had trouble with me own boy,' Hatto said. 'I know what it is.'

'Oh, but mine is a very good boy,' Felix said. 'He writes every week. Hullo, Bandy, what have you been up to?'

Bandy came sidling through the door. She did not answer her step-father, but kept her eyes fixed on Hatto. She was now fifteen, a strong, thin girl, very unlike her mother, with a skin like a dead beech leaf, pale and glossy; small features, a neat flat nose, a well cut mouth and chin.

She never took her eyes off Hatto while she sidled like a stealthy animal to Felix, squatted down against the wall behind him and lifted his arm round her neck.

Hatto was shocked by her confident familiarity. He said, 'She's a piece too.'

'Dinah wants me to marry her.'

'Wot, marry 'er own daughter?'

'It's common enough in Laka for mother and daughter to share a husband if he isn't the girl's father.'

'Don't you do it,' Hatto said with horror. 'Don't you do it, Mr. Corner.'

'Bandy here seems to think it a good plan.'

'Ye-r-r.' Hatto made a disgusted noise. 'She would.'

Dinah bounced into the hut. Her jealousy, like a pet dog's, made her know of a visitor's presence even from a distance. She began at once to shout at Felix, complaining that he neglected her, that there was too much work to do. 'Work enough for three wives, but I have to do it alone, like any poor man's wife.'

Then she turned her furious eyes on Hatto, who at once took his leave. He was afraid of Dinah, who was as different from Bobs as a forest pagan from the corrupt town people of the coast. Dinah's passions were real. Her love, hatred, anger and sense of importance were not to be controlled by fear or even prudence.

Dinah continued to abuse Felix. She was angry that he, an important man, should keep only one wife. She felt that she had a right to the dignity and leisure of a head wife.

'You're too lazy,' she declared angrily, and losing her temper because he did not answer, she pulled at his hair with both hands. But Felix was too heavy for her to move, her most violent tugs only rocked his head on its thick neck. She did not interrupt his reflections. 'What does he mean—going native.' He scratched himself pensively. He suffered from lice because he always forgot to change his shirt. It seemed to him that he never had time to think of changing it. His life was too full.

246

Bandy had shot out of the door. Already like a wife, she disappeared when some other woman of the household was quarrelling with its man. But she was not a wife, and so, like the other village girls of her age, she spent all her time in the game of love. In Laka girls were free till they married, and all the young men and girls, except in the farming season of hard work, were in a perpetual excitement; pursuing or being pursued; every day there were jealous fights, new couplings. As Bandy darted through the twisting alleys of trees, now at six o'clock in a grey darkness, giggles were heard in the bush, a boy's voice calling, not loud but urgent; and a quick rustle of hard-soled feet on dry earth. Bandy stopped, quivering, and threw up her head; tossing her broad nostrils towards the sound; then suddenly disappeared, like a melting shadow, into the bush. Two boys of fifteen, just initiated and carrying their first men's spears, swaggered past, both talking at once. Each had a hand across the other's neck. As soon as they had passed Bandy's head shot out like a vixen's from its earth, and remained motionless, staring with fixed, glittering eyes. Then suddenly she uttered a scornful laugh and as they turned with open mouths and raised brows, she strolled into the path, languidly working her hips in the bright cloth. One of the boys called to her. At once she flew off; she was in terror, and when she heard the pounding feet close at her heels, she uttered suddenly a scream of fear. She dived through the undergrowth, broke into the open ground, and darted among the huts. Cooking fires from the compounds threw long bars of light across the bare earth; heads turned in doorways where the village fathers sat discussing the badness of crops and the changes of the times.

Bandy stopped instantly, gathered up her flying cloth, and hunched her shoulders as if the glances of these older people had the quality of cold rain or wind playing on her bare back. She drew her head down between her shoulders and slowly tucked up the cloth. Her whole body quivered with the effort of not giggling.

A man's voice spoke her name, softly and cautiously, from behind a hut. She started, and walked in the opposite direction, but with extreme deliberation. As she stepped into the shadows again, he touched her arm; he had run round behind the huts.

He began to make love. 'You are the most beautiful of all the girls in Laka.'

Bandy walked on gravely, a pace in front. Who was this stranger who knew her name and called her beautiful? He seemed to be a grown man, his step was heavy, his palm rough with work. She felt surprised, and his compliments stilled her nerves into a tension; she did not want to giggle. She felt important.

She walked importantly and slowly, paying no attention to the man's pleading, the touches of his hand sliding over her arm and back; but

247

she was turning always towards the darkest corner of the village, among the scrub growing on the old yam fields within the stockade.

Dinah's rages always ended in an amorous fit, and when she was satisfied, she was lazy and affectionate, lying across Felix' legs like an enormous cat.

'But he's quite wrong,' Felix' reflections continued with hardly a moment's break. He gently tickled Dinah to keep her quiet and to amuse her. 'A white man can't go native; he can only go among natives and that's quite different. It might be better for me if I could go native, or better, go plant.' And he felt for a moment his loneliness in the world, a detachment so complete that he did not seem to be related to it at all. 'Yes, trees and plants are happy enough, I suppose,' he looked at the moon flowers against the door of the hut. The moon was rising and their petals uncurled, sending out their rich strong scent, 'but I suppose they're also struggling for something more, a richer, more complex sensation. They're never satisfied either. And that, I suppose, is why they go on being alive.'

His mind darted off to explore and enjoy this new rich province of idea; the connection between dissatisfaction and purpose; ennui and ambition, static and dynamic perfection; fatigue of the stimulated nerve or brain lobe; and the necessary instability of limited beings, narrow lives.

Dinah, stretching languidly, pushed herself against his fingers; her expression was that of a purring cat with half closed eyes and an air of inward contemplation. Felix looked down upon her with the pleasure of one who is on terms with a creature entirely without hypocrisy or plan; with nature itself. Her ugliness was charming to him like the face of a pug to the old retired diplomat, sick of finesse. He thought of Hatto's warning with a tranquil amusement. No doubt she was capable of poisoning him, but who could blame her for that? She was devoted to him.

Dinah soon persuaded Felix to marry Bandy; she could persuade him to anything; but then it was found that Bandy was already pregnant. This was a crime, for though Laka girls have freedom till marriage they are expected to avoid pregnancy. Dinah beat the girl, who ran to Felix for protection, and when he defended her, saying that it was a very natural accident, she beat him also and called him an immoral man. Laka was shocked by Felix' attitude towards Bandy's misconduct, and many of the elders pressed the chief to turn the white men out of Laka before they corrupted all the people.

It was of course true that the old society of Laka was breaking up at contact with the stores, but the old chief was more disturbed by the raids from the north which every year came nearer to his border. At the end of '98, the Daji Emir brought his war camp within fifty miles of Laka, and took slaves from villages in tribute to Laka itself. Hatto, who had sold Daji most of his guns, and the two other traders, now disappeared. Felix, warned by them that Laka itself was the next object of attack, passed on his warning to the chiefs, and began to pack his boxes; but he continually put off moving till they gradually became unpacked again.

Felix, seeing that the chiefs made no attempt to put the defences in order, repeated his warning, but they answered that it was now time for the festival of the yam planting, when they could not prepare for any war. The first shower had fallen, the calender of the year had begun, and peace was enjoyed for all the Laka tribes until the planting was over. The festival, they pointed out, was extremely important. The harvest of last year had not been good; the languid earth had given few yams; and many women had been barren. The columns of the palms had not put out so much fruit as usual and the fish were scarce. It was necessary therefore to stimulate and excite that power which causes things to grow and swell and to bring forth increase by dancing and love making. The excitement of the dance is contagious. When men and women drink and dance together, singing obscene songs, the air itself becomes drunk and maddening; and the ground grows hot; so that the seed germinates.

Orders had been given therefore for three days of drinking and dancing; when any woman should be free to any man; and for the sacrifice of ten young virgins to the yam spirit, ten to the fish spirit and ten young men in full strength to the palm trees.

Felix came every day to the council house with warnings. The Emir, he said, was actually on the march.

The chiefs now became alarmed. All the old men knew what a slave raid meant, torture, rape, murder. But they also knew that even to carry weapons at a yam festival was offensive to the spirit of fertility and that spirits were easily offended. All powerful rulers were touchy.

Thus commonsense said one thing; and religion another, each supported by fear. The chiefs argued night and day. Their problem was difficult because it was insoluble. The royal courtyard under a straw canopy was crowded all day with squatting thick bodies in bright cotton, all shouting together with such extravagant motions that their faces with rolling white rimmed eyes and wrinkled foreheads seemed like masks of rage and fright stuck upon comic actors. But after four days they could only agree upon one point; hatred of the white man who had brought this perplexity upon them, and continued to remind them of it.

For the people, in the security of the old kingdom, this was a time of holiday. All day the fish hunters splashed in the Laka river, now, at low water, reduced to a chain of long muddy lakes. At about half past five, on this last evening, when Felix, taking his usual place on the shelving beach of mud, filled his first pipe, a drive was just over. A crowd of hunters of all ages from three to sixty, were gathered at the far end of the pool, asking each other how the fish had escaped. Children of six or seven could be seen abusing and instructing their fathers with great indignation. Children in an old and settled civilization like Laka had much freedom and were seldom beaten or snubbed. They did not seem to need it, perhaps because, seeing their places in society already prepared for them, with a regular gradation of accomplishments to be acquired, dignities, pleasures to be reached in due time, they did not need to be shown their places. They were drawn towards them by a natural inclination. At this moment, far out in the pool, a group of two old grandfathers, knee deep in the water, and three infants breast deep, were arguing on equal terms with agitated gestures and serious, concerned faces, about the organization of the next hunt. Anyone could tell by the excitement, and by certain repeated movements of the hands spread apart, that a very large fish was supposed to have escaped.

Azai, now a boy of ten, was especially irritated by the confusion. He waded out close to Felix, dragging by the hand a fat child of two, one of his numerous sisters, and said angrily, 'The men spoil everything.'

Felix by now knew most of the children of the royal compound, Dinah's nephews and nieces. He was an old acquaintance of both of Azai and the little fat girl, whose name was Osho; both treated him with the same contemptuous familiarity accorded to a foreigner.

'How do they spoil it?' Felix asked, watching Osho joyfully fall upon the soft mud, and begin to dig herself into it.

'They don't do it properly. They just play at it.'

'But isn't it a game?'

Azai looked at him with disgust, but Felix was wading into the pool. Bandy, with the voice and gestures of a spoilt child, had summoned him. Azai turned away. He was tired of games. He wanted, at his age, to do something more important, something real.

Bandy, covered with sweat and mud, had been shouting and jostling among the boys for two hours. She now spent every day at the pools. She had no household duties and she no longer played at love. In Laka a woman with a child at breast is forbidden the man; and this religious taboo is so strong that she has no idea of lovers or men of her. Bandy, romping in the water, rubbed her muddy flanks against former lovers with as much indifference in both parties as if they had become impotent. She was once more a child, thinking of nothing but play.

As Felix approached, she unbound the baby from her back and held it out, 'Here, old beard, you take it.'

'Isn't it time you fed it?'

'No, no, you take it. It's in the way.'

The baby was a fortnight old; a small, wrinkled creature like a marmoset. Half a calabash had been placed on its head to protect it from the sun, and this enormous hat, larger than its whole body, made it absurd and charming to Felix who could not help smiling at the serious little face, crumpled like a mandarin's, and the claw-like hands gripping at his shirt. Loud yells broke out; fifty or sixty rods beat the water and the hunters splashed past him on each side, jostling him and wetting him from head to feet.

Bandy, screaming at the top of her voice, and lifting her knees almost to her nose, took great leaping steps in front of the men, eager to be first. Felix, streaming with mud and water, held out his thick elbows to protect the baby and when the hunt was past, waded quickly back to Osho. Felix was the usual baby minder. He was especially fond of children so small that they did not embarrass his conscience as an educator by difficult questions; or interrupt his reflections by a demand for physical exertion. Sitting on the bank with Bandy's infant sleeping in his arms, and Osho trying now to bury herself head first in the mud, in the evening sunlight which had already turned the eastern sky pale green, he felt that serene happiness of a man who recognizes a moment of complete satisfaction, not to be improved.

Azai wandered to his father's house and made his way through the courtyard into the inner compound. Here stood the tribal arsenal where new poisoned spears and arrows were kept; a hut forbidden to women and children. Skulls of enemies hung upon the wall.

Azai had passed the spear hut a thousand times with no temptation to enter, but something in him had meanwhile been watching it, simply because it was mysterious and forbidden, with a ceaseless curiosity and desire.

Now he found it unguarded. The guards were at the fence peering through chinks at the council where an old chief was making a speech. The councillors had ceased to shout and quarrel because they were exhausted and found that they made no progress. They were now discussing a suggestion from the king, who, seeing no escape from their dilemma, proposed, from his long experience of politics, a means of avoiding it. 'There has always been peace in Laka during a festival,' he said, 'and therefore we cannot be attacked.'

A dozen younger men, not so experienced, not willing to recognize inevitable fate in a conflict of ideas, at once protested that the Daji men, as Mahomedans, acknowledged no pagan laws or customs.

In this last struggle of words, no one saw Azai stealing into the warriors' hut.

He stood trembling with excitement in the dim twilight, feeling in every nerve the powerful spirits which filled the air and the walls; which stared at him from the hollow eyes of the skulls hanging from the rafters.

Azai knew that everything in the world is full of spirits as well as he knew that water was wet and fire was hot. He felt and heard the spirits all day, in the air, in the trees, in the ground. At night when he slept, his own spirit passed out of him and had extraordinary adventures; fighting, hunting; flying through the air; or galloping on the ground like an animal. He felt now the spirits of dead warriors watching him.

He put out his hand towards the fighting spears. The points, glittering with the black poison like varnish, seemed to radiate the spirit of their power. He held his breath when he grasped at a shaft, as if it might sting his fingers. It did not sting but he felt its power. Carrying it like a sacred thing, charged with energy, he slipped to the door.

The noise had died; his father's cracked voice could be heard speaking; the guards had disappeared altogether. He darted towards the gate.

The guards were attending the decision of the council. For it had been decided that no attack could possibly take place during a festival, and all saw that no other decision was feasible.

Orders were at once given for the feast, already postponed at great danger of offence to the spirits, to begin, and the sacrifices were brought out.

Azai at the pool found that the hunt had gone far away. No one was left but Felix, Osho and three or four small boys, paddling together. He ran among them with the spear and shouted, 'Look out—it's real.' They surrounded him with awe and envy.

Osho, now so completely covered with mud that her eyes seemed like living eyes set by a miracle in a clay model, pointed at the water and said, 'fish.' She did not know what the word meant; she repeated it for its sound like a charm. It had a powerful effect. The children, forgetting the spear, darted their sticks at the water and rushed away.

Nobody paid any attention to Azai. Osho was patting the water as if to ask, 'What is it good for? Felix himself now got up, yawned and walked slowly away with the baby. He was taking it to Bandy. He looked round once and called 'Bring Osho.' Azai made no reply. He was not a nurse, and he despised white men who minded babies.

'Look out!' he said to the air, 'I'm about to kill an elephant fish.'

But this, of course, was just what he could not do. It was the children shouting in the distance who were catching fish, and now they disappeared round the bend of the pool towards the town. Their shouts diminished.

Azai stood perplexed between the hunt and the spear. He had no admirers now. He seized the spear again and said in a doubtful voice, 'Look out, here is the great chief.'

At once he felt again the glory of the real spear. He shook it and cried loudly, 'Look out—look out!'

The sun had fallen below the edge of the high trees before he found himself tired and hungry.

He perceived that it was late. He ought to be at home. There was danger already of spirits and leopards.

He turned to fetch his sister. But suddenly he saw three men on the opposite bank of the stream, in long gowns, turbans, and carrying broad-bladed spears. As he saw them, they disappeared; they seemed to fall into the ground.

Azai was too young to doubt his eyes. If they had seen a god or a ghost he would have believed them.

He ran for Osho and took her by the hand. The ball of mud which was her head turned towards him; a crack opened in it in which could be seen a bright red tongue; the living eyes closed and she uttered a loud yell.

Azai could not pick her up. She was too heavy for him. But he tugged her through the mud until they reached the bank. She protested against each step; roaring. She was tired. She needed to go home; but she did not want to go home. As Azai's eyes rose level with the dry edge of the bank, he saw two more turbans sinking behind a bush close to the town path. They were between him and the town.

He was frightened. He wanted to run back into the river; traditional hiding place of children. He half turned away. But he still held the real spear and now he felt that this made it difficult for him to run away. Just as he had to walk with dignity and keep himself clean when he was wearing his best cloth, he could not run away from danger with a real spear. He raised it in a threatening manner and began to trot towards the town. A sob of fear broke out of him.

He tugged angrily at Osho. His right arm, unable to hold up the spear, fell and let the shaft drag along the ground. But it was still a real spear with a real warrior's power, descended from generations of tribal courage, and he did not turn back at the darkest bush. Azai knew that there was power in the spear because he could feel it in himself.

In Laka the old chief was performing the last sacrifice. Twenty girls had been thrown into the river; and twenty men buried alive in the yam fields. The last of those dedicated to the palms, chosen for his

253

great size and beauty, was now being fixed to the sacred palm, the largest in the village. Long spikes were thrust through his feet into the ground; and his hands were tied together round the trunk, so that as he died the whole power of his strong virility would pass into the tree.

The victim, overwhelmed with terror and despair, had made no sound until the spikes were hammered into his feet. Then he began to scream. Everybody in Laka knew the man, a young farmer. He had been a popular guest at a thousand dances and drum parties. An hour before he could have counted on a sympathetic answer to his smile from anyone in the town. Now the faces of the priest's assistants, of the old chief, of the watching villagers were as blank of feeling as those of builders or woodsmen carrying out some operation of their craft. The old chief fussing round the tree with a busy, intent expression, now tried the bands, now plucked at the spikes.

He knew by experience that a strong young victim often took three or even four days to die; and that even on the second day he was capable of vigorous leaps and jerks. He called the hammer men to give a few more strokes.

Then he raised his arms and intoned the last prayer of dedication.

> *O Great God who feeds us*
> *We thank thee for thy bounty to us,*
> *May it please thee to accept our sacrifice.*

This prayer was interrupted by the screams of the victim and also loud hysterical cries from his wife. The rest of the family, his mother, father, brothers and sisters were conspicuous in the front row of spectators. They joined in the song of sacrifice with ardent cries. This misfortune which had marked them out filled them with the sense of guilt. But the man's wife had been shrieking abuse and threats for an hour.

Nobody hindered her. It was felt that her conduct, though foolish and rash, had some excuse. It was natural. Her nerve had given way and she could not help behaving foolishly.

The song ended. The chief, supported on each side by slaves, walked back to his house. At once the drums began to beat; the dancers formed in lines; the townsmen, women and children began to walk about in the lanes; laughing, looking expectant. Every now and then they would turn aside into a hut for a drink of palm wine. In an hour all were drunk. All clothes had been taken off. Men and women naked, sweating, shouting love songs, reeled and pranced together between the huts, jostling each other; wrestling. Few were laughing. Most faces expressed fierce greed, solemn truculence. A small number, who were already too drunk to be interested in others, alone appeared reasonable beings. Their tranquil expressions smoothed out like that of sleep walkers, their far gazing eyes, made them seem like philosophers among a rout of lunatics.

The old chief was still watching the dancers. He had drunk half a bottle of trade gin, but it had little effect upon him. The councillors and sub-chiefs seated round him were very drunk. They bore a most dignified appearance.

The household was drunk and the favourite wife Hama, Azai's mother, had beaten her daughters and servants. She was in a rage because Osho was missing. She beat also Osho's mother, a stupid thick-set girl who could only howl and protest that she had left a slave in charge of the girl.

As head wife Hama called all the children hers and governed their mothers. She was a good wife and mother, but obstinate and cantankerous. She spoilt babies but abused the elder children; and also the younger wives, whom she treated like children.

One would have thought that she would do murder, as she shook the girl, who, for her part, with open mouth and stupid eyes, submitted without a word. She felt her guilt. Her hands unconsciously covered her breasts, but she did not try to protect her face.

'You bitch,' Hama screamed, punching her in the nose and lip. 'I'll kill you.'

Luckily at this moment a house slave appeared in the doorway carrying Osho. The child, from which the pale mud, now dry, was cracking in broad flakes, was uttering a long wail which had ceased to be grievous. Its eyes indeed were full of a sleepy curiosity as it stared about it.

Hama and the sullen mother burst out laughing together at the wide open mouth, the sleepy wail, the wondering eyes. The mother, suddenly changed from a stupid lump of flesh to a being full of sense and humour, flew at the child, tossed it, hugged it, pushed her nipple between the wet lips.

Azai was standing behind his father's stool in the porch of the royal compound. He plucked at his robes. The old chief looked round in surprise; it was a crime on Azai's part to approach him in public, especially to touch his sacred robes.

'What are you doing?' he said sharply.

Azai was frightened, but he did not run away from his father who had never struck him. He said, 'Father, I saw some strangers by the river. They had white head cloths and broad spears like the cow people.'

'What?' cried the old man. 'What do you say?' He half rose from his stool, opening his mouth as if to shout. He sank back again and looked sternly at Azai. The sweat on his forehead stood in flat connected drops like rain on a polished leaf.

'What do you say?' said the old man.

Azai knew at once by the tone of this question that he was doing wrong. He said in a faltering voice, 'I saw some strangers with white caps.'

'Many Laka people wear white caps.'

'Yes, father,' said Azai, cast down.

The old man seemed to ponder. 'But then you say they had broad spears.'

'Yes, yes, yes, big spears like this,' Azai held up his hands.

The old man, having done sufficient honour to the truth, looked sternly at Azai and said:

'But plenty of Laka spears are as big as that.'

'Yes, father.'

Azai perceived at last what was the right thing to say, 'Perhaps they are not strangers.'

The old man smiled affectionately and stroked the child's head. He was not drunk, but he felt the licence of the occasion. Azai, surprised by the caress, smiled up at his father and said in a joyful voice, 'They were Laka people.'

'Of course they were. Who else could they be. Now run and play, child. This is a feast day.'

Azai ran off, skipping at every third step. He had forgotten about the strangers in the happiness of pleasing his father, in the importance of being complimented by him.

Felix had warning of the raiders just after sunset from his own servants. They at once took to the boats while he went to the town to find Dinah and Bandy. But the two women, both drunk, refused to come back with him and laughed at this story of raiders.

In this dilemma Felix walked about among the dancers, pensively smoking. He saw that it was stupid to remain; but he could not persuade himself to go. Four hours later, when the first explosion of twenty or thirty dane guns told the Laka people that the Emir's gunmen were actually in the stockades, Felix was still in the town.

He was like one of those people, who, when their houses are on fire, and the firemen put ladders to their windows, turn back into the room and are found afterwards burnt to death with the remains of a photograph frame or the collar of a favourite dog still grasped in one blackened claw.

The great Laka raid was planned by a certain Audu, slave to the Emir of Daji. Twelve months before Audu, already forty years old, had been a horse boy, with a bad reputation for impudence and ambition. In all autocracies ambition is a crime. Audu's back had been torn by floggings into a network of scar tissue. But he continued to be ambitious and he had at last found an opportunity of commending himself to the Emir by betraying one of his chief councillors for plotting against him. The councillor had not plotted, but he was too powerful to be accused, and, as Audu had foreseen, he was therefore prevented from defending himself. The Emir was obliged to have him murdered and Audu became at one jump master of the horse.

He was a short, very black Arab from the edge of the Sahara, with the face of a Pharaoh, thin nosed and thin lipped; full of deep pock marks. He was short and thickset with the legs and feet of a negro.

Audu at once set about planning the southern raids. No other ground was open to his master, the great chief of Daji, because he had devastated all the rest of the country.

Audu found the path through the Laka swamps by torturing a slave from Laka, and he chose feast time for the raid on the information of the same slave, who told him that the pagan tribes there preserved a religious truce.

This made success so easy that Audu with the vanguard was actually two miles away from Laka when it fell. A few dozen scouts and gun men, finding the place undefended, simply walked in. The ease of this conquest was probably the cause of its cruelty, because the raiders, full of that natural boisterous contempt for a fool or a weakling, which one sees in children, began at once to kill merely for the fun of the thing.

Audu had forbidden the place to be fired, but already at three o'clock the vanguard, still in the forest tracks, saw a glow in the sky and at half past three, when Felix wandering in the bush was surprised by shots, compounds all round him suddenly flared. The dry hut roofs exploded like bombs. They threw up crimson tulips of flame which made the sky seem like a low dome of old copper streaked with dark green verdigris. Thick sausages of smoke, extending slowly from them sideways in the light ground breeze from the river, divided the pinkish earth into strips and patches which gradually but continually changed their shapes. In each of these, as in the parts of a fair ground, divided for shows by fences of old grey canvas, figures could be seen grouped in dramatic attitudes. In one, two horsemen pranced, and below them, two small black figures sank down together, as if in a rehearsed gesture, and lifted up their arms. In another, further off, which was slowly enlarging as some nearer hut burnt low, five or six groups were seen sitting on the ground with their heads inwards, as if playing some game. A woman carrying a baby in front of her was running in and out among the groups which paid no attention to her. Two tall men with spears were trying to catch her. One of them struck her with the spear in the thigh. She fell. The two men then turned her over with their spear butts. They were arguing with violent gestures. One of them still arguing placed his foot on the woman's throat; took the baby by the legs, dragged it from her arms and in the same continued motion, swinging up and outwards, threw it out of sight into the smoke. Neither watched its flight. Suddenly a small boy in a white singlet, carrying a drum, came running in. He was followed by a cavalier, a short man in a white gown and a blue turban mounted on a very small, fat, black pony. It was Audu. He made a furious gesture; the two spearmen ran off. The boy with the drum took the woman by the hair and kicked her with his heel. Audu charged the nearest group, which did not scatter or run, but simply fell apart under his horse's hoofs like a broken stook of corn. He began to lash at these crooked remnants with his whip; stooping down to reach them with the lash. They lay where they had fallen; only a twitching leg or raised arm showed that they were alive.

The upper dome of the sky was fading into dirty yellow; the crimson flames lost their solidity, became like translucent pink or yellow stains on the white morning air; the smoke turned silver and yellowish. The rim of the sun sparkled through the trees like the sparks of a flintlock.

In the daylight, what had seemed dramatic became business-like. The soldiers lining up the prisoners, sorting out the useless old men and women, carrying out from the granaries huge calabashes full of maize and yam meal, had the intent, calm demeanour of people doing necessary business.

Chiefs moved here and there, inspecting the new taken slaves and especially the slave girls; but they did not stop in their walk or come too near the groups. If any seemed to look too closely at a slave, Audu came galloping up, and thrust himself between them. Then he would at once lash at the favoured slave with his whip; and if a girl had been noticed, he would cut at her face, laying open a cheek or knocking out an eye. He would scream at his men to take these vermin away. 'They belong to my lord Momadu, the King of Daji, the King of the world, Possessor of the Sudan.'

He was exhausted. Sweat poured from him. His eyes were bloodshot with heat and smoke. But he never ceased rushing through the huge camp—giving orders, cursing the lazy, flinging himself out of the saddle, knife in hand, to drag some trembling old woman from the line, and cut her throat where she stood; shouting at the alarmed soldiers, 'Brutes, fools, can't you see which are fit for use.'

It was the day of his opportunity.

Loud trumpets, the kakaka of a great chief were heard. Their blast was like the noise of stage thunder made with cracked tin. The Emir on his white arab stallion was seen approaching from the west. The sun fell on his pale face and his high white turban of narrow rolls of cambric, tier above tier. He was followed by seventy or a hundred horsemen in a disorderly mass. Some wore chain mail surcoats and steel caps. Others

258

were in patched gowns like dervishes. At each side of the Emir trum
peters walked with their six-foot tubes of brass at their lips. They
stumbled and hopped; tripping at every step on the uneven ground. In
front the famous Jingler, a tall figure in a white blouse and blue skirt,
with long twisted hair, walked backwards with an adroit, practised
step, lifting each foot high before thrusting it backwards to a firm
foothold. He carried a small hour-glass drum under his left arm and
beat on it rapidly with the tip of a carved stick. By squeezing the strings
of the drum into its waist with his elbow, he changed the note. He was
singing at the top of his voice impromptu verses in praise of the Emir.

> *Eater of men,*
> *Destroyer of towns,*
> *Most glorious and majestic of rulers.*

The Emir was a high bred Fulbe. His cheeks were a glistening yellow
brown. His nose, curved like a scimitar, was sharp at the bridge but
extremely wide at the base. Its wings were as wide as his big, thick-
lipped mouth, closed in a firm sinuous line. His chin, disclosed by the
falling of the loose chin cloth, was extremely small, cleft and receding.
It was a vulture's face; all beak and mouth. But the brown eyes had a
joyful, good-natured expression.

The Emir Momadu was in fact a good-natured man; famous for his
hospitality, his mild temper, his piety, his justice, almost as much as
for his courage and his love of glory. He did not need or seek wealth.
He gave away, after every successful campaign, the greater part of the
loot to his friends and captains. Only his devoted servants prevented
him from ruining himself.

He fought only for glory; for a moment like this when he found
himself riding in front of his men among burnt houses, broken corpses,
pools of blood; rows of prisoners lying in the dust and crying for
mercy.

Audu and four or five of his guards were seen driving forward a
crowd of men, women and children; the Laka chiefs and their families.
They pressed close on the high chief as if for his protection. He in the
midst of them, hidden to the waist, was carried forward as if by an
invisible vehicle; and his expression was that of one who suddenly finds
that he is being run away with; that he can't stop the machine. Confusion, increasing apprehension were mixed with the remains of his
royal dignity. His forehead was wrinkled deeply; his thin old lips
parted as if to exclaim, 'But this is absurd, incredible.'

Hama and two of the younger women were in front of him. Hama
was carrying Osho and stooping at the same time to guide another
toddling child between her feet. Bandy walked beside her, with her
baby on her back. At the assault she had run by instinct back to the

259

family household. She was so terrified that she could barely walk and tottered automatically against Hama's thick shoulder.

Hama was shouting at the guards, 'Wait a minute, curse you, the children can't go at that rate.' She was furious with the guards for their inconsiderate and foolish haste.

In front of Hama and Bandy, all by himself, Azai was marching with his head in the air. He had received for the feast a full dress of royal blue, and he marched with his stomach well forward to show off the cloth. But though his walk was dignified as befitted his rank, his looks were childish. He had just been waked up, dressed, pushed into the open; and the burning huts, the spearmen, the shouts, the horses, astonished him. He gazed about him wondering, full of a curiosity which could hold so many objects that it could not fix itself. He had forgotten himself in his wonderment, so that the majesty of his look, the royal projection of his stomach were maintained only by the command of nerves and muscles, educated already, like a lower branch of the Civil Service, to go on with their routine jobs until further orders.

The guards were using whips and spears; shouting as if in the midst of a battle with dangerous enemies. The captives about the high chief did not even raise their heads and eyes. Even their senses perceived their helplessness.

'Down on your knees, pagan dogs, before the King of the world,' they shouted. To show their zeal they knocked the old men and women down on their faces before they had time to prostrate themselves. Hama, still protesting, was flung upon Osho; Azai, who had stopped in a last overwhelming surprise with his eyes turned up towards the Emir's horse, received a blow in the ear from a spear butt which knocked him down as suddenly as if the ground had fallen in beneath him.

Audu himself lay under the forefeet of the Emir's horse; throwing dirt on his head with both hands.

The Emir said to him, 'I thank you, Audu. Salute the chiefs for me and set them free. I spare them.'

A hundred voices of the horsemen at once shouted loudly, 'The King of the world salutes Audu, and says I thank you. He says, let the pagan chiefs be set free,' and then broke into a confused noise of congratulation, cries of wonder, 'Oh the merciful king. Hear his sweet words to the defeated. Oh mighty lord, most patient, most merciful— we see and hear wonderful things.'

The Emir was not a cruel man and he delighted in this name of the merciful. He rode past the little group of the chiefs, still prostrate, with a benignant gesture, like a blessing.

Audu turned to his men and said, 'Take out the girls.'

Several of the young women, including Bandy and Osho's mother, and the girl babies who could walk, were pulled out and set aside. Bandy's baby was taken from her and thrown into the bush.

'As for the men,' Audu said, 'the great King is merciful—he spares the lives of these pagan dogs—make dogs of them.'

A swordsman at once dragged out the old high chief and hacked off his hands and feet.

This was the operation, inflicted on pagan chiefs or rebels by the Daji custom, known as making a dog of a man. The idea was that he would be compelled to go on all fours and eat from the ground. But unless the wounds were at once cauterized, they quickly caused death. The high chief died in a few minutes; others not so quickly, either because they had more vitality or because their guards chose to torture them.

To four or five of these men, the finer and more nervous types, arabs from the north, Fulani high strung and emotional, cruelty was a delight. These were the torturers who played with their victims for the sympathetic thrill of their terror and pain.

One of them caught at the boy Azai. Hama, who had been crouching over Osho, at once scrambled to her feet and rushed at the man. It was like the charge of a leopard. The ferocity, the weight of her rage threw him down and scattered the whole party. The newly captured slaves behind, startled from despair, turned and bolted, and the surprised guards ran after them. Bandy and Osho's mother, carrying Osho, were seen twenty yards away. Bandy's thin, crooked legs and big feet were twinkling like the spokes of a wheel. The big spearman who had singled her out was trying to stab her. She doubled and darted into the bush. Two or three more joined in the chase; whooping as after a deer.

Hama with Azai in front of her was flying in the opposite direction. The big woman who seemed to travel slowly had the speed and momentum of a bush cow. She crashed through the scrub into tracks known only to Laka people, towards the deepest part of the jungle. But at last, near the roots of a great cotton tree, standing in a clearing, Azai fell exhausted and while Hama was picking him up, the Daji men closed upon her. They cornered her between the huge buttresses of the tree. She turned sideways, putting her body between the swords and the child clinging to her neck. One of the men tried to drag it away, and failing slashed at its wrists, so that with a scream, it fell to the ground. Hama flew at the enemy with teeth and nails, but came upon the swords. In a moment she was slashed to death. Her body fell upon Azai's. The Daji men pulled off her heavy bangles and ran on quickly to find other booty.

Azai's wrists had not been cut through and he did not bleed to death. After a long time he awakened from a faint and found himself lying against something warm and soft, the familiar breast of his mother.

261

The sun was burning upon his legs and side. It was morning and there was a deep silence. Nothing could be heard except the occasional swirl of a dust whirl, or the murmur of the taller trees when their upper branches caught the wind.

Azai sighed and moved. He was comforted but still he wanted reassurance. He said again, 'Mother.'

There was no sound but the whisper of the leaves, far over his head.

Azai struggled free and saw that he was covered with blood. His mother lay dead against the root of the tree which was soaked in her blood. Azai gave a scream of terror and threw himself on the body, clasping it tightly between his arms and crying, 'Mother, mother, mother.'

He screamed and cried out; weeping and imploring his mother's body until he was exhausted and fell asleep. He was awaked again, thirsty and stiff in the dark, by a movement of the body. Eyes like pieces of moonlight stared at him. He knew that they belonged to hyenas or jackals, and shrank silently into the shadow of the tree. The body, jerking as if alive, trailed out of sight beyond the buttress.

Azai crept away into the narrowest recess between the great projecting buttresses of the roots; he closed his eyes expecting to feel the beasts' teeth. The teeth did not seize him, but he dared not move. He pressed himself against the tree as if to get within its bark; his whole being was asking for its protection.

His ear, pressed to the tree, gradually noticed a murmur like a pulse. There was no doubt of the sound; it grew louder and stronger every minute. He clasped the bark in an imploring agony; listening with his whole power.

Had his mother's spirit entered the tree, upon which her blood had fallen? He listened breathless to the pulse of its life; was this his mother's own life; the life which belonged to him, Azai.

'Mother, mother,' he shrieked suddenly; and at once from the high up branches of the tree he heard a whisper, 'Azai.'

Felix, rushing about the compounds to find Dinah, who as it happened had already run off to the store, was knocked down early in the raid by a horseman who probably did not recognize his tribe in the dark. Afterwards in daylight, when he came to himself among the smoking huts, he was allowed to walk away without molestation. The preoccupied raiders looked with surprise at the bearded foreigner but they did not try to make use of him either for sport or trade.

When Pooley, sent with half a company of the Nigerian Regiment to avenge his murder, reached Laka, the first person he met on the Laka road was Felix, strolling from one of the ruined huts with his brass pipe in his mouth.

262

Pooley surprised the raiders, who bolted at the first volley, leaving most of their loot and slaves behind them. He then camped at Laka, for though the Government had not intended to advance so far beyond the Mosi, the French with unusual promptness, had sent in a strong protest and a demand that the troops should be withdrawn. As the French and the British peoples were then on bad terms, the French and British governments dared not concede anything that the other demanded. Pooley was therefore ordered to remain in Laka and the old royal compound was converted into the fort of the new station.

Bandy sat in the bush holding herself by the breasts which ached with milk. She had no idea about anything so that even the terror which filled her body seemed inert and senseless. She had no positive feeling even about the disappearance of her baby. It had been swallowed up into confusion like the rest of the world, which had ceased to mean anything. For a day and night she had listened to the shouts of the raiders, the shrieks of tortured victims; and now there were different yells and the sound of different guns.

Osho, lying at her side, slept, breathing easily. Osho had crept up to her as if by scent the day before, and Bandy had been glad to feed her. Osho's face was squashed into her thigh for though she had taken her fill she liked the smell of a mother, of the secure and happy world into which she had been born. Bandy had seen nothing of the child's mother; probably like most of the others she had been speared.

The undergrowth cracked; men were cutting into her hiding place with matchets on both sides. Suddenly four big Yoruba soldiers appeared, waist deep in the scrub before her.

Bandy caught up Osho and darted forward, turned aside and charged head first at the thick tangled scrub.

A soldier bawled, 'Hi, stop, we want you.'

Bandy butted at the thorns, tearing her way forward.

'Hi, we come to save you. We want you.'

Bandy fell through the creepers, ran head first against a tree and fell almost unconscious; but her legs and arms still crept away from the soldiers, like a dog's running in his sleep, and her right arm still cupped Osho.

The soldier, though he could not see Bandy, was still shouting. He was inviting her to come to the white man's camp. Women were wanted to pound yam and cook for the soldiers. He offered sixpence a day. He explained that the soldiers had come to save the Laka women and that the Laka women ought to make chop for them. Why did they all run away from the good kind soldiers, and the great white man, the great captain, Pooley?

But Bandy continued to crouch away from the voice. She crawled

263

until it was dark. She met others creeping, hiding from the new terror. There was a group at every big tree. Under the cotton tree there were twenty or more pressed among the buttress. Bandy crawled among them; pushing among their legs like a fox through a copse, seeking a hole. It was only when her head struck against the back of the stem, that she sank down, exhausted. Osho was crying. She put the breast in her mouth.

Something stirred against the warmth of her legs. She looked and saw the body of a small boy, dried up, with fallen stomach and sharp cheek-bones. He was covered with stains of blood; black on the pale brown skin. Suddenly he opened a slit of eye, looked up at her, then feebly struggled towards her.

Bandy looked at the boy with no thought or feeling about him at all; as he struggled, moving his dried, withered lips, and fell across her legs, she jerked him aside with her knees.

The people were chattering over her head, all round her. At each distant shot they all fell silent; and then they all cried out together, 'This place is no good—we must go——'

It was true that the cotton tree stood in a clearing, exposed on all sides; Bandy herself, seeking a hiding-place, had examined it more than once from the bush and decided that it would not do. It was a big tree and probably had a strong spirit; but it was too much in the open. No one could be hidden there. All these people had come like herself in the last hour, flying from the soldiers. There were other groups at the big palm tree twenty yards away; equally exposed.

'We must go,' the people jabbered, but they did not go. They were waiting for orders, for a leader, for advice; but there was no one to advise them.

Bandy felt a touch at her right breast. The dying boy was reaching out to it. She looked down and saw that he was Azai; she knew his hair, cut in the regal style with the central ridge. The wrist touching her was cut and the hand was twisted and shrivelled, like a parrot's claw. She shuddered with disgust at the touch against her sensitive breast of this cold dead hand, and thrust the boy roughly away. Azai was nothing to her; nothing to anybody now, without hands.

The boy fell back. He gazed at her. His lips moved but he could not utter a sound.

The shots grew faint, the cries small like bird calls. There was silence. Bandy herself grew sleepy. She slipped down against the stem, her cheek on the ground, and was at once asleep. Osho, half crushed beneath her, screamed. She was almost upside down. She wriggled and cried for ten minutes, then also fell asleep.

Bandy waked cold and stiff. Her head was aching. Osho was screaming; yet she felt a mouth at her nipple. She did not reflect upon this odd matter. She lay with a sulky expression, waiting for her brain to begin working; for some thought or impulse to move her. Osho's yells increased; the mouth continued to suck. A dim wonder formed in Bandy's head. She looked down beneath her and seeing Azai fixed to her breast, she gazed without thought, feeling him as a creature, and now she had no inclination to push him away. She looked at his hands, his body withered by thirst to the likeness of a little old man, but she was not disgusted. When her back began to ache and she changed her position, so that her breast swung away from him; and she saw that he was too weak to raise himself to it, she stooped, again putting it to his mouth. The wrists grasped her again, the eager mouth sucked; the eyes looked up at her and seemed to implore her. Once more she felt him, his lips; sometimes his teeth. She felt his need of her. She smiled and put an arm round him, lifting him against her breast. She stooped over him and murmured, 'Poor Azai, drink then.'

She picked up the useless hand and cried, 'Aie, aie, it's spoilt.' She pondered, watching him and after reflection, said, 'You were hungry then. But how could you feed yourself? Aie, aie. Drink then, my poor one.'

She felt suddenly pity and tenderness. She smiled down at the boy and cried, 'What, are you going to eat me.'

She pressed his head against her breast, as if its sensitive skin could express to him also this joyful love and protective assurance. She laughed at him 'Go on, bite it off, you cannibal. Don't be afraid. I shan't beat you.'

At last Azai was satisfied. He let the nipple slip from his mouth. For a few moments he clung to her with his wrists; and then whispered, 'Good Bandy.'

'You've had enough, have you? Then we'd better go away from here.'
'Why, you mustn't go.'
'All the others have gone. It's not safe. Anyone could see us.'
'But this tree will look after us. It is my mother. Hama the queen. Her spirit went into the tree.'

Bandy looked up with a startled face and said, 'Hama the queen.
'Listen and she will speak to you.'

Bandy listened. Azai said, 'She is speaking to me. She says, "Azai, Azai, rest now." '

Bandy listened and her mouth fell open. She breathed, 'It is a voice——'

'They killed her and her blood fell on the tree. There, you can see it.'

The leaves rustled in the morning breeze, high up. Azai interpreted, 'Stay, Bandy—stay with Azai.'

Bandy threw herself on her face. Osho gave a loud cry of indignation. 'You will stay,' Azai said, touching the girl with his wrists.

'Yes, I must—it is Hama then. I will stay. We must put a cloth on her.' She looked at the tree. A tree containing a recognized spirit was usually marked by a cloth tied round the trunk.

'Yours would do.'

'Yes, I could tear a piece from it.'

Bandy tore thin strips from her cloth and knotted them together. Then she clambered up a buttress, fixed one end in a crack of the bark and slowly worked her way round to it. The trunk was encircled. After this, Bandy felt perfectly safe at the tree. Also she became a collected and responsible person, like one belonging to an orderly household, with a head wife to give commands and a regular routine of duties.

Yet she gave herself the commands; she formed her own routine of duties, which were quite new and original. It was as though she needed only the notion of law, of order, to release her invention.

She began to devise schemes for feeding her family, and sheltering them. She left Azai with Osho and scouted through the jungle; fearless as a leopard with cubs. She discovered water, and a deserted yam store; left in its patch by the owner, killed or in hiding. She dragged yams and thatch to the tree and put up the thatch on bush sticks to shelter the two children from the heat. It was the kind of shelter that she had seen a hundred times in the yam fields made to cover babies while the women worked; but she had not before turned such a shelter into a house.

In three days Bandy had formed a household which was in miniature the household of a Laka native; with cooking hut, sleeping hut, yam store, water pots, a heap of firewood; and she herself like chief and junior wives in one, commanded, bustled, scolded like the head wife, pounded and cooked like a minor humble wife, gossiped and chattered like a daughter, from morning till night.

The soldiers were in camp among the ruins of the old town, less than a mile away, and often they could be heard chasing women in the bush. But they never came into the clearing.

This did not surprise Bandy and Azai who knew themselves under the tree's protection, speaking to them all day long, gossiping, scolding, murmuring affectionate speeches. At night when the dark was already cold, they crept into the cleft of the buttress, still warm from the sun, and slept as between warm, living breasts.

VIII

'The hour is dark, my friends, let us not deceive ourselves. Every-where Satan seems to triumph. Nothing is left us but faith——'

The little congregation in the tin chapel listened with upturned faces. Porfit was its favourite preacher and it was said that he would not be heard much longer in Porriton. He was known to be in debt all round, and there had been trouble about his articles in the *Gazette;* threats of libel actions by the brewers.

The preacher approached his peroration, his voice rose like a cry like a prayer.

'For in the desert of our hopes, we remember that spirit which led the children of Israel through deserts of despair as barren and hopeless seeming as this life of ours.'

It was a good address suited to the feeling of the moment, at a time when the Liberal Party seemed hopelessly beaten; in winter when most of the congregation, small tradespeople and artisans, felt a pinch.

Porfit received many congratulations after the service; sincere gratitude from those whom he had heartened for battles of life as dreary and thankless as any in the kingdom; and as he walked home he was greeted still by every second person with friendly or admiring smiles. He had the largest following of any man in Porriton; but his followers were poor, and as he had reflected often in the last weeks, their respect could not keep him in food, rent and clothes. He was deeply dejected; he saw no hope anywhere.

It was bitter weather; as he walked down the lane the mud cracked under his feet. The horse dung was frozen in the pools so that the old cripple who came every day from his cellar in Pynsant's Place, gathering it with his hands into a box, was obliged to scrape it up with the jagged edge of an old saucepan. The people coming from the Baptist chapel, in a cross stream, greeted Porfit. He saluted them with an easy wave; or suddenly, with a vigorous gesture, at sight of the women in their high bonnets and wide bugled capes trimmed with feathers, he raised his hat high into the air and jerked his body forward from the waist. It was a salute half gallant and half facetious. The gallantry was excused by the exaggeration, which made a joke of all ceremony.

But these bows and smiles, so adroitly performed, were motions as habitual to Porfit as the courtesies of royalty. He had been accustomed to the public eye, the sharp and attentive eye of the lower middle class, for more than ten years. But to what advantage? He had failed like a thousand others in the same place; aspiring young lay preachers and street corner orators, secretaries of the choir, and prime ministers in the mock parliament of the young men's temperance club. His own uncle had been the first Radical district councillor for Motcombe, but he had died in the workhouse infirmary. Porfit remembered that death. In fits of despondency he could still see the old man on his death bed, crumpled as if by some juggernaut that had rolled over his stomach, weeping senile tears for his own failure.

'Go you to London,' he had said. 'It ain't no good you're stopping here—you'll never get anywhere without money behind you.'

Porfit had not gone to London. He could not agree to be nobody in London after years of distinction in Motcombe. But now he was finished. The rent was three weeks overdue; and his only pair of boots were cracked through the toe cap. A hole in the sole did not matter, but the crack was fatal because he could not stand upon a platform, or even a soap box, with a cracked boot. He entered the little back bedroom, smelling of the cold close air and the cotton counterpane, and collapsed on the bed. Despondency overwhelmed him. He felt like weeping; and he thought, 'It would do me good.' He wept.

Then he sat still at the bottom of his darkness with sore throat and blank mind. He felt nothing; thought nothing. But gradually it became an effort to sit still; activity seemed to rise by itself within him.

'I'm done for,' he said, but now the exclamation was a challenge, it was as though he kicked himself. He straightened his back and looked up. His eye fell on a portrait; a large, coloured print which hung then in thousands of Radical households; Gladstone. For a long time he gazed at the deep eyes, the big nose and the bald head in its halo of white; the wide free collar; the face which to millions carried the recollection of Liberal triumphs, of an immense achievement over half a century. He felt a release so sudden that it was like a physical lightening. It was as though the tide of his energy rushed up into assurance. He felt that the world where such men existed and could sometimes rule, was God's world; that his Liberal cause, to free the spirit of man from political, religious and economic bondage, was the cause of God. God was for freedom and God must triumph.

He felt such a confidence in himself, in his success that his recent despondency seemed incredible. He could not believe it. He thought, 'I was just acting a part—and that's a fault of mine. It gives the impression of insincerity when I am really a sincere person. No one more so, God knows.'

There was a knock at the door. His mother's voice called, 'Robert, dinner.'

He quickly brushed his fingers across his face, to take away his smile. His mother was depressed and he did not wish to seem too cheerful. He entered softly into the kitchen and sat down at the table, spread with a clean American cloth, and sitting down, repeated in a melancholy voice, 'For all that we are about to receive the Lord make me truly thankful.'

Mrs. Porfit unclasped her short thick hands, grey with work, and looked at her son. She exclaimed, 'You've sold that article, Robert?'

'No, mother.'

'Why are you looking so pleased?'

'I don't know.'

The woman, short, thick-set, eyed him suspiciously and fiercely, through her small iron spectacles. Then she said, 'I hear they're skating at New Grange.'

'Not to-day.'

'They might, God forgive them. But they were yesterday, for Aunt May was there watching 'em, she says Miss Chorley was the best of the lot.'

Robert answered that this was very likely; Miss Chorley had been at school in Switzerland.

'Well then, if the frost holds, why don't you go and skate? It's free to all and you've nothing to do to-morrow.'

This was the first time Mrs. Porfit had shown any knowledge of her son's infatuation. He was not surprised. No child is surprised by that parental omniscience which first appeared to them before they could speak. But even though he was the best of sons, he did not choose to confess that his mother understood his most private feelings. He answered, 'I can't go in a frock coat.'

'Why not—of course you can. And your skates are in the ottoman.'

Porfit shook his head. But Mrs. Porfit was not surprised, after breakfast on the next morning, to see him cleaning his skates. He went out to call on a friend, and returned with a large parcel. At dinner he appeared in a knickerbocker suit of pepper and salt, with a Norfolk jacket and a barmaid's collar with a neat little bow tie. He smiled gaily at his mother's astonishment and disapproval.

'You're not going in those things?'

'Don't you like them?'

'Why, what will people think? And they don't fit. Wherever did you get such breeches? Everybody'll laugh at you.'

'Do you think so?' Porfit looked at his legs. The knickerbockers were certainly too large.

'I know it. You go and change at once. If you want to skate, you can skate in your frock coat, like a Christian should.'

'A frock coat for skating.'

Porfit always wore his old frock coat. He felt by instinct what royalty discovers by experience, that a popular leader should never be fashionable. That is to invite criticism from triflers in exchange for their condescension, which is the only form of their sympathy; and to risk the condescension of the serious, the envy of the mean, and the religious prejudice of the stupid.

As soon as dinner was over, he went to change into the frock coat. But he did so with a great reluctance, to which, though he did not understand it, he paid attention, as to all his impulses, since, as experience had shown, they might prove to be the first warnings of conscience or a direct hint from the guiding providence which had so often inspired his acts and speeches.

Lucy Chorley rose in his mind as he had met her once, after much contrivance, at a missionary meeting in Bellavista. She had come in late from some luncheon party, in an elaborate frock, and when gathering his courage, he had said, 'What a nice dress, Miss Lucy,' she had answered, 'I had no time to change it.'

'But I'm very glad you didn't. Young ladies ought to wear pretty frocks.'

He had been alarmed by his own rashness. He had felt Mrs. Chorley's eyes turned upon him with that fierce expression which meant, 'Oh dear, how dreadful these people are—you never know what they'll do." But even in his alarm his quick wits had seized upon Lucy's face an expression which again added to his knowledge of her, something which he could not formulate, a look part guilt, part confusion.

He saw that look now when he was in the act of peeling off the absurd knickers, and at once his feeling of stupidity, almost of sin, increased so strongly that he stopped. Two minutes later he appeared in the outer room of the cottage fully dressed in the knickerbocker suit.

Mrs. Porfit, who had been a schoolmistress, and who still had the sharp voice and sharp manner of a teacher, ejaculated, 'You've not changed yet.'

'I'm not going to change, mother.'

'You can't go like that.'

'Why should I trouble about such people and their laughter? The crackling of thorns under the pot. It is better that they should laugh than that I should offend an old friend like Jenkins who lent me his best suit.'

Mrs. Porfit made a face as if to say, 'Don't make your speeches to me,' but she said no more. She was a sharp critic of her son, to whom she had given her life and for whom she slaved, but she never opposed him.

'I'll wear my black coat through the streets.'

'I think you'd better,' she answered grimly.

270

A few minutes later he went out, in his black overcoat and bowler, showing only the black stockings and yellow boots beneath it, and carrying his skates in a brown paper parcel. But the stockings were at once noticed from a dozen windows in Chorley Street. It was a respectable street. None of its families gossiped at doors or shouted across from window to window. To occasional passengers, it seemed dead; inhabited only by passing rag and bone men, a street singer, two little boys with satchels and a tabby cat. But every one of its little houses with their shining door bells and lace curtains was explosive with life. An opening door poured out steam, the smell of cooking, rumbling voices, shrieks of babies. It was a street full of enclosed energies; like a row of charged shells; shut in their neat brass cases. People in Chorley Street spent much time at windows, behind the lace curtains which were intended to prevent overlooking and to permit outlooking; studying their neighbours and the passers by. But their discreet watchfulness was more intelligent than the bold staring of the slum tribe in Pynsant's Place. They had a grasp of politics and social relations which, although narrow, was inclusive and rational. From Porfit's stockings they reasoned that he was going to amuse himself, by walking or playing some game.

Porfit of course was not a minister. But the question remained, was he as serious as he seemed to be? It was debated in twenty houses before tea-time; not in any heavy or intolerant manner. Even those middle-aged men who had themselves preached and at Porfit's age had aspired to his distinction, did not make a serious crime of the boots. They said only that there was something a bit flibberty about young Porfit. There always had been, and they recalled that he had once appeared in a play, when Mr. Chorley gave theatricals at Bellavista for the Armenian refugees.

New Grange, built about 1830, was a long, rambling house with high pitched roofs, and Gothic casements. It lay in a valley, among the famous gardens, full of semi-tropical plants, which had been the General's hobby. There was no park in the usual sense of the word. The woods and fields beyond the immense garden were all Pynsant land, strictly preserved; but Stella, when she went riding, was obliged to find a grass field for a gallop.

In winter, the gardens had a strange appearance. The palms were wrapped in straw and many of the stone figures which stood in the French garden among clipped yews were covered in wood and canvas to prevent erosion by frost. At this time neighbouring landowners with Georgian houses and normal parks were able to despise New Grange, and to say that it was as ugly as a nursery.

But on the east side of the house the General had kept a rough grass lawn, among English trees; and a slope of rough grass falling to a chain of lakes, once the fish ponds of the old priory.

The smallest, below the house, had an island summer house, where Stella had often played at pirates; and it was joined to the next larger one by a narrow neck of water with a slight fall, which served at children's parties for the rapids of Niagara.

The view of the house from these lakes in winter, with snow on the highpitched roofs and the lattice of the windows, was Stella's favourite scene. It was like a Christmas card of old England.

When the lakes froze, Motcombe villagers, by old custom, were allowed to skate on the larger, and already by nine o'clock there were at least a hundred skating and sliding upon it. No one intruded upon the smaller lake now being swept by the gardeners; and a close observer could notice a further gradation of social privilege accepted by the villagers on their own ice; the boys and the collarless kept to the far end, where they shouted and wrestled. Few of these had skates. The next class, the barmen from the Green Man, a foreman carter, and three small-holders, with skates and collars, used the middle; while close to the neck itself, at the threshold of the gentry's ice, two farmers, a butcher and the second huntsman could be seen; one of them in breeches. No women were present. The village women did not skate. Even the grocer's wife who had leisure to amuse herself considered it unwomanly to do so.

Meanwhile Helen Pynsant, in the little private sitting room next to her bedroom, was sending out by a groom invitations to all those surrounding gentry who could not, since they were themselves owners of property, intrude upon hers without a formal invitation.

'But not the Chorleys, mother,' Stella said.

'Not the Chorleys,' Helen cried in amazement. 'What do you say to that, Theo?' She turned in her chair and regarded Benskin, who stood close to the door, with his cuffs turned back. He had been working for two days on a chair sledge, in white and gilt, to match Helen's new skating dress.

Helen was not yet dressed, except for her hair. She wore a dressing gown of white satin, trimmed with ospreys, and as she turned, she drew it together across her breasts with a gesture at once dignified and coquettish. Helen's modesty was a grace rather than a virtue.

'The Chorleys,' Benskin said. 'I'd as soon not. Chorley always has some bee in his bonnet about his blessed newspaper or the Kaffirs in the mines.'

'Oh, business,' with impatience. 'But how could we leave them out, it would be impossibly rude.'

Stella, looking sullenly on the ground, muttered, 'They've got their own lake.'

'Then Lucy can skate there, but Cobden is coming over in any case,' and dropping her eyelids she glanced at Benskin's hands, hanging from his cuffs. 'Your sleeves always seem too short,' she murmured. 'Who buys your shirts?'

Benskin's long arms and enormous hands on their bony wrists, now hanging from his turned back cuffs, certainly appeared abnormal; but he was surprised by the attack. It was seen that he was deeply hurt. This was absurd in a man of forty-two, but Benskin's childish and sensitive nerves always invited Helen to cruelty. She smiled and said, 'But of course, your hands are rather abnormal.'

Benskin put his hands behind him, and after a moment's reflection, left the room. Spitefulness in a woman always scattered his wits.

Helen, smiling, a little flushed, as if by an amorous pleasure, turned back to her table. Suddenly she caught her daughter's eye fixed upon her with a furious look. Stella was crimson. 'If I were Theo, I'd never speak to you again.'

'I must remember to write to Madame Paul about that finishing school for you.'

'Yesterday it was Mr. Nussbaum, to-day it's going to be that boy.'

'Mr. Nussbaum is a guest of the house, and I must ask you to be polite to him—I was ashamed of the way you looked at the poor man yesterday. He may be plain, but he's not a monster.'

'You know it isn't his looks——'

'Hadn't you better let me finish dressing?'

'You had him in this room nearly all night.'

Helen, who had indeed allowed Nussbaum to stay late in her room, was startled. She said, 'My dear child, what do you mean?'

'Only—it looks so queer. It's so undignified. People are laughing.'

Helen became pink, and made no answer. She was wounded and even frightened. For her as for Cobden attitude was highly important. Dignity, which was the chief virtue of Albert Edward as she knew to her cost, was also her own. It was something for which she acknowledged the need of self-sacrifice.

With a slightly tremulous hand, she patted the high rolls of her pompadour. She studied her daughter's sulky face in the glass. She knew, of course, that Stella had no idea of her real relations with Nussbaum. That was the virtue of her other defects as a daughter; an innocence which had cost, at a hundred guineas a term, already more than fifteen hundred pounds. She could see, too, that the girl was frightened by her own boldness. She need not be afraid of her.

But undignified! laughable! Perhaps she had better not ask Cobden.

Yet who else could push her sledge? Who else could not only admire her new winter dress, but harmonize with it. The idea of Nussbaum on the ice was revolting. He, certainly, would make her ridiculous.

273

And Benskin was even more intolerable; with his mind as obtuse as his fingers.

She turned her eyes to Stella, making them pathetic and said, 'Darling, I don't think you are very kind to me.'

Stella suddenly lost her anger. She flushed, her lips trembled and she drew her thick brows together. 'But I don't understand, Mamma.'

'Never mind, darling—I don't expect the Chorleys will leave their own pond.'

'But Mama, you won't——'

'My dear, I must really finish dressing.'

Stella went out. Helen threw her note into the fire. But a moment later, while her maid was lacing her, her eyes fell upon the white Huzzar jacket laid on the bed. She looked sadly at it; tears were in her eyes; then suddenly she pouted like a cross child, turned firmly to her bureau, dragging the maid after her by the stay strings. She sat down and wrote to Cobden, 'I will never forgive you if you don't come and give me an opinion on my new frock. Your poems were utterly lovely,' she paused, biting the pen; what could she say about the poems? The maid, who could not continue her work on account of the back of the chair, stood patiently holding the tags of the laces.

Brakes and carriages began to arrive immediately after lunch. At three o'clock the noise of skates was like the roar of a mill wheel.

The sky was full of snow clouds, coloured like the varnish of an old master; under their dull golden light, refracted and diffused, all objects and planes acquired great solidarity; and local colours were intensified. The black ice, marked already with white lines and figures, where Benskin, Lucy and her father made threes and eights, seemed a portion of some original geometrical earth, the smooth and solid globe of the original geometer, skinned of its ornaments. The withered grass on the banks, and the close set tufts on the slope toward the house, rising through the powder of dry snow, had more individuality, as grass in their brittle age, than when they had been part of the spring. The rough trunks of the elms seemed as solid and dense as old rusty iron, and their dull brown, rusty at the edge of each plate of bark, had a force of tint which caught the eye. Even the white of Helen's Huzzar dress, as Cobden pushed her here and there across the ice in Benskin's new sledge, was colour in this light like a white wine. Helen's cheeks, usually too pale, now had a radiance which made even the women glance at her with smiles of appreciation. She was a delight to the eye; and therefore to herself. Her smiles were like blessings given out of her happiness upon the worshipping faithful.

Benskin, circling to the bank to welcome his friend, Mr. Nussbaum, and to avoid Chorley who had several times attempted to open a conversation, said gravely, as one supporting an English institution, 'Grand sport and the grand weather for it. Real English weather.'

'A most beautiful sight,' Nussbaum said. He had been glad to admire its beauty, and not to look at Helen with Cobden.

Nussbaum was an Alsation of the second generation in England; but still northern French in manner, precise, reserved, rather sharp. He was extremely ugly. It was said indeed that his mother, still living in France, had refused to see him since his boyhood. His low-crowned head, his large ears, his enormous mouth and short thick nose, had given him the name, among Helen's smart friends, of the frog.

He was a man of first rate intelligence and the highest education; generous to his friends; a lover of all the arts. His prim, rather cold manner, was protective; his fierce gloomy expression was the device adopted many years before by the schoolboy when he first realized that his smile was hideous.

He turned to Benskin and said with gravity, as if to emphasize an important fact:

'This only was worth the journey from London. It is a perfect Breughel.'

'Pardon.'

'A Breughel. Don't you know him? A Dutch painter, a very great painter.'

'Oh, yes, I know the man you mean. So that's what you call him— Broy-gel,' Benskin repeated the name as if memorising it. He was just beginning to study the arts. He looked closely at the dark trees, the sky as low-toned as the ice, and the level ice with its flying skaters as if to see it in a new aspect. 'Broy-gel,' he murmured.

Helen Pynsant came from behind the island in her sledge pushed by Cobden, who, in a very long black overcoat, braided across the chest, looked almost like a Beardsley drawing. His face was so white by contrast that it might have been powdered. He bent his long neck towards Helen to speak in her ear, and she laughed heartily, showing her teeth. Cobden seemed about to weep.

'Breughel,' Nussbaum murmured, but his voice had changed its note. He, too, was staring at Helen and his small, screwed up eyes were full of such pain that Benskin, even in his own preoccupation, noticed it.

'She seems to have lost her head,' he said in a flat, helpless voice.

'No, no, it's quite natural. The pretty widow. It is a very old story, and always quite natural.'

'But you don't think she will marry the boy?'

'Why not? He is very good looking. He would suit her very well.' Nussbaum gave a deep, involuntary sigh. 'If she asked me, I should say, "Marry him, my dear."'

'Seventeen years older.'

275

'It would be a capital thing. The boy wants a profession—Helen wants a strong young husband to spoil her.'

'A profession?'

'A religious profession, then. Helen could be a cult.'

'I can't stand the chap—always mooning about like a puppy with worms.' Benskin spoke with unusual violence.

'A faith must have its martyrs—even the æsthetic faith—or how can anyone take it seriously—even æsthetic young men.'

'I see,' Benskin said, staring angrily at the martyrized Cobden.

'Helen would be excellent for the young æsthete.'

'In that case, I might think of your damned Klipspringer East Concession again.'

'Ah! if you would. What a chance.'

Nussbaum began to urge upon Benskin, as often before, that he was wasting himself in England, on local politics and parochial intrigues, buying a brewery here and a newspaper there. 'What if you do put a few more Liberal Imperialists into Parliament, what difference will it make?'

He understood Benskin's idea. He, too, had known Rhodes, to whom the Empire with its system of decentralized local governments was the nucleus of a world state. But to Nussbaum, with his Continental mind, this Rhodes imperialism was a dream. He was sceptical of all ideas of security; of lasting peace. He did not think of the world in the first place as a complex of powers, but of cultures, in which he savoured each, the French, the German, the English for its special flavour, not only in art but in all its character.

'And then if you must play at your English politics, play big. Start a London newspaper—buy cabinet ministers.'

'We don't do that here.'

'Yes, yes. of course you do. Not with cash, perhaps, but with little arrangements, with friendships, with sugar sticks—it is all the more interesting.'

'I think I'd prefer even prospecting,' Benskin said.

Chorley skated slowly past, looked at Benskin, hesitated, and swung away. Chorley had been trying to catch Benskin alone for the last two hours in order to ask him a question which he did not like to write, because in writing it seemed too rude, too insulting. Was he responsible for the canvassers who, in the last three weeks, had been offering space in the *Granport Advertiser* at half rates causing the *Gazette* already the loss of the greater part of its advertising income, and even some circulation. The rumour was that the Granport Advertising Company, which had sent out the canvassers, belonged to Benskin. Chorley could not believe it, and his wife was convinced that Mr. Benskin was incapable of such an act. They had discussed the matter for three nights and their conclusion had been that the rumour must be a slander; that it would be unchristian as well as unwise to accuse the new partner, a friend and a fellow Liberal, of such a stab in the back. But perhaps Chorley might discuss the matter with him, in a casual way.

Chorley had tried to do so for a week, but Benskin had eluded him; and now on the ice he was sure that this evasion was deliberate. The man had a guilty conscience.

Chorley was astonished and furious. He did not know if he could trust himself to speak to one who was capable of such treachery. He did not get the opportunity till tea time, when mats and rugs were spread on the banks of the lakes, and the whole house staff brought out thick bread and butter and tea in kitchen cups. For a moment Benskin, skating slowly along the bank with a thick white mug in his hand, was alone. Chorley intercepted him. The two looked at each other, Benskin out of his deep eyes, which seemed always withdrawn into their caves, like shy wild animals; Chorley with his angry, frank stare.

'Hullo, old man,' Benskin said softly. 'Have you had any tea yet, or would you like a drink?'

'Benskin, you spoke to me once of buying the *Gazette*.'

'Yes, three months ago.'

'I see, you don't want it now.'

'What is it worth now? What are you asking?'

Chorley, looking at the man's shelving head and sharp gaze, hesitated. He had suddenly the feeling that Benskin, even if he were guilty, would not be ashamed to admit it, that it was as dangerous and useless to quarrel with him as with a savage. Why then quarrel? He said with his easy grace, 'It's not for sale, of course, but I was going to ask you if——'

'Excuse me,' Benskin turned and called to Nussbaum. 'This is the man,' he introduced them. 'Mr. Chorley is interested in labour conditions on the Witwatersrand.'

Chorley smiled in his grand way. His anger against Benskin had disappeared. He did not want to be angry with him. His attitude became still more distinguished and grave. 'I believe you know South Africa well, Mr. Nussbaum.'

Cleeve's shouts were heard. Cleeve had never skated before, and after a dozen severe falls before luncheon, he had gone to buy new skates. Now seeing Lucy disengaged, he was calling for her. Both Lucy and Stella, who had been practising a Dutch roll in a corner by herself for the last three hours, at once came flying towards him, laughing and calling out their encouragement. It was as though he had released in

277

them some natural joy, which was young and gay and free from preoccupation.

'Try them,' Lucy called. It had amused her that Cleeve should blame his skates for his falls, and go six miles for a precisely similar pair.

'No, wait.' Stella shouted a warning. But Cleeve had already struck out boldly upon the ice. He at once turned a back somersault and lay with legs and arms in the air.

At once everyone, including Stella, Helen from the sledge, now drawn up on the bank, Nussbaum and Benskin, broke into laughter. All their faces, different in their various solemn expressions, assumed one general delight.

'Ha-ha!' Nussbaum cried, forgetting himself, opening his mouth like a cavern. He exclaimed, 'But it's that boy from Ireland. What a pity his eyes are so small. In colour they are beautiful. But I thought he was in Africa.'

'It's his cousin who had been distinguishing himself in Africa—Harry Jarvis.'

'You think then, Mr. Nussbaum, that a missioner among your Kaffir miners——' Chorley returned again to serious matters. On Nussbaum's face as he turned politely towards him there was that indescribable expression of the Continental freethinker, faced by an evangelical; a look in which boredom, contempt, and the consideration which distorts the faces of asylum visitors into a kind of fearful politeness, mixed and contradicted each other.

Benskin, empty mug in hand, seized his chance to escape. He cut a three, and came to the foot of Helen's chair, fifteen yards away. The group surrounding the chair, Cobden, a young soldier from Exeter, Lord Porriton, a short thickset man with a face like a John Dory, were still laughing. Benskin, however, did not laugh because he knew without turning round that they were no longer laughing at Cleeve. The laughter had a different sound. He glanced over his shoulder and saw, in the narrow neck, between the two ponds, a young man in a knickerbocker suit, much too large for him, and a bowler, much too small, staring towards the figure skaters. 'A Phil May come to life,' Helen said.

Benskin could not laugh at an aspiring young man, however absurd. His sympathies were with him. He cut short a turn, and called out to the garden boys who were building a fire of brushwood, close to their mistress' sledge, 'Stand 'em up—stand 'em up.'

He went to show them how to build a camp fire.

'But he's rather pathetic,' Helen said.

'Porfit,' Lord Porriton beamed. 'Is that the fellow? I thought you'd got rid of him. What's he doin' here?'

'On the pond of the oppressor,' Cobden murmured.

'But why,' the girl asked, 'do Radicals always have long hair?'

278

'Just to look different from other people,' Porriton said in a sour tone.

'Because they feel like John the Baptist,' Helen suggested, 'and then they're a little like artists too—they work by inspiration.'

'It's a complex idea,' Cobden said, 'in which you will find Rousseau as well as John the Baptist—nature plus providence.'

'Laissez hair,' Helen murmured, and Cobden congratulated her. 'Perfect, too perfect.'

The prophet craning forward across the invisible barrier of class, with his yearning eyes and mournful eyebrows, at this moment over-balanced and performed a quick shuffle on the ice, like an involuntary dance of the low comedian. The group by the fire burst into a shout of laughter. Benskin, quickly gliding in front of them, and turning towards them his roughly squared features, said urgently, 'Take care, he might hear.'

'But my dear Theo, it's Porfit.'

'Yes, but he's not deaf.' All looked at Benskin, the girls with surprise, Cobden with a faintly supercilious air, Helen with a little smile. Lord Porriton, suddenly recollecting that Benskin himself had an obscure origin, perhaps even from depths as low as Porfit's, as any Baptist agitators, suddenly burst out with a loud, panic-struck, 'H-rumph, no, of course—quite right, no fault of his—h-rumph.'

There was a short silence.

Cleeve, supported by the two girls, and gripping their arms, staggered slowly forward. Stella was in fits of laughter; Lucy was counting One, two, one, two; but at each step Cleeve's legs flew out sideways, his skates clattered wildly on the ice.

Cleeve had been practising all morning either with Lucy or Stella, and now in spite of his heat, exhaustion, bruises, he was supremely happy because he had both of them. Lucy's laughter enchanted him quite as much as Stella's sympathy, her grave anxiety to help, and now and then between his apologies, he also laughed, turning his agonized face towards Lucy and saying, 'But I'm getting on.'

He dived again; Stella, suddenly seized with her violent laughter, let his arm slip, the other arm jerked from Lucy's and, wheeling round twice, he fell crashing on his left ear. The two girls darted to pick him up. But the ear was bleeding. Stella, reproaching herself, full of a maternal anxiety, brought him to the shore and a footman, wearing a large grey muffler above his plum-coloured coat, was called from the lower pond and sent for a plaster.

It was now dark among the shrubberies, the house was a black silhouette pierced by the yellow lights shining through the lattices; but the sky and ice were grey. The ice was ash grey; and the sky, of the

279

same tone, was a smooth bright grey, like the iris of an eye, not luminous in itself but full of reflected light. Against this sky, the bare branches of the elms, fantastically twisted, and four poplars like skeletons of their own leaves, seemed like an enormous defensive hedge shutting out some giant enemy from the enchanted castle. The fire, now burning high, threw a reddish light across the grass stubble, stiff and brittle with cold; and on the group by the sledge, Cobden in his Beardsley coat, Helen raising her chin to him and to the ever-present imaginary audience, and showing her beautiful teeth in a smile, the young Grenadier with his muffler, his little cloth cap and his hands in his pockets and Benskin in front of them, now making a short circle on one leg or the other; now coming to a halt with a loud scrape, at Helen's feet, to say, 'Not practical politics, I'm afraid.'

'What is not practical politics, Theo—we were talking about the Baptists. Cobden was saying that it is not right of people to be good.'

'I beg your pardon, Helen, what I said was that the moral category is secondary to the æsthetic. For people to aim at goodness is rather as if a hunter should aim at shooting straight.'

'And never shoot anything.'

'Aren't Baptists allowed to shoot, then?' the soldier asked with gravity proper to a religious question.

'Happiness isn't practical politics,' said Benskin gravely. He was surprised that the group laughed, and explained himself, 'Hedonism.'

Benskin's knowledge was always surprising. It could be seen on five faces that no one had expected him to know or use this word.

'What have you been reading now, Theo?' Helen said. She had been snubbing Benskin all day. Benskin answered heavily, 'Hedonism wouldn't work, I'm afraid, you have to have religion.'

'If there were no Heaven, the police would have to invent one.'

Cleeve, sitting in the snow with a sensation as if his brain had been broken to pieces, gazed towards the ice with a look of astonishment; his eyebrows high, his lips parted in a fixed grin. He did not feel the snow soaking into his drawers; his splitting head and the sharp pain of his skinned ear, freezing in the night air, he was not existing in that place at all, but with Lucy as she whirled and swooped over the ice.

Lucy was a good skater in the English style of the day; without gesture, and without the appearance of effort. She carried her hands in a small round muff of white fur, her elbows rested at her sides; the movements of shoulder and hip by which she shifted her weight were made smoothly; she seemed to fly, turn and glide by some motive power in the skates themselves. The effort was that of a girl magically gliding through space, without the least effort.

Cleeve felt, too, the delight of that power, and of the artist making that beauty; and he could hardly breathe in his happiness.

The footman had brought a shaving basin full of hot water and a little black tin box with a red cover and the initials S.M.P., Stella's first aid case. She knelt down to wash and dress Cleeve's ear.

'Does it hurt?' she asked, solicitous.

'Oh, marvellous!' Cleeve exclaimed. 'How does she do it?'

Cleeve turned his head sideways to the right, so that it touched Stella's breast as she knelt behind him. Stella put her left hand to his left cheek as if to hold his head firm, and pressed his head into her breast.

Cleeve, twisting his eyes sideways, still gazed at Lucy. To him Stella was the nurse, and the firm grasp of her hand and arm, pressing him to her breast, was part of her nurse's duty while she plastered his ear.

'What a figure,' he cried. 'I never realized before how perfectly Lucy is made.'

Stella's heart throbbed in his right ear. 'Do you mind plaster?' she asked. She was in no hurry to complete her duty. She felt comfort in her sympathy. Comfort flowed from her breast through all her flesh, filling her with tenderness. She wanted to comfort Cleeve, too; to make him happy. 'Don't let me hurt you, Cleeve.'

'I'll yell. Lucy is a lucky girl. She can do anything in the world.'

'Why don't you tell her so?' The wise mother looked down on the foolish child in her arms.

'I have, but are you match making?'

'She's very fond of you.'

'I did propose, but she only laughed at me.'

This wasn't true, because Cleeve had never actually proposed to Lucy. He had forgotten to do so. Something in him had shied away from it as from a trap; a danger to his freedom.

'Perhaps she thought you were joking,' Stella said.

'Did she tell you so?'

'Ask her again.'

Cleeve raised his astonished eyebrows still further. 'Look at her— like a gull.' He scrambled to his feet, and balanced unsteadily with hand on Stella's shoulder. She looked up at him from the ground across the basin with a grave and anxious expression. 'You ought to go and lie down.'

'But what would we live on, Stella?'

'Lucy has enough for two.'

'Has she? I didn't know. I must really think of it.'

Porfit had not heard the laughter from the Pynsants; he would not have heard a clap of thunder while his eyes were fixed on Lucy. Now when he saw her alone, and the dusk falling, he went back into the large pond, stepped out on the bank, and walked through the undergrowth to a point behind the island. Lucy was just completing a backwards eight. As she came slowly to a halt on the outside edge backwards, she saw close to her a young man in a suit three sizes too large for him who suddenly pronounced her name in Porfit's voice.

She was astonished. Porfit was inconceivable to her in a norfolk suit.

'Excuse me, Miss Lucy, but I have wanted to speak——'

One leg of the suit was coming down. Lucy was seized with a violent emotion which would have been laughter if it had not flashed instantly into self-reproach and panic.

Porfit saw only a startled white face, an open mouth; then the girl flew away from him. But though he was a clumsy skater he had speed, and he was already between her and the fire. He cut her off against the island where a willow tree stood out across the ice like a cannon exploding into twigs.

'Miss Lucy, it's presumptuous and ridiculous of me——'

'Oh no, Mr. Porfit, you know you couldn't be.' Her words rushed out, tripping over each other in the eagerness of their reassurance.

'Without prospects——'

'But you're quite famous already, why even as far as Bristol——'

'But I shall never forget the bounty of God who in His goodness brought me to know in you what a lovely thing the human spirit can be—forgive me if I say too—what a lovely thing the human person can be. To know you and to love you has been the privilege of my life.'

'Please, Mr. Porfit, it's awfully kind of you. But really—I'm not like that at all.'

'I know very well, none better, the insignificance of my position. But if I had not taken up the political truths and feelings in which I was first instructed by your father, I would not be here now and I would not have known you. Therefore I can never repine at any failure.'

'But you can't fail, Mr. Porfit——'

'Forgive me for annoying you, but believe me that it is that very goodness, that true clarity of spirit that sets you so high above me which has given me courage to speak to you now—and that even if we had been on some equality of position—even if we had moved in the same social circles——'

At this moment Cleeve's voice was heard shouting, from close by, 'Lucy, Lucy. Where are you? What is it?' There was a clatter and a crash, he came charging from the darkness, almost hurled Porfit down, and saved himself from falling by seizing Lucy by the arm. 'I thought so,' he stared breathless at Porfit. 'What are you talking about? Are you bothering Miss Chorley?'

'I beg your pardon, sir—I don't know what business——'

'You're always pestering her. Don't you know how to behave?'

Lucy was protesting, but Cleeve had lost his temper. He was looking like a little dog which has been startled out of its great self confidence. 'Following her into private ground. Don't you know when you're not wanted?'

Porfit threw up his hand, palm upwards, as if to stop the traffic. 'Allow me to speak.' All spoke at once. Porfit declaring his old acquaintance with the Chorley family; Lucy defending him; Cleeve, still more angry and vicious, bawling that the Chorleys were sick of him; 'and I happen to know he told you so, after the Benskin speech.' This last bite took effect. The bigger dog snapped. 'Mister Chorley and I had a slight difference of opinion on a political matter.'

Several people were approaching in the gloom. Lucy, recognizing her father's and Benskin's voices, and terrified of a still more unpleasant scene, suddenly broke from Cleeve and skated towards them. A crash behind her showed that Cleeve had fallen.

'What is it?' Chorley asked her. 'What's wrong, my darling?'

'Nothing, Papa. Cleeve and——' She was silent. Benskin took her arm and guided her quickly and rapidly to the shore. He, more quickly than her father, perceived that she was about to cry or scream.

Chorley, looking round in surprise, saw close to him Cleeve being lifted up from the ice by the man in the knickerbockers. The group, except for the bowler and the knickerbockers, was very like that of the famous picture, one of Chorley's favourites, of the Good Samaritan rescuing the traveller, by Millais.

'Political,' he heard Cleeve's voice. 'But, you fool, don't you know they're partners, it's Chorley and Benskin.'

Chorley hesitated; then skated smoothly away to find Lucy and his carriage. Lucy was already in the carriage with her mother and Cobden. As he took off his skates, he could see Cleeve, by the bonfire, waving his arms and declaiming with great indignation. He did not say good-bye to his hostess. His going was like the flight of the guilty. Yet he could not see exactly where his guilt lay, and suddenly in the quiet of the carriage, as it swayed over the hills towards Porriton, he heard himself exclaim in an angry, peevish voice, very rare with him, 'All this Radical chatter about randlords is ignorant nonsense. Mr. Nussbaum is a most cultivated man.' His own voice silenced him, and no more was said, until at home the family separated for the night. Lucy, with her white, exhausted face; Cobden, with the expression of a correct attaché among the lower classes, wished their parents good night; received their blessing, and went silently over the thick carpets to their distant rooms.

The murmur of their parents' voices into the small hours could not be heard beyond their doors.

'I can't believe it,' Mrs. Chorley said a hundred times, and her husband answered gently, in his wise, firm tone: 'You must remember that Benskin has different standards. He's not what you call civilized. He doesn't even understand the kind of—what shall I say—the kind of values which are at stake in such a question.'

'But what can we do?'

'I shall have to teach him a lesson. I'm afraid an ultimatum is required—there's no other way in such cases.'

A thaw set in. All night snow slipped from the roofs and in the morning a thin sleet was falling, which seemed colder than snow. The white Huzzar uniform, after one day's triumph, was useless. Helen stayed in bed. At ten o'clock a groom set out for Bellavista. Mr. Nussbaum, with rings of lead round his eyes and hollow grey cheeks, had left by the first train to London. He was not even permitted to thank his hostess for his entertainment.

'I hope it didn't keep you awake,' Stella said to Cleeve. They were alone at breakfast. She came behind Cleeve's elbow and examined the ear. 'I'm not sure about that plaster—turn your head more.'

Cleeve, his head firmly gripped, said, 'What a hard-hearted girl you are Stella, or is it your stays?'

But Stella held him firmly, touching his ear with her careful fingers until she had decided that the plaster might remain.

'It's going to, in any case,' Cleeve said. 'What a beastly day. What shall we do?'

'I'll have to see about my things for Ireland,' Stella said, in the same absentminded and affectionate tone; a tone of general affection.

'Ireland—are you going to Ireland? What on earth for?'

'Fishing.'

'There's no fishing for a month, and isn't Knockeen shut up?'

'Uncle Theo thought we might go to the Slatters—Mr. Slatter is always asking us.'

'But what about me?'

'You can stay with mama. She'd love to have you—or better—go to Bellavista.'

'You dispose of me very easily; I suppose you know Cocky's at home.'

'Who? oh, Mister Jarvis, I did hear.'

Cleeve looked at her with suspicion. 'I thought you might like to avoid him.'

'I don't suppose we shall meet. It's not necessary.'

Benskin, coming in from the village with streaming mackintosh asked her if she would be ready to leave that afternoon. 'Oh yes,' she said. 'Of course I could be. There's nothing to keep us here in this horrid weather.'

'Right, then. I'll be ready when you're ready.' He flung the water from his hat brim upon the carpet with a jerk which said, 'Let's get out of this.'

'I'm ready now. Filkins is packing.'

'Put on your coat—I believe I know where that badger is lying up.'

They went out together arm in arm across the park. Cleeve, who hated wet weather like a cat, had avoided an invitation to join them. He watched them for a moment from the window, slightly curious about their friendship, so suddenly renewed, and then opened a novel. Cleeve had now ceased to write novels; but he had begun to read them.

At half-past ten he was startled by the appearance of Helen Pynsant in her white dressing-gown. She was greatly agitated; and also she looked confused. She was pathetic, tragic, like a woman roused from amorous and luxurious dreams by revolution. Clasping her dressing-gown across her splendid bust, she asked three or four times, 'But what does it mean—it's so extraordinary. I can't understand it.'

'I'd no idea you didn't know. Stella just said——'

'I never noticed it.'

'He never did this before,' and she cried in a burst of incredulity, 'But he can't go away now. There's a thousand things.'

Wheels were heard on the gravel. A footman announced Mr. Chorley. Helen, who since her friendship with Cobden had been on very cold terms with the Chorleys, cried sharply, 'Not at home. What on earth does he want?'

'He heard that Mr. Benskin was here. He says it's urgent, madam.'

'Mr. Benskin is out. He's going away. Tell him.'

But Chorley was already in the hall. His agitated voice was heard. 'But I must see Mr. Benskin. It's most urgent.'

Helen Pynsant, floating round the room as if pushed forward by a Versailles mob, dignified still in the upper part because the conception of her stay maker was dignified, but mere trembling flesh below, suddenly rushed to the door and called, 'Mr. Chorley!'

Chorley appeared with his grand air; his head and nose held high. But his cheeks were flushed and his forehead was indented with perplexed wrinkles. He did not seem surprised to find Mrs. Pynsant in a dressing-gown.

'Oh, Mr. Chorley, what is this about Mr. Benskin?'

'I was just going to ask you.'

'But he didn't say a word.'

'I had a note only an hour ago—I can't understand it.'

'A note?'

Chorley drew out an envelope. His movements were slow and calm; his fingers were visibly shaking.

The note was worded:

Dear Chorley,
*   I'm off and so's the business, if you like. The bank will foot your*
loan if you don't like my money—but he did not read this part, only
the postscript, *Letters won't be forwarded, I'm giving myself a breath*
of fresh air.

'A breath of fresh air,' Helen said. Her mouth hung open, her cheeks
sagged. Nothing was left of the high, noble poise but the chin, and of
course the stays.

But Chorley was still the grand duke. Only his voice faltered.
'It's most awkward for me—you don't think he's offended in any
way?'

Helen collapsed into a chair. 'He's never done this before.'

'He is perhaps a little impatient at our country methods of doing
business.'

'He was seeing my lawyers to-morrow—some stupid business about
my poor husband's will.'

The business, in fact, was to explain to Helen's lawyers why she was
already several thousand pounds in debt; and to pay them. Helen had
reason to be alarmed by Benskin's sudden rebellion, for he was now
her chief source of income. The widow's five thousand a year barely
covered New Grange and the little new house in Curzon Street; the
bare needs of food and shelter. For all the graces of life, for clothes,
travelling, for a proper appearance at Ascot, on the Solent and the
moors, she was dependent on Benskin. She thought bitterly how cruel
and unfair it was that such as Benskin, without grace, taste, or even
the appreciation of good society, should have money. What a horrid
thing money was.

She went to dress. She put on the coat and skirt, two years out of
fashion, in which Benskin had admired her. When he and Stella
returned, they found that Helen had resolved to join them in their
holiday. She was charming, gay, and there was something at once so
affectionate and so dignified in the manner with which she reproached
them for leaving her out of their plans, that Benskin was melted and
conscience-stricken. Only Stella, as her mother became more delightful,
withdrew into herself.

As for Chorley, after ten minutes with his partner in the small
sitting-room, he went away in very good spirits. Even his back, as he
crossed the gravel to his brougham, was distinguished.

'Benskin,' he said to his wife that night as they lay in the double bed,
'is an interesting type. Rather rough-and-ready but easy enough to
handle if you know the way. He gave way at once when I told him
plainly that I wouldn't have any interference with the policy of the

286

Gazette. Our business co-operation was one thing; but in politics we must agree to differ.'

'Oh, my dear, but can we afford to go on with the *Gazette*?'

'I'm afraid not. No, the poor old *Gazette* stops on Saturday.'

'After forty years.' Mrs. Chorley sighed; but the sigh was merely polite. She was much relieved that this drain in the family income was to be stopped up.

'All things come to an end and perhaps the *Gazette* has fulfilled its purpose. And at least it dies honest.'

'But the staff—poor Mr. Jones.'

'Benskin has offered jobs to the editor and two more. It seems that he owns several other papers—in the Midlands.'

'You must send Mr. Porfit.'

'Yes, Benskin mentioned Porfit. He particularly wants him. He authorized me to offer Porfit five pounds a week to go to Yorkshire.'

'But what a splendid thing.'

'Yes, I think we've managed very well; as I say, Benskin is not really difficult to manage, if you show the necessary firmness. That type of man thinks always in terms of force.'

Carnmore was thrown into turmoil by Benskin's wire. Maddy began a complete house cleaning; Coo, unable to settle down with her adventure magazine, wandered through the rooms and got in everybody's way; Slatter went about like a man in a fire, bawling orders and shouting for Philly. 'Philly, Philly, did ye send for the whisky? Philly, Philly, did ye order the claret? Philly, Philly, will they dress for dinner, d'ye think?' and sometimes with a wink and a poke with the elbow, 'It'll be your jawb to take care of the wee gyurly and she's a grand wee gyurly, too. They say she'll have ten thousand a year. Aw, dahm the money. I've enough for all of ye. But mind ye, Philly, a gyurl with money of her own has more weight and character in herself. There's more taste to her.'

On the morning when Benskin's party was expected, Philip was waked up at seven o'clock by a pleading, tender voice, 'Aw, Philly, if ye love me—not wan drink before dinner—remember she's English and these English will turn up their nose at a fella would so much as whisper them in the breath of a wet.'

Philip, who had as usual in the morning an aching head and a foul tongue, growled that the visitors could go to hell and turned his face into the pillow. Slatter, in consternation and sympathy, murmured tearfully, 'Aw, Philly, are ye feeling your head? Shall I mix ye a saline?'

Philip could not refuse a dose of salts offered with such affectionate sympathy, but he was in a bad temper. He objected to this visit which was upsetting the whole order of his life. Philip, in the view of Annish and his own view, had now settled to a respectable and sensible life. He acted as his uncle's agent and secretary, for which reason, or excuse, the latter had persuaded him to live entirely at Carnmore; he kept the accounts, went to markets, and took care of the cellar. He had grown out of youthful follies and he was even able to meet the country people without embarrassment. He would drink with any of them.

He drank about six whiskies a day as a central heater takes six scuttles of coals at regular intervals, to keep the warmth circulating from one apartment to another; the bedroom, dining-room, W.C., estate office. He was slightly drunk once or twice a week, or after fair days, when his uncle was also drunk and they were very affectionate. They remembered then all their old quarrels and sufferings; their reconciliations and confidences, and they clung together like babes lost in a wood, full of Home Rulers and murderers, swindlers and fools. Philip had discovered at last how to get on with life; but it was dull work. He knew of course by now that it had to be dull. It was dull in the nature of things and people, who were damned dull. He resented bitterly the need of entertaining Benskin, Mrs. Pynsant and especially Stella, who would need to be talked to. Nevertheless, he went to get his hair cut, and ran his eye over the newspapers to see what was happening in the world. He even glanced through the latest smart novel, borrowed from the castle, in order to have a subject for the English ladies. He did not, however, refrain from his usual getting-up drink; a double one to carry him through the boring ceremonies of the morning, after breakfast he took one slightly stronger.

Slatter's orders were that the whole family should meet the important visitors on Dunvil pier. They were to start from Carnmore as soon as the steamer's smoke rose behind Sandy Point.

Slatter was already on the watch. It was luckily a fine, clear morning. The sky was transparent after two days of east wind, and the sunlight itself seemed to be brighter and clearer as it fell slanting on the ground. This wintry light, acutely slanted. always made Annish seem unusually solid. The fallow fields like tarnished copper, the black and rusty bog banks, purple in shadow, the black wiry hedges and black trees, the pale gilded branches of the sycamores at the castle, had the weight of metal or heavy ores. The lough, too, undulating all over in smooth, small waves without a break. was more like quicksilver than water.

Cottagers were everywhere sitting at their doors in the sun. They also glanced towards Sandy Point; because the steamer was an event for them. It moved the imagination to the idea, 'That steamer was in Liverpool last night.'

Bridget sat at her door, high up on Knockeen with Finian in her lap, staring at the narrow strip of the Atlantic on a level with her eyes, which had the peaceful, thoughtless expression of a ruminating animal.

288

She had suckled the boy, now fifteen months old, half an hour before and her bodice still gaped undone to the waist. She felt the slow movement of the cool air, not strong enough to be called a breeze, against her bitten nipples. She put off buttoning her bodice and laying Finian in his cradle because she was enjoying the feel of the air on her breast like a caress and the warmth of the baby on her knees. Bridget would sit for many hours a day with Finian, for the enjoyment of that warmth and weight.

They said of Bridget, 'She's mad about that wain.' This was true in the sense that Bridget's feeling was excessive and unusual.

Finian was a plump fair baby with dark eyes and hair like fogged silver. When he crawled about the floor of the cabin, lifting his tail in the air, so that his smock fell over his neck and showed the creases in his pink backside, he looked like any healthy Annish child. But to Bridget he was Cleeve's son, a different kind of being from herself. She felt in him a quality which she could not describe; the thing which she had known and felt in Cleeve, in the castle, in the furniture; the glory of that first day when she had stood in the castle drawing-room on the carpet, which as Grogan said, had cost a hundred pounds. It belonged to a magic world beyond her imagination; but in Finian she felt it like an idea of the blood.

It moved in her now like the powerful elation of strong health. Finian was asleep. The smoke of the steamer had been rising behind Sandy Point for five minutes before her eyes, gazing at it, became aware of it and she thought, 'That's from England.' England was for Bridget part of the general idea or sensations to which Cleeve belonged, wealth, excitement and power.

To Stella, Connel's boat was already charming because it belonged to Annish. She could forget that Benskin had his arm through her mother's while they sat beside her in the stern. She already seemed parted from them; going forward from them to a new existence. She could not help smiling at the waves, the boatmen, and meeting one young rower's eyes she was surprised to receive from him a broad, friendly grin. She did not know how quickly an Annishman can acknowledge that special smile, a pensive, gay, and sometimes mischievous smile, which belongs to a young girl on her nuptial flight.

Stella ran quickly up the pier ladder as if to meet somebody. Her first view was of Slatter with a crimson face, roaring at a dirty looking young man with a large, ferocious black moustache:

'Dahm ye,' Slatter was totally indifferent to the interested crowd of fishermen and loungers, 'Ye're drunk, and look at your clothes. Is that the way to come before ladies? Anyone would take ye for a bloody chicken higgler and bedambut ye smell worse.'

Stella, standing among the fishermen, was laughing. How delightfully Irish this was; how perfectly Annish. It could happen nowhere else.

Maddy and Coo, standing on both sides of the men, with pale, anxious faces, uttered consoling speeches. Their hands made gestures as if stroking fierce imaginary dogs.

'He's all right, Pappy.'

'Ye're all right, Philly.'

All were suddenly transfixed by Benskin's voice greeting Slatter. The two girls stiffened. Slatter jumped round; Philip's offended dignity became still more cold and haughty.

Stella was touched and amused by this haughtiness. She felt a gay sympathy towards all the party like that of the child, who enjoying a party, runs about clinging to any hand and embracing the chairs. She gave Philip a special smile, a smile which said, 'I understand drunk men, I'm almost Irish myself.'

Philip started like an awkward piece of machinery, and bowed stiffly over her hand; his stiff mouth expanded into a smile; his eyebrows rose among his tousled hair. He had the expression of someone just fallen out of bed.

'What a perfectly lovely day,' Stella said, raising her face as if to kiss the air, and Philip also looked at the sky with his astonished face. 'Awfully nice—yes, we're lucky.'

The three Slatters looked on with fascinated eyes at this interview. Then Slatter exploded, 'That's it, Philly, look after Miss Pynsant. He's English, ye know, Miss Pynsant—all but the name—yes, and he was the cleverest boy at his school, too. Aw, ye'll get on famously together. I can see that. Aw, why wouldn't ye take her up by the fields, Philly? We'll be ten minutes getting all the bags up, even if that blaggard Connel hasn't rooned them with bilge water. Go wan and show her the road.' He made a motion as if shooing chickens, 'Go wan, take her along with ye—sure she wouldn't want to be faltering here with a lot of worn out dromedaries the like of us.' He turned from Mrs. Pynsant to Benskin with a broad hospitable smile, and then glanced carelessly at the fishermen to see if they noticed his easy intercourse with the great.

Philip and Stella were climbing the hill through Dunvil main street and Stella, finding her companion a little confused, was saying, 'I do love this place—there's nowhere quite like it, is there?'

Philip gazed round at the single wide street of little, flat-faced houses, as if he had never seen it before. 'Yes, it's not bad.'

'I wish I could come here every year,' Stella said. 'It's got such a special kind of beauty—the little fields all round the mountains—the cottages going right up.'

Philip looked up at the mountains and then glanced over the hedges at the fields. He said, 'Yes, it's nice.' He looked again at Knockeen and said with more emphasis, 'That's a fine view of Knockeen now.'

'How lucky you are to see it whenever you like.'

'Yes, my window looks right on Knockeen,' and he added, 'I once wrote a poem about Knockeen—when I was at school of course.'

At lunch time when Maddy with pale damp cheeks was flying from the kitchen to the dining-room, while Coo, still clasping the *Wide World Magazine*, followed her about to ask if her blue blouse would do, while Slatter was telling Benskin and Mrs. Pynsant how he had persuaded John Chass to consolidate three mortgages on the Castle property at six per cent, for a thousand pounds down and a cart mare, and Mrs. Pynsant was smiling upon him as if she had never before met anyone so clever and entertaining; Phil was looking out of his bedroom window at Knockeen with the eyes of a discoverer.

He walked nervously about the room, sipped a neat whisky, brushed his hair and adjusted his tie. Then he took another look out of the window. It was a beautiful view; he remembered that he had always admired it.

Philip came to lunch extremely flushed and talked during the whole meal with extraordinary animation. No one had heard him talk like that for at least six years. He quoted poetry to Mrs. Pynsant; he explained to Benskin exactly how the Jameson Raid had failed; and turning to Stella now and then with a little smile of understanding, he spoke of the sights of Annish.

'I know what you'd like,' he said with confidence. 'There's a lovely old cross at Cool.'

They went to see the cross after lunch and Philip, now eloquent, pointed out his favourite views as they walked through the fields. 'It's a beautiful country,' he said, 'and the great advantage of my work here is that I can always be about the fields.'

'I'd love it.'

'Yes, I suppose I'm lucky. In fact I know I am. As Harry Jarvis said to me the other day, "Philly, old chap, I envy you your job in Annish." I must say that surprised me from Harry. With his mention and so on he's a regular lion just now at all the parties. Not that he's conceited at all. No, Harry's a grand fella.'

'But I suppose he wouldn't leave the army now.'

'No, nor me Annish. Not for anything.' Philip looked round at the landskip. 'I know when I'm well off.' He smiled at Stella whose smile in return gave him a shock of happiness. He had never met anyone like this girl with her soft mouth and her brown eyes, who in an hour or

291

two had penetrated into his inmost feelings; and become a friend to whom he had already told more of himself than anyone before.

'It's a quiet life, of course,' he told her, as they came down the hill. 'But that's its advantage for me. The real secret, I suppose, is to enjoy your job—and to have a job that you can enjoy—something that's really necessary and important—and after all, growing food for people is rather more important than killing them, like poor old Harry. Of course I am lucky in doing such a job in Annish. You can't help loving Annish—and the people, too. Got to look out for them—but really they're the nicest kind of people. Of course, they seem rather a rough lot to you.'

'No, no, I love them, and the place.' Stella glanced round affectionately at the fields, the sky and the hedges and finally at Philip, who looked reckless with the sense of his happiness. It was the third time that she had smiled at him.

'You ought to be Irish yourself,' he said.

'Yes, I'd like that,' Stella said, and then stopping in the road, opposite the castle lodge she asked, 'The Corners are back, aren't they? Maddy was going to tea.'

'Yes, but it's only three.'

'I think I'll run in all the same.'

'Do, Mrs. Corner would like to see you, if you don't mind me not coming.'

'Oh no, Maddy will pick me up.'

Philip took off his hat and walked into Dunvil, smiling to himself all the way. He felt how wise he was, how happy, and how successful, and what a darling Stella was.

Stella turned into the castle drive. She had not been in any impatience to go to the castle. It was only now that she felt urgency, and her feet began to hurry.

Mary Corner was just going out on her afternoon sick visits and especially to see Kitty, when Miss Pynsant was announced. She was flustered by a call at such a time and cried out to Grogan, 'Who d'ye say,' just as Stella walked in.

They stared at each other, Stella at the little ugly woman in her wide-brimmed black hat, tied under the chin with a black scarf, her old sealskin coat and very full black skirts, Mary at the plump young girl, so full of life that she seemed to warm the air. Both faces took the expression of sympathy, as if Stella had thought, 'How old she is, how ugly and unhappy,' and Mary had thought, 'How young she is—how ignorant and exposed.'

Mary started into activity as if to fly to a rescue.

'Good gracious, m' dear,' she cried, 'it's you—I didn't know you with your hair up. Sit down and have something.' She pulled the bell and screamed towards the closed door, 'Grogan, the madeira and the plum cake.'

This order showed that she still regarded Stella as a child. Madeira and plum cake were given to all morning visitors at the castle, but it was only children who received them in the afternoon. Children under thirteen or fourteen were given grenadine or raspberry juice instead of madeira.

Mary Corner had a fixed notion that children would always eat and that they ought to be kept full.

Wheels crunched the gravel outside, a governess-cart passed from the yard toward the front door, and an old woman in a purple bonnet put her head through the window and exclaimed in an agitated voice, 'I'm ready, ma'm.'

Mary Corner jumped and cried, 'Good gracious, Susanna, go away.'

The old woman, muttering, took a few steps away and then returned to the window.

Stella got up. 'But I mustn't keep you, Mrs. Corner.'

'You're not keeping me, m' dear. It's very nice to see you. There's not enough pretty young gels come to the house. Have some more cake.' She seized the knife.

'Oh please, Mrs. Corner——'

'Now, now, we don't need compliments. I know what gels like,' and then catching sight of Sukey again at the window, she waved the knife at her. 'Go away, Susanna, you silly gel.'

Sukey made one stride away and one back again to the window.

Stella did not recognize the old cook in her bonnet and cape. Sukey had been transformed in the last months when Kitty Foy, now on her death bed, asked her to take Teresa into her care. She had at once given notice and taken a room in Dunvil. Almost every day she visited Kitty, to see the little girl; and then she would go to Dunvil and add some piece of furniture, a picture or a curtain, to the room.

Sukey had been sober for three weeks and in the kitchen she talked of nothing but Teresa, the room in Dunvil and her new life.

'It's what I'll be free,' she would say, rubbing her knees with a broad, ecstatic smile, turning away her face like a bride that can't hide her excitement but feels shy of it.

Everyone noticed the change in Sukey, including the blue yard cat, which after ten thousand attempts to settle itself in the kitchen and ten thousand flights in front of pans, boots, curses, potatoes, sods of turf, one day found herself permitted to stay. 'Ah, the poor creature,' Sukey

293

said, finding her under the table with a herring. 'There's no harm in her bating she's a cat, the murdering thief.'

Even Sukey's curses had a different tone; they were no longer revengeful weapons; she threw them off in her busy excitement like the poetry of gusto. She had no time within herself to distil poison in them.

'Oh, gawd damn ye, me poor Grogan, and your hump like Moses' ould camel, give me a week till I'm free and then ye may bury yerself in the cans.'

Nevertheless there was fluster in Sukey's exultation. She was off her balance; and now she kept putting her head in at the window and muttering till Mary exclaimed, 'Good gracious, Susanna, what a stoopid gel you are, but I suppose I must come with you.'

She turned to apologise to Stella, and to pour her out another glass of wine. 'Not a word now—good gracious, there's no one to see.'

A moment later the two ageing women in their shabby blacks jingled down the drive together; wagging and bobbing in the helpless and pathetic fashion of jolted travellers, who never seem to expect exactly the jolt that comes to them.

'Poor old dears,' Stella thought. Her tender sympathy followed them. Then she tiptoed round the room, as if in the presence of some sacred thing, examining the portraits, the small ornaments on the tables and the mantelpiece.

She picked up an old illustrated paper. It opened by itself at a photograph, marked in red ink, of Lieut. P. L. H. Jarvis, wounded in action against the slave raiders. She stared at the picture in surprise. She could not recognize the face which, with the little moustache, seemed to her at first glance comical, like that of the actor who in the Pinero comedies took the part of the silly soldier. But as she gazed, with arched brows, she saw that this first impression was wrong. The face was that of a hero; it was the most noble and beautiful face. She turned slowly red and her half-parted lips trembled while she stared fascinated.

A carriage drove up outside and John Chass' voice sounded in the hall. With one quick movement she returned the paper to its place and removed herself across the room from it. The Feenix girls, two other girls and John Chass came in together.

'Why, here you are,' Maddy said.

'But ye wouldn't want to sew,' Coo said.

John Chass complimented her on becoming a young lady, and she answered, laughing, 'It's only for the holidays.'

'What, are you going back to school?'

'Just for a term, Mr. Corner.'

'Oh, I thought the great day of destruction was not far off when:

> *She who provokes the storm may scorn the waves,*
> *Who by their ardour own themselves her slaves.*

Stella blushed and Maddy said, 'Don't mind him, Stella, He doesn't mean it.'

'Why would she mind?' Coo said. 'I daresay she's a dozen boys already.'

Stella did not mind. She was charmed. She had acquired the power of finding extraordinary pleasure in every event of life. She gazed with keen appreciation at Darcy coming in with a basket of half-made shirts, and in his right hand, as well as the basket handle, a long, silver-mounted state-carriage whip.

Old Jebb had had a stroke and Darcy was driving the barouche. He was not, of course, appointed coachman and not likely, with one eye, to be appointed. He was not in top boots. But he carried his whip everywhere, and now coming into the drawing-room, he had the air of one to whom all activities had acquired significance and importance. When the girls rushed at the basket, he said with anxious but tender authority, 'Wait ye now, misses, ye'll jag yourselves.'

He put the basket in the bow window and watching the girls throwing themselves upon it, he said to Stella, also in the background, 'Ye see— 1 wouldn't put thon ould creel on the cyarpet.'

Stella did not understand the words, but she felt an instant sympathy for something in the man. They smiled at each other as if they enjoyed together a whole history of private sympathy, and Darcy was still smiling as he backed away from her, carrying the whip like a bridal bouquet.

The girls were already dragging the basket across the carpet while they jostled each other, crying, 'Give me the one that's got the arms in it. I'll not do another neckband.'

The shirts were for the foreign mission, and the girls were the advance party of a sewing meeting; within half an hour there were twenty at work.

Stella, too, sewed. She said with enthusiasm that she loved sewing.

John Chass had gone out; the room was warm and full of chattering women, whose arms thrown up with movements like those of an orchestra seemed to play a domestic and womanly symphony; peaceful, but not sentimental or even sympathetic. All these faces, movements, were practical and unstudied. Maddy frowned at her shirt, and sometimes at a neighbour. Talk was extremely frank, and intercepted glances were sharp and cold.

At every moment someone raised her head and looked out of the window. It was not a gesture of escape, but of curiosity.

'There's that Annie Foy with a milk can. She could do with washing.'

'Hasn't Mrs. Corner gone to the Foys?'

'To Kitty—but Kitty was an Egan.'

'I'm told she won't last the week.'

'Indeed,' one said, biting off a thread. 'It's a wonder she's lasted the winter.'

'There's the trap now.'

'No, it's the butcher. What are they doing with the boat?'

Again the heads started up. Stella glanced out of the window behind her and saw Jarvis, with a pipe in his mouth, and a paint pot in his hand, walking past within ten yards.

Maddy Feenix put her nose to the narrow crack at the bottom of the window and called, 'You're not painting the wee boat?'

Jarvis took out his pipe and opened the window from outside, with great pains, to know what she wanted.

'What is it, Maddy?'

'You're not painting the wee boat?'

'No, we're blackleading the bottom to make her slip.' His eyes wandered over the heads in the twilight of the room, and suddenly meeting Stella's eyes, looking up at him, stopped. They looked at each other for a fraction of a second and in that time asked something and revealed something. But neither question nor confirmation could have been expressed in words. They were as simple and elementary as the dog's nose seeking a lamp post and the bristling of his whiskers at the sight, far off, of an eye turned towards him over a female stern.

When Sukey took her room in Dunvil, it was suddenly perceived that she must be rich. Annish calculated her fortune from thirty-four years' wages, paid regularly in gold. She never spent gold. She had clothes from Mrs. Corner and tips from John Chass who would often send her half a crown for a good dinner. She drank either Grogan's whisky, or poteen which she had from Breedy in exchange for the kitchen stuff. She must be worth four or five hundred pounds. The idea of this wealth to Annish was quite different from its idea of Benskin's, Duff's or Slatter's wealth. It admired Benskin's million as a child gazes at the moon; but it felt Sukey's treasure in its own veins.

On the next fair day Sukey's fortune was the most exciting news in the market. Rifty heard of it from a chicken dealer.

'Four hundred pounds,' he said. He couldn't imagine the money. It was a cold day, with a sky as bright and cold as the lake, from which a sharp breeze blew up the hill into the market place. Rifty, in his old, dirt-coloured overcoat, with his button nose blue and his ears red as the post box, stared at the lake with eyes like itself and said, 'Four hundred pounds.'

He shouted suddenly to Manus Foy, slouching past with a half sack of meal on his back, and his shirt falling through the seat of his trousers, 'D'ye hear that your Anty Sukey has a thousand pounds saved?'

Manus turned his old man's face, full of withered vices, to his brother-in-law, and spat through his rotten teeth. 'She may,' he said softly.

Manus had no feelings to give to anything. They were locked together inside him like starving wild cats in a snowdrift. He paused a moment, gazing at Rifty as if at a white-washed wall, and then lurched forward towards the grocery.

'A thousand pounds,' Rifty said and his eyes rounded like sovereigns. Rifty could never grasp a great thing until he had seen it reflected from another face. He plunged through the scattered, depressed crowd among the carts. It was a thin market. 'D'ye hear me Ant Sukey has a thousand pounds saved—she's richer nor John Chass himself—he couldn't raise two for a tinker's wake.'

When he came up the hill shouting about Sukey's money and sometimes turning right round in the lane to see behind him, the Knockeen people smiled as if at some innocent and foolish person. But Rifty was sharper than most of them. It was lack of settled conviction that made him seem childish.

When Bridget, sitting at the door, saw Rifty's active figure in the lane, jerking and hopping along as if all his limbs had a tic, she felt calm disgust. She did not like to be interrupted in her day-dreams. But she did not show any annoyance. She recognized a husband's right to come home when he chose.

Rifty and Bridget exasperated each other in many ways; Bridget knew that Rifty was not to be trusted, he was a liar and would play spiteful tricks; Rifty hated Bridget for her idle fecklessness; even now, at four o'clock in the afternoon, she had not yet made the bed or swept the house. But their marriage was a success because their idea of marriage was of a joint stock union for work and duty, in which each gave certain services laid down by the church, the law and the necessity of things. The pleasures of it, therefore, came to them like a stroke of winter sunlight to a worker in the fields; something delightful but not essential.

Rifty stood in front of Bridget in a dramatic pose, jerked off his cap and exclaimed, 'Did ye know that your Ant Sukey had a thousand gold sovereigns in her old black box?'

Bridget said nothing. She was stroking Finian's hair. The child, with his thumb in his mouth and one foot in the air, gazed thoughtfully past Rifty at the sky, whose pale clouds, like dry snow blown across an ice field, could be seen reflected in his eyes.

297

Rifty, enraged by Bridget's calmness, rushed suddenly into the cabin and clattered among the pots.

But Bridget was not calm. She was feeling the importance of the news and already excitement was growing within her; pressing urgently upon her. She felt the power of a thousand pounds even before she could grasp it; ambition grew in her flesh by itself, so that when at last, looking down at Finian on her lap, she thought, 'He could be a priest or a doctor or even an officer,' she was only discovering the idea already formed within her.

Rifty threw a bucketful of slops into the midden, splashing her bare feet, and said to her in his quick, friendly voice, as if he had splashed her by accident, 'A thousand pounds—and ye've thrown it away be your crossness. Never goin' near her.'

Bridget suddenly turned red with anger; it was for fear that Rifty might be right.

She glanced at him fiercely and said, 'I did not then—how could I know that she had it?'

The angry look startled Rifty. Suddenly he smiled and said, 'Ah, I'm not blaming ye, Bridgy, I wouldn't do that.'

Bridget, at once pacified, answered that she had not quarrelled with Sukey; it was Sukey who refused to see her. Then she went to put Finian in his cradle and to fill the potato pot. Her face was once more tranquil and pensive. But her brain was more active than it had been for a year past. She had an idea of action. The same afternoon she was at Sukey's kitchen door, bringing her aunt as peace offering a bottle of whisky for which Rifty had paid.

Sukey accepted it in these words, 'So you're wanting to be back in me kitchen and so ye may when I'm out of it come Holy Week when ye wouldn't be dirtying me floor.'

Sukey now wore her bonnet all day, ready for immediate flight, for Kitty was sinking fast. She was in her most excited temper, and fought the cans like a demon; she swore at Bridget whenever she saw her. But Bridget was not to be turned aside by a few curses. She came every evening; one day with a medicine bottle of poteen, of Padsy's brewing, the next with liquorice, good for the stomach, or a barnbrack. She would slip in at the door, a dark, thick figure hooded in a black shawl which also wrapped the baby, and put her gift, with a quick timid movement, at the far end of the kitchen table. Then she would sit on the form next the door, the bench of favoured tramps, in a roaring draught from the stone passage, and unwrap the baby.

She held the baby so that Sukey, if she looked that way, might see his beauty; and sometimes she would put him on the floor and push him gently behind to make him crawl towards Sukey. But Sukey took care not to see the child, though he crawled to the fender. She would not look at him even when, one afternoon, Stella and Cocky came to the kitchen and Stella, picking up the baby from under the table, kissed it and said to Sukey, 'What a darling baby, is it yours?'

Sukey turned her back and shouted for Molly to bring the collander.

Bridget, who had stood up by the door, made a bob towards Cocky. She did not dare to raise her voice to claim the baby. But Cocky did not see her. He was looking at Stella while she looked at the baby. Both of them had flushed cheeks and the same doting smile.

It was ten days since Miss Pynsant's first visit but already all Annish knew what she had come for and that she was getting it. Bridget could not help smiling in sympathy with their condition. Sukey, moved to hatred by the same nerve, scowled over her shoulder, muttering that her kitchen might be a fair for all the gomerils that stood about in the road.

Stella, because of her natural love, being tender and quick in her feelings, cried at once, 'I'm being in the way, Mrs. Egan.'

'We won't spoil the good dinner you're making us,' Cocky said. 'If you could let us have a candle for Miss Pynsant to see the dead cellar.'

Molly brought the candle and Cocky, lighting it, led the way through the scullery towards the old deep cellar under the north wing; called sometimes the smuggler's hole and sometimes the dead cellar, because in it, according to the tale, the rebels of 1641 had murdered and burnt the second Mrs. John and three of her children.

Stella, going out of the room, still turned back her rosy, smiling face to look at the baby, staring up at her from the floor. As soon as she was gone, Sukey, in a murderous passion, screamed at Bridget, who still had the lover's smile on her face, 'Will ye sit there all day? Did ye think ye'd bought the bench with your bottles of bog water?'

Bridget was suddenly eloquent. 'It was the real Fly at three and six, Anty. And I wouldn't give you less. Amn't I the oldest niece ye have and the ony one that's ever worked with ye?'

'Devil receive me,' Sukey said, glaring at the girl. 'If I know what false work she's at now. Does she think I'm going to drop dead for to steal me stockings?'

In the dead cellar, Cocky stood with the candle raised to show Stella the vaulted roof, but though he was telling her about the murders, both were smiling. She was smiling at the walls, covered with green slime, the wet floor and the dripping groins of the roof, as she had smiled at the baby.

'How many children were killed?'

'Three.'

'How awful. And that was the end of those Corners.'

'No, there were six more. But '88 was nearly the end of us when we were shut up in Dunderry siege. Only two small children escaped alive from that rebellion, and they were smuggled out of the town in creels, baskets you know, hung on each side of a donkey.'

'I wonder they ever came back.'

'They not only came back, but John Felix, the elder, who built this house on the old ruins, had seventeen children to make sure of the line.'

'And now there's only Cleeve left—I mean in the direct line.'

'There's some in America. Do you believe in big families?'

'I don't know. I haven't thought of it.'

'I do. I think one ought to have a lot. After all, it's the natural thing.'

He spoke firmly, looking at Stella with a stern expression. She knew already that the expression was merely his evangelistic face. He looked so when he spoke of the wickedness of Gladstone or the sins of the War Office; and she, too, when he spoke about serious matters of belief, became grave and severe.

'A lot of children together are rather quarrelsome sometimes.'

'But that's good for them, too. They bring each other up.'

Gradually Stella's colour had risen; her heart was beating violently, and all at once, she gave a deep sigh. She relaxed from thought or anxiety, from making any plan, and it seemed to her that her sensible answers to Cocky's speeches were being spoken by another person; by the well trained young lady from New Grange. She was like one pulse, beating warmly; in an enormous body of the world which included the baby in the kitchen and the cellar wall.

Cocky's voice, in the middle of a sentence about the advantages of a big family, faltered at this sigh, but he continued in the same argumentative tone, 'I can see how you love babies.'

Stella said nothing to this.

'Everybody ought to be married, don't you think?'

'Could everybody?'

'If they can, and you know that you could whenever you liked. But I've told you already what I think about that.'

There was another silence.

'I'd like to marry you, Stella. I think that to have you for a wife would be the greatest piece of luck that any man could have in the world and a great deal more than I'd deserve.'

Stella tried to speak and put out her hand. Jarvis took her in his arms and held her for a moment, kissed her once. Then she said, still holding his hand, 'Won't they wonder——'

'Yes, we'd better go up.'

The young couple showed their usual demeanour at tea time, and afterwards Stella was carried back to Carnmore by her mother, to write family letters. Helen Pynsant, though much preoccupied with her own matrimonial negotiations with Benskin, difficult and complicated because so many important points, such as her resolve not to have any children, were not at once acceptable to the other, was beginning to wonder if Stella were not again flirting with the Irish bo-hoy.

Jarvis at the castle was not seen again until dinner time, when John Chass, though both preferred whisky, insisted on champagne.

'It's a grand thing for a touch of fever, for any kind of fever.' He winked at Mary. In Annish all love affairs, engagements, marriages, were jokes, not only in cottages and kitchens, but in the houses. John Chass was in the old tradition of the Tudors who serenaded newly married couples with pans and blew water through the key holes of the marriage chamber.

Mary Corner was fearful that her darling Harry would see the winks. She screamed at John Chass, 'But it's very bad for your liver, you silly man.'

'I'm not prescribing for the liver,' John Chass said, 'but the heart.' He winked again in a manner which made even Grogan, coming with the opened bottle, change expression from the melancholy to the discreet.

But Jarvis did not notice winks; and if he had he would have ignored them, as a communicant seeing in church some frivolous visitor grinning in a corner, does not allow even his expression to change from its grave devotion. Love to Jarvis, like war, was a religious experience.

Now that Stella went every day to sew at the castle, Philip was left alone as before. But this did not seem to affect his spirits and when Maddy and Coo came back to say that Stella had spent the whole afternoon with Harry Jarvis in the stables, he answered calmly and with dignity, 'Why shouldn't she?'

'I never saw anything so bold the way she goes after'm,' Maddy said.

'But she might get'm that way,' Coo suggested.

'I never heard anything like the way you girls talk,' Philip said angrily. He turned red with anger and disgust, 'It's simply revolting, like children eating with dirty hands.'

The two girls stared at him in wonder and then Maddy said, 'It's not us that make the dirt in the house—I'm tired takin' out the mud ye leave in the cyarpet. The new cyarpet too.'

'Oh God, are you going to spend your life rubbing furniture.'

Maddy's face changed to a moment, her eyes widened as if she were gazing beyond Philip at something he had suddenly revealed to her; her forehead wrinkled. But the look passed in an instant and she said, 'Somebody has to keep the place clean and it won't be you or Coo. Now for goodness' sake, there's another hole burnt in your coat pocket. It's you men aren't fit to look after yourselves.'

301

Philip went to climb Knockeen and to take consolation in the view. But on the road he met a pig dealer from Dunderry; an old acquaintance, and he said to him, 'A grand day. I never saw such colour on the lough.'

The pig dealer looked at the lough which was as dark as blue black ink, and covered with white waves, which jumped up and down, over twenty square miles of water, in tens of thousands. They made a rustling noise in the air which reached far up the mountainside.

The pig dealer looked at this sight for a moment with mild interest, Philip looked at the pig dealer. He felt an overwhelming desire to tell him about his happiness, his wise aloofness from the world, to make him understand how he, Philip, had succeeded in avoiding the snares of ambition and egotism. He said to him, 'Come into Connell's and we'll have a wee one.'

'Thank you, Mr. Feenix, it's a cold wind.'

They walked down the hill into Dunvil. Philip, talking all the time about the beauties of the country and the advantages of an agent's life, kept turning his face to the pig dealer's with an eager smile, as if to say, 'You understand.'

The pig dealer understood. He met men in pubs every day who wanted a little encouragement to enjoy life. He kept on saying, 'What about another little one,' and at every drink Philip became happier, more benevolent and also more condescending towards those who did not know how to be happy.

Father MacFee took the holy oils to Kitty on Wednesday morning, but she was still alive on Thursday when Mary Corner went to her for the last time. She was lying flat on her back in the little room which was only two foot wider than the bed, gazing at the rafters. Mary had never seen such a look of calm triumphant happiness on any face. It filled her with such pity and grief that she could not speak for a moment. She sat down and took Kitty's hand in hers. Kitty turned her brilliant eyes towards her mistress and said, 'I'll be seeing the wee master this very day.'

Mary's lips were pressed together; she had a look of desperation as if turning her face towards a victorious enemy. Her hand crushed Kitty's. 'This very day,' Kitty said, 'will I see the wee false smile he had when he wanted something out of me.'

Mary said in a hoarse voice, 'You're a brave gel, Catherine, and I don't know how we'll do without you.'

Mary, in her Protestant heart, could not believe that death was the gateway of joy. She loved people far more than she ever loved God, and she could not bear to lose them or to see them lost from love. She felt now such a pain in her heart, like a spasm of the heart muscle, that

302

she did not know how to utter her grief and pity. She could only give her final recipe for all misfortunes, courage.

But in fact Kitty did not need pity. Her nerves, excited by the toxins of her illness, were in continual vibration and all their different excitements, like a poet's under a drug, rejoiced together in the single harmony, reconciling all their appetites in the one passion. Her love of Annish and her love of the Virgin were parts of one love in which Annish was the holy place of God, as much nearer to Heaven than America as the miles of ocean between them. All the Atlantic for Kitty had been downhill, and now she had climbed again to the clear air where, washed by daily showers, the sky itself seemed penetrable by the light of the blessed saints turning down their faces towards Ireland.

Kitty, gay and collected, was already living in a world so different from Mary Corner's that they could not understand each other. For Kitty, Con and Teresa were further off from her and less real than Shon. She had hardly noticed Con or Teresa for the last weeks, and the little girl, as careless of her, was now lying on her stomach, among the stones, with the rain falling on her mottled legs, while she watched a minute crab trying to climb up a branch of weed.

Con sat on a rock with his collar turned up. He seemed small and withered, as if most of his insides had fallen away from him. His face had fallen in, and though, having spent his last shilling, he had been sober for a fortnight, he had the dazed, senseless look of a soaker.

'I suppose you'll be going back to the States,' Cocky said to him. Cocky and Stella had driven over with Mary; Cocky to drive and Stella to be with Cocky and to begin her practice as a lady of the country.

Con raised his head to stare at Cocky; but his hollow, battered face had no more expression than the inside of a broken saucepan.

'You needn't worry about the fare,' Cocky said. 'Mr. Corner and Sir Walter will advance it to you.'

'Ah,' Con said. Six months or even three months before he would have felt that there was a deep plot in the magistrates' offer, and so he would have had the notion, 'They want to get rid of me,' but now he had no thoughts.

Stella had caught Teresa by the legs. 'But you mustn't lie there— you're getting wet through.'

Teresa did not protest, but she gripped the rock with all the surprising force of children who resist an interruption.

'She won't come,' Stella said to Cocky. In England she would have taken Teresa by force; but in this foreign land she was still diffident. She did not know yet what was permitted to her by local custom.

Cocky, glad to leave Con, came down and lifted up Teresa with one sweep, 'Upsidaisy, and what's your name, young woman?'

303

Teresa looked at him without anger; as she might have looked at a thunder cloud or a cow. Grown ups to her were irresponsible and foolish powers. She was a little, thin, white girl with a long nose, white as a birthday candle, and pale green eyes.

Cocky was beginning to notice and to enjoy children. He smiled at the child's solemn, blank look and said, 'Would you like a penny?'

Teresa made no sign. Mary Corner, coming from the cottage with her white crumpled face and inflamed eyes, hurried to the trap. Cocky gave Teresa a penny and took her to her father. 'She's wet, Con.'

'It's a soft day,' Con echoed, looking at Teresa with his empty face. Then he looked at the sky which was full of enormous trails of vapour, melting into each other, as if they could not decide whether to be clouds or fog, and said, 'To hell with it.' But his voice had no conviction; it was like a flake of old rust falling off the saucepan by the operation of long standing corrosion.

The trap drove away; Teresa was seen diving between two wet rocks on her head. She was already restarting her life of enquiry.

When Helen Pynsant heard that Stella was engaged to Jarvis, she was nearly as angry as Slatter. Stella was only seventeen, still at school; she would have four thousand a year and Jarvis had nothing but his pay.

She was, of course, charming to Stella, who wanted to be married at once in order to have two months' honeymoon before Jarvis went back to Africa. She did not abuse Jarvis even to Slatter when he shouted, 'Is it Cocky, the dirty little schemer, without a brass ha'penny. But I'll run him out of the country. I'll put the bank on ould Jawn and burst him. Why I could turn him out of the cassle itself, if I put on the screw.' She said that Captain Jarvis seemed a nice young man, a gentleman in every way.

'A funny kind of gentleman without any money,' Slatter exclaimed. He turned towards Philip, who was standing on one side with the expression of one quite uninterested in the affair. 'And there's Philly will have thousands a year, the best lookin', best hearted boy ye could find anywhere, breakin' his heart for her.' Slatter's own voice broke at the thought of Philip's unhappiness.

'Aw Philly, why didn't ye go after her—but it's too dalicate he is Mrs. Pynsant—too much of a gentleman. Not like that little murdering blaggard down below.'

'But it's not like that at all,' Philip exclaimed. He wanted to make them understand that he felt no disappointment, that his regard for Stella had been a noble and sympathetic friendship. He opened his mouth to explain all this, but looking round and seeing the tender sympathy in Slatter's eyes, the sisterly mournfulness in Maddy's, the curious grief in Coo's, and Mrs. Pynsant's little smile, he realized that

304

he would not be understood or believed. He left the room with dignity, and went out on the road.

Perhaps after all he had been foolish with Stella; too modest, too retiring; or perhaps he was a generous and high-minded person marooned among savages. How could one tell?

The morning was wet, the big clouds, rising from the west, seemed like great bags of dirty sail cloth raised up out of the Atlantic by a hand too weak to lift their weight of water above the top of Knockeen. Their rotten canvas struck it and broke into tatters; the grey green water fell across the black mountain so thick that the fields below looked like weeds under ice.

Philip stood looking at the sky and the hilltop; but he could not be sure whether this movement of the big clouds, the darkening of the rain, the changing of its thickness on the air, like smoke, were beautiful or merely ordinary.

It was a fair day in Dunvil. The country people were going down the hill in carts and on foot. As they passed him, they greeted him with the same words 'A soft day the day.' They looked at him with discreet curiosity.

A carriage passed, going towards Dunderry. He saw his father's umbrella suddenly at the corner of the rectory lane bobbing towards him with slow dignified undulations. Philip had not spoken to his father for several weeks. He was supposed to spend every week end at the rectory but his uncle usually found some reason why he should not go. Philip saw through these jealous tricks but he gave way to them because he was on the whole, glad to avoid the visits. He knew that his father was disappointed in him, and this made him embarrassed and angry.

The umbrella bobbed round the corner and they stood face to face. Old Feenix' pale eyebrows rose, his mouth opened, his long worn face, usually fixed like an official mask of patience, showed for a moment eagerness, diffidence, affectionate interest; the simplest feelings of an old, lonely man who is surprised by a meeting with an only child. Philip felt suddenly guilty. He stared at his father. Neither spoke.

The old man put out his hand and felt the boy's coat. He said in a solicitous voice 'You're getting wet, Philly.'

Philip answered shortly, 'It can't be helped—I'm busy on a fair day.'

He hurried down the hill. He thought angrily, 'He's no business to look like that at me—a busy man. I go in whenever I can.' It seemed to him that no one, not even his father, understood how occupied he was; overwhelmed with urgent problems.

What had he been working at when he was interrupted? He could not remember—but he remembered its urgency and importance, which still oppressed him. He felt crushed by the weight of it, whatever it was.

305

He turned into Connells. The pig man was there and he told him that he had been on the hill, only to admire the rain.

The pig man was a reliable friend. 'Aye,' he said at once, 'a grand thing when it's needed.' He would tell Philly by and by about his feats in the market.

That afternoon Helen Pynsant put on her smartest frock, took the Carnmore brougham, and drove to the castle. She had never liked Annish which was not even fashionable rusticity and now she hated it as if it had played a trick on her. She looked with disgust at the little tumble-down lodge at the castle gates and she almost lost her temper when the brougham was blocked in the drive by an unattended horse and cart. The horse was cropping the grass. Beyond, there could be seen a group of servants and country people about a large box, planted by the front door. On the top of the box a young woman in a shawl was suckling a baby.

Rain was falling heavily. Helen Pynsant refused to walk twenty yards in ankle-deep, wet gravel. She called to the coachman through the speaking tube, 'Go on.' He at once got down, hitched his reins to the lamp and joined the group at the box.

'Is it Sukey's box?'

'Aye, and the bottom fell out when we went for to lift it, and she's away to Dunvil.'

'Put some planks under it.'

'Or a dure,' Darcy said, placing himself next the real coachman, but with a modest air. He was carrying his whip, but of course he had no top boots. 'Wouldn't ye say a dure, Mr. Curtin—a dure has more stiffness within itself.'

The coachman frowned thoughtfully. Mrs. Pynsant called from the brougham window, but no one paid any attention to her.

'It's a quare thing,' Dow said, 'that Sukey would not take more thought for her box.'

'Aye, she'll never care for annything but the new ploy with poor Kitty's wain,' Foley said.

Bridget, seated on the box, continued to suckle Finian. She had been left in charge by Rifty while he ran to tell Sukey herself of the disaster. She paid no more attention to the group of councillors than to the drizzle of rain falling through the opening of her shawl into her breast, and the baby's round cheek. She only took care to hold the shawl so that none of them should see her breast.

The energetic coachman called for ropes and showed how they could be pushed under the box.

'Aye, but ye'll want a dure too.'

'But if the bags is broke within,' Padsy said.

306

'It wouldn't be in bags.'

'More likely an ould stocking or a bottle.'

No one spoke of gold or money, except by implication. It was felt that a direct reference would be gross and almost indecent, like speaking publicly of some intimate part of Sukey.

Helen Pynsant called again from the brougham; the coachman, after one irritated glance over his shoulder, went to the hall door and thumped the knocker. He then returned to the box and when Grogan's pale face appeared at the hall window, he shouted and jerked his elbow towards the brougham.

But Grogan disappeared. Even when John Chass, seeing the brougham from the drawing-room, rang and shouted for him, he could not be found. Peggy went out with the carriage umbrella.

Apparently Grogan, long-suffering as he appeared, could not bring himself to take the carriage umbrella to such a scarlet woman as Mrs. Pynsant.

Helen Pynsant found, of course, that both the Corners were delighted with the engagement. John Chass complimented her on her daughter's charm, and Mary on her beauty and manners. Mary called people beautiful or ugly according to her notion of their characters.

'Such a pretty gel and so happy,' Mary said. 'I like to see a young gel enjoying life.'

'She teaches in Sunday School at home, I believe,' John Chass said, projecting his leg, 'a very good thing for a girl. Nothing like a good grounding in Scripture.'

'Stella is a good girl,' Helen Pynsant agreed, 'but, of course, she is very young.'

This opened the battle. Mary Corner at once felt opposition and flew to the help of the young people. She was in mood for battle because of the trouble and grief of the last week; the death of Kitty, Sukey's bad temper; and especially her anxiety about Teresa.

Con was already on his way to America and how could Sukey look after a child? What would happen to Teresa in such hands? Mary always had a guilty conscience if any child in her neighbourhood were unhappy or neglected and she could not sleep for thinking of Teresa with Sukey. This had disturbed John Chass and still further troubled her conscience; so that she flew at Helen Pynsant as if she had been a natural enemy.

'If the gel wants to get married,' she said, 'the sooner the better. My mother was married at seventeen and she was glad of it.'

'But don't you think, Mrs. Corner, that a girl misses a great deal by marrying young.'

307

'She misses nothing that she had not better be without.'

'You think that a little pleasure might spoil her taste for matrimony?'

The argument grew bitter because the two women had no common ground, no common idea of things. Mary Corner was early Victorian; Helen Pynsant belonged to a society which would set the tone to a new age, and each had complete confidence in a position which was very strong. Mary Corner would have said from her own experience of life, 'There is no secure happiness anywhere, except in love, in giving.' Helen Pynsant would have asked, 'Why should anyone be asked to make sacrifices? You say, for civilization, for the next generation. But why should I trouble about something that doesn't even exist?'

'You think, Mrs. Corner, that it's a woman's part to be married at seventeen and to have a child every year,' Helen said.

'I would have thanked God if it had been mine,' the other answered with a force of conviction which made Helen colour with anger and contempt.

John Chass, greatly embarrassed by this argument, kept smiling at each lady in a hopeful manner, and agreeing with each in turn.

He was relieved when Grogan came to call his mistress away.

Mary went out and John Chass apologized to her. 'We are in a whirl to-day.'

'I hope I'm not in the way.'

'You could never be that, Mrs. Pynsant.'

They looked at each other, not smiling, but with lips ready to smile.

'Stella has changed,' John Chass said. 'I had hoped she would have been more like you.'

'I'm afraid you're an Irishman, Mr. Corner.'

The whole atmosphere of the conversation was altered. Something easy and careless had taken the place of a fateful discussion. Helen Pynsant unconsciously fell into an attractive pose; John Chass put out his leg and bent his foot, showing its high curve; he smiled at his foot as if chaffing its vanity.

'Stella is not strictly pretty,' Mrs. Pynsant said, 'but she is a very affectionate, good hearted girl, and I want her to have all possible happiness.'

'Of course you do,' John Chass said. 'There's not so much happiness that it ought to be wasted.'

'And she was certainly looking forward to her first season.'

'Yes, it's a pity for a girl not to have plenty of balls when she's young.'

'You see what I mean, Mr. Corner?'

'Indeed I do see.'

Helen Pynsant throwing out her fine bosom towards John Chass and raising her beautiful chin, said, 'Young people are so helpless.' Her glance complimented John Chass on his sagacity.

'We must see that Miss Stella gets her season,' John Chass answered, turning his leg.

Down in the kitchen, Mary Corner was looking with surprise at Sukey, who, very drunk, with her bonnet over one ear, was rattling the pots on the range. Molly was nursing Teresa. From the background, a dozen Egans, Foys stared inwards. The box, roped to planks had been pushed under the kitchen table, but Rifty and Bridget still held an end of the rope as if to show their dutiful wardership; and also their family connection with it.

Sukey was abusing Molly. 'Is that the way ye use my pots?'

'What's all this, Susanna?' Mary cried. 'What are you screaming like that for? I thought Maria was scalded.'

'I'm not stopping,' Sukey shrieked. 'Mind that, not another hour. Darcy came for the box.'

'You needn't stop a minute. Maria is cook now, and it's time that child was in bed.'

'There's no harm in the wain. What harm is she; you wouldn't be noticing her if she lived here.'

This remark startled everyone who saw its drift. Mary Corner had no answer; the loyal Darcy exclaimed, 'You couldn't keep a wain in the kitchen, Sukey.'

Sukey turned on him with her streaming white face and flourished a wooden spoon like a weapon. 'Who are you to say no to that?' she screamed. 'D'ye think ye're coachy already with one wall eye to drive all ways into the ditches?'

'Ah! Sukey, she'd be walked on—she'd be kilt with all the feet does infect this kitchen.'

'It would be the feet of a fule then, like your own feet.'

Mary Corner, suddenly recollecting herself, cried so shrilly that even Sukey was shocked. 'Susanna how can you speak so. Darcy is a good, sensible boy and a good friend to you. You're making yourself a miserable old woman with your tongue. Now that's enough, for I won't have such silliness. Go and get the trap, Darcy, and take Mrs. Egan.' Sukey was missus by courtesy.

Sukey turned red with rage, but she did not answer. Mary left with the honours of battle, but when she reached the drawing-room she found that the other battle had been lost. It had been agreed that Stella should have her season; that no engagement should be announced for the present, and Mary Corner could not oppose this scheme because her husband had already committed himself to it.

When that evening, at Carnmore, Helen told Stella that the

309

engagement was impossible at least for another year, she answered that it could not be put off. She must be married at once. She surprised even her mother by her calm resolution. But of course the girl was already beaten because Helen had seen Jarvis at the castle, and explained to him how unfair it would be to Stella to marry her out of school.

Helen understood young men in love; she knew that they never made conditions for themselves. She was not surprised at Jarvis' instant agreement with her. He felt, as she had foreseen, as if he had been saved from a crime and when he was sent for to make Stella understand that they could not be married in the next three weeks, he repeated Mrs. Pynsant's arguments with even more conviction than she had used herself.

Stella was obliged to give way. But she was depressed and full of apprehension. She was angry with Jarvis for his confidence and the air with which he said, 'What does it matter as long as we love each other?'

She could not tell him what her fears were, because they were not clear to herself. She felt only that what had been settled, and clear to her, a simple deep happiness, a plain duty, a life in which everything, even anxiety, had its dignity and appropriate place, was now once more confused and muddled.

To go back to school and learn French; to go to Paris and learn deportment; to find out what she ought to think about her mother's friendship with Benskin and about Benskin himself; all this seemed to her not only boring but disgusting.

She accused Jarvis of being stupid. 'Don't you see we're spoiling everything?'

'But, sweetheart, what does it matter when we love each other; it's only for a few months and we couldn't very well go against your mother.'

'Mother doesn't understand—she doesn't really understand anything.'

Slatter hearing from Benskin just before dinner that the engagement was put off, ran joyfully to tell Philip. But he could not find him in his room and so he ran to find Maddy. 'Where's Philly—what have ye done with Philly?'

'Goodness knows, Pappy, I've not seen him.'

'If I was Philly, I'd be drunk, too,' said Coo.

'What a way to talk, Coo—why would Philly want to get drunk to-day with the visitors here?' Maddy asked her.

'All the upset,' Coo said. Coo objected to visitors because they interrupted the flow of her ideas and her peaceful walks and sits with Maddy. 'I can't find me *Wide World* eether,' she said sadly.

Philip was then in the highest degree of drink, when the very whirl of his ideas had reached steadiness, like a top at high speed. He was walking among the crowd in Dunvil, between the pig man and Breedy Macan, who were both rolling drunk. Philip did not roll and as he looked about him he smiled upon the scene with the air of a master. It was still raining. The sky was so dark that the huge torn clouds, whirled along with great rags of vapour hanging from their lower edges, which had seemed dirty yellow in the morning, appeared pale and clear against black. The rain poured down the broad slope of the main street towards the lough which could only be distinguished by the melancholy dash of the waves on the pier and the grinding of boats in the harbour.

There was no light in the village except from the windows of the pubs and cottages which fell on the shining road in irregular patches; it picked out the group of carts and the little crowd of people standing round them only by sparkling lines at the edges of the wet shafts and sparkling broken drops on wet hats, noses, chins and shoulders. The body of the mass was solid black.

From all the pubs came out with the bright bars of yellow light a loud confusion of voices with the rhythm and pitch of triumph, as if a victory were being celebrated, but from the black mass in the middle of the wide street there was heard only the loud, despairing moos of a cow separated from her calf. The voices of the men out there, chiefly farm hands, talking together quietly, were drowned in the rain which splashed about them on the stones and poured down the sagging necks of their coats behind. Their faces, shadowed under their jutting cap brims, were thoughtful and indifferent to rain and the time, having no money for drink they were prepared to wait all night for their fathers, brothers or masters in the pubs.

Philip walking with the pig man was still in triumph. He perceived clearly and logically that Dunvil, if he cared to think it so, was the centre of the universe and that he was among the great men of the world; the dominators. He was not to be put upon or deceived by anybody; and the pretensions of an enemy or a rival simply made him laugh. By laughing at people one crushed them.

The pig man suddenly fell into the gutter and rolled on his back. Philip, smiling, looked at this object for some time, then carefully climbed over it.

A short, square figure in a very long overcoat reaching to the ground and a broken hat stood before him. He carried a big stick in his hands, holding it straight in front of his nose, like Punch, and rapidly bent himself into a series of stiff little bows like Punch beating his wife. At the same time he grinned broadly and cried out, 'Phillyphilly hallo phillyphilly hullophilphilly hallphil.'

Philip recognized Bob the Duker, a village idiot, whose custom it was to salute everybody with these rapid bobs or dukes. Philip was deeply touched by this devotion even of a poor subject; he gave Bob his hand and told him how much he esteemed his regard; that he was a good fellow.

Bob, on his side, who had a cheerful contempt for the whole world, continued his satirical bobs and grins and his chaff so that the group at the carts turning round saw Philip shaking hands with Bob's stick, amidst the duologue.

'Goofellowhellfelle.'

'Phillyfilly, phillyfill, hallophilly.'

Both were roaring with laughter.

The turn of the cap peaks and half a dozen pairs of eyes, glinting in the yellow light of the pub windows, caught Philip's attention and suddenly he became suspicious. He drew himself up and said, 'What laughin' at?' The caps at once flowed round him like attendant courtiers or a bodyguard, somebody pushed Bob Duker away and numerous grave voices assured Philip that he was all right, that he was doing grandly.

They soothed him like a dangerous animal. They knew that a man in the grand stage of drunkenness, when he feels like the conqueror of the world and is full of tenderness and gratitude towards his devoted subjects, is also highly touchy in his dignity. He sees treachery in the most innocent glance and then at once he turns into a ferocious brute. They carefully guided Philip away from the carts, complimenting him at every step. 'Ah, but you're the grand man to walk, sor—there's no one walks a straighter road. Ah, who'd laff at ye?'

Philip was silent. He was still suspicious; he knew how difficult it was to detect treachery; and he knew how much treachery there was. He proceeded with a dignified, slow step back to Connells and ordered another whisky. But he looked closely at the barman to see that he filled the glass.

Philip did not reach Carnmore till one o'clock when two of the tenants brought him up the hill in a cart.

Philip walked away from the cart without a word. His expression was gloomy but resolute. He suspected that the whole world was having a joke at his expense. The wind rushing among the trees and pulling out his coat tails, the gusts of rain suddenly dashed upon him were part of the plot to make him look like a fool. The stream of ragged clouds, grey-black and yellow, taking enormous leaps over his head from one side of the earth to the other, were all making mouths at him. They had no faces but their black mouths full of broken teeth twisted every instant into grins of painful malice. They were like the grins of prisoners or unhappy wretches whose laughter is full of spite, because they don't want to laugh at anything or anybody, because they have been made to laugh by their own grotesque misery.

The lights in the lower story and Slatter's hurried anxious shadow flitting from window to window told him that he was awaited; but he did not want sympathy or affection. It was time for action; for a definite statement, so to speak, of what he was and what he thought about things.

He took off his shoes and slipped in by the lamp-room window, his usual entrance when he wished to avoid notice. He took down the old sixteen bore and charged both barrels.

But suddenly he noticed that the fireplace was laughing at him. Its lower lip and sharp narrow chin under the bars were pushed forward in a jeer; its upper canopy was lifted and thrust out in an enormous silent spasm of laughter.

Philip, taken by surprise, lost his imperial dignity. He cursed at the fireplace, hit it in the teeth with the gun.

Slatter had been walking about for nearly two hours waiting for his Philly to come home. He was too excited to sit down. He took his drink from the hall mantelpiece as he passed, alternately cursing Philip for being late, and agonizing for fear of some accident to him.

The two girls, sent to bed long before, were sitting up in dressing-gowns in case Philip should come home drunk, Maddy would then have to run down and help her father, or to save her carpets, and Coo would of course go with her. The terrific crashes which came from the lamp-room together with screams of rage, made Slatter and both girls rush towards the same point. Slatter threw open the lamp-room door, there was a second's silence, and then he gave a yell of terror and bolted down the passage to the hall. Philip, dashing after him, aimed a blow at him with the gun, which luckily struck the top of the passage door instead of his head. This gave Slatter a small start and enabled him and Maddy, who had just reached the hall, to escape into the garden through the front door, which had been unlocked for Philip's return.

Philip chased them about fifty yards down the drive until they turned among the trees. Then he went back to the house and smashed furniture and pictures in the drawing-room until Benskin came downstairs and knocked him out. Hanna arrived ten minutes later, summoned by one of the frightened maids, and prescribed total abstinence for the patient.

Hanna, who himself smelt of whisky, was in fair day form. 'He'll kill some of ye yet,' he said, 'if he goes on with the whisky. There's too much poetry in his drinking.'

As he said this he grinned at Maddy in her dressing-gown as if to say, 'And what are you thinking about?'

Maddy had taken a dislike to Hanna and she used to put out her

313

chin and look at him with an indignant and perplexed air even on public occasions, like the church fête. She would say of him scornfully, 'That play boy.'

She felt, perhaps, that Hanna had not done his duty as a man; that he had not been enterprising or persistent enough in his pursuit, and Hanna himself no doubt had the same feeling and wondered why he had not yet married Maddy. So that when he laughed at Philip as a poet, he contrived also to take a jaunty air with Maddy and to express even a genial contempt for Slatter and his ambitions for Philip. Yet Hanna still sang his ballads, with even more sentiment than before, and when he was almost tearful, he would say, 'Give me a come-all-you, to promote the flow of the vital juices.'

'You'll have to cut off Philly's whisky, Mr. Slatter,' he said. 'He's the kind that gets carried away.' He gave Maddy another grin, and picked up his hat. When he went out, Maddy gave a little sniff to herself, but she still looked perplexed.

Then immediately she took up duty. 'Where's Coo?' No one had seen Coo. But luckily before Slatter could become hysterical again she was found under her own bed, asleep.

She had taken refuge there and finding an old cardboard box against the wall, had experimented with it as a pillow.

'It was those Japanese tea girls made me think of it,' she explained. 'The Geeshas.'

Philip was still asleep when the English visitors left on the next afternoon for home. If Slatter had not run about all morning with tears in his voice saying that Philip would never have treated him so if he had not been mad, they would not have referred to the night's disturbance. They had thought it nothing uncommon in Ireland. As it was, Helen said with a smile that everyone knew what happened at an Irish fair, and Stella left Philip a friendly message by Maddy.

Mary Corner had defeated Sukey, but it was found the same night that though Darcy had harnessed the pony, Sukey had refused to come upstairs. She had slept on the floor.

The next morning she put on her old print frock and took up her duties as if she had never left them. But her temper was, if anything, a little worse than before; and she was drunk almost every night. She referred to the episode only once, when she said gloomily after her first evening glass, 'I'll tell ye what brought me back—it was me feet, gawd damn them—me feet, and may they burn the first of me in the last day.'

Sukey paid little attention to Teresa. Yet she was very jealous of her. Since Mary absolutely forbade that the child should be put to sleep in Sukey's cellar, it was sent to Molly's attic for the night, and Molly took it out in Shon's old perambulator twice a day; but it spent the rest of the time in the kitchen under Sukey's eye.

It was usually anchored to the kitchen table by a stout blind cord. Even Mary Corner could not alter this arrangement for Sukey would scream at her, 'If ye want her to drink the kettle and put her hand in the boiling soup, I'll loose her this minnit, ma'am.'

She was especially jealous of her mistress and whenever Mary, coming to the kitchen in the morning, would stoop down to play with the child, and to guide its hand into her sweet pocket, she would furiously rattle her pots on the range, and turning a bloodshot eye over her shoulder, growl, 'Ye'll sicken her, ma'am. Ye have her stomach destroyed with them lozengeys.'

Luckily Teresa was a good child. Her two years' experience of the world; in the steerage of an emigrant liner, in a one-room cottage with a dying mother, had taught her to be quiet and self-sufficient.

She would sit perfectly still under the kitchen table for five or ten minutes at a time; a habit that greatly irritated Sukey, who thought that it betokened a slow brain. 'All the Foys were like that—Con and Padsy—they would sit still and stare like the fules they were born.'

It was Mary who perceived that Teresa was always looking at something; a fly, a cockroach, the blue cat, Peter, stealing away under Peggy's skirts with the desperate plan of reaching the drawing-room hearthrug: or a bird, half a mile away in the sky, seen in two inches of dirty window between the edge of the table and the wall of the moat.

'What are you looking at, Teresa?' she would say, putting down her crumpled face beneath the table top, on the opposite side from Sukey. Teresa would then shift her piercing gaze to the old woman's face. The face would crumple still further till the long, bony nose almost touched the projecting chin; the red-rimmed eyes would close in a sly look. Teresa at once scrambled across the floor, grabbed the old black skirt, hauled herself up, and thrust her hand into the sweet pocket.

Sukey's growl, like distant thunder, over the table top, did not trouble her at all.

'A regular Foy—no proper feeling for anybody,' Sukey complained.

It was true that Teresa did not show affection or gratitude and this angered Sukey. But Mary Corner was not looking for affection and so she did not miss it.

IX

Jarvis, who on the strength of his famous map was considered an expert on the Laka and Daji districts, was reappointed to Pooley's company, at Laka. It was suggested that he might do some more mapping, as there was talk of a treaty with France to fix the limits of each nation's sphere of influence.

It was said that France was to receive Daji in this division, but the very notion threw Jarvis into a rage against the Government, for, as he wrote to Stella, 'What right had France to it?'

Jarvis had received only one short note from Stella. He had written every day, sending off budgets from every port of call. He was surprised when the mess sergeant at headquarters gave him one thin note containing a single half sheet, signed 'ever yours affectionately.' It was the first letter she had ever written to him. He was surprised but not hurt or even disturbed. In one moment, his active love had turned this strange coldness into a charm, 'She's shy.' This was a charm for Jarvis, as for many of the pagans round him, who expected to be scratched on their wedding night. As he journeyed along the Laka road, half running in his eagerness, with two carriers to a load, so that they, too, could trot all day and half the night, he was full of tempestuous excitement in which love and ambition and mere galvanic released energy could not be separated. 'Ah, the darling,' he thought, 'with her bog pool eyes— by Christ, if the French get away with Daji, I'll write to the papers and show up the whole bloody lot of this so-called British Government— she can't write, the sweetheart, but she can love, God bless her, the truest heart in the world. Oh, if Pooley wasn't such a damned Englishman, I'd know what to do.'

Pooley did not expect his second-in-command till Thursday, a week ahead, and for that day he had planned to shoot a guinea fowl for dinner. On the Friday before he sat down to his usual meal of chicken and yam. He was living in the old chief's compound; Felix also, since the final destruction of the company station, had his quarters there.

Felix had not yet joined his friend at table. He was walking slowly up and down the compound, in old native boots turned up at the toes; smiling to himself and occasionally scratching himself fiercely through the breast of his shirt. He was in deep and happy meditation. Dinah screamed abuse at him from her hut. Dinah had been bad tempered and quarrelsome since the loss of the store, because she had nothing to do but eat and be jealous. Felix was her only occupation and lately he had been absent-minded.

Dinah, following the invariable rule of her kind in the same difficulty, had ordered a love potion to put in Felix' soup; but the juju man, living like a wild beast in the sacred grove, had been difficult to approach. The medicine had not arrived.

Meanwhile she was enraged with Felix, especially when, as now, he was so absorbed by his thoughts that he did not even notice her screams.

Pooley's boy came to him and said, 'Chop live for table, sah.' Felix gazed vaguely at the servant and then slowly approached the table where Pooley, in crumpled grey pyjamas, was reading with one hand a new magazine and feeding himself at random with the other. Pooley, ill as usual, looked like a condemned man who had passed beyond suffering.

The rickety table, covered with chipped crockery and old sauce bottles and lighted by a hurricane lantern, stood opposite the guard room, where soldiers and a few women prisoners squatted by the light of a small fire.

Everything in sight was dirty, broken, cheap, ugly; all the faces were strongly marked. Resignation was savage despair; mildness looked like imbecility; detachment had the lines of cruelty. Dinah's savage screams were like the cries of some bewildered creature protesting against the mud hole into which it had wandered.

'Good mail?' Pooley said. The mail had come in the day before, bringing Pooley his *Christian Intelligencer*. Pooley was always extremely happy for the week after he received his magazine of prophecy.

'It's this question of antichrist that's the trouble,' he said. 'But there doesn't seem any doubt that Prince Louis Napoleon is the man. His name works out exactly to 666. That gives us another six months.'

'Before the end of the world?'

'Yes, or six months from April.'

'I must have a look at that,' Felix said. He always took Pooley seriously; because there was nothing else to be done. Moreover, Pooley listened to his ideas, and it was only fair that he should listen to Pooley.

'Six months,' he murmured. 'That will be interesting.'

Meanwhile his mind was full of Cleeve who had suddenly begun to write letters such as Felix himself might have written thirty years before; full of familiar names and arguments; the same discoveries, the same tricks, the same enthusiasm. The reasons appeared quite simple, that the boy's æsthetic friend, Chorley, had left Oxford and that he himself had just started philosophy and discovered all at once

317

a great many new and fascinating ideas; above all, a play of the mind which was at once amusing and exciting.

Since the beginning of these letters Felix had been a different man. For the first time in years he was eager to go home, and chafed at the impossibility of it. The Mosi Company was bankrupt since the Laka raid, and Felix at that time could barely pay for his food.

Pooley looked up from his magazine, reached for the sauce and said, 'Of course you know, we'll begin with Satan's dominion—Satan will get a clear run for three and a half years.'

'That will be a lively time.'

'England and America, they say, will get the worst of it—the general idea is that volcanoes will blow up under the chief towns—Edinburgh is on a volcano.'

'That sounds reasonable.'

There was a commotion among the huts and a shriek. No one paid any attention. Every day forest women were caught prowling through the compounds to steal food. The sergeant of the guard reported, 'It's the one that we caught on Saturday—she escaped the same night. That's three in a week.'

Pooley was still looking at his book in which he read the exciting sentence, 'The little toe of the left foot is undoubtedly Bulgaria.'

He said, 'Put her in the guard room.'

'But, sah, she's a very bad thief, this one—she ought to be whipped.'

'Keep her in the guard room.'

'Yassah.' The sergeant saluted and returned to the guard room where Bandy stood naked between two soldiers. Her body, oiled to slip out of a captor's hands, caught the flicker of the fire under the breasts; and a single steady reflection on the belly was the light of Pooley's lantern.

Bandy herself stood sulky, with hanging lip. She expected a flogging. She could see from where she stood Felix' thick back, but she would rather be flogged than appeal to him. She had avoided Felix and Dinah for two months for no reason except the instinctive logic of a domestic creature gone wild, that, having hidden its litter in the wood, avoids its former owners. She was afraid of being held, afraid of the soldiers who caught women, afraid of everything that might prevent her from flying back to her helpless family at the tree.

The sergeant began to shout at her; if she ran away again, the sentry would kill her with his gun; the men, angry that she was not to be whipped, punched her in the ribs and the stomach. Bandy, limp and sulky, said nothing and made no defence. She allowed herself to be knocked into a corner where she lay crouched among the other prisoners. Her sulky eyes already examined the guard room windows; the doors of the porch and the little straw canopy beyond, under which the sentry stood at ease.

The sentry threw his gun to the order and shouted in one word, 'alt-oo-go-dar. Pass, friend' with a slap on the butt for fullstop. He had recognized Jarvis coming through the clearing and he did not wait for an answer to his challenge.

Jarvis was through the gate before Pooley and Felix could look round; pouring with sweat, he exclaimed, 'Thank God, I've caught you. I was sure you'd be off.'

'Where to?'

'Daji.'

'Daji?'

'Yes, they told me that the Emir had been raiding again—raiding the Islanders. I thought I'd missed the show.'

'I believe there has been a raid up among the islands, but they're outside our beat, you know.'

'A raid, and you stayed here. But don't you see that it's the biggest chance we've ever had, to hop in before the French.'

Pooley was calling for drinks, ordering a dinner for Jarvis, a bath and clean clothes. He did not want to argue with him about politics. His orders were to avoid a clash with the French and to keep out of Daji, and these orders were definite and peremptory. The Government did not want any more incidents like Fashoda.

Jarvis had now recognized Felix. He shook hands with him politely and asked him how he did; but without waiting for an answer he said, 'Did you know about this treaty?'

'I did hear that we were going to make a boundary treaty with the French.'

'Yes, and they're asking for the whole of Daji, right down to the Niger.'

'My orders——' Pooley began.

'Oh, Government orders. We know what they mean—for God's sake take care of our Government skins—everything else can go to the devil. Look here sir, do you think we ought to let the French steal Daji from us under our noses. Why, they're laffing at us already.'

A boy appeared. 'Bafu live sah.'

Jarvis waved him away; he didn't want a bath, he could barely be troubled to put drink and food in his mouth. 'Where's the map?' he called. This was his own map preserved in the company office box. It was brought from the office and spread over the sauce bottles and the dirty plates.

'Here you are, sir, not a hundred miles from here to Daji and nothing in the way except a few swamps—we could do it in four days.'

Felix and Pooley looked at him with their bland faces which hid the opinion, 'This man is absurd.' They could not believe that he seriously proposed an attack on the Daji Emirate, a country rather larger than Wales, with half a company of half trained infantry; against the strictest orders of his Government.

'But what's stopping us?' Jarvis cried.

Pooley smiled and Jarvis turned white with anger. 'Well, what then? What's the objection—what in God's name—here we are—there's the men—we've got legs and arms, haven't we?'

Felix slipped away to write his letter for the mail which was to return with Jarvis' carriers. In the little hut, stifling and filthy, Dinah lay on a heap of frowsy blankets, bored and malicious with idleness. She looked sullenly at Felix and said, 'I'm going away from you.'

Felix sat down on a box in front of two piled boxes and wrote:

Dear Cleeve——

'I'll go with the sergeant,' Dinah said.

Felix reflected upon his letter. He wanted to warn Cleeve against certain traps into which he himself had fallen; to point out that philosophy was not a set of facts, much less a set of tricks; but a certain kind of training. It was worse than useless unless it changed a man so that he took the same kind of pleasure in finding truth as others took in defending various kinds of lies. Such men might not be common but no other kind of man could be called free or received on equal terms by other free men.

'I'll kill you,' Dinah said.

Felix paused in his second sentence. 'I must be careful,' he thought. 'Philosophy is only a kind of game to him now and he finds it amusing. If he thought it was going to change his character, he might run away from it. Nobody likes the idea of losing his self, however foolish or unhappy it is.'

'I'll kill you, I'll kill you,' Dinah screamed, scratching at his face. Felix noticed her and his conscience stirred. He felt his responsibility to Dinah, for whom he was so important. She needed him. He smiled and carried her to the blankets. 'It might be better to stick to Plato this time—something about the good life.'

Dinah gave a shriek of pleasure and Felix, smiling down at her, enjoying her sensuous delight as one enjoys the purring and the wriggles of a tickled cat, thought, 'The good life—the good possession, that is, after all, the solution of all the problems, religious and political,' and tickling Dinah to keep her happy, he imagined long conversations with Cleeve under trees, in the college garden or Addison's Walk, while they discussed authority and freedom, tradition and progress, democracy, and efficiency, change and security, and he would say, 'These everlasting conflicts have produced all the miseries, tyrannies, revolutions

320

and pogroms in the world—they have smashed up every nation, race and church since the beginning of time. But there is no reason why they should do so—the fundamental problems are quite simple.'

A black form appeared in the doorway, thrusting in his head, one of Dinah's suitors. He made an exclamation at the smell of the hut in which the full stink of dirt and sweat was brought out by the heat of the walls, and then, at last distinguishing Felix, gave a loud laugh and said, 'You got him there.'

Dinah, embracing Felix, gave a shriek of laughter and cried, 'Go away, you black man.'

Felix reflected. 'It simply boils down to the question of the good life.'

At the dinner table, Jarvis' angry voice was asking Pooley what he was afraid of. It could be heard that he wanted to quarrel with Pooley, and Pooley's mild, languid tones had a soothing sound, 'Orders are orders, I'm afraid.'

'That's the trouble—you funk it.' Jarvis, standing over the map, threw this out with such fury that the chatter in the guard room suddenly died, and Pooley, lounging in his chair on the other side of the table with his pipe in his mouth, looked at his subaltern with a startled expression. He was at last annoyed. But he remembered that Irishmen were a childish people; they must not be provoked; and that if Jarvis, who had been turned out of his British regiment for insubordination and rejected since by two company commanders for the same reason, were to make another failure in Laka, he would be finished.

He began patiently to explain again the danger of a clash between French and English troops in Africa at that time, just after Fashoda. It would probably start a European war.

'European war, be damned!' Cocky exclaimed. 'You know they wouldn't dare.'

Everyone in the compound was watching the quarrel. Heads blocked the door of the cook house. The Laka women in the guard room turned their mournful eyes towards the white men. The soldiers, including the sergeant, had come out into the compound and sat staring as if to listen with their eyes. They knew that there was talk of war. Bandy, left alone in the guard room, edged along the wall to the outer porch, and stood peeping at the sentry.

The moon had risen. It shone on the sentry's canopy, two tattered mats propped on four crooked sticks, on his right shoulder in its yellow jacket, on his polished legs, and on his rifle. A yellow flame from the guard room fire danced on one side of its muzzle and on the top a round glittering star.

Bandy gazed at the rifle.

321

The rifles were devil's rifles. The white men's bullets followed you wherever you went, until they caught you and blew your heart out. She trembled with horror at the feel of it. Her hand went to her breast.

'No, I can't, I can't,' she breathed, imploring, arguing, as if someone had ordered her to go to her children, even if her heart were blown out. 'I can't, I can't,' her legs trembled before that ruthless power which was, however, herself. She knew that she must go and she was terrified to die. She gave a deep sigh of despair.

'Pure bloody funk,' Jarvis shouted in the compound. He was in a blind rage. It seemed to him that something precious and even holy, something immeasurably more important than trifles like his life or Pooley's, was being sacrificed by this Englishman's stupidity, the honour of an Empire which was also his own honour, and his own glory.

'Pure bloody funk, because we might get into trouble,' Jarvis' voice rose to an incredulous sing-song. Pooley, much embarrassed by the scene, for which he blamed himself, got up and knocked out his pipe. 'I'm going to bed.' he said. 'Good night, old man.'

A quarter of an hour later, when, having taken his medicine, and carefully cleaned his teeth, he was creeping beneath his net into bed, he was startled by the appearance of Jarvis, dressed only in his shirt, now dried, and a pair of mosquito boots.

Pooley, seeing that his night load could not have arrived, was about to offer him a pair of pyjamas, when he suddenly began an elaborate apology. He said that he had behaved like a brute, and that Pooley was a gentleman. More than a gentleman, he was a Christian. Though, he continued, thrusting out chin and nose as if about to attack the bed, some people might be shy of the word, it meant a lot to him, and he meant a lot when he used it. He then pushed out his hand. Pooley, overcome by embarrassment, had at last lost his presence of mind. He gazed, and did not perceive what the hand meant. There was an agonizing silence.

In the midst of the silence a shout was heard, then a shot, and a piercing shriek; but such was the sensitive Pooley's embarrassment, and Jarvis' concentration, that neither paid the least attention to it.

Suddenly Pooley understood Jarvis' attitude; pulled up the net in a fluster; and grabbed the hand. He shook it with force. Jarvis marched off. Pooley, perspiring, fell back on the pillow and said, 'No, that's a bit too much—that's going too far. Damn the fellow.'

The sergeant of the guard entered and saluted. Pooley gazed at him with alarm, as if asking, 'Is this another lunatic?' Then recollecting himself, he said, 'Oh yes, who fired?'

'Sentry, sir—prisoner go for bush.'

322

'Prisoner, what prisoner?'

'I don't know, sir. Sentry see him run, he shoot; prisoner shout. I tink he hit him.'

'It sounded like a woman. I told you not to shoot at the woman.'

'Oh no, sir. Not woman, sir. Run too fast.'

'Very well, sargy.'

'Good night, sir.'

'Good night, sargy.'

Bandy had chosen to run when the sentry was yawning. His shot was late; it passed through the girl's shoulder muscle without touching the bone, and though the wound was large, and Bandy flying to the tree shrieked, 'I'm killed, I'm killed,' she did not die. She was only more frightened of the soldiers. But this did not prevent her stealing their yams the next day.

Suddenly the soldiers left Laka. The tall captain and Corner were taken ill and went away in hammocks with fifty men. The officer Jarvis on the next day marched north with the rest of the soldiers.

The half a dozen women who here and there in the forest had children to feed were in camp within the hour, pushing their noses into every hole, but they found little to eat. The Laka rains had now begun; bringing fever and making the swamps impassable; and none of the yam fields had been planted. It was a time of famine and despair for the Laka people. They did not know how to start again the broken wheel of their lives, and strong young men who four months before had been full of energy and purpose could be seen now, with swollen stomachs and hollow ribs, wandering listlessly through the scrub or lying in a puddle with a cloth over their heads. The languid young girls died every day, too indifferent to feed themselves. Bandy and the other mothers with young broods alone were active and purposeful; they did not ask how or why or wait for instructions, and they could not despair because they had no more thought for themselves than the leopards and hyænas, which with their own young to feed, hunted beside them through the forest.

Like the leopards, too, Bandy was at war with all the others. With the pain of her wound and her stiff arm, with days of fever and weakness which terrified her with the fear that she would not be able to forage, she was even more fierce and dangerous than the rest. She robbed them when she found their hiding places unguarded but they dared not rob her at the sacred tree. At the howl of a leopard in the night, when she would sit up and look across the clearing, putting out her flat skull and long jaw through the mat walls of her shelter, her savage eyes said already, like a leopard's from its den, 'Keep off, this is my place which I have made and these are my children.'

'My heart's blood,' Jarvis wrote to Stella. 'My C.O. and Uncle Felix ate something that didn't agree with them and had to go to hospital. Uncle came off best because he was only sick but the C.O. nearly died. I'm told Pooley is to be relieved by a certain Captain Figg. Figg and I are not fast friends. We had a difference about politics; but that's not the reason why I won't turn out the guard for him. It won't be here, and neither will I. Sweetheart, I've got the chance of a lifetime. It was the blessing of God that sent the cramps to Pooley and left me in command here. But I daren't tell you what kind of chance I mean— only that it's a great one—the biggest kind of a chance that a soldier could ask for. Pray for me, my darling, and God bless you for ever, your loving husband, Harry.'

Cocky always signed himself husband. Why, he did not know, and Stella was not the girl to ask.

It was true that Captain Figg had quarrelled with Jarvis. They had differed, at the headquarters mess, about the Irish regiments. Figg maintained that they had no discipline. Jarvis declared them to be the finest and smartest regiments in the world; and added that if they had no discipline it was because they did not need it. It was only Figg's regiment that needed to be drilled into a machine to keep it from running away. Figg answered with some rude speeches about Irish rebels. Two days later he was found dozing in his long chair, after a mess night, with his nose painted bright green and on his shirt front, 'Erin Go Bragh,' in letters six inches long. A pot of green paint was missing from the store.

Jarvis did not deny the deed. He offered to pay for the paint. Luckily the colonel, though he found Jarvis a nuisance, admired him as a polo player and a soldier. He was a thoroughly English colonel, as far outside the continental tradition of soldiering, as a forty-niner from Oxford. The English army of the last century was a frontier force. It thought in raids, reliefs, sudden attacks, cross-country gallops; not in campaigns. It did not value learning, but dash. Colonel Y—— far preferred Cocky, as a soldier, to Pooley or Figg. He was therefore let off lightly for this joke.

But Cocky and Figg remained bad friends, and when Figg reached Laka and found that Cocky had marched off to the north with half the company, he began at once to threaten courts martial.

His first dispatch to headquarters was not taken seriously, because Jarvis' own letter had arrived first. Jarvis wrote that he had marched north to take action against Daji raiders in the neighbourhood of Laka.

This did not frighten anybody and Figg's report that Jarvis was already across the Daji frontier was not believed. His feat was as much beyond headquarters' reach of idea as Cezanne's pictures in that same year were beyond that of the Salon jury. Both were original and simple acts of imagination.

Thus when the French cabled to Paris, declaring that a British force had invaded the French sphere of influence; Paris to London, threatening to move troops from Dahomey; London to Lagos, requesting explanations, and Lagos to Lakoja, demanding the facts; there was a panic. No one knew what to do. Figg was ordered to go after Jarvis; and then ordered to come back again. Runners, including the local intelligence agent, were sent north and then recalled. But they had already gone, and nobody knew where they had gone to, because the only map of Daji was Jarvis' own, now printed and distributed from the War Office. By this map the most experienced African travellers continued for years to lose themselves.

Intelligence agent Jingler knew Daji very well. He visited the Emir's court at least twice a year, taking news from the south, about movements of troops, the intentions of the British; and then moved on to Dahomey, where he gave the French any information about Daji, Laka, Lokoja, that they might choose to pay for.

Jingler, making due north, soon struck the trail; on the fourth evening, in the middle of a Daji desert avoided by all roads, he came upon the party. At first he thought that the men were dead. They lay like corpses, twisted and flattened among the short, twisted trees which were still bare of leaves. In Daji no rain had fallen.

Then Jarvis started up from a hollow and came rattling towards him on the iron ground. He, too, looked like a sun-dried corpse, his skin a dried, hardened mask on his bones.

Jingler held out his letter stick, and Jarvis read an order to return, or face 'the most serious consequences.'

He did not smile, but threw the paper away and said to Jingler, 'There ought to be a well here.'

'No water, sah. I tink you come back, sah,' Jingler had no wish to see a good customer massacred.

Jarvis' face showed his indecision. The march had been a disaster. Of forty-two men, nine had deserted in the terrible Laka jungle, two had died. If there was no water or food found within the next two days, the whole force would die.

Jingler swung his stick with the nonchalance of the independent.

'You no fit come Daji this way, sah.'

Jingler, as it turned out, was right, but meanwhile the physical shock upon Jarvis' strong, tense nerves had produced the physical reaction. A fear, greater than of death, the fear of failure, produced strong faith. He was suddenly full of resolution and confidence. He looked at the sky and said, 'Rain comes to-morrow.' The twilight sky was a bright

325

green, like sea water seen from below. Jingler grinned at the sky and said, 'It come next month.'

Jarvis was impatient. He talked about rain but his faith did not need any support. He said sharply, 'Where are you going then?'

'You give me answer, I go back.'

'There's no answer.'

Jingler grinned and walked off with his dancing step. Jarvis turned and darted towards his men, his energy renewed.

A sergeant staggered up and exclaimed in a cracked, angry voice, 'Well no here.'

He should have reported all present, but Jarvis paid no attention to this breach of routine. He answered cheerfully, 'No, Sergy, the well is a little further on. We'll have to manage on our water bottles to-night.'

The sergeant muttered in an audible voice that he didn't agree for this. Voice and look were mutinous.

Jarvis was careful not to notice the remark. He had known for two days that the men were on the edge of mutiny. They were too dejected and worn out to care what he might do to them; let him shoot them if he chose. The only reason why there had been no mutiny, only desertions, was that Jarvis did not seem to notice disobedience, or provocative rudeness. When the sentries went to sleep, he himself kept watch. He had watched all last night and slept at the midday halt. When a man threw away his rifle, he carried it. The idea of discipline was still present to these men because no one and nothing had made them notice that the reality had disappeared; and the instinctive idealist in Jarvis knew the power of ideas. The men groaned, 'I can't—I'm dying,' and of several of them this was true. But when Jarvis set these dying men on their feet, and turned them towards Daji, they moved forwards because his hands had given them direction.

So he had moved them twenty-three miles that day, with the loss only of two rifles, and now, smiling pleasantly at the mutinous sergeant, he said, 'Now we make chop.'

'Men no fit eat anything.'

'Oh yes, they are. Come on, what about a fire?' He walked among the tumbled bodies. 'Come on, get wood, make fire. Then you'll have chop.'

They did not move a finger. One or two, opening their eyes, looked at him with hatred; but sidelong, as if at a demon.

Jarvis looked round, and picked his man; young, strong, a sulky boy that nothing could kill. He pounced on him and dragged him to his feet, pushed him towards the nearest tree. 'Go on, boy—you want your chop.' He knew that here he could use authority. Men do not mutiny when they are urged to feed. He shouted at them, 'Fire—chop—then sleep.'

326

In a few minutes a few tottering grey shapes could be seen feebly moving among the trees; among them Jarvis, shouting, joking, jumping at the branches, and ripping them away. He was like a white demon among tortured shades. But in an hour the fire was lighted, the food was cooking, the men were chatting together, and the company singer was intoning through his nose a long-drawn song of arrived travellers. Somebody made a joke and there was a short laugh, surprisingly loud. The shades had come to life. The demon, for his own ends, had resurrected them.

Jingler, meanwhile, was making his way at full speed to Daji. He was a good judge of the value of news. The Emir knew already that British troops had crossed the frontier; the invasion had been discussed for a week in all the markets of Daji and Dahomey; but he did not know where or how many they were. Jingler gave him exact particulars and pointed out how easily the small force could be overwhelmed in the bush.

The army was at once called together by sound of the trumpet; the Emir's green war banner was set up in front of his palace; Audu and a numerous party of slaves plundered the villages for fodder and corn; southern traders, including two white men, were arrested and their goods confiscated. In Daji it was understood that war abolished all laws.

The white men were traders well known in Daji. One was a Syrian who dealt in aphrodisiacs and scent; the other was Hatto, who had lately sold the Emir twenty-four Tower muskets, and forty pounds of gunpowder. The guns were not paid for, and Hatto had spent three months in Daji trying to get his money. The Emir said that the guns were bad; two had already burst, killing a man and maiming two more. Hatto answered that they had burst because his men overcharged them with the wrong gunpowder. He demanded his guns back, and one thousand teresa dollars compensation for the two damaged and for breach of contract.

He continued to make these demands even after his arrest; and the crowd in the market place were surprised and scandalized to hear him shout, as the guards led him through to prison, 'Tell your king that he's a dirty swindler, and I'm not going away till he pays me, either.'

Hatto's insistence had irritated the Daji people for some time. They were used, of course, to his type, common in all the large northern market towns. But though they could understand why a man's self-respect should urge him to be a nuisance; they couldn't forgive him for giving way to it. Now they lost patience with Hatto and put him in the stocks.

The stocks in Daji market were in the full sun. Prisoners frequently died there within a few hours. But Hatto could not be subdued. He kept shouting at the market people, 'All right, but don't think you're going to get away with it. I'm here till I get my money.'

'Go on then,' he said, 'have a good look. Don't mind me. I like it.'

Sometimes he shouted threats. 'You wait, that's all, you wait and see wot's goin' to happen to your majesty the lord high welsher.' He used a particularly offensive word for welsher. 'You wait till the Queen of England gets to know about this.'

Once he asked for water, and when it was refused he said, 'Beer, then, I'm not particular.' He also asked about an hour later for a mat to shelter from the sun. When the mat was also refused, he appeared for the first time a little dejected. He said to the guards, 'All right then, but you can tell your silly old king that if he goes on like this, I'll chuck the whole business and he won't get any more guns.'

The Emir, by that time, with his whole army, was twenty miles away on the southern road.

It halted for the night, and the scouts went on alone. They found Jarvis' camp on the next evening, two days' march from Daji, approaching so close that they could count the soldiers; and one of them, creeping up to a sleeping man, brought away his rifle.

The scouts, returning, met the army on the road, and led them forward to a suitable battle-ground.

Jarvis had brought no loads. He slept on a mat like the men and his net was hung from the branch of a tree. He slept deeply, but on this night he suddenly waked at two o'clock with the sense of urgency so strong that he believed the sentry had challenged.

But there was dead silence. It was his nerves, which, knowing what he wanted of them and performing their duty even while he slept, had called him. He pulled on his boots and went to the sentries. The first had collapsed. He lay snoring, flat on his back. The moon shone directly into his broad nostrils, illuminating their hairless, red-brown channels. The other stood upright against a tree. From the back he appeared stiff with watchfulness, like a hawk that has closed its high-shouldered wings to fall on some prey. But Jarvis, walking round him, found that his eyes were closed. With his wrinkled, drawn face, thin and covered with yellow dust, his look of bitter experience and mournful resignation, he resembled a mummy dug out of the sand and propped against a tree.

Jarvis did not wake the men. He would watch for them, and let them wake. He began to walk up and down. The moon, nearly full, poured through the east side of the sky a pale blue light which seemed to have the tension of an electric fluid. It was like lightning dissolved and suspended in dry air, so that each particle was a blue spark of it.

328

In the black sky in the west, the stars seemed white hot with the energy of their still projection, firing their rays a billion miles through the solid tension of space.

The landscape, mean scrub, scattered upon little stray hills, like a petrified ocean extending every way to the horizon, was now a broken pattern of white fire and blue-black shadow, like a crucible of melted steel on which slag floats. Each tree coiled upwards like a tongue of flame and its branches were like the spread top of a flame pressed down by a back draught. But the fire was the cold burning of electricity. One expected the trees to crackle at a touch. Their hair was standing on end.

Jarvis, as if suddenly arrested by this violent beauty, stood still and looked at the sky. In fact, he did not notice it. He had not consciously observed any object for its own sake in the last week. His brain was a calculating machine, planning, arranging, with the foresight and refinement of an insect. Yet he felt the tension; he knew that this was a time of concentrated life, unforgettable, and that the danger increased it as the solid opposition of the ground made the light seen. Life was felt like power against the danger, the stubbornness of material.

'It's a poor chance,' he thought, and found himself grinning, exultant with some secret energy of purpose and ambition.

The rattle of a rifle on the hard ground told him that the upright sentry had awakened. A moment later a wavering voice said, 'Halt, friend. Who go dar?'

'Friend.'

The sentry, who was dead within three hours, answered him in an exhausted voice, 'Pass, friend, and all's well.'

The Emir with his chief captain Audu, halted in a shallow depression about a hundred yards from the Daji road. It was an excellent place for an ambush.

The chiefs, on a front of about half a mile, took up positions in this valley, which hid them completely. The gunmen, fifty in number, were ordered to lie close to the road on either side, in patches of scrub and behind ant-heaps.

At half-past six, in bright, early sunshine, the enemy were seen; creeping along the road in a close bunch. Some carried their rifles on their backs; some carried two rifles; others had none. The white man could be seen moving rapidly from back to front and then back again. He was running among them like a dog driving goats.

The chiefs, seeing this small party of crippled men, less in number than one of their own households, were impatient to attack. But their orders were strict not to charge until the Emir's gunner fired, and the gunner, by Audu's advice, had been ordered to reserve fire until the enemy had reached the centre of the battle front.

329

However, the discharge, when it came, from fifty muzzle-loading guns made a noise like cannon. Several soldiers fell.

At the first shot, Jarvis shouted, 'Form square.' His reaction was so quick that the order seemed to be at the same time as the shot, and quicker than the smoke. He jumped forward and grabbed the barrel of the maxim gun from its carrier's head. The other carrier, with the tripod, was still gazing open-mouthed at the enemy. Groups of horsemen, yards apart, were rising as if from the whole plain, In four or five seconds these groups became a line of which the ends could not be seen. They diminished on the right and left into clouds of dust. A high, rolling wave of dark horses, surmounted by a foam of white robes, and the glitter of swords and spear blades, rolled across the whole visible earth. The ground fluctuated under the tons of its weight and the pounding of its hoofs.

'Put down that stand,' Jarvis yelled at the maxim-gun carrier.

The men were in confusion. This was due to their surprise, which, upon many of them, already sick, acted like an anæsthetic. Drill and discipline obliged them to go towards their places, but nervous apathy caused them to move with extreme slowness.

The charging wave was now so close that the whites of the horses' eyes, wide with panic, could easily be seen. In the middle, slightly in front, the Emir, marked by a green turban, rode a horse of unusual height. He was followed by a standard bearer carrying the sacred green flag. None of the soldiers had fired at the enemy. They were still scattered; limping towards Jarvis to form square. Jarvis was fitting the belt of cartridges into the gun. The first two cartridges were uneven; they were not in line with the rest. He noticed this, and adjusted them. He felt the mastery of a man who, in a crisis of seconds, can think quickly and act with judgment; this feeling of detached power in judgment was the happiest moment of his life till that time. Happiness was not the word for it. It was a concentration of nervous life.

He put in the belt; sat down on the tripod; put his thumb to the trigger. The horsemen were twenty yards away.

Jarvis pressed the trigger; the gun fired and in his relief he smiled. He traversed the gun. Horses and men fell; the charge divided into two parts and the wings, without objective and unable to change course, galloped past on either side. Enormous clouds of dust at once obscured them.

The Emir was among those, whose horses, terrified by the rattle of the maxim, swerved aside; but at once he pulled up, turned and charged from the right flank. He was followed by Audu, by the little black standard bearer, and at a long interval by seven or eight swordsmen.

330

As he charged he rose in his stirrups and shouted, 'In the name of Allah.'

Jarvis could not swing the gun because his own men were in the way. But by now they had formed a rough square with about six rifles to each face. The sergeant shouted an order; the men took aim and opened rapid fire on two faces.

This was almost as effective, in noise and execution, as the maxim. The two wings of the native army, now convinced, chiefly by the fact of their motion away from the scene of action, that they had lost the battle, disappeared helter-skelter towards Daji, leaving about a dozen horses and men scattered on the plain.

The Emir's party, however, charging straight at the square from a short distance, was not all shot down until the leader, the Emir himself, was within ten yards. The men lowered their rifles. Jarvis stared up from the sun.

Suddenly the Emir scrambled to his feet, sword in hand, and rushed at them on foot, with a shout of 'God is Great.'

The sergeant yelled, 'Fire!' and at the same moment Jarvis ordered, 'Don't shoot.'

Four rifles went off. The Emir fell like a rabbit, rolling head over heels in a billow of white gowns, and lay on his back, kicking and struggling.

The men on the north face of the square, seeing that the Emir was alive, once more took aim, deflecting their rifles. But at this moment, Jarvis, who had been running round the outside of the square, appeared in front of them, holding up both arms and shouting, 'Don't shoot.'

One rifle went off, but the bullet luckily passed under Jarvis's arm into the ground. The surprised firer exclaimed, 'Haice!' in a tone of extreme surprise.

All the men were gazing with surprise while Jarvis went up to the Emir and held out his hand.

The Emir, who had raised himself on one arm, tried to reach his sword, which had fallen from him, and failing to do so, glared at Jarvis with the expression of a broken-winged vulture. His eyes had the ferocity of a beast that does not conceive mercy.

Jarvis, exclaiming, 'Are you hurt?' stooped towards him. The Emir, by a sudden convulsive effort, scrambled to his feet. Blood could be seen on the ground and on his white gown but he stood rigidly, with his wide, yellow-ringed eyes still fixed on the enemy.

Jarvis, in his admiration for the man, his sympathy and natural respect for royalty, struck the attitude of one about to make a fine speech; but as he knew no Hausa, he could only shake the Emir's hand, and say, 'You no fit be afraid. I your friend. You good brave soldier, I soldier. We friends.'

331

This speech, even when interpreted to the Emir by a Hausa sergeant, did not seem to explain the situation to him. His expression remained suspicious and hostile.

Jarvis, therefore, made another longer speech, explaining that he had no hostility to the Emir and no wish to take Daji from him. He hoped that he would continue to be Emir of Daji and he, Jarvis, would ask the Queen of England to make him so. The Queen, he was sure, would agree to this suggestion, because she, too, admired so brave a man who knew how to fight.

The Emir's expression now changed to one of bewilderment. He looked wildly about as if suspecting himself among lunatics. Suddenly he began to collapse into himself. The robe bulged out. Jarvis cried out, 'Catch him,' but already he was on the ground. He had fainted.

The examined him and found a large, torn, flesh wound in his right thigh, pouring blood. Jarvis himself bandaged the Emir's wound, and had him placed in a temporary shelter.

Meanwhile the men had already gathered food, water, great heaps of loot; embroidered saddles, swords, turbans, robes. A crowd of natives watched their motions from a distance, apparently without fear. These were traders and camp servants of the Emir's army, who were now prepared to serve the conquerors. They waited only for an invitation.

Jarvis was surprised at first to see these people gathering on the outskirts of his camp. Although war was still an adventure, the English idea of it had already changed from that of the eighteenth century, when English travellers in Paris, during the Franco-English war of the seventies, confidently asked for the passports which they had forgotten, and were entertained by the best French society. Nationalism had made way since then even in the upper classes, and so it seemed odd to Jarvis that the Daji traders should not run away with the Daji army; or at least, feel hatred against its conqueror. He ordered his men to keep them at a distance. But the men found this precaution so ridiculous, and the traders' neutrality so natural and reasonable, that he perceived his mistake. The traders were allowed to enter the camp. From this time it was well supplied with all requirements.

Yet Jarvis could not help feeling a little contempt for these traders who set private gain above patriotism.

He camped two days in the bush to give a military funeral to his dead; one killed by a slug, the other dead of fever, and to recuperate the survivors. On the third he set out for Daji. He was prepared for a triumph. The men, such as could walk, had oiled their legs. He himself had mended his breeches and whitened his helmet. He had chosen the biggest horse he could among the loot and rode through the main gate, with the Union Jack carried before him.

But the people were busy. They paid very little attention to the soldiers. In the market-place, indeed, crowded with buyers and sellers, a mass of old women, round a dried fish stall which was selling off at low prices, blocked the road, so that Jarvis, the conqueror, and the conquering army, had to wait for five minutes; and at last, since the women would not clear the road, to take another one.

The only cheer received by the conqueror was given by the skeleton of a white man, Hatto, who, released from the stocks ten minutes before, dragged himself forward on hands and knees into the way of the procession, and as it passed him, shouted out from beneath clouds of dust, 'Gawd save the Queen.'

Hatto saluted the flag with deep emotion, quite separate from that appropriate to his own rescue.

Afterwards, he was picked up by two of the soldiers and carried to the palace where Jarvis, astonished and pleased to find a white man in Daji, put him into his own bed, and carefully nursed him. In return, Jarvis was asked to admire Daisy's picture, he had a full inventory of the marriage chamber, including the bedroom china, decorated with primroses. 'I used to say sometimes when she got up in the night, that the primroses were wyting for a spring shower. Har. Har. But you couldn't pass that kind of tweezer to Dysy in dylight. She's a real lydy in her feelings.'

Jarvis failed to like Hatto, but Hatto admired Jarvis. 'I guess you syved me life,' he said, 'and if you want a real good tip, I'll put you on to a gold mine.'

'I'm afraid I haven't much faith in gold mines,' said Jarvis. 'My uncle lost a fortune in them.'

'I didn't mean a real mine—something better. New Mosi?'

'What's that?'

It proved to be a plan for amalgamating all the Mosi river companies. 'Look at all the country round here,' Hatto said. 'Daji and Laka, just opened up. Wot you've opened up, sir. We're going to get all the ground nuts and the palm kernels in Laka down the Mosi. The traders are there already. All we wants, captain, is a few 'undred for expenses. I don't mean thousands, 'undreds. To get in touch with the right people and print a few circulars. Promotion expenses. It'll pay you a thousand per cent. It's the biggest chanst you'll ever have.'

But Jarvis, whose whole capital at the time was not more than two hundred pounds back pay, would not give it to Hatto.

'But don't you want to see the country opened up?'

'Yes, I should like to see a trading company in Daji—but I wouldn't put money into it even if I had the cash. It's not allowed.'

'Go on, sir. Nobody'd know or mind.'

But Jarvis had grown an official conscience. He was a responsible

333

ruler. Every day he issued proclamations, laws. He rose before dawn to write his dispatches and from then till midnight he was examining markets, inspecting nuisances, hearing grievances; he had never worked so hard in his life and all this work was for the benefit of other people, because he thought of them as his people. He loved the chattering mobs in Daji, like a first born, and often after sixteen hours' work he could not sleep for thinking whether this or that would be the best way to cheapen supplies or prevent disease.

He dug public latrines, abolished the cutting off of hands for theft, two reforms equally detested by the Emir's late officers. The Emir, slowly recovering from his wound, did not give him any assistance. The Emir had never loved his people; but only his wives, the children of his body, glory and righteousness. The idea of the fond ruler, invented by poets, had not reached Africa, and therefore African rulers could not love their peoples in the same way as European monarchs.

Jarvis took special pains to assure the people of the Queen's love, which they would now share. He promised them his protection in their work, peace and justice throughout the land. The people, however, were already at work. They had to be. They did not care who ruled them, black or white, so long as he let them alone. Peace and justice they had never had; and they did not expect them now.

The people paid no attention to Jarvis and neither did the Government. His dispatches announcing the treaty of peace with Daji and his intention to remain in possession of the emirate until further notice, were not even acknowledged. The Government was in the same difficulty that affects all imperial governments in such a crisis. They could not disown Jarvis without danger of trouble at home; or support him without danger of trouble abroad. So they did nothing and waited to see if France would take the first step, which, under the circumstances, was almost bound to be a false one, because the position itself was false in its very basis.

The first news of Jarvis' march, conveyed in a four line paragraph in *The Times* and a long letter to Stella, of which two pages were marked, 'For family circulation,' made small impression, even on the family. It arrived when everybody had other preoccupations. Benskin, who had married Helen Pynsant a month before, was still on his honeymoon in the Mediterranean. In Annish everyone was excited by the Irish Councils Act, just passed, to set up district and county councils in Ireland. These were to be the first councils ever known in Ireland and everywhere nationalists were standing against the landlords and magistrates.

Thus suddenly the farmers had woken to the fact that the Conservative Government might be giving them a kind of home rule much nearer to their pocket interest than a Dublin parliament. They began to hold meetings and the green flags came out of dusty cupboards where they had lain since the Liberal defeat.

Breedy Macan went about with a grin of delight and when he came to the castle yard for the kitchen stuff, he shouted at Darcy, sunning himself at the pump, 'Them wull be the grand boots for Padsy's ass cart.'

Darcy had been wearing top boots for a month; Old Jebb was dead and John Chass and Mary had agreed that Darcy, whether he was a safe driver or not, had the first claim to the coachman's post, on moral grounds.

Darcy had been accused of pride in his new post and it was said that he slept with his whip. But it was an undiscriminating charge. Darcy carried his new boots with pride, but it was the honest pride of a young wife wearing her first baby. God had blessed him with increase.

Breedy could not upset that dignity. Darcy looked at him with surprise and said, 'Why would I be driving Padsy's ass cart?'

'There'll be no more horses here if Jawn Chass loses the election, and no sarvents neether.'

Darcy looked at him with a serious expression and remarked only, 'He knows well that I could do the gyarden. I could cook too.'

But he was looking thoughtfully at his boots when Breedy, in search of better game, went into the kitchen. He took his place on the beggars' bench. 'And where will ye go to Sukey when Flash Jawn is run out of his cassle.'

'And what'll ye do for your kitchen stuff, Breedy?'

Breedy laughed. He enjoyed revolutions more than business. 'Ah, but I tell ye it's one thing to be Jawn that gives out the contracks and another to be Jawn that has nothing to give annybody but the ould chat. Aye,' he spat again, behind Bridget, next him on the bench, 'it'll be the bailiffs in before the year's out and who's caring.'

There was silence. The malicious little man looked round the kitchen and twisted up his white face in a grin. Then he nudged Bridget and pointed at Finian crawling beneath the table, 'Did ye think he'd be king of the cassle on his anty's money. Faith, maybe there'll be no more cassles in Ireland by the time he's breeched.'

The speech was like an explosion in the room. The silence that followed it was not that of disapproval but shock. Sukey, at the range, stood still with a wooden spoon in one hand and a pot lid in the other.

Bridget, who rarely flushed, turned a dark red and a look of terror and entreaty came into her eyes. She had never formed such a plan in her head, but now that Breedy spoke of it, she found it in her actions. She knew that she wanted Sukey's money for Finian as well as herself; for a compound which was herself and Finian as one living need.

335

As for the phrase, king of the castle; that passed over her mind, terrified and confused, like a scented wind, leaving only a memory of some faint unusual tremor of the sense, whether pleasant or unpleasant she did not enquire.

She turned her frightened, sulky eyes on Sukey, but Sukey had formed the habit of ignoring Bridget. She did not seem to have heard. Bridget looked at Finian, who having reached Teresa's outstretched leg in his crawling, was patting it with both hands.

Teresa, grasping a toy cart, a present from Mary Corner, in one hand, stared at the baby. The hand holding the cart stood still in the air, as if all its nerves had been suddenly withdrawn into the green eyes, staring at the baby.

Finian, to whom the leg was a natural obstacle, having judged its consistency, climbed over it, with great difficulty, and then, obviously delighted with this feat, advanced with the gait of a hackney, kicking up his legs behind and slapping down his hands in front.

Bridget came quickly and smoothly to the table and, whipping out a little crumpled paper, offered Teresa a piece of seed cake. She smiled and wheedled, 'Ye wee darling, arn't ye the loveliest wee gyurl.'

This was new for Bridget to make love to Teresa. It had been thought that she was jealous of the child. Sukey turned round to the stove, Breedy sniggered.

'A penny, then. Would ye like a penny? Ah, did ye ever see such eyes, like the sea itself. Your Anty Sukey has right to be proud of ye.'

Finian had reached Sukey's carpet slippers. He patted them carefully in preparation for another feat. Sukey started forward, throwing him a yard away on his back.

'There's your bones,' she shouted at Breedy, 'and now go wan out of my kitchen.'

Finian, finding breath at last, sat up with a yell of rage and astonishment. Bridget flew to snatch him up.

Sukey paid no attention to either of them. But she beat at the fire bars of the range with such violence that the red hot coals flew to the middle of the floor, filling the air with the smell of singeing.

'The smell of hell for ye,' Breedy said, going out with the bucket, 'and faith ye wouldn't look far for a damned soul.'

It was Benskin who, as soon as he saw it, first understood what could be done with Jarvis' letter. He took it to town with him and asked some of his friends about it; some Members of Parliament, a few of the big financiers in the African market. He returned to New Grange by the night train, in unusual excitement.

'I tell you what, Stella, this may be a big thing for Nigeria if the papers take it up.'

336

'There is a piece in *The Times*.'

'You have the photograph of Cocky in uniform, haven't you?'

'It's not a good one.'

'It can be touched up and we ought to have a picture of the battle, too. What a nuisance this shoot is to-day.'

Pheasant shooting had begun and a large party was expected for that day. Both he and Stella were in tweeds. 'I'll have to go up to-night.'

He looked thoughtfully at Stella. 'What about some of the other letters?' but seeing her surprised expression, as she buttered a piece of toast, he said, 'Oh, of course, nothing may come of it after all. You never know how the public will catch on to things; but I'd like to do your young man a good turn.'

Benskin was both more affectionate to Stella and more confident, more paternal in his manner. He had been married to Helen for three months, and this triumph, which still seemed to him a crowning stroke of luck, had given him the aplomb and confidence of a happy man.

Happiness had quickened all his feelings, ambitions; his friendships and his generosity. He had given Helen forty thousand pounds worth of jewels, and Stella pearls which she would not wear, as she said they were too valuable.

Benskin was now a county councillor, but he had no political ambition for himself. He was not ambitious for power or glory except as a priest wants it to extend the faith. If he had been an Italian or Irish peasant he would have turned naturally to the priesthood or some humble Christian brotherhood. Since his spiritual faith was imperial, in a spirit which he called the English spirit, his feeling now while he joined the ranks of country gentlemen was of one entering upon a quasi-religious vocation; to support and maintain the traditions of the hierarchy; as magistrate and councillor; to use his influence for the faith; with a wife of the true breed at the head of his table worthy of her responsibility; children to carry on his name, and a house to take its place beside New Grange and Porriton Hall, in the ranks of country houses.

The house had been building already for the last year, on a green slope bought from the Corners. It was to be called Motcombe Manor, for though there had never been a manor house at Motcombe, Benskin's experts had discovered a reputed manor of which the Corners had perhaps been lords. John Chass had cheerfully conveyed this nominal lordship for a hundred pounds.

Benskin had wanted to build a Tudor house in the old English style; but his art advisers at the Royal Academy hinted that it was a vulgarity to imitate the Tudor. Let him build, as the Tudors had built, a work of contemporary art, expressive of the spirit of his times.

Benskin had at once seen the force of this. Motcombe Manor

designed by an R.A. famous for his country houses in the English style, was being constructed in red brick, with terra-cotta ornaments, and a red tiled roof which could be seen fifteen miles away.

This raw red roof could be seen between the trees even from New Grange and Benskin's eyes turned towards it from the window. 'And I tell you what, Stella,' he said, 'we ought to have a photograph of Castle Corner—you have one. The public likes the idea of an Irish castle somewhere in the background.'

'Do you mean for a lecture?' Stella asked, thinking of the village hall.

'A lecture? No, for the papers. This is bigger than a lecture.'

Stella flushed with surprise and indignation. She jumped up and came towards him, holding out her hand for the letter. 'But you can't.'

'They'll jump at it. I know half a dozen men in Fleet Street, who'd—'

'But you can't. It's private. You couldn't without asking him.'

'Take too long. It's now or never.'

Stella, by a quick unexpected gesture, snatched the letter out of his hand. Benskin, surprised, said, 'But Stella, it might be the making of him.'

Stella went quickly out of the room. Benskin was astonished. He went to Helen who was breakfasting in bed.

She was amused by his agitation. 'Yes, I'm really afraid she's in love.'

'It's a funny way to show it when I'm trying to give the boy a leg up.'

'But love's a funny thing, isn't it?' She smiled. The smile and implication together conveyed all that mixed meaning, with a trace of the improper, which had made her talk interesting to princes and charming to men of the world.

Helen was once more mistress of all that peculiar grace and fascination which marked her out even in the society of that time, full of beautiful, dignified and charming women. For she was rich again. She felt such kindness towards all the world that even with Benskin, a rough and clumsy lover, she had been complaisant. She had endured much discomfort and even a little pain to satisfy him.

She was charming now. 'Poor Theo, has she been silly.'

'I can't understand what she's objecting to.'

'All girls make sacred relics of their letters, some of them even hide away old chocolate boxes and dance programmes.'

'But I'm not stealing her letters.'

'You're profaning them. Stella has a strong religious instinct, you know. She always had, poor darling.'

'I've got to have the photograph, at least.'

'I'll do what I can, but she's not very easy to manage just now. She's always had a bit of a temper.'

338

Stella, having escaped to her room, locked the letter into her cash box, with all her other letters, with a native charm, given her by Cocky, a faded bunch of white heather in an envelope, which he had picked for her on Knockeen, and a brass star from his uniform coat. She had found it in his bedroom after his departure, and she had meant to send it to him. But now she would not have parted with it to anybody, even himself. She needed it. It had become a sacred possession.

Stella was not a demonstrative lover. She did not talk about Jarvis or ask for sympathy from her friends. Those who had seen her during her first season, dancing, calling, flirting, driving in the park; a little too much the country bred; heavy footed and plump; too ready to blush, too ready to perspire at a ball, too energetic in the lancers for London taste, too silent with stupid young men and too talkative and noisy with amusing ones; too easily exhausted and when exhausted, too vulgarly collapsed, put her down for a solid rather stupid young woman, highly unromantic and commonplace. She would make, as a friend told Helen, an ideal wife for a county member who needed a good breeder, an efficient warming pan and a suitable exhibit at church bazaars and agricultural shows.

This was true. Stella was an ordinary girl with ordinary feelings. Her lover's letters were sacred to her; and now when she sat on her bed, breathless as if she had escaped from a great danger, she felt the same kind of anger against her stepfather as a nun or a mystic against a blasphemer.

Love was now part of her religion, so that when she went to church, she thought of it; not of her lover, but of loving, of being in love, of being married, of having children. And this love, with its code, its relics and its god, was a much simpler and more effective religion than the church religion.

Stella, without knowing it, was already removed from her mother's set and her life of charming egotism; not because she criticized her, but simply because she was in love. If her mother had been the most unselfish and admirable of women, she would still have felt separated from her by an immense distance.

She looked at the clock. There was just time to write to Jarvis before the shooting guests began to arrive. She sat down and wrote:

'*My dearest Harry*,' and sucked her pen for ten minutes.

She never knew what to write to Jarvis; and the odd thing was that she could always write four pages to Cleeve. But then she was not in love with Cleeve. He was only a friend.

In Stella's idea of things, love and friendship were as distinct as religion and games. The one belonged to the sphere of mystery and emotion; the other to reason, study, mutual forbearance.

The guns were lunching at Motcombe Manor, for though the plaster was not yet dry on the walls, Benskin could not forbear any chance of showing off his darling. A trestle table, set up by the paper-hangers in the large empty drawing-room, was used for the meal. The eight guns sat down at one o'clock, for though the ladies had not yet arrived, they were too hungry to wait for them. Since it was a shooting lunch, the males felt entitled to consider themselves first. They were the workers. They expressed themselves eager, after shooting two hundred birds in the morning, to return to duty. But at two o'clock, when Helen, Stella, Lucy Chorley and Cobden arrived, they were still drinking champagne and discussing the cost of pheasant shooting. This, a favourite subject with preservers, had proved so much more exciting than the shoot that they had not been able to leave it.

The ladies were received with very careless politeness, and at once ignored. Servants had come from New Grange to wait upon them, and the shooters did not need to do so.

'It costs me about two pounds a bird, first and last,' old Lord Porriton said.

'You're badly poached though—too near Porriton.'

'Yes, the new factories are ruining the whole place.'

Only Nussbaum, who hated shooting almost as much as his friend Benskin, paid no attention to this important matter. Sitting next Helen, he said to her in his precise, clipped voice, 'You have my sympathy, Helen. Shooting is not very interesting.'

'Oh, I don't mind pheasant shooting. It is the grouse season which is so terrible. I sometimes wish that August had never been invented.'

Cobden, who had not succeeded in sitting next to her, but who was cut off by his sister and Lord Porriton, leant forward his pale countenance, and murmured, 'The Scotch are quite too barbarous—their knees alone are perfectly Gothic.'

'It is not the Scotch, Cobby, but the evenings. I always tell girls never never to marry a man whose grouse moor belongs to one of the real Highland chieftains.'

Lucy suddenly broke into her silent, helpless laughter, which caused everybody to look at her with disapproval. All of them knew that she was a suspicious character, a Nonconformist, almost a Radical; Lord Porriton, beside her, turned his large eyes sideways upon her with an expression of alarmed suspicion.

Helen herself was not disconcerted. She went on, 'They never allow driving, you know—and the men come back so tired, after walking after the birds all day, that they're not fit for human society.'

This remark was successful in attracting the interest of the shooters. Porriton exclaimed, 'What, what, hrumph! Human society! Ho, ho!'

Benskin said gravely, 'But, Helen, you never told me of this.'

340

'My dear Theo, have you never seen the agony of wives after dinner in a Highland lodge. But no, how could you, you're always asleep. Even at Knockeen you sleep.'

'Hrumph! Ho, ho! That's one for you, Benskin.'

'The curse of Eve,' Cobden sighed, but the remark, like Lucy's laugh, produced an uncomfortable sensation. He was stared at, except by Helen, who gave him a dazzling smile of the understanding friend.

The smile, like most of Helen's social gestures, like her frocks, her jewels, her friendships, her parties, was designed for a double effect; to produce admiration and jealousy at the same time. It would charm Cobden and wound both Nussbaum and her husband.

She was fond of Cobden. She more nearly loved him than any of her men. He excited her curiosity as well as her nerves. His tragic airs were charming; all the more so if he were really tragic.

She was sorry for him even while she felt the pleasure of his wasted hollow cheeks, of Nussbaum's sharp bitter jealousy, a French jealousy like corrosive acid, and her husband's quite different feeling of perplexity and helpless anxiety.

Felix said of Helen and her set that its art of life, by which it produced its special kind of enjoyment, was founded upon a two-sided sensuality; on the one side, various forms of lechery; on the other, of spite. Both were civilized by dignity. But the dignity itself belonged to an age of decadence. It was not from within, from an idea of life in itself great; but from without, from the custom of society. There were still great ladies in England at this time, headed by the old Queen; but they were few and Helen laughed at them.

The guns went out again, at the earnest request of the head keeper, at three. Nussbaum, who attempted to excuse himself on the grounds of a blistered heel, was not allowed to escape. He was carried away to his stand in Helen's victoria.

Helen did not care to have Nussbaum and Cobden together at Motcombe because they quarrelled so bitterly about new wallpapers and fireplaces that they could pay no attention to her.

Stella, who had been silent throughout the meal, was sent to show Lucy the latest development of the gardens; Helen and Cobden, carrying a large book of wallpapers beneath his arm, went up the grand staircase to the bedrooms. Helen suggested that they might look at some of the servants' rooms. 'It is so difficult to choose servants' wallpapers.'

'Rose trellis would be best for country girls, but in London I always recommend something more pious.'

'Are these pious wallpapers?'

'I have seen a design in church windows but I was thinking of something more ordinary, lilies or forget-me-nots.'

They were in the attic corridor, far from the remotest workmen on the ground floor. Helen let her elbow touch Cobden's arm; but he did not answer the signal. He even withdrew a little. He had never cared for flirtation. The very word expressed to him something ignominious; a surrender to the meanness and vulgarity of the world. Indeed since that scene in Portland Place, grotesque and horrible in his memory, Cobden when alone with Helen had always been uneasy. He preferred to write poems to her; to adore her among a group; to form, as it were, part of a ceremonial adoration for her beauty.

It was said that Cobden's passion for Helen was a pose. Her young soldiers laughed at his attitudes. But what is sincerely felt is not a pose and Cobden in his adoration of Helen's beauty and grace, or what he made of them, was as sincere as any devotee who cuts himself in front of an idol, enjoying the thrills of his painful sacrifice.

'This kind of room,' Helen said, stopping at a narrow door leading into an attic behind the balustrade of the room.

'Yes, very difficult.' Cobden looked round at the dark little room, in which there was nothing but a bucket, a new iron bedstead with the legs still bound in straw, and an iron tripod washstand holding a tin basin.

Helen plumped down upon the new mattress and gave a cry, 'Oh dear, I didn't know it was so hard.' She smiled up at the boy with an expression which was childish in its ingenuous wantonness and mischief.

Cobden was staring at her with an extraordinary look. He had obviously understood her meaning. But his expression was almost of terror; his cheeks had turned red in patches like a consumptive's.

'Well, Cobbie,' Helen began to giggle. She was simple in the flesh, perhaps even coarse. 'It's quite safe.'

The boy dropped the roll of papers and fell down beside her on the bed. But he still looked terrified. He made a face and muttered, 'It's such a beastly room——'

Helen suddenly kissed him and his hands began to fumble at her dress. He had lost all his airs: he muttered angrily and almost tearfully. His hands were violent and greedy, so that already she felt herself flushed and hot; but at the same time he was protesting; his flushed face was jerked by a strange agony. Helen felt suddenly as if she were seducing a priest. Nothing could have been more attractive to her senses.

The door sprang suddenly open behind Cobden's back, and a young man with a pale, thin face, a blue chin and small black whiskers, rapidly projected his face and body into the room. His black eyes were already turned towards the bed.

342

Helen exclaimed, 'How dare you?'

'Beg pardon, madam, I didn't know anyone was here.' The young man disappeared as quickly and silently as he had shown himself. There was no sound of his step retreating outside.

Cobden turned half-round his perspiring confused face. 'Who was it?'

Helen was already on her feet. She was pale with rage and surprise. Her chin was thrust forward pugnaciously, but her lips hung apart, weak and querulous. 'He was watching us——'

'Who, what was it?' Cobden put his face between his hands.

'That new man of Theo's. He was following us—he had rubber on his boots. Theo must have got him to spy.'

The boy said in an exhausted voice, 'This is becoming impossible.'

'There's nothing to be afraid of,' she turned on him angrily.

'I'm not afraid—but it's so horrible'—his hysterical voice and look gave her pause for a moment. She gazed at his damp face and shaking hands. But then at once she forgot him again. She began to feel alarmed.

'I can't believe it.'

Suddenly she lost her temper and rushed furiously across the room, chin up, bust thrown forward, her petticoats rustling like dry leaves in a storm. 'I won't stand it—I won't be propped—I won't be propped.'

Cobden got up slowly. His composure, his priestly dignity, was returning. He put his hand to his tie, to make sure that it was not absurdly misplaced. 'You're risking too much for me, Helen,' he said sadly. 'I mustn't see you again like this.'

That night, when the last of the guests had gone, Helen lay in bed, listening to Benskin in his dressing-room. He was changing his clothes to go to town by the last train. He had not yet spoken to her alone and she was both contemptuous and frightened. Helen was not a coward. If Benskin had been a man of her own kind, she would have attacked him and defied him. But he was a strange species, and she could never exactly forecast his conduct. He might do something extraordinary, he might even try to divorce her, and that would not only destroy her position, it would ruin her. She perceived suddenly her complete dependence on the man to whom she had condescended.

He came in suddenly, wearing his morning coat which, displaying his immense chest, and prolonging his long back, made him seem even more simian than usual.

She pretended to be asleep, looking under her eyelids. But his expression was affectionate, sympathetic. He came to the bed and kissed her forehead. 'Tired, my darling?'

'Porriton was rather exhausting.'

'Yes, my poor girl—these shoots are a trial.'

343

She returned the affection. 'Must you go to town to-night?'

'I must, worse luck. Got to catch Fleet Street early. Did you see Stella?'

'See Stella?' She did not understand. Then she remembered, as it were from the far past, that she was to ask Stella about a photograph, and that she had actually spoken six words to the girl, on the way to Motcombe. She looked tenderly regretful and shook her head. 'No go. She's very obstinate, you know. And I don't think we're in favour, either.'

'Why not, she's been charming.'

'She's annoyed with us—you can tell by her mouth.' Helen's confidence had returned. She thought, even if he knows something, he's not going to speak.

Benskin was surprised, and a look of distress appeared in his eyes. 'But why——'

'Because you married me, perhaps.'

'But she was charming.'

Helen decided to be affectionate. She put out a beautiful arm and took his wrist. 'Now you can stay with me.'

He shook his head. 'Got appointments.'

'But you haven't got the letter.'

'Oh, that's all right. I had a copy. The thing will come out, anyhow.'

'Stella won't like that.'

'No, she won't.' He turned his haggard face towards the bed. 'But what could I do—it might be a big thing—something of real importance—permanent importance.'

'Permanent!' She chaffed him about his Empire.

'I don't see why the Empire shouldn't be permanent. It gives people something that they all need—peace and federation.'

'So did Rome, I suppose.'

'Rome hadn't got machine-guns.' He paused, and his mournful expression, beginning to excite Helen's sense of humour, caused her to smile at him. 'You're not so sure.'

He jumped up and said, 'I was thinking of Stella. I must make it up to her—I'm not going to let her quarrel with me. Good-night, my dearest. Be good.' He kissed her suddenly and went out.

'Be good.' From Benskin that was undoubtedly a warning.

Three days later the illustrated papers were full of Jarvis' name. The chief of them had a full page description of the march to Daji, a full length photograph of the hero in tropical uniform, and a double page drawing of the assault on the Emir's stronghold. Jarvis was named 'The Conqueror of Daji,' and compared with Clive, Wolfe, Kitchener, Lugard. 'He has added to the Empire a territory larger than the British

344

Isles and richer than Ceylon. It is also the key of the Niger Valley, securing it for all time against the aggression of a certain power whose unscrupulous ambitions in Africa have already threatened the peace of Europe.'

Jarvis' name was heard during the next week in four different music halls. Six girls at the Empire, in khaki tights with union jacks tied round their bottoms, sang a new verse to their patriotic song, 'When Kitchener said March.' When Cocky Jarvis marched. This with three high kicks brought down the house.

The effects were even better than Benskin and his powerful friends could have expected. The Foreign Office, badgered by their minister who knew well the weight of money and influence behind the Jarvis boom, replied to French protests that Daji had never been within the French sphere of influence, and ignored the French reply that neither had it been within the British sphere of influence. Both sides were so much alarmed to find their troops within striking distance of each other on the Daji frontier that a boundary treaty was concluded within a few weeks.

By this time Jarvis' fame had been superseded by a murder and a fashionable divorce case, except at Castle Corner, where John Chass had his picture in oils, copied from the photograph, hung in the hall between that of old John the Recorder and William of Wickham, who was kin to all the Corners. To John Chass, of course, as to the Rev. Feenix, the sudden glory of his nephew was due to an irresistible outburst of popular appreciation, earned by his extraordinary merit.

He spoke the words 'Harry' or 'my nephew' with a new respect; and his tendency, noticed first about the time when Harry went to Africa, to take imperial views; or, when presiding on the bench, to speak on matters of imperial importance, such as the irresponsible conduct of the Dunvil boys in breaking the dispensary window and the necessity of good education and self respect to a ruling race, was slightly increased.

The remark about the ruling race produced some rude comments in the *Annish Gazette*, which pointed out that John Chass would not rule much longer if the people did their duty in the new council election. 'These elections,' the editor wrote, 'mean the end of feudalism in Ireland. For three hundred years the landlords have ruled this country from the bench, but in the new year, when for the first time Irishmen can vote for Irishmen to control their own local affairs, their power will be broken in a day. Let us see that Mr. John Corner, at least, shall not pollute the chair of the new democracy with the blood-stained shibboleths of the Saxon imperialist or sit upon the new council with such tried patriots as Mr. Joseph Giveen.'

John Chass laughed at this editorial and said, 'A fine piece of

MacJefferson Brick.' He enraged Slatter by his jokes about the election and his refusal to canvass.

On the evening before election day, instead of addressing the Unionist meeting at the Orange Hall in Dunvil, he gave a dinner party at the castle. Slatter came down after dinner in a rage. He found the drawing-room full of whist tables. Whist was still played in Annish. A clear coal fire burned in the little marble Adams grate within the shining brass fender. Two tall lamps in pink shades threw a soft sleepy light on the solemn company. At one table John Chass, Feenix, Mary, and Lady MacEwen, who had played at least ten thousand rubbers of the game which the two ladies detested, were at their third rubber of the evening. At another Maddy, Coo, Phil and Hanna sat with the faces of people who follow a routine, better than nothing but still without interest. Maddy's forehead at twenty-three was already full of small, fine wrinkles; and Coo, holding herself very upright, and pressing her cards against her breast, looked out of the window at the calm, black level of the sea with her eyebrows raised in a thoughtful expression. But she was not thinking of anything.

When Hanna opposite her said in his rough, chaffing voice, 'Play, partner,' she started as if out of sleep.

Maddy would look indignantly at him, and throw her card on his like a challenge, and if the card had beaten his he would peep at her out of the side of his eye, roll in his chair with enjoyment, and say slily, 'Good for you, Miss Maddy.'

He loved to chaff Maddy and he was always peeping at her. His little eyes would drop to her round, high bosom and he would raise his eyebrows and purse his lips as if at a daring display.

Slatter, stalking among the tables in his yellow tweeds, shouted that this was no time for anyone to play cards when the Nationalists were holding three meetings a night.

John Chass laughed and said, 'Did you see the paper to-day?'

'What paper?' Slatter shouted at him.

'Mosis are up threepence—that's sixpence in the week.'

'W-h-hat!' No words can describe Slatter's contempt and anger. For the last month John Chass had been advising all his friends to buy various West African shares, including Mosis and Transport. 'They're going up,' he would say, 'there's going to be a merger of all the old firms to open up the Laka country. Felix tells me that they're going to raise half a million new capital. His friend Hatto is behind it, one of the biggest men on the coast.'

Felix in fact had not only advised John Chass to buy Mosis but he had sold him his own holding at one and sixpence a share. 'I need the money to bring me home but I'd like to keep the shares in the family,' he wrote. 'You can have every confidence in them because

Hatto himself made me an offer, proof by itself that he is up to something.'

MacEwen, Feenix, and Duff had all bought Mosi shares, but Slatter, who owned already five hundred one pound ordinary, quoted at one and sixpence, flew into a rage at the very name. Slatter, it seemed, about the time of Benskin's first visit had had a fit of buying shares. He was the early speculator, who as somebody said, gets left in the basement. He had bought Mosi because he saw Benskin and Felix together; and he had bought gold shares in one of Benskin's mines at a top price which they had not touched since.

'That swindle,' he would shout. 'It's Benskin's gang that robbed me before.'

But the very word Mosi changed the expressions of MacEwen and Feenix. Something came to life in their eyes as they looked round at John Chass; and MacEwen, with his grave voice of the philosopher and the retired proconsul, said, 'Do you think it's too late to buy?'

'Not a bit of it,' John Chass answered, 'I'm buying all the time. The more you buy, the better.'

'The more you buy, the better,' he said, examining this statement.

'Because then they go up,' John Chass said, laughing as if at a good joke. 'The more you buy, the dearer they get, and the more they're worth to you.'

'Within limits, I suppose?'

'Oh, within limits. But Mosi have a long way to go from one and sixpence, or Transport from half-a-crown—James, I'll give you two shillings each for your Mosi.'

But Slatter could never bear to sell at a loss. He answered with an exclamation of disgust, 'A-ach—you and your play games. While Joe Giveen there is tellin' your own tenants that he'll drive the Queen out of Ireland in a month. I'll tell you this, Jawn,' he leant over Mary's shoulder and struck the table with his fist so that the cards jumped, 'if ye lose the election, it's because ye didn't take the trouble to win it, and if we're all rooned, every man jack landlord of us in Ireland, it's because of the likes of you that would rather be playin' yourselves than fightin' traitors and rebels like Joe Giveen that lives by England's trade and slanders the hand that feeds him.'

John Chass threw down a card. 'Is it Joe—they might do worse.'

'The biggest thief in Annish,' Slatter spluttered.

'Oh no, James, I know six would beat him.'

'And you let him in.'

'Ah, what's the good of meetings?'

'They'd listen to you, Jawn—the only wan they would listen to.'

'They'd listen, but how would they vote? According to the little black father on the hill. Come now, James, take a wee glass and be easy. It's a poor heart that never rejoices.'

But Slatter was in a panic. His face was long and creased; his cheeks sweated. 'D'ye know this, Jawn—that this election will be the roon of ye—and every wan of us.'

But John Chass was not troubling about what he could not help. He continued to play his cards with great enjoyment.

The kitchen, like Slatter, was excited by the crisis. There was no patience or boredom on any face there. One saw on the old, battered features of Sukey's visitors, faces that looked like clods of dry mud thrown off a fork, every shade of hope, greed, wonder, calculation, and the expectancy of children who wait confidently to be amazed.

Padsy, who for some reason was in his Sunday clothes, had formed the idea that the castle grounds were going to be divided up. 'It's Egan ground,' he shouted. 'From the ould ancient times of King Fergus Macegan—and wasn't me mawther an Egan.'

'How could Joe give ye the land,' Rifty answered him angrily. Rifty was flying round with a knowing grin; contradicting himself every minute.

'Didn't he promise to divide up the land?'

'He's not in yet.'

'Sukey, isn't Joe to get in?'

'The hell with the lot of ye.'

'Oh, Sukey, ye'll tell us.'

Sukey had not told the future for two years but she, too, was excited and when they put a plate of herrings in her lap and sat her over against the corner beneath the sea windows, she called out, 'A melt for Joe.'

Sukey told fortunes with herrings. She would take out the strips of brown meat, which she called the melts, and throw them against the wall, where they stuck. The shape of the melt on the wall told the fortune.

'Look at thon crooked devil,' she said. 'Isn't it the spirit of Joe, and watch now—he's peelin', he's peelin',' the melt fell off the wall. Someone uttered a frightened exclamation, 'It's what he'll go high and then he'll go low. It's what he'll cheat ye annyway and fall down to hell.'

The crowd pressed round with eyes glistening in the red fire and in the pale glitter of the small moon from the windows, with parted lips and bared teeth points. Sukey had a great name as a fortune-teller. As each melt struck the wall, gasps and groans were heard, or faint protests, as if against fate.

'There's Darcy and see the grand house he's in—as big as a king's.'

'A King!' Darcy was startled for a moment. But then his expression cleared. 'It would be for to drive him. Ay, that could be.'

'It's the workhouse,' Sukey said.

'Is that how it is,' Darcy murmured, accepting this fate as readily as the other.

The watchers could scarcely breathe for eagerness and terror of what they might hear, and those like Grogan, who walked away with scornful faces, came suddenly back when their own names were heard. Padsy, glaring at the wall, kept muttering to himself like a man in pain; half drugged. Bridget in the dark corner behind the kitchen door, which in those days was as far as she dared to come near Sukey, was pushing forward her face with the expression of a wounded creature dying in a hole that stretches up its neck to the light.

To her even more than the rest the world was a mysterious confusion where anything might happen; more confused and fantastic even than Padsy's because it contained stranger, more glittering, visions. For Bridget even religion and morals were dark and confused, where Father MacFee sometimes appeared like an avenging god as big as the world itself, with hands and eyes in every corner of it; and sometimes like a little black spider running about distracted in a broken web.

Finian had crawled away from Bridget. She could hear him crowing and stamping at the back stairs which he was forbidden to climb. They were dangerous stairs, iron-edged with a turn at the middle landing, and the child was only just beginning to walk. But she could not leave the door crack, and she could not call for fear of being heard in the kitchen.

Finian, now two, a stout and fat little boy, had staggered after Teresa towards the stairs. He had made all his discoveries by following Teresa, who having explored every crack in the lower story, was now absorbing the stairs and cupboards. Unluckily she was restricted on this side. The stair bend was the limit of the kitchen and therefore of Teresa and the blue cat, Peter. She stood now at the bend, by the door of Grogan's pantry cupboard, staring upwards at the object which had fascinated her for the last week, the tea urn, placed ready on Grogan's tray-table for the evening tea at eleven or twelve o'clock.

Teresa had visited the stairs every afternoon to see the urn, at afternoon tea-time; but she found it even more beautiful and mysterious by the dim light of a bedroom candle. She wanted to know about the urn, how it worked, why it was the shape of an egg, what that great mass of silver felt like; she was greedy for knowing; she stretched up her neck towards it like a young bird asking for a worm.

Young Finian paid no attention to Teresa. He followed her only as a little dog runs after the bigger dog because it has left behind a track of dog feeling; continuing meanwhile in its own course of sensation. He had long forgotten the reason of his direction, and now, on the third step, he was alone. He uttered another crow of triumph, stamped his foot on the conquered step, and looking affectionately and condescendingly on the fourth, patted it with his hand. The pat was also a warning; almost a slap. He was about to possess this step, too, to triumph over it.

Finian in the joy of perpetual triumphs had forgotten the danger from his mother; but his loud crow caused Teresa above to look apprehensively down into the greenish shadow of the corridor. The look was an unconscious expression of a guilty idea already forming in her mind. But Bridget had disappeared, stealing into the kitchen. Teresa looked again towards the urn, and stretched out her yearning neck so far that she nearly fell. Her feet were still obedient. They held back strongly as if, being unprovided with eyes and ears, they felt no inducement to break their customary respect for authority.

Sukey's face was twisted as if in a spasm, her lips protruded and all her cheek muscles jumped and worked; so that they flowed into wrinkles like pools in a shower. She was excited by her own prophesying. 'It's a death,' she screamed. 'It's a ryal death.'

Bridget was pushing her head past Padsy's Sunday coat, smelling like his mountain hovel of turf and sweat. She strained her neck forward like a starving animal for food. What was to happen to her? What was the truth? Her cheek touched Sukey's greying hair, sticking out all round her head like smoky flames.

'I see a woman in a golden coffin.'

Wee Dan the gamekeeper, standing beside Bridget muttered, 'Glory to Gawd. That will be the ould Queen.'

Grogan came quickly down the room, listened a moment, picked up a muffin dish from the table and asked Bridget, in a reproachful voice directed at the whole affair, where she had put the big milk can. Bridget had brought milk from the farm.

Bridget made an impatient jerk of her right shoulder; Sukey's arm was in the air; Grogan stood with a pale, anxious gaze.

The melt struck the wall and stuck. Sukey screamed, 'A black crow—it's a black crow, waiting to pick out the old woman's eyes that fed it. But see now, its wings is spread. Wee Dan has it nailed to a board. And its neck stretched. It's what he hanged it first, the murdering thief, and there, now,' with another throw, 'look at that one, it's a nun, it's a holy nun praying for the old woman's soul, that took her out of the dirt. Look now if she hasn't the lovely eyes to turn up to the blessed Mother of Gawd—eyes like the green say.'

There was another silence, so that everyone heard a baby's loud, triumphant whoop from the back stairs.

'A black crow,' Sukey muttered, and then she screamed like a whistle; a piercing yell that made half a dozen faces change colour. 'It's a black Foy that wanted to see her anty dead.'

Bridget gave a loud cry, and fell on her knees. 'Anty, anty, for the love of Gawd.'

'Aye,' Sukey shrieked, 'and the polis have got her—she's hanged—the devil. She's kicking on the rope.'

Bridget threw her apron over her head and ran out of the room.

'See the feet of her then,' Sukey screamed, pointing at the wall, 'hanging out of the black skirt they put upon her.'

Bridget snatched up Finian from the stairs and flew out of the house. It was a mile before Rifty caught her. He was breathless and confused. 'Ah, don't mind her, Bridgeen, she's drunk. She couldn't see straight. It was another wan she saw hanging. It wouldn't be a woman, annyway. There's no woman ever killed annywan in Annish.'

Bridget walked on in silence, towards the mountain which grew smaller as they climbed, so that the clear pale sky seemed to expand. The moon was at its height and though its curve of reflecting surface was narrow; it seemed to throw off the light in a continuous agitation, which could be seen like a foam or mist surrounding the outer face. The sky below was clear grey space, but on the fields and walls there was the same halo of energy, in which the black tangle of winter hedges and the bare, wind-twisted branches of the spindle trees or the dwarf oaks seemed to bathe like creatures absorbed in their own sensations.

Bridget felt the moon, the silent, still mountain without perceiving them. She felt a confused excitement so strong that her body was congested with it. Her thought and separate feelings had no room to move. She scurried like an escaped prisoner whose legs are in a hurry because he doesn't know where he is or what to do with himself.

There was a shout. A brougham came bowling along through a dip in the lane. Rifty and Bridget fell into the hedge on opposite sides of the road. Slatter, thrusting his head out of the carriage window, bawled at Bridget, 'Dahm ye, why wouldn't we go over ye the next time?'

Maddy's voice said, 'Is the door tight shut?' and Coo answered, 'He hasn't a hat, either. You'll catch your death, pappy.' The words, muffled in the carriage, were like disembodied voices from the ghosts of girls, coming from another world. The carriage rolled away so suddenly that to Bridget and Rifty it was hard to believe that it had existed.

They walked on in silence, pondering, still on opposite sides of the road. Rifty's brain was a whirligig of surprise, alarm, wonder and petty expenses; Bridget did not think at all; but she felt like a murderess, she felt that already she was waiting to kill, and that the fate that had

351

seized upon her was whirling her forward through an endless series of extraordinary events.

There was neither fear, hope, nor wonder in her heavy body, only stolid endurance. From Finian, sleeping in her arms, a warmth came like the ambition of her soul.

Joe Giveen won the election by three hundred votes. The Annish Press wrote in two columns headed 'Downfall of the British Empire.'

Ireland, from whose green shores the ceaseless tide of saints and scholars has flowed through more than twenty centuries, carrying to all nations of the world the message of her ancient wisdom, the tradition of her art and the purest inspiration of Christendom, yesterday struck a blow, which, in the opinion of Europe, marks the end of British Imperialism.

It was perhaps true that John Chass' defeat was the end of the landlords' power in Annish, so that the imperial filibuster of Old John Recorder and the rest of the younger sons from the West country, who cut out for themselves Irish principalities about 1610, came to an end in eighteen ninety-nine, when their descendants were already ranging through Africa on the same kind of enterprise; but this, much more than the fall of the British Empire, was what interested the farmers. They saw the fall of a dynasty. Home Rule to Padsy and Dan and Rifty was talk, but all of them knew John Chass at the castle and Joe Giveen at the store. Now Joe Giveen was suddenly the man in power; the dispenser of jobs, contracts, cottages, relief; to be capped and wheedled.

On the day after the election, when John Chass drove Grey Lady and Dapple into Dunderry, the people rushed to the doors as if they expected to see upon their old master's face some appropriate mark of his downfall. But they saw him apparently in the best of spirits. He had a new tandem cart and the new patent harness, with a swingle bar for the leader. He was wearing a new grey hat curled up at the brim like a stage coachman's. As he tooled flashing and sparkling over the wet roads as pale as new leather, through the puddles full of winter sunshine which made them glitter like the new silver buckles and the new wheels of his cart, with his hat cocked up on his brown curls, he seemed more like a man on holiday than a deposed chief. He sat as usual with his back hollowed, his shoulders square, his elbows down, and when they gazed up at him with their curious, sharp looks he laughed down at them as if he knew very well what they had come to see.

John Chass having seen defeat to be inevitable, did not mind it. In fact, the day after the election found him in unusual spirits, because

352

Mosi shares had risen another threepence and Felix had written from Africa:

> *Get as many as you can afford. I have it on good authority that financial interests in London are buying for control. Possibly Benskin himself is behind them. When firms of that quality are buying for control, it's safe to follow because they aren't frightened to spend money. They know they can go through with the scheme. Don't be alarmed by temporary setbacks.*

John Chass saw the force of the argument. He had made three hundred pounds in the last five weeks. This, of course, was nothing to his debts. He did not know how much he owed, but the secured debts on the property, including mortgages, amounted to seventeen thousand and he had borrowed at different times four thousand from Benskin on I.O.U.s. His credit was exhausted and immediately after the election the banks began to press for repayment of their loans. But John Chass felt more confident in his position than he had done for years; partly because it was so bad that strong confidence was necessary to avoid depression; but chiefly because he was making money. He was not only making money for the first time in his life, but he saw no reason why he shouldn't continue to make it.

Mary Corner was sceptical of this kind of prosperity, of all shares; not as Slatter was sceptical, from mere hatred of the Mosi Company and of Benskin the Home Ruler, but as women are sceptical of every new thing that their men do, until they have grown so used to it that they need not trouble about it. Besides, Mary Corner's God was not one who gave benefits or saved spendthrifts from ruin, but an emperor who inflicted hardship and suffering on his servants, in the interests of a secret policy which no private person could hope to understand. Why had he killed Shon and Kitty? She did not ask. She knew her duty. No one took less pride in her house and more trouble about it than she. But like a soldier picked by lot for the storm troop, she did not grudge others their leisure and safety. Coo Slatter, who never did any work, used to come as usual during spring cleaning, almost every day, and follow Mary through the house, talking in her soft voice about anything that dropped into her head.

'Pappy says Philly ought to get a wife.'

Mary in her own sitting-room washing the Dresden service in a basin placed on a chair, a duty never delegated in those times, screamed out, 'Bridget, Bridget, the soap,' and then to Coo, sitting on the couch with her hands in her lap, reflecting deeply on the strange nature of things, 'Good gracious, yes, of course he ought.'

'It's Doctor Hanna thought it would be better for'm.'

'Bridget, what's the gel doing?'

'But ye know, Anty, Philly was mad with the drink this last year.'

'Now, I won't have you call poor Philip mad.'

'He was d.t.s and he took a knife to Pappy.'

'D.t.s is not the same thing. It's not at all the same thing. People have no right to call Philip mad because he took too much drink for a time. Plenty of men do that, very good men.'

'But how will he get a wife now—the gyurls is all afraid of him.'

There was a pause. Mary Corner, with her face of set despair, an expression which seemed to be stamped upon the flesh as a design is stamped upon metal, without affecting the quality or the active secret character of its atomic composition, closely examined the handle of a cup to make sure that no dust lingered in the joints. Her thin fine hands, half boiled in the hot water, and glazed by soapsuds, glittered like the cup in the sunlight darting through the windows out of the clear fresh sky. Outside the lake was all in movement with small waves, sparkling with a million miniature suns, while as if at from an immense distance, the hills of County Derry floated like another island, a calm and solid Atlantis in a universe composed solely of air, light and water, with a few excited joyful birds for inhabitants.

Neither Mary nor Coo noticed the glittering commotion outside; Mary frowned at the cups, Coo mused with her curious tired face, which seemed already exhausted by futile thoughts. On the small patch of green below the window, in what was called the lady's garden, Teresa sat motionless, stroking the blue cat. The movement of her hand was full of enquiry into the nature of fur and possibly cats.

Teresa liked the lady's garden because when Mary Corner saw her there she would open the window and give her a penny or a sweet, forbidden in the kitchen by Sukey's jealousy.

'It's a queer thing,' Coo mused.

'What's queer? Bridget! Good Gracious, has the gel gone to sleep?' Bridget came in quickly with the can and a towel.

'I couldn't find the soap, mam.'

'Didn't I tell you in the rattantoo?'

'I didn't think for to look there, mam.'

'But I told you to look there.'

Bridget's face, as always when she was reprimanded, fell into wooden indifference. Her eyes, directed out of the open window, fixed upon Teresa; and the child, as if feeling them upon her, looked up. The two stared at each other with a curious intensity. Teresa was wondering why Bridget always hung about her; Bridget was feeling, with terror and fascination, 'Is she the wan that will hang me?'

She did not want to kill anybody. The notion was fantastic, but she felt already that there was murder in her fate.

'What are you saying, m'dear,' Mary said to Coo. 'What's queer?'

354

'Getting married.'

'Good gracious, what nonsense you talk, you gels nowdays. I don't know what the world's coming to. What's queer about marriage?'

Coo was also surprised at herself. She opened her eyes widely What there was still in her mind was the tail of her sudden feeling, like the last fleeting glow of laughing gas at the dentist's, that not only marriage, sex, men, girls, life itself was a queer and mysterious business, but that she herself, bewildered in the midst of it, was a queer fragment of matter. What for was this collection of hair, skin, teeth, arms and legs, all elaborately washed and dressed and getting older every day.

There was a sudden loud crash. Mary jumped and nearly dropped a cup; Coo gave a sharp cry, Bridget, with a crimson face, stood back from the window and said in an astonished voice, 'I didn't go for to do it, mam. It was me arrum.'

A flower pot holding nasturtium seedlings had fallen out of the window and lay now in fragments at Teresa's side on the iron grating. Teresa, whose lap was sprinkled with earth and broken pottery, looked up with an air full of mild interest, as if falling flower pots whizzing past her nose were no more than drops of rain. The blue cat had disappeared. It understood fear.

Mary Corner gave Teresa a penny, for though the child had not been frightened, she might have been so, and Sukey could not growl at her mistress' self-indulgence.

John Chass was certainly insolvent. The difficulty was to make him admit it. His bankers, about June, finally stopped his credit and the mortgagees, including Slatter, finding their half yearly moieties in arrear, threatened foreclosure. But he would not answer letters, and when he was challenged face to face, he would laugh and say, 'Haven't I paid that yet? Wait-a-bit does no one any harm.'

Slatter, losing patience one day, shouted at him, 'Ah, Jawn, you and your wee smiles. What are ye waiting on, for Mosi at two a penny?'

Mosis were back to two and sixpence. John Chass smiled and answered, 'Do you know how Rothschild made his fortune?'

'It wasn't lending you money, begob.'

'By buying in the hard times and selling in the good. Take a tip, James, this is a time to buy.'

Slatter could only stare at him in a state between apoplexy and wonder and shout at last, 'Did Felix tell ye that?'

'Felix is no fool, James.'

'What are fools then. Aw, Gawd, Jawn, ye'll roon us all before ye're done.'

Towards autumn, when even the tradesmen began to refuse goods on order, John Chass' own lawyers advised him to meet his creditors

355

and avoid a bankruptcy by private arrangement. As business men they urged this resolution, for John Chass' own sake. But he paid no attention to them, perhaps because he understood his own business better than they did. For no one cared to take the next step. Old friends like to break up a man in a good-natured way across a glass of whisky; and it was felt even by the bankers, who had often shot over Knockeen that any other course would expose them to moral odium.

Slatter found patience more difficult than the rest. He had always been an eager and impatient man and now that he saw himself at last owner of the castle, he could hardly keep his eyes off it.

He would stand for half an hour at a time gazing from his own windows down the side of Knockeen towards the castle chimneys in the dark square of their wood; sending up their pale blue smoke which against the blue lough became grey; and then he would turn to Philip and shout, 'What'll ye bet, Philly, that we're not in the cassle for Christmas?'

Philip, who had been lying in his chair without movement for an hour or more, did not stir. Slatter rushed down on him. 'Here, you—what's wrong with ya at all—have ye got a pain, or what? Not a word out of ya the whole day.'

The boy got up startled and turned his melancholy face towards his uncle. 'I beg your pardon, uncle.'

'Ah beg your pardon,' Slatter mimicked. 'Gawd sakes, a corpse is better company. What are ye made of, boy? and ye twenty-seven.'

The girls in their distant corners made faces at each other as if to say, 'Again, what a nuisance.'

Philip tried to speak and instead a noise came from his mouth like a child sobbing against its will. Slatter crouched down beside him, half kneeling, and put an arm round him. 'Aw, Philly, and what's wrong, man. What d'ye want—ye know I'd give ye annything ye like, for anny money.'

'I don't want anything.'

Slatter was anxious about Philip. By close vigilance he had kept him sober for four months; but the boy did not seem to benefit. On the contrary, he grew every day more listless and melancholy. Slatter consulted a specialist in Dunderry, and he also got a herb medicine from a wise woman on Knockeen. Hanna came in every day and slapped the patient on the back, saying, 'How's the poet to-day—I never saw ye better. Man, I wish I had half your constitution and three-quarters of your time.'

To Slatter he said, 'What he wants is something to keep him amused —a hobby.'

'Aw, I got'm a fretsaw and he wouldn't use it.'

'A wife would be better.'

356

'And where would ye find a gyurl for him in Annish? These bawg hoppers don't know how to talk to a man of real education like Philly.'

'Talk, it's not the talk,' Hanna said, breathing whisky. 'It's the company and the taking him out of himself. He wants to have somebody else to think of. Why, don't we all know,' here Hanna was growing serious, his voice more chaffing, 'that marriage is the salvation of man, whoever he is. A good wee wife to keep him warm at night and warm his ears if he takes anything else to warm him. Ah, you don't need anything much—any nice simple gyurl that's been reared for her job like your own gyurls.' Hanna hesitated here with his mouth and eyes open as if surprised to find himself at this point; then suddenly he grinned in his most derisory fashion and said, 'Maddy there would be the good wife for'm. She's made for it.'

'Maddy!' Slatter roared with laughter. 'Thon ould maid.'

Nevertheless, after a week's reflection, he asked Maddy, who, with a duster tied over her hair, was in the middle of the important task of turning out the drawing-room. She answered absentmindedly, 'I never thought of it, Pappy.' Then she shouted with the angry voice of her father at the housemaid, 'That's the way, go wan, break the legs off it.'

'Ye know, Maddy, Phil would make ye a grand husband.'

Maddy had no time for nonsense. 'If he didn't murder me,' and dashing among the piled furniture at the powerful maid, she cried in despair, 'Ah, will ye look at the scratches on me legs, and they were all new polished, Monday was six months.'

'And ye wouldn't have to leave home, eether,' Slatter said.

'Unless I went out in my coffin.' Maddy turned on him her distracted face. 'And perhaps I might want to leave here, too, after twenty years of it without so much as a trip to Dublin.'

Slatter then grew angry and began to shout that Maddy was an ungrateful girl who had no proper feelings. But Maddy was not persuaded to marry Phil, she did not like even to be alone in the room with him for fear that he would bring out a knife and cut her throat.

'If Pappy wants to marry Phil off he'd better get someone from England,' she said to Coo, 'where they don't know he's a lunatic.'

'Or Germany?'

'Why Germany?'

'I don't know,' Coo said, having already passed on from the idea of a rash and belligerent nation.

'And it's not only the way he might knife you, he'd give you the creeps.'

Coo shuddered at the notion and squeezed Maddy's arm. They were walking in the back drive, under the bare trees.

'Do married people have two pigs?' she asked suddenly. A pig in Annish was a stone hot-water bottle.

'I suppose it's what they'd like. Why do you ask a thing like that?'

'I don't know.' Coo had forgotten already the impression that Philly's feet would be cold in bed. 'Don't you want to get married, Maddy?'

'Aw, I might.' Maddy raised her eyebrows in a little perplexity.

'There's no men, annyway.'

'Then why talk of it?'

'They're all gone away. Cleeve went away and so did Harry. Why do they all go away?'

'What would they be doing here?'

'What are we doing here, Maddy?'

'Haven't we enough to do with Pappy to look after and the servants the way they are?'

'You used to want to go to Paris.'

'And I will, too, when I've time.'

'I should think a French girl would marry Philly.'

'Why French?'

'I just thought so,' Coo said, but the impression of the boldness of a French girl in pursuit of a man remained with her. She considered it for a long time while they walked along the drive. She pressed Maddy's arm tenderly, asking for sympathy. 'Really, Maddy, there's no other man but poor Philly.'

'If ye call'm a man the way he is now.'

'In Paris, they'd have him.'

'If Pappy paid them enough, but a decent gyurl couldn't marry for that.'

'No, not for that,' Coo murmured, and then hastily, in case Maddy was shocked, she said, 'It's the different education they give them to scheme at things. Look at the way Mrs. Corner talks.'

Maddy said, 'There's ould Dan now with the fish and I hope it isn't pollock for Pappy says he'd as lieve eat cotton wool.'

'If we'd been French now,' Coo said, 'we'd take Philly and thank you.'

'We couldn't both.'

'But Philly'd have to be in Paris, too.'

Coo was interested in this subject. She talked about it often and in the middle of the night, Maddy would hear her voice in the darkness, from the other side of the room, asking, 'Do gyurls go for to get married in Japan?'

'Aw, go to sleep.'

'It will be the way they're taught. The world's full of customs; I suppose now that we have customs too.'

X

Felix reached England in September. He was met by a bankruptcy petition against the Mosi Company, but this did not trouble him at all, compared with a letter from Cleeve, saying:

> *I have been looking at your book about Schopenhauer and Darwin which I'd never seen before. It was in the college library. I think you're absolutely right about the fundamental activity in the universe. It must be something like will, but with a certain character. Darwin, as you say, took it for granted that the will to live explained everything: the struggle for existence and the evolution of species, but as Schopenhauer's critics proved, a bare will to live is impossible,*

and four more excited pages about will, purpose, life, mind.

Felix was most alarmed by this letter. He knew the dangers of such ideas to undergraduates, seeing that they had ruined his own career. His first words to Cleeve were, 'That was an interesting letter of yours about the will.'

He paused. He scarcely liked to say, 'My dear boy, I want you to get a first class, and the best way of doing that is to give the examiners what they want—good sound Plato and Kant. Stick to the beaten track.'

This approach might produce that cynical attitude which Felix detested, and which would prevent Cleeve from obtaining any real good from philosophy. The problem was a subtle one. He therefore marked time and discussed the will for the rest of the evening.

The Chorleys, with whom Cleeve was staying for the end of the vacation, were much interested in the discussion and charmed by Felix who impressed them at once as a man of the highest ability. Felix indeed, prematurely aged by the coast, with fallen yellow cheeks and almost white hair, was now a figure of such distinction that people, by involuntary association of ideas, would rise from their seats when he came into a room. His height, his enormous nose, his thoughtful gaze directed on a level with his nose, his immense white beard, won the respect even of young ladies and the awe of children.

Mrs. Chorley congratulated him on the sagacity with which he had brought up Cleeve, and thinking of her own Cobden, she said, 'I only wish I had been able to get your advice years ago when my own boy was at school.'

359

'I've done what I could,' Felix admitted modestly, 'but you must give the chief credit to Cleeve. He's always been keen.'

But this modesty seemed only to increase his reputation as a father and an educator. It was, Chorley suggested, part of his method. He was asked to speak at two meetings, got up by Chorley for young Liberals in the constituency, on faith and freedom, and though he declined to speak, his presence on the platform lent weight to Chorley's arguments. Chorley was now the accepted candidate for the Porriton division at the next election; and he was extremely busy with anti-war meetings. Every day eminent Liberals, M.P.s, journalists came to Bellavista, and at the end of the month there was a garden party, the largest within Porriton memory, to which all Liberals and especially all ministers and their wives were asked.

Benskin as a Liberal had his invitation, but he did not come. He was for the war. The fact that many Liberals were for war was one reason why Chorley said frequently, 'War is impossible—it would be too great an infamy.' He was in excellent spirits at the garden party.

Stella who was included in the family invitation, came because she wanted to play tennis. Tennis had been arranged to amuse some of the guests who had never seen the game. Stella played with Cleeve against Lucy and her father. It was a tribute to Chorley's magnanimity that he played against the advice of the Liberal agent, who warned him that many of the ministers would consider the amusement too worldly for a Liberal candidate.

Cleeve missed everything, but encouraged Stella with loud cries. When they were two sets down, he laughed to see her breathless and said, 'You're better than I am.'

'We'll have to play up.' She put back a lock from her forehead.

'Oh yes, we're going to win. I say, I've been asked to the pro-Boer meeting.'

'Are you going?'

'No, I've got a tennis party. Besides, I'm not really a patriot.'

'But didn't you say it was a pro-Boer meeting?'

'Oh well, I suppose if I did catch the disease it would be the Boer kind. In Paris, I did actually carry a flag one day. That's to say, I touched the staff. I gave it moral support—the only moral support it had because the lady who actually did the work, though of the highest republican charm——'

'What sort of a flag—a French flag?'

'They said it was a Boer flag—but don't tell Cocky.'

Stella said nothing.

'I suppose Cocky is coming home in hopes of another good war,' Cleeve said.

'It's your serve.' She handed him two balls.

360

Cleeve served a double fault far beyond the serving lines and said, 'I'm not blaming him, you know, it's his job.'

Stella, passing behind him, gave him two more balls and said, 'Not quite so hard this time.'

Cleeve served twice into the net and exclaimed, 'But what rot all this fuss is, it's so stupid.'

Stella privately agreed with him The war talk annoyed her and also for some reason it alarmed her. She did not like to find that the Chorleys and Benskin took different sides. She did not like the feeling of a war fought apparently for the benefit of rich financiers whom she thought of as vulgar climbers against poor farmers who might be her own tenants. But meanwhile she was playing tennis and she was not ready to think of anything else. She handed two more balls to Cleeve and said, 'Never mind, the great thing is not to lose your nerve. Hit a little harder.'

Cleeve served a double fault ten feet over the net and exclaimed earnestly, 'I wonder has Cocky ever heard of the categorical imperative.'

'A little harder this time. Love forty.'

Cleeve served one ball into the net and then a let. He turned to Stella with an animated expression, 'You see, that's why all this patriotism and fuss is such rot.'

'Go on, another.'

'But I've finished that one—I served two.'

'No, it was a let. Just a little harder. But be careful, we're love forty.'

Cleeve hit at the ball with great force, but managed to strike it on the extreme tip of the racket. It flew thirty feet into the air, and while Cleeve was still gazing wildly round, it fell into Chorley's court on the other side of the net; Chorley returned it to Cleeve, Stella by a complicated and skilful stroke, pushed Cleeve off the court with her left, hand and drove the ball to Chorley on the back line. He returned it with his old-fashioned style in a high lob. Stella, frowning, stood till it had reached the top of its bounce and slammed it at Lucy. A furious rally had begun. Stella was in fighting mood. She flew about the court, and at each stroke of her racket, like the blow of a weapon, she turned her rosy, excited face and sparkling eyes towards the enemy like a bomber who looks for the bodies to fly from the opposite trench. Cleeve meanwhile had sighted his father under the trees, in conversation with Cobden Chorley. He approached with a serious and expectant look, and hearing the word Plato, at once entered into eager discussion about the republic.

'Plato saw that education was the secret.'

'You have to decide first what to teach them,' Cobden said, with his distinguished, melancholy air. Cobden and Helen Pynsant since the last year had agreed that it was unwise for them to meet. Since then

Cobden had been broken-hearted and the rôle suited him very well. It gave depth and reality to his feelings and leisure for their realization. It was in this year that he produced his chief work, the first act of the *Suffering Pierrot*, which some people prefer to anything of Dowson's, and published the sonnet sequence, *Necromancies*, which had already made his name known to discerning critics.

Cobden's family, delighted and relieved to see him settled in life, had good reason at that time to hope for the completion of the *Pierrot* within another year or two. But that famous play, of course, remains unfinished to this day.

'Religion for instance,' Cobden said.

'Of course you must teach them the truth—things that everybody agrees to, the universal things.'

'Rome invented a universal creed some time ago.'

'My dear Cobbie, you'll end as a priest if you're not careful.'

'No hope,' Cobden said mournfully, 'I was born five hundred years too late. But life is a poor thing without faith.'

'It's easy enough to get faith—but you want a true one. Aquinas is all very well, but he doesn't prove that his first cause is a moral agent. Besides, he simply borrowed from Aristotle, didn't he father?'

'Yes, Aristotle. I suppose you'll be doing some Aristotle next term.'

Felix was extremely happy. To walk in the chequered sunlight with birds twittering overhead, and to hear Cleeve talk with enthusiasm of his own favourites, was such a serene happiness as he had not enjoyed since his own time at the university thirty-five years before. To see in Cleeve the same happiness, to feel in him the same interests, was to know a triumph which had no drawback of egotism. It was an essential glory belonging to the sympathies of nature itself. Felix was ambitious for Cleeve. He was already calculating on his chances of a first in greats, and it seemed to him that in that triumph, he would also be victorious. His mild gaze, dwelling on the solemn Cleeve, was full of parental self-satisfaction not the least impaired by the recollection of bankruptcy. John Chass had been paying Cleeve's fees for the year past and he supposed he would continue to do so.

But suddenly the word Schopenhauer came to his ears. Cleeve had rapidly travelled from Aquinas' first cause to his own favourite subject of the moment, 'Schopenhauer was wrong there——'

'H'm—h'm,' Felix muttered. 'But Schopenhauer—H'm, rather off your beat just now. I suppose, by the way, your tutor gave you a good deal to read.'

'Just the usual old stuff.' Cleeve, excited by his enquiry into what seemed to him at the moment the most important secret in the world, the very nature of its life, paused as if enquiring of the nature within himself. Suddenly he exclaimed in excitement, 'A will to will is simply absurd—the will must want something outside itself—a kind of experience.'

'The usual old stuff!' Felix protested.

'The æsthetic experience,' Cobden murmured to Cleeve.

'Much more than that—what do people want—what do all living things want—to be happy.'

Felix shook his head in his alarm. 'My dear Cleeve—of course there's something in what you say—but I'm afraid your tutor——'

'But father—what else can life be for—even Christians see that happiness is the only logical object—they put it in heaven, of course, but they still make it the end of life.'

'The Christian martyrs were happy on a gridiron,' Cobden murmured.

'An unnatural happiness,' Cleeve said impatiently.

'Oh, if you're bringing nature into it,' Cobden said mildly disgusted. 'Besides you can't deny it was happiness.'

'Nature can enjoy pain,' Felix suggested, 'or any other kind of nervous stimulation, anything, I suppose, except boredom or frustration.'

'Yes,' Cleeve cried, 'there you are—it wants pleasure.'

'Does that get you any further?' Felix said hastily. 'Does it give you anything material?'

'It's the material of happiness,' Cleeve insisted. 'Rich material— why is there colour, scent, music in the world, or sex, for the matter of that—except for happiness. Sex is an extraordinary idea when you think of it.'

'Beastly,' Cobden said.

'And why did nature invent it except for enjoyment, all kinds of enjoyment?'

'Enjoyment,' Cobden murmured.

'Of course nature must be the foundation, the raw material.'

'Too, too raw,' Cobden sighed.

'Rich, splendid material,' Cleeve said, 'the very stuff of happiness.'

'But as you remember, Cleeve,' Felix firmly seized the opening to bring Cleeve back into orthodoxy, 'the utilitarians got nowhere with the happiness principle—it was too vague. They were pushed back into ethics, into absolute standards—and once you get there, I don't think'— he paused as for impartial reflection—'no, really I don't think you can do better than Kant. I'm sure your tutor would agree with me.'

'Act as if your action could be made a universal law,' Cobden murmured. 'Not a very appetising programme.'

'Happiness, after all, is always social and co-operative,' Felix said. 'Even Bismarck, in his career of nationalist wars——'

'Or Joe Chamberlain,' Cobden murmured.

'Oh let's keep politics out of it,' Cleeve said. He looked round with disgust at the groups of excited Radicals chattering on the bright lawns beyond their shady grove.

'Merely as an illustration,' Felix apologized for bringing in anything so foolish as present politics, 'I was going to say that the fallacy of national glory is simply in that, that it needs co-operation but depends on competition. so that——'

They strolled on. Felix and Cleeve had the same expression of absorbed and lively happiness.

Loud cries of 'Cleeve!' were heard and Stella, flushed and perspiring, came from among the trees. 'Where on earth did you go, Cleeve, we've been hunting the whole garden.'

Cleeve was in the middle of saying to Cobden, with a slight air of condescension, 'Of course Kant is not picturesque.' He looked in surprise at Stella, 'I'm awfully sorry—I thought we'd finished.'

'We won the point,' her voice exulted in her triumph. 'Didn't you see the rally? Come on, that's fifteen forty and if we win the game we're bound to win Lucy's serve.'

Cleeve made a face at his father which meant, 'One must humour these children,' and uttering polite apologies, returned to the tennis. But as he was still engaged with philosophy, as the movements of his racket were either polite gestures or the expressions of the arguments which he intended to bring against Cobden, he and Stella did not win either the game or Lucy's serve. Stella, when she refrained from losing her temper at the end of the match, achieved a high degree of self-control. 'I'm sorry I was so bad,' she said to Cleeve, and Cleeve answered affectionately, taking her arm, 'Yes, you weren't up to form to-day. But I don't really mind losing. What I like is a good game.'

'Hullo!' He stopped.

'What is it?'

'That little beast, Porfit. Where on earth has he dropped from?'

He looked with disgust at Porfit who, smartly dressed in a frock coat and a new top hat, was talking to a group of ladies from the step of the garden door. He had plainly just arrived. He stood between Mrs. Chorley and Lucy who, with face still shining from tennis, was looking at him with a startled and watchful expression, as if wondering at a conjurer.

The Radical ladies on the lawn below the step were smiling up at the preacher with expressions which showed that he was not forgotten in Porriton.

Suddenly he saw Cleeve and Stella. He raised his hat and came down the steps. Stella was surprised to find her hand shaken. She was still more surprised to find herself alone. Cleeve had gone.

She asked him later why he had disappeared so suddenly. 'I can't bear that chap,' he said angrily. 'What's he doing here?'

'He's come to speak against the war.'
'Damn the war.'
'I don't suppose there'll be one, after all.'

Jarvis reached Porriton on October 17th. A deputation of the mayor and corporation, John Chass, summoned from Ireland, Benskin and Nussbaum, and a detachment of the Boys' Brigade awaited him on the platform. A band was drawn up in the road and a second had been playing for an hour in the town square. Over the town hall balcony, from which Monmouth was said to have addressed his Protestant levies, a great white streamer was being hung, with red letters a foot high. WELCOME TO THE CONQUEROR OF DAJI.

This streamer, prepared in great haste by a sewing bee at Motcombe, was received with loud cheers by the waiting crowd. They did not know where Daji was and they had long forgotten its conqueror's name, but it was a pleasure to feel any sentiment and to cheer anything or anybody.

The streets were hung with flags Always after the Jubilee Porriton possessed flags and since there were flags, there was more public feeling and patriotism.

At half-past twelve when five carriages appeared carrying Jarvis and the deputation to the town hall, for an address of welcome and a ceremonial luncheon, even the women uttered shrill cries.

Luckily it was a fine day and the hero, in an open landau, could be seen by the enthusiastic crowds who filled the pavements and the upper windows of shops. It was a disappointment that he was not in uniform. The country was at war and uniforms had been as exciting to the people as vestments to nuns. But they were scarce. The only distinguished soldier in Porriton on the active list, a colonel, had gone away to the war in a bowler, carrying his umbrella.

Even Stella and the Chorleys who were watching the entry from the second story window of the draper's shop opposite the town hall, were disappointed by the absence of uniform. Chorley, who hated the war to whom the idea of bloodshed was so terrifying that he could not bear to think of it, said with disgust and contempt, 'A very drab affair—they've bungled their own silly show.'

'But he'd no warning except a wire,' Stella said. 'He only arrived this morning'

'I expect he's too much sense,' Chorley said for Stella's comfort.

'I'm sure he hates it as much as you do.'

But she did not speak with conviction and Chorley's look was sceptical. Then suddenly his expression changed and he said, 'It's not his fault, after all.'

'He wanted to leave the army once.'

365

Again there was a little silence. Both felt that there was something false in all their remarks. Stella had never before made excuses for Harry's soldiering, and Chorley, like most of his party except the Radical tail, was in great confusion of feeling.

'Nussbaum,' he muttered. 'All our patriots, in fact.'

The deputation was descending from the carriages.

'Uncle Theo really arranged it,' Stella said, and Chorley was again silent.

The cheers rose up and made them both blush with their unexpected force. Stella was so much moved that she could not speak. Yet she frowned and Chorley said angrily, 'They were cheering the footbal team last week.'

Just then the mayor, Benskin, the town clerk in his wig, and Nussbaum appeared on the balcony of the town hall. Behind them John Chass, taller than any, stood looking round with such frank pleasure in the grandeur of the occasion that he received a cheer for himself; a perceptible wave among the last ripples.

Jarvis stepped out between the mayor and Benskin. The crowd approved him with a shout such as, to royal ears, means loyalty. He was there to be cheered; he was in fact the necessary excuse for that pleasure. Moreover, though he was not in uniform he looked pale and wasted like a hero, and he had the true Napoleonic nose and chin.

The mayor made a long speech in silence; Benskin spoke two sentences; and finally the hero himself, in a clear, small voice which nevertheless carried far over the silent crowd, said, 'Mr. Mayor, my lords, ladies and gentlemen, I didn't expect this at all, and so I haven't been able to make up a speech.' He paused as if looking for words, but he did not seem shy or at a loss, and hundreds of the listeners murmured to each other smiling, 'That's what they always say.'

But it was true. Jarvis had not expected a reception. It was more than a year since his march, and during that year, having been first threatened and then ignored, he had earnt how governments can revenge themselves on the private person who flaunts them even with popular support. As soon as the treaty had been signed and Daji had become part of Nigeria, he had been recalled to duty at headquarters and treated like an office boy who had robbed the till. All his measures in Daji had been reversed by a civilian resident, the Emir exiled, the new station and gardens abandoned. It had seemed to him for the last eight months that he had both thrown away his career as a soldier and been robbed of his credit as a pioneer. No one had received him at Plymouth, and acquaintances on the boat had treated him with that tact and quick agreement which is accorded to the failure.

He was deeply touched by the faithfulness of Porriton, which had remembered his services to the Empire, when everyone else had for-

366

gotten them; and he was not only at a loss for words to express himself, but for speech itself. The cheers, the kindness of these people, strangers, gathered to do him honour, made his throat swell.

His silence was so long that Benskin began to look anxious, and Stella put down her head and twisted her hands together. It was as though she, too, felt the crowd waiting; as if Jarvis was part of her and that part was in pain. Behind she could hear Lucy talking, 'One good thing, it will finish this government,' and Porfit's voice answering, 'That's what we have to make sure of, Miss Lucy.'

Stella looked angrily aside at the interrupter; but Lucy was looking at Porfit with an eager and friendly expression as if to ask for his approval. She did not even notice Stella.

Stella shrugged with irritation. She knew that Porfit was now an important person. His name was in the papers, even the London papers, which called him a traitor for his speeches. He was staying at Bellavista to organize the local campaign against the war and everywhere he was received with cheers and boos. All over England the same thing had happened; new, obscure men among the Radicals had suddenly become famous for their violent anti-war speeches; and already it was seen that they were the coming men in their party. They had rallied it in its confusion, raised a battle cry, while the Chorleys, the men who saw the difficulties, who thought first of what was the right course of action, were eclipsed. In a week of war dozens of reputations had been lost and made, as if by luck; not only of the soldiers but of the politicians.

So much the worse, Stella felt. How she hated all these politics which had suddenly produced such confusion, had turned her friends into lunatics so that Chorley contradicted himself and Lucy hung upon Porfit's words; which had thrown a shadow even on the triumph of Harry.

Suddenly Jarvis' voice sounded again, small and far off. Stella gave a deep, silent exhalation of relief.

'I haven't been able to make up a speech, but I can tell you that I won't forget to-day or your kindness as long as I live. I've only tried to do my duty to this great empire which all of us are proud to serve, and I know if any of you had been in Africa with me, you would have done as much as ever I did to save these poor people from their oppressors and to give them some of the freedom and peace and justice which we all enjoy as a birthright. Now when new enemies, oppressors worse even than the slave dealers we fought in Daji, have dared to challenge us, I feel that I have done little enough. We ought to be thinking of the men who are meeting, perhaps this minute, the attack of the Boers upon our peaceful colonies in South Africa. And so I say God bless our soldiers, God bless you, and God bless the Queen.'

367

This speech had a powerful effect; Benskin was flushed; Nussbaum smiled once; the crowd cheered like thunder, drowning even the band which played with all their might God save the Queen. Many of the women in the crowd, who had relations at the front, or were moved simply by the voice of any public speaker, were in tears. Everywhere one saw open, yelling mouths; sparkling, excited eyes; and heard cheers, shrieks, howls, broken words of the royal hymn. Hats jumped up and down above the bobbing heads, like the balls at a shooting alley; and the tumult went on, even increased, when the hero, after repeated bows, turned with the deputation and guided on each side by the affectionate hands of Benskin and Nussbaum upon his arms, disappeared into the town hall for the state luncheon.

'So he is for the war,' Lucy said and her father, thinking of Stella, said quickly, 'My dear, as a soldier——'

Stella had tears in her eyes. The speech had made her cry. Through an irregular, glittering brightness like a wet window-pane, she saw the waving shapes of Chorley, the grey-bearded draper, who was also a Methodist preacher, and little Porfit. Porfit was speaking loudly to Chorley, gesticulating with both hands, shoulders, even his body. 'The greatest crime in history and it won't go unpunished. It's a crime that can't be hid under a bushel. The whole world sees it and knows it for what it is, the foulest betrayal since Judas sold his soul for gold.'

He was obviously quoting from one of his own speeches. His voice had the ring of a preacher, and his chin was thrown up like one addressing an audience. 'And what a good thing Nussbaum was here.'

The pale, clever face changed from the grand aloofness of the apostle to the pawky, genial shrewdness of the politician. 'That's a bit of luck I didn't expect—what we've got to do is to make people understand that Benskin, for all his fine talk, is just another of the money-grabbing gang, and five thousand have seen them together all the morning. It's a point we've got to drive home at the meeting to-night—that this is a grabber's war, an assassination.'

Stella's eyes cleared. She looked, frowning slightly, at Porfit and Lucy, and said in an abrupt tone, 'Where's Cleeve—we ought to go, I suppose—it's lunch time?'

Lucy coloured slightly, as if Cleeve's name had made her ashamed, and said that she thought he had gone out.

Cleeve was at the next window hiding among the wax dummies. He had retreated as far as possible from Porfit and Lucy. He could not bear to see Porfit and Lucy together, even to hear Lucy speak to Porfit. Her enthusiasm seemed to him false, and he thought gloomily, 'But of course it's easy to make a hero of him and she's doing it—she wants to make the best of him.'

'Cleeve,' Stella called. 'Where are you?'

Cleeve appeared suddenly alongside of a magnificent dummy, in the style of the period, of a gentleman with a six-inch blonde moustache, and a full-breasted frock coat.

'I'm being a hero—it seems in the mode.'

'What do you think about it, Cleeve?' Chorley asked.

'I suppose they started it,' Cleeves said irritably, with his eyes on Lucy. He noticed that she would not meet his eye. The wretched girl was already as good as lost; meat for Porfit.

'So that's how you see it. Do they all see it like that?' Chorley turned round as if asking a congregation.

'Ah, but that was the real triumph of Judas,' Porfit said, 'that his treachery did not appear, that he did not need to offer violence. It was the betrayed who first unsheathed the sword. Judas was not seen.'

Chorley interrupted with a sarcastic tone as novel as the disorder of his beard. 'Even without comparing Kruger with Christ I should have thought our position was obviously impossible. We're going to murder these people, men are being killed at this very moment, and what for? Gold.'

'If it was only copper,' Cleeve murmured, appearing now between two ladies in extremely low ball dresses.

Chorley looked disconcerted. Porfit suddenly whirled round and cried, 'Oh, Mr. Corner, I was looking for you—I want you to come to our meeting on Saturday—I have a Cambridge representative.'

'I never go to political meetings.'

'Oh, I quite understand your feeling. I know you find better things to think of in your classical studies. But in a case of special urgency like this I ventured to suggest your name.'

Cleeve turned red with annoyance. He had not expected this answer and yet it seemed that his nerves had been expecting it, and that it was exactly what he had been afraid of, the charge of aloofness. He answered sharply, 'It's not that at all—it's simply that they're so boring.'

He turned to Stella. 'We ought to be getting on,' and she went out.

Lucy had stepped out of their way; she was pressing herself back among a row of silk petticoats hanging from a bar. Cleeve stopped and muttered angrily to her, 'It's a grand thing, war, isn't it. Lucy?'

Her face wrinkled and turned pink; she glanced hurriedly towards Porfit. She had been terrified that Cleeve would say something like this before Porfit; would betray her old disgust of the man. But luckily Porfit was already speaking to Chorley and the draper; making another little speech. Her face became calm and pale again, she looked boldly at Cleeve as if to say, 'Think what you like.'

'When did you get so fond of Mr. Porfit?'

'He's a very brave man,' Lucy said.

'Yes, it's a grand war—its solved all sorts of problems.'

Lucy looked pensively at Cleeve from among the petticoats and said, 'You don't understand, Cleeve.'

'But I do understand—only too well.'

Both knew the truth of this and Lucy once more turned pink. Her lips trembled and her eyes suddenly had the bright look of tears. She fowned at Cleeve. She wanted to say, 'Then why didn't you marry me—save me.' Cleeve himself turned red and stuck out his lips with a sulky, obstinate expression, meaning, 'Oh, damn it all.'

Porfit glanced round as if surprised to find a gap at his side and she went quickly forward, smiling already her approval for what she had not heard. Cleeve plunged down the stairs after Stella. He did not feel victorious over Lucy, but defeated, and this made him still more disgusted. He said to Stella, 'I feel like the only sober man at a freshman's blind. I think I'll go and get drunk.'

Stella made no answer. She walked on with flushed cheeks and bright eyes; probably she was still listening to Harry's war speech.

John Chass had brought with him a pocketful of letters and papers about the Mosi Company. At luncheon he pulled out a circular from Hatto, proposing a merger of three companies on the Mosi.

'Have you seen this, Benskin? Hatto is a good man, I believe, my brother knows him in Africa.'

'Never met him.'

'Are you buying Mosis?' John Chass smiled at his friend as if to say, 'What scheme are you up to now?'

Nussbaum, knowing that Benskin would not like to answer this question, put out his hand and said, 'Excuse me, is that a prospectus?' He read it carelessly, holding it sideways as if it was scarcely worth the trouble of holding at all and frowning as if to say, 'What nonsense is this?'

In fact Nussbaum, like Benskin, had already seen the circular sent to all members of the African market; and he and Benskin had bought since, in consultation with Hatto, large blocks of shares in half a dozen companies on the Mosi river. Mosi and Transport were, of course, very minor concerns to the syndicate of which Nussbaum himself was not the predominant partner, and he really did not know much about the companies. But he knew that the Colonial Office was favourable to the scheme.

Nussbaum did not think of himself as a speculator. He had inherited a fortune and his chief pleasure was the enjoyment of it. He regarded money as a squire regards his land; as the necessary foundation of his existence but not its first interest. He bought such shares as Mosi only as a squire puts a fiver on a horse, for a passing amusement, in the interests of the sport, or simply as a social art, because not to do so might imply a criticism of friends.

Nussbaum's business, the financing of prospecting expeditions, the floating of new gold companies and the rebuilding of old ones, seemed to him an important and serious profession, requiring great technical knowledge, and the widest acquaintance with men, politics and world conditions. To make a hundred thousand pounds in a year by the combination of two properties with a million capital each into a company with a capital of two millions, pleased him as much by the skill and coolness with which he could carry out the operation, as by the profit.

If anyone had asked him, 'But where has your hundred thousand come from if you have not swindled somebody?' he would have answered, 'These two companies, badly organized, competing for transport and labour, duplicating posts, had between them nearly double the overhead expenses of the amalgamated company which I made out of them. I saved them more than ten thousand a year in salaries alone—that is, capitalized, two hundred thousand pounds. My one hundred thousand is not a quarter of what they owe me altogether.'

No one had ever asked him 'What happened to the men who drew the salaries'; and if they had, he would have answered coolly and reasonably, 'The object of business is not to provide jobs but certain products at the cheapest rates, and it works by competition, for goods as well as jobs. That is, as you know, good Liberal doctrine, free competition. It is also science, nature—the fundamental rule of life.'

Nussbaum, like all philosophical, free-thinking Frenchmen, believed more profoundly in Darwin even than the Darwinians. For the idea that lurks in Darwin, the unconscious philosophy of Darwin's age which impregnated all Darwin's thought, of inevitable progress based upon a natural providence, was natural to the French mind before Darwin was born. It appeared in Rousseau.

As Felix used to say, the Frenchmen's economics will be those of nature and providence even longer than the evangelical Americans.

The mayor had risen to propose the toast, 'Queen and Empire.' Nussbaum handed back the pamphlet with a grave face. He did not believe in the Empire any more or less than he believed in God, but he considered that both deserved the support of intelligent men; like the police force and the gold standard.

Nothing more was said about the Mosi Company or Hatto's schemes until in the carriage, driving home, Nussbaum suddenly asked Jarvis if Laka really had a population of a million.

Cocky was startled by the question, in the midst of these powerful emotions of gratitude and victory; of his own success, assuring him of worth; and of affection for those who had so generously given him this

371

assurance, which had exalted him for the last three hours. He answered abruptly, with a look of unconscious sarcasm, 'You think there's money in it?'

'That depends on so many things.'

'And people,' Benskin said.

'Business and politics—they are mostly people.'

'And people are mostly rascals,' John Chass said, with his loud laugh like two blasts of a trumpet. He was saying what he supposed would please the business man, but to his surprise Benskin said, 'I wouldn't say so.'

'Not so much rascals,' Nussbaum agreed, 'as, let us say, dilettanti.' Nussbaum himself had been called a dilettante.

'What about this prospectus?'

'I should call that a work of imagination,' Benskin said.

'Yes, yes, that's the trouble. It's not that all men are liars but that they are not interested in truth—they are poets.'

Jarvis said suddenly, 'I see Buller is commander-in-chief.'

All turned hastily and respectfully towards the hero. Their quick deference, like that of children caught eating sweets in church, expressed their feeling that business was hardly a suitable subject of discussion, in this warlike time.

Motcombe Manor had been completed in the last year. As the carriages topped the hill the party had a view of the new house, standing on the opposite slope in the midst of green fields, beautiful in shape and line, which had belonged to the old Corner lands.

Benskin's head turned automatically towards the view which still gave him the keenest delight. The huge square house, ostentatious in the very forms of its elaborate, expensive detail was all that belongs to the ideal mansion, a name which seemed to have waited till that age for its realization. Its colour was such that the very blue of the sky, the green of the fields, the amber of the trees fading in autumn, the smooth curves and broad planes of the hillside were changed on the eye to the coarse thin appearance of a drop scene.

But it was a contemporary masterpiece, acknowledged by all authorities, and Benskin's pride in it was very little less than his delight in his son, born in the masterpiece three months before.

It seemed to Benskin that he had succeeded beyond his hopes. The modesty which had marked upon his face the characteristic expression of suspended judgment, was not affected. He was always surprised by his triumph in marrying, against so many competitors, a woman of family, beauty, wit and distinction.

Helen, it was true, was not a good mother. She had bitterly resented her pregnancy for which Benskin, of course, who had undertaken precautions, accepted responsibility. He admitted carelessness. But Helen had not even accused him as he had fully expected, of being careless on purpose. She had behaved with that good sense and grace upon which her reputation was perched. She had made, as Benskin had foreseen, a charm of her misfortune, asked for congratulations, and surrounded herself with admirers. She played the affectionate mother to perfection, in public, and when she was at home, made a point of visiting the nursery at least once a day.

At that moment she was in the day nursery. The baby in its long clothes ready for an afternoon walk lay in her lap gazing with vague absentminded stare at her glittering ring finger waved above its nose. It was in a condition of sleepy drunkenness after its meal; floating in a daze of visceral excitement. Cobden, sitting beside Helen, gazed at her with hollow eyes. He seemed even more like the mystic in contemplation of a holy vision; in fact, he was panic-stricken.

Helen had been pursuing him for the last month. Having officially loved her for years, he could not refuse her invitations; that would be absurd; but he was terrified by some new recklessness in the woman. What did she want? What was going to happen to him? He had done no work for weeks. He could not sleep for apprehension. Sometimes he feared some horrible dénouement; a divorce case, or worse, more undignified, a kick in the backside. But deeper and stronger was the terror which he could not define, as of disintegration; as if his very essence and self, so painfully formed, was threatened by a fate too horrible to imagine; a kind of luxurious dissolution, a falling apart into the nothingness of daily satisfactions.

In the last few days Cobden had lost many pounds in weight; he had become still more the picture of an ascetic.

Helen turned her laughing face towards him, raising her chin in the style of the grand coquette; then suddenly skittish put out her lips like a child asking for a kiss. Cobden looked round with involuntary caution; an abject movement which brought blood to his own cheeks and made Helen mischievous.

'Afraid?'

'The nurse is just outside.'

'What about nurse?'

'I've got to think of you.'

'Never mind me.' She laughed and tossed the baby 'gee-ho.' Helen enjoyed her baby, and she noticed, as Benskin had promised her, that having the baby had done her good. It had even increased her beauty, rounding her figure, plumping out her hips, to the great satisfaction of her corsetière. Helen was a good natured woman, too self-indulgent to be revengeful. She knew that Benskin had tricked her, that for him such a trick was justified not only morally but by its success, but she was ready to admit that he had been right in wanting a child, and that she had been wrong. She felt no spite against him. She was too busy enjoying the moment. Every day she looked afresh on the same problem, how to amuse herself, and any change of circumstance, of fashion, or moral standards, of her own position, which offered a new opening to a new kind of pleasure, immediately caught her attention. She tossed the baby again, laughing at its solemn, foolish look, then suddenly putting her face close to Cobden's said, 'I'm not afraid.'

'But she's just coming.' His face was damp with sweat.

She smiled at his complicated misery. She did not understand quite why Cobden had such an ecclesiastical attitude towards the sins of the flesh; but she knew that it made him an exciting lover. She had not forgotten his tearing hands in Portland Place.

'Poor Cobbie,' she put her face close to his. He made a face like a child taking medicine, and desperately kissed her. She pressed against him, holding his lips, till the door handle turned.

He sprang away, white and frowning, as the nurse came in; a middle-aged woman in uniform, with a long severe face. Benskin himself had engaged her.

Helen smiled at her. She took up the baby from her mistress' silk lap and said, 'You shouldn't have tossed him, madam. He's been sick in your lap.'

Helen gave a cry of annoyance and disgust. The nurse going out said, 'I don't know how you didn't notice it, madam.'

Cobden gazed at her with a furious perplexed air; like an unhappy humiliated little boy who doesn't know whether to cry or to storm. 'She saw.'

'Poor Cobbie, are you afraid he'll shoot you?'

He jumped up and walked away. His legs were trembling. He muttered, 'Let him—it's not that.' He looked at her with an expression very like hatred. Helen, laughing, crossed the room and took his face between her hands. 'Don't be afraid, darling—I'll arrange it properly this time—no more servants' bedrooms, and all quite safe. Now I must go and change my dress to receive the hero—the other hero.' She smiled at him. 'We're going to be happy, aren't we?' She held out her warm, greedy lips, 'Kiss me, Pierrot.'

She went out with the look of a little girl with a jujube; Cobden fell into the nurse's chair. His face expressed despair almost as eloquently as his famous play.

In the great hall of the manor, larger than the parish church, hung with pictures of the English school, a Reynolds, a Romney, portraits of Clive and Rhodes, the celebrated Lady Mary Boodle and children by Lawrence, guests were arriving to meet Jarvis. They were received

374

within the great door by Helen and presented to Jarvis by Benskin, who now and then gave to his friend a little apologetic smile or murmured, 'I'm afraid this is rather an imposition.'

Jarvis, who had but five days' leave before joining his old regiment, made no answer. He did not think it necessary to explain that he felt an obligation rather than a burden, in the honours paid to him by all these people. He pressed each hand with a new gratitude, and a perpetual surprise. He was still astonished to find so much altruism, so much generous and disinterested feeling in people.

Now and then in a pause of the stream, while Benskin with his deferential respect pointed out the objects of interest, the mahogany panelling, the pictures, the carved ceiling, he looked round with an expression of enquiring patience.

He was looking for Stella whom he had not yet seen. He had not been surprised to miss her among the town councillors, but he expected to find her in her own house.

'A beautiful thing,' Benskin said, looking across the room at the picture hung in a strong light. Lady Mary was represented in a landskip with three children clambering over her. Children, mother, dress and landskip, had the quality of romantic art which shows life as sentimentalists would like to think it. Nothing was falsified, but every detail, the children's eyes, clothes, the mother's complexion, the grouping, was of a perfection seen usually in a glimpse, and in isolation. As a picture, it was a fine romantic piece; but as Benskin saw it, as a record of English family life at a country house, it was as absurd as any of Ouida's guardsmen.

'Yes, I like it,' Jarvis looked at the picture. 'Fine kids.'

'The mother's expression is so good.'

'She reminds me of somebody—Miss Pynsant. It's the eyebrows. By the way, she's all right, is she?'

'Stella—yes, she's somewhere about.' He glanced at Jarvis, and feeling with his quick sense the young man's surprise and longing, he said, 'I don't think she likes a crowd—she has moments of shyness—her feelings are sometimes a bit too strong for her.'

'Yes, she has strong feelings.'

'Right feelings, too. You can trust her feelings. She'll grow into a fine woman.'

'A real woman,' and then because Benskin had pleased him, he tried to please Benskin, 'She likes you a lot.'

'I'm afraid she prefers you,' with a smile.

'Oh no, not a bit of it.' Jarvis looked serious. He insisted on his compliment. He was fond of Benskin. He felt that Benskin was sound; that his heart was in the right place. 'Stella's as loyal as the day—I know that—she never changes.'

'May I say, Jarvis, that I think you and she ought to be a very happy couple.'

They shook hands, greatly moved. In the background a man's voice was heard saying. 'But de Beers might be a good lock up.'

The butler shouted, 'Lord AND Lady Porriton, Mr. AND Mrs. Pumphrey.'

The stream was running again, this time with greater continuity and pace. Towards four o'clock it had become a broad tide. Benskin, who was still a Liberal in name, had asked constituents from all classes. It was as though he had opened a sluice upon the broad slow flood of local life, which ran now across the sill of his doorstep, carrying its flotsam with it, bald heads like turnips, round polished ones like wet potatoes, hats like old birds' nests. Ladies were seen borne along in the midst of a tangle of relations, with the resigned, white, short chinned faces of lost sheep.

These, too, shook hands with Jarvis, not knowing who or what he was and afterwards, slowly revolving in the corner eddies, among strange green women, cylindrical as cabbage stalks, last relics of the æsthetic eighties, tubby rural councillors in fancy waistcoats, like empty tomato cans, crumpled girls, with startled eyes and flattened figures like drowned kittens badly done up in sodden brown paper, they could be heard bleating now and then, 'Who was the young man with the red moustache,' or 'those curtains cost a bit, I lay.'

Felix with his new, happy smile was standing on the bottom step of the stairs talking to Cleeve and Stella two steps above.

'It's like a game of poker between six card sharpers with marked cards all round—the only thing for a sensible man is to keep out of it.'

'I've no temptation to get into it,' Cleeve murmured.

'One thing at least one learns at Oxford is to suspect labels— Imperialism, Democracy and all the rest—what do they mean when they put China and Germany in one pigeon-hole and the U.S.A. and Paraguay in the other?'

Cleeve stood with bent head and thoughtful, pondering air; the look of a man of judgment, of the scholar who values the truth above all things. Stella gazed at the sage with a frown of attention. But in fact she had ceased to listen. Cleeve was straining his ears to catch the voice of a young man just below him in the crowd who was waving an evening paper and saying something about a battle.

Felix smiled on his pupils. 'And the reason our Liberal friends are in such a muddle is that they're always obsessed by this idea of a moral providence—it messed up their economics and it always messes them up in a war. Liberal democracy collapses in the presence of violence because it has never faced the problem of force.'

Cleeve thought he could distinguish the words, 'a hundred killed,' and his heart seemed to jump. A hundred killed—men perhaps were dying at that moment. He looked angrily through the banisters at the young man who sank his voice at all the interesting parts. Stella suddenly and accidentally gave a deep sigh as if she were going to weep. She had seen Jarvis' blond head coming towards her through the crowd. She said in a voice of extraordinary passion and bitterness, 'Why are politics so dirty—I do absolutely hate them.'

Jarvis was two yards away. She pretended to see him for the first time, and quickly hurried to him. He took her hand. 'Where can we go?'

She led him through the crowd towards a study where they could be alone. She thought, 'How happy I ought to be now—how happy if it wasn't for all this.'

The fashions were military that year. When Maddy and Coo went to Dunderry to buy winter coats at Pollocks' in the Diamond, they found all kinds of shakos and braided jackets.

Maddy refused them all. She wanted something in last year's fashion, but while she was arguing with the assistant, Coo quietly put on the most fashionable and absurd of the new modes, and insisted that she would have it. Maddy could storm; but the girl only looked more frightened and obstinate; she went home in the coat and though she never wore it again, for Slatter sent it back by the mail car, she continued in an unusual and excited state of mind.

Coo herself did not know what was wrong with her. She used to gaze for ten minutes at a time at the war map hung up in the hall, stuck full of Union Jacks to show the advance of the troops, and then she would feel such excitement that she could not sleep. She took a hatred to everything ordinary, like stirabout, cod, egg sauce, table cloths, carpets and bedroom china. She clattered her jug so savagely one night that she broke it, and when Maddy warned her at breakfast that the tea was boiling, she scalded her throat to get it out of the way.

One day, seeing Philip quietly stealing into the lamp room, Coo had a bold thought which suddenly sprang to her attention. As soon as she had it, she knew what to do. There was nothing else to do. She went to Philip and still terrified and pale, breathless, as if she had stormed a kopje in face of the enemy, she proposed to him in these words. 'Ye know, Philly, that Pappy says that Hanna would like ye to be married for your nerves. How would ye like that?'

Philip said nothing but he looked grand and savage. He had been sober for five months and his life was at a low ebb. He had, in fact, no ideas on any subject and he had not thought about anything for several weeks. He felt an enormous, bored misery.

'I'd like it well enough myself,' Coo said, 'if ye'd have me, and ye know, Philly, we like each other well enough this long while.'

Philip said nothing and Coo, looking at his rough, savage expression and red face, which grew every day more like his uncle's, felt terror. She thought, 'He'll kill me.' But she was also brave and resolute. She felt that she could not run away now. If she did, she would be worse than an old maid, she would be a coward. She said, 'Ye know, Philly, I might be a good wife for ye, even if ye had them to pick, because now I've asked ye, ye needn't be so nice with me as an English gyurl.'

Suddenly Philip had an idea. He looked at her and said, 'Don't ye think I might kill ye?'

'Oh no, Philly.' Coo was turning green.

'But I might, too. I've been mad once.' He got up, towering over her; he could see that she was terrified but this did not give him any great satisfaction. It was however something. For the first time in many weeks he had a distinct sensation of accomplishment. He went out of the room in a dignified manner.

Coo sat down. She felt faint. But how could she turn back now? She was afraid of turning back in case something worse should happen to her; a self-contempt which would spoil all her peace and comfort.

She saw now that she had cut herself away from all her peace, the safety of sleeping with the strong, brave Maddy; the security of the iron shutters and the double locked door; and even the delightful peace of walking in the back drive with Maddy and allowing her mind and tongue to wander as they chose without fear or responsibility.

She went to bed and refused all meals. She wanted to feel the desperation of her state, until it pushed her into some desperate action. At last she told Maddy that she was prepared to marry Philip.

Maddy was astounded and horrified. But she told her father. The same night uncle and nephew, after a battle lasting two hours, had hysterics together.

The engagement was announced the next day and the banns were called that week. Annish was surprised by this event. No one knew what to think of Slatter's marrying a daughter he despised to a nervous wreck who had already had an attack of homicidal mania. But Slatter himself was delighted and took all credit for the plan. He asked for congratulations everywhere. 'Coo's the very gyurl for Philly—she knows how to look after'm. And mind ye, she's a grand wee gyurl, too, whatever ye may think. Aye, she's no fule.'

He took Coo to Dunderry and bought her an enormous trousseau, choosing everything, even the nightdresses, himself. He was particular that the nightdresses should be like Mary Corner's, frilled to the neck. For Philip also he ordered suits, hats, a new frock coat and nightshirts. 'Aw, man, ye can't go on a honeymoon with they pyjamas—they may do for Injuns, but they're a dahm nuisance to a Christian—always in the way—naw, naw, nightshirts for a honeymoon.'

378

The wedding took place on the earliest possible date, on November the twentieth. It was a brilliant success. Nothing fell short of Slatter's hopes except the absence of Mary Corner who sent the excuse that she had to take Teresa to Belfast to see a specialist.

Teresa had had an accident. She had been found one evening at the bottom of the kitchen stairs with the urn on top of her; with a broken arm and scalds all over her face and body. No one had seen the accident except Bridget, passing at the moment along the upper hall passage on her way to the mistress, where she came almost every day to ask for a job in the rooms, since Sukey would not have her in the kitchen. But Bridget could give no account of it except that she thought perhaps Teresa had pulled the urn down upon herself.

The burns had become septic and the left eye had been infected. Mary sat up all night for a week nursing the child, and now, when it had proved impossible to save the eye, she was taking a specialist's advice about its removal.

But Slatter was convinced that the sickness of a servant's child could not be a true excuse for anyone to stay away from so grand a wedding. 'Don't ye believe it. It's what old Mary doesn't like to think of Coo and Philly at the cassle. Aw, she's a quiet wan, but don't make anny mistake, she's gye and proud in her bones.'

John Chass had been prevented from the wedding by business. Immediately after the reception at Porriton, Transport dropped a shilling, and Mosis, having touched ten and threepence began their final decline from which they never recovered.

John Chass and Felix went to their brokers, Messrs. Sling & Cardew, who found themselves in a difficulty because neither of the brothers showed their minds.

A broker likes to tell a client what the client wants to hear; and especially with speculative shares, he has to find out, before he gives advice, whether the client is the kind of man who knows what speculation is; whether, for instance, he would be more angry at losing his money in a margin gamble, or disgusted by missing a profit. He must know what a client means by such words as investment, safety, reasonable security, a fair chance, a good return. For old ladies, an investment is a share; any share. For country gentlemen like John Chass, it might be anything from an outsider in a selling plate with a shot of ginger essence in its sphincter to bullion in a safe deposit.

When Mr. Sling, a tall, heavy, red-faced man, well known with several packs near London, saw John Chass' whiskers and covert coat, his horse-shoe pin, and his curly hat, he was inclined to the first view and began, 'Of course, Mr. Corner, West Africans have always had

379

their ups and downs—though I must admit this recent down in the Mosi river group is rather sharper than usual.'

He then waited for enlightenment. But John Chass sat tapping his beautiful hat with a gold-headed malacca; with the cheerful air of a man consulting his doctor about a rich relation from whom he has expectations; and Felix, dressed as usual like a seedy professor, gazed dreamily out of the window at the opposite side of Lombard Street. The truth was that Felix had warned John Chass not to show his own inclination to the broker.

'They are, of course, speculative,' Mr. Sling said, as a doctor might remark that earache was sometimes painful. He paused, but the brothers were silent. 'And there has been a good deal of realization in the last few days.' He paused again. Neither brother spoke. 'On the other hand, a reaction may be due in the opposite direction.'

There was a long pause. Mr. Sling's clerk tapped at the door, and he glanced at the clock. He looked again at John Chass with a penetrating gaze, and then sidelong at Felix. He said to Felix, 'Are you interested in West African yourself, sir?'

Felix was wondering if it would be wise for Cleeve at this stage in his education to spend the Christmas vacation in Germany. His German was weak so that he had missed something essential of Kant; the striving, anxious quality of his mind; on the other hand, the boy had no time to waste. 'Perhaps I'd better consult his tutor,' he thought. 'I could run down this afternoon, and then if I stayed overnight, I could dine in hall and see Cleeve in his place below.'

Mr. Sling repeated his question. 'Are you interested in West Africans, sir?'

'The shares are worthless, of course,' Felix said briskly.

Mr. Sling made up his mind. He spoke with confidence, 'Well, Mr. Corner, taking everything into consideration, I think, on the whole,' and he was going to advise John Chass to sell, when Felix, mistaking his pause, which was on this occasion not an enquiring pause, but an impressive one, broke in, 'But of course that doesn't matter on the Stock Exchange.'

'Yes, Mr. Sling,' John Chass said politely, to excuse his brother's interruption.

'I should hold,' Mr. Sling said, 'quite definitely. The shares are something of a gamble, of course; but powerful groups are interested and I see no reason why they shouldn't recover from their low point of last week. At least we might wait until to-morrow and the beginning of a new account.'

'Just what I say,' Felix said, greatly relieved by the end of the interview. 'I wonder if you have such a thing as a railway time table?'

On the next morning when John Chass opened his paper he saw

380

that the Mosi shares had fallen with increasing speed. They had closed at about one and sixpence. He had lost seven thousand pounds in a day. This gave him a shock, but not such a severe shock as he had felt some years before at the loss of his wallet, containing four five pound notes, at Ballyarnet races. Notes were real money.

The post brought a note from Mr. Sling, requesting instructions before the opening of the market at eleven; and a letter from his wife.

Dear John,

The Slatters are passing through London to-morrow, the twenty-first, and I hope that you will contrive to see them, for I fear that Mr. Slatter feels slighted that neither of us will be able to attend poor Constance's wedding to-day. His direction in London is to be Wilkins Hotel, Strand. Margaret accompanies the young couple as dame d'honneur, a very suitable arrangement though I am told it is old-fashioned: and Mr. Slatter goes with Philip because I suppose he cannot be parted from him. Hardy tells me the mortgagees have a right to foreclose at the end of December and that they intend to do so. Perhaps you will speak to Mr. Slatter about this. It has been a surprise to me and I should like to know what you would have me do, supposing it is not convenient for you to return. Henriette is now in Touraine and I'm sure she would be glad for us to stay with her as long as we liked if we gave her notice. She tells me the shooting is much improved. I think in any case poor little Teresa Foy needs a change. The specialists would not take out the eye and it has a very ugly appearance: the country people are saying that she is unlucky. I am teaching her ABC and her needle. When she grows up she will make a good lady's maid. She is so quiet and quick and looks do not matter to a lady's maid———'

The rest of the letter was concerned entirely with Teresa, and John Chass skipped it. He looked at his watch. It was a quarter past ten. There was a telephone in the hotel and he thought, 'I'll speak to Sling by telephone, and go straight to Slatter. I must see him about these instalments.'

John Chass was then two months behind in his interest payments to Slatter's lawyers, on the former's consolidated mortgage. This had not given him any anxiety and it did not trouble him now; he would find the money somehow before the end of the month. But he had a fine excuse to see Slatter, and a strong disinclination, at that moment, to see Sling. He feared bad news from Sling. When he reached the telephone in the hall, he felt such a strong dislike to hearing Sling's voice that he said, 'Well now, what does it matter when I'm seeing him, in half an hour—and I hate these telephones, anyhow.'

Thus absolved, he joyfully took a hansom down the Strand.

He congratulated himself on this promptitude when he saw the two girls, across the pavement, on the hotel steps, in the act of going out.

'Poor Maddy,' was his first thought. He saw at once that Maddy was exhausted; that she looked pale and sad, that her dress was even shabbier and dustier than usual. Coo, on the other hand, standing beside her, was wearing an elaborate coat, almost military in cut, of serge braided and scalloped, with sleeves up to her ears. Her hat with upturned brim was like the basin of a fountain with three ostrich feathers rising from the crown to a great height, like the plumes seen at Versailles when the grand waters are turned on. This hat, perched high on the top of her small, pinched face and big, alarmed eyes reminded John Chass of a monkey on an organ dressed for some farce. He felt at once that tender sympathy for Coo which he gave to all small animals.

They were astonished and delighted to see him, but their looks of delight were only momentary. Anxiety creased Maddy's forehead before she had finished shaking hands. 'How far is it to St. Paul's, Mr. Corner?'

'As far as your own back gate to the corner of the bog. A quarter of an hour with a horse, but with these animals in London I wouldn't like to guess.'

'To walk, I mean.'

'But why walk it, my dear?'

Slatter, crimson and perspiring, rushed towards them from the street. He was dressed as usual in yellow tweeds, with bulging pockets; and he bawled across the passing Londoners, as if they had been cattle at a fair, 'Where is he, oh Gawd, isn't it the pair of ye—who'd bring a gyurl on a holiday.' He rushed past them into the hall, shouting, 'Philly—Philly, dahm ye. Oh Gawd.'

Philip appeared suddenly from the hall. He was smartly dressed in a frock coat, new top hat, fancy waistcoat; with a flower in his buttonhole and a huge diamond pin glittering in his blue satin tie. Only his long patent leather boots, dusty as Maddy's and Coo's, spoilt his magnificent appearance. But he carried himself like a prince.

'Dahm ye!' Slatter shouted. 'Where've ye been—I can smell ye from here.' He seized the boy by the arm and pushed his nose up to his lips. 'Be Gawd, it's smokin' from him.'

'Ah, Pappy,' Maddy said, 'how could he get it without any money, and you tellin' them all not to give him any liquor.'

'Ahm trusting no one but me nose.'

Slatter turned to John Chass at last and held out a hand. 'Begob, Jawn, ye'd better have come to the wedding for all the good ye've been doing here.'

'Well now, James, I was wanting to ask you about a little matter—certain payments, I'm told, are a trifle overdue.'

An expression passed over Slatter's face which was like a veil; the look of the farmer when the other party to a bargain puts a vital question. 'Aw, dahm business. This is a honeymoon, and we've only got three hours for St. Paul's and the Mint, too. D'ye know how we get to St. Paul's?'

'You're not going to walk there?'

'What else?'

'But the girls are worn out. There's poor Maddy ready to faint.'

'Aw, don't ye believe it. She's legs like an allephant, all ways.'

'But James, what are cabs for—and a few shillings on a cab saves time that may be costing you pounds.'

'It's not the money, don't think it. It's them swindling jarveys on the box that'll never tell ye what to pay. Lave it to you, sir—and how are ye to know they go straight except ye know they'll take ye all round like Phil the Fluter.'

'Let me stand poor Maddy a cab this time.'

'Aw, if ye like, and Coo can sit on somebody's knee. Not on Phil's, though, in his new trousers, and I have me rheumatism.'

'I shall be honoured to support the bride.'

The cab was called. Coo was placed on John Chass' knee; she at once took hold of his wrist. Slatter, entering last, banged the door behind him and shouted at Philip, 'So ye thought ye'd get away that time. But begob if Coo hasn't the sense to keep ye sober the day, I'll do it meself. This is their weddin' night, Jawn, ye see, because on the boat, I took the boyo in with me.' Then at once thrusting head and stick together out of the window, he shouted at the driver, 'What's that, Pat?'

It proved to be merely a bank building in Holborn. Slatter sank back with a sigh and said, 'I thought it was historical. It was dirty enough.'

'You'll like the old historical buildings in Paris, Maddy,' John Chass said.

'I would so,' said Maddy, 'if it wasn't for the new gyurl,' and looking at John Chass with confidence in his sympathy. 'Ye know what it is, Mr. Corner, with a new gyurl coming in the very day before we left and not there ten minutes before she made me a dint in the bust with the handle of a bissom.'

John Chass, who knew Carnmore as well as the castle, said, 'Not Fishy.'

'Psyche,' Maddy reproached him for levity with her treasures.

'Ah well, that lady's wounds can never be too bad for plaster to mend.'

'Aw, dahm your statues and your bissoms. Can't ye think of

383

annything clsc? And look at Coo with a face like a plate. Gawd, what a pair of ould maids to take on a honeymoon!'

John Chass changed the subject by pointing out Staples Inn, which caused Slatter to hang out of the cab for five minutes, staring hard at it. The others did not even turn their eyes towards it. They had other preoccupations.

John Chass was enjoying himself so much that his anxiety about business, never very deep, was entirely forgotten. The cab was like a piece of home to him, and he felt an affectionate sympathy towards all these people, as if crisis and excitement for Annish people was different in kind from any other; as a sensation in his own nervous system was different. Coo's nervous grasp of his wrist, James Slatter's fluster, Maddy's exhaustion, and the unhappy Philip in his beautiful clothes, without a sixpence in his pocket; he felt them all like his own life with its mixed sensations, amusing, sad, apprehensive. They were parts of his life in which the loss of any part would impoverish the whole, and when he smiled at Coo on his lap and said, 'Many a time you sat there, m'dear, when you thought more of sweeties than bridegrooms,' he was enjoying a sentimental memory which belonged to him much more than the young woman. She made no reply, except the same faint absentminded smile John Chass had seen on the faces of many new married brides, a little anxiety mixed with a little firmness, but never such fear and resolution as in Coo's eyes and small set mouth.

'Haw, haw!' Slatter laughed. 'Now Jawn, no squeezing. She's a married woman, remember—partly, annyway.'

Maddy turned pink and looked out of the window, but Coo continued to stare in front of her with a desperate expression.

John Chass was so reluctant to go away from the rich life of Annish into the thin and poor marionette show which was all that London could give him, that he was persuaded to tour St. Paul's with the party and even to climb to the whispering gallery, where Slatter, listening to the whispers, alarmed his family by ejaculating, 'A whisper—thon Jew's harp.'

But even John Chass realized, when he heard that Slatter intended to climb to the cross, that he could not spare the time to go with them. He said to him again, 'I must go now James—what about that little business of ours and the moiety notices?'

James thrust him back with a long arm and stared upwards at the high spiral ladders rising through the timbers of the outer dome towards the upper gallery. He was very angry. 'Look at them,' he shouted. 'They take your shillin' and tell ye to go up that monkey's walk. Begob, I won't do it—I can't. It'd kill me.'

They stood in a narrow stone cell at the bottom of a high shaft.

Maddy leant against a sloping breast of stone and took off her shoe. Coo stood beside her holding her by the puff of her sleeve and gazing furtively at her husband out of the sides of her eyes. Philip, withdrawn as far as possible from the party, stood with a grand despair. He was ashamed of it, but he could not get rid of it.

'Then let's go back, Pappy,' Maddy said, 'and we'll rest our poor feet before we see the post office this afternoon, They say it's two miles through.'

'What!' Slatter shouted. 'Go back from the dome of St. Pauls'. Aw, I'm ashamed of ye, for Gawd's sake—who'd take a gyurl on a honeymoon.'

'But Pappy——'

'Look at 'em, Jawn. There's not enough spunk between the whole lot of 'em would push a flea off their own noses.' He stared at his family with perplexity and disgust. It was true that beside the girls and Philip with their sad eyes, expecting nothing from life, Slatter with his boundless nervous energy, inexhaustible as a force of nature, his eager ambition, anxiety, seemed like a different kind of creature. He gave an ejaculation of disgust which was like a spit of contempt; then turned and seized John Chass by the coat, 'Come awn, Jawn, we'll show 'em.'

John Chass excused himself. 'I have to go back at once—I take it that it's all right about that interest, James.'

'Aw, to hell with the lot of ye. Good-bye. Here, Philly, up ye go— I'm not leaving ye behind. Up with ye now, me bucko. Ye won't find free drinks in the cross, that's wan thing.'

Philip marched to the stairs like a king going to execution and climbed rapidly out of sight. Slatter made a rush after him and hauled himself up the first short spiral, panting and gripping the rails. His bulging eyes stared upwards, his mouth hung open; he muttered to himself, 'Look up, look up, ye fule, hould on, ye fule, gawd, it's shakin'.'

After a long interval he reappeared on the tall flight above. His voice was heard rising with the stairs in a chant of terror. 'Look up, ye fule, dahm ye, ye fule, look up.' Suddenly he looked down, clung to the rails and screamed, 'Maddy, Maddy, for the love of Gawd.'

Maddy gave a loud cry and, carrying her shoe, flew up the stairs; Coo closely and silently followed. Philip, stirred from his apathy, was heard calling in anxious tones from above, 'Hold on, I'm coming.' He rattled downwards and caught Slatter under the left arm; Maddy seized him round the waist, Coo slipping behind, gripped his coat. All gave advice and consolation.

'Oh Pappy darling, for God's sake, it's not safe.'

'Shut your eyes, Pappy darling,' Coo said.

'Come down now, come down at once, oh God, oh Pappy!'

The group, bound together like one frightened, trembling creature, swayed up and down the narrow staircase. Slatter, grasping the rail in his knotted hands, hung forward panting. His crimson face dripped with the sweat of his terror.

'Come down, Pappy darling.'

'Oh, he'll be killed, he'll be killed!'

'I won't come down,' he panted. 'I've paid me shillin'. I won't come down—so ye'll have to get me up. Don't push,' his voice rose to a scream. 'Don't push, Maddy—have ye no sense at all.'

He climbed a step slowly, slipping his hands along the rail, then paused again to take breath and courage. His eyes suddenly noticed John Chass looking upwards from the well forty feet below and he shouted to him angrily, 'I'm doin' no business on me holiday.'

'But James, I don't want Mrs. Corner to be worried.'

'It's a holiday, I tell ye, a holiday—hould me Philly, quit tuggin', Coo. Aw, for Gawd's sake—it's what I suppose if ye paid a pound, they'd make ye walk the plank.'

John Chass did not reach the broker's office until half-past eleven. Mr. Sling was then in the market, but being fetched, he said that the collapse in Mosi shares was now complete. They were unsaleable at any price.

'But why is that?'

'Of course, as you know, Mr. Corner, there have been powerful interests at work.'

'Buying for control,' John Chass quoted Felix.

'That is the rumour, and it looks now as if the rumour might be true, and that control has been secured.'

'But why then have the shares collapsed?'

'Because the syndicate do not need any more.'

'But if it paid ten shillings for Mosi last week, they can't be worth nothing to-day.'

'That depends on the policy of the syndicate, Mr. Corner, and the market is not disposed to deal until the policy is known.'

'And the shares are unsaleable?'

'Half an hour ago I might have obtained a price, but not now. The rumour is that the syndicate will write off the whole ordinary capital.'

'Can they do that?'

'Certainly, they have control—a company, you understand, Mr. Corner, is a democratic institution. Anything can be done by a sufficient number of votes.'

John Chass sat gazing at Mr. Sling with an air of mild interest; and

Mr. Sling looked at John Chass with the calm but austere face of a doctor who wrestles with a layman's ignorance.

'I'm afraid, Mr. Corner, you have held on too long—I think I warned you that the shares were highly speculative.'

'Oh, yes,' John Chass said, 'it's my own fault. So there's nothing to be done?'

'Nothing—I'm afraid.'

'Good morning, Mr. Sling, I'm sorry to have wasted your time.'

'Don't mention it, Mr. Corner. I'm always glad to do anything for a client.'

John Chass was still smiling when he walked through Cornhill, he could not take this affair seriously. It seemed to him, not exactly fantastic, because of course he knew that all this business of buying and selling shares was perfectly regular and highly respectable; but romantic and also comical. He knew that his own position was serious, that all these people hurrying in every direction, in their top hats, were highly serious people, heads of households, props of Empire; but he could not feel that their business was serious, or that the place in which operations like those of the last few months, or the catastrophe of the last few days were usual, was in the same kind of world with Annish, where his father, for instance, laying out two thousand pounds on the drainage of Knockeen bog, had spoken of the money as an investment for his grandchildren.

There were eight farms on the new Knockeen including Rifty Regan's, and though their united rent was less than eighty pounds a year, they were there to see; real property. These farms were already feeding thirty or forty people. But what had he been buying during these last three months, and what had he now lost, without even knowing it? Control of what? It was no doubt a kind of power, but it was a strange kind of power, quite different from that of old John's to drain Knockeen and to put eight families into land.

It seemed to be power over values; John Chass had thought himself to be gambling, but he saw now that the transaction was not like a bet; it was more like a battle in which the defeated enemy could expect no quarter.

He looked with interest at the preoccupied, solemn faces around him and he thought, 'But they don't look like a lot of blaggards. They're more like church-wardens.'

He noticed suddenly that he was being examined. Two young men, bareheaded, were smiling at him. He returned the smile broadly, as if to say, 'Good day to you, gentlemen.' He was quite prepared, in his wide overcoat, his curly hat, his London gloves grasping an immense gold-headed malacca; with his rosy country face and beautiful whiskers, already old-fashioned, to be stared at in the city. It seemed to him still, like a white man among Zulus, that his was the correct dress for a rational creature, even if he was the only one in a wild and barbarous land.

Maddy and Coo were terrified of Philip, because, having lived close to him for years, they felt the nature of his despair; his confused bitterness which could not even find an enemy. They felt without reasoning that he was always capable of murder, out of the same spiteful misery.

That night when Slatter ordered the girls to bed, saying, 'And Philly will be up in half an hour,' Coo was in such terror that Maddy was afraid she would faint. She could not speak, and she could hardly move her arms and legs. Maddy had to undress her, wash her, and put her to bed like a baby.

Even Maddy with her unromantic commonsense, which accepted all things as they came to her, was moved to an imaginative sympathy by this dumb, helpless terror. She said, 'Come to my bed, Coo, and I'll put him off. I'll tell'm you're not fit. Pappy can eat me if he likes.'

Coo shook her head.

'You're not fit, darling. Ah, why did ye do it? I warned ye—didn't I tell you how it would be?'

Coo, as white as the sheets, whispered, 'I'm glad I did it.'

'Ah, Coo, ye needn't pretend to me. Come along to my bed and I'll tell them. Philly himself will thank ye.'

Coo knew this also; that Philip, who had not spoken to her for a week before the wedding, nor since, loathed the sight of her. But though she was in extreme terror, and too exhausted to fight it any longer, she knew also that she had deliberately produced this situation out of which there was no escape. She had bound herself to get a man or die and in all her terror she knew that she would not choose to go back into her old drifting life. Even the terror itself was something she would not be without.

Maddy was crying and begging her, 'I'll not let him near you.'

Coo shook her head.

Slatter burst in at the door. 'Here's Philly now, and out ye go Maddy. This is the end of your ould maid's cracks. Away with ye, gyurl. Haven't ye any sense of decency at all?'

Maddy ran out of the room, crying loudly. Slatter came over to Coo, kissed her forehead, and said with emotion, 'Aw, m'dear, ye've got more spunk than Maddy, annyway; and we'll make a man of Philly yet between us, won't we? or make another wan, begob. Gawd bless ye, me wee gyurlie. Now then, Philly, I'm goin' and I've no doubt ye'll think better of the wee gyurlie by the mornin'. Do your jawb man, and leave the rest to Gawd. He's the fella that knows how to work the oracle—and faith, I've seen some that would as soon have gone to bed with a baboon on their weddin' nights that got up as lovin' as Castor and Pollux.'

He went out, but after closing the door, he pushed in his head again by an afterthought and said, with tearful emotion, 'Aw, the blessin' of Gawd on both of ye, for I love ye, me poor children, and mind when ye get me a boy, he'll be the richest man in Annish by a good thousand pounds a year, if not more.' The door closed softly.

Philip, dressed in his new silk dressing-gown, and the long night-shirt chosen by Slatter, came to the bedside and said, 'Well, you've got what you wanted—but aren't you afraid I'll cut your throat?' He spoke with an English accent which showed that his temper was at the worst.

Coo, too frightened to speak, shook her head.

'You aren't?' Philip was insistent. 'Then, my God, you ought to be. Do you think I'm afraid of being hung?'

Coo again shook her head. This pleased Philip, who said with great dignity, 'Oh, you do know something about me, after all.'

Coo reached out her arm and tried to catch his hand, but at her touch, he jumped back. 'No, no, none of that. I'm not such a fool.' He reflected a moment, glancing gloomily at Coo. Then he said, 'Have you got any money?'

'No, Philly, ye know that Pappy never gives us any money.'

Philip's gloom became deeper. He said angrily, 'Ye think I can't be trusted not to make a beast of myself.'

'Oh no, Philly.'

'I don't even like the filthy stuff.'

There was a long silence. Philip stared at Coo with silent hatred, a general hatred concentrated on the nearest human creature. Then he said, 'I've half a mind to do it now'—he stepped forward and took her by the hair, pulling her head back and raising her chin. 'I'll cut your throat as wide as a melon.' He put his finger across her neck, and Coo lay looking up at him with fixed eyes.

'I don't need to be drunk,' he said, and then, 'Has Pappy a flask?'

'He has a flask in his bag.' An idea struck Coo and she said, 'Would you like a drink, Philly?'

'No, and you wouldn't give it to me if I did.'

'If I had it I would.'

'If ye had it——'

'Aw, Philly, I'd do annything to make ye happy.'

'Then why did ye marry me?'

Coo began to cry. 'Aw, Philly, I can't bear to see ye so unhappy—and in your new dressing-gown.'

'Don't cry, for God's sake. We've got enough without it.'

389

Coo swallowed her sobs and then, with an heroic gesture, she jumped out of bed and pulled on her dressing-gown. She turned her pale and tear-stained face towards him, 'I'll get ye a drink, Philly.'

'I'd believe it if I saw it.'

'Wait now, only wait a minute.' Coo rushed into the passage. She had no idea where she could get a drink, only the feeling, generated by desperation, that it was possible for her, at that moment, to do the impossible.

She ran towards Maddy's room. But suddenly she recalled the dining-room and the side table on which, as in most small commercial hotels, there stood a row of bottles marked with the names of their owners; half finished bottles of port. brandy and whisky. She turned round and flew down the stairs. The dining-room was empty and dark, but a faint light came from the street lamps through the dirty lace curtains on the windows.

Coo made her way to the side table and snatched two bottles. One proved to contain vinegar but the other was half full of brandy. In three minutes she was back in the bedroom, watching Philip take his first drink.

He drank with great dignity, sitting at the dressing-table and as he raised the tooth glass to his lips, he said, 'Not that I need the beastly stuff. but why shouldn't I have it?'

He looked grandly at Coo, who had crept quietly into bed. 'This won't save you.'

He attended then to the drink, pouring it through his throat every five minutes in half tumblerfuls. After each gulp he sat gloomily waiting for its effect. It had not the bite of poteen, but it warmed him, it quickened his blood, his cells, and from the drunken, excited cells, the stimulated blood, rose up the passion and the optimism of nature itself, the peacock's vanity, the monkey's curiosity, and sentimental tenderness. the energy and life of the fungus under a cellar which splits the pavement to reach the light and air.

Even as Coo watched, Philip's pose changed from pompous self-consciousness to the swagger of self-confidence. He relaxed in his chair and after half an hour, when the bottle was almost empty, noticing Coo with surprise, he said with good natured condescension, 'What are you thinking about?'

'Aw, Philly, ye could do annything ye liked.'

Philip was surprised by this mark of penetration in Coo, and it touched his heart. He smiled upon her and approached the bed. 'That's very nice of you Coo, but ye know, I haven't done very much.'

'But look at all the prizes ye won at school.'

'Oh school prizes, that's not saying anything. No Coo, I haven't done much—not yet.'

'But ye will, Philly.'

'You're a nice gyurl, Coo.' He was speaking Annish again.

'Aw Philly, I'd do annything for ye.'

Philip was slipping into bed. He said, 'But between ourselves there's not much I couldn't do.'

Cleeve, though he talked treason to Stella, had no intention of being involved in the pro-Boer campaign. He had too much to do. He avoided Porfit, therefore, and took a detached attitude to the war. When he met a patriot, he made rude jokes about the army, and when he met a violent pro-Boer, he attacked Boer nationalism. One day, however, the Liberal agent for Porriton, Captain Rankin, meeting him in Motcombe, told him that he was expected at the next meeting. Porfit had put down his name for the platform party, as representative of Oxford University.

Captain Rankin, a retired sailor with a wooden leg; a man as broad, heavy and red as a Devon bull, was enraged by some battle in which the British had been victorious. He shouted, 'I'd go out and fight for the Boers myself if it wasn't for this damned leg.'

'Yes,' Cleeve answered in his high, fluting voice. 'It's an attractive idea, though I suppose one would need one's Keatings. How odd it is, Captain, that no one wants to fight for the Kaffirs and the Zulus. I suppose it's because they haven't got a flag. What do you say to one black bottom reversed improper, on its native ground, triumphing in passive resistance over one sjambok gory. Motto: Divided we stand, united we can stand anything.'

Captain Rankin, a Wesleyan preacher in direct line from such western heroes as the Earl of Granport, concluded once more that Oxford University was the destruction of young souls. He was not sure that he wanted such frivolous persons on the Liberal platform. But Porfit's recommendation was already all powerful in the division. He shook hands warmly with the boy, three days later, when the platform party had gathered for the meeting. He felt then the comradeship of heroes on a forlorn hope.

They stood in a small vestry, full of music stands, listening to the yells of the enemy from the road outside. There were fourteen present, but they still waited for Porfit, the speaker, who was driving from Porriton.

Captain Rankin, hearing the yells, spread out his chest towards them, like a hero, and on all the faces of the committee, even on Chorley's, could be seen the consciousness of the heroic moment. Chorleys' beard had assumed a Cavalier angle; Rankin's blunt nose stood up like a bulldog's, displaying its broad nostrils. Only Cleeve, who was wearing a large chrysanthemum in his beautiful suit, had an easy and natural smile. But it was obvious that Cleeve did not feel himself concerned either in the heroism of his party, or the screams of the enemy.

The hall belonged to a Methodist chapel. It was a small tin building in a muddy lane about half a mile from Motcombe village. It held two hundred. Captain Rankin, after his week's canvass, after seeing all his posters torn down, and after being abused by one of the staunchest Liberals in the village, a woman who screamed that he was a traitor to her poor boys in khaki, had expected a small audience. He hoped for fifty and feared to see half a dozen.

But it was Saturday afternoon. Already two brakes had arrived from Porriton, with Union Jacks on the box rails, and kegs of beer among the passengers' legs. The local train to Motcombe had brought a hundred from Granport, all town workers; and all from the poorest classes. It was these people, twisted, short legged, hollow cheeked, with greasy skins full of blackheads, dressed not in the rough earth-coloured corduroys of the natives, but in shabby blues and greys, worn out Sunday suits, who swarmed into the Motcombe pubs that afternoon, and afterwards, with a forest of Union Jacks, set off for the Methodist hall as if on a religious crusade.

Stella had not promised to attend, because she was giving all her time to Jarvis for the few days of his leave. But Jarvis was still much sought after, and that afternoon he had been carried off to shoot at Porriton Hall. Stella was therefore free to go to the meeting.

Stella's own political convictions were still indefinite. She had avoided all discussion of the war with Jarvis. But he had talked much of it; he was enraged by the first defeats and eager to be at the front; and since she could not feel with him, she was still more disgusted with what she called politics.

She went to the meeting only because Cleeve was going to be there and he had asked her to go.

She went early to get a good seat from which she could see the speakers. She could never take interest in a meeting unless she could see the speakers, how they looked, dressed and behaved themselves.

She was surprised to find the hall full, but a young farmer in the front row, one of her own tenants, got up at once to give her a seat, "'Ere you are, miss.'

'But I can't take your seat.'

'It's all the same to me, miss,' a speech truly gallant because it was intended to relieve the lady of all obligation. Stella thanked him with the broad, dazzling smile which she gave to her favourite tenants, and he disappeared on creaking boots.

There were soon loud shouts from the back of the hall. 'Down with the traitors!' and a boyish voice cried something about 'old Kruger's bloody bastards.'

Stella turned red with surprise; and several of her neighbours, farmers, gamekeepers, turned round with raised eyebrows. They were good Radicals, but in their manners more conservative than Stella herself. One of then called out, 'Hush there, none of that,' and added that there were ladies present, but he was answered by rude shouts and a remark about the redness of his nose.

Ten minutes later, Rankin and Chorley, warned by the police that the crowd was getting out of hand, decided to open the meeting at once, and to keep it amused until the chief speaker should arrive.

They filed out upon the platform and took their seats upon a double line of cane chairs. The minister, a tall dark man, very like Henry Irving, advanced to the table and solemnly gazed upon the audience. There was at this moment a complete silence. Probably most of the audience was holding its breath. The minister opened his mouth and said, 'My friends——'

Immediately such an orchestral roar, screech and bellow of sound burst out that it had, by violence of shock, a physical effect on the hearers. Stella turned as white as her blouse. She had never heard such a terrifying sound before. Chorley also turned pale; and Rankin, scarlet. The minister glared fiercely; Cleeve smiled and crossed his legs with arrogant nonchalance. But in fact Cleeve did not know what he was doing. His smile was like the unconscious grin of a terrified puppy; he was shocked out of his senses.

Chorley now rose beside the minister and held up his hand in a gesture of commanding authority. In the same instant, every window in the hall was simultaneously knocked in and a shower of stones and bottles fell on the platform.

A policeman was heard shouting from the back door of the stage and the committee began to file out, but Captain Rankin, Chorley and the minister, not seeing or hearing the policeman, kept their places.

Cleeve jumped up and pushed forward beside the minister. He was still grinning, but the grin, by a natural nervous reaction, was one of rage. The puppy had flown at the offensive monster. He did not even notice the stones. The noise had already lessened, partly because the mob outside, now that the platform party was in the vestry, had turned upon the vestry; partly because the country people, enraged by the stones, had risen and thrown out the strangers at the back of the room.

Cleeve's high voice, like Cocky's, had the penetration of a woman's. Phrases reached Stella in her front seat, 'The patient and attentive hearing of both sides—the sense of fair play, so truly English.'

Stella could hear that Cleeve was talking what she called his nonsense, and she thought suddenly, 'How like Harry he is.'

393

It was true, not so much because of Cleeve's colouring, but of his pose, and at the moment of his fierce contempt for the mob.

Stella was suddenly more afraid for Cleeve than for herself. She was in agony for him.

The fight at the end of the hall was nearly over; the townsmen were being thrown out. But they were a quick-witted lot. They ran round to the windows and in a moment they were jumping down upon the platform itself. Before Stella's eyes, a little yellow faced man in a blue suit grappled with the minister. Captain Rankin caught hold of Chorley and dragged him through the back door. Then a mass of yelling hooligans charged across the platform; and Stella, knocked down by a flying body, was tangled in a chair. Something struck her a heavy blow in the back and she tumbled forward on her hands. A man crept past her on all fours, lifted the fringe of curtain at the edge of the platform, and disappeared. She crawled after him into the dark low space between the stage, full of carpenter's work. A boy's voice, close above her head was screaming, 'Set the bloody place afire; burn the swine.'

Stella felt sick and exhausted. What exhausted her was not the noise and the danger but something quite novel to her experience; the presence of cruelty. She could hardly move forward; she was fainting.

A voice said, "'Ere you are, missy.' Hands lifted her upon a chair, and put a glass of water to her lips. She smiled her tenants' smile and said, 'Thanks awfully.'

She was sitting in a small vestry behind a matchboard partition. Dusty music was piled against the wall among chairs; a cottage piano stood beside her. Ten or a dozen men were crowded into the narrow space remaining; they stood for the most part in silence with the peculiar resigned gloom of men in a tight corner. Their voices when they spoke could only be heard in gaps between the thumps and yells outside. Two or three in the background were talking excitedly together; somebody near Stella said in a flat, gloomy voice, 'A put up job—Granport chaps.'

'Yass and Porriton—and 'oo paid for the brakes?'

The noise was now at its maximum; it was like an avalanche mixed with thunder claps and the screams of a horse fight. The happy warriors of Granport were smashing the iron sides of the hall with forms.

The men scattered from in front of Stella to push the piano across the door. She saw suddenly that one of the excited youngsters in the corner was Cleeve. He was lying across a chair with his head stooped forward sideways. Blood was trickling down his forehead and his long fair hair hung down to the end of his nose. But he was talking all the time to the two others who were also talking among themselves.

394

Stella went over to him and dabbed the wound with her handkerchief. Cleeve, looking up and recognising her, said "Scuse me, I can't get up, it's my leg.'

'Never mind—you'll be all right.' She had to put her lips close to his ear to make herself heard. Cleeve exclaimed in his angry, mocking voice, 'Your friends' arguments were distinctly *ad hominem*.'

'They're not my friends. They're just hooligans from Granport.'

'Well, patriots then.' His excited, angry gace was full of amazement. He could still scarcely believe that such people existed in the world; dangerous and spiteful people capable of answering reason with stones. 'It's so damn silly—what did they think they were doing—there's no sense——' Suddenly, to Stella's dismay, he gave a sob. But in his furious excitement and rage he did not even notice it. He had forgotten himself. 'But if they think they're going to get away with it, they're damn well mistaken. It's what Porfit has been saying all along—the Empire's simply a lot of money grabbing millionaires and War Office generals, looking for somebody to try their new toy guns on—it's got to be smashed. Its murder.'

Outside the flimsy door, already pierced by a fence rail, the voices of the attacking party could be heard. 'Now then, boys, this ought to do it, all together.'

It was obvious that the young factory hands were having the most glorious holiday of their lives; sport and pleasure combined.

A terrific crash carried the door off its hinges and made the piano stagger. Two young men, with cheering, laughing faces, were suddenly seen behind the piano. Both were instantly knocked senseless by the defenders.

'It's so s-silly,' Cleeve muttered. 'Really, you know, Stella, it's absolutely mad. It simply can't go on.'

Another charge threw the piano on its face but luckily the police reinforcements arrived two minutes later and cleared the hall.

Cleeve and Stella went into the minister's house, where the platform party had already taken refuge. A doctor was found to bandage the wounded, and Cleeve was carried off at once to be put to bed. Benskin, who arrived with a carriage to rescue Stella less than half an hour after the riot, found that she had already gone to Bellavista with the Chorleys. She felt that Cleeve needed her, because no one else would have the sense to keep him in bed, no one else, certainly not Lucy or her father, knew how excitable and sensitive Cleeve was; how much he needed looking after.

But she found the Chorleys' drawing-room crowded from door to door, chiefly with Radical ladies who were all talking at once. She could see Cleeve, still bleeding through his bandage, standing beside

395

Porfit in the midst of an admiring group, making an excited speech. He had forgotten that he was to rest; that twenty minutes before he had been unable to walk. His high voice reached her, with it's bantering tone and quiver of rage. 'It was the patriot's flank attack that won the day and cut off our line of retreat—the thing was a neat bit of tactical work.'

'Who planned it?' somebody asked near Stella; and somebody else answered, 'Of course old Porriton—or Benskin.'

'Benskin, I should think,' Cleeve cried. His mind jumped at the name as a hand flies to a stick when the fight begins. 'Obviously Benskin, the noble patriots were all from the shipyards and the printing works—he's a director of both and he paid for the charabangs too.' Porfit smiled affectionately at his new disciple.

Stella, unable to approach him, walked impatiently up and down near the windows, waiting for Chorley or Lucy to arrive. She felt disgusted with all this noise, confusion, the political chatter; all the distraction and confusion which had ruined her time of happiness, so long looked forward to, with Harry.

On all faces round her she saw the exaggerated expressions of people drunk with excitement; and she heard Cleeve's voice again.

'The first thing to do is to smash the Liberal imperialists—people like Benskin—they're the worst.'

Her brows drew together in a frown. She felt a furious impatience with all these excited people; but her real anger, growing within her, as it seemed for a week past, was a general hatred directed simply against the cause of her frustration. It was like a hatred of her body so that she was aware of it not as anger but as a violent, fretting discomfort. It was like the protest of her womanhood against the interruption of its calm, leisurely purpose.

Suddenly she saw Harry Jarvis threading his way through the groups with his agile, quick step. His face was set in an expression of cool contempt. He felt himself among the traitors, and now that Britain was suffering defeat, now that she was friendless, he was fiercely loyal.

He saw Stella and came towards her. 'Are you all right?'

'Yes, but Cleeve was nearly killed.'

'Why on earth did you go to a pro-Boer meeting?'

Stella's anger burst out of her. It found its natural object in the man she loved, because she loved him, because her whole being was always concerned with him. 'Because I'm sick of the war—the sooner we stop it the better.'

'And take a licking from the Boers.'

'I don't care. It ought to be stopped. It's wrong. You don't like war, do you? You don't want people to be killed?'

'The Boers started it.'

'No, they didn't—it was people like Uncle Theo. It's a disgusting war. Against a few poor farmers.'

She was carried away by her rage against the war and against Harry who stood there with his surprised, angry stare. Now that she had given rein to her secret anger, she remembered all the arguments against the war that she had heard from the Chorleys and Porfit, and seized upon them for the expression of it. For Stella political ideas were weapons or solaces. 'Anybody can see that it's a mean war—what would you say if the Germans said they wanted our coal mines and therefore they had the right to conquer us.'

'But Stella——'

'Oh, of course you won't admit it. You can't expect a soldier to see the biggest truth.'

Her fury astonished Jarvis and now, seeing that it was directed against him, his expression changed. He looked at her with a kind of mournful and humble surprise. He did not know what to say. But this, of course, only increased Stella's pathological rage which required perhaps, according to nature, a punch on the nose; or words of equivalent violence to the nerves. 'You think I'm a fool, but it's you who are the fool to have anything to do with this war.'

People had begun to notice the scene. Heads turned towards them and Jarvis said nervously, 'Hadn't we better go?'

'You can go. Go and tell your friend Theo that his plan to smash up the meeting was quite successful.'

Nevertheless she went out beside him and they got into the Manor carriage where Benskin was waiting for her. Then she had to be silent and her anger swelled up once more. She stared at Harry on the seat before her with furious contempt. How silly he looked in his perplexity. What a fool he was to be used by men like Benskin.

Jarvis' orders were to sail on the twenty-fifth. He was to take charge of a detachment. Stella, Benskin and John Chass went to Southampton with him. Cleeve excused himself.

The little party in the railway carriage was embarrassed. The two older men knew that there was a quarrel between the lovers. The announcement of the engagement, which was to have been made that morning, had not appeared. It had been stopped by wire. Stella had spent last evening, Jarvis' last evening in England, with the Chorleys talking treason. She had suddenly become violently anti-war, and even now, while she sat calmly in her corner, she had an angry, obstinate look about her lips and forehead.

On the other hand, neither she nor Jarvis had spoken of their affairs to anybody, and their attitude did not invite question.

'Well now, I hear Cleeve is going to speak again to-morrow,' John Chass said.

Stella looked sharply at him and said that Cleeve had been asked to speak.

'I thought he had to go back to college.'

Stella was silent. She disdained to talk about Cleeve or the war with John Chass, who could take neither seriously. She had, in fact, begged Cleeve not to speak at the next meeting, until his head was healed. But Porfit was anxious that he should appear at once while he was still in his bandages. It would be good for the cause.

As for Cleeve's returning to Oxford, Stella troubled about it as little as Cleeve himself who had written to the college authorities to say that he was not well enough to return at the beginning of term. 'And I don't care if I never go back at all,' he told the Chorley party. 'What rot it is to talk about the meaning of justice and the ideal state while people like Benskin make wars to put money in their pockets.'

'I hope you won't go to this meeting, my dear,' John Chass said. 'The last was bad enough. Politics are dirty work for ladies.'

Stella, feeling as if Cleeve had been attacked, fired up. 'What about business?' She struck at both the older men but John Chass cheerfully agreed with her, 'Or business either.'

'Cleeve is honest about politics,' she said.

'So he is—why not, it's an exciting time—but I hope he won't get into any more trouble.'

There was a long silence. Stella looked cautiously at Jarvis, opposite her, sitting forward with knees apart, chin up, arms crossed, as if riding the train, and she thought angrily, 'He's enjoying his war—he thinks I'm not serious—but he'll find out that he's wrong.'

Her throat swelled with the revengeful bitterness of a woman against the enemies of her happiness. Her very cells seemed to say, 'What have we done to be hindered in our peaceful needs and honest desires.' She felt that somebody must be punished. She thought, 'How I hate men.'

Jarvis was not conscious of enjoyment, but only of a great moment. Just as he had been astonished and exalted by his unexpected triumph, his sudden greatness; not only for his own sake, but because it was a tribute to the moral dignity of that scheme of things in which he trusted, so he now felt the war, not only as a chance of glory, but as a stroke of redeeming providence, bringing the country back from foolish extravagance, foolish æsthetics, to stern duty and responsibilities. Men were being killed. No one could go on playing the fool in the presence of death.

His arms tightened across his chest; his body stiffened. He thought, 'I'm seeing this perhaps for the last time—and Stella.'

His eyes turned to her with an intense, longing devotion. He thought

398

bitterly of the foolish quarrel which had spoilt their last day. Naturally the poor child had been upset by all the talky-talky. He should have had more consideration for her. What did women know of politics?

The train rolled into Southampton. Rain was falling.

Benskin and John Chass said good-bye in the cab, and left the lovers to be alone on the quay. They stood in the pouring rain while the men already wearing their incongruous white helmets above glistening overcoats, mounted the steep gangways. All round them good-byes were being said. Stella had wondered how she could bear this moment. She did not know what to say to him. She supposed that he might be killed and that then she would feel like a murderess. She did not know whether the acute pain in her breast which she felt now standing beside him, so ridiculous with his little moustache, his gallant attitude, his absurd, childish ideas, was from a love which nothing could break, or from pity.

They talked of indifferent matters; the weather and the mails. They were still involved in their quarrel; deeply embarrassed.

A small, dapper sergeant came to attention close beside Jarvis and saluted; causing the rain drops to fly from his nose and the trim points of his long, waxed moustache.

'Someone wants you,' Stella said, and she saw in Jarvis' face, turned towards her with humble adoration, the flash of resolution like steel stiffening a sheath. His very mournfulness changed its nature to the acceptance of a soldier ready to challenge his fate. He said to the man, 'Just coming, Sergeant,' and turned to her. "Fraid I've got to go—it's been good these five days.'

Stella felt a sudden explosion of feeling, terror, pity, a confusion which nearly overwhelmed her. She stared at Harry in silence.

The lilt of the band came to her.

Cook's son, Duke's son, son of a hundred kings,
Twenty thousand fighting men off to Table Bay.

The tune brought her back to the moment; her nervous agitation did not take the shape of misery but heroic tragedy; men were being killed; and on the idea of tragedy, she rode like a warrior going to war.

'Good-bye, my darling,' Harry said; the sergeant turned discreetly away.

'Good-bye, Harry, and don't get killed. It's not worth it in a war like this.' She defied him to think her views unimportant.

They looked at each other, hesitated, but they did not kiss. It was too soon after the quarrel. Their quarrel had been deep because they really loved.

399

In the cab John Chass had seized his chance to obtain information. Felix, who had been expected also with the party, but who seemed to have missed his train, had strongly advised an enquiry of Benskin himself. 'Go to the fountain head,' he had said. 'In business it's just as easy to get information from a good source as a bad.'

'I'm told,' John Chass had said, 'that the Mosi syndicate want you and Chorley for directors.'

Benskin's face became blank. He had been expecting some appeal from the Corners for the last week, and he was surprised that it had not come through Jarvis. He said, 'I know very little about these activities.'

'Nussbaum is coming to see you to-day.'

'Yes, but he hasn't seen me yet.'

'The shares have collapsed.'

'Have they?'

'My broker says that you mean to liquidate the old companies.'

'If they're already bankrupt, I suppose that won't be difficult.'

Benskin's cool tone surprised John Chass. His eyebrows rose slightly; he looked at his friend with a humourous pursing of lips, as if to say, 'What's he up to now, the rascal.'

'If they're worth nothing,' he said, 'it rather looks as if I'm worth nothing.'

Benskin was silent. He might have been stone deaf.

'Or less than nothing,' John Chass said with the voice of a man who examines a strange natural phenomenon with detached interest.

'A pity they couldn't have a fine afternoon,' Benskin said.

'It is indeed,' John Chass agreed. His good humour overrode the least appearance of humiliation at a snub. His social flair was still unimpaired. 'We'll hope that the next war is in June, for the sake of the ladies' hats, anyway.'

Both gazed out of the window at the wet streets and bedraggled crowd. Southampton was full of soldiers' relations come to say good-bye. In spite of the rain, all these people had an air of enjoyment. Even the women with tear-stained faces and swollen eyes were grave with that kind of excited solemnity which one sees in people taking part in great events, in pilgrimages. Only the small children and the dogs, unhappy little animals dragged through the rain and mud, seemed to know that they were tired, cold and wet.

Stella appeared at the cab door and Benskin jumped out to hand her in. She was crying so violently that he was embarrassed. He did not know what to say or do. But John Chass began to talk about the war; saying that it was going better at last; thank God for Roberts and Kitchener. He did not look at Stella and his talk was not directed at her, either by obvious avoidance of her case or obvious reference. John

Chass did not say that victory was now sure and that Jarvis would soon be home again. He knew that consolation at that moment would have fallen on her nerves like scent on a raw cut. But his speech filled the cab with the idea of marching, fighting, the idea of enthusiastic armies under competent leaders, and the girl, looking out of the window and discreetly wiping her nose, felt her own part in a time of glory. But she did not think of the warlike operations of Cocky in Africa; but of Porfit and Cleeve and the Chorleys in England. When John Chass said the words, campaign flank attack, generalship, they called up to her imagination little Porfit standing in the Bellavista drawing-room, with his shrewd face full of energy and cunning, while he spoke of the tactics of the opposition, the campaign in Porriton, and the need of leadership in the Liberal Party.

Meanwhile her tears, careless of unrelated enquiries, continued to flow for the cruelly used Cocky, until finding leisure to attend to them she noticed that they were not required, and stopped them at once.

Benskin said to her with timid sympathy, 'You'll be glad of your holiday to-morrow.'

'What holiday?'

'I thought it was to-morrow that you were going away?'

'Oh that! I'd forgotten about it. What a nuisance.'

Helen and Stella a month before had accepted an invitation to a house party near London.

'But I can't go. I've got to be at the Chorleys' every day for the next month at least.'

'At the Chorleys'?'

'Yes, I'm working there—Lucy and I are doing all Mr. Porfit's correspondence.'

'Your mother will be disappointed.'

'She won't mind. Cobbie's going to be there.'

Stella did not speak with contempt, but she made the statement as a busy person says of a child, 'She's got her toy.'

Benskin, looking at the girl's face still tear-stained, still flushed with a mysterious excitement; at the thick eyebrows and thick lips set now in resolution which would have seemed brutal if it had not been for the high raised chin; her mother's gestures changed from the insolence of the flirt to the arrogance of the rebel; knew that argument or expostulation would be stupid. It was a time when no young person could be expected to hear reason.

At Motcombe the Chorleys' brougham was already waiting in the drive. Cleeve and Lucy sat in it. They had not entered the house and when Benskin asked them to come in to tea, Cleeve said with the same important grown-up air of Stella, 'I'm afraid there's no time.'

Cleeve had a bandage on his head; but when he jumped out of the brougham to hand Stella in, Benskin had never seen his narrow face look more animated.

'How is your head now?' Stella asked him anxiously; and Lucy, half-leaning over him from the carriage, said, 'He oughtn't to be rushing about like this.'

Cleeve laughed and said that he was perfectly well. He was the centre of the group; the wounded soldier among his admiring friends. This was the first wounded soldier that any of them had seen in their lives.

'But we're expecting your father.'

'Mr. Porfit is waiting for him at the village,' Lucy said like the aide-de-camp defending a General from importunity.

'We must go,' Stella said decidedly, climbing in. 'Why did you wait for me?'

She was so much disturbed to think that the commander-in-chief, Porfit, should have been kept waiting for his tea that she forgot to say good-bye to Benskin. As the brougham drove away the three voices inside were heard together in a chatter of excitement. Benskin and John Chass climbed up the steps of the Manor. They both had a pensive air, alone with each other and not confident of anything.

Helen had been entertaining Nussbaum, Ingles and Cobden for the last hour. She was in the highest spirits in the presence of two lovers, and Ingles, more exciting than either, because he was a stranger to her and because he was one of those men whose very voice and glance tell women like Helen that they are womanizers.

She thought him vulgar; one of those city men who had begun to appear about the beginning of the gold boom, with a self-assurance and a smartness of dress peculiar apparently to the type. But she delighted in the vulgarity of brassy men as she delighted in the sensitive nerves of Cobbie. Each thrilled an appropriate nerve, like the tuba in the orchestra which always made her tears flow, even when she laughed at herself, and the violins which stirred tremors in her flesh.

Benskin and John Chass were two more instruments, making possibly a new theme. There was Benskin's jealousy, simple-minded as a watch dog's, glaring out on all sides; and John Chass' absurd mid-Victorian gallantry, to be played upon. She was inspired; she had never been more beautiful, witty, charming; more skilful in those changes of voice which serve a clever woman to display the peacock feathers of her mind, as the turn of her waist, arm or thigh shows off her frock.

'But haven't you seen our latest masterpiece, Mr. Ingles?'

'I congratulated Mr. Benskin at the christening.' The brassy young man curled up his lips at her. Helen's quick smile and side glance at once approved his jape and made it a private joke between them;

402

caused Nussbaum to look down at the ground, wrinkling his nostrils in fastidious disgust; Cobden to stare at the intruder with a kind of hollow, timid rage, while she was already saying with a grave and enthusiastic voice, 'I meant the Lawrence.'

She approached the picture with the steps and pose of reverent delight which gave the bust and hips their best projection and by raising the chin and eyes, showed off mouth and eyebrows. 'The children are such darlings.'

Suddenly she turned, skilfully throwing back her frock, so that it twisted round her knees; she stood in the pose favoured by the court photographers, in the shape of a thistle wineglass, narrow below, wide at the hips and breasts, the figure of contemporary admiration. She looked at the semi-circle of her men. 'Family groups are always so delightful,' then with a change of voice, not satirical but meditative, 'At least, in that period.' Smiling at Ingles, she added, 'Rather fast, I suppose you'd say,' but quickly turned to Nussbaum, 'You can feel the woman under the muslin, can't you, but I suppose she wasn't wearing much in those good old times.' A slight emphasis on the first you changed the expression of all the men in a characteristic manner, making Ingles' grin sidelong, Nussbaum turn a shade yellower. more wrinkled about the nose and mouth; and John Chass slightly raise his eyebrows. He was actually disconcerted. Benskin turned sharply on his toe, a half turn away, as if to leave the hall; a half turn back, as if pulled by a string.

To him the exhibition was disquieting. For the last two months he had noticed a change in Helen, a reversion to her merry widow period. She had begun to flirt again, even with Cobden. Benskin had cured her once before of that folly, and he had no doubt that she would be checked again by the least appearance of danger to her position and her comfort. But he felt always a sickness in his heart when he saw this beautiful, accomplished woman, who had realized for him the great lady of his imagination, practising on such as Ingles or Cobden.

When the dressing-bell cut short Helen's comedy and the party dispersed, he went into Helen's room. She turned to him with a look of comedy surprise and asked, 'Not now, Theo?'

His grave look reproached her. At once her smile became timid, pleading. She looked like the village maiden, dependent on the cruel lover's whims. She said, 'Do you mind my going to the Kellys'?'

Benskin hesitated. He wanted to say, 'Not unless Cobden is there,' but he saw or felt in Helen an expectation of some such question; and his instinct, in such a conflict, was not to do the expected.

'I suppose Mrs. Epps will be there,' he said.

'But I won't play bridge with her—not again. I'll have a good excuse in baby.'

Benskin was startled as if by an explosion. His eyes shifted quickly, staring at his wife's less than a foot away. They regarded him with a calm look of power. She did not even defy him.

'You don't mind if I take baby? The poor little mite wants a change of air—and of course both the nurses will go. Lady Kelly has very good nurseries.'

Benskin felt like a commander brought to a decisive battle on ground of which all the maps have proved wrong. He said mildly, pensively, 'It's rather a new idea of yours, isn't it?'

'Well, Stella isn't coming, you see—that made room for nurse, and I never liked being separated from baby for a whole week.'

Benskin did not ask why, in that case, she had arranged the visit, because he knew that she would have a dozen plausible answers. Besides, it did not touch the real strategical problem. That lay deeper. He could not yet grasp it. He looked again at Helen, who, still tender, affectionate, put out a hand to take an imaginary fluff from his lapel. She said, 'I must really speak to Harris. He doesn't brush you properly.'

'Is it wise to take Foley on a journey like this at three months?'

'It's only that I don't like to leave him—while he's so small.' She kissed him suddenly. 'Don't look so blue, Theo. It's only for three weeks.' Her voice was chaffing and skittish. Again he looked at her and felt the same profound uncertainty. Her bold, gay look seemed to triumph over him; not crudely, but with a cheerful, friendly manner of one who wins a game. It increased his disquietude with a sensation that he did not analyse. But he could not say any more. He went thoughtfully to his dressing-room.

The sensation was very like that which had once assailed him when, in floating his first company, he had been told that his assayer had been in prison for a trivial fraud. It was something larger than fear of failure; a doubt of himself, of his aims, of the very nature of possibility. He had thought that assayer secured by self-interest as well as professional honour. But it seemed that the man was full of mysterious weakness and irrational motives, that you could not depend on him even to look after his own interests.

He felt rather than understood, while he stood in his dressing-room, hearing through the door Helen's polite but condescending voice as she spoke to her maid, the sense of instability deeper than superficial change. It was as though everything, which he valued in the world had begun to slip, to crack, to bulge; so that he could not get a firm hold of any part of it. Stella had eluded him. The girl whose firm sound character had seemed as dependable as English oak, had suddenly become mysterious; so that he could not even argue with her. He had no hold there at all. What was Helen's real nature? Had she anything solid; anything constant in her, except appetites, tastes, passions, wrapped up in a bag called the fashion: the fashion in frocks, and the fashion in morals, which changed every day. It was obvious that she meant to use his son as a weapon against him, but his sense of insecurity went deeper than that new anxiety.

He felt uncertain even of himself. He, too, seemed to be losing something essential to his quality as Theodore Benskin; the very character and purpose of his energy.

He was silent and preoccupied all the evening; and in the morning, after Helen's departure with the baby, her maid, the nurses, two carriages full of luggage, he walked about the gardens instead of attending to his work. Now and then his secretary or Ingles came to him for some instruction, but he answered always, 'Don't ask me to make up your minds for you. I've heard quite enough arguments on all sides.'

He examined the house from different angles; carefully inspected the gardens, with a critical and enquiring air.

Felix Corner appeared in the drive on foot and extremely dusty. He had written to Benskin, suggesting a meeting to discuss the Mosi, a note to which Benskin had as yet sent no answer.

Felix was staying at Bellavista and he had walked over from Porfit's committee-room in Motcombe. Felix had intended to appeal to Porfit on behalf of Cleeve, pointing out that the boy's education would be ruined if he rushed about the country addressing political meetings instead of going back to college. In fact, the college authorities, if they heard of his pro-Boer speeches, would probably take a severe view of his absence. But he had not yet made his appeal for various reasons upon which he reflected now as he strolled thoughtfully under Benskin's avenue. 'Porfit, I suppose, would say his cause is more urgent.' He stopped on the fresh gravel, gazing mournfully at the clear, pale, English sky, neither blue nor white, in which clouds as formless as milk drops in a pail of water hung suspended, clouds without edge but a definite middle, a body, an individuality. It occurred to Felix that the affair was immensely complicated, that Porfit would not understand his arguments, that Cleeve, caught up in the first ideal excitement of his life, would pay no attention to them, and that he was not quite sure if his own sympathies did not lie the same way.

He walked towards the Manor. He felt that kind of despair which is the intelligent acceptance of futility; a calm hopelessness in which a man, having no sharp pain on which to centre his courage, feels lassitude and death in every cell.

'Good morning, Mr. Corner.'

He stopped, surprised to find himself already under the trees of the park. Benskin was standing at the side of the drive, looking at him with a sharp expression. The fear of a petition, an appeal, interrupting his train of reflection, annoyed him.

Felix, who had forgotten his purpose in coming to the Manor, gazed solemnly at the financier and said, 'Good morning.' He reflected, seeking for a polite remark, 'I admire your avenue.'

'It must have been planted by some of your people for a manor house.'

'Very likely.' Felix raised his head, looking down the avenue at the house. He stared at it through his spectacles.

Benskin came to his side and followed his glance. 'What do you think of it?'

'A period piece,' Felix said.

'That's what I wanted.'

'It's strange how a period shows itself even in a thing like that—you could write a volume on that house.'

'There is a booklet—perhaps you would like to see it.'

'The confusion of ideas,' Felix murmured over his beard. 'The vague, imbecile egotism—the attempt to look important—the all-pervading vulgarity. You could even write a description of the architect's mind. You can see his idea of architecture is not something constructed according to certain laws for a certain purpose; for use and for beauty; but self-advertisement. You can see him when he got the commission, saying, "Hooray, here's a job to build a millionaire's house It will make my reputation if I'm careful. Now what is my problem? To produce a work of contemporary English art, such that everyone will say as soon as they see it, a typical what's-his-name. So the house has got to be contemporary, it's got to be art and it's got to be English and it's got to be me." Then he threw himself into a kind of trance and allowed that monstrous chunk of ugly nonsense to bulge out of his inner light, a work of the age.'

Benskin stood with a little smile. He was not attending because at the first words of depreciation he had ceased to listen. Here at least he could feel confident and secure, for he had had the best advice in England, from the R.A. itself, and the house was undoubtedly a masterpiece.

In a question of taste he felt the solid ground beneath his feet and the experience was encouraging. He was suddenly cheerful and benign. He said to Felix, 'Won't you come in and take something?'

'Thanks, but I can't stay.'

'What are your plans? I hear you're retiring from Africa.'

Felix had not thought of plans. He reflected and at once perceived that he could not retire from Africa; that he was waiting to return there. He said, 'No, I shall go back as soon as I can.'

Benskin reflected that Felix' services certainly would not be required by a new company but he said, 'I hope you will find conditions improved '

'The new companies will be a good deal worse than the old ones—the natives will have no chance against a monopoly.'

'You ought to look for a Government post, Mr. Corner.'

Felix made no answer; he was thinking of the Major; Pooley, who was said to be back at Laka; and Laka itself; the huts, the river and the steep banked river where the children had played. He felt suddenly like an exile. He wondered if Dinah had been faithful, and the notion amused him. But Dinah had her own faithfulness; she was true to her nature, herself, and her needs, and her nature was as firm and dependable as the ground. A man could rest there, at least.

In the morning room, Nussbaum and Ingles, surrounded by heaps of papers, had been arguing for two hours about a question which, as Benskin had said, no argument could solve; whether to liquidate the Mosi companies or to merge them.

Ingles was for liquidation. The shares were worthless. 'I don't see why we should consider the outside holders—they've made us pay ten bob or a pound for shares not worth fourpence and now you propose to make them a present.'

But Nussbaum wanted a merger. For two hours he had advanced arguments supported by figures, reports, opinions, to show that a merger was the right business policy. His real reason, however, was nothing to do with business; it was his nervous dislike of anything like violence. His hatred of any kind of disturbance was like a cat's objection to a thunderstorm. The secret, unconscious motive of all his political and business thinking was to let sleeping dogs lie; to avoid disturbing by any sudden brusqueness a condition of temporary equilibrium which alarmed him by its shakiness.

But Ingles wanted to do something forcible and striking. He was full of contempt for the big men, these elders of the financial church, who were always preaching caution and respect for tradition.

'There's Benskin,' he said, looking out of the window. 'Shall I tell him we're stymied?'

Nussbaum frowned, wrinkling his nose, and shuffled among his papers. He did not know what the word meant and therefore he did not like it. He said, 'In any case, he must decide. We must have him on the board and we want the Chorley contract.'

They walked down the drive to Benskin, still strolling with Felix.

'It's up to you, sir,' Ingles said.

Benskin, keen, revived, looked at them sharply. 'Which is it—liquidation?'

'I'm for liquidation.'

407

'So am I. I don't see why we should consider the speculators.'

'A lot of fly-flats who thought they could beat us at the game,' Ingles said.

'I'm not considering the outside holders,' Nussbaum began.

Felix had stood a little aside, thoughtfully gazing at the ground. He was smiling in his beard at the recollection of Dinah and Bandy.

'But surely as a matter of business——'

Benskin smiled and said, 'What an old maid you are, Alf—very well then, we'll merge. It's not such a big business, anyhow. Or I tell you what, toss up for it.'

'No—no.'

'Yes—yes.' Benskin was cheerful. His faith had returned to him; from where he did not know. He was full of confidence, resolution.

Ingles tossed up a penny and Benskin said heads for merger, tails for smash.

'Heads it is.'

'That penny understands business,' Nussbaum said. He smiled, forgetting in his relief the enormous size of his mouth. 'Yes, it is the best for everybody.' He suddenly looked fierce again, drawing his lips together.

'Nonsense, Alfred, it will cost us a hundred thousand pounds even if we write down the ordinary to five bob and make up differences.'

'But what you both forget is that this business can't be treated in isolation. You can't separate it from the general situation. For instance, the Colonial Office is notoriously nervous about the newspapers. Now suppose some of your speculative gentlemen, say, for instance, old Porriton, chose to write to the papers and accuse us of anything they like—you see—the problem is just as much political and social.'

They strolled on, discussing the business. Felix, suddenly finding himself alone in the drive, wondered how he had got there, turned and made his way back towards Porriton. He calculated how soon he could be back in Africa.

He was received at Bellavista, still more muddy, by the anxious Chorleys and John Chass, an hour late for lunch.

John Chass asked him as soon as they were alone, 'What about it?'

'I didn't say anything to Porfit after all. It wouldn't do any good.'

'But Benskin——'

'Oh, it's too early for a decision there.' Felix threw up his beard. 'They can't do anything in a hurry—but I'm hopeful. Yes I think it will be all right. Benskin is not the kind of chap to let us down, he's more civilized than he looks. H'm, all the same, I think I'd better be getting back.'

'What, are you going back, my dear Felix, what about the doctors?'

'I must.' Felix shook his head. 'It's all very well, Charley, but someone has to attend to things at the front.'

The word had jumped into his mouth out of the air. He gravely repeated it, 'At the front,' and it called up before him, by some extraordinary associations of ideas, a pair of full brown breasts.

Felix, as usual, was justified in his wisdom. At the end of three weeks John Chass, still in retirement at a cheap London hotel, had a letter offering to write down his shares in three separate Mosi river companies to five shillings; to amalgamate them into a new company, the Mosi River Company, and to give him extra shares of the same value as adjustment between the valuation of the original issues. He joyfully accepted this suggestion. He owned then a hundred and forty three thousand shares in three companies, bought for the most part, at Felix' first suggestion, for less than three shillings. It was true that he had also bought some at seven shillings, but luckily they were few. The banks had refused credit before the price had risen. Moreover, as everyone knows, this flotation, like that of the Royal Niger Co. ten years before, was an immediate success; with such directors as Benskin, Nussbaum and Chorley, who had contracted to take a regular annual tonnage of palm kernels, there was no fear of a narrow market. The shares were at a premium on the day of issue, and went to nine shillings before the end of the year. John Chass found himself with a sum that varied every day, but never sank below forty thousand pounds.

This seemed to him amusing and he told stories about his various adventures, interviews, his trepidations and hopes, at every gathering in Annish. But though he had made money, as he put it, out of the air, he spent it upon solid objects. It had taken form already as new lodge gates and a new north lodge; some expensive toys for Teresa, new liveries for servants, a new suit for Grogan, more horses and an increase in all wages.

This was the beginning of the castle's time of splendour when John Chass gave his most celebrated parties. The African gold fountain which had been playing upon England and Europe for twenty years, now began to throw a sprinkle of sovereigns as far as Annish, so that even old Dan, dragging his rheumatism along the shore with a string of dabs or glasson, found that his market had improved. There were dinner parties every week and Sukey never haggled about a price. Sukey herself was richer by two pounds a year, though she took no pleasure in the sovereigns, even when they clinked in the bottle behind the broken fire-back which was her safe.

Coo's baby was born in August, a son to whom John Chass was godfather. He was christened James John. Slatter was so delighted with this event that he bought Coo a fur coat. He thanked God ten times a day for the boy, and he began at once to plan his education as a gentleman fit to inherit an estate.

His only anxiety was Philip, who had been extremely happy since his marriage, friendly with everyone and devoted to Coo, but who often smelt of drink.

Slatter was bewildered to know where Philip got his drink. He gave him no money, he locked up his whisky, he forbade Maddy to lend him money. Coo, of course, he suspected; but she strongly denied it, and he did not see how she could find whisky for Philip when she had no money, and while she could barely walk with her bigness.

But Philip was always slightly drunk and on the christening day, when he could not be prevented from drinking with the guests of the house, he swallowed whisky by the full glass. He entertained everyone with his gaiety and his stories, especially a new tale of how he had sold a cow with a blind teat to a dealer from Dunderry.

'Ah, that fella thought he'd made a hare of me, but I knew one trick better.'

Since his happy marriage Philip had been still more like his uncle. He talked broad Annish, told the same kind of story and sometimes, by pushing out his neck and letting his jaw drop, he even achieved the look of him.

'Ah tell ye this, too—some of the Dunderry fellas need watchin'.'

Slatter, himself in drink, burst out laughing and put his arm across the boy's shoulder. 'Philly's the wan that knows his way about.'

'And who was it taught me?'

There was great laughter from the christening party, especially Hanna, but when the last guest had driven away just after three o'clock Philip was discovered smashing an empty bottle against the mantelpiece because, he said, it wouldn't milk, and when he was urged to lie down and rest, he turned upon his uncle with the jagged bottle end in his hand and said in a sulky voice, 'Look at this—it would take your eye out. That would be a good trick, too.'

Everyone was relieved when half an hour later he went to sleep on the floor. Slatter and the butler put him to bed.

Slatter had been frightened by that sulky threat. He rushed to Coo in the drawing-room and shouted at her, 'Look at what ye've done now—there's Philly mad with the drink—I suppose it's what ye want us all killed.'

Coo, who seemed diminished in all proportion since her delivery, as if the baby had drawn away half her substance, sat gazing at her father from an arm-chair with a pensive expression.

It was true that she smuggled poteen for Philip. She got it usually from Manus Foy who would bring it to her at the edge of the fir wood above the house. She paid in kind. A pair of her father's woollen stockings, one at a time, had kept Philip in paradise for a month. Coo, like her father, was mistrustful of the country people and Manus since his imprisonment had been distrustful of everybody, so that this method of dealing in pairs suited them both. The pair was useless until it was complete and so Coo had a hold on Manus. But equally the remnant of a pair was useless to Coo, and so Manus felt sure of his pay. He had even advanced during Coo's lying-in two quarts against the left foot of a pair of shooting boots, laid aside for the summer, of which the right had been delivered by Coo a few hours before it. Her first pains were actually squeezing her when without a word even to Maddy, she had crept up through the trees one evening to the wall and given Manus his signal. She wanted to make sure that Philip would not lack for comfort in the next weeks.

But she did not know how to explain to her father her conviction that she owed Philip all the happiness that she could give him.

'But it would be the whisky, Pappy, that he had with the colonel and the rest of them.'

'The colonel be damned—he's always at it and if it isn't you that got it for him, then who did? Gawd, look at her, who could ask a gyurl to have sense?'

He ran upstairs to listen at Philip's door. No sound came from there and he sighed. 'Aw, Philly, why wull ye do it—why can't ye be happy like annyone else?'

He went out to look for Hanna and sympathy. He stopped Mac-Ewen's car outside in the road to tell him that Coo had been giving drink to her husband, and to ask him if he had ever heard of a stupider girl. At six he was at the castle shouting at John Chass, 'What can ye do with the young people these days? What's come over them?' His voice was full of wonder. Slatter always meant what he said; his words were the product of a real discovery. 'What's come over the world?' he asked John Chass in amazement. 'What's happened to the childher?'

But in a little while he began to peer curiously about; he said, 'I see ye've a new rug there—polar bear is it, naw, polar bear—begob that cost ye somethin'.' His eyes began to shine; he delighted in each new purchase at the castle, in all John Chass' extravagance, which was at once right and proper in the great John Chass, and encouraging to his own ambition. He knew that John Chass was already exceeding his new income, and that he had not troubled to pay off even his bank debts; all the mortgages remained. Money was flowing already in a dozen new streams, the African fountain was trickling into a hundred cottages.

'And I'm told you've another gyurl in the house, that's three more. Man, ye'll be ruined with your parties.'

'It's only Bridgy Egan to do the washing up.'

'Aw well, that keeps it in the family, annyway. Haw, haw!'

Bridget had been admitted once more to the scullery soon after Teresa's accident, for though Sukey still abused her, she had not troubled to continue in hatred of her. Now that Teresa was banished from the kitchen she even allowed Bridget sometimes to bring Finian there and scowling at the boy she would say, 'The spit of a Corner—to hell with him.'

Teresa was never seen in the lower part of the house. She was completely cured; a strong little girl of five, active and good-tempered; and the red marks of scalding had faded from her pale, waxy forehead. But her left eye, though bright, was a bluish milky globe. Sukey could not bear the glance of this eye turned towards her, and many of the country people would cross the road or look the other way if they saw the child coming, even with Mary Corner in the governess cart. Teresa had always looked fixedly at things and the fixed gaze of her white eye made even John Chass uneasy. It was a natural thing that the country people should be frightened of her. They said already that she was a starer, who gave bad luck.

A starer in Annish is much feared and Sukey could not endure Teresa in her kitchen. The child spent all her time either in the lady's garden, or in Mary Corner's own room, which had become her day nursery. Here she spent wet afternoons quietly playing by herself, and here she had her morning lesson after breakfast and her evening hour before bed when she expected to be read to. At the moment, she was sitting on the old, broken, horsehair sofa with one hand in Mary Corner's apron, listening to a story.

'Once upon a time there was a cat——'

Teresa gave a light sigh of pleasure. This was her favourite story of the cat's clever triumph over the world.

She felt already that the world was queer and dangerous; it was full of people who stared.

'And this cat's master was very poor, so that he could not live in his own house.'

Teresa glanced nervously about her and took a grip of the apron.

'But this cat was a clever cat—good gracious—what a cat—she was cleverer even than blue Peter from the kitchen, that is always trying to get into the drawing-room.'

Mary Corner had the old-fashioned nursery style, the dramatic, and when she threw in a 'Good gracious,' she looked at Teresa and met the child's unwinking gaze; the one eye which seemed to ask, 'Tell me what really happened,' and the other with its ghostly appearance of watching without sight. To Mary, of course, with her training, this eye, because it was ugly and frightening, excited her nerves to tenderness and sympathy so that when she saw it a little colour came into her cheeks, and she smiled at Teresa as if she would like to kiss her. She did not, how-

412

ever, kiss Teresa because she felt that it would be wrong to treat her as a daughter seeing that she was to be brought up in her own station as a lady's-maid.

Slatter's voice could be heard beyond the window and the hedge of the lady's garden. He was no doubt going to look at the harbour work with John Chass. She thanked goodness that he had not come before to keep her from this time with Teresa, the happiest in her day, the hour which justified all the hard endurance and bitter disappointments of her life. Mary Corner felt no grievance against a world in which there were children to love; and though she did not expressly thank God for Teresa, because she felt with her strong senses that it would be indecent to suppose that so great a King should contrive to throw a little girl downstairs and put her eye out, she had a sense of gratitude so strong within her, day and night, that all her feelings were of obligation.

'And so the Marquis of Carabas had this magnificent castle for his very own——'

Teresa looked round at the shabby, crooked little room with its dingy wall paper, its old, calf-brown books, its sticking-plaster miniatures; the engraving of the Meeting between Blucher and Wellington at Waterloo; and that other, still more fascinating to Teresa, of a pyramid composed of egg-shaped shields, each inscribed with the name of a Waterloo colonel.

To Teresa the word castle meant this room and the lady's garden; and the word magnificent, since it was obviously a word of highest praise, meant secure, peaceful and safe from people's eyes.

'Good gracious, Teresa, wasn't that a clever cat.'

Teresa looked sharply at Mary and her grip tightened on the apron. She was waiting for the last important assurance. She held her breath.

'And so they lived happily ever afterwards.'

Teresa let out her breath in a noiseless sigh of relief. She was safe for ever.

There was a knock at the door and Grogan thrust in his head through the opening in his usual lizard-like manner. 'It's what there's a message for Mr. Slatter, mam—they say Mr. Philly is for doing murder up there at Carnmore.'

'Good gracious, has he killed anybody?'

'I don't know, mam, but he was shootin'.'

Mary put down the book and hurried out to find Slatter, exclaiming at every step, 'The poor boy—the poor boy.' If Philip had been older than Slatter she would probably have felt for Slatter. Slatter had already been found on the shore and was running towards the yard. Two minutes later he drove off with John Chass at a bucketing canter. His expression, as he bounced up and down, showed the highest degree of

413

terror possible to the human face, which, combined with the desperation of his grip on the hand rail, formed probably an exact picture of his contradictory feelings.

Philip had got up almost as his uncle had left the house to go to Coo's wardrobe where the poteen was hidden. Then he came downstairs and charged a gun. His intention was to shoot Coo at least and perhaps everybody in the house.

Coo was still sitting at the drawing-room window with the baby in its basket close to the chair. The baby was asleep and this pleased her because Maddy was out and she did not know what to do without Maddy if the baby cried. Coo was not a responsible mother.

It was a warm, sleepy afternoon. The lough was a very pale blue streaked with broad, glistening bands, like the marks on watered silk; the sky was empty except for a few thin, high clouds like shreds of cambric, through which sky could be seen. Nothing moved except the upper leaves of a lime tree, which moved as if of themselves, as if the tree were restless, and the gaily rising smoke from the castle chimney pots.

Coo, gazing outwards, had the feeling of the veteran who has survived the forlorn hope; who has fulfilled his duty to the world and is entitled to sit in the sun, with trees and grass, enjoying like them a private life.

She was herself part of this luminous serenity, in which her anxiety about Philip, how to keep him happy, was no more than a flutter of nerves like the lime tree leaves, over strong-rooted security. She was beyond criticism, completely unnoticeable; a wife, a part of social nature. She didn't want even her magazine.

She was almost in a trance, a kind of vegetable state, when Philip came into the room with the gun and said to her in a gloomy and pompous manner, 'This has been a good joke while it lasted, Mrs. Constance, but it's lasted long enough. I suppose you didn't know I was seeing through you.'

Coo was frightened, but not greatly frightened. She was always slow to grasp a crisis and she had found Philip an easy husband. She said mildly, 'If ye go on the mountain, Philly, ye could remind Manus or Padsy that there's another quart to come on the left boot. And ye know, dear, ye might be needing it in the night.'

'Buttering me up,' Philip said in an uncertain voice.

This phrase seemed to throw him into a frenzy; he screamed, 'Buttering me up,' and raised the gun.

This yell however, heard through the lower part of the house, brought the monthly nurse from the kitchen. She was a dry, pompous little woman, full of importance. When she had rattled to the door and

414

met Philip's gun aimed at her, she gave a shriek and bolted down the back passage.

Philip hated the nurse who had always treated him as if he were of no account. He chased her into the yard, and fired after her from the back steps just as she threw herself past the gate.

Philip knew that he had missed the woman but he hesitated to pursue her further because he had only one cartridge. He was still hesitating when the back door crashed behind him, making him jump. There was suddenly an outburst of noise from the quiet house; windows closed, another door crashed, probably the front door, pans cascaded in the kitchen and in the distance a pony was galloping down the drive. Then there was silence again. He saw half a face, a forehead, a mob cap and two round eyes rise slowly above the bottom edge of the kitchen window It disappeared again with great rapidity as he met its stare.

Philip stood where he was, in the bright afternoon sun of the yard, and pondered, with the gun under his arm. He appeared so deep in his pensive contemplation that the groom, who had been washing the gig in the middle of the yard, tried to steal away, sponge in hand.

Philip, noticing the man's terrified eyes, turned towards him, raised his head and said mildly, 'What do you want?'

The man stood as if frozen in the act of a Red Indian drama. Philip looked at him with mild surprise, and then returned to his meditation.

He was too preoccupied to trouble about the conduct of lunatic grooms. He had an important job on hand; a really important job. For whatever else might be confused and uncertain, it was clear that killing was important. No one could explain a corpse away; turn it into a joke and make it seem like something else; for instance, a wedding cake. But whom to kill? His first idea had been the best. Coo deserved punishment for her deceitfulness in praising him all these months, in stealing for him and amusing him.

Unluckily it was too late to do justice on Coo. He had lost his chance there. He must be careful, too, that the police did not catch him. That galloping horse had no doubt taken a message. No more judges for him. They wouldn't understand a situation. They would want to make him fit into some of their legal notions and if he did not fit, they would pull and drag him about until he was broken out of his own shape and ready to be pushed into one of theirs. They would make him look like a fool and he was not a fool. He protested.

Confused voices were heard calling beyond the house; somebody had arrived. He gave the closed house a contemptuous glance and walked with dignity across the yard and paddock into the fir wood. He knew the wood well. Half a mile along the hill face there was an old clearing; a thicket of brambles surrounding half a dozen stumps. He found it in ten minutes, picked a low stump, sat down and took off his boot and sock. Then he put the gun barrel against his chest and pressed the trigger with his toe.

He heard a loud explosion and felt greatly surprised. Was it possible that he, Philip Feenix, had performed this bold, this terrible deed. Something struck him a heavy thump on the back and then he was falling; he reflected in ever growing astonishment, 'I really have done it—I'm killed.' Triumph and consternation filled him.

John Chass returned at seven just in time to prepare for dinner. Philip had not been traced, but Slatter was convinced that he had gone to some mountain shebeen for more drink. As he said, there was no harm in the boy—he wouldn't hurt a fly.

Everyone in the castle was relieved to hear John Chass' voice in the hall, for ten people had been asked to dinner, and it was too late to put them off. It would have been a pity, they felt, if a silly freak of that lunatic Phil Feenix, had spoilt all the thought, plans and hard work which had gone to the organization of the party.

But the party, like most castle parties, was a success. The young soldiers from the garrison found themselves next pretty girls. Duff, who liked claret, was on the same side of the table as his wife who could not therefore frown at him when Grogan filled his glass; old Feenix, more blind and deaf every day, was next his beloved Mary, who alone did not mind screaming at him and who was ready to discuss his subjects.

John Chass' art was hospitality and at ten o'clock when he got up from a second rubber of whist, for tea, he could feel the pleasure of an artist in a sound composition. One of the soldiers was still on the terrace with the prettiest girl; the other was deep in an album with Laetitia Duff. Old Duff in the largest arm-chair was beaming with happiness after two bottles. His wife was scandalmongering with the English Dean's wife. Feenix, the Dean and Mary had got upon the subject of Church Government.

Old Feenix, with his hollow white face marked with those firm deep lines of the man who lives with suffering as a familiar; the good-natured Dean and Mary full of lively enjoyment, demolishing from their shaded corner the Machiavellian despotism of Rome; and deploring the slight confusion of Protestant doctrine, gave John Chass more pleasure even than the flirtations. The English Dean had been the inspiration there, for though he said the same things as Feenix and Mary, he was a new voice and a new ear.

When Grogan, weary and untidy looking as usual after a dinner party, with his tie crooked, his collar sagging, his new best suit already spotted with grease, and on his pale face the expression of a pilgrim in

416

the slough of despond, brought in the tray, John Chass gave him a shilling for Sukey.

'That's for the soufflet—tell Mrs. Egan she never did a lighter one.'

Grogan took the shilling in silence and dived out of the room.

Sukey, worn out like Grogan by the evening's work, sat crouched in front of the range, with her stockinged feet in the fender. She was three parts drunk and when Grogan brought her the shilling, she said fiercely, 'The soufflet, damn him, of course it was good, didn't I make it?'

Sukey had the ticklish pride of a great artist, ticklish to praise as well as to blame. She brooded for a moment, 'Get the hell with him and you too. Put it on the table. Naw, give it to me before that murdering Bridgeen there puts her hand to it.'

Bridget's handsome, pale face appeared in the scullery door with an expression of protest. Grogan dropped the coin into Sukey's lap, poured himself out a cup of tea, black as porter, from the old blue enamel pot stewing on the stove, and went eagerly to his pantry. He still had to count the silver and to read his Bible, and these, marking the end of the day and so a day nearer to the glorious resurrection into eternal joy, were, with the tea, the chief pleasures of his life.

He propped the book against the handle of the plate basket, and slowly, with deep calm appreciation, indulging himself in his weariness, he read his favourite passages; a piece of Jeremiah, Job, the psalm beginning, 'Oh God, my heart is fixed,' and his chief delight in Revelation, 'And the building of the wall of it was of jasper, and the city was pure gold like unto clear glass——'

The blue cat, gazing up from the floor with eyes like topaz, suddenly stretched herself to the shelf, put up a paw and knocked down the teaspoon out of the saucer.

Bridget had disappeared again. She had thought better of protesting. She knew her luck and she was content to be abused by Sukey while she was accepted in the kitchen without a rival, the acknowledged niece. She could penetrate now into every corner of the basement. She had explored Sukey's own room, and putting her hand down at the back of the fireplace she had touched the bottle that held the gold. Were Sukey to drop dead at any time between seven in the morning and six at night, or twelve on a dinner night, she would be on the spot.

Rifty called her lucky. But was it luck that had brought her back to the castle? Was it luck that had moved her arm and sent the urn tumbling on Teresa; that had made everyone say that Teresa was always at the urn; that had made the child a terror to Sukey?

Bridget, surrounded still by a mountain of dirty plates, pots and pans, with two more hours of rinsing, wiping, and scouring in front of her among the thick fumes of the zinc, knew that her career was too wonderful for luck; it was the working of a fate, a secret power.

She did not know what power this was among the various powers controlling her world. God with whom she communicated through Father MacFee; the Blessed Virgin to whom she prayed; blessed St. Bridget, who kept her in special charge; but she knew it and felt it every day of her life; a providence in her very brain and flesh, guiding her to Cleeve, thrusting her arm against the urn. She felt it now, simmering inside her like the joy of her strength and dexterity, as she deftly slipped the plates into the rack. Bridget never broke a plate from the house; a real china plate. She felt for them, expensive fragile things, the same tenderness that she felt for Cleeve's pyjamas, and the smell of scented soap upon his skin; that she felt for Finian. There was reverence in her fingers and a triumphant reverence in her soul. She was at worship.

In the kitchen Sukey twiddled her toes at the fire which was singeing her old stockings. She looked at the half-empty cup of poteen on the cold end of the range but she had not the heart to put out her arm for it, even though it would lay her dead for the night.

The drink poured through her, making her nerves quiver and her veins swell and throb; and all this energy was turned to the life of her despair. It seemed to her that all the loneliness in the world was thumping through her like the feet of condemned men in the prison yard. She felt amazement at this terrible pounding misery which did not shake her to pieces but only beat the floor of her heart into a harder clay; a closer, denser ache. How had she, the lively, pretty Sukey, with a dozen boys, the rich woman with nephews and nieces in every village, come to this state? How was it that she was still sitting in this kitchen which she hated and from which she could not escape? She reflected but her thoughts whirled and flapped like disturbed rooks; no sooner had the vision of Bridget, young and eager, coming to learn the kitchen maiding, or Teresa tied to the kitchen table, appeared with sharp outline on her memory, than it whirled away in a turmoil. What had she done to suffer such loneliness? Hadn't she worked; no one harder; hadn't she paid her dues? Had she ever stolen so much as an egg, or told a lie or broken any of God's commandments? She had not.

Whose then was the fault? Who or what had brought her to despair? She stared at the fire with eyes that themselves seemed to be red-hot, her grey hairs waved in the draught of it like thin flames. What was it? Her sudden loud muttering brought Bridget on tiptoe to the door. She peeped in with eager eye, expecting the next turn of her fate and Finian's; Sukey in a fit, Sukey mad or only Sukey drunk again.

Sukey uttered a loud furious croak, 'Me feet, the Judases.'

A prefatory essay by Joyce Cary
written especially for
the Carfax edition of *Castle Corner*

CASTLE CORNER

|

★ ★ ★

C astle Corner was to have been the beginning of a vast work in three or four volumes showing not only the lives of all the characters in the first volume, but the revolutions of history during the period 1880–1935. Much of it was carried into the second and even third volume. There are in the attic whole scenes written even of the last volume, showing the end of the work, and the final condition of the persons. But I could never bring myself to finish any beyond the first. Partly I think this was due to lack of encouragement. Critics can easily depress a writer, not so much by abusing him, as by mis-comprehending him.

The criticism of Castle Corner (even the praise for which I was grateful) made me wonder if I had found the right means of saying what I had to say. I had learnt enough to know that the same general theme can be expressed in many different forms, but I had not fully realized that the very virtue of art, of which the power is that it can give experience, on that same account, limits its scope in argument. It cannot state the case, in all its qualifications, because to do so is to appeal to the intelligence alone and to break the emotional continuity.

This is so even if one invents 'raisonneurs,' characters like Peter in War and Peace, to discuss philosophy; for a character able to discuss fine points (which is what you need to get

421

any value out of him) however real in himself, and firmly placed in the action of the book, if he state the case, will at once come out of it and appear like a lecturer on the platform. For the reader perceives at once that that is what he is for, and is rightly offended. And the more carefully one hides such a purpose, the more offensive it is. Ingenuity, in fact, is always disastrous, if it is meant to deceive.

You say that many writers have stated cases, for instance, Tolstoy in *Resurrection*, Dostoievsky in the *Brothers Karamazov*. But these great books do not state the case, they weave a spell; they leave out all those qualifications, those relativities which, in the real world, affect conduct and opinion. They state not the case, but a case; they see everything from one angle; they are 'true' only for their own characters in that situation, carefully chosen and limited to drive home one moral slogan, and excluding all these complex issues which in real life would make it possible to say 'but Aloysha's solution is wish-fulfilment.'

To do myself justice, I did not mean to write crude social philosophy into *Castle Corner*. I meant to create characters and leave them to act; characters conceived with those springs of action which seemed to me most important in all character, working out their fates in a world charged throughout with freedom and individuality, and the consequences of that inescapable freedom, where moral principles must be like those of an army on the march, inventive, flexible, for ever balanced between the immediate circumstances (this man's nature, this crisis) and an ultimate end (the good, the true, etc.) and a final judgment is final only in the sense that it is the best (however bad) solution of an immediate problem. Think of Oates' suicide in the Antarctic, or thousands of 'mercy killings,' which are technically murder.

But I had to ask myself if anyone would notice that the book had any general meaning; if, in fact, it did mean anything; if the contrast of different characters, though all making their lives, seeking fulfilment of one kind or another, did not result in that very neutral tint which we find in the events of real life. For life, as it occurs, has no meaning. It is too full of chance, too stupid. We give it meaning by choosing from it what we call significant patterns. I don't mean that we make those patterns, we find or think that we find them among the mass of nonsense as a man sees from a plane the track of a Roman road under crops, and chicken runs; or a beach-comber goes out for drift wood to a certain bay at a certain hour of a certain month. What I had to ask was if the pattern would come out from a mere tale of currents, winds, moons and rocks.

The question was especially complicated for me because my subject was personal character working in a medium which was also personal (but I suppose final) character; that is, universal values. I meant to raise such questions as, Is there a final shape of society, to be founded upon the common needs and hopes of humanity?

The answer was that the final shape, if it ever arrived, would be one not of peace and justice, security and comfort, but of limited insecurity, limited physical misery on the one hand, and on the other, richer possibilities of experience, both in fulfilment and despair. The tragic dilemma of freedom is incurable; that it can't have either security or justice, which belong only to robots, to machines; that because it has the power to know goodness, it must also suffer evil. In fact, those who have the keenest intensity of happiness, in love and achievement, are those most exposed to suffering in loss and defeat.

And this too would have to appear in the book. But how could a story which is strictly concerned with persons, answer universal *political* questions. Would not a reader say, 'So that's what happened to Jarvis, or Bridget (who became a rich woman in England, but a drunkard), or

Cleeve, because they were what they were. The better I drew my characters, the more they would fail as illustrations of general laws. And in the upshot I abandoned the whole enterprise, and turned to write about the simplest of characters in a simple background, with the simplest of themes, Mister Johnson, the artist of his own joyful tale.

Yet I still regret the loss of my characters in *Castle Corner*, and their adventures, their development through another fifty years.

J.C.